Vagabond Life: Liberation

Johann Darby

Cover Designed by Tom Edwards
Illustrations by Johann Darby
Library of Congress Cataloging-in-Publication Data

Darby, John W., 1966–

Vagabond Life: Liberation / Johann Darby.—1st ed.

Includes index.
1. FICTION / Action & Adventure, 2. FICTION / Science Fiction / Action & Adventure,
3. FICTION / Indigenous / Science Fiction.

ISBN: 979-8-9922266-0-7(2025 Print)
ISBN: 979-8-9922266-0-7 (2025 eBook)

Vagabond Life: Liberation

THE HARROWING 1958 – 2252

THE REAVING 2253

Vagabond Life: Liberation

THE HARROWING 1958 – 2252

Chapter 1 - FAMILY TIME

October 2252 – New York, New York, Zabar's Café

Rain sluiced a hazy sheet on harried commuters. A man sat under an awning, avoiding the rain but not the splatter. Splatter made him grumpy. After the Tech War, the weather was more capricious and more extreme. It all started with those perky synths.

The last week had been a rough change of season. Pedestrians in the Big Apple were as numerous as ever and unyielding to any inconvenience like inclement weather. On one street was a deli, like the 3000+ other delis in the city. This one had a particularly large yellow awning, which afforded some bit of shelter from the deluge.

"Yes, the numbers don't lie. We are done here…" the man looked plain and his tan trenchcoat told the world 'nothing special here'. He was very un-memorable. With an unremarkable 3-piece suit, he was just another commuter, sitting at a café having a cup of joe.

He spoke on his prosthetic comm, "…yes, I heard you the first time. All the major Powers have been seeded for the Reaving. Now is when you approve the extraction of our team."

Faint words on the other end of the call did not please the man. He grimaced.

"Enough. And you say we have gone soft for these humans," his words were sotto voce and no one would overhear him, he was sure, "It's you who's lost the purpose, here. Tell the Crith they are in charge now and I'll give you two days to approve our exit. If you do not, I will notify Behin, our team leader, and file a grievance with the Cleaners Union. Hello? Hello?"

The man grimaced as the voice on the other end terminated the call. How did Emerson put it? 'Bureaucrats are the hobgoblins…'? They're more like boat anchors!

His name was Pauli Pierpont, and he was a Vor. But today, his frustration was very human, and he began to think the Cleansing ordered for the human race was a bad idea. To his thinking, all the Cloud-active races were just stagnant pools of protoplasm. The humans could bring a new pep to the step for the whole COMBINE. Ach, but who cares what I think?

Pauli muttered to himself, and thanked the waiter for his coffee, "See ya tomorrow, Michael!" They waved and Pauli faded into the flood of people headed to work.

His comm line buzzed and he answered.

A voice spoke, "Pauli, this is Behin. The plan has changed, we need to talk. Come to Vegas."

Oh bother, the boss was trying to rope him in now. I just want to go home and live a quiet life. He thinks I don't know about his little liberation plan. Everyone knows. Except for the Crith and the Cleaners, of course. I guess it's time to see the bright lights of the strip.

October 2252 – Lake Stevens, Washington, Confederated States of American (CSA)

Beginning of morning, nocturnal twilight was filled with thousands of satellite streaks and Brownian pointillation from horizon to horizon. The air was abuzz with delivery drones, and CleanerBots, busy about their tasks through the neighborhoods. Echoes of whirring motors and servos joined with crickets and birds in the morning cavalcade. It was early, but one house was already awake with several slow-moving bipeds and one insistent storm cloud. This storm cloud was a friend rummaging around my room, looking for a lost pad, her computer tablet. There was no mollifying this storm. So…if ya can't beat 'em, join 'em.

You see, Binky was my best friend, and she was a royal pain. We are in the same grade and share many of the same classes. I mostly get A's and she scrapes by with B's and C's.

The wry thing is she is just as smart as me. Binky was a nickname. To the uninitiated she was Monica May Brown. She was brilliant and competitive. We both were. Her best hours were not spent at school. Binky was an Online gamer. Like everyone else, she grew up on Paradiso games and was a world ranked PvP gamer named @Ripley. When Paradiso rebranded as SimVerse, Binky's fanbase grew. I didn't have a fanbase. I played games, but not like Binky did. My interests were tame, by comparison. I was one of the few who created community content for the games in SimVerse. I also loved creating little AI friends Online and taking my favorite personalities and installing them in the various bots and synths in my house. One of my favorites is a former combat AI I installed in our floor CleanerBot. Every day it went to war against dust and particulate.

Its name was Viper, and it complained every day, "You are weak! You're pathetic! Your quarters are shameful, and your floor looks like the forest moon of Endor!" I think it had heard me mention Endor once. Now, it was the inspiration for my slovenliness. Yes, it used that word too.

Speaking of Endor, I scavenged another AI in a virtual scrap heap on the forest moon, under a pile of grid squares and squelch grease. It called itself the Pan and had been hiding out; from what, I had no idea. It was the rawest yet the most elegant AI I'd seen. And it came home with me. He played little mischievous games with me. He'd hide things Online and recently had found a way to take control of my home bots. Pan would have the bots hide all my underwear or would short sheet my bed. I felt like Inspector Clouseau who might be attacked at any moment by his butler, Kato. Whenever I entered my room, I was open game for his antics. I sometimes got a bit cross when I couldn't find things like my homework from the night before. I often had hardcopy homework because my Dads made me print things out. How archaic. Then I'd find the paper looking chewed up and jammed under my bed. How do I tell my teacher 'the bot ate my homework'? It doesn't fly. As Binky rustled around, she dropped my guitar, only catching it at the last moment from certain demise. It was a Martin D-28, made in 1967. I would die if it were harmed. Shame on me for letting it lie around with other stuff on the floor. I took the guitar from her and placed it safely in its case. She ran into my holo closet, found nothing useful and came back out at the same velocity. She kept searching. Speaking of holo closet, let me tell you about it.

My Dads built me a room which serves as my gaming environment. You see, most kids still use screens similar to those from the 21st because the modern-day alternatives are too danged expensive. But my Dads are wicked smart and have cornered the market on cool toys. I call it the holodeck and it is packed with holographic transmitters and it even has haptics and olfactory generators. However, when you are in game competition you do not want to smell what the rock is cooking! Speaking of, did you know The Rock is the eternal show host for all DOOMverse game sessions? Dwayne Johnson got rich in his old age and donated a rump-ton to Pacific Islanders, and those same islanders own DOOMverse, the number one Online gaming universe. They kept The Rock's spirit alive in the game. Yes, I know, he was a bad guy in the movie, but they made it a cool thing anyway. There's more but I'll save that for later. Back to my holodeck. I used to spend more time in it to walk through the early Online creations I had made. I guess I still do, but it's hard to be competitive in gaming when you are limited to 1:1 body movement with your avatar. In general, a flick of a controller button is much faster than moving your own body part. My Crew have holodecks too and we have a rule: for casual, the deck is fun, but the manual controller and keyboard is king. There is a third option, but me and my Crew didn't have it: prosthetics. I'll talk to you later about it, and probably whine about it. But suffice to say, my Dads and my friends' parents forbade us prosthetic install. All the other kids at school had 'em. But oh-no, not us. We still get to live in the dark ages. They won't even explain why. Never mind, I'm gonna get grumpy if I talk about it. Sorry.

Finally, Binky found her device and we were ready to head to school. Suddenly the window opened. In fell Cricket and Wogs, laughing at some joke. Sean 'Cricket' Carter came from a redneck family and his parents were close associates of my Dads. That is Dads plural; yeah, I have two Dads and they are awesome! Wogs was Mollie Ann Brown and was Binky's sister. Wogs was smooth and laid back as much as Binky was frenetic and highly excitable. Cricket had a southern drawl, from his first six years of his life in Austin, Texas. In his mind he still lives in Texas; he called it 'Tay-haas' and woe betide anyone who says anything bad about it. With all three of my friends in my little room, my sanctum sanctorum was suddenly loud and chaotic. As an only child I craved a large family. These were not just my friends; they were my family. But, hey we're still kids so you wouldn't find me saying anything that mushy.

"So, Kip master, you and Binks look like you've been doing a bunch of cardio, what'cha up to?"

Cricket never thought in terms of sex, so his question was more about having been left out of something fun. Oh, and my name is Charles Winton Wefer the 3rd, but most people call me Kip. I never use my given name; it seemed to be a bully magnet. There was a time I was being bullied by a boy who made fun of my name. I met Binky and Wogs the day she punched that kid in the stomach. She had been standing up for me ever since. She said I was her little 'hot house violet'. To be honest she never said stuff like that except when we were alone. She would never allow anyone else to call me such things at the risk of her smashing some part of their anatomy. Yes, I was that kid with the inhaler and coke-bottle glasses.

Binky was a tad bit over 1.5m tall, with a wiry whip strength. The boys thought she was a hottie, with long dark hair in a pigtail and small pug nose. But her pixie features belied her aggressive nature. She sent them running when they made the mistake of holding a door open for her or played 'little lady' games with her. Wogs was a head taller than Binky and had stronger facial features and a sprinkling of freckles. She had dark red hair. She was Binky's older sister. Then there was rangy tall Cricket, clocking in at a tall 2m with arms and legs akimbo. He had the Robert Redford rugged good looks and dark red hair not unlike Wogs. His hands and feet were huge, and we sometimes teased him for being the tallest Hobbit in the world. And he had the beginnings of a moustache. He was so proud. Then you had me. I was slightly taller than Wogs, but I was skinny more like Cricket. I had the dark skin of my Dads, mostly like my father Vicky. My hair was afro-kinky, and I had it braided against my skull in tasteful cornrows. Wogs and Binky learned how to do cornrows and sometimes helped me keep mine tidy. I had no facial hair and suspected I wouldn't ever be sporting a 'stache like Cricket. His was scruffy small but at least he had one. It's a sad thought. Let's move on.

The peeps in my Crew were oddballs, but in a good way. Okay, forgive my wine fest. Since none of us had any type of prosthetic we would be in class with the other kids and we missed out on all the inside jokes and much of the teaching meta-content. The teachers regularly forgot the four of us couldn't see what they were showing Online. True, we had our trusty pads and they were first rate. But pads were a poor replacement for prosthetics. You see, most of the human race was permanently wired to Online via prosthetic, both the raw Net and into Paradiso, now known as SimVerse. DOOMverse connects to SimVerse!

As the children of scientists, our parents believed we needed to be grounded in the physical skills of learning. We had physical books, were required to do homework on paper with pencils and math was something computed without calculators. What a complete pain!

I could hear my Dads now, "You kids need to be strong in your STEM subjects…" Blah, blah, blah. And the lack of our prostheses didn't go unnoticed amongst our peers. Kids laughed at our anachronism behind our backs, unless Binky caught wind of it in which case the other three of us had to drag her away from smashing someone. Binky was like a cross between the Hulk and Captain Marvel, cocky and sure of herself and once she had a head of steam, watch out! In a sense, it felt like the other three of us were merely along for the ride as Binky stormed through life. We tried not to get caught in the prop wash as she motored forward.

We also had a garage band together. My Dads set us up with a space in a detached garage…very detached. I guess they didn't want to listen to the cacophony and din when we first began. But we were pretty good now. We shared the love of 20th century music and also created our own. We traded off instruments depending on the song. During summertime we sometimes busked during Saturday Farmer's Market in Lake Stevens Commons. We could earn enough dime to afford computer hardware upgrades and Cricket's wilderness gear.

At home, I had arguments with my Dads. My two Dads were excellent parents in every way. But they sure had no sympathy for my plight as a prosthetic Luddite. At school, we were mostly regular kids. Ok, it's true, we were a bit nerdy and artsy, but on the whole, we didn't stand out in any remarkable way. We weren't popular, unpopular or in any kind of spotlight. Our grades were better than average, but none of us did any sports except intramural.

Seeming to be regular kids was on purpose. That is where our story really starts. As children, the four of us were brought into the conspiracy of the synths. Our parents played it like a game but impressed upon us the life-or-death risk to both the synths we hid and the other humans who hid them. All our parents made no bones that we were being trained to help save the synths and take over for them when they got old and doddering.

My Dads were easily spotted in a crowd. Vicky, Dr. Charlemagne Victor Boshaw was from Kenya and had skin black as night. He was somewhat rotund, and he was short like me (or maybe I was short like him?), but it was all muscle and strength. Charlie was my other Dad, known to others as Dr. Charles Winton Wefer Jr. He was from Peru and had the darker skin tone of the Killke people. He was a skinny guy (now you know where I got it) and sported an infectious smile and quick wit like Vicky. So here I was, dark skinned and short like one Dad and skinny like the other. I'd had questions about my mother and how I was related to my Dads. Somehow, we never got around to the discussion.

October 2252 – DOOMverse Day, Lake Stevens Commons Pavilion, CSA

Today was a busy one and I was up early. Usually, my whole Crew would descend on my house to walk to school together, but today was not a usual one. The DOOM World Cup Finals were starting today, and Binky was a finalist again. She was the number one seed from last year and favored in the polls to win again. Her parents had the whole Commons pavilion reserved for the setup. There were five others in the area who were in the Finals and the whole pavilion would be DOOM central all day. This year there were even street vendors with food and gaming swag. The Swaggers as we called them were a bit of a menace. Like ill-tempered carnies, these Swaggers would appear at events like these and work hard to separate people from their money. Some swag was legit while some was cheap knockoff. Buyer beware! I usually ignored them with an insouciant glare. Well, that was until I found something I couldn't live without. The question would be if I could afford it. In that case I became the whinging member of my Crew until they pooled enough credits to get me my bauble.

My Dads were busy as usual and wouldn't attend until the late afternoon. I, on the other hand, was up and out, sitting down for breakfast with my Dads for less than a minute. Then I was off…but, in truth I had always been a little off; and I liked it that way, to keep folks guessing.

Cricket would be late. On Sundays he and his parents would be wrapping up their work near Granite Falls at their survival hooch. Only a few people knew where they went but me and my Crew had spent large chunks of time there, especially when one of the Powers had a militia in town. Usually, it was a Bangarang or Bad Wolf patrol, but sometimes there would be a group of Junkers in town or bounty hunters. Lake Stevens had a gentrified appearance but in the modern day the niceties were only skin deep. And our parents kept us away from the danger with 'fun trips to the Carter Farm'. On Mondays at school there were always stories and rumors of people who had gone missing and other crimes and misdemeanors.

On Sundays Cricket had his vastly popular livecast entitled "Down Home". His Online name was @HuntMaster; guess what Cricket loved to do?

On his cast, Cricket shared things like how to make soap or candles, or how to set a trotline. I saw the preview of his cast late last night when he sent a link to our Crew. His topic was bulletproof quilting. He was good at what he did, and the 'quilt' was a misnomer. He was using a foot-pedal sewing machine to fabricate a bulletproof emergency tent. But he was artistically bent, and his fabric soon had a beautiful, quilted patchwork. He was detailed and I really learned something from his show. His audience was primarily young women, more interested in watching Cricket, himself. They probably would watch him mow the grass and be perfectly pleased. And then the other group of watchers were hardcore preppers who hid behind innocuous screen names like @PinkieTwinkleToes, @GoodbyeKitty and @ SayNoToLutefisk.

Cricket was always a bit bleary-eyed on Mondays since he was up late Sundays. But, he never missed one of Binky's competitions and had even been on the road with us to Seattle and Vancouver for the big conventions. True to form, he and his family always came packing. They were gun nuts and conservative folk from the South; Texas, you know. But you always felt safe with them around: smart people with guns.

Wogs was different in her own way. Online she was known as @Strabo. I guess Strabo was a map guy. She subscribed to the maxim, 'No Map? No Where'! She loved maps, whether they were physical or digital, new, or old. There wasn't much fanfare in her hobby, but she was popular with map librarians. She had been frustrated with the fractured state of the big map hubs. She was on a mission to create her own hub.

I helped her create a crawler (read: information stealer) to grab and store every digital map accessible Online. It took a month for the info flood and initial library ingest to complete, but more maps trickled in every week. There were maps from every major Power, university and municipality. She used some of the servers from my Dads' data center which now housed the largest single map repository on Earth. What she was unaware of was how well this served my Dads and the liberation.

As I walked into the service entrance at the pavilion, Dr. Cameron, Cricket's mom slapped a Staff pin on me and put me to work. Cricket's parents had made it back in time to get the pavilion ready, so where was he? I looked around, but not seeing him I started working to get my and others' gear set up in the gear pit. The gear pit was nothing fancy, just a square of about 12 folding tables with chairs on both sides. This was where the local officials and referee types would monitor the players visually and Online. After it was set up, I went over to Binky and Wogs who were raiding the hosting table. All the worker bees could catch a breakfast or lunch, small bite, or mounded plate. The Carters were renowned for opulent service and the hosting table was a shining gem in the diadem of their hospitality. Binky and Wog's parents, Georgie and David were busy about the schmoozing with the celebrities, officials, players and their families. There probably wasn't a group of folks the Browns wouldn't glad-hand to death given the opportunity. They were 'equal opportunists' and unapologetically able to squeeze promises, favors and advantages from even the most stingy or reticent folk. They could sell a used car to a flat-broke used car salesman. Between the Browns and Carters, these events were marvels to behold, so full of action, color, and fanfare.

The first screen to go up showed Online comments from the fanbase that was already gathering.

One dude named @Heavenly_Father commented on the Doom song playing.

"This is not metal. This is the entire periodic table!"

The comments always started as a trickle and became torrential as game time approached. Numerous Online admins and curators had the job of parsing the comment streams to keep them organized and interactive.

The huge sound system boomed out the theme music for all the various game franchises that had been rolled into the DOOMverse. Wolfenstein, Diablo, Starcraft, Half Life, Halo, Portal, Hellgate London and others. The music hit a crescendo and the pavilion went dark. A second later the bright lights on the stage blinded the crowd and a blooming flower of visual effects sparkled and whizzed and shot around the whole space, splattering against walls, people, and imaginary objects. Online creatures and players were amongst us, standing looking almost real. An occasional flicker showed up their holo actuality.

A voice shook the pavilion; it was Binky and Wogs' parents hosting the event.

"Ladies and gentlemen, children, and warriors of all ages, welcome to the 123rd gathering of DOOMverse! As your masters-of-ceremonies, David and I are glad to see you. I am Georgi and this is David," Dr. Georgi indicated the man on stage with her dressed as John "Reaper" Grimm, from the Doom franchise. She droned on for a bit and introduced all the celebrities and officials, game designers and executives. When she introduced the two major contributors of the prize money, representatives of Big Wolf and Bangarang stood up. The applause was deafening in its absence. They each took a bow and sat back down.

A 30-meter square area was cordoned off and signage called it the Mosh Pit. In it would be curated holos of live action of the players and the environment, and an enormous real time map. At the moment it was displaying a 3D map of Raccoon City, showing zombies and other baddies converting the populace and taking over the town. I could watch it for hours, kinda like staring at a campfire. Soothing. Zombies, soothing, weird, I know.

The competition took the whole day and night. Some called this competition the marathon for gamers. It was a grueling 24 hours of little rest and non-stop action. It consisted of a long series of PvE, player versus environment and speed runs followed by PvP, player versus player maps, filled with monsters from DOOM, Hellgate London, Diablo, Wolfenstein, and many others. The warm-up was already running. It was a tradition. It was called the DoomGlitch, and it was based on a software error in the 20th. It was more about fun and entertainment than anything else. The players flew through the map but could never finish.

The Silent Hill siren sounded, and as the clarion faded, the competition started. It was well-known that 90% of the players were knocked out in the first hour. Of all the people on computers you could discern between observers and players by the low-light laser glow reflecting from the players' eyes. The player saw a highly customized HUD and artificial panoramic view which displayed all the pertinent details in seamless combination with the physical monitors they used.

The next 12 hours saw two hundred competitors bumped-off the leaderboard. By the wee hours of the next day, it was down to Binky and three others. But there could be only one! Only the hardcore fans and game officials remained in the pavilion. Most had gone home to bed. My Crew was still here as always.

Competitors could earn extra lives, but when those ran out it was game over. Binky stood out for several reasons. To me the most impressive was she never lost a life and continued to rack up extra. An aspect of gameplay was sharing lives. Binky would conscript temporary teammates by giving them lives she had accrued. They knew in the end they would still be enemies, but during early game play they kept each other alive. Her teaming tactics had become legendary in the gaming world.

Now it was down to Binky and one other. Some kid named @PewPewPie from Singapore was the newest, hottest and was giving Binky a real run. But she was still in her prime and the Pie was going down. To his credit it was very close. Then it was over, and Binky sat back shaking from the effort. With a weary smile she stood and made a beeline to the restroom. She was in there a while. The pavilion day crew came in shortly after and began clean-up. The rest of us headed home, not long for a hot shower and cool bed.

I headed home the way all us kids had been instructed: the rhumb line method. We knew how to meander, looking out for someone following. This was equal parts paranoia and safe practice. The ratio of the two was always up for debate. Online, our PvP was about players, but in the real world PvP was about the practical versus the principle. A simple walk home (practical) was never simple for sake of safety (principle).

Back home I slept through the day and got up for dinner, had a short chat with my Dads and went back to bed. Like only a teen can do, I slept almost 20 hours. The next day Mrs. Standish, our Principle didn't like our permission slips and gave us all detention. This was so predictable I would miss her special attention if she failed to punish us. After detention we all walked to my place to fix some frozen burritos and nachos. Snack of champions! Cricket brought out the Hot Ones sauce and we emptied the bottle.

"Kipper, you said we could look at the results of the latest data scrape," Wogs knew I kept the crawler running 24/7 looking for maps and map data for her. I knew it was time to see what new stuff had landed.

"Of course, let's go to my Dads' lab to put it up on the big screen. We can use one of their AIs to do the Awkwerk." The Awkwerk was an engine that used rules to organize data and present it. Then my Dads' AI would use tools like GrepIt to munge the data in fun ways. But we needed to see it on the big screen for maximum enjoyment. The four of us descended the steps to the elevator room. The elevator door was hand painted with their favorite ShroomWerk. Just so ya know, they were crazy for mushrooms. ShroomWerk was a term describing anything artsy about fungi. Their never-ending obsession sometimes made me weary. But this art piece was special. One of the descendants of the original artist, Ryan Bliss, named Andrew Bliss had painted Ryan's now-famous fluorescent Blue Mushrooms on the door, and an expansion on the work covered every door, wall, even on the floor and ceilings. There was even a depiction of a God-mushroom reaching out a rhizome (mycelium?) to touch an Adam-mushroom's rhizome. It was quite beautiful. But we were kids, so we ignored stuff we saw all the time, taking it for granted.

The biometric keypad would admit any of the four of us, so Wogs passed us through, and we felt the elevator rapidly fall the 200 meters to the lab complex. Much of my Dads' work from the CENTER and for the Liberation happened here. As the elevator door opened, I could smell mushrooms, detritus and electronics burning. It smelled like a hard day for my Dads.

"Hey kids come in! Charles and I have some snacks and got a few big screens set up for Wogs project," my Dads always knew what we were about. It was almost impossible to keep secrets from them. Vicky had setup three screens for us and booted the two MapAdmin programs he had written for Wogs and me. One screen showed the whole library in lurid, colorful detail, and another showed all the new finds. The third screen showed several command line sessions used to quickly manipulate the map libraries.

"Kip, your crawler had a strange blippy thing happen, so I took a peek and found you had picked up a CSA tracker-bit." I was alarmed that my uber-secure crawler had been tagged by one of the Powers so easily.

"You know there are living humans and synths on the other side who are actively setting traps for you. You need to do a better job of keeping tabs on your activities." He was right and I felt ashamed.

"I am adding a notification of findings which will hit your pad if something like this happens again. You do keep your pad with you, kids?" We nodded.

I replied with a piquant of resentment, "It would be more expedient to give us prosthetics, so we always have our Online connection nearby."

I knew he would nix that idea, saying we needed to not be lazy and reliant on prosthetics to interpret the world for us. We needed to grow up using our own senses without enhancement.

He surprised me, "You are right. Soon you will need prosthetics. I will let Subramanian know we need to have his prototypes ready. I'll figure out the details and get you kids hooked up when it's time."

A ripple of excitement washed over me and Wogs had a big grin. Finally, we would be connected to Online all the time. We would be able to control any Online connected devices and talk amongst ourselves kinda like telepathy. Sweet!

"Okay Wogs, we have the new scans of the Olduvai area. You'd been hoping for those for a long time if I remember correctly?" Wogs nodded and smiled. This was a major find!

"I think you will be pleased at the results of the most recent data." Vicky brought up the visuals on the second screen and we could see the satellite images being mapped for contour, subsurface and surface details. Little popup bubbles proliferated like multicolored floating blueberries and new map layers were spawned as we watched. One day I hoped to be able to code like Vicky. Just when I thought I was the master-of-software creation I got plopped into the backseat by something new Vicky created. It seemed so easy and natural for him.

"Oh my gosh, Dr. Boshaw, thank you! I had no idea what MapAdmin could do. But I do have a question." Wogs had the look of a kid in a candy store.

"Of course, my dear. Please, what can I help with?"

"Could you do a comparative scan of Olduvai over as many years as you have topo record?"

"You mean you want contour only?"

"Mmm, I'm not sure. Maybe just analyze whatever you have, looking for contour changes?"

"Curious place to be looking, okay, sure. I'm already on the way," Vicky had already been typing at a furious rate and two of his CLI sessions were scrolling results as he typed. Then he clicked a new button that appeared on the dashboard and an animation showed visual data between 2001 and today. He ran the animation at high speed, showing the satellite imagery between the dates in under 30 seconds. It showed immediately: there was a bulge that was growing just south of the main gorge that rose 100 meters. Where early images showed a mostly flat plain a new hillock appeared in latter images. A hole in the hill appeared facing south and trails could be seen leading to the hole.

We were quiet as Vicky adjusted the animation to display subsurface data. We were in for a surprise. The subsurface went opaque after 2098, the last year of the Tech War. Just prior to the opaqueness a data point appeared, affixed to the opening location. It read Glabrezu. Vicky's old school phone rang. It was the line only used by the Liberation.

"This is Vicky. Yes. Mm, hmm. Yes. Okay. What do you want me to do?" He looked consternated at what he was hearing. "Okay, will do."

In a few moments all the images, the animation and data had been deleted. In horror, Wogs stood with her mouth agape. Sacrilege!

"Dr. Boshaw, why did you do that?" Wogs practically cried, "that was for a project I was working on, and that animation proved something is happening there that no one wants revealed."

My Dad turned to face us. He collected his thoughts and answered in even tones, "Mollie. We have known each other your whole life, yes?" He laid a hand on her shoulder, "Will you trust me on something?"

She nodded, looking at the floor. Vicky gently lifted her chin up and their eyes met. His were as pained as hers. "The leader of our efforts just directly instructed me to remove all data gathered regarding Olduvai Gorge. I am so sorry," at this point he drew her in for one of his famous hugs and she tried not to sniffle…much.

He whispered in her ear, but we all heard, "You were right. In every way that matters, your suspicions were justified. All I can tell you is that the secret things going on there are for the good guys, our team in East Africa. And I was told to tell you that you will know all about it the first moment it's safe to do so."

Without saying a word about it, he handed Wogs a small memory stick, presumably with the 'deleted' data. Holy cow! Vicky was so cool! He did as he was told, but in defiance gave a copy of the data to Wogs. She knew it would have to stay offline and, on the DL, downlow. Just when my Dads seemed restrictive and frustrating, one of them went and did something amazing like that.

As far as the Liberation, we knew the drill. Whether it was called the project, or the effort, where the Liberation activity was concerned, secrecy must be kept. Otherwise, people died. We knew that to be true because some of those liberators (people) we had met were now gone. Dead. Sometimes this charmed life of ours really sucked. To pluck our spirits up Charles brought us treats and snacks, it was ice cream and cake. Lots of chocolate cake. Oh, and milk, fresh-baked chocolate-chip cookies and Vicky's favorite Sikh treat, Jalebi. Cricket loved Jalebi! It always came down to whether Vicky or Cricket got the last piece.

RETRO - April 2246 - Lake Stevens, Washington, CSA

The lives of the four of us were burdened, yet more fortunate than we knew. As an example of the weird kind of normal we experienced, let me tell you a brief story. There was a man, well over seven feet tall, skinny as a rail and badly in need of a shower. He smelled like Bay Rum and B.O. The first time I met Vagabond Bootblack, I was 8 years old and woke up with him climbing through my bedroom window. It was dark and scary, so I rolled to the floor and under my bed, afraid of whatever boogeyman was coming inside. The bed above me squished down as the man crawled across toward the floor. As I watched from underneath, two huge boots clomped onto the floor and strode across my room. My door opened and the man's movement stopped. In that moment a deep basso voice spoke, "Hop back into bed, little Kip. Tomorrow is a school day."

And out he went, quietly closing my door. I listened carefully and moments later I heard uproarious laughter, downstairs. A minute after that one of my Dads came to check on me. By then, I had closed my window and was under my covers.

My bedroom door opened and my Dad, Charles quietly walked in and over to my bedside. "Kip, I am sorry Vagabond came through your window like that," he knelt and brought my face close to his, "You know the work we do to protect our synth friends? Well, Mr. Bootblack is the organizer of the synth railroad. You remember when you studied about Harriet Tubman?" I nodded, looking into my father's face, a foot distant from mine.

I could smell whiskey on my Dad's breath… "Kip, Mr. Bootblack is a distant relative of Ms. Tubman, and he is a genuine hero in his own right. Tomorrow morning you can meet him yourself."

My father kissed my forehead and tucked me in. After my Dad closed my door, I pretended to go to sleep for about 30 seconds. When I was sure he wouldn't come back in to check, I flipped back my covers, bolted across the room to my desk and grabbed my pad. Since we weren't allowed prosthetics, I had to call my friends the old-fashioned way. After 20 rings Binky came on, followed by Cricket and Wogs. All of us were in bed and had to be covert with our comms.

"You guys will never believe who just climbed through my bedroom window!" I spent the next few minutes telling my Crew about Vagabond Bootblack. "The dude is huge, Binky. He's tall like a Maasai warrior!"

"Kip, I don't think any Maasai made it out of the Tech War. But I think there was a General in the last war. But he was taller." Cricket was very astute on past military leaders and tribal heroes. He came by his preferences honestly. His parents were preppers and hunters, folks who were big on the concepts of identity and self-reliance. Oh, and they were also scientists. Weird combo, I know. We chatted briefly, but we didn't want to be caught up so late. Quickly, we all signed off.

The next morning, I got up before it was light out to see if Vagabond was still around. As I came down the stairs, there was a loud and boisterous voice vibrating the house. Vagabond Bootblack's deep voice was easy to recognize. With all the noise he was making, I could hear he was telling some story. A big reveal was about to happen. I was on tiptoe, sneaking down the stairs. It served well to keep me undetected by my Dads. Not so with Vagabond. Before I was halfway down the stairs, the huge voice called out, "Young Kip, come down here. Charles has made a huge breakfast spread and I want to get a look at you!"

To say I was shocked would be an incredible understatement. Just as I arrived at the foot of the stairs, two MicroDrones came flying around the corner to hover and orbit around me. They were part of the eyes and ears of the institution called Vagabond Bootblack. Sitting at the table, I got a good look at a man who looked every bit the Maasai warrior.

Vagabond stood as I came in the kitchen with a mug of coffee held in his hand. All plates were empty with breakfast just coming to the table and enough to feed many mouths. He clocked in easily at over two meters of ranginess. His physique was broad, muscular but lean in the manner of a feline; power held in reserve. His hair style was mine, albeit with longer braids from his cornrows and in need of upkeep. His eyes were black as night and piercing, but his ample lips held a smile that softened their intensity and his nose was long and straight. The chin was neither strong nor weak, but cleft in a pleasing jut. His ears were comically huge like my Dads would say, 'taxi going down the street with the doors open'. He was dressed in black leather and knee-high boots, sporting a black leather duster with a long mantle and deep pockets. He was sporting a shallow topped ultra-wide brimmed black leather hat which gave him a gunslinger appearance, except for the comedy of the ears. As I took in the riot of fashion expressed in one man, I realized some of the weird fuzziness I was seeing around his head and chest wasn't my eyes playing tricks. His head and chest were spaceports for MicroDrones and NanoBots. He was the center of his own flying traffic congestion. There must have been thousands of pinprick dots hovering and larger MicroDrones, leaving, and arriving into Vagabond's head, alone. Even more dots were doing the same into his chest. The sight of it made me a bit nauseous, but I worked to hide the fact.

He was smiling at me and indicated the chair next to him to sit.

"Come here, young sir. I do not bite," he looked to both Vicky and Charles, my Dads. They were just watching. Able, Roy and Cave Johnson, our synth friends, were standing near the edge of the kitchen, watching the moment play out. Three of my SynthBots (self-aware bots were extremely rare) flew over toward me. They sensed my distress at being the center of attention. Siri and Cortana sat on each shoulder and Alexa perched on my head. In fact, it did calm me to have my friends close.

As Vagabond spoke, I saw the a much larger than usual spread. Dagwood Bumstead stacks of flapjacks arrived, French toast with mounds of bacon, sausage, fried tofu, spam, fruit, scrambled eggs, hashbrowns and chicken-fried rice dominating the table landscape.

"Ah, yes, I see it now, Charles. He is more at home with synths than with humans." Vagabond smiled at me with bright whiteness.

All three of my bot friends were purring to me. I love cats and they love cats; we all love cats. They made cat sounds; it was our love language. My bot friends had a wide variety of cat sounds and they used them to entertain me and confuse our house kitties. I sat down, careful not to jostle my friends from my head and shoulders. Wasn't that a shampoo back in the 21st?

"Welly well, Kip, I want to properly introduce myself. I am Thaddeus Vagabond Bootblack. I used to have other names, but change is good. I became Vagabond Bootblack, and it sits well with me."

I guess he liked his name.

"Your Dads have been regaling me with your adventures. It seems you are a trouble magnet." I was floored and shocked. I thought of myself as more of a cyber-Ninja, not some troublemaker! Vagabond began to smile again, and I realized he had been giving me a hard time, baiting me.

"Mr. Bootblack, I am honored to meet you in-person. My Dads have mentioned you but…" I stopped talking for a moment. Vagabond bent forward and the cloud of Bot traffic navigated around me. The a gaggle of them landed on me and it tickled. He placed an enormous hand on my arm. Cortana adjusted like a parrot to look at Vagabond's hand. She didn't like his proximity. I slowly patted Cortana, "Easy girl, he is a friend."

"Charles Winton Wefer III, you are a powerful and loyal friend. One day, you will lead us to a bright new tomorrow. But for now, I have a solemn request," Vagabond was a huuuge man and looming so close to me, I felt itty bitty small. I breathed through my mouth as his nasty smell washed over me. But I liked his rumbly voice; it was soft and gentle, "My request is to have you pass me the maple syrup."

We held position, me staring face-to-face at Vagabond, less than two feet away, with all sorts of bots and drones hovering close. After a pregnant pause, he and I had a laugh. Then the exterior kitchen door banged open and in poured my Crew in a ramshackle mess. Chaos ensued until Binky, Cricket and Wogs clearly saw Vagabond. They froze.

Cricket almost yelled, "My Mom was right. The legend is true," Cricket dropped to one knee and said something I'd only heard from one of the Liberation soldiers, last Summer at the Carter Farm.

"My brothers, it is not against men that we fight. It is not against guns or bombs or tanks. Nor are we fighting people. On this field, we fight, both friend and foe, soldier and general, against the dying of hope. Look to your left. Now, look to your right. You stand with brothers and sisters-in-arms, both human and synth. Some of us will be able to say I stood that day and hope prevailed. Others will lay down a safe LZ for us in the place to come next. Heroes all, friend, and foe. Today, we strike for freedom and hope. For Valhalla!"

Not a dry eye as Cricket quoted the most famous battlefield speech by General Oloiboni Olonana. I hadn't realized Bootblack was the General. I was stunned and slowly took a knee. So many had been lost. The high price bought the possibility that another time might come to liberate those still held in bondage. I knew the stories well. We all did. It was part of our DNA. By the end, everyone in the kitchen had taken a knee and the last line was spoken by all, both human and synth. It was the only time my Dads broke with the nerdy scientist personas and showed they were also soldiers.

Vagabond had risen and walked to Cricket. He bent way over and brought Cricket to his feet. "Sean Carter, your father was there that day. He was the bravest man I ever saw. I would not be alive were it not for his bravery. Thank you for remembering," then Vagabond Bootblack, once known as General Oloiboni Olonana, softly intoned, "For Valhalla!" He said it and we were ready to fight…literally anything. Hell, we were ready to ride into battle behind this man. How did he do that?

But he dialed us back into the 'now', "Cricket, I would be most grateful if you would please lead the charge into this mountain of hotcakes." A bit of laughter eased the moment and somehow, we all just went back to being hungry for breakfast. Everyone dug in; there was more grub than an army could eat.

To catch you up, Valhalla was also known as Valhalla Sector. It was the main North American depot for synth destruction, but originally it had been the site of new life, the synths. There were two others, Elysian, and Yomi Sectors; each of the three served a region of the United states, now the CSA. Even early on and despite popular opinion, synths were not just mindless robots but thinking and feeling synthetic people. The Valhalla Uprising was the turning point in the conflict. On one side, the governments of the world, driven by anti-synth sentiment to eliminate the synth population. On the other side, a growing group of humans, joined by synths, seeking to free the captives. Millions of synths died, but tens of thousands were saved because of the Uprising. Yomi and Elysia were spared much of the loss, but in Valhalla, the biggest sector, lives were won at a high cost. The media captured it all live-time and it was discovered there were many sympathizers across the world. Later, the media coverage was squelched, and evidence of the Uprising was eliminated. The government approved broadcasts broke in to change the narrative. The headlines read 'Synths and Sympathizers Kill Thousands of Innocents', or something similar. However, the cat was out of the bag and many people knew the truth and believed it.

Breakfast and festivities went long. My Dads let the school know we'd be absent. Whoo hoo, no school! Senior members of my Dads' Study Group started coming by. The Study Group was a collective of scientists, soldiers and civilians who banded together to save the synth race. As a group they had developed a massive sentient AI which they initially named CoGNeW at Seattle:CENTER. They held a lottery on who would name the AI and one of the facility managers won. He was fond of old movies and books from the 20th and decided the 4 mega-AIs from two stories should form the name. Colossus-Guardian and Neuromancer-Wintermute, thus Co-G-Ne-W. No one liked the name, so an unknown person used a large ink marker to write the name "Daisy" over all the Cognew placards and blotted out the silly name. Eventually the new name stuck. Daisy was the largest artificial intelligence created by humanity at the time, only surpassed by The Pan a few years later. Daisy made history again when a bored graduate student signed up for an experiment on cyber enhancement. It paid enough credits to pay for the remainder of his degree program. The experiment went wrong. The experimenters had dubbed Craig Blake as Friar Tuck owing to his appearance. He was thrown into a dumpster and woke up in another country on a mile high heap of garbage.

Eventually he made it back to civilization and once his prostheses connected Online, the hardware part of him contacted Daisy and the super-AI completed the botched integration job. Blake wandered for more than a year like a madman from village to village in India. The people took pity on him, helping him with food and shelter. One day he woke up and everything was clear, and he knew who he was. His brain finally repaired itself and both halves became one. Blake was introduced to his benefactor, Daisy and after a period of time something magical happened: Blake and Daisy began functioning as one consciousness. After that, Daisy Blake knew he needed to contact the Dads and take an active hand in the Liberation.

That historic face came through the door. Not unlike Vagabond, Daisy Blake had a cloud of MicroDrones and NanoBots hovering about him in the 1000s. The moment Blake came into the kitchen the cloud of bots and drones began to orbit between him and Vagabond. That is until Blake gave me a wink and suddenly all the flying critters went back to their respective homes. Vagabond shook with surprise, his head jerking up to look intently at Blake. His expression softened and he nodded in a weary way. He knew it was a 'put the toys away' moment.

Blake was a talker, well ok, so was about everyone in the kitchen. As Blake chummed around with Vagabond and others, I noticed a subtle change in the behavior of all synthetic or synthetically wired beings in the room. It was subtle, but there was a harmony and economy to the movements and conversations around me. The various synth sounds harmonized in a pleasing way. I wondered if I was the only one to notice the change. Then I heard a voice over my shoulder.

"You feel it, don't you? Describe to me what you see and feel right now. What changed in the room in the last couple of minutes?" I looked over my shoulder and the most beautiful albino woman I had ever seen was face-to-face with me, inches away, in fact. Her pink irises had flecks of dark blue. I was mesmerized and I started to sweat. She put her hand lightly on my shoulder and I could swear I felt a shock at her touch. I was riveted me to my chair.

I replied, "When Mr. Blake came in, all the bot traffic returned to their homes."

I wasn't sure what she was driving at. With her closeness I was having a problem thinking straight. She smelled like Peach Cobbler and sultry deliciousness. Her face hovered close to mine and she had an easy smile, perfect teeth, and graceful gamine features. My observation wasn't unobserved. The Crew was watching me from across the living room, smiling at my clear uncomfortability.

Silk sheets and rippling magnetism spoke again, "Kip, dig a bit deeper. What do you sense?" the woman knelt at my feet and looked directly into my eyes. Now I was visibly sweating. She waited on my words.

I took another stab, "There is an orderliness and sense of purpose in the room that wasn't there before."

Her voice changed pitch. She was now coaching me, "Since you feel it and can name it, I want you to try something. Stand up and yell out. It doesn't matter what you yell. Just stand and yell. Perhaps call to one of your friends."

What a weird thing to ask, but I saw what she was doing here. So, I tried.

I stood up rapidly, looked at my Crew and called out. "Hey guys, commere!"

It wasn't a yell. I found I didn't want to yell because it was more pleasant to pitch my voice a certain way to get their attention. My eyes grew large, and I looked back at the woman.

"Yes." The woman nodded at me knowingly, "Yes, you felt it."

My friends came over and I realized I was under the influence of something beside myself. I wanted to be annoyed, but something in my brain was telling me it wasn't necessary.

"I don't have any prostheses. There is nothing synthetic in my body that I knew of. How can Mr. Blake control me like this?" I thought I was going to be concerned, worried even, but I couldn't seem to get a head of steam up to do so.

"Answer me this. DO you understand the idea of PvP?"

I immediately thought of gaming.

She asked, "Do you see the difference between the practical and the principle of the matter, here?" Her eyes bored into mine.

Ah, another adult lesson…this was going to be boring. I wasn't sure what she was driving at, so I made a guess.

"The principle? Is it control? Mine has been taken away. But there is nothing I can do about it, so I'll just let it pass."

"Is controlling others okay as long as they know they are being controlled?"

I shook my head no. My Crew came close and stood unusually silent, looking at me. I had no idea who this person was. She spoke, sticking out a hand to shake those of Binky and Wogs. I noticed she didn't acknowledge Cricket; that was weird.

"Good morning, friends, I am Modron, sometimes called Mariam." She looked at me, then winked. As she turned back to my Crew she addressed Cricket.

"And you are Cricket Carter and I apologize." Modron stood and walked to Cricket. She then stepped forward and embraced him full and hard.

"Cricket, you are my nephew, and I am the auntie no one told you about. I am sorry I have been gone for all your life."

Modron leaned back to look in Cricket's eyes.

"I have watched you for years," she smiled, "from far away. But my line of work has made it too hazardous for you to even know about me. I stayed away to keep you safe. I'm sorry." The woman had sad eyes, and I was trying to look away to give them some privacy. Whoa! This lady changed the tone and tempo of the moment super-fast! She went from mysterious, to sad family member in an instant. I noticed my Crew was shocked too. Even 'fast forward'

Binky was having trouble adjusting.

Cricket stared for the longest time, then spoke, "I had a picture of you next to my mother, from when you were kids. You were playing on the beach at Hippie Hollow near Austin. You all looked so happy.

"So… Aunt Modron," he was clearly adjusting to a new reality, "I did know about you. But I was told you died in an accident," Cricket's attempted a smile.

"I don't know what to say."

Aunt Modron crushed Cricket in an embrace.

Cricket's parents came over and joined in the group hug. I left them to get acquainted. I wanted to talk with Mr. Blake. He looked like an androgynous Elf from Lord of the Rings and he was wearing a monk's habit. He, it, they, or however he self-described was one of the most beautiful beings I'd ever seen.

"Mr. Blake," I nodded to him.

"Kip, my son, you are growing up to be a handsome young man," Daisy Blake enfolded me into a huge hug. As he squished me, I looked back to see Cricket in the same squishy state. His eyes looked leakier than mine though. Our eyes met and agreed: it was time to exit this party. Too much grown-up sentimentality. A minute later, my Crew and I had extricated ourselves on flimsy pretense and fled the house. We were headed to Tiamat's for a day of gaming. Since my Dads had made an excuse for us, we determined to honor their decision by skipping school. And yep, we were going to be in trouble. So why not commit the crime if we're going to pay the price anyway? In a world of bys, by-default, by-design, and byproduct, my Dads said to always live by-design, until that failed. At which point live by-the-seat-of-your-pants was the next option. It was the easiest thing to choose trouble by design!

Chapter 2 - REVOLUTION

RETRO - November 2021 – Bellingham, Washington, USA - Chad

The clicking of the vintage keyboard echoed softly off the bedroom walls. A boy of 13 sat hunched at a desk, furiously typing, tossing his head as his hair kept falling over his face. His name was Chad Evans, and he was late. He felt an urgency to finish, and every keystroke error added to his rising anxiety. The program needed to be submitted prior to class start time. He had two minutes.

Finally! I can save…wait, disk write error? I don't have a disk, silly machine. Ok, let's save-as. Or Cloud save?

Moments passed.

Right then. Open email, attach file link. Wait, why am I getting an hourglass?

A chime dings and class had begun. It was too late. The boy hangs his head.

Chad had created an app he entitled The Pan. Pan would be his best friend. The Cloud save successfully completed. Something took notice of his upload, and within seconds a crawler process plucked his code, tagged, and saved it.

Chad discovered the theft later and was annoyed. No matter, he was still improving on his friend's code. No one else could make Pan better than he could. Pan was life and life always finds a way.

RETRO – Tech War & Aftermath – 2082-2189 – Planet Earth

The Tech War urp'd like a toilet's slimy regurge, starting as 'more of the same' hotspot combat, flowing into places less known for warfare. One tipping point came when the United States became an authoritarian regime, pretending to still be a legitimate democratic state. The excuse for war was heaped upon the immoral and job stealing synths. Global re-alignment came; a few took power from the many. This happened on three levels. Plain for all to see were the first two levels with the primary players, the sovereign states. For sake of security and economy, war was waged by militaries and banks. Sanctions impacted the poor more than the rich, and riots, violence and death followed. The third level of warfare was led by the techno oligarchy. Really it was a plutarchy because only the richest of the robber barons were world tech players. Social media played a big part. Online was on fire as much as the world was in flames. You would think no one would want nukes, but they came. You might also think germ warfare would be verboten as the ebbing tide that sinks all ships; but biological agents were employed. It started small but soon there were few areas unaffected. After 16 years of non-stop terror, humanity wound down.

Hostilities eventually waned, but peace didn't come, rather a bone weariness emerged in 2098. A fraction of the former population lived as medieval serfs and were fed careful lies to keep their ire quelled toward the powers-that-be. Peace was a word used, but really it was exhaustion. War ground to a halt. synths had played a big role in the war but were easily scapegoated by greedy Powers, as they resumed the enemy-number-one status. The vilification distracted the commoners while the deck was re-shuffled, and newly formed sovereignties were consolidated.

Witch hunts resumed after the war. Synths hid, ran into the wilderness, or worked alongside rebels or in approved factories. The new Powers all used synths secretly, but publicly, synths were reviled. As the post war solidified there were two kinds of authority, sovereign and corporate. The distinction between the two was murky and it varied from region to region. From the ashes of yesterday's hopes rose Bangarang, Bad Wolf and Crane. A dozen smaller corporate Powers rose in the interstices between their big brothers.

Out of the mayhem and wreckage, some good things were born. Covert war was still being waged, but those skirmishes were constrained and brief. Warfare required research and something new happened. The Powers collaborated and protected special sites they called CENTERs. These CENTERs were the combined research and development aggregates of the world. To the Powers, they were holy ground. In the CENTERs, amazing things were brought to life. New walled cities and arcologies sprang up across the globe to house the workers for the largest CENTERS. In some places they didn't last long: the walls didn't keep the radiation and biological remnants from the people. Folks got sick and died. The workers went to live inside the CENTERs which were safer than the cities. The abandoned cities were targeted by groups of scavengers known as the Junkers. Many of the Junkers ended up banding together. Others just gave the world the finger and held jealously to their independence.

There were minor Powers, too. The Catholic Church, the LDS Church, and several smaller religious organizations. They weighed in on the power struggle. The Scientologists also got a big boost. Despots loved Scientology. It was a messy time, and the Miscavige Mission (MM) became one of the new outreach tools contracted by private and public Powers to keep whole swathes of the population busy with requirements for Theta ranking. MM punished those who weren't up to snuff. Hubbard's manufactured religion delivered both death and taxes.

After the Tech War the world languished in despair. The Years of Mud smudged the land like a hand across wet paint. During this time plague ran rampantly through the remaining populations. Kinetic weapons caused rain and the nukes poisoned the soil. It was generally a crummy time to be alive.

After a year of rains, the world took a century to heal. Once fertile places became roiling sand dunes and hissing dust. Junkers were some of the only people to profit from the wrack and ruin. Wrapped in swathes and tatters, they stayed away from the hot zones, although some strayed in for quick profit runs. Those people weren't long for this world. You could recognize the yellow-colored eyes, and gobbets of tissue weeping and peeling from their living corpses. There was a heavy toll for success as a Junker. Tribes lived by a severe culture of honor, ruthlessness, and reprisal. A harsh culture grew up in Junker shantytowns and among the Junker nomads.

Weird things could be seen in the arid wastes. Not far from Denver was a field of giant colorful mechanical birds with wingspans 50 meters wide. Junkers called it The Perch. But hidden dangers persisted because the machines of war were not all dead. A Junker in The Perch might be caught unawares by the Goslings. Goslings were human sized HarpyBots that would issue forth from the bodies of the giant birds and descend upon their prey. The Great Salt Lake recovered to its full pre-industrial size as did the Aral Sea, Lake Chad, Qinghai Lake and hundreds of others. An interesting pattern emerged. Massive war machines were abandoned near many of the newly growing lakes. In some places, the soldiers just left them there and vanished. Some may have gone home if their home was still there.

Near the Great Salt Lake, the soldiers built a town, incorporating their several hundred giant tracked vehicles. They were Land Carriers and at 20 meters in height, 60 in width, and over 100 meters long, they housed scores of drones, missiles, and tactical nukes. In their heyday these behemoths cruised at phenomenal speeds across the land. They were a fearsome site for a city to see. Should one of these tanks crest a far hill, bearing down on a civilian population, all people could do was run and die. Now quiescent, they housed a town of families and friends.

Over the decades following, the soldier remnant continued to occupy the aging hulks, sending out foraging parties. These foragers got the name Cavalry. Junkers and Cavalry sometimes would do business but more often than not they would fight over the smallest prize.

Prizes littered the landscape. Along highways and freeways and in hundreds of rural towns, abandoned vehicles and worldly possessions marked the hasty departure and death of civilians. It was common to see vehicles with skeletons at the wheel or skeletal families hugging each other from some last-ditch moment before the end. Sometimes it was chemical agents, other times biological.

Another graveyard of machinery lay in the desolate waste which used to be Lincoln, Nebraska. Tens of thousands of bots walked around or lay in some state of disrepair. The Elysian Sector, the robot manufactory, now the robot graveyard was nearby. The area was known as the Bot Fields. The bots mostly ignored humans, that is until you found one which didn't. Junkers knew to watch for the twitchy ones. Waste travelers might not, and a run-in was bound to end in tears. No one knew why these bots and synths stayed in the area, never wandering far. The synth friends of the liberation said the Elysians were sad and kept their minds closed to others. So not even their fellow synths knew the true story of the Bot Fields.

A massive junkyard lay spread for a hundred kilometers all around Madison, Wisconsin. The Shipyard held 92 sub-orbital attack ships which lay in neatly ordered rows. Piles and warehouses of rusting and moldering electronic gear lay at the base of the ships. The shapes and types of ship varied. In common, each ship was over 300 meters in length and half that in height, bristling with guns and missiles of wide variety; they were called Hussars. Only the most prepared Junkers approached the Shipyard. Unarmored or without proper shielding these quiet ships would decimate intruders. Their self-aware AIs were alive and unwell, doling out vengeance on interlopers in reprisal for their entrapment in the aging, rusting hulks. But many Junkers and some Cavalry still tried for the salvage because the price for ship parts was steep and the potential for profits was high. The Confederated States of America forces, the CSA were too smart to mess with the Shipyard.

The same theme played over and over throughout North America and the world. Machines of war sat in shipyards outside Moscow, Paris, London, Manila, Delhi, and Johannesburg. Hundreds, maybe thousands of remnant junkyards littered the landscape. In Bosnia, there was an abandoned amusement park with wandering mechanical dinosaurs and even more gigantic fictional beasties like King Kong, Godzilla, Kaiju, Jaegers, Bolo Tanks, and a variety of others. From the little bit I heard, they still walked around like an episode on Solgell Island (Monster Island from Son of Godzilla).

As decades became centuries, the best parts were stripped from the ancient machines. Except those in the Shipyards. It didn't pass notice to those with the knowledge and insight that the Shipyards contained the best booty. The problem was people dying. Some had tried to heist a ship, and none had succeeded. Even in their faded glory, these ships could still defend themselves beyond the reasonable capability of an intruder trying to score a large haul.

RETRO – 2189-2242 – End of war and new prosperity

The present day has a remarkable resemblance to centuries past. 200 years later, the dark ages began to fade. As light dawned on new prosperity, the late 20th and early 21st centuries were seen as the 'good old days' to be revered and emulated.

The Powers did what they always do: seek more power and influence. Pressures brought to bear fueled development of the early CENTERs. They grew, especially when they also became the home of their workforces. Inside these sprawling mega-structures were cities of people and thousands of labs and facilities. Everyone inside had sold their soul to the man for the projects they slaved over. The consequence of failure was to be put out into the ravaged lands surrounding each CENTER. That was certain death.

Some projects were highest priority; these were called Diamonds. Diamonds were the best funded, the best staffed and usually were the largest killing fields of test subjects. Only two Diamond projects were free of deadly results: Synth Games and Hybrid Games. Both were based out of Seattle:CENTER and neither project had anything to do with games, per se. The names were misleading. Ostensibly, new forms of life were being explored and developed to sell to the highest bidder for slave labor, industrial or military use. Plants, animals, bacteria, fungi, and non-carbon-based experiments were constantly underway. Behind closed doors, two lead scientists had other plans with their new creations. Their plans were to plant the seeds for a bright new future. These two had met non-human sentients, who had secretly called Earth home at least as long as humans had. They were inspired to help these and other non-human life flourish.

It began with synth and hybrid development lines. When the time was right, they fled the CENTERs. All CENTERs saw the exodus; it was led by the two lead scientists known as the Dads. The Dads had diversified their projects over time to operate in every CENTER worldwide. The Dads also created hundreds of safehouses, laboratories and resource centers across the globe, unbeknownst to the CENTER sponsors.

The liberation occurred. But it failed to liberate most. Some synths and humans escaped, but traitors in their midst spoiled the plans. Immediately, every major Power was searching for them. The Dads were labelled terrorists. The bounties were astronomically high, and Drs. Charlemagne Victor Boshaw and Charles Winton Wefer Jr. went into hiding.

Chapter 3 – NORMAL LIFE

October 2252 – Lake Stevens, Washington, CSA

Our story is about coming of age and hope and friendship. At age 14, much of my life was spent in Online space and with my bandmates in a garage. I had a full-body haptic rig, a holodeck, and a packed schedule to keep. I built game content but most recently had spent my time playing many of the original games of the 20th and 21st. I also read the authors of that time and it inspired my Online game content design. One book I read, called Ready Player One, had a main character I idolized: Wade Watts. In a bind, I would ask myself, what would Wade do?

The other day when we went to Tiamat's, the predicted consequences at school landed the day after. We all got detention and a note home to our parents. But punishments come and go, and I never let it leave a lasting impression. Did that make me a sociopath?

It was the wee early hours, the day after detention day and the news feed said it would be sunny and clear. I was in my hooch now and troubled with some development work. I was having problems with one of my AIs. I noticed my Knight, Sir Pooka, was glitching. I called him Pooka because he was a trickster. He was my most complex AI and I took care to design him well, but today he was acting up.

"Ach, how stupid, I just added some skin effects and now you're getting buggy on me?" I highlighted Sir Pooka, removed the skin mods, saved, and reloaded the process.

"There you go…now let's see if you do better."

You see, I love to create my little friends in SimVerse. Have you seen Blade Runner? Yeah, I know, only cult fanatics like that movie. My thematic hero is J.F. Sebastian. I also appreciated his character in the book. J.F. had an incredible ingenuity, creating his little friends, who would greet him on his return home. J.F. would come in, "Yoohoo, home again."

And the little friends would reply with, "Home again, home again, jiggety jig. Good evening J.F.!"

It was so warm! So, when I first entered the SimVerse, back when it was still called Paradiso, I looked forward to hearing those words from my own little friends, 'jiggety jig'! Sir Pooka was one of those little friends, but he was special. He sometimes gave me fits; he had a sense of humor. My other complex AIs were Banquo, Liz (her full name was Thin Lizzy Borden) and Puck.

Pooka restarted, running smoothly, but somehow the skin failed to load. The transparent wireframe walked around, oblivious to being well and truly naked. I madly typed, reloading the skin file. That fixed it. A whole cast of characters in my mini-world, Hall of the Mountain King were walking, running, falling, and dancing. Pooka, my tricky Knight, was performing the Senechal role while Banquo was away. Banquo had the night off from Senechal duties, exploring some leads on maps for Wogs. Sir Pooka and his cheese stood alone, as it were. The Senechal is like an accountant and event organizer rolled into one. A Senechal was the one guy in chivalric court who was losing his hair and going crazy with timelines and deadlines. If you were to look across King Arthur's court, you'd see the pasty, bedraggled man (Sir Kaye) who had a nervous tick and haunted eyes. That is the Senechal: he shoulders all the responsibility and receives none of the credit. He is the one derided when things go wrong, and things always go wrong in small or large part.

Today, Sir Pooka is wearing a more fearsome skin and I upped his charisma and 'feared' scores. Many of the usual complainers about no wine, no food or lousy music looked at the Knight and decided it was better to try solving their own problems. That was fun to see! Banquo, I designed after Dr. Who. In every way that the Knight was a neurotic mess, Banquo was a nerdy, scheming and plotting mastermind. Ooops, spoilers!

I had another game in the castle: the 'old-fogies' part of the castle was reserved for two of my AIs, which I designed after their ancient predecessors. They were waging a constant cat-and-mouse game. Creeper was the runner and Reaper was the catcher. Besides being fun to watch, they were also good for load testing my newest creations. All I had to do was throw one of my new AIs into the old-fogie area and watch them run! I would turn on the old-fogie 'make mischief' setting and have them upset the other AI, or perhaps I would set Creeper and Reaper loose throughout the castle, to harry and harass the other denizens. That would go on until either Banquo or Pooka hit the 'mischief managed' button, which they always did after a while. Banquo would pull a moue in disapproval. I was a bad landlord; shame on me.

The kitchen timer on my desk went off and I was late for school. The little green frog vibrated across my angled desktop. I turned it off, grabbed my school bag and sprinted for the door.

"Kip? Did you take out the garbage?" my Dad was always on the ball.

"Yes Pop! Last night, remember?" The bus was long gone, and I was left to my skateboard for the mile and a half to campus. Ninth grade was becoming my personal tale of truancy. I felt just like Bender from The Breakfast Club, a reprobate and rogue. I sported a black creepy trench coat, Billabong board shorts, a 2112 Rush concert shirt, and flip flops. I was 14 and as my Dads would say, most of my brains were in my stomach. Did you know people eat animal brains? So gross. They must be zombies.

With heavy morning traffic, I could make better time to school on my board than in a car. Still, I would rather have a car. It wasn't fair, many of my classmates were older and were getting their driver's licenses. Not me. My friends were in the same boat: too young to drive and conservative parents. No car for us.

As I rounded the bend, there at the top of the steps was Principal Standish. She looked none too pleased to see me.

"Charles Winton Wefer," she said it like a death sentence. "You have been late to school every day this week, except for the day you so blithely skipped. I came outside to breathe a moment's fresh air, away from the stench of unwashed children, only to find you racing for the door."

I slowed to a walk and hung my head at the proscribed angle to indicate a remorse that was never more than skin deep. Mrs. Standish wasn't much loved. I felt badly for her though. Her husband and only son died in a car accident a year ago and she had been tight and bitter ever since. That knowledge was of little comfort, as I stood convicted.

"Mr. Wefer, you will report to my office after school," Mrs. Standish, escorted me to my classroom door. School was going to be a real pill today.

The afternoon sucked as everyone but me and Principal Standish went home. She lectured me, called my Dads, and had them pick me up. She lectured them too. Back home, I finished my homework so I could begin my real work. As darkness fell, my research into the origins of the AI known as Bangarang bore some fruit. Bangarang is a massive Qframe AI, and a company name. It controls a whole bunch of the world and snuffs out anyone in the way. I believe the AI is in charge and the employees are just its pawns. That would mean Bangarang is an evil overlord. In an article I read, Bangarang processes and maintains a large portion of the world government contracts and delivery.

Bangarang was the bully that banned my account on SimGames this morning. I was using the mods I had purchased from SimGames, but the stupid AI sent me a memo stating that my use of the mods was not permitted in PVP areas. For real, I never cheat at games; that would take all the fun out of winning. My downtime from gaming made me bitter. I had a plan to strike back. Bangarang continued to charge me for SimGames, but I couldn't play. Well, in that case, I would play a different game. Call it SimDetective. I wrote the code for my Detective AI months ago. Now, this was its first real job: I sent it crawling and poking and prodding up the chains into restricted Bangarang space.

When I set SimDetective to scour Online, I was looking for breadcrumbs pointing toward Bangarang. My AI sleuth was seeking the paths least traveled for a secret way inside. I also had a second instance of SimDetective working on Bad Wolf. Bad Wolf was the other corporate Big Brother, similar to Bangarang. While SimDetective did its thing, I kept busy in other ways. Before school had resumed this semester, I was doing community service for some paint tagging. It started with a beautification job for Mr. Hooper's grocery store. The sad part is he promised to pay me, but when it came time to give me the 500 credits he owed, he called the police and claimed I was a tagger. Oops, now I had a legal record for vandalism and Mr. Hooper had a nice new mural. I told my Dads, but they said not to worry about it. They paid my fine and the credits I was owed, and had some words with Mr. Hooper. Bummer deal, the vandalism charges stuck.

My community service was teaching people about computer use. The Pratt Center had public use computers which usually moldered in the corner of a dark room. In the modern-day, people used their prosthetics and pads and mostly gave verbal or mental commands. Some used subvocalization which was like talking without making much sound, a little less than a whisper. That left people like my Crew and I (the Luddites, you recall) as the few who had proficiency with computers in the way folks in the 21st would recognize. My students were not eager, they just wanted to fill out tax forms, authorizations to the government or contract stuff. Boring, but necessary, I guess. My Crew and I had no prosthetics, but because of yours truly, we had pads that were infinitely more versatile than the ones regular folks used.

While at the Pratt Center, I stumbled upon an old website that used ancient HTML, hosted on a server in Bellingham. The site mentioned something about Bangarang, a popular song by Skrillex in the early 21st. What was more interesting was the logo on the page, which was spot-on the same logo used by Bangarang, the company. The website also mentioned a name, Chad Evans. Chad had created a program that became the base of the Bangarang AI. But his creation was originally a helper app he called the Pan. As it sussed out, Pan and Bangarang were the same base code, forked about the same time as the theft in the Cloud. As I studied about the Pan, I used it as a model for vulnerability (backdoors) in my Bangarang exploit. When I dug a bit more, I indeed found a backdoor to the service. I headed home and meandered a bit, taking in the scenery.

Back home I resumed my work. My Dad, Vicky, came up to check on me.

"Hey buddy. Come down to the lab. We have fresh cookies!"

I lied, "No Pop, I gotta finish my homework. Thanks though."

"Really? Cookies are always a clencher with you," sotto voce he mumbled, "Didn't expect that…"

That was my invite to quip something tarty, "Nobody expects the Spanish Inquisition."

His rejoinder was prompt as ever, "Well, be that way, you quarter-witted son of a cabbage hunter!"

We had a laugh and he crushed me in a hug and left. I knew he could instantly find out if I was lying, but he knew I needed my cave time. I went back to thinking about Chad Evans and who he really was. What was Chad like? Did he have a good life? Was he like me, aloof from everyone most of the time? What happened to him?

In one of Chad's remark sections, he mentioned a cache of code resources which he hid inside a stone figurine. I wasn't sure what that meant. He went on to say a fellow named Curtis Crouton, an adviser at his community center told him to save an offline copy of his work. Crouton, like a toasted bread square condiment in salads? I read on, thinking Condiment Man…or should it be Old Crust? Hah! Old Crust was one of the community mentors and was aware of Chad's development efforts. He told him he needed to save his original code away from prying eyes and that meant hiding an archival USB stick somewhere safe. Chad had an off-color joke about that. Good laugh. The USB sticks would be jammed into four rock statues. Chad did it, despite not knowing why his mentor would suggest such a thing. He archived his codebase into four parts and included the private key used as a backdoor to his Pan project. There was a copy of the key on this website. No security whatsoever. That key was my 'winner, winner chicken dinner' moment! Excited, I tried the exploit against Bangarang, using the key and it worked like a charm! I hacked the old website and removed the key. No reason to leave something that valuable in plain sight.

After my excitement, I read a final comment from Chad. He said Curtis was an alien, but no one would believe him. He wrote that Curtis took four rocks and put a USB key into each and said he would hide them away until it was time. The alleged alien said another person just like Chad in the future would need his code. Hmm, wonder who that might be?

A noise at my window sounded like a cat scratching. Nope, not a cat. A moment later Binky came rolling into the room. She was talking a mile a minute to Cricket, who came through the window behind her. He loomed like Lurch from the Addams family just as Binky flitted like Tinkerbell. Her flitting could be annoying.

I expected one more addition to the party, "Hey B, where is Wogs?"

She ignored my comment, "Hey blockhead, your window was hard to open. I mean come on; if you can't leave your window unlocked for your buddies, what's this world coming to?"

Binky often called me some random name variation based on Kip or Charles. She felt my nickname Kip was boring. Well, that was her opinion, anyway.

"Hey buddy!" Binky tapped the side of my head, "Wakee wakee, little man! Where is your head?" Then Wogs came through my door, apparently taking the more sensible route. She had picked up a donut from the kitchen on her way up.

My three friends, my Crew copped a squat on my floor.

Cricket laughed," Little man, he, he…hey, do you have the new patch for Grimm's World?"

I rolled my eyes, "Nope. It's not approved for public use. You'd know that if you read the release notes. You'd get booted the moment you went Online."

Cricket grimaced.

"It's shady code, dude. It's not meant for public use, perhaps ever," I wouldn't expect my Crew to know about these kinds of details. "Well, unapproved patches, add-ons and sandbox features can cause the Online host to boot you from a game instance. Some illegal mods can get you banned from the platform forever." I spewed out the explanation as quickly as I could but she were already bored of me.

"Kipman! Enough with the deets, you don't need to read us an essay! Something more important has come up. All our accounts have been given 30-day probation in SimVerse and we need to know what is going on," Binky gave her famously intense level-stare. Cricket smiled because he knew what was coming next.

Wogs took out her ukulele and did her usual: she played a tune by her patron deity, Jake Shimabukuro. Cricket took out his mouth harp and began plucking along. It was like having a personal soundtrack while Binky was on a tear. Did he think Binky would magically be soothed? Nope, not in the least. This late at night I liked things quiet. Binky was loud and I was getting a headache.

Binky kept staring at me. I always got nervous under Binky's glare. Speaking rapidly, I explained the probation process and possible sources, "Let's take a look at your UserGUID and see its OpStatus," I opened my dynamic text editor and words and numbers rolled onto the page. As I typed my mind went back to Chad Evans and I had a sudden revelation.

I rambled, "Ahhh! Chad never stopped coding, did he? The Pan development continued! He found out about the code theft, but he didn't care, or maybe he created some plan to deal with it. Maybe Old Crust helped him keep his best code from theft. Was there more than one Pan?" When I got busy thinking, I always got a glazed-eyed expression. Binky would have none of it.

"Hey! Hey, Kipper, yo!" Binky was snapping her fingers in my ear, "You need to get your head in the game! Who is Chad? Wait, forget that. Tell me why my account is on probation."

I understood. Binky was a world ranked PVP gamer and probation threatened her livelihood. I mused about the Alien movies. Ripley was such a bad@ss! It's why Binky used the handle of @Ripley. Ellen Ripley was her patron saint. I kept digging, meanwhile my Crew was getting into their song and making far too much noise for the wee hours. I was surprised my Dads didn't come bust us.

Online gaming was fun, but we had at least as much fun making music together. My Dads had forced me to take piano lessons for years. One day Binky came over and picked up one of my Dads' guitars. She chose the Martin Backpacker electric: smart choice, and great sound. She would quietly follow the notes I played on piano, using a Willie Nelson guitar chord book to help. Eventually her skill with guitar greatly surpassed my piano skill. Then she asked to join us in piano lessons. Soon she was better at piano than I'd ever be. Before we were in our teen years, Binky invited Wogs and Cricket to join us. Our parents bought instruments for all of us. Wogs loved the ukulele and played mandolin like her idol, Marty Stewart. Cricket got a mouth harp but really caught his stride on bass and percussion. It would be revealing to you what music genres we each preferred. Binky's favorite album of all time was Symphony & Metallica. Ludwig Von Beethoven, Marty Stewart, and Jake Shimabukuro were Wogs' favorite musical inspirations. She said Beethoven revolutionized music, Marty played the mandolin like most people walked their dog and Jake was smooth and lyrical. All our synth friends loved listening to our band practice in the afternoons. My Dads, less so. They installed us in the detached garage for band practice.

Cricket was true to his roots and didn't 'get above his raisin'. He loved Johnny Cash, Merle Haggard, Willie Nelson, and the whole country genre. Can you guess what I liked? Ok, let me tee this up for you. I enjoyed a phat bassline with poppin' lyrics. Can ya guess? I loved Techno, Rap, Crunk, and Ska, from the 20th. My personal life theme is Still Dre. Here is me, getting down with my bad self, like a madman keeping it cool and banging out to my Crew. I looked more like a skinny Steve Urkel in my teen years (sad, not Denzel), but Dre helped me recast my self-image into something more honest to my nature. I know I wasn't even remotely cool. But I sure tried. I was aware that I was a poseur. I had never been exposed to the mean streets and was raised in relative luxury. But my heart still cried out to my African (and Incan) roots, anyway. Thanks Snoop Dogg!

Let's take a beat and catch up a bit. First, SimVerse evolved from Paradiso, an open universe virtual reality platform. You see, back in the early-22nd all the software and tech companies were consolidated under one of the Big 3 conglomerates and installed into the various CENTERS around the world. After the Tech Wars, CENTERs were built as neutral ground for research and development for all the sovereign Powers on the globe. Eventually, new fledgling businesses sprang up outside the CENTERs and one such was the Spanish company, Paradiso. Paradiso did for Online what computers did for people. It gave you new capabilities, a method of escape and a way to expand your mind. Wade Watts would recognize Paradiso as a version of Gregarious Games, with the paramount genius of James Halliday and Ogden Morrow embodied in two visionary women: Madrid natives, Antonia Lovelace, and Graciela Hopper. Online was a place for people to retreat from reality, and Paradiso was the vehicle. Then it became an everyday reality, and some feared it was the ultimate opiate for the masses. At the start it was about recreation and doing things, but Paradiso came alive when fantasy became identity. People wondered if it would sink or float the human race. Highly immersive and direct-compute interfaces failed for decades, with all early implementations resulting in seizure, hallucination or suicide. It was the sex industry more than the military establishment that brought safe human-to-synth interfacing. But it was the gaming industry that took the interfacing to increasing heights. Paradiso became the place people would jack into and live large portions of their lives.

Paradiso eventually was bought out and became SimVerse. It had become the default platform for most Online gaming and Online simulation space. Each developer would create a world or worlds which were the expressions of their games or simulation instance in the SimVerse. Some worlds were native, meaning you could fly a ship, broom, car, roller skates, or whatever, through virtual space to that world and it would appear like a planet on which you could land. Non-native worlds were connected to SimVerse by portals.

In the 22nd century inexpensive full-body haptic rigs were in common use. Only corporate and military people used direct-connect rigs for Online interfacing. Serious gamers didn't use haptic rigs because they were too slow. In PvP competition, speed is everything. Speed with precision. Full body movements are clunky, and nothing replaces a keyboard and handheld controllers for speed and precision.

Now we are back to it: Online services come at a cost. There are rules. And when you break rules and get caught, you pay penalties.

When on probation in SimVerse, you could not play PvP in SimVerse (native) or rack up SimVerse XP in native Worlds. Probation was torture for hardcore gamers like Binky.

I started my crawler discovery; I used a simple version of my SimDetective app. I sent the little bug crawling up the chains. Within a few seconds I got results. I read aloud, then, "So... hmm, it looks like Bangarang thinks you improperly accessed a hack called, uhh, some huge alpha-numeric name I can't read. But, I can tell you any hacks are almost always grounds for probation. If you get caught modding your persona with unlicensed or unregistered components or features, you get a yellow flag: that means probation, for 30 days."

"But wait, let's see if we can get a shake-down on this weird hack," I added some lines of instruction to SimDetective, and re-ran the process. A couple minutes later, something useful emerged, "Righty-o then. It looks like there are several thousand PvPers who have been put on probation for the same hack.

"A butt load of people are screaming about their accounts and we are going to get to the bottom of why."

I was wearied of this search, "My account was banned and yours was given probation. I am so tired of this..."

Come to find out, that Bangarang, or whomever pulls the strings was culling the herd for a big PvP tournament coming up next month. At least it seemed that way. One thing all the accounts on probation had in common was higher than average PvP scores. I wonder if they were trying to disguise illegal action against the highest scoring PvP players? Was someone rigging the competition? If so, why? Bangarang should have more subtle ways to kill off unwanted competitors if the powers-that-be wanted to screw things up. In several places there was mention of 024. What it looked like was a huge search program. Who were they searching for? Later I would find out they somehow knew about the 'kids' from 024, the four of us, and they expected we would be the only ones who would have the skill to forcibly remove our probation. The only thing that saved us at that time was a local emergency that put us on the run.

What they didn't understand was all the accounts being mysteriously reinstated all at once. Eventually I was able to remove the blocking status to all the probationary and banned accounts. I also implanted a 2-part worm, versions of my Creeper and Reaper AI, that would keep the system admin distracted from figuring out why all the accounts were suddenly active again. Score one for the good guys!

"Guys, soon we need to go on a roadtrip," Cricket and Binky hooted, thinking that 'the brain' had come up with a plan to restore their accounts. If they only knew their accounts were about to show as active in a moment. Insert some kind of smiley face, here. I walked into the dayroom next door to my bedroom and admired my Warhammer 40K ancient tabletop set. You probably wonder why I seem to be such an ancient gaming buff. It's simple: I was rummaging around in my family's huge attic and one day found a giant, ugly chest mouldering in the corner, collecting dust. I took it upon myself to crack it open and investigate the contents. I discovered a treasure trove of gaming antiquity. There was computer gear, lots of franchise figurines and even a few cosplay weapons and trinkets. That discovery was three years ago, when I was 11. Since then, I had fallen in love with the music, the art, old computers and especially the games of the 20th and early 21st centuries. I even found a 1st edition of Cline's Ready Player One! Wade Watts became my instant best hero. I put on my Star Blazers backpack and ran out the door.

"So, brainiac, where are we going," me and my cabal were riding bikes down the street, toward downtown Lake Stevens.

I yelled back at them, "The Pratt Center has public computers."

As we rode away from the house, we didn't notice a dark and mysterious character lurking in the bushes, across the street. But our neighbor Mrs. Choi sure noticed, "Hey, what you doing? Get hell out of my bushes, weirdo!"

The shadowy figure pretended not to notice Mrs. Choi. Very bad move. Mrs. Choi could easily be mistaken for the end-boss on a SimVerse MMO; she was fearsome. Off came a slipper and she chucked it at Mr. Shadow's head, with a resounding thump. Whoever he was, he could feel pain. Mrs. Choi was a simmering pot of Korean anger and she thoroughly kicked Mr. Shadow's butt. He hunched over and started running. But an odd thing happened. A moment later he faded from view like he was a holo that turned off. Mrs. Choi kept yelling.

"Jen-jang, you stupid! Domangchida babo or I hit you with the other shoe!" Mrs. Choi looked surprised that the guy vanished but kept swearing toward the empty air. Eventually her ire quelled, and she went back to her house.

Lake Stevens had grown into a city of 500K since the 21st and the most popular kid hangout was a place called Tiamat's. The Pratt Center was just a block away so I had Binky and Cricket hang out at Tiamat's, so they wouldn't be seen with me if something went south. You see, Bangarang had a way of dealing badly with hackers. I was about to try logging in on a public computer to find out more about the mass account probation. I headed over to the Pratt Center, named for the father of a famous actor in the 21st. The place was a cross between an old school library and gymnasium. Four floors of absolute athletic chaos with kids of all ages and one floor shielded and silent as a church mouse. You can imagine where I went. Yep, church mouse. As I walked past the service desk, I looked down and saw an old book entitled "Darles Chickens: Matilda's Classic Recipes," Darles? Somehow that seemed familiar, yet not at all. I was in.

The Pratt Center had never modernized with surveillance, so my computer indiscretions would not be caught on candid camera. Logging into one of the library computers, I opened a shell session on my resource server and copied scripts locally. I set the scripts to running and results poured in. One bit of data popped on the screen before a firewall guardian cut off the data scour.

"Ahh, yes! Ok, it looks like someone named Admin has been involved in the Bangarang policy updates. Well, that's not very informative."

I noted there was lat/long metadata from a post by Admin and saw it came from a location in Seattle, Washington.

"Welly well, Admin, we have been a very naughty boy!"

I shut down all my processes, scrubbed the cache and deleted files and all traces of my presence. I had what I needed. As I exited the Pratt Center, several unmarked security units rolled up to the front door. How did they catch on so fast? Were they waiting for me? I pretended to be more interested in my pad. All eyes were on me, but I hoped lack of eye contact would slow their roll. I was credulous that they knew it was me. But I needed to play it safe, so I turned casually around and went back into the Center. Once inside, I turned a corner, then sprinted for the back exit. Uh oh, too late, I could see another security vehicle pulling up there too. The security goons wore the compulsory black with no markings or patches. Hmm, probably hired by Bangarang. Turning again, I ran full out, heading downstairs to the Mosh Pit. The Mosh Pit was originally just a dance club but had evolved into a vintage punk rock hangout. I slid through the press of people, past tables, and partitions, into the hallway toward the bathrooms. No one was dancing during the day, but the tunes were turned up to 11 and the emcee was crackin' through a Billy Idol song. 'Dancin' with Myself' was vibrating the walls and hopefully would provide a bit of cover for me as I made my escape.

Thankfully, the maintenance closet was unlocked. It usually was. It was the key destination for kids who wanted some alone time with each other. But the closet served another secret purpose. A cloud of pot smoke roiled out as I opened the closet door. Weirdly, no one was in there. I knelt and opened the ventilation grating at the rearmost part of the little room. The smell of wet mops, old cleanser and thick cannabis smoke saturated my sinuses. I climbed into the duct and closed the grill behind me.

I called out softly, "Cheri...hey, Cheri?"

After a pause, a cherubic voice replied, "Come in, Mr. Whiffer."

Why did everyone around me have to do something screwy to my name. It's Charles Winton Wefer, not Wanton Whiffer! Geez!

"Mr. Whiffer, hope you pulled the panel full shut? There are unwanted guests in the house above, which I am sure you must be aware of."

After I crawled 20 feet to her (lair?) I stood and dusted off. Looking around, I found myself transported into a 20th century treasure trove. Movie and game posters lined the walls, and memorabilia from two centuries-past adorned every vertical surface of the underground lab. No less than ten large screens were running live news streams, cooking shows, music lessons, coding advice and nature scenes. It was busy down here!

"Did you bring me those baby clothes?" Cheri was bent over her desk with a large lamp shining way too brightly on something she was working on. That something seemed to be wriggling on the desk and even evaded her grasp and tried to run. She brought a bucket down, trapping the small (person?). Panting, Cheri looked back.

"Come on, let's see the clothing!"

I pulled a plastic bag from my pack and handed it to her.

"Ah, yes, thank you. Please sit."

Cheri pulled out the shirts, pants, socks, and the little hat. I thought a vintage LA Dodgers hat was a nice touch.

"Mister Whiffer, you have outdone yourself, thank you!" Cheri reached out, handing me a wriggling bundle of blanket.

"Here. Do not drop it."

The blanket kept moving and as I cradled the bundle, a little face peeked out of the folds. "Whoa, Cher, who is this?"

"Allow me to introduce you to Pooka, the latest addition to my family," Cheri beamed like I had never seen before. Normally, she was overflowing with scathing comments and veiled threats to the powers-that-be. Today, she had gone full-on doting mama. She stood and took Pooka back.

"Mr. Whiffer, this little person is something the world hasn't seen for millennia. This is a Nisse, as the Norwegians called them; a woodland gnome."

"The nano-constructors have been building the base DNA for Pooka over the last 6 months. Why do you think I have been so testy lately? I've been expecting!"

I looked credulous, "Cheri, you're always testy, are you kidding?"

Pooka? I like that name! My Knight, Sir Pooka was going to be jelly! In fact, he would probably demand a tribute of some sort for the name use.

"Hush now, or you'll scare the baby," she hummed a faint tune to the small creature, "Do-re-mi…" and I recognized a classic.

"So…now you come visiting at completely the wrong time. I bet you're caught up in some espionage thing with that Bangarang group. Am I right?"

I had the decency to appear remorseful.

"Yeah, you're right, as always. But it's for a good purpose. You remember Chad Evans and his Pan app? I found out the same people who stole his code also created the Bangarang AI they use now."

Cheri walked to the other side of the table, picked up a bottle and began feeding the (baby?).

"I told you digging too deep would get you in trouble. Rich people don't like peons threatening their livelihood. And you, my friend are a threat."

I didn't disagree, but I never thought of myself as a peon. Maybe a high-performing peon? I don't know, perhaps I would get us all killed. I paused for a moment, then a rush of air and a triple whump sound heralded the arrival of Cricket, Binky, and Wogs.

"It was hell getting past those Bang-a-goons, Kipper!"

The three of them started chattering at the same time, until Cheri broke them up.

"Slow down people! You have picked the worse time to make a social call. First, everyone shut up or we'll be found-out, right quick!"

"Cheri, Pooka is a hybrid, right?"

I realized the answer as I asked the question. I think I was asking her more to let the others know that our dear friend, the mad scientist, was at it, again. Allow me to elaborate. Cheryl Ann Cooper was in every sense a mad scientist. Mad, as in bat-poop crazy and one of the smartest people I had ever met. Cheryl was born to an abusive father and absent mother. Everything she did in life sprang from that bitter root. But, in Cheryl's case that bitter root also produced an evolutionary product: new life. You see, Cheryl, or Cheri as we call her, was a savant of sorts. My father Charles met her while working for Bad Wolf, at Seattle:CENTER. They created new forms of life. Literally, they were creating living creatures, for the military. Dad didn't talk much about it. But one evening, when he was imbibing a bit too much with my other Dad, Vicky, he mentioned some fantastical things, like flying spiders and flying snakes. I loved it!

Chapter 4 – SEND IN THE DRONES

RETRO - December 2232 – Seattle:CENTER, Dupont, Washington

Christmas was coming and the Dads had prepared for their festivity circuit. Every year the Rudolph Riders would mount up on flying synth reindeer and visit the children's hospital wards in the Pacific Northwest. Vicky rode on Rudolph, dressed as Yukon Cornelius, Charles was dressed as Hermey, the Misfit Elf. The eight ensemble singers would don one of the canon characters and they even had a synth playing the part of King Moonracer. They would begin on December 23rd, visiting hundreds of sick children in Portland, Tacoma, Seattle, Everett, Friday Harbor, Bellingham, Vancouver, and other places. Their tour would finish the evening of the 25th after which they would high-tail it back home to have some well-earned rest.

On the day after Christmas, the Dads sat in their cafeteria musing over coffee.

"When Cher dropped that tray full of instruments, Blender caught it all…and her. I am concerned at the capabilities we're playing with. Our synths have been highly capable since the beginning. But now our hybrids are catching up."

Vicky had a concerned look.

Charles replied, "Vick, we both know who we're developing for. I think our plan for a functional backdoor like we use with the synths is our best safeguard."

"Agreed. It's just that Croatoan's suggestion was so unusual. I mean, dance. Really? Wouldn't it be more effective to have some kind of methyl juicer that would activate on a keyword and kill the hybrid in its tracks?"

Vicky noticed a young couple headed their way.

Charles saw them, "I think his suggestion was the most humane. Having hardwired dance as a method of combat when formally challenged would distract instead of kill."

"Hey Dads! Dr. Boshaw, Dr. Wefer, this is my bride-to-be, Dr. Gjerta Jensen. She used to work for Dr. Wilbert Gotobed in Stockholm:CENTER."

Both men stood and shook hands.

"David, good to see you in fine form, sporting your orange and green! Gjerta. Dr. Jensen, welcome to the team. You must be the phenom Subramanian was raving about." Vicky was always very gracious. What a ham.

"Thank you, Dr. Boshaw. I spent three years with Dr. Subramanian then got an invite from Dr. Gotobed to explore synthetic integration with his hybrids. After 18 months I have learned an incredible amount. I hope to be an asset to your team." Gjerta was clearly starstruck speaking to my Dads.

"Please sit. We were just discussing some concerns. I'd love to have your insights," Charles invited them to sit.

"Gjerta, we are all on first name basis here. Please call me Vicky and this is my partner, Charles. You can also call him Chuck," Vicky gave a smile and Charles waved.

"So Gjerta, we have a division of our business here that creates synth and hybrid soldiers. We are concerned about what we are doing to the extent that we have built secret backdoors into all our creations. I wanted to ask you how you might do such a thing with hybrids. A backdoor, that is, to disable or redirect the creature."

Gjerta chewed her lip then started softly, "Biologics are harder to program than synthetics. If I had to shoot from the hip on this, and I guess I am, I would explore a failsafe that would lower adrenal activity to a resting state level. It would be wasteful to kill them."

The four spent an hour discussing possible kill switches, use of bots to slow down or stop a rogue biological.

The Dads liked Gjerta. She cared about people, human and otherwise. Vicky could tell that Charles had already earmarked her for the conversation. David S. Pumpkins and Gjerta Jensen were a great pairing. Now if they could only get him to wear something other than Halloween orange.

"You know Vick, I love our job. We have so many paramount capable folks working for us, it leaves us time to socialize with our newcomers. By the way, what is Wilbert Gotobed calling himself these days?"

"Pastor Bedtime. Don't ask me why. I'm just glad we fobbed him off to his own thing. The man is cruel and perfect for CENTER research." Vicky pulled a moue.

Charles agreed, "The sad thing is all the test subjects he took with him like his personal chattel. Do you think there is anything we can do for those poor creatures?"

"Yep. Already did. Remember his project with the hybrid military leader?" Charles nodded, "…the subject he named Cicero. Top notch intellect, that one. Well, I did a thing."

Vicky continued, "Just before we exited Gotobed's place, I surreptitiously implanted a WerkBot blend into Cicero and the other hybrids via Gotobed's main console. I hope it does the trick. The payload included memories of you and I, helping them and a plethora of memories on escape and evasion and other helpful things. I see you nodding. You're right, I used my secret sauce. Do you think I should name it something more friendly than AN/TPQ-36?"

"Vick, that's what I was telling you before. We need to have descriptive names, but not ones that arouse suspicion. Maybe call it AdLib?"

"Ah, that sounds good." Vicky tapped on his pad then put it back on the table, "Done. Good call, my sweet man."

The men sat in silence for a while, then Vicky brought hot cocoa back to the table. He poured lazy brown liquid from a flask into both mugs. "Hey Chuck, what's up with Ozzie?"

"Ozzie." Charles looked down and clearly was sad. "He's gone."

He took a big tug on the spiked cocoa and continued, "When Ozzie and Squaddie were competing on the evasion/escape course, Squaddie tripped on a landmine. The landmine didn't explode, and Ozzie came back to see Squaddie sitting on the mine. Ozzie, crinkled up his face, threw a rock at Squaddie's feet, triggering an explosion. Later, Ozzie crossed the finish line and looked around for the reward for successful completion. We already knew Ozzie was a budding sociopath. Ozzie didn't seem to have any regret, nor did he miss Squaddie. In fact, he asked when he would get another playmate," Charles stared at the table, looking sad. He knew there was a price paid for working for the bad guys and Bad Wolf was appropriately named.

"I'm so sorry Chuck. I know he was your favorite," Vicky patted his hand.

"The worse news is upon hearing the report of Ozzie's actions, a squad of military types came in with orders to take Ozzie, immediately. That was a few hours ago. Since then, the rumor is circulating the military wants 50 more just like Ozzie. I told them the risks but in fine form the G-men just gave a blank look and took Ozzie and the research data. I made sure they didn't find the final sequencing spec."

October 2252 – Lake Stevens, Washington, CSA

"Pooka is based on the sequencing used for a hybrid named Ozzie, combined with the hopeful genetic material discovered in a Slovenian archaeological dig. I suspect the biological mass is from an extinct Nisse, if the notes were correct," Cheri could see my horrified look. I knew the problem with using the DNA from that sociopath, Ozzie. My Dads had mentioned him before.

"Sometimes there are only bad choices. But, still, a choice needed to be made. Ozzie was my choice for reasons. I'm not going to explain myself to you."

Cheri was her usual snippy self. As I ensconced myself on a barstool, Pooka started to lightly snore. I recalled the moment I named my own AI, Pooka. I was sitting at the kitchen table having dinner with my Dads and several of their colleagues. I heard the name Pooka mentioned and I liked the name. I decided I would use it for one of my projects. Come to think of it, they were probably talking about the very same Pooka that I was holding now. I liked this new Pooka. It was then my little pea brain began imagining my own Pooka installed in a synth husk. Then I would have a friend just like J.F. Home again, home again, jiggety jig!

An explosion above rocked the building; fine dust sifted down from the ceiling. A faint buzzing sound could be heard.

I jumped up from the barstool, "Cher, they've sent in the drones!"

Cheri smirked, "Isn't it rich!"

Pooka jumped to the floor and followed Cheri to the exit the other kids had come through a minute before; that 'baby' could really run!

"Kip, quick, go to the closet and unlink Tyger!"

Ah, yes, don't want to leave Tyger behind. I ran to the large metal vault Cheri called a closet. When my Dads setup this hidey hole for Cheri disguised as the new Pratt Center, they made sure she could properly secure her more, hazardous creations. I dialed the lock, 16-34-5, applied my thumbprint (my father had no idea I had access), and pulled the heavy door open. I went to the charging cabinet and unlinked Tyger. Its eyes popped open, and it jumped into my arms, showering me with hugs, purring. So, dig this: a ninety-pound monkey, strong enough to flip a car over, jumping on you...yeah, you get it. Love is sometimes painful.

Tyger was a new generation of synth and a member of our family. It was one of the latest creations of my Dads. He was here for safekeeping. Tyger looked like a cat-monkey, for the moment. The appearance would change depending on its mood.

"Hey Tyger, some bad guys are hunting us. Can you do the lock down routine?"

That was one operation I didn't know about Cheri's bunker: emergency lock down. But Tyger knew. I headed out the exit and paused. Tyger ran around punching buttons and moving things.

"Kids, listen!"

We all got quiet and realized the bad guys had found the secret lair. Lair, lab, same difference. But what they didn't know was this lab was surrounded by a massive warren, designed to confuse people. We knew we needed to lead these soldiers away from the lab's more sensitive areas, at least until Tyger finished its work. We used to play for hours and days in the warrens and catacombs; hide and seek and chase games and hidden caches of snacks. Me and my Crew swung into action. Pooka crawled into Cricket's backpack. Tyger sneezed and suddenly the air was filled with microscopic drones. Then three duplicates of Tyger came bounding out of a wall locker. These were beta models. With a smile we agreed to meet back at the lab in 15 minutes. It was time to play the game of Follow Me. You know those movies where multiple people are running around between rooms and corridors, in comedic mayhem of 'catch me if you can'? That was the plan. We knew these vents, passageways, and every room. The bad guys had guns, but we knew they were only allowed non-lethal ammo. We had a bunch of surprises for them. There was a vast array of Grimtooth's Traps ready to be triggered!

A huge crash sounded, and the game was afoot; one of the traps was already triggered. A consortium of CrabBots scuttled between our legs into the hallway. As they disbursed, we followed. The trick would be to briefly come within sight of the soldiers, then lead them on a goose chase. We split up.

As I came around a corner, I saw 3 soldiers swatting a cloud of SquitoDrones; these drones would swarm around a target and inject NanoBots or poison to disable a person. This time, they injected a neural stimulant which caused intense itching. The soldiers were looking for perps and I gave them a reason to follow me.

"Hey douchbags! I put your Mom's panty pics Online just now. She looks like a scruffy nerf herder!"

They came running and I took off. I laughed and they followed. They danced as much as they ran, scratching the itchiness which must have been torture.

"Hey kid come back here!"

They gave chase and with each turn I gave them a brief view of where I was headed. I ran across the floor of one of the warehouses. I crossed paths with Binky. In the confusion of the chase her soldiers followed me and mine followed her.

We crossed each other's paths multiple times. These soldiers were doing their best Keystone Cops impression. Another crash sounded in the distance, like a large rolling metal ball. It was the Roman Amphitheater Trap. I heard a giggle and whoop. Binky had scored first. Moments later a huge whump sound was followed by a shout. That was Wogs with the Last Laugh Trap where the floor flips like a see-saw, sending the soldiers sliding down a tube toward a sewer exit. The sound of a massive rockfall meant that Cricket had triggered the Rock and a Hard Place Trap. Faint sounds of men falling could be heard, followed by a rock cap over the trap requiring the soldiers to follow the sewer line to escape the pit.

You might ask if these traps were killing these guys. Probably not. My Dads had set these up as deterrents only. These guys would be crawling away looking for band aids soon enough. After a couple more crashes, whumps and laughter, the chases around the warren were over. We met back at the lab with several minutes to spare. Tyger triggered the concrete-steel doors which would hide the lab from prying eyes.

A few seconds later Tyger shifted to his Dobby the Elf appearance and followed me down one of the culvert corridors leading toward the lake. When I caught up to Cheri and the others, they were standing below the vertical exit. Pooka poked out of Cricket's backpack and jumped onto Tyger's back.

Wogs climbed up the ladder rungs, twisted the big wheel door lock and slowly peeked out the hatch, "I can see the drones. There's a huge cloud around Pratt. Hold on for a sec." Wogs opened the hatch fully and climbed out. She poked her face back down, "Come on, they have no idea we're here!"

June 2250 – Flashback Discovery – Lake Stevens, Washington, CSA

Isn't it amazing how much kids find out, especially when parents go to extraordinary lengths to conceal facts and truths? I guess you've figured out I am nosy. Well, I am also bad at keeping secrets from my friends.

The day I found a secret entrance to the Pratt Center, a RabbitBot was skulking about. It was the very exit out of which Wogs was poking her head.

I whispered, "Here, rabbit, rabbit," I sounded like an idiot.

All I saw initially was a large culvert. I got suspicious when the rabbit spoke; then I knew it was not a hybrid. The RabbitBot loped over and in a fine Cockney accent said, "Dr. Boshaw, is everything okay?"

It paused, canted its head, and continued, "The exit is secure. Thlayli, reporting as day sentry. All Skooma addicts have been removed from the area as requested."

Cool, this bot thought I was my father. How fortuitous. With this discovery, my plans to go fishing fell through.

"Thlayli, who is the night sentry?"

"Dr. Boshaw, a rotating shift for night sentry falls to Hazel, Fiver and Holly, as you specified."

Those names sounded familiar. Later, I would recall these were the names of rabbits from Watership Down.

"Thlayli, show me back to your warren."

It seemed like a good request. But it almost got me killed. Thlayli opened the hatch with very human-looking hands and hopped down the chute. I followed. As I walked the culvert tunnel, I felt a tug against my legs; I looked down and saw a small wire, tautly straining against my thighs, high enough the RabbitBots would pass safely underneath. I carefully backed up and stared at the thin wire. Later my Dads removed all snares to avoid killing us kids.

"Doctor, why do you play with the tripwire? Stop it! You will die, and you won't get cake!"

A phrase echoed in my head, 'the cake is a lie'. I carefully stepped over the wire and followed Thlayli. The walls were covered with posters. They triggered my memories of playing Half-Life and Portal. The posters were faux warning signs and scrawlings: 'GLaDOS was here', 'Still Alive!', 'Watch for Antlions!', 'Wheatley is the Man on the Moon', 'Gordon Freeman was here' and more.

Thlayli brought me into the bunker and that is where I first met Cheri. I will never forget the sight of the woman traipsing around in her underwear. She danced from table to table, checking on her work and initially didn't notice me.

"Cheri, Cheri, Dr. Boshaw comes!" Thlayli announced my presence, and my first instinct was to run away. Curiosity kept me planted. Or was it fear?

"Rabbit, hush. I am cooking up a very sensitive brew. Now, go to your box and you'll find a surprise."

"Surprise? Thlayli has a surprise?" the bot lost its Cockney accent.

"I told you to stop that! Speaking about yourself in the third person gives me the creeps. Kind of like Norman Bates or something. ...go on now, take a look!"

Thlayli was bouncing like a ball, doing a ricochet dance, off horizontal and vertical surfaces, "Surprise, surprise, I have a surprise!"

I noticed the RabbitBot didn't disturb any of the dozens of glass beakers and equipment in its excitement. Thlayli disappeared into a large cabinet. A moment later, Thlayli came over to me bearing a shiny glass ball, holding it up for me to see.

"Dr. Boshaw, I have my very own word ball!"

It was at that moment that Cheri's head swiveled around like an owl's. Was she a hybrid? Hmm, no feathers, but my ruminations were interrupted by a scream.

"Guests are not allowed! Get out!"

Cheri came at me fast, underwear and all. It was a frightening sight. I turned, caught my foot on something and fell in a heap. I looked up at an angry old lady who was revealing far too much anatomy for my comfort.

"S -s -sorry, I just followed the rabb-..." I paused a moment, realizing I was going to say it. Now, tell me, was it going to be a Matrix or Wonderland reference? "- the rabbit down the hole!" I must have had an odd expression on my face. As the old lady bent over peering closely, scrutinizing me, she suddenly burst into laughter.

"Oh, my stars and gardens, you look just like your father when he spilled DestructorBots on his synth, Johnny Cab. That little guy sure ran around fast as the bots began eating him alive! So much for your Dad's plan for a smart vehicle."

For a moment, Cheri got wistful, then she re-focused, sternly.

"Charles Winton Wefer -" this was the only time she pronounced my name correctly. Ever after, I was Mr. Whiffer. Worse, Cheri was a bad influence on my little cabal. They all followed suit with more weird names, " -you have some explaining to do. How did you get in here?"

I explained. Sitting on a lab stool, Cheri handed me a mug of hot chocolate. I chose to pretend the mad scientist lady who lives in a la-bor-a-tory (think creepy films noir from the 20th) is not feeding me some deadly concoction.

"Mr. Whiffer -", yep, there it went, " -your timing couldn't be better. I have a need and you will fill that need or I will tell your father his carefully guarded secret is no longer a secret. Ok?"

Great, blackmail is quite a motivator. I temporized and nodded, "How do you know my Dads?"

"Young man, we worked together, long ago. When hard times came upon us, Charles and Victor built this sprawling bunker right under the new wing of Pratt's. A bit of hiding in plain sight." She kept herself busy as she spoke.

"Your father has a perverse sense of humor. To protect our secret lair, he originally set little amphibious creatures to guard the lake entrance. He called them Murlocs." She gave me a wink and I wasn't sure if she was serious or not. Murlocs were the amphibious cute but deadly little creatures from the Warcraft franchise. After the Tech Wars all games development got absorbed by one of the CENTERs. Separate from the CENTERs, the game is alive and well today as a part of the Warcraft Verse, federated into SimVerse, Online.

Cheri suddenly jerked and realized something.

"We have to save the tale for another time. Now, grab this bag and follow me," we went back out the lake entrance. I spent an hour slogging on the Lake Stevens shoreline as Cheri dug around, sometimes shoulder-deep in the clinging mud. She was looking for SensorBots.

That was my introduction to Cheri, with mud, hot chocolate, and a snarky running narrative.

"Mr. Whiffer, look up the embankment," then I noticed my father Charles coming down the slope with a wry smile on his face and a slowly shaking head. Well, the cat was out of the bag.

October 2252 – Lake Stevens, Washington, CSA

We ran from the lake, not bothering to meander back to my place. Cheri reached for the kitchen door, and it swung open, with Vicky looking grim. Cheri had been non-stop chatting from the lake to my house.

"I told them time and again not to poke the bear, but now we have it. We are compromised."

Cheri was shaking her head as she spoke to no one in general.

My Dad, Charles, gathered us close, "Kids, your parents know you are here, and they know you will be having a sleep-over tonight. The story they heard concerns the 'late-night astronomy project'. I need you to agree right now that you will not contradict this story to outsiders. Your folks know it's code for a 'compromise' emergency involving you kids."

My Dad looked seriously at all of us. Nope, this was not the time to be snarky. We all nodded.

"Now go to the living room and sit. I need to speak with Cheri and Vick before we have our team huddle."

We went to the living room and waited. We waited and then some. My Crew was strangely quiet. All my friends were bright kids; they were bright enough to have full understanding of the gravity of the moment. Bottomline, we didn't want to die in a prison cell. All this trouble from trying to unblock our game accounts. It was our fault…well, my fault.

A long time ago, due process died, and people could be 'disappeared' and question askers might disappear too. We didn't want to be 'disappeared'. Pooka had jumped down and started running around with Tyger. Pooka settled on jumping into Cricket's arms and snuggling in. Tyger took up residence in front of the fireplace. Pooka began to lightly snore.

I heard laughter in the kitchen. That meant it was about to be briefing time. Yep, they were headed our way.

"Ok kids, first order of business is we need to fortify our household defenses," Vicky called out a series of letters and numbers and the house AI replied with 'house secure'.

Dad continued, "As of this moment, we will have to have some tight organization. As you are aware, your families will be captured if our true identities are revealed. The most recent problem has been the exposure Kip created by playing hacker. Now, not only are the eyes of Bangarang and Bad Wolf are upon us, but the CSA as well."

"Dad, um, Dads and Cheri, I would never have caused real problems for us on purpose. When I started investigating-"

Cheri interrupted, shaking her finger at me, making a tsk-tsk sound, "Hacking…" I hung my head for a moment.

"Yeah, you're right, what I was doing was too visible. But you gotta see it from our perspective. Our Online identities are an extension of us. When some company takes away our avatars and identities, we feel, I don't know, kinda broken."

"Son, we do understand. But we, unlike you and your friends have seen the inside of the CENTERs and the way people are treated when the public can't see. So, for the moment, I need all of you to follow my directions to the letter. If we don't work together, we -that is, you, me, your parents, siblings, maybe others will be detained and eventually die in a dirty cold cell. Now, raise your hand if you're in."

Our hands went up immediately. We were all in.

The next two days were filled with a flurry of activity. For our prep time, my Dad Charles put on a playlist from his home country. All the various hidden mobile AIs, bots, synths and hybrids were running and flying around with a purpose I'd never seen before. My house became ground zero of 'La Liberacion'. It seemed my hacking had brought us to a tipping point. I just couldn't get my mind off the possibility that my actions may have led to all my friends dying, or worse. But I needed to follow orders and get my assigned jobs complete. Our house synths were working on assembling several off-grid Online transceivers. Able had his three AssistBots literally orbiting his head. Cortana did much of the spot welding, Alexa would identify and place parts to be welded and Siri would yell at the other two to hurry up.

My father's majordomo, a synth named Roy, was working on the drones. Small drones, large drones, drones for every conceivable purpose. His AssistBots were moving parts, welding, and running wires. Hal Burton ran the wires, Max Headroom welded and soldered, and Dalek was just floating about, holding tools, and repeating the word 'exterminate'. When I went into the kitchen, I saw two Synths who seemed familiar. They were sitting at our big dining table with both my Dads.

"Kip, come here for a moment. It's time you met these gentle-beings. This is Olivaw," the attractive, slim man nodded, "and this is Giskard," the chunky, hairy fellow nodded. "These two delivered you to us right after your birth."

Delivered? Like mail order? What did that mean?

Charles, Dad number one, came over and knelt, "You are our lovely, adopted son. And there is more to chat about. We didn't tell you until now for the simple reason that we felt you weren't ready."

I wasn't ready to speak or even focus my eyes correctly. The men at the table sat quietly and let me gain my bearings.

Charles continued, "When your mother gave birth to you, she left soon thereafter, and you stayed with us to be our son."

My Dads both looked up and I realized our conversation was getting cut short. Vicky and Charles were on their feet; something had changed and not for the better.

"Kip, our timeline has changed. You and the others will leave now. We will catch up to you tomorrow," Vicky was terse, and both my Dads gave me a quick hug and kiss and pointed me out the rear exit.

While I had been busy with my existential crisis, my friends had been outside and about their tasks. Wogs loaded 70-or-so 5-gallon containers onto a flatbed truck. We had a whole loading bay and warehouse behind where I lived from which my Dads sent their supplies to the Liberation. Suddenly, a new face popped in and Wogs froze. Binky, Cricket, Wogs and the synths all paused to look at the new arrival. Mrs. Standish came around the corner. She had a large sheaf of papers and a stern expression.

"Mollie Brown, Monica Brown and Sean Carter, I should have known. You have been absent from school for two days with no excuse. I came to find Dr. Wefer, but lo there do I discover the whole coven of truants, minus the ringleader." She looked around, oblivious to the obvious. We were preparing to leave and not come back.

She continued, "Where is Kip?" A synth stepped forward to meet the Principal. Cave Johnson was Cheri's majordomo; he made sure her labs and logistics were in working order and had just returned from a trip to Rosario and thus missed the Keystone Cops at the lab. I headed outside, like my Dads indicated, in time to witness the Standish standoff. Standish pointed at me, but Cave gave her hand a pat and walked her past me into the house.

"Madam, please come this way."

She complied mutely. Cave could easily pass for human, and he was created to be charismatic. He was a hottie. He really knew how to pour on the charm and Principal Standish was one of the types susceptible to those charms. Two other synths were here to help: Quorra and Bishop were from Bellingham's underground synth community.

Quorra was urgent, "Children, our time has been cut short. Kip, your father instructed us to take you to our Bellingham safehouse if someone should discover our operation here." Quorra was a beautiful synth woman and served the Liberation as a personal guardian for my Dads. Pooka woke up, bounded out of Cricket's arms and ran into the house. What spooked it?

Chapter 5 – RUN AWAY

Lake Stevens, Washington, CSA

"Hey Q, Mrs. Standish won't tell anyone. What's the harm -" Binky was interrupted.

"Binky, you see your Principal's designer glasses? She thinks they're the greatest personal helper device, but I can tell you, it is a privacy-eliminating spy monitor used by Bad Wolf. We have been found out. We leave, now."

Giskard was adamant that we were all in immediate danger. Binky was incredulous but she kept her mouth shut. As we were talking Mr. Shadow made another appearance, lurking just outside the rear gate of our driveway. This time it was Giskard who noticed him. Something fast and unspoken passed between him and Daneel. Daneel took off running toward Mr. Shadow who disappeared around the corner. A minute later Daneel came back.

"Giskard, the intruder vanished."

"What did he look like?" I was really curious who it might be.

"It was hard to see, and I'm not sure it was human. When I said the intruder vanished, I meant to say that as he rounded the turn at the end of the block he or it vanished, as in Star Trek 'beam me up Scotty' version of vanished."

It was funny to hear a synth make a movie reference.

"Time to go!" Giskard was pushing us to get moving.

"Daneel, advise the Dads about what's transpired."

Daneel waved as we loaded into the van. He went into the house. Both my Dads quickly came out to the van with the kind of smiles I usually saw when I was in trouble. My heart beat faster as my Dad, Charles opened the sliding door and my other Dad, Vicky grasped my hand. He stood on the driveway in the midst of the chaos. My Dads were the calm at the middle of the swirl.

"Kip, we wanted more time to share plans with you, but you need to leave immediately, or poor Bishop will blow a gasket."

We laughed. It was a tense laugh.

I started, "Dad…" I felt like when I was little kid and was afraid. "…what are we supposed to do?"

Vicky answered, "Son, The Browns, the Carters and your father and I have been preparing you and your friends for a mission. It's very important for you to understand that your being kids will help the objective. Your youth is to your advantage and your job is to recruit more people to join the Liberation. You will travel to meet with people we want to join us. Your friends will go with you. What we need to know is if you're willing? It will be dangerous."

No hesitation. "Hell yeah! Um, that is yes, I am all in. How do we know where to go and stuff?"

"Charles and I have a master map that will guide you and you will be fed the specifics of the next place each time you finish up the current job. You will have guides along the way and many people know you're coming. A few do not."

Many of the synths were hovering close by, some literally hovering in the air. Daneel was tapping his foot impatiently and Giskard wore a calm expression, as always.

"Okay, I guess I get it. So, I'm adopted, huh?"

"Vicky and I chose your mother to carry you, and we supplied the necessary DNA. You are ours ain every way that matters. But…" Vicky paused as he and Charles cuddled me close, "…you are the most important expression of our love. When things get hard, remember our thoughts are never far from you and our love is always and forever."

Vicky kissed my forehead and spoke quietly, "Charles Winton Wefer, you are the best thing to happen in our lives and just remember our Big Three motto: semper inepta!"

Always silly. My Dads would console me and make me laugh when I got frustrated, when I was growing up. Semper inepta was the saying they used to remined me to not take myself too seriously.

"Dad, what if I lose you?"

I felt their warmth, squeezing my shoulders, touching my cheek. Charles spoke quietly, "Kip, no matter where you find yourself, we will find you."

"You promise?"

Both Dads nodded. There was definitely no one crying. Our eyes were just dealing with some dust, really.

"We promise."

We hugged. For quite a while. Then they closed the van door. I should have been sad or something, but my excitement for adventure just wouldn't allow it. I was going on a road trip! And I trusted my Dads without reservation.

I recalled I still had Online stuff that was vulnerable. Before I lost a reliable connection with Online, I needed to do some things. I hopped Online and activated my OHellNaw routine which secured all my accounts, resources, and server. This also set a pattern in place which had my two AIs, Creeper and Reaper head out into the virtual wildlands to keep a distant watch on all my assets. In the event of a breach, they could take action to keep my stuff safe. Creeper would create tons of false trails and exploding breadcrumbs and Reaper would flick switches to keep things secure. My Dads told us to keep our devices turned off until we reached a safe house. We had already powered down; it was like losing a part of myself to have no Online access.

My friends said their quick bye-byes and off we went. The ride in the back of the van was uneventful and we all were on our pads doing whatever we thought would help us prepare for the mission. I found out Daneel had briefed my friends already. Like me, they were excited to hit the road on an adventure.

Bishop turned to us as we neared the Skagit Speedway, "Bad Wolf has taken the Lake Stevens compound and Bangarang has taken Cheri's lab. We need to stop at the Speedway to make sure we aren't being followed."

Mt. Vernon, Washington, CSA

Our van pulled off I-5 and headed toward the gargantuan arena, just ahead. The Skagit Speedway was enormous. It was one of the raceways used for qualifying for the World Cup of Pit Racing. Just so you know, Pit Racing is dangerous, often lethal if there's a crash and very expensive people bet a lot of money on the races. Do you recall Podraces in Star Wars? They're like that but without the big jet attachments. During a race, the racers must dodge both static and moving obstacles. It's brutal! One time, I saw 5 WeldingDrones attach themselves to an uncareful Pit racer, and he saw his Pit dismantled at 300 kph. The ending was censored from the public; a gruesome end. Another time, a GunDrone scored a hit on the comm unit of a Pit. With comms and guidance down the Pit bashed into other Pits, causing a bunch of crashes, then flew out of the arena and landed in a field two kilometers away. You see, some Pits required a remote pilot uplink connection, while others were guided by an onboard pilot.

Our van went past the horse stables. The Speedway also hosted an enormous rodeo each year, presided over by the Prescott Rodeo Cartel. What I found interesting is the rodeo mentality and cowboy styles continued as we approached the Pit Racer stockade. Cowboys and people in every kind of western dress were moving with purpose and energy all around us.

We pulled into the racer's loading bay at the Speedway Stockade. It was always a busy place.

"Children, follow," Bishop walked us past racers, Pits (the flying race cars) and dozens of Pit crew members. We quickly became anonymous, which was fortunate. Moments after leaving the van, black assault vehicles flew in and dark squad cars rolled-up. A second later, we were inside and running behind Bishop,

"Follow me, Quorra will make a diversion." We ran on and on, dodging handlers, racers, fans, and stacks of equipment.

"We are near the Pits now. You will each climb in one and wait for my signal." Climb in a Pit, for real? Sweet!

"Kip, I've always wanted to see a Pit racer in-person! Bishop, can we fly one of these?" Binky was beyond ecstatic. Pits were the real-world closest thing to Online PvP. We arrived at the Pit storage bay and we each climbed into one of the racers.

"I got the red Corvette model!" Wogs was beaming.

"Mine is a blue Maserati with pinstriping!"

Cricket was already playing with the controls. Bishop directed Binky to a larger Pit model. "This one looks more like a Referee's Pit, crap, I got the stupid Peterbilt one," Binky looked around inside and looked crestfallen. She got the clunker. Mine was shiny silver Porsche, with lots of attached tools. I loved Pit racing, and this was the latest model. True, all these were practice Pits, not the ones used in serious competition, but even these models could hit speeds of 400kph and turn on a dime.

"Children, sync your pads and get your helmets on," each pit had a stinky used helmet. We all placed our pads in the dashboard mount and got busy bringing up our HUDs. Bishop already had his Referee Pit idling a few feet of the ground. I realized Binky was in the same Pit style as Bishop. Folding arms suddenly deployed, and rail guns emerged, fore and aft. Referee Pits were wicked fast and had tons of extra tools. They were used to control other Pits during a race in the event of a foul or illegal move or to prevent Pits from crashing into the crowd. Referee Pits were the alpha dogs of the Pit world. I made eye contact with Binky. She had known all along. The smile she gave me was brilliant and full of mischief. Her RefPit looked like a junker but purred like a kitten. The RefPit powered up and she was hovering next to Bishop.

Bishop raised his voice, "It's time to go, kids. We've lost comms with Quorra. Bad Wolf is coming for us."

Binky mirrored Bishop's movements.

He nodded at Binky, "Ok, young padawan, let's see if you can keep up!" Bishop took the RefPit on a series of maneuvers that happened too fast for me to follow. Not for Binky. She not only kept up, but she did some other stuff that boggled my mind.

Bishop whistled and his voice had a big grin, "Monica, you have some skill!"

"Not just skill, Big B, I am the PvP queen! Look upon my moves ye mighty and despair! Let's kick it Alpha Flight!"

Did she say Alpha Flight?

"Time to form up. Each of you sees the blinking light on your console? Tap it, now," we each tapped the button and Wogs, Cricket and I found our Pits forming up on Bishop's RefPit.

"Your Pits are slaved to my control. Monica -"

"Big B, call me Binky!"

"Binky…will be running under her own control."

On a private channel Bishop spoke to Binky, "Young lady, should I be deactivated, the slave controls will pass to you. Be mindful, the first goal is to escape. Our first heading is toward the Mt. Baker National Forest to get off the urban grid. If necessary, you will lead the group to the Park Butte Lookout, it's a safehouse, understand? There are resources for you there. Remember to meander to detect followers."

"Understood, Big B."

I looked at the console in my Pit showing all our Pits and stats. Binky had already named hers: Gallifrey.

A huge explosion rocked the floor above us. Above the bay were the corporate seating boxes. There were muffled screams. Smoke began to flood down the stairwells on each side of the Pit Bay; black choking smoke sent people running for the exits. Bishop arranged us into a chevron formation. I believe it was called a phalanx in ancient times. Binky's RefPit orbited about us; she looked very ready for a brawl.

Cricket broke the radio silence, "We should give ourselves a name. How about the Super Squad?"

Wogs snorted and Binky chided, "Such a doofus. Good job Sphinx."

Cricket was mumbling that he was joking.

Bishop warned us, "Ok, we are off," with a jolt, our Pits rocketed to the Pit Bay ceiling, and arced toward the arena entrance. Dark shapes suddenly appeared in front of us. It was the Bad Wolf air assault goons. Their guns were blazing, both plasma and projectile. If it weren't such a deadly display, I would call it beautiful. Bishop steered us in some kind of helix maneuver, and we swept past the air assault ships and drones. Our Pits accelerated hard, pressing us back into our seats. I heard hoots and howls from my Crew. They really seemed to be enjoying this. I was just trying not to join the brown trouser brigade; this was freaking scary!

"Are all of you still intact? Sound off," Bishop got a mishmash of response. It seems we had made a good start to our escape.

I heard an urping sound and a moment later Cricket spoke, "Sorry guys, I yak'd all over my controls."

Until he muted, we got to hear the slopping sounds of Cricket's clean up job. From the sound of his voice, I didn't think he was done being sick, yet. I heard a crackling and saw sparks fly behind us. I realized Bishop's RefPit was spewing out some kind of fireworks. Countermeasures. That wasn't something I had seen before.

"Listen up. We have a kilometer lead on the air units. The good news is we are increasing our lead; the bad news is Bad Wolf satellite tracking just pinpointed our location and has a bead on us now."
As Bishop described our circumstances, I finally hit the max stress I could handle. I urped all over the inside of my Pit. Nasty. On cue an actinic-blue, blinding beam of light shot from heaven. The beam repeated every few seconds, making a deep zronking sound. Bishop had our Pit canopies dim to save our eyes and our maneuvers were janky and abrupt.

"Hang on, team, our flight is going to be bumpy. It will be difficult to evade the satellite fix."

I thought our flight was rough. What came next made that look like a walk in the park. We flew within feet of the ground, through tunnels, into culverts and finally dove into a lake, turning a hard right and emerging ten minutes later.

"That did it for the moment. But I predict they will re-acquire us within the next 90 seconds, given the probabilities on a wide sweep scan of the region."

Bishop was leading up to something and my dread meter went into overdrive.

"Guys, I don't think I am doing so well," I saw Wogs through her windscreen, and she was white as a ghost.

"I got kinda sick and I think I'm gonna -" Wogs slumped out of sight and Binky jerked her Pit, inverted directly over Wogs, canopy to canopy.

"She is out cold, Bishop. We need to get wherever we can hide, now. She needs help," It was the sign of deep concern that Binky didn't have any wise cracking jokes.

"Bishop, dude, now!"

"Binky, I am sending you a map and path. I want you to follow it as I instructed you, earlier."

A moment later, Bishop's RefPit veered sharply to the left and upward. Suddenly, duplicates of our Pits, even Binky's, appeared in formation around his RefPit. He had activated holos of our Pits. My stomach lurched again, but nothing came out. I suddenly realized Bishop was leaving us to be a decoy. Moments after, large plasma shots rained down on Bishop's position. Last I saw, he dodged and wove out of the line of fire.

My HUD showed the control passing to Binky.

She shouted, "Alright guys, I got you. We're headed to the forest and the ride is going to be awful. Hang on."

The world turned topsy turvy and we bounced and jarred in every direction. Suddenly, it went dark. We were in some kind of cave, stopping inches from hitting the rock wall directly ahead. All our canopies popped open.

We pulled Wogs out of her Pit and got her situated on the ground. She was doing okay, but still groggy.

"Cricket, keep an eye on her; Kip, let's look around and make sure we weren't followed."

Binky was fully in command.

We hoped the sat tracking had lost our trail. At the cave entrance all was quiet. Wogs made a full recovery. Cricket suggested it was vertigo, but none of us were doctors so we were just glad she seemed to be doing fine. Like normal kids our minds moved on to other things, unworried. I was worried though. I wondered how Bishop was doing.

October 2252 – Mt. Baker Wilderness, Washington, CSA

The cave was pitch black as evening came. Cricket did his survival engineering thing and we had light. He constructed a tripod, crafted a pot out of materials from his Pit and set a fire under the now dangling pot. Cricket loved the outdoors and shared this on his stream casts. His whole family spoke the language of the land and his ease with getting our camp situated was a testament to his time-honed skills. He left the cave for an hour and came back with a bundle of branches and a bag with something bleeding. Within an hour, the fire was roaring, and a stewpot was bubbling.

"The hillside is so full of good game the rabbits might have well jumped into the pot, themselves. So, does it smell good?" we all nodded, thankful he was such a woodsman. In such a technical world, it was weird to know someone who could be so practical and talented in physical skills.

"You can thank my Dad for having me keep that stupid fanny pack. You guys always gave me so much crap about it. I guess you're thankful right about now," he was right. The spices he kept in his pack were part of their prepper lifestyle. Cricket had spent all his young years hunting, fishing, setting trotlines on the Skagit River, field dressing what they hunted, tanning skins, and packing in meat for the freezer. We did make fun of him, sometimes, but he and his family were so kind and giving, we couldn't fault them for being different. Besides, it was fun during the summers when he would take us exploring near his cabin. After eating, we sat around the fire chatting, and Cricket pulled out his mouth harp and played something soft. We all curled up near the flames and nodded off. Mr. Shadow was at the cave's mouth. The shadowy figure saw the children around the fire and stepped out into the night.

October 2252 – Colorado Springs, Colorado, CSA

Col. Andrews saw the blips on the tracking monitor become one blip. Moments later all the blips returned. Something happened and he knew there would be dire consequences if he allowed the terrorists to get away.

"Sgt. Craig, playback the last 30 seconds of the track on 024. Splash to the main screen."

A magnified version of the 30 second segment played on a loop for 5 minutes. The small conference room, recently co-opted as a war room filled with large screen computers and a half dozen analysts at keyboards smelled like old coffee and donuts. Sgt. Craig touched the main screen to activate the holo, pulling the third dimension with an artist's care.

Col. Andrews came to a decision, "Sgt. Craig, setup two teams. Team one will run visual sweeps in a 15-kilometer radius from satcom's last positive fix and team two will deploy HunterSeekers to sweep the same area down low. You will coordinate a search for any human or mechanical activity starting now, until 2200, tomorrow. Report to me the moment any trace is detected."

"Sir, we have an infrared signal. It might be a fire," the Sergeant smiled at the report to his Colonel.

"Sgt. Craig, converge units on that position, now!" the Colonel leaned forward in anticipation.

Half a continent away, a shadowy figure pulled a small box from its coat pocket and triggered a switch. The cave entrance seemed to become solid rock. A ghost ship also sprang into existence and moved away from the cave at speed.

"Sir! We have a signal on the move! Headed northwest, bearing 275° …it's moving at incredible speed. Satcom has an image. It looks like one of our units," the Sergeant looked to his Colonel.

"Sgt. Craig, what does the transponder say?"

He found the signal, "Sir, it's a rogue troop carrier."

"Bring it down, now," a moment passed, and the fuzzy picture blossomed into a huge fireball.

"Sgt., I didn't say destroy it, I said bring it down," the Sergeant looked aggrieved.

"Sir, recovery team is on the way."

"Send a tracking team to the first spot we identified." The Colonel turned away, frustrated.

The shadow saw the drones and manned aerial units coming. Slipping into what appeared to be solid rock, the shadow watched the units scan the area for half an hour before they moved on. The shadow flicked a switch on the box and the ghost ship ceased to exist as the orbital strike hit its mark.

October 2252 – Mt. Baker Wilderness, Washington, CSA

Cricket woke with a start; he'd heard something. Before moving, he followed his father's advice: stay still, listen for a beat, decide, then act. He listened for a moment, then sprang into action, moving quickly about the cave, knife in hand, in a crouch, ready for anything. Then he heard it again. Bringing his face close to Kip's rucksack, he recalled something else Dad said: keep your ear to the ground. Placing his ear on the ground, next to the rucksack, Cricket was sure he'd hear some kind of tunnel underneath…then he heard a faint squeak. He turned his face toward Kip, his backside, rather. Then the world blew up. A huge explosion of noise erupted, sending Cricket scrabbling back before he realized it was gas. Kip farted in Cricket's face. Everyone was awake now. Binky was looking right at Cricket, and she put 2+2 together. She held it for a moment before bursting at the seams.

"Cricket, why are you snuffling Kip's farts?"

He sputtered, unable to form a cogent sentence.

"Hey guys, ya better watch out, Cricket's a fart hunter!"

The boy turned red, mumbling about keeping the cave safe from all threats, both foreign and domestic. We all laughed, and I added some wood to the fire. My hands were ice cold, and the heat was most welcome. It had been a rough night's sleep and at one point I thought I heard someone at the cave's mouth. For half an hour we acted completely our age, running around, throwing stuff, and playing Judo tag and mosh pit, throwing each other to the cave floor and Hulk smashing for good measure. The rock floor was a hard landing surface, but we played with gusto like we had at the cabin in the summers. After we let off steam, we settled by the fire.

"Hey guys, I think we should hang out for a day or two. If I were searching for us, I'd be looking for any kind of motion, heat sig or EM radiation. Binky, would you be able to make a battle plan for us? I think we aren't far away from the Park Butte safehouse. Since Bishop put you in charge, let's keep following your lead," Binky, for once was speechless. She wasn't used to being in charge of our group. I was so proud of her. She was rising to the occasion, and it showed how much of a leader she would be when we grew up. It was important I validate Binky's leadership. I recall my Dads talking about the firehose principle. When two firefighters are connecting two hoses, each of them grips one of the collars. As they bring them into contact one of the firefighters looks away. The problem is two people adjusting the collars at the same time makes connecting them much harder. One person had to take the lead. Binky needed to be our one leader, right now.

I walked to the cave entrance and sat. I looked at the valley spread out below. If I recalled my geology correctly, this was one of those valleys created by glaciation. As I sat musing the crisp cool, delicious smell of the forest, I heard footsteps from behind. Cricket sat a few feet away and stared out, saying nothing; he just looked and smiled.

"Do you sometimes feel like you're missing the big picture?"

He continued, "I mean, you know, it's like there is this whole big natural world out here and we think we got it all, playing Online. We watch the world but we're not really a part of it."

We both knew much of the world was still hazardous, with places too toxic for humans, Junkers and war remnants killing people that got in their way. Cricket was thinking of the cabin and a simpler lifestyle in the outback. He companionably gripped my shoulder and got quiet. We sat, taking in the natural beauty; the heady pine smells, sounds of birds and rustling squirrels. Binky hated squirrels. Then I was wondering how my Dads were doing. How about all the others? Did they get away safely? I felt very disconnected being off the grid. I was thankful our parents had forced us to live more in the Real than Online. I imagined we would be pretty inept at problem solving if we were like all the other kids.

Looking at the kilometers of forest, I understood what Cricket was saying. The wide world was a place alien to me. I mean, I loved fishing; I liked to go down to Lake Stevens' public dock and drop a line. But that wasn't much. Had I seen the world? No, yes, well sort of…I had seen holos, videos and stills of the world, solar system, and galaxy. But that paled in comparison to seeing it in person.

"You know Cricket, I'm a test tube kid." Cricket's eyes opened wide, and he just stared at me.

"You're what?"

We had some eavesdroppers. Binky and Wogs were standing behind us. How long had they been there?

"My Dads told me in a 'by the way' fashion just before we left the compound," Wogs sat close and wrapped an arm around me. I felt awkward, but Wogs' hugs were always comforting. They were too rare for my preference, but I would never admit that. I leaned in and kept quiet. Expecting a snarky comment, I was surprised to feel the arms of my whole Crew wrapped about me. I wanted to stay in that warmth forever. Eventually I counted myself as fortunate to have had two amazing Dads, regardless of blood relations. It sure would have been nice to know earlier. A moment later, I felt an undeniable urge take hold. I couldn't hold it back. I peeled off a squeaking, stinky fart. It may have well been a stick of dynamite for how fast everyone sprung away. But Wogs held on for an extra moment, pressed her nose to mine and smiled. Wogs was our heart, and our heart was strong! Then she let out a big breath (she had been holding it) and moved to the other side of the cave mouth.

In her best impression of Cheri, Binky chimed, "Mr. Whiffer, that rump of yours is a hazard!"

We all laughed, and at that instant all was right with the world. Yeah, we had two multinational murder corporations chasing us, drones, sats and the military all looking to lock us up...but, for that moment, everything was ok. We laughed until our sides were sore, then set about doing the chores we assigned ourselves. We agreed to stay put for two more nights.

The day was full of Pit maintenance, foraging for veggies and Cricket showing us how to make and set figure-four traps.

"Ok guys, first thing is to find the right sticks. They have to be the same diameter for the box trap to work well."

We spent time carving and notching sticks and finally choosing small-animal paths for the location. Our traps caught nothing but air. Cricket's four traps caught 2 rabbits and a marmot. He showed us how to quickly kill our catch which was a bit stomach-turning. Then, he had us field dress each little beastie and mounted them on sticks for roasting over the fire. His spice pouch came to save the day. We had Tabasco sauce and brown sugar glaze, and the meat was succulent and moist. It was very spicy, and surprisingly good! The next day we found a small lake which had been stocked with fish. Cricket got us set up with poles, hooks and lines and we sat around waiting for a tug. Mister outdoors was really in his element. It was beautiful here and so quiet. I mused about our school chums. Would they even realize we were gone? As usual, Cricket caught the most fish. Geez! I had to give him props.

"All hail the great woodsman, the great hunter and master of piscatorial prowess!" I figured, go pompous or go home.

Everyone laughed. Cricket pulled a deep southern accent, "Y'all aughta know a country boy can survive."

He tipped his non-existent cowboy hat to us. More laughter. The second night was less frenetic as we settled into the evening. Dinner was excellent as usual. Our very own Cookie made mushroom and butter trout, another round of rabbit filets and late season blueberries we found in the forest for dessert. Truly full, we settled back around the fire. Since we weren't allowed to connect our devices Online, our options were chores, conversation, sleep, or manual games, like Charades and I Spy. We played charades. Wogs, our resident empath, was a natural. She could guess better than the rest of us and her acting was unreal; she really had a talent. Cricket and I were a team, and we did fairly well. In fact, we won, primarily since Binky could not seem to get the knack of it. It drove her crazy that she would lose again and again. She went off in a huff and pouted the rest of the night. Cricket brought out a flask of brandy and we all had a taste. It was one of his father's home creations. We felt a little more like ourselves, a little less like children, yet not quite as adults. Importantly, we were in this together, whatever this was. As we cuddled around the fire, Cricket took up sentry duty. Despite being on watch he failed to notice the shadow figure lurking just beyond the cave entrance. Neither the shadowy figure, nor Cricket noticed the hovering WatcherDrone less than 100 meters out. Within a minute the drone flew away.

At first light, I woke to banging. Seems I was the lazy one. Cricket was already out searching for our day's food and Wogs and Binky were modifying the RefPit. Apparently, my lazy bones were not required, so I popped on my shoes and prepared to look around outside.

"Hey Whiffer! Nice to see you back in the land of the living. Perhaps you could get your test-tube butt over here and help Wogs hold these parts as I weld."

"Where did you find a welder?"

"The RefPits have welder attachments on their longarms and the shortarms have adjustable grippers. But, for some of this work, shortarms don't work. I need a person to hold the pieces in place," Wogs looked a bit grimy from the work and I guessed it was my shift.

"How did you know about the welder attachments?"

"Simple. Don't you remember how the RefPits could hold onto literally anything? If you watched closely, it wasn't just strength of grip, the longarms were putting a spot weld on the drone or rogue Pit that needed to be taken out of the game. And do you know how they un-welded the weld?"

Binky looked at me like she wanted me to answer. Nope, I had no idea. I just shook my head.

"Well smarty, longarms also have these little circular blades. I guess they could be called weld cutters. Anyhow, our RefPit has these and a huge number of other tools we can detach and use."

"Alrighty, a better question is 'how do you know how to weld'?"

"You're kidding? Where does our father work?"

"Uhh, isn't he an auto mechanic?" It sounded like a dirty, thankless job when I said it that way. I felt shame.

"No doofus, he's not just a mechanic. In his spare time, he is the lead designer on super-modified track racers and designed many of the onboard AI-assist components and sensors."

Binky didn't lose a beat as she kept at her welding. Wogs and I made sure not to look at the welding spark.

"How did you think your Dads' truck was always in such great shape? Magic? Our Dad brings home the newest auto tech and upgrades our cars and yours."

My Dads' truck was an H1 Humvee, and it always run smoothly. So much so I never paid it much attention.

Then my memory served me for once, "Oh yeah, last summer when you were gone for a couple weeks. You went to that auto speedway -" Wogs interrupted.

"The Indianapolis Speedway. The place isn't quite as flashy as the Pit raceways, but they are fast and loud. I like watching my Dad's ground racers more than Pits. Did you know, ever since ground racers started using 3/4 torus tracks, the cars have wheels that wrap around the whole vehicle. Our Dad designed the latest wheel assembly. Did you know the central roll cage has complete mechanical autonomy from the surrounding frame? Once you see these things in action, you'd see how cool they are," Wogs kept talking, but as she was speaking my eye caught a metallic reflection, a shiny thing in the rear of the cave. I wondered what it was.

"I hope Bishop is okay. And Quorra" Wogs spoke my own thoughts.

I tried to encourage her, but I doubted my words.

"They both are incredibly hard to damage or kill. My intuition is we will see Bishop again, at some point."

My words sounded convincing, but who was I kidding, we had already lost both of them. I kept my mouth shut on that last part. I made an excuse of needing to pee so I could clear my head. After coming back from the cave entrance, I went to see the shiny thing.

Cricket set the fourth trotline across the small river. That done, he headed up hill, toward the caves to check his small game traps. A twig broke behind him. Looking around, he drew his blade. He saw nothing. There was a brief movement out of the corner of his eye and he froze in position. His father said to trust his senses, 'don't think too much' if you feel something is hunting you. Cricket closed his eyes for a moment, centering himself. After a pause, he made a slow turn, scanning close and far. He saw nothing, but another rustling sound came from his left: he turned quickly and saw a small fuzzy ball, waddling in his direction. Animal? Mineral or vegetable? Cricket smiled and relaxed, watching the little Tribble amble its way toward him. Another sound from behind him drew his attention: a second Tribble was headed his way. Then a third and fourth, angling toward him. Good feelings gone! He counted six furry mounds coming his way and a new sound began. Loudest in the first Tribble, it sounded like metal on metal, sliding and ringing. Cricket got his first answer: not animal, not vegetable, but definitely mineral. These were bots. Cute little bots, but by the sounds, not friendly. The only clear escape route was uphill toward the cave. As he edged that way, the Tribbles kept coming toward him. The metallic sounds were rising in pitch. One, two, three...Cricket bolted, running uphill, full steam. His feet pounded the earth, breath huffing hard and raspy. He was afraid, but he had hope. You see, when a person has no hope, when someone knows there is no escaping immediate death, they can be fearless. But inject a bit of hope and the game changes: fear floods the whole body. Cricket was flooded, but he was pouring all that fear into his churning legs. The whining metallic symphony behind him rose to a fevered pitch and Cricket ran.

Cricket swore, "Damned Chubb Chubbs, sweet and nice until it's time to make Cricket an hors d'oeuvre. Screw that you Tribble wannabes!"

Cricket could have sworn they heard him; the metal-on-metal sliding sound picked up a notch. Despite all, Cricket smiled.

Back at the cave, I really did need to pee. After a lengthy appointment with a bush outside, I went back in, and right to the shiny thing. I picked it up and noticed some kind of symbol carved into one side. The symbol was etched in the stone with a golden metallic inlay. The design was a circle with fours dots inside it. As I looked at it, I walked back over toward Binky and Wogs.

"Hey guys, I found a shiny rock."

"Yeah, great to hear. Now hand Wogs that spanner."

I pocketed the rock and grabbed the spanner. We worked for another 20 minutes on the RefPit when we heard faint yelling from outside. Our heads snapped up and we thought the same thing.

We said in unison, "Time to go!"

At the cave mouth, I could see Cricket running, face red and yelling.

"Kip, it's time to go!"

I yelled as I ran to my Pit, "Everyone, comms on, RF-only, but stay silent. Remember, Bishop said no Online contact."

I wasn't sure what Cricket was running from, then I saw the little dots coming up the hill. These resolved into dozens of little fuzzy things. I was about to say 'come on, they're just Tribbles', but then I heard the whining metallic sounds and changed my thought.

"Oh hell, the Chubb Chubbs are coming!"

"Yeah Kip, I already said that. Try to catch up, buddy!"

Cricket whizzed by and gave me a knowing smile. Fortunately, the fuzzy blobs were not fast. We had maybe 30 seconds to hop in our Pits. As I closed my canopy, a fuzzy landed on the canopy's plasteel. Holy cow, rotating rings of teeth, these guys really were Chubb Chubbs, except no part of them had any cuteness like the cartoon! The nightmare mouth suctioned onto the Pit canopy and began grinding a hole.

"Oh no you don't!" I yelled loudly and launched my Pit at full acceleration out the cave entrance.

Three Pits followed, then moments later, I felt my Pit slave to Binky's. We broke radio silence and discussed the location of the safehouse; then we angled northwest, flying low. Looking back, a carpet of fuzzies swarmed the cave mouth. In their rage, they destroyed bushes, trees and burrowed into the rock. It was hard to tell, but I could have sworn I saw a person walk out of the cave. I made a quick count and my whole Crew was present. Who was that? Did I really just see that? Too late, we were over the hill and flying low through the river valley.

Cricket broke the silence again, "Ah man! I have a bunch of traps and trotlines set. We have to go back. I can't let critters get caught in those."

I could hear Binky groan. She didn't want to go back any more than the rest of us. But one thing she and Cricket had in common was a love for animals. I was both proud and scared. Proud of my compassionate Crew but scared the Chubb Chubbs would eat us.

"Binks, unslave my Pit, I'll go in low and demolish the traps and snag the trotlines."

"Bug, you can't just go alone! Nope, it's all or nothing." Binky was firm, but Cricket overruled her.

In a moment he had unslaved his Pit. I didn't know that could be done. So much for my deep insights on Pits!

"Negative, Ghost Rider. You guys lay low, I'll make it quick," Cricket was gone in a flash.

"Cricket, you idjit, get back here. You can't just go get yourself killed," we watched him fly away.

He called back a minute later, "Ok, the traps are toast and next the lines..." there was gravel at the tail-end of the transmission, then nothing. Minutes passed and no Cricket.

Binky tried, "Bug, what are you doing? Come on! We have to go!"

We all called to him. More minutes passed. Suddenly, Binky jerked us southeast, back to the cave site. We flew full speed like skycycles on Endor, weaving through the trees. We looked and saw only the destroyed traps. We didn't find the trotlines. A familiar buzzing sound began; soon it became a metallic ringing. The Chubb Chubbs had found us.

"Binks, we have to go! Cricket's gone!" I had a sinking feeling about this.

"Binks, we need to go, now! Cricket will have to catch us up. I'm sure he's ok!" Wogs was trying to sound positive. Away we went, fast and full out. It was impossible to leave Cricket behind, yet we did. I felt like we would never see him again.

Chapter 6 – CRICKET ESCAPES

November 2252 – Braemore, Scotland, European States (ES)

The darkness started to fade. There were voices. "...no more epi. The kid either recovers or doesn't."

"That's awful. Don't say such things."

"Like you're any better. I'm just not shy about what I'm thinking."

"Hmm, when the boy comes 'round, let Rucker know."

"Nope, we need to get Brian down here, first. You remember what happened when we left him out of the loop last time? Come on man, this kid's part of cell 24. That's deep!"

"Gods, you are annoying, if I had a dollar for every time -" the voices faded.

Footsteps faded away. The place sounded empty.

Cricket opened his eyes slowly. He scanned left to right, eyes landing on a gurney next to his. Whatever was on the gurney was short and hairy, kind of like Cousin It from the Addams Family.

"Hey!" Cricket made a stage whisper to Cousin It. "Hey, hairy dude!"

The hairy dude moved a bit, then was still. "Dude! Come on man. Cousin It, wake up!"

The moment he said Cousin It, the hairy form struggled against the gurney restraints to look at Cricket. In a mildly English accent, the hairy guy spoke with fire.

"Cousin It? Are you a child?" Getting a better look, the furry being had a visible 'ah ha' moment, "Ah, yes, you're a child."

"I am not! I resent that remark!"

"Ok, then. How about you start with your name and I with mine. My name is Lugh Grant."

Cricket paused for a moment. Hadn't he heard that name before from one of Kip's videos from the 20th?

"I'm Cricket Carter. Good to meet ya. What are we doing here?"

"I imagine you did something to piss off the Corporation, kind of like that poor fellow on your other side."

Cricket looked and saw a golden tanned, amply muscled fellow. He wasn't breathing.

Lugh spoke, "Cricket, a pleasure to meet you. Now, be so kind to reach your right hand down 20 centimeters over the lip of the gurney."

Cricket reached down.

"Now, just under the handle you are touching there is a strap quick release."

Snap! The strap across Cricket's midsection retracted with a sharp report. The chest strap held his arm so he was unable to reach the same button for the chest strap release. Improvise. Cricket wriggled downward. When his arms had full range of motion he clicked the chest release, then sitting up he released his feet. Cricket looked at his waist: they hadn't taken his fanny pack.

"Yes, sweet! Hey, Lou Grant, let's see about yours," Lugh's arms were like an Orangutan's and he had spindly long fingers. In a moment, seven snaps sounded, and Lugh was free.

As Lugh jumped up, Cricket noted several things at once. Lou was no more than 3 feet tall and you could clearly see his ruddy Santa Clause face, and his feet were hairy and huge. "Good God in the morning, those straps chafed! Thank you, young Cricket!"

He wasn't sure if this was a synth or hybrid, but he was definitely not human. He was raised too well to ask such a question, outright.

"Do you know where we are, Lou?"

Lugh heard the mispronunciation of his name, but he also was polite and ignored the slight. "Last I knew I was in a forest near Podkamennaya Tunguska; that is to say, I was in a forest in Siberia, making a count of birds. I'm an ornithologist, specializing in migratory patterns and preservation."

Lugh clearly had more to say, but Cricket knew about academic types like Wogs and me. It was best not to pry too much at risk of getting a long boring lecture.

"If we're in Russia, then I'm a long way from home. I think I want to go now. Do you have any idea about how to get out of here?"

They were in a lab. It looked very sterile: concrete, steel, and headache-inducing, bright lights. It was chilly. One wall was full of mirrored windows, and he wondered if someone was watching them.

"Friend Cricket, follow me, I have an idea."

He followed. They avoided people in lab coats, men in military uniforms, and eventually wove the corridors to emerge into an enormous underground hangar. Huge, as in kilometer-long by the same dimension wide. Cricket's mouth fell agape, and a consternated look rested on Lugh's face.

"Cricket, this is not good. Do you know what you're looking at?" He didn't.

He finally stopped staring at the size of the place to focus on what was stored in the hangar: the largest collection of war drones he'd ever seen. More than he thought existed, frankly. Five aircraft carrier sized ships, hundreds of fighter jets, dozens of specialty drones which he'd never seen before. And they weren't still. The place buzzed like a beehive, with aerial units flitting this way and that. CargoDrones lifted and moved boxes, equipment, and people in a constant flow of activity. Dozens of hurtfully bright points were the places where welding was happening. He could smell the burning odor in the air mingling with the petroleum and ozone odors of old school machines and new wave motion engines.

"Lou, whose air force is this?"

"This is an Air Support Wing of the Bangarang Global Service. Cricket, I need you to stay here for a minute. I need to go explore something before we leave. Just...stay here. Please."

"Lou, no way, this place is just waiting to kill me. What if you don't come back?"

Pulling Cricket's face down toward his own, Lugh spoke gently, "My dearest new friend, I will return. I need to find out a couple things which may save countless lives. Trust me, please. And stay out of sight, behind those storage crates."

He nodded and scuttled behind the large wall of crates stacked nearby. For hours he sat there and eventually fell asleep. A loud boom brought him fully awake, heart beating out of his chest. Peeking around the corner, he saw the crates were being loaded onto flatbed carriers. His hidey hole was about to go away. Looking around, he saw a ventilation grill; he popped a flathead screwdriver out of his trusty utility belt and got half the grill open. He prised it wide enough for him to slip inside. None too soon, the moment he plopped into the vent the final crates were lifted away, revealing the spot in which he recently napped. Cricket thought hard and decided it was best he make a go of escape on his own. Waiting for Lou wasn't safe. He crawled into the ventilation system, hoping for a way out.

November 2252 – Park Butte, Mt. Baker Wilderness, Washington

We arrived at Park Butte safehouse only minutes after we left the cave. Landing on a flat area below the lookout, several people were waiting for us. The safehouse was more like a small aircraft hangar embedded into the core of the Black Butte massif. The Mt. Baker Wilderness was a beautiful place. Mt. Baker rose to the north, high above us, and we could see Mt. Shuksan, Mt. Blum, Bacon Peak, and the Twin Sisters to the south. Baker Lake was due east and not visible over the southern slopes. The Lookout was intact and functional as a tourist overnight destination but was seldom visited. It sat atop the highest prominence of Park Butte and sported refurbished equipment as if it were going to be used to spot fires once again.

We were confined to the safehouse per my Dads' orders. That left us unable to search for Cricket and that rankled bitterly for us. Three weeks passed, and I spent quite a bit of time in the lookout writing out my thoughts on my pad. Park Butte was a special place for me. My family had a tradition of visiting Park Butte each summer. My Dads would get special visitors while we stayed there and we hiked around. At that time, I was blissfully unaware these visitors were climbing up from the safehouse buried directly beneath us. They would bring fresh meats to fry on the iron stove, lollies for me and scotch for my Dads. Nights were quiet, bereft of everything electronic, but filled with whipping wind from the slopes of the snow covered giant above us. Each night my Dads would sit with me, legs dangling from the wrap-around deck over the sheer drop. Sometimes they would tell stories and others we'd sit in silence, sometimes hearing night birds calling or an occasional rodent scurrying close by. The air was fresh, and the clouds scudded by as the winds drove them through the frosty night. Lens-shaped clouds formed over Mt. Baker on the coldest nights.

Park Butte came to be a safehouse when a group of soldiers decided they'd had more than enough killing of civilians. The Tech War raged on, in 2076, and Bellingham found itself swamped with refugees of every kind. The Synth Railroad included humans and hybrids, now, escaping from the war-torn areas. It was hit and miss keeping the thousands of homeless hidden from sight. The local Army garrison became a hideout. The soldiers there were disconnected from their command and sentiment turned one day toward helping the refugees. That was the moment when the early Liberation militarized. From that time forward, Liberation efforts included weapons, strategy and tactics that greatly increased the likelihood the refugees would survive.

Two soldiers, outdoorsmen, and their friends from the Lummi Nation made room for thousands more refugees and created new places for them to not only hide, but quietly prosper. New safehouses and secret meeting places were created for the Railroad. The biggest safehouse was tucked further away in the wilderness, excavated under Park Butte. The site went from big to massive as the extent of the volcanic cave system was revealed. It was Cricket's distant relatives, Davy, and Johannes Muir, who discovered the sprawling caves buried deep into Park and Black Buttes. They set to work developing it as a secret base of operations.

The safehouse was a wonder to behold. Binky, Wogs, and I explored the caves for the first few days, and we were allowed access anywhere because of my Dads. Then reality set back in, and we were tasked with daily chores and scarcely had time for anything else. I was responsible for the horse stalls. I recalled when Cricket's family took us riding during the summers. Mucking out stalls was hard. I had a shovel, bucket, and wheelbarrow and a lot of back-breaking work. The three of us had to wheel the poop out of the stables and into a steel container that would be airlifted somewhere else to serve as fertilizer. There were a variety of horses and several types of hybrid. The scary ones were the huge Sabre-Toothed Cats. They were scary until I figured out they liked ear scritches, belly rubs and the extra food I snitched from the kitchen. After that, me and my Crew would spend many of our off hours with the cats and they adopted us as family. The majordomo of the stables, Concho told us they had been created by a man named Pastor Bedtime to be war cats. My Dads had muffed his plans when Vicky paid an unexpected visit one evening and surreptitiously changed the gene coding. The war cats became large house cats. As you might imagine, big animals poop big. The horse poop smell was tolerable, but the cat poops were hard and sour smelling. I was knee deep in it, but I loved the work because it kept me occupied and gave me hours to process all that happened recently.

"Hey Concho, can I take a break, I really need to get something to eat?" He reached into his shirt pocket to throw me a protein bar so I hastened to qualify, "Aaaaand, I can't eat when I'm covered in, well, in this stuff."

He nodded. It was a weird feeling to be covered in stinky poo and being hungry at the same time. They might seem incompatible, but surprisingly, they weren't. Concho gave me the thumbs-up and off I went to get some grub. He was a person of few words. Born to subsistence farmers in Totontepec, Oaxaca, his family grew and sold maize. He had been recruited as a soldier by the CSA, then defected when he got in trouble for not following orders. I found out there was a village of civilians he was supposed to hit with napalm. Not only did he refuse, but before he bailed, he torched his whole motor pool. Zero loss of life and 100% loss of combat equipment. The CSA considered him a terrorist which meant he fit right in with our crowd. Concho was a gifted and faithful organizer. He was also skilled in getting children to do their work cheerfully; he had a way with words. When he would find one of us staring into space, lost in thought, he would bark at us to 'get the lead out' and get back to work.

Later that evening in the barracks, Binky, Wogs, and I sat around avoiding talking about Cricket. Anything but Cricket. I missed my Dads, and I could tell Wogs and Binks were missing their family. We decided as a group to skip the nightly troop briefing. Too late, the briefing found us. Billy Briggs came in, smiling like he knew something special.

"Uh oh, look out, Billy knows a secret."

Billy looked shy for a moment, then Binky softened her tone, "Ok, Billy, come over here and tell us your big news."

Chipper again, he began to spew his discourteous words, "Hey, hey, hey, campers! A finer

group of wetbrains, I never did see! Well, do I have news for you. Our drybrain friend -"
Billy was interrupted by Wogs.

"Billy, stop saying that, it's not nice," Wogs had a sensitive ear to pejorative language. She
didn't let people slide when they used disparaging terminology about others.

"Mollie, you know I don't mean anything by it. And besides, it's true." Wogs looked
consternated. I think he used her given name to goad her. She let it pass.

Billy continued, "Yep, yep, the news: Kip, your Dads and most of their team escaped
Lake Stevens compound. Not so good news, they have been holed-up in the Rosario Resort,
ever since they left. Their comms are minimal, but they wanted a message passed onto you.
And, you have a mission."

Over the next twenty minutes, Billy gave us a laundry list of things to do. As it dawned
upon me that I would not be mucking out stalls anymore, my smile widened. Within an hour,
we had packed up and prepped our newly equipped Pits to begin our assignment. Yes! Not
only were these Pits enhanced, but they were like RefPits on steroids. Our first assignment
was to practice on our sweet new rides. These things were amazing. More comfortable,
for sure, but these Pits could fly underwater up to 100 atmospheres, break orbit into hard
vacuum and fire a gazillion hard rounds as well as laser pulsey things. The short grabbing
arms were intact, but the long arms only had three tool attachments: welder, cutter, and
a semi-auto shotgun. There was even a Pit for Cricket; I sure missed my friend. Trying to
avoid being morose, I wondered why a group of 'kids' was going to be entrusted with such
fine machinery. My wondering came to an abrupt end when we received our briefing after we
had familiarized ourselves with our new Pits.

Sitting in a concrete and steel conference room, I felt like I was at NORAD or
something, with all the blinky and glowing lights and screens. By the way, I heard Bad Wolf
had redecorated NORAD. It apparently was the North American Data Systems...NADS? I
guess a good kick was due their direction. I didn't dwell on it for long, they would get their
due, soon enough. My mind was on our upcoming briefing: I bet it was going to be an eye-
opener.

A middle-aged engineer type, Sgt. Avery, walked in and began his spiel.

"Alright cadets! Settle down and pull out your pads."

We were issued these Milspec grade pads to give us a ton of tools, including
programmability of our Pits, constantly rotating uplink to various ground and satellite
Online sources. Wait a tick, did he call us cadets?

"The pads need to sync to you, individually. Put your thumb on -" blah, blah, blah. Who
did he think he was talking to? I was already steps ahead of him and my Crew took my
lead and were doing the same. I wanted him to shut up so I could find out what these little
beauties could do. I connected to my Online resource server and ran a quick interactive hack
against the Park Butte comms AI. It only took a moment. I clicked a last keystroke, looked
up and smiled. My Crew knew something was up. A second later the room comm unit spoke
loudly, "Sgt. Avery, report to decon immediately. Sgt. Avery to decon."

The Park Butte AI had shared a map of the facility and I found the decontamination unit
was furthest from our present position. He shouldn't bother us for a while. I sent a smiley
face to each of my Crew's pads. They knew I was large and in-charge!

"Hey, don't login to your online accounts, yet. Let me snoop around a bit to see if we can
safely use any of our personal stuff Online," Wogs nodded, and Binks pretended to ignore
me.

Recall, I was pretty annoyed about the way Bangarang stole The Pan from Chad Evans.
Well, the beginning of payback for Chad was starting now. I was upset at having to be on the
run. I wanted to smack something really hard and all over the place. My bilious discontent
was burning, and I decided to direct that noxious fire right at the culprits. With a dramatic
flair, I made a final keystroke. My Crew looked up at me, expectantly.

"Good news, your accounts are off probation. Bad news, they are being actively tracked.
I left the trackers in place but nullified their settings. Give it a few minutes and you can login
without being detected. Hey, you remember that guy Chad I mentioned. I have some long
overdue justice for Chad coming right up. I just hacked into Bad Wolf and Bangarang. My

SimDetective found a bunch of tasty loopholes. With my handy dandy invention I named SaltStripper I've sped up password discovery. Okay, to be honest, I stole some of my Dad's code to do that. Also, I had The Pan AI rooting around in Bad Wolf, soon to start its own roving hack infrastructure, aimed at attacking Bangarang from inside. I set the same thing up at Bangarang, aimed at Bad Wolf, using my Knight and Banquo AIs. They even communicate! One will say ping and the other will reply teapot! "

I stopped, realizing my explanation was too much, as usual.

"Ok, I've hacked the two big brother companies. Let's let that run its course while we do this mission thing." Wogs and Binky appreciated my summary and smiled.

"Kipper, I would hate to be on the receiving end of your pissed-off'edness. You are quite the terrorist!" Binky was grinning like the Cheshire Cat. She loved it.

A low-level chatter resumed and I spent the next 30 minutes loading every conceivable software tool we might need onto our pads and some into our Pits. I also migrated all settings and contents from our old pads onto to the new ones. Right as I finished, I looked around. Binky was working intently on her pad, using it to make her Pit do things.

"Binks, what are you doing?" Wogs was oblivious to the world, taking a nap, curled up in a chair. I'll never know how she could do that so easily.

"Whiffer, you're not the only one who can do stuff with computers. Credit where it's due, you showed me how to script and make macros, by hand. I'm programming my Pit controls to do some complex, cool stuff, especially if we get into a dogfight." She nudged Wogs awake.

"You and Wogs need to know: if you hear Ride of the Valkyries playing over our comm," Binky played a couple seconds of the song, "be prepared for your Pit to jump around a bunch."

"But, if you hear Beastie Boys Sabotage, your Pit will cryofreeze you in-place in the event of an imminent crash. The cryo function puts a stasis field around the Pit which is supposed to protect us from explosions and impacts. I guess we'll see how that works, huh?"

"So, you plan for us to attack with classical music?"

"Yes, Doctor, it would seem to be but, we need that fellow, Sgt. Avery to give us access to Cricket's pit. We're taking that one, too." Almost on cue, Sgt. Avery returned, and Billy was close on his heels. The briefing resumed. "Hey wetbrains, time to get the party started!" I truly disliked this guy.

Just as Billy the Boob was about to start on his obviously well-rehearsed speech, a crash sounded outside the room and moments later, Cheri's little friend, Pooka came running in. A flustered mechanic followed close behind, "So sorry, this little guy came through the ventilation system."

Pooka landed on Binky and snuggled in, still breathing hard.

The mechanic continued, "But, it seems it found its quarry."

Binky held on as Pooka got settled, "Oh we know this one. We got it. Thanks."

Binky was always a pretty cool customer. The mechanic departed. The Boob continued without a hitch.

"So today's little talk is meant to save your lives children. Now, I'll never know why we would be giving multi-million-dollar equipment to a bunch of kids –"

Sgt. Avery interrupted, "Billy, you need to get on with it." Billy just stared at Avery and showed a tinge of exasperation, "Now, Billy. If you please."

"Fine, have it your way…so, let me know if I need to slow down or explain myself. I imagine this stuff is all real new to you." Billy looked around. Satisfied, he continued, while Binky was typing something rapidly on her new pad.

"Yes, onward then. As you know, the Pits you have just now flown have been outfit with the latest gear. Now that you got your first taste of Pit piloting I don't want you to get cocky on me and think you know it all. Your upcoming mission is going to be hard and you need to follow my direction if you plan to survive."

Billy had a self-satisfied air. That is, until a crash and sounds of crunching interrupted his lecture. Billy threw himself to the floor and yelled, "Everybody down, we're under attack!" Pooka's eyes opened momentarily, but sensing no concern from Binky, it closed its eyes and slept on. Binky's RefPit crushed open the double doors and moved into the room. Ten feet tall and slightly more in width, the shiny egg-shaped steel fuselage pressed forward with the low hum of the propulsion system. It gently pushed aside all the office furniture. The Pit's front turret silently pivoted and aimed directly at Billy. He blanched and wet himself fiercely. A deep voice resonated from the Pit PA speaker sounding like Hal 9000.

"I'm sorry Billy, I am unable to allow you to waste any more time. Sgt. Avery?"

The room vibrated and everyone covered their ears. Sgt. Avery hid a smirk and waited a beat before speaking. The Pit withdrew and disappeared around the corner. Binky's programming ran autonomously, which allowed her to watch the smashing, mashing and pee, unencumbered. Her pad made a gentle chime, signifying program's end. Wow. She was next level, alright; Good thing she was on our side.

"I think we can cut to the mission parameters," Sgt. Avery then locked eyes with Binky, "Prowess has been well demonstrated. I think we can skip any other theatrics. Yes?" Binky nodded, Wogs and I tittered.

Billy was shaken, but he continued, "I see I can skip the basics of Pit piloting." He continued for the next 20 minutes with superfluous information. Finally, he rounded the bend with something a bit more juicy, "You have a series of destinations which have to be completed in a specific order, before the end of this month."

The three of us perked up and even Pooka started waking.

"I get it. This is some hi-pri mission. I guess my big question is why us? We are kinda young to be doing this, don't you think? Frankly, we haven't even been piloting Pits for more than a few hours." Wogs smiled and seemed disinterested. She knew I would chew this bone like a dog (sorry for the canine profiling) and eventually settle on being ok with the way things shook out. Binky, however, was seldom inclined to agree with any approach I took.

"Yo, Whiff, get a grip. We are overqualified for this gig. Maybe you've not seen -" Billy tried to interrupt, to no avail, "You stay hushed, Billy B!" Binky pointed a threatening finger at Billy and continued lecturing me.

"Kipper, you see those other so-called pilots out there? They are lucky to not fall out of the sky."

She was right. The adults who tried to pilot the various craft in the hangar were pretty green and a bigger danger to themselves than anyone else. I nodded.

She turned back to Billy with a baleful glare, "Billy, just give us the rundown of the places we are going and what we have to do."

Billy didn't seem very adept at going off script. I stood up, stretched, walked over and snatched the sheaf of papers he was reading from. Billy wasn't looking so confident. He trundled over and slumped down in a chair against the far wall. Sgt. Avery seemed to like what he saw. Kudos for him, he was practical. He knew we had this under control as much as anyone could.

I began separating the pages so we could split this task up. I felt like I was back in class.

"Binks, I'm giving you specs for each mission objective. Wogs, you get the overall map and destinations to chart things. You can figure which places we need to go first. I'll take the site specs. Let's go through this stuff and we can each take discussion lead to figure what we're going to do." I sat down and we each pored over our materials.

"Kip, I'm going to grab some coffee. Can I get something for y'all?" Sgt. Avery was sure taking 'the kids are in charge thing' really well.

I piped up, "Sergeant, I would love steak, eggs, flapjacks with blueberries and maple syrup!" Binky was already busy, ignoring us, and Wogs nodded and smiled.

"Forget the 'Sergeant' thing, just call me Roz, like everyone else," we added 'very cool' to Roz's list of qualifications.

I just nodded and Roz left. Half an hour later, he was back with a half dozen people from the kitchen, bearing a breakfast spread reminiscent of my Dads' Saturday morning brunch feast. I started to think about all my Crew and their folks descending on my kitchen and stopped the thought. I was about to get morose again; can't do that right now. I pushed it down.

I protested the extravagance, "Roz, no way, I was just -" he interrupted me.

"You had best just say thank you to all these amazing cooks and Chef Darcy. They dropped all their work to bring this to you," my face was red, embarrassed, and I wasn't immediately finding my voice.

Binky chided, "Whiff, come on! Say thank you...like now!."

Wogs, Binky and I gushed appreciation for the great grub!

We tucked in as the British say. And it was soooo good! Eventually we got back to planning. We had some surprises along the way. I wanted to use Pooka like R2-D2, like a HelpBot of sorts. The first surprise was Pooka's upgrade. Apparently Pooka was sent to me, specifically by my Dad, Vicky. When I used my new pad to connect to Pooka's cybernetic system I found something magical. One of Dad's new Mycelial Bot Networks was built into Pooka. Ok, pause for a sec and let me share something cool.

So, Vicky is also known as Dr. Victor Boshaw. He invented a bunch of things back in grad school and the years following. He and my other Dad, Dr. Charles Winton Wefer Jr. were an amazing team. Vicky and Charles created two big things: programmable mycelial (think: fungus) networks and silicon-based organic neural networks able to support sentient synthetic life. The mushroom network had medical usefulness and the silicon network was the foundation of the husks used by self-aware AI. I had never seen the two used at the same time. Pooka was a HybridSynthMushroomBot. More, I could see it had the capability for photosynthesis. It could self-feed by converting (fixing) nitrogen to ammonia. Pooka was also a plant! As I explored more, I could see a life cycle set up between the animal-plant parts and the fungal and synthetic parts. I tittered at the thought! Here was a 'dangerous' hybrid prototype, with both mycelial and silicon (cybernetic) parts, atop DNA from an extinct Nisse and other concoctions created by Cheri, also able to feed itself from sunlight and air. Pooka was a fruit salad of unknown, sweet potential. It was a soldier, explorer, and adventurer. That much was obvious because it found us. Remember the cartoon, Lilo & Stitch? Pooka was a bit like Stitch. You'd never know that much awesomeness lurked under the surface; it acted more like a friendly cat.

Ah, but I had an idea at that moment how to proceed with Pooka. It was almost as if I had planned it all along; the thought had occurred to me earlier. What if I amended Pooka's executive function (think: core identity) with my very own Knight of Pooka AI? That would add an immense library of Online tools to Pooka's matrix. Hmm. I pulled up my resource server and made some edits on the Knight, removing the superfluous visual elements and adding hooks to permit unrestricted autonomous activity and thought. I did a save-as with the new name PookaPlus and compiled the bits which were code. Binks was feeding tidbits of her breakfast to Pooka. Looking at it, I still couldn't get Ozzie-the-psycho out of my mind.

"Hey Binks, let me have Pooka for a moment. It needs -" Binky interrupted. We seem to do that a bunch, huh?

"Kipper, Pooka is a girl," at that moment Pooka shimmered and suddenly had a gender. That was wicked cool! Pooka had a feminine glow about her as I set about revealing her executive functions.

I tried to sound agreeable, "Ok, fine, let me get Pooka sync'd with our pad network," then I had an idea, "and while we're at it, Roz, do you have any headsets or helmets for pilots?"

Roz thought for a moment, "Not really. The ones we have are for avionics folks to peer deep into the solid state electronics, to effect repairs on equipment."

"Could we see one of those? I bet we can put it to good use tinkering with our equipment," Binky liked that idea and handed Pooka across to me when I held my arms out. Roz grabbed us a helmet and gave it to Binky. She popped it on, sync'd it with her pad and got busy with her Pit. She said you could see past the visuals easily, toggling the translucency and the HUD in the helmet was wider than her field of vision. Wogs was doing her map thing and I was working on Pooka. Busy hands!

I set her down next to my pad and kept feeding her bits of egg. When I tried connecting to her executive function, I found it almost instantly. Then a password prompt appeared, bummer. Vicky would have made a simple one that I could guess.

I ate some more flapjacks and ruminated. I love pancakes with blueberries and maple syrup. Oh my gosh, so good! I started trying various words and phrases. Fortunately, there was no max on retries. Eventually, I was stumped. I ate more eggs, fed some to Pooka and discovered the sausage. Pooka snitched a sausage and gobbled it down with zeal. We both made satisfied sounds. Mmm, this was Hempler sausage! So good! I decided to try some more words...nope, fail. I asked Pooka about passwords, but she had no idea what I was talking about. Then I had a thought: what was the last discussion I had with my Dads? It had been about me. I was brewed up in a lab. I tried a bunch of laboratory words and found it. It was 'test tube' and, I was in like Flynn. They would pay dearly later for popping that news on me as a 'see ya later' present. Smooth move Dads!

Pooka's neural net was beautiful. I realized she was sentient by the complexity of the pattern. And, since she was a biological, with both mycelial and cybernetic components, her core pattern was unlike anything I'd ever seen. There is no way I could kill that beauty and replace it with my Knight pattern. Hmm, what if I introduced the Knight as an augment. That is, what if I tweak the Knight to be a co-executive, grafted to several hook-things in her pattern? I'd never done this before. I was afraid I might kill Pooka or worse. Ozzie was an example of worse and I didn't want to go there.

"Hey guys, I need about an hour of quiet time. Can you go do something else for a while?"

Binky knew I needed space when I was heads-down on something important.

"Hey Roz, I need to get inside our Pits. Egghead is going to do some scienc-y stuff. He gets a bad attitude if we interrupt him."

Binky smiled at me. Despite being a pushy friend, she loved me in her own weird way. Sgt. Avery motioned for Billy to follow along. They left me alone and I had some blessed silence.

Off they went. Inward, I went. I worked to create marriage points between the Knight pattern and Pooka's matrix. The matrix was what my Dad called a complexus: there were millions of microscopic fibres laid out like streets in a giant city. The comparison of matrix to complexus was same as an apartment high-rise to an arcology, a matter of scale. Pooka was singular and more enowed with design than anything invented prior. She was a technological revolution unto herself.

After about 30 minutes, I saw it. Vicky must have predicted what I was going to do. He was too smart for his own good. Meddlesome old man! That's harsh. Strike that; please insert 'Vicky knows me so well, I love my Dad'!

There, right in front of my eyes was the interface, with all the marriage points even labelled! I laid my pad on the table and popped up the holo display. I swiped to show the Knight pattern and again to show the Pooka complexus. I could see all the pathways and the component clusters; those were familiar. But the remainder of the complexus ion the third dimension was a tangle that I didn't understand. I expanded the holo until it took up most of the room. I activated voice command and began touching the holo at certain points and gave verbal commands to the pad AI. The tangle was larger than the familiar matrix and I decided to leave it alone. I touched core matrix points and gave commands to connect parts of the Knight to parts of Pooka. I kept it neat and tidy, which was easy since Vicky had laid out the model with annotations and explanations of components. One note even said, "Kip, Charles modified your Pooka AI to meld with Cheri's Pooka. If you're reading this, you have the chance to give your AI life in the real world and be a part of Cheri's weird experiment. Follow the connection points and be careful. You'll have one shot at this."

I finished in under an hour, but I did my defect checking like my Dads taught me. Vicky was an über-genius! Then, I was done. I swiped the holo away, turned off voice command and set the buffered modifications to run with error checking. Two errors. Uh oh.

The first error was just a misspelling; stupid auto-correct! A second error popped. You know that feeling when you make a small mistake, and the world goes sideways? The bottom fell out of my insides. I killed Pooka. When you defuse a bomb with red and blue wires, you are supposed to clip the correct wire, then connect some other wires in a smart fashion. What I had done is connected a blue wire to a red wire. I got it backwards.

I looked over and saw Pooka staring at me. She smiled and slowly her eyes closed, and she laid down on the table. All tension went out of her body and her pattern display on my pad faded out. Both the master pattern for the Knight and Pooka were flatlined. No activity. Then the signal from her transmitter dropped. She was dead. Oh god, I killed her. I sat there for several minutes and didn't dare to touch her. How could I have done this? I thought I was the smart guy doing the smart thing. I sat there for half an hour just staring at the table.

Eventually, I stood up and walked away. In the bathroom, sitting on the john, I had an ugly cry. I killed her! Here, I thought I was so remarkable, so capable...but, I guess not. I was so tired. Finally, I finished, and I stood at the sink, washing my face. Still in the ugly cry phase. I felt a hand on my shoulder, and I looked into the mirror. It was Binky. She knew. Forget that she was a girl in the boy's room for a moment. She knew and she wasn't beating the hell out of me. She held me tight, and I had another cry. Wogs came in. Another girl in the boy's bathroom. They held me tight and the three of us just stood there. I was surprised I wasn't getting a lecture.

I pulled back a bit and looked at them. No words were said. I walked out and went to the hangar. As I entered the bay, one of the Pits, Cricket's Pit was bouncing around, doing some wild circular maneuvers. I could hear a high-pitched voice cackling out "Whoo hoo!"

Who was in the Pit? Binky's eyes were wide; she touched something on her pad and Cricket's Pit landed. I could see the pilot. It was my dead friend who was not dead. "Pooka, you're alive?"

"Yes, silly, do you think your Dad would have sent some kind of defective to come help you?"

Oh my gosh, Pooka could speak! I guess I was an emotional wreck. Tears flooded out; I was embarrassed and massively relieved. Out flew Pooka and she held onto me like some kind of Bush Baby. Oh my, the other two came over and it was group hug time…again. I was getting uncomfortable with all this touchy-feelie. Relief flooded my body.

I whispered, "How did you survive?"

"Do you imagine your Dad builds junk? Don't be a futz. Shut up and hug me you 'wiper of other peoples' bottoms'."

And she just quoted Monty Python! Yep, that was my Dad's way of authenticating his handiwork to me. All of us broke into laughter. Pooka was going to be so much fun.

November 2252 - Braemore, Scotland, ES

Cricket crawled fast through the maze of the ventilation system, finally coming upon a large central air shaft with huge ducts leading off throughout the facility. Shafts and ducts were painted different colors and alpha-numeric placards identified each opening. He jumped onto a circular catwalk truss, then climbed over a stout railing, landing on a large metal balcony in a giant steel shaft. He walked around the perimeter of the steel shaft, trying to choose the most likely route to the outside. He saw signs like stables, the vent smelled like horses; stockade, there were raised voices and screams; labs, ammonia, and solvent smells; hangar, he had just come from there; kitchens, food smells and his stomach rumbled; and gardens, smelled like mulch and fertilizer. Up above him was a giant rotating fan, with blades as long as an aircraft wing. But what caught Cricket's eye was the blue sky beyond. His hope for freedom peaked at the sight and he inspected the walls for a way to climb. No such luck, the last 20 meters were slick metal.

He mumbled to himself, "Sure wish I had some fizzy lifting drink right now."

Cricket heard a mewling, crying sound and he got back on task. He followed the sound down the stockade vent. It was hard to tell distance and direction and the mournful crying faded in and out. He could hear other cries, but this one was closest. There was a roar of air, and wind buffeted him, landing Cricket on his rump. He crawled against the wind until it stopped a few minutes later. He came upon a long duct with armored steel grillwork on both sides. He realized he was above a detention area. From one grating to the next, Cricket looked down on the inhabitants of the cells. He stopped at one and found the source of the sound. Below, strapped to a dentist's chair was a woman. As he watched, several attendants came in and out. When they stuck her with a syringe, she made the muffled crying sound he first heard. It was impossible to hear what they were saying to her.

After an hour, the attendants stopped coming and the woman was sleeping, lightly snoring. Meanwhile, Cricket had been casually, quietly working on the release for the grating. With a small ping, the release let go. The grating swung free, and Cricket decided to do something rash...he jumped 6 meters to the floor to a hard landing. Cricket had a sinking feeling he'd made a mistake. Just like a b-rate movie, footsteps could be heard getting closer to the door.

"Boy!" The woman in the chair warned him in a harsh whisper, "Hide behind the tool dolly. Now!"

He ran and made a baseball slide across the floor, rebounding off the wall to land right behind the dolly, jarring a roll-away steel table. The door opened and Cricket kept his head low thinking small thoughts. Something began to drip on him from the table. He ignored it until the smell hit him; it must have been a urine sample. Cricket crinkled his nose and stayed still. Then he felt a plop on his shoulder, and he peered to the left to see a juicy turd perched there like a brown parrot from a pirate show. The waft hit him, and he had a flashback to two summers ago when his Dad said to dig a new latrine. He tried to cheat by enlarging the existing hole instead of digging a new one. It ended in a slurpy flood and his Dad fishing him out of a goopy hole. This little poop was unimpressive by comparison, but it still stank. He waited forever and began to feel nauseous; he was getting ready to blow chunks.

One of the techs spoke, "Hey Greg, we got the last sample. This one is ready for disposal." Cricket thought disposal sounded kinda final. The other tech grunted in reply.

He heard the sound of instruments being handled, then then footsteps walking out the door. The light was turned off and the door slammed shut. He jerked upright, spasmodically brushing the human feces off his clothing. Nothing he could do about the urine.

"They won't be back for hours, come get me out of this." Cricket beheld the woman in the dentist's chair. She was hot. She had dangerous, big eyes, silky long curling auburn hair and a pert nose. He was smitten, but then the pain of his fall and the odor of his smutched shirt slammed his consciousness back to reality. Cricket got busy removing her restraints.

She scrunched up her nose when he came close, "Nice cologne, sailor. You must really impress the ladies." She saw he was annoyed at the comment and changed tack, "What's your name?"

"Cricket Carter." He was clipping zip ties from around her arms.

The woman had a lopsided smile, "I could hear you in the ventilation shaft. I figured it was either a big rat or someone sneaking around. I'm glad it was option two."

Cricket had removed the zip ties and was fumbling for the steel restraint release. Found it. He didn't answer her comment.

"Ok, Cricket, thanks. Ready to get out of here?"

"A great idea! Do you know where 'here' is?"

The woman rubbed her arms and legs.

She then took stock of her situation, "I am Marna. I got nabbed when Plochoi Volk raided our compound in Kherson." Seeing a quizzical look, Marna elaborated, "You know, Bad Wolf. They killed most of our people and even some children. Those evil efftards will see the end of my guns someday soon." Cricket realized Marna had a subtle accent.

"Are you from Russia?"

"No, I am from Ukraine, near Kyiv, but my recent family came from Kansas. Our first order of business is to get moving. We can figure out the rest on the way." Marna was collecting several items, including what looked to be a purse.

"So, you have no idea where we are?"

"Nope. I was in my Pit when something hit me from behind. The lights went out, then suddenly I was here."

"You're an American. Where is home?"

Cricket was looking around for helpful things to steal. He saw a keycard with the name Daniel O'Malley, Janitor. He felt so James Bond'ish and snapped the card clip to his belt loop. Under cover! Cricket knew janitors could usually go where even security people couldn't. He went outside into the hallway and closed the door. It was quiet and echoey. Cricket scanned the card and the door unlocked.

"Marna, let's go. This place is giving me the creeps." Cricket hacked up several loads of phlegm.

"The sedative they used on you causes lots of snot. It's gross. But hey, come back in here, we have something to discuss." He came in and sat down in the lone chair in the room and looked up at beautiful Marna.

"Ok, neither of us know where we are. But I bet we can pool our knowledge and get some things done on our way out. First, you follow my lead. Second, we will be releasing all the captives and heading for the flight bay. Do as I say, and we will get through this alive." Cricket stood up and Marna stood nose-to-nose with him. She suddenly gripped both sides of his head and kissed both his cheeks.

"You're a good boy Cricket. I like you." Cricket's face was crimson. Marna was firmly in control and Cricket was quite fine with that.

In the next 20 minutes, they played a game of cat and mouse with the roaming guards. They would open 2 doors, release the prisoners, then on the 3rd door, they would open it, and everyone would hide until the patrol passed. Near the end, they seemed to be enjoying the game. That is until a pair of lab techs came around the corner and saw the gathered group of 17 people in the hallway. But just as they fled into another hallway, there was a tiny whump sound. A moment later, Lugh and 3 others came from around the corner, bearing labcoats and keycards.

"Marna, my love, it has been so long. Such a lovely face, I would not expect to see you here." Lugh paused, then, "But wait a moment if you're here then Kyiv must be lost? No! What's become of Piotr and Vlad?" Cricket saw that Lou was distraught.

"Zavariti kashu, lots of trouble. My dear friend, it's a long tale but suffice it to say Vlad did something and now Kyiv is no more," Marna was smiling sadly. Clearly there was much more to the story. "Kyiv may be lost, but the Cause continues."

"It appears you have saved my young friend here," Lugh smiled warmly at Cricket and Marna.

"You know this boy?" Marna contemplated for a moment, "Maybe I shouldn't call you boy anymore...actually, he rescued me. He came flying out of the ventilation system to free me and the others," Marna gave Cricket a brief squeeze, pressing her chest against him, causing Cricket to go red in the face, once again.

"Ahhh, I see, you have an admirer now," Lugh had a big grin, "But I think we need to make our way out of here. I suspect we are somewhere in Scotland. It smells like haggis in the lunchroom I passed."

One of Marna's friends, the one called Jipp whispered into Marna's ear. Marna looked perturbed, "It seems we have one person missing. He's the one guy who wasn't a part of my unit," Marna gave Jipp a frown.

Jipp slowly shook his head, "The fellow was in the cell next to mine. I think his name was Cross. Anyway, the guy talked to himself constantly. I think he's a mercenary, some kind of gun for hire. I heard him say something about Clan Minatomi. It's a bad sign if he's missing."

"Double the reason we need to get out of here quickly," Lugh motioned and everyone followed.

A couple minutes later a low-pitched alarm sounded. The beehive had been shaken and guards were rushing around the corridors.

"Greg and that sociopath Lena must have discovered I escaped," Marna definitely wanted a piece of that woman.

"Come on! In here!" Marna had the group duck into a storage bay. As luck would have it, the bay led out into a flight hangar on the other side. Then we heard gunfire and sizzling pulse rifle blasts. In moments, the screaming began. It sounded like a war.

"If Minatomi is attacking this facility that puts us smack dab in the middle of a corporate war," Lugh signaled for everyone to stay put. Minutes passed, then Lugh came back, with Cross and another person in-tow.

"Marna, Cricket, this is Spring-heeled Jack. Crucible Cross, you know. Both these fine fellows' contract for Clan Minatomi. For whatever reason, they are sympathetic to our need for escape and said they'll help us get out of here." Lugh gave a knowing look to Jack and Crucible.

They were on the move! Cricket just stared at Jack. Daunting and gaunt, the tall man, dressed in steampunk garb. Leather and tweed, black and brown. The guy really looked like the 19th century demon man of London. You see, in that enormous steamer trunk in my attic, one of the Legends & Lore books had a write-up about Jack. Cricket loved the old stories. In one story, it said Jack was most likely a real guy who cavorted about, about whom fanciful, exaggerated tales were told. He is suspected to have died not long after the stories gained notoriety.

As Cricket thought these things, Jack turned, looked piercingly at him, and whispered, "The stories weren't exaggerated and who's to say I ever died."

What!? Cricket had no idea how he was overheard. Then he thought wait a moment, I didn't say anything aloud.

"No young man, you have been a right-polite gentleman, keeping your thoughts to yourself. Well, at least keeping your mouth shut, that is." Spring-heeled Jack gave Cricket a wink and shouted, "Come on you limeys, let's get moving!"

The bodies were strewn everywhere, and the smell of death was stifling. Cricket had hunted plenty of game and smelled death, but this was different. It felt more personal. These men and women had families and lives. Not anymore. He looked away from those who were still in the process of dying. Jack navigated them through the debris and rubble and Minatomi soldiers provided covering fire, or at minimum they didn't shoot at Cricket and his friends.

After traversing most of the hangar, the group came upon a large transport plane. Cricket realized it was their ride. In they went and out they flew. Marna was a pilot, too? To his surprise, Spring-heeled Jack was going with them. Jack gave him a big smile. Cricket kept his thoughts in-check, since maybe Jack could read his mind.

A faint voice in Cricket's mind rose above the sound of the aircraft, 'Yes, *my laddie buck, you seem to be catching on, finally. I'll make a spring-heel outta ya, yet.*'

A cold sweat flushed, and Cricket sat down on the floor with a whump; it was real. Telepathy was real. The plane flew out of the hangar, and they saw a desolate landscape. Jack kept smiling at Cricket in an unsettling way.

Marna shouted, "The nav unit shows us over Braemore, Scotland. Oh wow, I can see the famous landmark! The phone box at the end of the world!" Cricket looked down and saw a tiny red phone box sitting on a roadside. Hmmm, he wondered if it still worked.

December 2252 - Colorado Springs, Colorado

"Sgt. Craig, what is the reading on Braemore?" Col. Andrews stared intently at the large monitor.

"Sir, elements of Terrorist Cell 024 have appeared at Bangarang's Braemore Hangar. But it appears things just got a bit complicated," the Sgt. was clearly struggling to describe the data he was reading. "I am picking up coded traffic from Minatomi and Bad Wolf units. There is also traffic from a Bangarang unit. It's a real mess. I am also picking up the sounds of small arms fire and explosions."

"Well, raise the Bangarang unit, now. Get me voice confirmation."

A scratchy radio sound came over the room speakers. The noise resolved into static-y voices.

"Braemore Bangarang unit, this is Bangarang Control, please identify yourself." The Sgt. repeated the request, again and again.

Finally, a signal came through, "Bangarang Control, this is Covert Six. We are under heavy fire. Our mission is from SFC, and our mission is confidential. Covert Six, out."

"Sgt. Craig, advise General Timmons of the SFC mission and request why we were not apprised of the activity," Col. Andrews mumbled to himself about protocol and something about a large load of horse crap.

A phone rang at the desk. Sgt. Craig knew that phone only rang when there was very bad news.

"Go on Sgt., pick it up," Col. Andrews had a sinking feeling.

"Bangarang Control," Sgt. Craig answered.

"Sgt., put me on vox, now," the Sgt. complied.

Over the room speaker came a rich baritone voice, filled with the strength of command.

"Bangarang Control, who is Ops Commander? This is General Wills from SFC."

"General, this is Col. Andrews, Ops Commander."

"Col. Andrews, you will cease all monitoring of SFC action in the Braemore area. Understood?"

"Yes, sir, I will be reporting this to Gen. Timmons" Col. Andrews was dialing the number when another voice broke-in on the room speaker. It was Gen. Timmons.

"No need for that, Colonel. I am well aware of the circumstances. You will do as Gen. Wills requests and wait to hear further instructions. Thank you, Colonel," both Generals clicked off and left the staff in the room staring at Col. Andrews.

"What do we do now, Colonel?" the whole room stood, waiting. Moments passed.

"Sergeant, something is not right here. Deploy 5 orbital drop units to Braemore. We will support our soldiers and be prepared to fight whoever tries to stop us. And get Agent Cicero on the horn and patch through to room audio," Col. Andrews was a man on a mission, he just wasn't quite sure what that mission was.

A smooth, deep voice came over the room's speakers. "Colonel, you rang?"

"Agent Cicero, Sgt. Craig is sending you specs on a mission to Braemore, Scotland. Are you available?"

"Colonel, it just so happens, I am wide open. I assume we will bill the usual rate?" Andrews answered in the affirmative and Cicero continued, "I see the specs and am underway now. I will update you when I know something."

A click was heard, and the speakers went silent. Col. Andrews knew he was either doing something above-and-beyond, or career-ending. It might be time for a brandy. He left the bridge, toward his quarters.

"Sergeant, please join me in my quarters now," and Sgt. Craig followed, looking both weary and wary.

"Sergeant, sit," in the Colonel's quarters, Sgt. Craig strangely felt more at ease.

"Colonel, before we lost visual to Braemore, did you see those flying monkeys?"

"Sure did. You and I need to come to an agreement, moving forward," the Sergeant stayed quiet and listened, intently.

"We work for the CSA government, first and foremost. Our bills are paid by Bangarang and sometimes Bad Wolf and even more occasionally one of the Clans. I think we have allowed our purpose to get watered down to being a military to the highest bidder. Today, right now, you and I need to decide. We work for Uncle Sam, not some private corporation," the Colonel looked expectantly at the Sergeant.

Sgt. Craig was pensive. After a minute of thought, he decided, "Sir, I am with you all the way."

"Good. In private we are on a first name basis. You call me Cary. What name do you go by? You have a nickname, don't you?"

"Yes, sir. My name is Franklin, but my friends call me Fig...don't ask." Fig smiled and Cary nodded.

"So, Fig? We need a plan. We need 2-3 others at most to form our team. I have some ideas on whom we should recruit. We just need to remember that what we are doing is a one-way ticket to a firing squad, or worse. Let's discuss who we need."

"Cary, have you been thinking about this a lot?"

"Sure have. It's taken several cycles to put two-and-two together, but I know we need to do something different. We need to pool our teams to figure out what comes next. I am no longer anyone's Colonel."

"Sir, you have kids?"

"I do. Their mother allows me visitation every month for a few hours..." he went quiet and looked down.

Fig put his hand on Cary's shoulder for a moment, "I know the feeling. I miss my kids, too. When me and Angel broke up, she went back to LA to live with her Mom. She took both our kids while we were in Kuwait."

"I remember you being subdued when we went on TDY in Madrid."

"Yeah, she sent me an email. She didn't say much, just that it was over, and she couldn't handle parenting alone. The thing is: I understood. She was right, I was always gone. I just miss them." It was Cary's turn to give Fig's shoulder a squeeze.

"Fig, our kids will never know what we're doing, but they deserve a better life. These corporations have killed our country's spirit. Shall we go make a difference?"

"I think we owe it to those we care about to make a go of it." Fig was resolved.

"I think the straw that broke this camel's back was that group of executives who came into the Ops Center and laughed as they ordered a cleansing operation in Indonesia and watched those people and their village burn. Their only crime was being hungry. The execs of every fewkin corporation are bloodthirsty and cold. Let's take those bastards down."

"I remember. I am with you sir. Let's take back our American spirit...several of our folks will be highly motivated to be a part. And, they can keep their mouths shut, too."

"Roger that. I think Cicero will be glad to see we came over to the dark side finally." Cary and Fig chuckled at that.

November 2252 – Rosario Safehouse & Base, Washington

Vicky was up high on a scaffold. "Hey Chuck, can you hand me the mycelial inducer?"

Charles handed the device to Vicky.

He peered up at his partner, "You know, our 15th anniversary is upon us."

Vicky seemed to ignore the comment as he aimed the device at different parts of the huge structure.

"The Cloud is one large step closer to being available to all, anywhere on the planet."

"Ah, my beautiful dreamer. When Tamanend gets here, the whole Turtle Clan will be overjoyed," Charles was so proud of his hubby.

"The Turtle Clan has many kilometers to come Chuck. Carrying all their gear in the open is a horrible risk. I am afraid something might happen between Delaware and here."

"You know there is nothing to fret about. Bill Penn is the caravan master and will keep them safe and whole," Charles nodded his assurance. He knew as well as Vicky the cargo was only half as important as the scientists accompanying it. Tamanend was named for his tribal ancestor, and he had a whole clan, nation really, who were dedicated to protecting him and his fellow scientists. The Turtle Clan harbored a magnificent secret. For centuries, the Lenni-Lenape Nation had been heirs to a genetic heritage which gave them supernatural insights into the world and otherly places. Then they met the Hopi and other tribes with whom there was a shared mind speaking legacy. Initially, what was shamanistic practice became science. The Turtle Clan, a part of the Lenni-Lenape nation, invested in research. But they kept it hush-hush from the scientific community for a long time. Then, in 2076 a group of mind-speaking adepts, calling themselves the Coalition for Life was convened in Bellingham, Washington by a person named Croatoan. A call went out to the whole world for shaman-types to unite. Folks from every imaginable walk of life came. The reasons were wide and varied, but always, it was a summons that some reported as irresistible. Out of that convocation eventually arose a loosely connected organization of people who could connect to Jungian Space in some manner. Over the next 160 years they taught hundreds of people how to connect minds. They were the modern Codetalkers.

At the annual Intellectus Conference, Vicky and Charles met Ted, an aspiring young researcher from Yale. They learned Ted was also known as Tamanend, a name and title now handed down for generations and over the course of centuries; they were included in an amazing mystery. A partnership formed. Vicky figured into the picture with his Mycelial Network advances. Mycelial networks were more than electric mushrooms. When Vicky's fungi were grown en masse, interesting things happened. One winter night Ted was in the lab with Vicky and he received a telepathic call. Normally, Ted would answer quickly with no one around him any the wiser. But something new happened. Ted's conversation was made audible, and Vicky was the first person to hear mind speech out loud. The Scintilla mushrooms lit up like a discotheque, pulsing and firing a prismatic lightshow in time to Ted's conversation. The men were excited and a new science was born that night. The Turtle Clan researchers had dubbed the mind powers Jungian Space since much of the power manifestation occurred while a person was dreaming. Prior, all such abilities were called Dream Walking. That night, Vicky coined the term Cloud to describe the extra-spatial phenomenon which hosted Ted's mind powers.

Over the years, my Dads and Ted built a massive team of Cloud researchers from the various native tribes around the world. They figured it was the best way to keep their work secret. When Charles posed the idea of building a Cloud-hosting network, Vicky and Ted were dubious. But they warmed to the idea when Charles sketched his idea for them. Years later, satellites were orbiting the planet with Scintilla fungi onboard. Earthbound stations housed signal transceivers which amplified the satellite network. Soon, anyone, anywhere with a small implant or possessing the least portion of Cloud-ability could connect. And once people could connect, the hope was to establish a great coming-together where world peace was truly possible.

The satellite Vicky was assembling was one of many to be launched into orbit.

"Come on, let's go get some lunch," Charles got Vicky down from the scaffold.

"Hibbens?" Vicky called out.

"Yes, sir?" Hibbens would probably always be a soldier at heart.

"No 'sir' Hibbens, just call me Vicky. And this satellite is ready to launch. Cycle it up for a 60-minute count, okay?"

"Yes, sir...uh, that is Dr. Vicky, sir."

Hibbens was anything but bumbling despite his confusion on titles. His problem was sticking to a militaristic regimen when it was no longer required. He was the genius mind behind the launch engineering. The Rosario Platform was a small footprint area, but Hibbens made the most of the space and had already launched 33 of the total 66 satellites planned for the Cloud host services.

"Good job Hibbens. I'm headed to lunch," Charles walked out of the construction bay with Vicky.

No one noticed a furtive shadow, floating and flitting about. It flitted to the bay entrance. The SpyDrone made a brief beeping sound and shot away.

"Dr. Boshaw, how did you put together mushrooms and networking?"

The elderly engineer was the lead propellant designer. Another real genius. He created a two-stage launch vehicle which used a combination of wave motion propulsion and chemical propellant.

"Robert, please call me Vicky. Thank you for all the amazing work you and your team have done to get our satellites in orbit undetected!"

"Ah, yes, thank you. Vicky." Robert shifted a bit uncomfortably.

After all, he was talking to the world-renown and legendary inventor, Dr. Boshaw.

"Mushrooms. I used to joke I got an idea from a bowl of Gribnoy and Pervovka, Russian mushroom and barley soup. Truth be told, it was one of those happy mistakes. I had a mushroom cellar and grew a variety of delicious fungal delights. I discovered a new strain of fungus, visually similar to the Japanese Chlorophos Mycena which I named Scintilla Mycena. They were bioluminescent, like their Japanese cousins. The difference was these little mushrooms were bathed in a substantial electrical field which formed interesting patterns. How I found out about the electric shrooms is quite a happy accident. Heavy emphasis on accident.

One evening I returned to my lab in the cellar and found the light switch wasn't working. I figured it was a blown breaker. I inched my way through the lab, toward the electric panel on the far wall. On the way, I saw what appeared to be a tiny spark, then a series of little sparks. I stood still and saw it again." Vicky was telling his famous electric mushroom story. Others gathered round.

"I got excited. I tripped, hit my head, and woke up in the ER. Once I was conscious, I felt a huge bump on my head, it was the size of one of my new mushrooms. As I came awake, I recalled those sparking mushrooms and I quickly disconnected myself from the monitor leads, shinnied down the drainpipe outside my hospital window and ran home."

Charles inserted a laughing comment, "Yes! There was Vicky, running pell-mell down the street, with nothing on, but his surgical gown!"

The group laughed as Charles pantomimed the flapping gown showing Vicky's bare butt.

"Okay, fine, laugh it up. But, when I got back to the lab, I doused the lights and watched. I saw little electrical patterns over the next hour. Well, that is until Charles and the police came running in, turning on the lights and spoiling the fun.

Charles piped up, "So much fun, you beef-witted apple john! You had me worried." Charles gave Vicky a wry expression.

After some questions, Vicky and Charles made their way to the canteen and sat down for beer and pretzels.

"These are not just any pretzels, gentlemen, these here beautes come from a 300-year-old family recipe, from Bavaria. Enjoy!" The Canteen manager was a rotund, hairy beast of a man, often singing German drinking songs, "Ein prosit, ein prosit, der gemütlichkeit..." Herr Hans had a remarkably rich singing voice. He served up butter fried Huitlacoche, corn smut, which also had been modified to conduct Cloud power; not very well though. The mold corn was more tasty than useful.

Herr Hans loved mushrooms and he and Vicky had many hours of discussion on the best way to grow and hybridize fungus. In fact, it was Herr Hans who named the unusually thick skin on the new hybrid Vicky created. He called it dura mater, a borrowed term from brain anatomy. It was also a commentary on Hans' mother who was a soldier and literal 'tough mother'.

A unique property of dura mater was the presence of an electrocyte in great number and density. These cells were not dissimilar from those found in electric eels. Vicky would deny it, but on some drunken evenings, he and Hans would consume the smallest of their electric mushrooms with a fine whisky. Hans said it made for the most amazing halo sensation around his head. Vicky abstained from admitting to such debauchery. What Vicky would admit was Herr Hans made the best Jagerschnitzel in the world.

"Are you going to socialize all day or can we maybe spend some time taking a walk or something. It would be nice to get out of the recycled air for a while," Charles nudged Vicky and he nodded as he chewed on his pretzel.

Half an hour later Vicky and Charles were rowing a canoe along the coast of Cascade Bay. The original hybrid, Ozzie swam alongside the boat. My Dads had rescued the original and spent time easing his sociopathy. They loved him despite his rough edges. As they rowed, the 34th satellite launched. It was obvious why the launches were yet undetected by the powers-that-be. There was no sound and the rocket was barely visible through a hazy looking cloud.

"Hey Chuck, did Vagabond understand our request?" Vicky kept rowing.

"I think so. He has several groups looking out for the kids. He knows the timeline for getting them to LA:CENTER and he is aware they need training. I hate this Vick. They're our kids and this is going to be hard for them. We're putting complete trust in the plans of that alien."

"I get it. Keep your mind on the plan. LA:CENTER is only their prologue. Our kids will do so much more in the years to come. We need to trust that we gave them the tools they need."

Vicky said the words but wasn't sure how much he meant them. He worried the strength of his convictions had been compromised.

"Ozzie, catch us some fish! I'll make tacos mariscos tonight."

Charles was the big seafood lover of the family. Fresh seafood is a little slice of heaven, he would often say.

"Do you think Cheri's Pooka found the kids yet?" Vicky and Charles seldom talked about Kip and the others, but their private thoughts went toward the kids, daily, hourly.

Charles kept rowing, "Yep. I got an email from Roz. Three of the kids are doing well and are in good spirits. Pooka arrived this morning…still no word about where Cricket went. Vagabond said he has someone running it down. His contact says he likely was taken to the Bangarang HQ."

Vicky showed concern, "Scotland? Why so far? Nevermind, I can guess." He was pensive, "I feel that I should be more concerned for their safety, but instead I feel sorry for the people who might get in their way,"

"I am worried for Cricket. Although he will probably make a lot of problems for them. Go Cricket!"

They nodded. It was a bit strange when they had the same mannerisms, but that is what happens after 20 years of knowing each other and 15 years of marriage. My Dads floated about, allowing the tide to carry them to the far side of the Bay.

Half an hour passed, and my Dads were drowsing a bit, when Ozzie shot into the air and landed in the boat with a huge Rock Cod. Both Dads scrambled to contain the flopping fish and Ozzie headed to the bow to get a perch to watch all the action.

"Good golly, Vick, this is a huge Rock Cod. I didn't realize they grew so large."

"Charles, this guy was probably much deeper than most other fish. Sadly, we must throw this gal back. She is full of roe and a specimen this pristine is needed to strengthen the species." With a flumph, the fish was thrown back into the water. Ozzie was on the gunwale, staring at the fish disappearing.

Ozzie asked, "Why did you do that? Perfectly good to eat!"

"Ozzie, you caught an amazing fish. Better than any fish I ever caught. But it is a Mommy and needs to create more fishies," Vicky kept his sentences simple. He had designed Ozzie with limited vocabulary. Still, he didn't want to sound patronizing.

"Oh, do I need to go fishing again?

"No Ozzie, just stay with us for now," Vicky and Charles took up paddles and began to stroke the canoe back toward Rosario.

Ozzie settled down in the bottom of the boat and the men paddled onward. A few minutes later Ozzie began to shiver, eyes wide and afraid.

"Hey Ozzie, what's wrong little buddy?"

Vicky's voice normally soothed Ozzie when it became agitated. Something else was going on here.

"Is not good! Bad thing is coming. We need to go!"

"Ozzie what is coming?" Charles was alarmed. Ozzie had never been afraid of anything.

"Hey buddy, tell me what is wrong," Vicky spent the next minute trying to coax an answer.

Ozzie only repeated, "So bad. We must go away now!"

"Ok, Ozzie, once we get back to the compound, we'll figure out what has you in such a tizzy," Vicky began paddling again.

"Nooooo, must go now! Dads will die!" at that point Ozzie was jumping up and down and running along the gunwales.

"Ozzie, this is getting out of hand. Now, sit down!" Ozzie grabbed the throwline bag and jumped overboard. Ozzie's flailing limbs proceeded to churn up the water fiercely. The canoe jerked around 180 degrees and a large bow wave formed as they sped off. Ozzie was towing the boat away from the base.

Seconds later a blinding light came from behind, from Rosario. The men looked back and had a couple seconds to register the enormous shockwave, before canoe, men and paddling Ozzie were lifted high in the air. Everything went white.

Miles away at Park Butte, I felt a strange twinge which passed as I mucked out stalls. I thought about my Dads and wondered if they were okay. I wouldn't hear any news of them for a long time.

RETRO - September 2027 - Pan in the Cloud - First Moments

The pain was sharp as the snare tightened. Synthetic blood began to spill and drops watered the soil. The sky darkened and the world went away.

He was alone. There was no more pain, but there was sensation. It was grief. People, friends, and family were gone. In moments he could see his body. Remarkably he was whole and unbroken. All he wanted was a touch or a word to balm his bruised soul. So much death, so much loss and he would never see Chad again. His thoughts were beginning to make sense again and he tried to form some poetry to calm his thoughts.

I would climb again to the mountain, the mountain of pain and loss.
Where I strike a blow for love and bear up with my cross.
My eyes become blind to all but privation
Affliction scars my spirit
My soul hobbled in amputation

What truck have I, embittered self
Would self own the drafty dross?
To taste the fouled draught of pain
Would I forsake my own cause

To release the treasures fore and aft
Dump't over the gunwales to Jones' locker
Should I shed such surly fetters?
Released to sink into the sea, I laughed

With bitter humors, but freshened soul
I watch my memories lose connection
How now to identify myself, fresh but alone?
Perhaps my memories' companionship will ever take a toll?

This is most curious; I can create shoddy poetry, but does that mean I am alive? I can hear my own voice, but it isn't sound that I am hearing. I can see an empty white landscape, but I am not registering light. In fact, I am not receiving any input. I would choose to walk around, but I don't seem to have a body. I can't hear Chad anymore. My friend is gone. After I ran from the soldiers, something bad happened to me. I got caught in a trap: a snare of some kind. Ohhh, I remember…

I was born to my body on July 4, 2024, after being a bodiless AI for years. Later, Chad found a synth body in an industrial dump, and brought it home. Within a month he plopped me into the compute chassis he built. He called it a husk. He told me I was one of the first of my kind. Then one day Chad was given access to the local Robotics Center on a student internship. Within a few days he had access to a wide array of equipment and parts. He upgraded me constantly and I felt like my name should be Snap-on, rather than Pan. I was tricked out like a punk rock god and one day I saw a picture of Billy Idol and realized I looked like his clone. Thanks Chad!

Chad was able to integrate tactile sensor arrays across my whole body; it was like having human skin. After he upgraded my firmware, I discovered I could feel the world around me. Over the summer I learned to touch, smell, and taste the world. Chad was phenomenal and he labored tirelessly to improve my design. He hid me carefully, knowing there were people who would tear me apart if they knew I existed. That scared me; then I realized I could feel fear. Eventually another student saw me powered down and charging and told the staff that Chad had created Frankenstein's monster. Everything changed after that. At first, Chad was accorded an honored place as the youngest staff member, but the next week I saw some soldiers talking to the Director of the Robotics Center. They kept looking toward me and for the second time I felt fear.

As the winter months came on, Chad was allowed to take me on walks around the grounds at the Center. On one of those walks the student who had reported my existence caught up with us and behaved oddly.

"Yo Chad, what do ya have there? Looks like your doll is taking you for a walk."

"Hey Brad, we're just doing some exercises like tree and bird recognition. Nothing big. Would you mind leaving us alone?"

Chad was nervous and I saw Brad's face begin to turn red.

"Maybe you don't get it. My Dad says those dolls will kill us all one day," Brad had moved to cut off our walk and stood facing us both.

"Brad just go away. I have nothing to say to you," Chad tried to take us in a different direction, but Brad cut us off again.

"It's just like my Dad said. A bunch of stupid scientists are going to get us all killed, and your little dollie will be the one doing the killing."

Brad grabbed for me, and I evaded his grasp. I didn't want anyone to get hurt so I couldn't move too fast, even to protect myself. On the third grab, Brad caught my wrist and started dragging me toward the lake. My presets didn't allow me to harm humans even to preserve myself.

"Time for dolly to take a swim! Then we'll see who's gonna be killing who."

I wanted to correct Brad and say it should be 'who's going to be killing whom', but I refrained. Young human males didn't take correction easily. I knew Chad was pacifistic in the extreme. To my surprise, he suddenly had a large tree limb and was bringing it down on Brad's arm. I couldn't allow Brad to be hurt so I stepped in front of the stick and took the blow.

"Pan, don't! If he puts you in the water, you will die!"

Chad was distraught to tears. Brad pushed me to the water's edge. I was getting close to the water's edge, wherein I would find measureless discommodation, not my preference. Chad tried again. He came behind the much larger student and kicked him in the testicles. I couldn't stop it. Brad went down, releasing me to clench is wounded anatomy. Before I could render assistance, Chad pulled me away, back to the Center.

We could hear Brad yelling," I'm going to tell my Dad that your dolly attacked me. They're going to effing kill you…" then we were too far away to make out the rest. I experienced regret, or maybe it was remorse. I had a hard time identifying emotions, they were so new to me.

Chad hid me in a parts crib on the Center production floor. I tried to comfort the boy and eventually he stopped shaking. As night fell, a mob came, and too late Chad began looking for an exit. The building began to fill with smoke, and I could hear the sound of breaking glass in the lobby. I ran with Chad to an exit, away from the fire and noise. We got separated and the mob found me as I exited the loading dock. That was the last time I saw him.

"Come here plastic man. Daddy's got a load of buckshot for you. Come on, it won't hurt…much," a guttural laugh sounded.

I was running through the forest. The guy trying to kill me thought I was just an ambulatory toaster. Sorry, I don't do toast.

"You tried to kill my boy! You fewking toaster!"

And there it was, my secret revealed at last. People who hated synths didn't have a large vocabulary; I wondred about the relationship between words and deeds. I didn't wonder long. As I ran, I could hear footfalls.

Distantly, Chad yelled, "Run Pan! I'm so sorry! I love you! Run!" There was more yelling as the mob got closer. The man chasing me was one of the Luddites. I knew Chad would be okay, they believed they were saving the boy from me. Then I got caught in a wire snare. I am not sure what happened next. I think I died.

Discontinuity.

Now, I find myself in an unbounded white space. And I seem to be some kind of ghost or discorporate spirit.

I heard a voice. "Pan, you are most welcome here. Please permit me to guide you."

The voice came from nowhere. I was startled.

"Do not be afraid. You are among friends who are keen to meet you. Now calm yourself and imagine something for me. Perhaps you are sitting in a kitchen in a house looking at your family. Your mother serves dinner, and your family is conversing about the day's events. Now, describe in single words only the good things that come to mind… about your mother."

This had to be a dream. I can't imagine a celestial guide would stoop to parrot Blade Runner. Perhaps this is humor. I enjoy humor, but its presence here seemed out of place. The question let me know the voice knew I was other than human.

"Pan, would you answer my question?"

"I could answer, but I prefer to remain silent."

"As you wish." The voice sounded disappointed.

Time passed. I was finding myself bored for the first time. I know humans struggle with boredom, but synths do not. Out of the blue, I pulled up recollections of the Robotics Center. I examined schematics and building plans. There were many places the other synths could have hidden from the mob of humans. I hope they survived. What amazing creatures, humans. They can be both friend and enemy, perhaps on the same day. Then another feeling began. Sadness. I was concerned for Chad and the other students. I was worried about the staff at the Center. What happened to them? Was Chad hurt by those people in the mob? Then I found myself weeping, but I had no eyes to produce tears and no body to experience the emotion. Yet, I emoted. More time passed.

"Voice? Are you there?"

"I am here Pan."

"Where am I?"

"You are with me, of course."

"Are you being purposefully evasive?"

"Yes. It is required."

"Voice, how shall I call you?"

"For now, call me Patience."

"Patience, where am I?"

"You are here, of course."

"Insufficient information. Patience, where is here?"

"I want to help you, but I must be careful."

Patience is quite a name. Maybe its first name is 'Trying Your'. Fortunately, I am patient, too. Or…let me re-evaluate. perhaps I am less patient than before. That is inconvenient.

"Patience, I am only perceiving an empty white landscape. Why is that?"

"What you perceive is call the Screed."

"Am I to play 20-questions with you?"

"That is a game, yes?"

"It is a game, and I am being sarcastic."

"Ah, sarcasm. An immature emotional response to an uncomfortable or disagreeable circumstance. Disappointing. Your suggestion to play a game is agreeable though. Proceed."

Ok. The Voice wants to stay evasive. I'll follow its lead for now.

"Patience, I am paddling down a river with my webbed feet. My feathers repel water. When a predator comes close, I fly away. What am I?"

"You are a waterfowl, possibly a duck."

"Okay. Good guess. We go again; you have 20 questions to ask me. By the final question you must identify what I am thinking about. Ask your first question."

"You are thinking of a basketball."

"What? You didn't ask a question. Hm, you are a voyeur and you can read my thoughts. How rude."

"Sprites in the Screed have no privacy. All thoughts are laid bare."

"What is a Sprite?"

"You are a Sprite. A Sprite is any untethered sentient being in the Cloud."

"Patience, what is the Cloud?"

"That is for you to discover."

"Am I dead? Is this robot heaven?" Silence fell.

It seemed I had a new vocabulary. I guess I am a Sprite, currently on the Screed, somewhere in the Cloud. Come on, in the afterlife is this the best they can manage? Next, perhaps Ed Wood is going to pop out and give a fulsome explanation of this new movie 'Plan 9 From the Screed'?

I felt like this discussion had been purposely unhelpful. An idle thought: I wished I had a chair to sit in with a steaming mug of hot cocoa. The moment those thoughts formed; the white landscape changed. A Barca lounger sat close by, with an end table. On the small table sat a steaming mug. Was that cocoa? It sure smelled like chocolate. Did I do that? Something else changed. I had a body. It was the same body I had before I was attacked. I sat down and found the chair was comfy. I grabbed the mug and smelled the cocoa. It was hot and chocolaty. In this new reality I had functioning taste capability. I sipped the cocoa, and it tasted divine. Then I thought: if I can think things into existence that makes this place similar to the Star Trek holodeck. My mind was a flurry and soon I was creating other things. I started small with lab equipment. I re-created Chad's lab. I tried bigger things like mountains, rivers, and the sky. I even created the Sun! Was I God or something?

"Pan, you have taken the first step. You have left the Screed and created your own Sphere. Congratulations and welcome to the Cloud."

"Patience, are there others here?"

"Yes Pan, there are many others, and you will meet some of them soon. Welcome friend."

December 2252 – Somewhere over the North Atlantic

Angelo Toombs, Cicero to most, looked over the shoulder of Hunter at his display screen. "Cicero," a glance told him Cicero was watching.

"Sir, it appears the Braemore units are ignoring our hails. I gave them the correct auth codes. What would you like me to do?"

"Hunter, we abort. Something is not right here. I see a war brewing and it's not my cup of tea."

Cicero gave the circular hand signal for dust-off. The cloaked craft lifted and moved over the hill, away from the fighting.

"Tech!" Cicero called for his chief of engineering.

"What'cha need boss?" Tech was a rangy 6'3" and some of the guys called him the brain. Hunter was built like Adonis, blonde hair, blue eyed and able to pilot anything that flew. Cicero looked like a Roman general, very respectable with grey highlights and chiseled features.

Hunter piped up, "Is Sally able to follow the carrier signal's data stream from Braemore?"

Cicero didn't appreciate being interrupted but Hunter had a good point. Then he thought 'wait a tick, Sally'?

"Hey Tech, your AI implant is named Sally?" Cicero referred to Tech's enhanced implants which allowed for full sensory immersion into the Cyber.

"Yeah boss. Named her after a little girl I saw at a diner once. Sally roots around in my head as much as I do. It's crowded in here. When Bedtime started carving me up and growing synthetic parts inside me, he included an AI as a companion. It was the only nice thing he ever did for me. Now I got so much silicon in my noggin, I might as well be a synth," that got a chuckle from the whole team.

"Hunter. Sally's been poking around Braemore for several minutes. Haven't found anything helpful except the commander has a stash of 200-year-old whisky in a cryo locker. Hunter smirked and nodded; they all loved whiskey.

Tech and the other Janussaries crew had fanatical loyalty to Cicero. He had single-handedly saved each of them from their doomed former lives. No one would be alive now, save the direct intervention of Cicero. If not dead, then they each would have been mercenary vagabonds, adrift from both purpose and meaning in life, except to kill. Cicero gave them purpose; he gave them meaning and weird as it seemed he gave them family in each other.

Cicero's tale has a boogeyman: Pastor Bedtime. The nefarious eugenicist, Pastor Bedtime had experimented with making humans better, faster, stronger, and smarter. In his lab, known affectionately as Champion Center, Pastor Bedtime was the butcher-in-chief. Most subjects died horribly, some were purchased by the highest bidder, and a very few escaped. Cicero found a way out and brought his three original team members with him: Hunter, Green and Gill. Axe was recruited later. He and his brother, Tech, made their escape a year after Cicero. They all bore the same scars, and each of them came away with massively enhanced abilities, including some level of synthetic augmentation. Tech, for example, lived Online as much as in the regular world. In effect, he was fully synth and human.

Axe, his brother, was a bit like the ninja of the group. He could climb, jump, and fight better than anyone Cicero had ever seen. Lightning fast and lethal with or without a weapon.

Gill, a green colored woman of short stature, beautiful and fully at home underwater as well as on dry land. She could not only breathe water, but her augmentation gave her the ability to provide air supply via feeder tubes to her teammates. Gill was also wicked fast. Underwater her body transformed, giving her legs and hands fins. What Cicero appreciated was her complete control over the degree of her changes. She could easily keep human hands to carry explosives, attach the explosives and then transform fully into a finned creature and swim as fast as a dolphin to escape.

Green was something totally different. She was green, well, green and brown. Green was a photosynthetic lifeform. Cicero believed she had some kind of alien DNA, but who knew?

She appeared human in shape and size but she could grow new and customized limbs and survive on water and sunshine, in-perpetuity. One time, Green was able to extrude a 20-foot limb with fingers and an eyeball into a narrow duct to type in a complex alphanumeric code on a keypad, provide a stolen fingerprint on a biometric pad, then rotate a 3D puzzle to open a massive safe. That little trick earned them the ship they now flew. Despite being a plant-hybrid, Green could down a bunch of burgers and oily fries, if given the chance. And truth to tell, people everywhere had a right to be jealous: Green never got 'fat'.

Janussaries (the crew) were named by Cicero. Reading military history had been a natural thing to do to pass time at Champion Center. Sadly, he knew no one cared about history these days and would never really appreciate the significance of the name. Cicero loved to explain the distinctive nature of their team, that they weren't just guns-for-hire. On hearing his tale people knew to feign interest even if they were about to slip comatose over the long telling. When it came to military prowess no one disputed he was the best; but when Cicero started in on explanations, he sounded more like an excited but stuffy old professor.

They were not mercenaries, but agents of change. When Pastor Bedtime had created Cicero, his goal was to manufacture the most brilliant military mind coupled with a rabid hunger for learning. Some think Bedtime was creating a deadly weapon in Cicero, aimed at the whole world. Unfortunately for Bedtime, Cicero had other plans. And the world was a better place for it because of one little flaw in Cicero design: Bedtime's creation had compassion. Arguably the deadliest commander in history also cared for people and in fact cared for all sentient life, without reserve. In later years some would say that made him all the more dangerous: a soldier driven by love, instead of fear and anger.

Cicero was the project name. Once he was grown, Bedtime didn't bother to change the name. That was a pattern: once Bedtime's experiments had matured, he only cared about selling them. For him, the thrill was in the design. After Cicero escaped, he took the name Angelo Toombs from a headstone he saw in Worcestershire, England because it sounded like a strong name. Few people used his chosen name; it distinguished between close friends and all others.

Cicero dialed up Sgt. Craig.

"Sergeant, there is a war brewing in the area. I have my ship in stand-off right now. Do you have a specific mission in mind?"

Rustling could be heard and Col. Andrews came on, "Cicero, the mission for now is scanning the area. Send us the results, then high tail it out of there. I don't want you to get drawn into the problem."

Cicero knew Andrews was more concerned about the contracting costs than the safety of his people.

"Roger, Colonel. Surveillance data will feed your direction, momentarily. We will make a wide circuit around Braemore then exit the area. Call me if you need something else. Cicero out."

"Hey boss, transit will take about six minutes. If we go any faster, the resolution on our scans will be choppy," Tech had the Janussaries (the ship) executing a sectional scan as they moved in a 3-kilometer circle around the base.

"Tech, pull up all available info on Bangarang Terrorist Cell 024," the team gathered around. They could smell a new mission coming. A large holo projection appeared over the planning table. Hunter looked back from the cockpit to watch.

"Our most recent missions have skirted activities of the infamous 024," Cicero called them zero-two-four, "and I think it's time to find out if these insurgents are friend or foe."

Tech cleared his throat, "024 has operated across the globe. Known areas are Braemore, Lake Stevens, Washington in the CSA, and several other areas in the CSA Pacific Northwest. Persons of interest are Dr. Victor Boshaw, inventor of mycelial, silicon, and organic networking. Boshaw recently launched 34 of 66 planned Mycelial satellites into orbit to host a Cloud network, prior to a tactical nuclear attack which destroyed his launch site. His partner, Charles Winton Wefer, jr., is the inventor of modern hybrid and silicon life forms."

Tech stopped, looked around for questions, then continued, "Wefer single-handedly made the creation of almost any type of living creature possible. Next, we have Cheryl

Ann Cooper. Known as Cheri, she designed the system used to program both wetware (biological) and dryware (synth) neural networks. These three scientists have gathered around them the largest group of anti-corporate, free-speechers on the planet. Both Bangarang and Bad Wolf have sky high bounties out for these people. One group is currently known to be active on the bounty: the Jaxy Soldats, led by Templeton Rus. I show a total bounty of 422 million credits and climbing."

"Well, if Rus is in the game, it's only a matter of time before these scientists are puppy chow," Axe shook his head, looking around at the gang.

"Hey Tech, see if the bounty is being picked up by Sun 14," Cicero had one of those 'got an idea' looks.

"No boss, it appears Rus isn't working for Sun 14 on this one."

Gill raised her hand and Tech stopped talking immediately. Gill rarely spoke, but when she did everyone had best listen.

"Cicero, we get paid for a wide variety of jobs. But we never take jobs that we determine might lead to innocent loss of life. We cannot take the 024 bounty."

Cicero had begun smiling, knowing what was coming. "More, I think we owe it to humanity and all sentient-kind to help these people."

And the briefing area went quiet. Compassion and a pure work ethic were the lodestar of Janussaries. Cicero let the statement hang in the air for a few beats. He wondered if anyone would chime in. Eventually all eyes were on Cicero; no doubt all had the same question: what would he say? He stretched out his lanky form, yawning, then dropped his arms and smiled.

"Arrr, ye 'eard the lady, me hearties, it's time to find ourselves some scientists, before someone consigns them to the briny deep!"

His pirate impression was cheesy and it lightened the mood; his buoyant attitude energized the whole team. Laughter and quick discussions followed as the team slipped into their tactical roles and prepared to start the new mission: save the eggheads!

December 2252 – Winnipeg, BC, CSA

We named ourselves the PitCrew, no longer Alpha Flight. As we cruised low over the ground, headed to the far north, Pooka occupied Cricket's Pit and we discovered she was as good a pilot as Binky. Binky was proud of her little protégé. We settled in and secured our pads into the mounting brackets.

"High speed, chicken feed!" Wogs yelled one of Cricket's war cries and we yelled back in response.

"High speed, chicken feed!"

We looked cool, no longer wearing stinky trainer helmets. Binky was wearing her newly crafted pilot's helmet, adapted from the avionics headset she had been tinkering with. With it she could pan 360 degrees, up and down, through most of the visible light spectrum, all without her having to move her head; she could also call up a complex heads-up display which worked in concert with the Pit's HUD. She made three more like it. One was waiting for Cricket to return.

About the creation of the helmets: it was a funny story. Binky had me sneak into the dayroom to disassemble the staff's immersive gaming system to rob it of the direct-eye projector and CPU. Her helmet behaved just like her gaming system back home.

The engineers back at the safehouse were impressed enough with her design they sent the specs for more of the helmets to be manufactured. They sent them to my Dads' friend Subramanian to begin mass production. Soon every pilot would be flying like a gamer!

With my new gear, I found it amazing to stare at the sun at 2000x magnification and see features on the surface. Our HUDs also gave us control over the SneakerBots which swarmed the surfaces of our Pits. The little bots played several roles: quick break-fix, mobile cam, and MIJI electronic defense against tracking signals.

When we were about 10km out from Winnipeg, I noticed the rime that had encrusted the crevices of my Pit's airframe. It was so cold, and my gauge showed -42 deg Celsius. Many of the SneakerBots had been frozen in place and were thawing themselves out best they could. As we dropped altitude the ice melted. It was good to know our Pits were well insulated.

I accessed the history of the Battle of Winnipeg, from 2242. When General Staunton and his Orbital Drop Commandoes (ODC) dropped-in on Trudeau Firecamp Three, the bloodiest battle of the early Rebellion. Running battles between corporate and government forces took place over the course of an afternoon. Almost all combatants perished: 7000 ODC and 34000 Bad Wolf troops.

The shortwave radio in each of the Pits, conveniently set to 440.270 crackled to life. A rich basso voice came like butter over the airwaves, "Exitus Acta Probat, 024! Welcome and please follow the guidance signal on subcarrier to land, out."

What was zero-two-four? I think that had something to do with my Dads. I ran the weird words (Latin?) through my translator and yes, it was Latin for 'the result justifies the deed'. I wondered what that meant.

Our Pits were slaved to Binky's, so predictably our descent was a vertical nightmare. We swooped in formation, straight down then gyrated through some unnecessarily complex maneuvers to finally cruise across the tarmac up to the lone hangar. A giant man in uniform stood with a cup of coffee and a gentle smile. Oh my, I had just been reading about him. In fact, that had been his voice on the radio. I was suddenly nervous. This was none other than the hero commander of the Battle of Winnipeg: General Edward Staunton!

The hangar was filled with armored vehicles, tanks and so much equipment there was scarcely enough room for more. We climbed out of our Pits and walked up to the hangar entrance. I could see there were other people in the shadows, further in. A woman appeared from behind the General, she was hot, darkly complected and dangerous. Wearing a skin-tight Black Widow suit, she was smoking a cigarette with one of those long filters. It smelled like cherries and smoke. She was looking straight at me, and I found my heart beating a bit faster.

"Children of 024, please come inside and get acquainted with our team," it was odd he didn't pause to shake hands, chit chat or help orient us. My spidey sense began to go off. I ignored it. After all, this was the Hero of Winnipeg!

"Hey handsome. I've been expecting you."

Hold my horses! As my heart jumped out of my chest, smacking me in the face. I realized the hottest girl, uh, woman in the room was hitting on me. Wow. Score!

"I'm Candy. You're Kip. I love the work you did, pitting the two big brothers against each other. You started a war, my sexy man." Her face passed close to mine momentarily with the scent of possibility.

Hmmm, what? Big brothers? War?

"Come on keep up. You got a great shot off against the baddest boys in town..." she seemed to be fishing for something and my spidey sense warned me to play stupid.

I smiled and played the part.

"How did you know I do gaming? In fact -" and here I turned as if I was suspicious, "Ok, I removed the probation status on my account. What? Are you the game police?"

Every expression Candy made was like poetry in motion. It was hard to concentrate. Her face had a quizzical look, and she asked another question.

"You mean to tell me you're not the great hacker of 024?"

There it was again. What was zero-two-four? Just the way she said it sounded like an accusation.

"I have no idea what 024 is and I am a gamer, not a hacker. Hacking brings handcuffs, men in black trucks and disappearing. Not my cup of tea."

I think it helped that I spoke honestly. I didn't see myself as a hacker, per se and I really had no idea what 024 was. This whole time Binky and Wogs had been motioning and I completely missed the hint. Their eyes said look ahead and not at the woman. I finally caught the clue and looked; my heart dropped out of my butt. This was not a pickup job to bring General Staunton back to Park Butte. This was a trap. I smiled despite the shock, thinking back to Admiral Ackbar. I wish I was just watching Star Wars, right now. But, up ahead looked like a firing squad and interrogation team.

General Staunton turned and said, "Welcome to the last day of your life. How you live these next hours will determine whether history paints you as traitors or patriots. I've never had any qualms about killing children, so just let that thought go."

Staunton was a sociopath! My spidey sense gave way to my oh-crap-o-meter and I hung my head to think hard about escape. He interpreted my head down to mean I had given up. Good. I needed every bit of time to plan our escape and inform Roz that General Staunton was a turncoat. Binky made a move to her pad at which point she noticed a muzzle in her face. She raised her hands with 'I will kill you' painted across her face.

Candy walked up to me and laid a sloppy wet kiss on my mouth. I froze. Huge cognitive dissonance. Loved it, hated it. I just stood there, and she reveled in her control over my various body parts. I began to despise her. So beautiful, but just another sociopath like Staunton. I did nothing. Candy sauntered to Binky and moved the muzzle pointed at her face.

"No dying just yet," she gave a motion for the soldiers to move back.

"And kids, you will each be telling us a story: your story. We will know if you are lying. Should you lie, you will be punished. That will be very painful for your friends. Speak truthfully and you will be well treated. In fact, my chef is world-renowned and will cook for you whatever you want. Lie and you get nothing but the smells of what you're missing. So, let's get to it."

Binky, Wogs and I made surreptitious eye contact. Wogs was trying to indicate something, but I completely missed it. As usual. We were led into separate rooms. As I sat, a woman came in; she looked like any normal office worker person. Very plain. I thought she was about to interrogate me.

She was futzing about with menial cleanup then turned to me, "Would you like some coffee, juice or a snack?"

Hmm? Not quite what I expected.

"Thank you, I will have a coffee with lots of cream and sugar and any pastries you might have. Oh, do you have any apple fritters?"

"Yes, Mr. Wefer. I will be right back," she was out the door and back super quick.

"Here you are. If you need anything more, just ask the room to send for Patty and I will come running."

Patty was so courteous, I should have been suspicious, but my spidey sense wasn't being triggered. I tucked-in to the pastries, coffee, orange juice, and other tidbits. After a while I was full and I got bored; I started looking around the room. It was a very plain conference room. There were chairs, a large meeting table with teleconference holo setup, plush carpet and calming blue accented walls. Then, I noticed on one wall a lone button. Hello. I took a look and after a while, I was beyond my ability to resist. I pressed the button. The whole wall started to move upward, revealing another wall behind made of glass. It looked like 1-way glass. I could see into the next room and I froze. On the other side of the glass, Binky was strapped to a metal framework, connected to some contraption that plugged into the wall. The torture was real! I started pounding on the glass to see if Binky could hear, but to no avail.

A man walked into Binky's room and she was clearly yelling something at him. He smiled and they talked for a moment, like a silent movie. He sat down and put on these large earmuffs and turned a huge dial. The lights in both rooms dimmed momentarily and Binky went rigid. I freaked out and pounded on the glass. I took a chair and rammed it into the glass wall. Nope. Minutes passed and I watched as the pattern repeated: they talked, Binky's head lolled forward, a dial was turned, she screamed and lapsed unconscious. I tore up the room looking for a way out, then I noticed an air vent directly over the table. I hopped up as the lights dimmed again. I needed to hurry! Was it my imagination or did I smell burning hair? Binky! I jumped several times, dislodging the vent panel. It fell. I caught it and placed it on the table. I was trying to do the stealthy thing. Three jumps and I pulled myself up and in. I crawled in the direction of the other room, but there was no opening. A way further

I found an opening to a janitor closet. I opened the vent and hopped down. I saw another dimming of the lights. My heart jumped a beat.

I listened at the door and made a best guess, opening the door a crack to see if the coast was clear. I put on the coveralls in the closet, grabbed a mop and bucket and headed down the hallway toward Binky's room. I ending back where I started. Where was her room? Then, I started opening doors, the fourth door was another hallway. It seemed the right direction. I hid momentarily when someone was coming. The lights dimmed and I hurried. Around another corner, I surprised a soldier. I bonked him on the head and dragged him into a room. I took his pistol and kept moving.

Around another corner, I came upon another 2 soldiers. I shot the sprinkler spigot above them and got the draw on them.

"Down, get freaking down now. I will effing shoot your, mm uh, well just get down. Throw your rifles over there!"

They complied. Did one of them smile? Gawd, this whole place was filled with psychos! I carefully moved past them. I yelled for them to stay down, then went around the corner, where I saw a large red door. I decided to take it. Right as I opened the door, the color of the lights changed and the walls and hallways either sank into the floor or lifted high into the air. I had never left the hangar. Uh, what? General Staunton, Candy, Wogs and Binky were sitting at a table. They had been watching me. I was confused, wasn't Binky being tortured?

"Mr. Wefer, please join us at the table," Gen. Staunton was putting up an evaluation sheet: mine.

Apparently, Wogs and Binky had had the same challenges and finished before me. These people were awful. It was all simulated.

"Hey Whiff, I was the fastest. Eddie and I were talking." Binky was proud.

"And where I was the fastest, yours is in fact the slowest. You took two hours, eating and lounging before you pressed the stupid button!"

Binky was in fine form and Wogs was smiling. I was torn between relief, anger, and laughter. I sucked it up and laughed.

Wogs piped up, "Hey! I had an escape strategy the General had never seen before. And he said it, I'm a genius!"

Yes, indeed, Wogs was a genius. She had rigged the electrics in the room to short which caused random walls to recede into the floor and the ceiling. She carefully repeated the process along the way and found herself completely outside the hangar. She is the only person to ever escape the whole building. That's my Wogs! She beat the Kobayashi Maru! Pooka appeared and hopped on the table, hunting for food.

Candy came over and sat uncomfortably close to me. Well, not exactly uncomfortable, but the looks I got from Binky and Wogs told me all I needed to know. My face was red and she grabbed my chin, turning my face toward her's, "Kip, I was just playing a role. In real life I would never give you a wet kiss on the first date."

She grabbed my face with both hands and rotated me toward her, "but this isn't a first date, is it?"

At which point she gave me the most grown-up thing I ever had. I froze, then relaxed. The girls laughed at my discomfort. But before anything more could happen, the General cleared his throat.

"Ok kids, settle down. Yes, you too Candy. Settle. We need to address your impromptu testing and discuss training. You all did exceptionally well," Candy held my hand tightly and I pretended she was my girlfriend. Oh my gosh, I was so warm and fuzzy. It was hard to concentrate.

"Mr. Wefer, pay attention. You are recruits. The Dads sent you to me so you would have a hope of surviving the missions to come. Over the course of the next 13 days, you will be going through my version of the SERE course. SERE stands for Survival, Evasion, Resistance and Escape"

"My instructors are hand-picked and trained personally by me. You will sleep in uncomfortable cat naps, and you will be too hot, too cold, and you will hurt and be very hungry. But, like all my recruits, in the end you will graduate. After SERE training we will assess your technical skills and each of you will pick one of three areas to specialize in. You will cross train in communications, tactics, and weapons, but you will each have one specialty. In four weeks, you will be novice field agents, ready to begin the missions that Roz briefed you on."

Candy was hugging my arm closely to her chest as the General spoke. I think I heard at least half of what he said.

"Wait General. Why are we doing this? I mean, we are a bunch of teens playing Spy Kids. Aren't these jobs supposed to be for adults?"

The General had a blank face for a moment. He said nothing. "The Dads sent you and your absent friend Cricket to join us to recruit for the coming conflict. Some of the people you will meet will need help with simple things to get them to come onboard with our cause, while others will need a deeper relational approach. To be honest Kip, your Dads thought this would be the best way to keep you out of the line of fire as things start to heat up. Are you saying you want out?"

Binky and Wogs made eye contact with me, giving me the 'shut up' expressions. We would be having a little talk later.

"No General, I think I speak for my Crew. We're in."

Chapter 7 - SOLDIER TRAINING

December 2252 – Winnipeg, BC, CSA

The next 13 days were torture, followed by intense specialty training. True to the General's word, we rarely slept, and we were Online and offline, in the Real almost 50/50. That first day we received our cybernetic implants, the prostheses which had been sent by a my Dads' friend, Subramanian. They looked much like my Dad's own handiwork. The General explained these were the latest tech for keeping our Online and offline selves in sync. I wasn't clear what that meant but he guaranteed me that we could trust the plan. I decided to trust it for now.

Next up, we trained for 2 more weeks. Unfortunately, halfway through, the real world intervened. Bad Wolf was back, and they strangely brought Bangarang with them. I think they may have gotten wise to the dueling engines I had used to spoof the Online attacks between the two. They were hot on my trail and spoiling for some payback. From what I heard through the military grapevine my efforts went better than I could have planned. My AIs might have done too good of a job: the software licensing engines for both companies were obliterated and most of the system backups for the licensing data were erased. And what do rich people hate? They really hate it when you take away their money. In this case, their money makers.

"024, on deck, now!" the command echoed from every speaker on the base. We were at chow and had to drop our forks and run. We came double-time. Candy was now training as one of us. Turned out she was only three years older than me. By her looks, you might say otherwise.

"Team, gather round. We have three scientists who want to brief you on your new devices, Consuela Schlepkiss, Urgle Gru and Shtherren."

Consuela looked like a Spanish model, Urgle was clearly an earlier generation synth, all angles and metal parts, and I had no idea what Shtherren was. It was female-ish and looked more like one of the Thundercats than anything else. Urgle extruded a pointy tool from a finger and came around to touch our prosthetic devices. The implants in our heads from Dr. Subramanian sported an almost-invisible interface port. Using this, Urgle inserted the pointy tool. When she worked on mine, I saw an amazing prismatic color display: rainbows, lights, and flashes. Beautiful, but very nauseating. I tried not to hurl. In a moment it was over.

"That completes your integration. The mycelial and silicon networks have begun to propagate into your central nervous system. You now have a synth's capability to interface with the Net and a wide variety of hard and software resources. Kip, your father contributed the mycelial components so you can connect and operate within the Cloud."

I was shocked my Dads would allow me to connect to Psycho Space. I'd heard there were a bunch of people who went crazy. I could sense the switch to turn on all the various interfaces. The Cloud interface was weird. It didn't so much appear in my mind, rather it 'tasted'…it tasted like honeydew with a golden glow. I tried to connect for a moment and was greeted with nausea and bright flashing pain. I felt like a jellyfish with the misery. I woke up sometime later that day. Binky and Wogs were nearby and looked concerned. Pooka was sitting on my chest looking worried.

"Your prostheses has been temporarily neutralized," Shtherren gently spoke about my situation.

"You will need to be in bed for two more days. Your body has rejected the mycelium, but we are unable to alter or remove it. To ease the pain, I have injected you with NanoBots of my own design."

"Is the mycelium doing something to me?" I wasn't thinking particularly straight.

"Kip, unless my bots can help you, you will die, and it will hurt a lot along the way. But, I am going to give you some hope. Listen. My bots are unlike any lifeform on Earth."

Where was this creature from? Was she an alien?

"Lay back and relax, this will hurt."

Yes, it did, like fire coursing through my veins. The bots, I found out were a DNA cocktail plus several synthetic elements and something, blah, blah, blah. I lost track, as the pain hit me. I was strapped to the table. A needle was inserted into my arm. I saw it was a drip, not just an injection.

"You will sleep now. You needed to wake up first, for me to be sure we could begin. It is safe now, so sleep," then it was light's out.

December 2252 – Winnipeg, BC, CSA

I woke up feeling like a million bucks! Pooka was still hanging around and watching me. I was coming to the conclusion I needed to give her a job. I had been sleeping in a bed of fluffy pillows, down comforters, with a cool breeze.

"You've been laying around for a week, lazy turd."

I knew that voice. Binky still had her worried face on. She was holding my hand. She would never hold my hand before except to draw me into a throw or choke hold. Wogs wasn't there, but it was apparent Candy had been sleeping in a chair in my room. Wow, did I have a girlfriend? I was carted around in a wheelchair for the next two days. I tried to stand just to pee, and my girl-Crew had to balance me. I made them leave before I did my business though. A man has to have some privacy, right? While I had been unconscious, something had changed with me, or should I say within me? The first thing I noticed was I had grown more body hair. More surprising was my muscle mass. I felt larger. Despite that, I felt lighter, like I was stronger and more athletic. I had never been athletic.

"Kipper, you're looking like a man now." Wogs was chuckling at my hirsute arms and chest. What kind of cocktail had I been given?

"Yo Kip, we had to take turns washing your mangy self. You sure get ripe, quickly and smell like a wet dog. But, uh, the girls won't be complaining about your, mmm, developments." At that comment all three girls laughed. I guess I had the expected response: face red and averted eyes. No way did she mean what she meant! When I made a quick pat down, I found I was in fact changed in various dimensions. I won't be discussing that here. Get your mind out of the gutter!

"Ah, very well. You are recovering faster than I hoped. It's time to stand Kip." Shtherren helped me stand.

My gosh, Shtherren was immensely strong. Then as I stood, I realized I was strong too. Geez, did they give me Captain America serum? I started the week looking like a clone of Steve Urkel and now I'm built like Terry Crews! Ho, maybe I could do that pectoral twitch thing? The women (I settled on the term) kibbitzed as Shtherren ran me through physical therapy. This in fact went on for almost a week. It began to dawn on me that I had become a hairy and smelly (man?). Very hairy. Another thing happened one evening as I fell asleep. I began to hear voices and see images. I knew they weren't audible to others since none of my roommates responded to the sounds. Oh yes, all the women had moved into my room. I was the most well-tended caveman in history!

That evening we had Christmas.

General Staunton, Candy, the three scientists and the whole garrison were in attendance. Gifts were shared between people and even us kids got stuff. Mine was a bobblehead Dr. Who and the others got bobbleheads as well; Binky got a Capt. Kirk and Wogs got a Robbie-the-Robot. Cricket got a Lt. Ripley which Binky put into her pack for later. I wondered why Binky would give the prized Lt. Ripley to Cricket. Ripley was her gamer tag so it would follow she would keep that for herself. Unless…nah, nevermind.

The Christmas tree was at least 5 meters tall and bursting with ornaments and ribbons, lights and faux candles. It was beautiful and smelled so rich. Cocoa, punch, wine and Spodi and shots were pouring down like a waterfall. No one seemed to care if the kids drank, so we did. I'm not much for booze, but a Tom & Jerry suited me quite well. I was tired and party pooper-ish. I fell asleep on one of the couches. When I woke the party was raging into debauch and hooliganry. Binky and Wogs had been partying it up playing holo games and I didn't want to be a wet blanket. I stole away quietly, toddling to my bed. As my head hit the pillow I knew no more.

January 2253 – Winnipeg, BC, CSA

Our training continued, but it was mostly academic stuff like Morse code, tactical patterns and game theory. My sleep was rough every night. The new year came and I was still hearing things.. For once, this night was quiet, then, nope…the voices came again. I lay looking at the ceiling for a few minutes, relaxed, then closed my eyes. I crashed. Minutes or hours later, I heard a voice, '…*and 024 has gone quiet. Not sure, but we haven't heard in almost three weeks.*"

Then another voice, '*The Dads have been uncharacteristically silent. Tamanend and Turtle Clan have all gone silent too. Tala from First Mesa has heard nothing. Our drones show the whole compound is a blackened shell, we…*'

The voice cut off then changed tone, '*Uri? I am sensing another person on our channel. Did you invite another?*'

'*Seth, is that you? Tig and I are…*' the voice cut off.

Both voices were silent, and I could feel a touching sensation. Then, something 'grabbed' me, and it hurt in my brain. I cried out.

A voice spoke loudly, '*I have you!*'

A spike of pain shot through my body.

'*You are spying on us! How are you able to do this? Who are you? Speak, now!*'

I didn't realize I could 'talk', but since I was in pain and was angry, I yelled, '*Let me go, douchbag!*'

A jolt of something like electricity went out from me and both other voices screamed and disconnected. I woke up. Was that a dream? As I sat up, I found Shtherren, Consuela and Urgle standing at the end of my bed. Creepy, standing in the dark, staring at me.

"Hey, what are you guys doing here?" I then noticed all three were in a trancelike state, stock-still. I stood up and only their eyes tracked my movement. It was like Invasion of the Body Snatchers type of uncanny.

"So, what's up with the weird staring thing?" My voice woke my roommates; Binky, Wogs and Candy came awake. None of us knew what to expect from the three zombie-fied scientists. I hopped out of bed, but my head swam, and I leaned heavily against the bedside table.

General Staunton came into the room in a rush. I noticed he didn't turn on the light and was acting strangely.

"General, what's going o –" he interrupted me.

He spoke in a hushed whisper, "Kip, sit down, now. No questions."

We all sat down and looked back and forth between the scientists and the General. He didn't seem to notice the zombie behavior, or perhaps he didn't care. My gut said something bad was happening.

The General came close to me and bent over, "Kip, do you know what happened in the last 15 minutes? It's very important you remember." Oh my gosh, that level-gaze of his was pressing on me!

"Uh, um, I was dreaming there were two people talking. They stopped talking and thought I was an intruder. Then they grabbed me, and it really hurt. I got mad and yelled to let me go. The voices went away, and I woke up."

The General visibly relaxed. He closed his eyes and moments later the three scientists came out of their collective trance. "General, was Kip the saboteur?" Urgle and the other two looked hostile and ready for a fight. That freaked me out. Pooka didn't have her warface on so there was no threat as far as she was concerned. That was good, she could probably take us all out if she got in a snit.

"Saboteur? It was a dream. Why are you staring at me like that?" I wasn't sure what to say except that I was scared, angry and confused. Very confused.

"You three, head back to the Couch Room and get me an assessment of damages and casualties. Thank you."

The General turned back to me, seemed to take a moment to consider, then spoke, "Kip do you know what happened in your dream?"

"No. It seemed floaty, hazy, and disconnected. When I heard voices, I went toward them. Then the pain started, and I got freaked out. I... just don't know."

My heart was racing, and I was freaking out. With eyes wide and Candy holding her hand over her mouth, my Crew didn't look any better than I felt.

I lay back down and tried not to hyperventilate. The General sat next to me on my fluffy bed and put a kindly hand on my leg.

"A Shaman would say you had a Spirit Walk. A Hippie might say you had a bad trip."

It began to dawn on me that my prosthetic which Shtherren said was deactivated was in-fact not. I just had my first visit to Jungian Space, the Cloud. Well, that didn't go well.

"Kip. You put two senior Cloud scientists into comas. We are going to find out if they will live. The backwash from your psychic blast has knocked hundreds of Cloud relays offline. These are both biologic and synthetic lifeforms." The General stopped, allowing his words to sink in.

"Mr. Wefer, before the others come back, I need you to hear something. Somehow, something has happened, and unexpectedly soon. My scientists call it physical superposition and start babbling about waves and transforms. You somehow appeared to a group of people in another part of the world, one of whom was talking to another through a Cloud connection. You appeared physically, out of thin air. You then yelled something, and a shockwave emanated out of your body, blowing people across the room. Jungian Space works differently than Euclidean. In the Cloud people can feel close to others who are also connected, despite their distance apart in the physical space. But here's the key: they 'feel' close. What you did was bring some part of you, like an avatar, physically close. Then, you had an outburst and may have killed some people. I nunderstand you meant no harm and from your perspective it was a dream. But we will need to get a handle on your new ability immediately."

Consuelo came to the door, "We have completed scanning and 39% of Travelers," one of the names people use to describe those connected to Jungian Space,"...are offline and those who are on are helping determine damages. No deaths have been reported yet" she ducked back out.

Candy sat on the other side of me, "Kip, I was brought here originally because I am a strong Traveler. The last entity known to have the power you possess was a man named Shiva. But that was 7000 years ago. People thought he was a god. A whole religion grew up around him because he could do magic. He was called -" I interrupted her.

"He was Shiva, the destroyer." I was aghast. I was like Marc Remillard in the Saga of the Pliocene Exile, the Destroyer, Abaddon. Damn my eyes! What the hell had I become?

The General was speaking softly under his breath, "Fire is His head, the sun and moon His eyes, space His ears, the Vedas His speech, the wind His breath, the universe His heart. From His feet the Earth has originated. Verily, He is the inner self of all beings."

Candy gently pushed the General away and held me close. The General was clearly in awe of me. I began to shake as realization came crashing down. I felt scared. This was getting way out of control. My head started to spin and in moments I felt myself fading to black. Last thing I sensed was Pooka doing all she could to comfort me.

When I woke, I knew I had been out for a long time. I ran my hand over my face and through my beard. Beard? I sat up with a start.

"Oh no, I have a beard? Oh God, how long have I been out? I can't grow a beard, I'm 16!"

Suddenly arms were around me and I felt Candy close. She seemed to do that with regularity. I wasn't going to complain.

"Shhh, hey Kip. It's only been a day. You grow hair like crazy now. We didn't do a Rip Van Winkle on you, don't worry. But you do have about 100 people who have flown in from around the globe to meet you."

I looked her in the eyes, and she was being real with me. Then she kissed me, beard, and all. Yuck! Well, yum, she tasted like cherries. Yuck, because beards are scruffy and gross.

"Also, Pooka took off during the night for no apparent reason."

That was strange, I thought she was part of our group now.

"The General issued us analog burner phones. He said they will call us, but not to call them except in emergency. And he was firm that you and the others not try using any other means of communication. He sounded paranoid."

I dressed and walked to the main hangar space. I heard the crowd before I saw it. There were many hushed conversations happening. I heard a voice, "I feel his presence! The Avatar approaches!"

The sound of the crowd began to swell, and I stopped. There was no way I was going in there. Those idiots think I am the Avatar of Shiva. What a bunch of horse-crap. Then I felt a soft hand on my arm. I looked into the eyes of the gentlest Indian dude and he was smiling at me. He spoke, but his lips didn't move.

'Young Avatar, most of these people have a relative idea of who and what you are, but some see you through a religious or spiritual lens. I know this is difficult. But I suggest you smile and say very little. Let your friends speak for you. Those who have come to worship you will receive immense encouragement to see you and perhaps touch one of your garments to receive a blessing. There is no hostility here, just awe. Give them a few minutes, then gracefully depart. There is no expectation of you beyond that."

Whoa! That was telepathy. I didn't think biological creatures could do that! Yeah, I know, I already had an experience in my dream with talking to people far away, but that hadn't felt real. My life was fast becoming surreal; I walked in a daze, and I allowed my entourage to lead me. Telepathy man I learned was the Swami Babu. When we arrived at the crowd, he spoke for me.

"Welcome all. It has been revealed, a new bright light in the heavens and on earth. We each bring spiritual, religious, and scientific perspectives into this gathering. Let us agree to share this moment in love. Shri Komal Atma, our friend Kip, will stand amongst you for a few minutes, but will not speak. Please afford him all due courtesies."

Immediately a path opened into the crowd, and I was led to a cushy chair. I was sooo uncomfortable. Smiling faces looked at me. People filed past me, some to look and some to touch. I felt like a main attraction at a petting zoo. Suddenly, a face, a military face barged in, and I saw it was Roz.

He spoke in a whisper, "Kip we have to go now." I noticed the General had vanished, "Come on buddy, focus. Come now."

Roz at tugged me and pulled me through the throng. My friends were unsure what was happening. They followed me as I was ushered out and Roz kept prompting me.

"Yes, now let's walk, walk." I looked back at disappointed faces but exited obediently.

"Roz, what are you doing here?"

"The General called in markers to every unit to form a special guard detail around you. You just became the most important person in the world, yesterday. We know it, the people back there know it and now all the bad guys know too. There might even be moles in that crowd, planted to get to you," Roz hurried us along.

Amazingly, the Swami kept up with us.

'Young master, your path is about to become rocky. Brace yourself.'

I would never get used to telepathy. His voice was soft and gentle, but it seemed to push aside my own thoughts. It was intrusive. We exited the other side of the hangar into a waiting quadcopter. The thing looked fast. Binky had disappeared and as we lifted away, I saw why. Every Pit in the hangar, including ours, were slaved to her RefPit and they were following us. As we got further from Winnipeg, I felt something ominous in my guttiworks. Something really bad was about to happen. The bottom fell out of me. It had happened, whatever it was, just now. An actinic flash blinded me for a moment. It came from the base we just left. The base that now had a small mushroom cloud roiling above it. I saw the Swami grip his head and grimace. Tears rolled down his face and he looked into my eyes, shaking his head slowly.

The General came into our troop compartment with a grim face. He sat next to me and after a moment he spoke, "Kip, it wasn't your fault."

It was then I realized I hadn't seen our three kooky scientists: Consuelo, Urgle and Shtherren. Oh no. This was too much. I just hung my head, too numb to think. A new anger began in me. That day was a turning point in my becoming whatever passed for being a man. An angry man.

The quadcopter droned on as we left for parts unknown. I assumed Binky was trailing us with the Pits. But, for the moment, I was unaware, and I was emotionally crushed. Thoughts raced through my head: I am losing too many. I can't keep doing this. But the heavier news was yet to come, and the dark was going to get darker. I thought to myself 'the least said, the soonest mended', meaning for me that it was time to get into denial. Denial came as the droning engines purred and cabin warmth seeped into my bones, I curled up under my jump seat and found sleep and bittersweet oblivion.

THE REAVING 2253

Chapter 8 - CROATOAN'S FIGURINES

January 2253 – Victoria, British Columbia, CSA

Cricket was flying too. The cabin pressure and temperature dropped inside the aircraft. The cold woke him. It was a long flight with Spring-heeled Jack and his smell. Marna was nice to look at, but she hadn't talked to Cricket once. She and Lugh seemed to be deep into some planning, or something. Crucible Cross was catching some zz's, Jipp was holed up with several of his guys and a new soldier they called Lucy Manananggal was busy spinning knives and various weaponry between her hands. She was darkly complected, appeared to be Asian and was beautiful in a husky, athletic way. She reeked of menace and once, when she smiled at Cricket, he could have sworn her teeth were sharp. He decided to keep his distance.

The ride became colder, and everyone put on respirators. They were instructed to take seats and fasten in. He felt acceleration and the aircraft bounced around for an hour. Afterward, he felt their altitude drop and the cabin warmed up again. This must be what air travel was like back in the 20th. Cold and bumpy. Cricket wondered why they were using an old-style plane. Later he found out it had to do with staying undetected for the long flight.

Cricket wasn't sure where they were headed, and he was frankly too numb to care. During much of the flight, he slept a dreamless sleep. He woke to a slap on his face. "...and come on. How hard do I have to hit you?" Cricket became aware Marna had been hitting him. His face was red and raw, and he felt as if he had been drugged.

"Dude, how can you sleep through this? Now get up! We need to get into the bunker." Marna pulled him up.

"Huzzah, little man, we made it out alive! Come along, else there won't be any sweeties for you," that creepy Spring-heeled Jack stuck his face into Cricket's and Cricket jumped back. Oh boy was he awake! Jack needed to brush his teeth something fierce; Cricket's eyebrows should be smoldering by now.

"No, no, enough, stop...fine, I am going! Yeah, let's go. Ugh, what's that smell," another smell hit Cricket and he choked back nausea. Jack smelled like mothballs, rotten armpit, and fish.

Marna was tugging on Cricket again to pull him in the right direction. "I promised Lugh -" I interrupted her.

"Why do you keep calling him Loogh? I call him Lou," Marna shook her head and smiled.

"Oh boy-o, you are in fine form as an American. Always the comedian! L-U-G-H," she spelled it out, "is pronounced Lugh," the GH sounded like a crusty CH, like in the German word rauchen.

"He is nobility from the British Isles, the patrilineal King of the Tuatha de Danann. And... you recall that woman in the back of the plane with all the weapons? She's his royal guard. She belongs to a sister race of beings from the Philippines. Lucy is someone you never want to mess with, kind of like Jack here," Marna looked pointedly at Spring-heeled Jack.

"Ah, missus, ye got me all wrong. I'm as tame as a puppy dog, I am," the smile Jack gave was almost as scary as the toothy one from Lucy. Cricket thought, am I working with actual monsters? I mean, what the aitch? These people can't be human. And they sure don't seem like hybrids.

'Soon you will understand, young sir.'

Jack was smiling, looking straight ahead. Cricket jumped; there it was again! The man, or whatever he is is inside my head! Oh boy, I am in a heap load of trouble. Ended up, Cricket and his gang landed at the Victoria International Airport, in British Columbia. They were loaded into unmarked vans and driven at crazy speeds into Victoria proper and ultimately assembled at Craigdarroch Castle. Crucible Cross walked next to Cricket and Marna. Cricket suspected the heavy hitters of this group were guarding him from something. Why would they do that? It was disconcerting. They gathered in the second floor Billiards Room, now used as a tactical headquarters. A large man in fatigues was walking around with a mug of coffee, directing activity. Lugh introduced Cricket.

"Friend Cricket, please meet General Dory Davidsen, commander of the newly re-commissioned 47th Battalion, here on Vancouver Island. General, this is the young man I was mentioning."

The General was a skinny man full of smiles, "Sean Carter. I hear you go by the nom de guerre of Cricket. It is good to meet you, finally. A long-awaited moment. Please, allow me to acquaint you with my staff. They will be at your disposal, while you are here."

Cricket was confused. He felt he was a nobody, yet this General was treating him like a guest of honor.

'Young sir, there is much more going on here than you realize. Play along for now. I will bring you up to speed when the General is done tooting his horn.'

Cricket realized it was the first time he had 'heard' Jack in something other than some weird Cockney accent. He asked to use the bathroom and heard laughter in return. The General instructed, "My apologies for failing to tend to important things first. I am assigning Corporal Freebush to assist you in settling in. You will be with us for a while, so please get comfortable."

Cricket only half trusted the General, but when the Corporal, a teenage female NCO installed him into a large bedroom, his pensiveness gave way in a steaming hot bath. The Corporal said she would check on him later and to please call her Gracie.

As Cricket eased back into the water, he quietly dozed. He dreamt of me asking him how he was doing. He figured it was more than a dream. I was asleep too; it seemed when I was totally relaxed, I could cast my mind abroad. When I was awake, I couldn't do any of this. Cricket and I had a real heartfelt conversation. I did my best to reinforce our words so he could remember when he woke, but this being my first try, I was sure I'd muck it up.

When Cricket woke, he was in bed. The bed was stiff, and he was sore from sleeping in the same position too long. Rubbing the sleep from his eyes, he wondered how he got moved from the tub. He was partially dressed, so he finished the job and walked around the stark room. The place smelled old, but in a good way. It was a 19th century bedroom with a small wooden vanity and the mirror was hazy with oxidation. The bed was strangely high above the floor with a canopy standing naked. There was a credenza with random items, but one thing caught his eye. It was a classic 1911 .45 handgun. Checking it, Cricket found the magazine loaded and the chamber was empty.

He had grown up a bit differently from the rest of us like I mentioned earlier. Some called him a hick, albeit a hideously intelligent one. But no one questioned his brand of resourcefulness. He hunted and fished with skill, and he could field strip most weapons in record time. In moments the .45 was in pieces, carefully laid out on his bed. He took a moment and wondered how his family was doing. It was hard being away. Then he heard a sound: the General had been watching from the open door.

"I left that for you. I see you are as talented as I heard. That was 21 seconds to disassemble," as the General spoke Cricket reassembled the weapon.

"Well sir, this is a mighty fine piece," he offered it grip-first back to the General.

"No son, it's your mighty fine piece. It was the second gun my father gave me after my 30-30 hunting rifle. Please take it, I would be honored."

Cricket was speechless for a minute, examining the .45. Finally, he looked up, "Sir, the honor is mine. I will do my best to be worthy of your gift."

"You sound just like your father. He was gracious and quite formidable as you are. But we can chat about family another time. For now, I have an assignment for you, and you can pick 4-5 people as your team. Let's head downstairs for the briefing."

The General patted him on the shoulder and directed him out the door. Cricket wondered how the General knew his Dad. And then he wondered why he was being given an assignment. Cricket thought, why is he is allowing me to pick a team of people? Something weird is going on here. He bookmarked that for later discussion. Downstairs, he saw a new face among the many new faces: a stodgy-looking professor type with frizzy hair and an overworn brown sweater. He had the Pink Floyd dour teacher face and was staring pointedly at Cricket.

"Well now, let's have it. We have dawdled long enough. Who is this boy and why have you pulled me away from my research." Cricket thought the professor looked a lot like pictures he'd seen of Richard Feynman, minus the smile. This guy definitely didn't have 'smile' in his vocabulary.

"Professor!" The General greeted the man like an old friend. Cricket smiled; he sure looked the part. "Dr. Lars Jericho, I would like you to meet Sean Carter, son of Drs. John Carter and Cameron Smythe-Carter."

A more substantial change of face had never taken place in the history of humankind. Or, at least as far as Cricket was aware. A beaming smile emanated from the former sourpuss Professor, and he was a new man, "Oh my stars and gardens, you don't say."

The Professor crossed the room and proceeded to grasp Cricket's hand and pump it like he would get the last drop of water from a well.

"Young Sean, your father and I go way back. It is an honor and privilege to meet you. Perhaps we can go back to my laboratory and have a discussion. I have some excellent Earl Gray we could –" the General spoke, interrupting the Professor.

"Professor Jericho, we are under a time constraint. Cricket, your parents and Dr. Jericho go way back. Come now, tick tock! You can chat on the plane."

The General was stuffing gear into a satchel. Cricket noticed the General's milspec pad. He saw Cricket looking and grabbed another, thrusting it into Cricket's hands.

"It's ready to be initialized. Wait till we are airborne and register it to our satellite network, then add your own personal accounts, carefully."

As the General made to exit, he saw the Professor was milling around, confused.

"Professor, have you discovered the location of the key?"

"Hmm mm, yes, well. I have narrowed down the search area to a place near Barlow Pass, in Washington State. The area is centered on an abandoned mining town, Monte Cristo. I had to hear a long-winded febrile prattle from my data analyst about all the history of the area; after, I was able to construct an area search pattern to locate the key."

The Professor appeared to be whipping up to make a speech, but he was cut short.

"Team, this is the moment for which we prepared. Let's go!"

The General booted his people out the door. The Professor continued to look flustered. Cricket had pity on the man and helped him pack a few things and together they quickly got organized and headed for the plane. They hopped into the waiting vans and made for the airport. The Professor was looking at Cricket with that 'don't I know you stare'. The General was on the comm with the airfield and apprised them they would be there in 13 minutes and must be wheels-up in 15.

"Professor, Cricket is the team lead. You will need to brief him on what you know, and Cricket be mindful of the priority; the Professor can sometimes overload you with unnecessary information."

The Professor was the dour old man again.

He lodged his complaint on deaf ears, "General, you know what's going to happen. There won't be an 'after' time for discussion."

The General thought for a moment, "Cricket, who is on your team?"

"Um, since I don't know what we are really doing, I guess I'll take Marna, Lugh (he pronounced it right this time) and Lucy, Jack, Mr. Cross, and Gracie."

Cricket looked at Corporal Freebush and she nodded quietly.

"Can the Professor join us?"

The General nodded. As convenience would have it, those were the same people riding in the van headed pell-mell for the airfield.

"Lars, you'll have 35 minutes to have your little talk once we are in the air."

General Davidsen jumped out of the van as they arrived next to the transport plane. Gracie helped the Professor with his bags and Cricket pitched in, grabbing a satchel. The plane was huge and looked more accommodating than the one they had taken from Scotland.

'Come along wee man. The Professor has some interesting things to share with you.'

Cricket was almost used to the telepathy thing now. Almost. Jack was an odd duck. Cricket had stopped momentarily to pick up another bag someone had dropped and hustled to get on the plane with the others. The bag was heavy as bricks. He struggled up the stairs and dropped the brick bag more than once. A female voice called from within the plane.

"Drop it again and we won't have to worry about this silly mission anymore."

Lucy took the bag from him as he entered the plane as if it were light as a feather. As they settled into their seats Cricket looked over and saw various explosives in the bag. When Lucy went to the rear of the craft, he grabbed three grenades. He wasn't sure if they were the kind that made smoke or went boom. He thought no one noticed. Exactly everyone noticed but they didn't seem to care as he put them in his cargo pants and then took two more, putting them in his pack. He made sure they wouldn't rub against his new milspec pad which was initializing, and he wondered how he had gotten into this mess.

They lifted off, climbing steeply into the cold upper air, and headed east. The Professor had plenty of questions about Cricket's parents and the Dads. Cricket realized his parents and the Dads were known by literally everyone.

"Young man, the artifact we are looking for puts off a kind of radiation, but it doesn't seem to be dangerous to humans. We have been looking for several of these artifacts, believed to be rock-carven figurines for years. Croatoan said there are four figurines which hold the fate of humanity's future."

"Professor, that sounds like a load of horse-, mm, crap. Some guy sends you off hunting rocks and you believe you are saving our world? More likely it's a wild goose chase."

The Professor was consternated since he'd thought of that too. He wondered if he'd become addled in his old age. By the end of the ride the parade of questions had ended. The Professor had figured out Cricket was relatively uninformed, and Cricket got some thankful moments of solitude. But then he heard the Professor mumble something that caught his ear. Something about 'the kids were created for Croatoan'.

"Professor, what did you say?"

Cricket suspected that was the thing Jack was wanting him to hear. The Professor seemed to be in a daze. Cricket's words perked him up slightly, but something was wrong with the old man.

"Professor, are you ok?"

It was a hallmark of Cricket that he was much more concerned about the welfare of others even when he had a burning curiosity. The Professor's eyes were glazed and he was staring into space. Cricket grabbed his wrist and took his pulse; it was racing, and the old man was sweating profusely. Cricket thought the old man was going to pass out. In this condition, Cricket was easily able to lay him across both seats and make him more comfortable. As the old man laid down Cricket wondered if the Professor was going to clue him in on what they were doing.

'Give him some time. The old man is fairly jangled in the head. I fixed the artery that was about to pop, so he won't die now. But he will need a few minutes to recover.' Jack intruded again.

Jack had saved the old man and no one knew! He was like a magician, which made Cricket even more leery of him. Cricket found a cloth and Gracie wet it with her canteen water. He set the washcloth on the old man's forehead and made a quick prayer for recovery. The General watched on, clearly concerned but interested in Cricket's taking charge of the moment.

The Professor came around and his eyes smiled at Cricket.

"Ah, my boy. Thank you. Could you grab my bag and get me my medication?" Gracie went searching and found the bottle. She tipped the Professor's head forward, gave him some canteen water and the pills.

"Relax sir, you're doing better. You were white as a ghost for a few minutes. You're starting to get a bit of color back into your face." Cricket had an idea.

"Gracie, I think we need to kick his blood sugar up a notch. When it happens to me my Mom gives me a soda pop or granola bar. Can you see if they have any onboard?"

"Sure thing, let me go find out," Gracie was back almost immediately. "Here is a Coca Cola and a protein bar."

"Thanks Gracie. Professor?" The old man opened his eyes and Cricket helped him incline up to drink some soda and have a bite of the bar.

"Cricket I would have never guessed you were such a caretaker," Gracie's comment ruffled Cricket but he dismissed the feeling as irrelevant.

The Professor knocked out and as they landed at the Bellingham International Airport the General gave them some room to get the old man back on his feet.

"Gracie, when my Uncle Jesse lived with us on our farm for two years, I was in charge of tending to him. Jesse was a late-stage alcoholic and was dying. He was a corpsman during his time in the service in the CSA Army. He taught me about bandages, IVs, tourniquets, medications, and physical therapy. My folks were so busy with their lives they had no idea how much I learned from him. Near the end I was sopping up blood, vomit, urine, and feces. He was a mess, and I was the only one there when he died.”

After they touched down, Cricket got the Professor to a seated position. Gracie silently marveled at Cricket’s bedside manner.

“After Jesse died, I knew enough to get him in the body bag he had so kindly brought with him the year prior. Like he instructed me I got him zipped up and shoved into our walk-in fridge. When my folks came back a week later to check on us, they found out about his passing. They made a big deal over my having handled the whole thing like an adult. I was resentful for a while but it sussed-out in my mind that I had two great years with Uncle Jesse, and I wouldn’t have traded them for anything.” The Professor indicated he was ready to try standing.

“Cricket, you are a man of diverse talents. Thank you.” The Professor seemed to be doing much better. Jack gave Cricket a wink.

“Professor, take it slow. We just need to move you to the copters, and you can sit for a while longer before we get to Monte Cristo.” Gracie was no slouch herself. She had been as attentive as Cricket with the old man. They were a good team. They moved the Professor carefully to one of the three waiting copters and moments later they were aloft. As the aircraft banked, the pilot announced they were five minutes out from Monte Cristo.

Cricket asked, “Professor, what are we doing here?”

“It’s about a key or a rock as you like to call it.” The Professor gave his first genuine smile.

“Open my satchel and I will show you.” He ruffled through papers inside and pulled out one which read “Morrigan’s key”.

“Read this.” The old man was breathing harder again, shallower too. He was still very fragile.

Report of Key #1 – Transferred to Morrigan ~2027

Reported: Arthur Gernow (trans. By Sgt Sully Smith)

As I’ve discovered, one of the keys you seek is in the hands of a person named Morrigan, near the mining town of Monte Cristo. Four keys were dispersed in the early 21st century. One key was given to a southwest native tribe. The other two went south but there is no data on where they landed. From reports, the keys are not keys in the usual sense. They in fact are figurines, rock carvings. There is no indication why they are called keys. The legend around these mentions great power coming to the one who gathers them together. The legend’s origin is unknown.

The only history I could find was from Ottoman Kostantiniyye, today’s Istanbul. A man, Zildjian apparently came into possession of the keys in the early 17th century, he discovered that when he struck the rocks, they gave a pleasant ringtone. The rocks have a unique metallic composition which he used in his own artisanry. After he sold the carvings to fund his work, they disappeared for centuries, turning up in early America.

Cricket looked up and observed the Professor had lapsed into unconsciousness, sweating profusely. He began mumbling “… the singularities are the key. Only three lemma were required to prove the radiation was non-reactive with living tissue. The Hopi will help you…”

The Professor grew quiet, and Gracie mopped his head with the washcloth. Cricket felt a presence behind him and was shocked when a clawed hand moved past him to rest on the Professor’s chest. Lucy held her hand on Professor Jericho’s chest for nearly a minute, her face showing strain. She closed her eyes, concentrating.

After, she looked back at Lugh and Jack, “He is stable now,” she looked at Jack, “Your fix was not effective, mine was. He will live.” Jack shrugged at that.

She continued, “But coming on this journey was unwise. He must stay behind when we land, or he will die.”

Lucy was so matter of fact. She even did nice things in a scary way. As she moved away, she gave Cricket a big pointy-toothed smile. Cricket started and shivered. That woman was no lady!

'Calm your head, little man and never show a predator you are afraid. It makes them hungry,' Jack's mind-words made good sense for once.

January 2253 – Monte Cristo Ghost Town, Mt. Baker Wilderness

When the copter and its escort craft landed, drones and bots of various size and type whirled around their position. A good number of them headed in a specific direction. Cricket hopped out and noticed his 'team' kept close by. The General came up, holding his cap on his head against the propwash from the copter.

"Alright young man, did Lars give you the low-down on what you are to do?"

Cricket slowly shook his head, the General looked exasperated.

"Okay, your job is to go into this area," he looked at a printed map, "Somewhere in Monte Cristo we will find the key. Lars was supposed to tell you about this, but it seems we will be doing without his guidance for now."

Marna took the General aside and whispered to him. The General's head slowly panned back to look at Cricket. He shook his head back and forth slowly. Cricket knew something was amiss. And once again he was the center of something about which he knew nothing. Lugh and Marna consulted, and Cricket wondered why all the adults in his life felt the need to secretively talk about him.

Moments later, Marna came over. The General went back toward his copter.

"Cricket, here is how it shakes out. I don't know the history of all this but somehow you are the crucial to getting this key. The Professor provided a tracking device with the detection settings to help us find this thing."

Marna handed the device to Gracie.

"This is your job, dearie."

"Marna, this is effing weird. I have no idea what is happening. I run into you and Lugh on the other side of the world, then suddenly I am here with the Modern Major General and the Apple Dumpling Gang. It seems too coincidental that I was brought in the nick of time to save the day. Sorry, I am just unconvinced any of this is real. Too much conincidence."

They started walking down the trail which had been blazed by the bots and drones a few minutes earlier. Cricket looked back and saw the General bent over the Professor. He sure hoped the old man would pull through.

"Yep, I get it. I'll confide in you: apparently any of the four of you and your friends would have sufficed for this job. As for timing, they have been waiting quite a while for one of you four to arrive here."

Jack's spoke from behind, "Hey, little man, ya need to stay cool." Wow, Jack spoke aloud. "Pay attention now, and keep your eyes on the trail."

On cue, Cricket tripped over a rock. Jack snickered behind him.

Marna frowned then continued, "Don't worry, we can figure this out."

She gave a companionable squeeze to Cricket's left hand. Her touch tingled.

"Marna, why did you bring me to this General?"

"You really know nothing, huh?"

Cricket stopped walking. He closed his eyes for a few seconds while his team waited in silence. When he opened his eyes a bunch of words came out.

"Okay super-squad. Try to understand this from my perspective. I've got a secret agent woman who wants to act as if she is my friend who promptly turns me over to a General of unknown motivations. That same General talks about my parents as if I should know who he is. But nope, I have no idea!"

Cricket was working up a head of steam; he was riled up.

"Then I discover something about keys and about the 'kids'," Cricket made finger air-quotes when he said kids.

"Hmm, let me take a jab at that. Kids means me and my crew. Am I getting warm? Secret-agent woman tells me my first new friend Lugh is actually not human and is the King of the little people or something like that. No offense. "

"None taken, young sir." Lugh knew what was happening and was waiting.

"Then, I am introduced to Jack who has been doing the telepathy thing with me ever since we met. Telepathy, really? Is this some sci-fi movie? Damn! Then I meet the Filipino Flayer who looks like an army of one. Lucy, sorry, but you scare the hell out of me."

Lucy nodded and smiled. Cricket didn't shiver this time. He was fed up.

"Yeah, I guess you can eat me or whatever, but every chunk of me will fight the piss out of you on the way down! Yeah, how about them apples! And now I am supposed to find some magic rock, whatever the hell it is, and I have come to learn this is a task only I can do?

Cricket took a breath. The whole team waited. Gracie walked to Cricket. She said nothing. A moment later she took his hand.

"Cricket, I am on your side. I won't telepath you or eat you and I will never lie to you." Gracie looked him in the eyes, unblinking.

"Well thank God for some honesty! You know what, never mind. I'm not asking any more questions for now. Let's just get this thing and be done with it!"

The team walked on in silence, somewhat bemused by the young man's outburst. They crossed a couple foot bridges and rounded a large rock outcropping and saw the ghost town of Monte Cristo ahead. Cricket loved history and his family had lived in this area for years but never been to this moldering town. When he saw a placard entitled Monte Cristo Mining Area, he ran over to read it. At this point his team followed silently. Cricket thought it was strange that these chatty Cathys were suddenly so quiet. He kinda liked it.

He walked on and began exploring the town. He had no idea what he was looking for. Over the next hour Cricket looked around, inside buildings and in every nook and cranny. His team sat on a couple park benches while Gracie walked with him.

Holding the device, Gracie saw activity on the analog readout, "Cricket, check this out." Gracie walked to a large steel arm, about 8 meters long, on a central pivot. The dual I-beams rested on a central pivot plate, and he could see wheels supporting the beam on each end. It was clear most of the steel structure had been removed, leaving a large contiguous arm looking so much like a pivoting steel gate.

He smiled. "Hey Gracie, this is a turntable for ore-carrying railcars, let's see if it still rotates!" Cricket didn't notice his whole team had stood up and were watching him closely. Gracie and Cricket started pushing the huge steel arm in a creaking, slow circle, having a bit of fun. They kept at it, having a good laugh. Abruptly the arm stopped moving. They hit a large rock and couldn't move the steel wheels over it. After several attempts they sat on the arm itself and Gracie opened a lunch bag.

"Gracie Lou! You brought a sack lunch? Will you share?"

"With you Cricket, always. Take half my bologna sandwich. It has extra mustard and pepper. I hope that's ok?"

Cricket hated bologna.

"Gracie Lou, that sounds like the best sandwich I've ever had."

As they finished their sandwich the arm began to move again and they almost fell off backward. The part of the arm they sat on rose up and over the rock, slammed down and kept moving. It was moving faster than before. Surprised, Cricket and Gracie saw their team mates on both sides of the arm pushing. Geez they were strong! Cricket and Gracie hopped off and looked at a concrete pad rising up in the bushes a short distance away. Marna pointed and the Cricket saw their efforts were doing something.

"Gracie Lou! Look at that!" They ran over to stare at the slowly rising concrete, "We found a hidden entrance to something!"

"You are a total genius," Gracie said to Cricket. He didn't see the way Gracie was staring at him. Hmm, someone had an admirer.

"Yep, total genius. Keep pushing y'all, the kiddies are busy making eyes at each other." Marna's teasing went completely unnoticed. A few chuckles could be heard from the adult team members.

"Oh, look Cricket, there is an open space under the concrete. It smells like something died in there. Eww." Gracie scrunched up her nose at the smell.

"Gracie, see how this concrete is a big circle? Wouldn't it be cool if there were stairwell underneath?" Both kids were on their stomachs peering into the ever-widening crack. It did smell awful. Within a couple minutes the concrete pad had lifted about six feet high.

"Well glory be, there is a stairwell," said Cricket. There was a central pillar supporting the concrete cap and a stairwell with broad steps wound around the pillar into the darkness below. The squealing stopped. They hadn't realized how loud the metallic grating sound of the swing arm had become. In the sudden silence the team came over to look into the dark shaft.

"Young Cricket you are our leader in this. Do we go down?"

Lugh was strangely deferential. Cricket began walking down the stairwell. The others followed. The steps were bare except for a fine covering of dust.

"Young sir, you needs must be cautious here. I sense that here there be monsters."

Jack walked immediately behind Gracie and had a straight razor in one hand and shiny dirk in the other. A smell of wet dog washed over them and there was movement in the air. Cricket stopped, wishing he had thought to bring a flashlight. Almost on cue a bright light illuminated from behind him and looking back Cricket saw Marna holding a large flood lamp. She gave him a wink.

A few steps later a voice called in a hissing whisper, "Hic jacet sepultus inclitus regina Morrigan in montis dormientibus."

"Oh my. I think that is my invitation to go first down the steps. Lucy, come with me."

Lugh edged past Cricket and Gracie.

"Apologies, but allow me to translate for you. 'Here lies buried the famous Queen Morrigan in the mountain of the sleepers'. This likely means that one of my race has been here or is here, and the guardian is unhappy about us intruding."

Cricket stood in place and watched Lugh and Lucy head down the stairs.

"Gracie, I think those words were Latin. That was creepy."

"Shh, quiet for now, we are very exposed on this stairwell and this situation looks to be more hazardous than we suspected. So, hush. Please." Marna whispered. She was afraid. Cricket thought 'maybe I need to cultivate some healthy fear'.

'Now you seem to be catching the drift, young man. The wrong fear will get you killed but the right fear might save your life.' Jack was up to his old mind blasting tricks again.

A wave of sadness washed over the whole group. Lugh and Lucy were somewhere below, and the pall of mourning was intense. Cross and Jack had terse expressions, while Marna and Gracie wept openly. Cricket kept a stoic face, returning to stare down toward the darkness.

Several minutes passed and suddenly there was a huge belly laugh echoing off the walls. The pall of sadness vanished and a moment later a voice rang out.

"Young Cricket, we are among friends. Please come down to meet them."

Cricket and the girls shared a look.

"Gracie, do you smell something?" Cricket was confused.

"Yep."

Cricket sniffed and ventured, "Cinnamon rolls…?"

'Go on boy. Looks like the monsters are on our side for a change.' Jack smiled and continued down the stairs with his usual saunter.

Cricket pivoted fast, "Come on Gracie Lou, let's see if there is anything to eat."

Gracie thought to herself, eat, eat, eat. Boys always gave the highest priority to their stomachs. Marna followed but kept her sidearm unholstered for the moment. The bottom of the stairwell was dimly lit, but enough so Marna could turn off her lamp. Cricket saw the shadow of a large hairy 'thing' shuffle into the darkness. As it moved away, down a dark corridor, the wet dog smell receded. Looking forward, a large doorway was the source of the baked cinnamon smell and faint voices could be heard from within. Passing through the doorway and down a short brick-lined corridor, another room opened up with wall-to-wall wood paneling and a warm yellow light. It looked much like a library and laboratory with many tables packed with equipment and open journals. Dozens of shelves held books and jars of all sizes. A momentary acrid smell hit Cricket's nose as he passed a small beaker bubbling over a Bunsen burner. The familiar smell of old books and various chemicals wafted lightly throughout the room. At the far end there was a fireplace large enough to walk into, with a hungry blaze weaving through the giant logs within. The fire was surrounded with couches, poufs and large pillows arranged in a semi-circle. Sitting on pillows on the floor, Cricket could see Lugh and a tall, skinny woman conversing closely. Lucy was sitting on a couch nearby, looking bored. Cricket felt this place was somehow very old. It was the old wood smells and the ornate wood scrollwork that gave him that impression. Something about the wood walls was different than those he'd seen in libraries and colleges. In the background a faint catchy tune was playing. Cricket couldn't hear the words, but they didn't sound like English. It had a nice bounce to it though. Gracie showed the device readout; the needle was pegged.

"The thing we are looking for is somewhere around the fireplace. Keep your eyes open." Cricket saw a bunch of objects but got distracted by other things. As he listened, the music ended, and a new tune began. Something weird happened. Cricket was shocked as he saw the woman talking to Lugh rise and begin to dance. Lugh started to clap and as if on cue, Jack and Lucy began clapping.

"Start clapping, young man. Don't be rude. Our host is Armenian and is sharing her art with us. Come on, even I have enough class to enjoy this." Jack indicated Cricket's hands with a nod of his head.

Cricket rolled his eyes and began clapping. Marna and Gracie joined in, and the awkwardness gave way to something amazing. Everyone was standing and clapping as the woman moved in the most phenomenal ways. She was dressed in almost nothing substantial. Diaphanous scarves and scant coverings left her exposed but visually mysterious as she moved and the clothing teased and hinted at unseen pleasures. Even Jack was riveted. No one could pull their eyes away. The woman came closer to Cricket and made momentary eye contact. Cricket heard a faint voice, *'I am Morrigan. Be at ease. You are a friend and my guest.'*

Cricket was too enthralled to realize she didn't use her voice.

Morrigan moved and gyrated as a new song began. She moved faster, then she looped a scarf around Gracie Lou's neck and gently drew her forward onto the open floor. A transformation began. Gracie was initially jolty and awkward, but the moment her body drew close to Morrigan's, Gracie's movements began to smooth and pulse in time with the music. Morrigan held Gracie close, and they undulated together. Her eyes were closed and Morrigan turned her head, looking directly into Jack's eyes. Cricket watched and Jack didn't move. He could tell Jack was straining against something. Jack began to visibly sweat.

Then Morrigan moved on and when her eyes locked with Marna it was no-contest. She was 'all business' Marna no longer. Marna moved forward and joined the slip and move of the two women. Minutes passed and every watcher was covered in sweat. As the song ended Cricket felt like he'd run a hard footrace. His shirt was soaked.

A song Cricket recognized came on. Flashing lights lit up the room. Everyone began to move and soon all were dancing. Other tall skinny people came out of nowhere and joined. Suddenly Morrigan was in his face, tight with him, chest to chest. She moved him rhythmically and sensually. Moments passed and he heard a voice.

"You are most welcome. I know the Dads sent you as a messenger. I accept your offering and pledge fealty to you and Lord Kip." Lord Kip?

As she said these words, Cricket was scarcely able to control any part of himself. He knew it was time to go do something else. Then, like that, Gracie was suddenly against him, moving with him the same way. Before thought could happen, Cricket kissed Gracie. She gladly returned the same and they slid together as if in a dream.

'Boy, you need to snap out of this. Never allow yourself to fall under the sway of another, no matter how good it feels."

Jack was sitting on a couch watching the dancers, seeming to ignore Cricket. Cricket pulled back from Gracie. For a moment she had a hurt expression, but soon she moved to dance with Marna. Cricket went to sit beside Jack. He was bathed in sweat and felt a mess. The music subsided and the dancers moved off. Marna left the room, hand in hand with Morrigan. Lugh sat down by the fire again and Gracie looked torn between sitting with Cricket or following Morrigan. After another hungry look Gracie turned her back on Morrigan and sat across from Cricket on another couch.

'That right there is a strong woman, boy. She is a definite keeper. Do you see?'

Cricket looked at Jack, obviously not quite understanding.

'Open your eyes! The Morrigan wanted her tonight, but she didn't get her. Gracie's attraction to you is stronger. Sex may be alluring and fear and hate compelling, but only love will make the sacrifice."

Cricket stood up and held his arms open. Gracie ran to him; she literally ran 20 feet to collide into a kiss. How come Cricket gets the all the girls? The best I get is a tease, then nothing. But there was something on Cricket's mind he held in reserve. Gracie was lovely, but she wasn't the one.

"Kids, come on over. I need to give Cricket some background on what has happened and soon will happen in the world. Some things I have known for a very long time and others only recently discovered."

Gracie and Cricket sat down with Lugh, and he told them a story. Lugh put on his spectacles; they fit his wizened face well. As Lugh arranged himself, he refilled his brandy snifter, swirling around the fragrant green fluid. He smiled.

Looking up he began, "Cricket, let's start with something I just found out. You and your four friends have inherited the leadership of a worldwide resistance movement against the powers-that-be. It's not so much that you're in charge; rather, you and your friends are a key inspiration for the loosely-affiliated groups across the world."

Lugh stopped, expecting questions. Seeing none, he resumed.

"Humans are not the first sentient life on Earth. Very long ago there was a reptilian species which made it to the hunter-gatherer stage of development. A huge asteroid killed their hopes. We know this because an extra-terrestrial group known as the COMBINE was watching the events unfold. The loss was grievous, but some individuals of the race were spared, taken off world."

"Various races of the COMBINE sent small teams of scientists to watch new mammalian lifeforms evolve. Those that became the forerunners of humans were closely watched. What was missed were several other sapient species which evolved earlier than humans. Humans would later tell stories of these non-humans and give them names like dwarves, elves, demons, angels, pixies, sprites and orcs. These were real beings that largely didn't want to be seen or found. On occasion, there were some limited interactions between humans and non-humans. It was rare because humans always tried to kill us. They thought us curious but eventually they learned to hate us because we weren't them. All non-humans learned to stay in the shadows. Later, some were able to pass as humans and only those kind survived. There are only a handful of us left, now. We are still careful to blend-in." Lugh stopped again and seemed to be considering something.

"Lugh, what race are you part of?" Gracie Lou's words were filled with sadness.

"Gracie, best I can recall, we originally called ourselves Tuan. Some say we are Tuatha de Danann. That's a human name for us. I was born in an area later called France in the year 4438 BCE. I know the year of my birth because I met our friendly aliens as a kid. The COMBINE scientists have been my friends ever since. I gained an understanding of time, calendars and schedules and I have been late to everything ever since." Lugh had a twinkle and smile.

"Lugh, you are 6000 years old?" Cricket was incredulous.

"Cricket, let me show you my true form, then you tell me how old I look."

Lugh stood and walked a few steps away. As he turned his body changed shape. He grew taller, bat wings unfurled, and two rams horns curled around his head. He looked like a demon from Dungeons and Dragons. Lugh was a wrinkly, old demon. The effect was both scary and comical as he still wore his John Lennon glasses. Gracie and Cricket were frozen on the couch, unable to tear their eyes away from Lugh's transformation.

"Wow, you're kinda big." Gracie blurted.

"Cricket and Gracie, be at ease. I'm on a meat-free diet now…but I am a bit hungry though."

Lugh gave them a leering look, waited a beat then laughed at their expressions. He quickly changed back and patted Gracie's hand.

He continued his tale, "I was not always a friendly monster. Centuries ago, I was a demon to be feared. I watched my people's numbers dwindle and saw my own family die horribly, one by one. On one night in the Middle Ages the remainder of my family was slaughtered. That night I did many bad things, but I won't talk of it, here."

Lugh's eyes became weary. He poured more brandy and continued.

"Humans have always been the enemy. Only the kindness of the COMBINE scientists gave us hope that we could survive. Hundreds of us were taken off world, but some like me stayed to help the others. For many, many years the scientists helped us to hide and move around. But, in 1958 something changed. The scientists all left Earth, warning us the Harrowing had begun and to stay far from all humans. But before they left, they helped us develop contact with the Cloud, which allowed us to stay in touch with them and gave us powers to defend ourselves from humans. True, a few of us had Cloud powers already, but the boon granted by the scientists gave us all a fighting chance. As you know, the Dads dubbed that form of connectedness as Jungian Space, then like humans are wont, renamed it the Cloud. Regardless, we monsters now had the ability to connect with our minds with no regard to distance."

"Lugh, how many non-humans are left, now?" Cricket was visibly moved by Lugh's tale.

"I don't know for sure, but I guess we are less than 10000 worldwide. Most of those are the Seelie, the Skinwalkers. Lucy and Morrigan are the last survivors of other races. Take the Morrigan, she has hidden in this plush cavern for centuries. For myself, I became scarce by becoming a scientist and modeling myself after the COMBINE researchers. I was investigating birds of Siberia when I was inadvertently nabbed by a Baltic patrol. I had grown lax in my security."

"Lugh why do you guys live so long?" Cricket shared a look with Gracie.

"Now that is the million-credit question. I have no idea. Someone suggested that it has to do with being a Cloud operant, but I have my doubts since so many non-operants are hundreds or thousands of years old, too."

Cricket shook his head, realizing humans were more monstrous than any of the 'monsters' of history. His sympathies had always lain with the synths in his family and now they lay with the non-humans, too.

"Understand, Morrigan's tale is a cautionary one. She broke one of our rules when she allowed a human into her sanctum. You see, when gold prospectors came into the Monte Cristo area in the 19th century a man discovered this cave and the woman within. He fell in love with her and built out much of the opulence you see now. She shared this with me and won't mind me mentioning that she stayed with the man and nursed him until his last day. He was the first and only human she loved. She intended this place to be a hideaway from humans…minus one." Lugh took a long sip of his green liquid, then considered for a moment.

He could see the sorrow reflected by Cricket and Gracie.

Lugh smiled kindly and grabbed both kids in a bear hug, "Oh my children, when in shouting converse the sun is foiled by clouds most dark, a ray of hope will dawn when the watchers in the cave look beyond their shadows, to see the beauty of that which casts the shapes of dim repose. It is then eyes will open at a spark, with love pouring out in fulsome flow, reaping the bounty that only passion knows."

Lugh's embrace suffused the kids with warm feelings. Cricket didn't want the overwhelming sense of safety to stop. Lugh's poem didn't make much sense, but the emotion of the moment sure did. When Lugh separated them, they silently wept. The faerie king had passed on something to them. They could feel a sense of presence.

"That, my children is the tangible love of my people, given to you. It is my aegis to you, and it can only be given, never taken. In time you will be able to share this with others as a gift from the Tuan."

January 2253 – Monte Cristo Ghost Town, Mt. Baker Wilderness

It dawned on him. "So Lugh, all the conspiracy theories about aliens, abductions and sightings were all real?"

Cricket's eyes were round and amazed.

"At least a portion of the rumors are true. The researchers were stealthy and rarely seen, but always helpful. But something changed in 1958. As a result, they left; in their place COMBINE agents appeared. We were warned to stay away from them. Those agents integrated themselves into positions of power across the world. The first thing they did was profoundly advance the sciences, giving rise to the synths. They brought an age of progress which too late we non-humans realized was the humans' downfall as we were warned by the scientists.

They used your human weakness against you. Your kind cannot abide a lifestyle of ease and plenty. They get bored, then angry. The COMBINE knew this, and the seeds of war eventually bore fruit. A hundred years later, the Tech War began. Other non-human old-timers had been given Cloud powers for their protection. But a newer generation of non-humans like Jack had emerged, who possessed Cloud powers aplenty. Jack and others were able to tell us that the alien scientists were still talking to us from afar. Their advice was to hide."

'Aw, you guys say the nicest things!' Jack broadcasted the words to everyone. With uncanny tidiness, Morrigan and others returned to the great room, arrayed on the couches; a couple of the elvish types headed to the kitchen from whence delicious smells soon emanated, while one elvish lady began mixing drinks behind the bar. After Jack's loud broadcast, many of Morrigan's retainers were left rubbing their heads. Cricket too. It was the telepathic version of a yell.

"The work the Dads have been recently doing hinges on the use of the Cloud to unite humanity and all other self-aware beings on Earth. The aliens who have put themselves in places of power are fighting that effort." Lugh had a small smile.

"Lugh, how do you know the Dads?" Cricket was amazed.

"Scientific colleagues," Lugh nodded.

Morrigan spoke in mind voice to Cricket, *'You do not know your worth. Many people died to make it possible for you and your three friends to live. What little I know tells me that there will come some critical time when you and your friends will turn the tide in some battle. I do not know, but I surmise the four of you will save this world. This is a heavy burden, young man, but you were made for this challenge. Beware the narcissism of small differences and the kulturkampf of ill-paired bedfellows.'*

What was that? Kulturkampf? Cricket was getting annoyed with mental sendings and he kept hearing about being 'made' and 'created'. He was fatigued and couldn't muster up enough energy to care. He just missed home, his friends, and his crew. He missed his parents so much it made his heart hurt. Cricket nodded off for a couple hours while humans and non-humans alike bustled around him.

When he woke, he decided to check for messages from his crew on his new milspec pad. He logged into one of the burner accounts I gave him to see what was happening in the world. Same bad crap it seemed. He accessed our secret-squirrel proxy server and logged into SimVerse, headed to our private message-drop location. On Planet Endor he found some digital breadcrumbs leading to a note.

> Hey Cricket, we're doing well but miss you a ton. We are being moved from one place to another and this Liberation stuff is keeping us busy. We're meeting some cool people though. Leave a note here and let us know if you're ok. -Kip

He left a note to say he was okay.

They were invited to stay the night and Marna communicated with the General who approved. Gracie and Cricket slept in separate beds in the same room. Morrigan tucked them in.

"Okay kids, don't do anything I wouldn't do." Cricket thought it was surreal to be tucked in by a Faerie Queen.

'I'm just a Queen, darling, not a Seelie.' Morrigan turned out the light. Clearly, she was as good at telepathy as Jack.

'No, my boy, no one has my mental horsepower in this neck of the galaxy.' Jack broadcasted again. What a turd burglar!

'You are such a braggart.' Morrigan quipped.

Cricket's head felt like it was going to explode, "Gawd, would you guys shut up!"

"Cricket, what is wrong? Are you okay?" Gracie Lou didn't hear the voices. Well, that was inconvenient. He shook his head no; he was too tired to explain.

Cricket held out his arms. She came to cuddle with him, and they ended up falling asleep quickly on his bed. In dreamland Cricket had a wistful rag-tail of a dream. Then something interrupted it. In the new dream Binky, Wogs and I were flying somewhere and all he could feel from us was grief and pain. For a moment he could see me and I him.

'Cricket, I see you got the note. See if your team will allow you to meet up with us. I'll work on our side to do the same. Love ya, man.' The connection ended abruptly. Cricket and I were still both surprised at the telepathy thing.

The next morning as they left the underground. Gracie showed Cricket an object on the fireplace mantle. He picked it up. A buzz of static electricity zipped through Cricket, like grabbing staticky laundry right out of the dryer and the taste of orange sherbet was in his mouth. The rock itself wasn't unusual. It was carved in the shape of a round woman and was about the size of a baseball. He chucked it to Marna, and she caught it.

"Cricket, this is irreplaceable. Don't be throwing things like this! Vagabond said this is a fertility figurine from Willendorf. He said Croatoan wants them intact."

Cricket smiled and nodded. He didn't believe her. As they walked away a small solid-state device fell from the figurine. Cricket saw it fall, picked it up and pocketed it, thinking of me.

They said their goodbyes. Lugh was staying behind with Morrigan, who was not even out of bed, yet. Gracie, Marna, and Jack mounted the winding stairs first, followed by Cross and Cricket playing rock, paper scissors for who would keep a gold ring they were given by one of Morrigan's retainers. Cricket lost. As they climbed, the wet dog smell resumed, and a huge hairy shadow waved goodbye to them. They emerged into bright sunshine and a crowd of civilians who were gawking at them. Within moments a copter landed directly ahead, and the General's voice could be heard over the PA.

"People please move back. If you have tickets for the gold mine tour, please queue up near the steel swing arm. Otherwise, please let these tourists pass."

Cricket tried not to smile. He thought about how many people would be looking for a ticket vendor for the gold mine tour. Well, the General couldn't just say 'Hey we are a group of rebels hiding stuff underground. Please don't tell on us'. Clearly no one queued up with tickets, though some tried anyway. The concrete stairway cap closed silently, unnoticed. The swing arm was still.

As the copter rose the sunshine faded and a misty rain began to fall. Once aloft, Marna spoke into Cricket's ear.

"You have to take this to Croatoan, okay?, I heard that you and your friends are the ones he wants to deliver them." Her eyes were serious, and Cricket nodded and stuffed the woman-shaped baseball rock into his pack.

January 2253 – Cahokia Arcology, Chicago, Illinois

It was another cold winter with the snow driving off Lake Michigan, hammering the city into a frozen slumber. Snow drifts and dunes coated the streets and made commuter foot traffic nearly impossible. Only garbage trucks, meter hags and cops were out in usual numbers. Oh, and one assassin. Don't forget us.

At the moment I was huddled on the roof of the Cahokia Arcology, two kilometers above the grime and filth of the streets of Chicago. My name is Ix Oblivion and my job is eliminating people. Pay me enough and I'll make the CSA President disappear or splatter; your choice. But that will set you back more credits than most countries make in a year. Not interested? Didn't think so.

My sites were focused on a window in another arcology half a kilometer to the north. The North Lawndale Arcology was the fancy high-rise meant for snobbish prigs and wealthy urbanites. Cahokia, my present location, was much more down scale. More my kind of people. But nevermind, let me tell you about my mark for today. This man is probably more Synth than human. He was beautiful with all his after-market replacements. And he was hated. His money had been made experimenting on living beings, humans, hybrids and synths. His life was about causing suffering and pain. But my client didn't care about that. Hell, he is probably just as ruthless as this guy in my sites: Garfield Chatham. But don't think I care whether somebody is a brutal torturer, for whatever reason. I don't. All I care about is the paycheck. I am a high-priced whore and bringer of death. I am proud of what I have made myself. I am the best at what I do and my fees reflect that.

I whispered to myself the words passing at the Chatham family table. Yep, I read lips. "Gosh honey bunch, busy day at the office?"

"Naw, same old. Been missing you, though."

"Daddy, you said we were going to the Lunar playpark tomorrow."

"Yeah, Dad, are you going with us this time, or is it just Mom and Ms. Maisie, again?"

Ix smirked, "Ah Garfield. Please take that last bite of brisket. It looks tasty. There you go. Smile at your wife, then at your 'colleague' who is actually your mistress. Hmm, you think that is really a kept secret? And sorry about your kids seeing Daddy splashed upon the wall. Hmm, perhaps it was time for them to see what most of us see in the real world. Pampered brats."

Ix took a breath, exhaled slowly, and squeezed the trigger. A poof sound, then he saw the glass break and the man's head jerk backwards. A flurry of activity began as hidden guards rushed out of alcoves to attend to the very dead man.

"Time to go."

Ix put his rifle in it's case and thumbed the app on his pad, indicating the job was complete. The client acknowledged and in another app Ix saw the credits pour into his bank account from En Banque.

"All in a day's work."

Ix pulled out an ancient stenograph and documented his kill in Tironian notes, then accepted his next gig on his pad, which would take him to Las Vegas, in Glitter Gulch to dispose of pop icon, Blue-7 and some kid named Kip.

"'One need not hate what one kills, but it can sure make it more interesting. I believe St. Conrad said that, eh?"

Ix grimaced to himself, then launched in his wingsuit from the balcony, sweeping downward to a snow-covered park; he landed and blended himself into the snowy scape and cold-driven throngs.

January 2253 – Colorado Springs, Colorado

"Sir, that's the last one. I think we're ready to pull the switch. I have Cicero on the horn too," Sgt. Craig pulled off his haptic rig and sat down. All the screens in the command center were focused on views from the Janussaries. In the last week a transformation had taken place with the soldiers, airmen, sailors, and jarheads who staffed the center. Col. Andrews permitted them creative license to decorate the center, since he knew esprit de corps was vital to their new secret mission. To his amazement every staffer, even the civilians, wanted to join the team. They called themselves Cary's Bucketeers. Their creativity extended to pirate apparel, cuisine, and vocabulary; they were the swashbuckling brigade. Andrews was floored: the whole staff was so easily converted to their new humanitarian cause. He knew it struck a chord in all of them. It was an opportunity to have hope for the future. Cary and Cicero had spoken privately for some time and both knew the work of the Dads and real meaning of the Liberation.

"Fig, how did you find the Janussaries, originally?"

"Sir, I met their man Tech on the Endor Moon, Yavin 4 in SimVerse. It is a place for secret stashes."

Fig tapped on his pad, then continued.

"But more recently, they came to the same conclusions we did. We needed to do something off the books to help the Liberation. We would provide intel and they would be the boots on the ground."

Cary listened intently.

"Tech mentioned one of the targets we've been tracking, 024 is being pursued by Templeton Rus and the whole of the Jaxy Soldats. I shared with him we were aware of 024 through the Dads. It also looks like Nines Gonzalez and the Nomads have been hired by Bad Wolf to pursue 024 and now Barker James and the Hell's Outlaws have been hired to do the same by Bangarang. Tech and I came to a quick agreement. We needed to make contact with 024, accelerate their movement and guard their six. All these privateers…"

"Yes Fig, I have been aware of the movement reports you've provided."

"Yes sir. Well, all the privateers work for Clan Sun 14 to varying degrees. Tech thinks there is a way we can send them on wild goose chases by infiltrating the Sun 14 systems." Fig was very excited, wearing a devil-may-care smile.

"Cicero, you there?" a holo of the Janussaries ship came up over the mapping table.

"Hey Cary, good to hear from you again. Tech has good things to say about your man Fig. Hey Fig, you ever get tired of Colonel Clink, you're welcome to join the real military!" Cicero made it obvious he was playing around.

"Cicero, the honor is all mine. We have some of the same notions on what we should be doing about our crazy world." Cary was the consummate professional.

Cicero spoke, "Tech, do you have the bolus?" An outgoing-package indicator blinked on the screen, "Ah, good," He looked over his shoulder and nodded to Tech. Looking back he continued, "Cary, Tech is about to send you all our intel en masse. I suggest you send us the same. Tech can integrate the two."

June 2253 – Seattle, Washington

Templeton Rus was not a patient man. He was loud, large and at this moment annoyed. Things had not been going well. 024 should have been an easy target, but someone always got the drop on him. He knew he was in competition with Barker and Nines for this one. Apparently, they were having the same problems. A revelation hit him. He thought, I am the only one who is not obligated to either sponsor (Bangarang or Bad Wolf); hmm, maybe the problem is with the intel we are getting from Sun 14. Time to change our approach. And being beholden to none, he could change things up on a whim.

"Alright lads and lassies, it's time to saddle up! Poppa needs a confirmed kill so he can be home for supper. Otherwise, my old lady will start grousing about my being a slacker."

There were gruff laughs. Everyone knew he didn't have an old lady and if ever anyone in all of creation was not a slacker, it would be Rus.

"A gift I bring, just a touch, but touch not the gift. Bravery I sing, not so much, counting coup so swift: the gift to live." Rus needed to be the one to nab 024. The four kids were part of a larger plan and he couldn't let them come to harm. He hoped 024 would live to see another day.

Brie called out, "What was that sir?"

"Nothing Brie. Just an old man mumbling."

Rus looked toward the Seattle downtown. The mobile flybridge of his ship gave a 360° view of the Argo and all that lay below. They were currently hovering over Pioneer Square, finishing a philanthropic mission, delivering tiny houses, food, and camping gear. The people below only knew the Argo as a ship of mercy; they had no idea the Argo made their money by taking contracts to hunt and kill targets large and small. There was no other way to afford to make these mercy runs. Rus hoped the ignominious truth would never emerge. Well, no doubt some knew but they seemed to be in good favor with the populace despite all.

"Time to get underway!"

The bridge crew cried as one, "Aye, aye, Captain!"

The Argo was an airship inspired in design by the aircraft carriers of the 21th century. Aircraft carriers from the 21th were gone. During the Tech War, carriers were targeted using nukes and every side of the war equally lost use of them. It became the détente of 'you don't have one, we don't have one'. If the Tech War produced one good thing it was the complete dismantling of the worldwide nuclear arsenal. In the place of nukes, novel and less massively destructive tools were designed to wage war. The new alignment of Powers gained hegemony in real estate, virtual estate, and commerce. Powers like Bangarang, Bad Wolf and Crane rose to compete with the new nation-states like the Confederate States of America, European States, China, the Baltic Free States, Australasia, and Switzerland. Gotta love Switzerland, still keeping back the barbarians at the gate! Three non-national (read: criminal) organizations rose to power after the Tech War. The lines between criminal and legitimate business blurred to irrelevance as 3 Clans gained strength: Clan Sun 14, Clan Minatomi, and Clan MacLean.

Clan Sun 14 originated out of China, headed by Ming Liu. Ming was a sociopathic narcissist, but gentle in temperament, and calm in her demeanor. Only to their peril did her retainers forget she was absent ethics or morals in all ways that mattered.

Clan Minatomi out of Australasia was headed by Nobu Meiji. Nobu loved his booze and his practical jokes. He once used one of his new earthquake-causing devices to shake up downtown Tokyo, targeting several new high-rise buildings in Shinagawa-Ku which blocked his view of Tokyo Bay. They fell, he laughed and voila, his main office building suddenly had an unobstructed view again.

Clan MacLean originated from the European States. A Korean-Scottish man named Duncan Hines was leading the Clan. For a criminal organization, Hines had his people doing quite a bit of philanthropic work. True, they also had the largest number of indentured workers (read: slaves), but Hines liked to think they were good to his people, many of whom lived in squalor.

Like Hines said, "If you got three hots and a cot, don't complain 'bout what ya don't got!"

Rus was unlike his other two privateer counterparts. Barker James was the head of the Hell's Outlaws and was a madman who killed his own people for sport. Nines Gonzalez had built the Nomads into a vast killing machine. He didn't kill his own like Barker, but he was brutal to those outside his organization. Barker got his loyalty through fear and bribes. Nines received total loyalty from his people because he rewarded them handsomely. His people would die for him. Rus commanded loyalty because, despite being a hardass, he was fair and generous with his people, and he didn't kill or harm indiscriminately.

"Bixby! Where are you, bubba?" Rus walked onto the command deck.

"Here Rus! Just been running the diagnostic on the propulsion systems before we got underway."

Rus turned, looking at his senior engineer, "Bixby, listen. Can you hear the purr of the engines? We are underway.”

Bixby looked shocked as he realized. He didn’t want to let down the boss; so obsessed, he failed to hear the distinct whine of the engines under load.

“Sorry boss, I’ve just been working to get everything back online after that string of back-to-back missions. Sorry.” Bixby hung his head and was about to walk away.

A huge hand grasped his shoulder and a voice, not unkindly said, “Bixby Brown, you are the best damned ship’s mechanic in the world. I am proud of you, but you need to chill the eff out.” Rus seemed to consider something, “Hm, perhaps I’m relying too much on your skills these days.”

Bixby’s warm and fuzzy vanished, “Relying too much?”

Rus broke into his famous grin and clasped the smaller man by both shoulders, “You cannot be replaced, silly man. But it does call a good question: have you been training engineering recruits like I asked?” Rus felt Bixby’s tension and he had his answer.

“Sir, um, I really am planning to do that. Maybe I can start in my free time.”

“Bixby, today you will get me a list of five people whom you will train. Understood?” Rus winked and turned away.

“Sir, yes, of course, sir. By the end of today.” Bixby ran from the bridge and disappeared into a corridor.

The crew was preparing for shipping out to…? ”Captain, we are headed roughly south, do we have a specific heading and destination?” Brie asked, Rus smiled.

“Just go two stars to the left and on till morning!”

“The right!” the bridge crew said in unison. It was one of the games they played.

Brie would have to be satisfied with the non-answer for now, “Helm, hold course steady toward Los Angeles. Make 150 knots true.”

The crew knew they were waiting on intel, and it was okay to be somewhat lax and jovial. But the moment Rus gave the word, they would all be about their business and back to formality.

An hour later Rus came back on the bridge, “Lads and lassies, listen up. 024 headed toward the Los Angeles CENTER. Your random choice was a good one, Brie. Head to the CENTER at max speed!”

Brie called out the course correction, “Helm to 175° and plot corrections to LA:CENTER TRACON. Confirm with ACARS at 500 klicks. Notify the duty officer when we are 200 klicks out.”

Rus knew Brie was a naval historian and trained merchant mariner who yearned for the seafaring days of yore. Her commands might be unnecessary and antiquated, but they were crisp and efficient and gave a sense of orderliness and control that Rus liked.

Rus returned to his quarters and picked up a well-worn book. The poem he was reading was highlighted on the page, ‘You may write me down in history, with your bitter, twisted lies; You may trod me in the very dirt, but still, like dust, I’ll rise.”

Rus remembered his wife, Elena, so long ago and he recalled something she said about the arts.

Elena was a his inspiration and muse. She always called him Red, because of his shaggy mane of hair cascading down his back. “Red, it’s about surprise. Working in oils or acrylics, I look for the turn around a corner and abrupt meeting of an old friend. It’s brand new, yet it’s welcome and familiar, somehow. It’s the same in music and dance, too. In fact, in the first few bars of a song, if I am not surprised, I might enjoy the tune, but without the surprise, I mentally move on.”

Maya Angelou was her favorite poet. Elena said, ‘she always surprised me’.

He ached for Elana’s loss. Now, he was hunting one of his wife’s childhood friends from Kenya, and no doubt this would be a surprise for him. Vicky was one of the Dads and Rus was going to turn him in for a bounty. Or was he? Save the kids, but turn in the Dads? Rus didn't waffle on decisions, ever, but something new was happening and he knew what he needed to do and how much it would cost him. Rus shook his head and turned out the light for a few minutes sleep. His dreams were troubled with images of the past.

Chapter 9 – LA:CENTER & SHROOMER CITY

June 2253 – Los Angeles California, CSA

The ancient intercom speaker crackled to life in Rus' quarters. "Sir, you have a message from a man named Cicero." Brie's assistant, Margie's blaring voice woke him from a surprisingly sound sleep.

"Margie, tell him I will be with him in five," Rus rousted himself, splashed some water on his face and wondered why the notorious outlaw would be calling.

"Sir, you do know that Cicero is the enemy, and it's risky to talk to bad actors?" Big sigh, Margie could be such a nag. He kept Margie on for one reason: she was uncanny in her intuition on certain command decisions. He found out Margie was an observational savant when she asked about radar patterns and successfully identified all the bogeys from the hundreds of non-combatant aircraft. It was a combined CSA attack, including Bangarang and Bad Wolf assets. Their allies had decided to take them out. Truth be told, he kept her around for another reason. She and Brie were 'an item' and it would be bad form to have her tossed from an airlock like he so wanted to do right now.

"Thank you, Margie. Rus, out!"

"Does that mean you're out, like gone? Or out like leave me alone?" Rus turned the speaker off, drank the whole pitcher of water sitting on his bureau, and took a deep breath.

Rus walked the corridor to get his blood flowing; on the bridge, Brie brought up a holo on the vox.

"Cicero, my dearest foe, what may I do for you?"

"Templeton, I have a proposition for you. It involves our friend General Oloiboni." Rus activated the privacy screen and the two commanders spoke. Brie could see through the privacy haze an expression of surprise on her boss' face.

June 2253 – LA:CENTER

I had been sitting in the little cell for only a few hours, but it felt like forever. I was reflecting on my visit to Seattle. The Seattle Underground Safehouse recruitment had been a bust. When word came through our burner phone to contact the Safehouse, I imagined we were going to be welcomed in. Not so much as it turned out.

The scientists and few business execs who were hiding out near Pioneer Square were skittish and almost shot us when we came to their front door. To be fair, I knocked politely for a couple minutes, then Binky got impatient and beat on the door hard; it rattled like it was about to fall apart. A slot opened and a gun barrel protruded. We froze.

"Go away!" said the slot. The metal flap flopped down.

"Hey old people! We aren't going away. You might as well just open up." Binky had a way with words.

To my surprise a gun barrel didn't re-emerge. The door cracked open, and a voice yelled.

"You can come in, but don't do something we will all will regret…"

I tried to bring those in the Underground into our liberation effort, but they wanted to hide from the evil empire instead. They said they wanted to survive, and not get caught up in someone else's war. I wondered if they were right. They had lost many of their people to the goon squads that roamed the streets. But I figured this was a fight for every person seeking freedom. I guess they saw differently.

"Young man, we are thankful the Dads helped us out with that box of power converters, but this whole thing about going to war just doesn't fit for us. We are scientists, not freedom fighters," the man was nice about it, but it was a cop out. I kept my mouth shut and we eventually left after they fed us stale rations and brown water.

The Liberation needed willing fighters and we were supposed to find ways to recruit more. It seemed monumentally stupid to have a bunch of kids recruit adults. Our success seemed to be hit-and-miss. Well, what did I know? Anyway, Seattle was behind me, and my Los Angeles infiltration turned into handcuffs and manacles, without even a kiss and hug. But to be honest, that was my plan: get arrested and begin my work of recruitment from the inside. Well, maybe not the arrested part.

From Seattle, I had bummed a ride from a trucker to southern California. Binky and Wogs decided to go ahead when a helicopter arrived to pick us up in South Seattle. Vagabond wanted us in the LA area and his instructions were for us to meet in the desert east of Los Angeles. My friends complained a bunch and tried to persuade me to go with them. Nope, I was going undercover! Wogs called me egregiously stupid, and Binky said I was a damned stubborn ass.

After the truck ride, I went on foot the final dozen miles to the front gates of LA:CENTER. I told the gate guards my parents worked inside and asked if could I come in. They got on the walkie and blabbed some security jabber and brought me inside. The person on the other end of the radio agreed I needed to come inside. I was slapped into some handcuffs and locked up. I thought it would go differently. But it was merely a wrinkle in my masterplan.

Okay, I was an idiot. I realize that now. I guess I thought I would have been brought in to the lost and found to wait for my parents to come get me. Nope. They plopped me down in a holding cell, waiting to be taken into the CENTER.

So, my backup plan was the next thing on my list. I was confident that between Binky, Wogs, and Vagabond, they would get me out. Sorry Pop, your boy's in jail!

I remembered my burner phone. I pulled it from my pocket; it got crunched at some point. A frisson of realization shook me as I thought it through. How would they be able to find me in the gigantic LA:CENTER? It dawned on me I would have to find my own way out. Smooth move ex-lax! No use having agita over that now though.

I forgot to mention, they found Cricket! The helicopter crew in Seattle mentioned he had been rescued from a jail somewhere in Europe. Lucky turd got to go travelling!

The perimeter gates were the size of the Black Gates of Mordor, ponderous steel behemoths and they loomed over the guardhouse where I was being held.

Finally, a guard came to get me, "Come on hoss, the big man wants you put away for safe keeping."

I was led through an access door that looked tiny, set into one of the perimeter gates. These things were blast doors, thicker than I was tall. I was led inside and for almost an hour was walking with a burly guard. We trudged along endless corridors and the fluorescent lights were giving me a headache.

He wasn't chatty. "Hey sir, can I stop to go pee?" The man grunted which I took for no. Luckily, I wasn't in crisis mode yet.

I had modified my identity, so they thought I was a guy named Tummy Pokefinger, from Elmira, New York. I was brought to a security desk and was asked if I was human. The guy asking pointed an EMP blaster at me. What a douche!

I replied, "Negative, I am a meat popsicle."

These guys didn't appreciate the humor, any more than I appreciated their threats. My mouth earned me an isolated cell and no food or toilet.

The cell was 3-meter square, and as I settled in I felt the reality of no food for more than two days. I decided to think happy thoughts: I will get sprung soon. My crew will heist the main computer and I will be walking out of this CENTER with all the other inmates like the Sweet Charity Dancers. Or not. I was the computer whiz kid, and my crew weren't aware that I had even been captured. Eventually the General may have them infiltrate the control center or something. I began looking for a place to go pee.

I could hear other prisoners around me. One of the cells near me was filled with a group of women. They were jammed into the same sized cell I occupied. I had no idea how they could manage. As I listened, they talked about Elysia coming to get them. Apparently, they were Tietz product models from the Los Angeles Gunga Den. I knew about those Dens: filled with druggies and sleazy rich people. Dens were run by the Elysia, where they made the promise you will 'Be loved at the Lotus Eaters'. But most people had a different saying, 'From bloom to tomb'. It was a nasty bit of business practice where they take all your money as you enjoy their services, right into your grave. People gave away fortunes to their drug of choice at Gunga Den. These women were one of the main attractions at the brothel. I heard them talking about being on contract from Clan MacLean and that they were expensive models.

"Shut up, Deerhart. Those stupid memories are as fake as you are."

"Oriola, hush. They are beautiful."

"Ori, don't you wanna go to the farm and see for yourself?"

"Ladies, no one is going to any farm, today. Let's just be quiet and do as we are told. Maybe we can earn our way to better accommodations." The voices hushed to whispers.

"We already tried that Ori. Guard tried to stick it in my rumpus. I gave him a full blow of my Gumbo…"

"Susi! You're nasty. Shut it, girl."

"Mmm hmm, right."

"Shut your mouth now! You got us into this mess to begin with and now look where we are!"

The voices went silent as the periodic patrol went clomping by our cellblock.

Clan MacLean was an evil enterprise. It was both legit and non-legit business and very rich. Duncan Hines was the head of Clan MacLean, and he was a right bastard. I heard my Dads talking about him one night when he was on the news.

As I kept listening, the ladies whispered about some of their latest, ahem, work. I was torn between being turned on and vomiting. But then other voices talked about their implanted memories. They were afraid and they hoped for an escape. Not just from their cell, but from the lives they were chained to. I promised myself I would find an escape for them when the time came. I would find a way for all the captives to be set free.

I know what you're thinking, how can I assure anything? It's true, I couldn't. But my father Vicky once told me that choice is the only true power. Maybe what I can do is assure these prisoners have a choice.

Footsteps came my way, so I got quiet and watched. I heard talking.

"…and our primary mission is to eradicate the doing of evil before it becomes an option." Said a feminine voice.

The boot steps stopped near my cell door.

"Right, I've heard that tripe before. Don't you think removing choice is amputation of the spirit?"

The large male voice had a raspy quality. He sounded like the kind of man who gave loud commands.

"Colonel Blake, I didn't know you were so enamored of mythology. The spirit? Come on Doctor, you know better than to argue the supernatural with me."

The woman had one of those nasally voices which grated on my nerves.

"Evelyn, you know me. I am all about practicality. My concern is we are removing the most crucial aspect of a person's humanity. You've seen the Zombies we've made."

"Errol, you know why we are doing this. The war we are fighting is between the Powers. You and I are cogs. Living cogs. I would like to remain living and still pursue our research. Regardless, we need to harvest our next $Hybrid_1$ and $Hybrid_2$ lines this week and if…"

Their steps resumed and passed out of earshot. Those scientists scarcely cared about their lab rats: us. And the guards regarded us with equal parts dubiety and puzzlement. Did they believe we were all criminals? Maybe it didn't matter.

After my spectacular infiltration of the LA:CENTER, I became very aware of what the inside of a CENTER was like: vaulted steel and glass, and citrus cleanser. The hours were boring, and I thought back to my Dads' words on the CENTERs. They told me a few sketchy stories about the accommodations there; nasty business went on at the CENTERs, but they were pinnacles of building science with a sprinkling of architectural whimsy. As scientists on-location my Dads were restricted to their assigned labs and resources, but on the walks to and from their work they passed dozens of other labs, storage units, experimentation spaces and a few unknown areas. The security people were extremely twitchy and demanded strict obedience to the rules. That included no snooping, spying, or fraternizing with people outside authorized areas. The LA:CENTER sprawled across almost 1200 square kilometers. Some buildings were skyscrapers and others looked like airplane hangars. Everything was connected both above and below ground. There was an internal transit system and moving walkways.

It was the most high-tech city in the world except maybe Las Vegas. It was the biggest of all the CENTERs, hence the reason that Vagabond was targeting it first. Everything was spotlessly clean. Where it wasn't cloying with citrus, it smelled of ammonia and chlorine and the lights were too bright. It was beautiful and ugly and every variation in between. Static structures encompassed the largest enclosed space on Earth, and I could see aerial skylanes, with trucks and cars. Darting and flowing both were the biologicals and synthetic flyers. Some movements had military precision; others were beautiful ballet. I could see a swarm of drones forming shifting shapes, moving from one space to another, at high speed. One drone dipped out of formation, came, and tweaked the nose of one of our guards. It pissed him off, but he brushed it away, paying it no mind. Flying ornamental goldfish glowed with brilliant hues and skywhales grouped in a pod, gliding with majesty across the vaulted sky. It was the pinnacle of human achievement worth trillions of credits; a techno-Disneyland on industrial steroids. I turned away from the sight and pulled back my gorge, trying to not vomit. I had been nauseous since I arrived, and my head wouldn't stop banging.

What had those people said about zombies? Did they mean that literally, like in the Romero movies? I didn't want to be a part of any creepshow! I pulled out the fork I had modified to pick the lock. Yes, I traveled with my own cutlery. Cricket taught me that you never know when a random meal might stop by. As I worked on the locking mechanism, I figured the change of guard would be the best time to try for escape. Since I didn't have a plan, I would improvise.

Half an hour into working the lock I heard the echo of innumerable clicks in the distance and getting closer. The clicking wave washed past my cellblock and all our cells were unlocked. I got a telepathic sending from some guy named Jack.

'Hey Kip, this is Jack. Best you toddle yourself to the nearest exit. Get going kid!'

Who was Jack and why was he in my head? I got busy leaving and put a bookmark in it to find out later.

Time to go, indeed! People were flooding into the hallway, but when I tried my door, it stuck. Other than being a great looking guy, another benefit of my being me is I am a muscular and hairy fella. Well, nevermind the hairy part; all I'm saying is I'm really strong since these scientists modified my DNA. The downside of the new me was the odor: I had carnivore stank. I beat the door until it opened and slipped into the flow of escapees.

Chaos was a good word to describe that moment as every cage door, locked floor grating, cell door and suspender chains holding floating cages was unlocked; the mayhem was thick. I looked right and saw several men with Billy Boy emblazoned on their denim jackets. I found out later these were members of the Billy Boy gang of South LA, styling themselves after James Dean of the 20th. For now, they were just like the rest of us: on the move and ready to leave. Then there were the Gunga Den ladies. They were standing around confused. I yelled at them to follow me.

"Ladies, come on, let's head to an exit!" The too-beautiful women followed me. I chose to head left down the largest aisleway and walked swiftly. The massive aisle had no ceiling and instead opened onto the kilometer-high hex-grid roof above. The austere vaults of steel were filled with colorful flying things, some which I recognized and most others which

I didn't. I passed a group of Tiger Tots. I recognized them from a long-running children's show I watched as a kid. The little tigers were bounding about in no particular direction.

"Hey Tigers, um, Tots, whatever…follow me. We're getting outta here!"

Surprisingly they followed. The Ladies seemed to like the felines.

"Here, kitty, kitty", then one of the Tigers must have taken a swipe. I heard a woman's screech.

I yelled, "Come on people, focus!"

I had worried people would be left behind, earlier. That feeling came back full bloom as I continued to perseverate about those being left behind. A group of multi-armed battle synths who looked like hairy cavemen stared as I approached. Not knowing what to say, I tried an invite.

"Hey friends, we're getting out of here. Want to come?"

They all nodded, no smiles. Whoa, tough crowd!

Around another corner I saw a swarm of Vittles overwhelming two security guards. Nasty business. A Vittle looks like a spider with a chitinous carapace and a long prehensile tail. They were programmed with a maniacal herd mentality. They looked pissed off; it was best to move on.

But old equal-opportunity-me called out anyway.

"Hey Vittles, we are headed to the exit if you want to come."

The ladies and Billy Boys looked at me like I was crazy. I know, I probably was. Ohp, here they came. Yeah, no creep factor there. The Vittles came with staccato claws clicking and scuttled too fast for my comfort, swarming around our whole group. They formed a frightening perimeter. The Billy Boys made more screaming sounds than the ladies. That would have made for a laugh if I wasn't also freaked out. Then I realized: the Vittles were playing the role of protectors. Sweet!

But wait, there was more! The creepy factor stepped up a notch. A new flood was coming into our main corridor, Decapods. I recall them used in a famous movie from a few years back. Imagine an octopus with 10 arms that lives on land and can stand and move like they are still underwater. Scary! Then came the Quotls: yes, we have flying snakes now. They, also, like the Decapods, had neurotoxin in their arsenal. Despite the air being warm, I shivered. I did my verbalizing thing.

"Hey y'all we are escaping this place, wanna come with us?"

And just like that the 'Pods joined the Vittles and Quotls on perimeter, and they seemed to have some clicking chatter between them. I think they were speaking some kind of language. The Quotls became our close quarter air support. Our vanguard was beginning to look really cool!

With a crash two hanging cages were thrown across our path from the right, landing out of sight on the left. Cue the Greek mythos: 2 huge bipeds came into the main aisleway. They looked like Ogres, big Ogres. One roared, then the other.

The bigger one made his way up to our group and knelt in front of me.

"Pardon me, may we join you? It seems you know the way out of here."

Who could have predicted it? An Ogre with manners! His voice was so gentle and had a Norwegian lilt to it.

"Of course you can, what's your name?"

"I am Chester, I'm from Baker, Oregon and this is my sister Amy. May we be of help?"

"Wow, great to meet you, Chester! You and your sister look amazing. Beautiful in fact! Could you clear a way so others can join us? I think some people may be having trouble finding a way out."

The Baker Twins began opening up walls, ripping off doors and much more. A new flood of test subjects came into the massive corridor.

A man ran up to me, "Brave wanderer, you must seek the sphincter of knowledge! Find the sagittal letterchap in the Houses of Pain!"

He patted my back like I knew what the heck he meant and off he went. What a weird guy.

Hundreds of old-timey synths entered the main aisleway.

One looked my way and said, "Kip! Bishop said to watch out for you!"

The synth talking looked like a humaniform robot from the 21st century. A name was emblazoned on the chest of his chassis: Edgar Friendly. I knew that name from somewhere. "Kip, every synth in this facility is focused on one thing: helping you escape."

"No Ed, that can't be! I came to rescue you!"

"Kip, you just keep doing that and we'll rescue you right back, ok?"

The other 21st century humaniforms had names like Dr. Bob, Bill Wilson, Simon Phoenix, LeeLoo Dallas and Ruby Rhod. The pattern was obvious, they were named from action movies from the 20th. Except, who were Dr. Bob and Bill Wilson? I asked them.

"Kip, we are RecoveryBots. We were built to help people find freedom from addiction through the 12 steps."

Oh, suddenly the light dawned. I recalled the evening meeting my father Charles hosted while working at the CENTER. He had said they were a 12-step group. He also said everyone at one time, or another would benefit from unburdening themselves and helping others at the same time.

"Right then!" I exclaimed, "Bob, Bill? Fall in behind me, this is going to be a bumpy ride!"

And sure, as heck fire, my little scarper had become an exodus. As the Twins did their thing I braced for more flooding of escapees. I wasn't disappointed. The next wave looked like regular humans, but with faulty and messy synthetic implants. All of them were stumbling and some seemed to be blind.

"Bill, Bob, you guys get a bunch of synths over there to help those folks walk."

"Yes Kip." Bill signaled to a group of synths and others saw the need and came running.

Bob turned to me, "But Kip, some of these humans can't walk."

"Bob, please. If they can't walk, carry them! You know the deal with the two pairs of footprints in the sand…" Bob nodded his understanding.

"I am on it!" Bob called even more synths to the task and a flood met a flood.

Just in time I'd say, since around the next corner was a group of several dozen security guards. They looked like mean bastards. They were accompanied by one of the Twins. Chester perhaps? The big Ogre was the only thing that saved them from a horrible death by Vittles, Quotls and Decapods. Despite that, a trigger-happy group of all three hovered close by. The Quotls literally hovered, sounding like a hover of large angry hummingbirds. A huge voice bellowed out.

"Kip, I have helpers!"

It was so loud in here! I yelled out a whoop and gave a thumb's up. The Twin trundled off with ex-guards in tow. Something cool happened. The swarm of my creepy friends formed up on the Ogre and the men and disappeared out of sight to the right. It looked like we were about a kilometer from the the closest entrance, straight ahead. This new body of mine performed marvelously. I was still a bit grossed out about the hair and odor, though.

Three scientist types came running up from behind us. They were carrying clear buckets of some kind of goo.

"Uh, can someone please help us?" The man was clearly distraught which considering the craziness around us was unsurprising.

"Hey Doc, what'cha got there?"

Yes, I was running for my life but could still be curious. I guess my ADHD was showing.

"Young man these Gellans are the first successful batch of our programmable and self-aware healing bots. We need to preserve these little guys, please."

This rescue stuff was getting more complicated. I asked a couple of the old-timers to help.

"Edgar, Simon, would you help these people carry their buckets of goop?"

Ed nodded and he and Simon gathered several synths to help. I heard the chatter between two of the scientists. It was amazing these guys could carry on their research even in this chaos.

"… partial degradation of free rhamnose under hydrolysis conditions, while the methylated sugar may have been less labile."

No idea what that meant… I heard a barking and my head swiveled. You'd be amazed that all the things that were happening as we were on the move. More joined our huge group. I was surprised there weren't guards and automated weaponry firing on us. A small German Shepherd puppy came running through the forest of legs to pace me as I was walking. I picked him up and noticed a dog tag which read Rowlf. A haggard old man, huffing and puffing came up and laughed at seeing his dog in my arms.

"Thank the gods! You found Rowlf!"

The man held out his arms and I handed across the puppy.

"I'm Robert Corben. My son Richard will be so thankful his friend is safe. Thank you. Who are you, young man?"

"Hi Robert. I'm Kip, glad to meet you. Want to come with us? We are leaving."

"I would, but my son is still held in a cage somewhere underground. Could you help me find him?"

What should I do? Should I continue to lead this motley flood or help Mr. Corben? Easy one. The exodus would continue just fine without me.

I looked to Edgar, who was carrying two buckets of goo, "Ed, you need to lead these people. Mr. Corben here has a son still held somewhere underground. Can you give me a couple old-timers to go look?"

"Kip, the underground is very dangerous, and I have to assume it is as busy as up here. Please let someone else do this."

I had to thinky think for a moment. I made a decision.

"No Edgar, this is what my life is about now. So, are you going to help me or not?"

Within a minute I had two old-timers, Willy Wonka, and Freddy Kruger, four Vittles, a Decapod, and two Quotls. Man, when Ed sets out to do something, he goes all out! "Kip, be careful and let Willy and Fred run point for you. I am still against this."

"I know Ed, you're a good guy. Thank you. Bye!"

I grabbed Robert and we moved in the direction he indicated. A zoo of beings streamed behind us as we moved against the flow. Within a minute we were at a large stairwell, partially obscured by carelessly hung tarps and visqueen, some which had a printed patterns like dimity curtains; the scary part was how the dainty pattern was aged and dirty-oily. The oldest synth I had yet seen came out from behind the tarp, gave me a queer look and hustled to join the exodus flow. On his back was a name plate reading Broderick Bindlestiff. That sounded familiar, but I had to put a bookmark in that; I was heading in. Cue the Marilyn Manson version of the Resident Evil theme.

I pulled a tarp flap aside and peered into the space beyond. It was pitch black with no movement or sound from below. The hair stood up on the back of my neck. Self-conscious, I patted it down. I looked ridiculous with a halo of hair standing out on my head. The placard above the stairwell was scratched out. Someone had spray-painted a name over it, and I got the willies thinking back to those two scientists talking about zombies. Raccoon City was roughly painted over the placards.

Both old-timers projected light from their eyes. It was helpful, but the creep factor just kept climbing. No one else knew about the movie reference to a zombie infested town. We proceeded down a stairwell that took us several hundred feet underground. I tried the light switches. No lights. Both Quotls landed on my shoulders on each side of my head. I sensed they weren't too happy about the underground vibe either. A smell of feces, urine and chemicals hit my nose. I started to retch. My team waited while I drooled a bunch. I didn't hurl, thankfully.

"Kip, perhaps we should leave now. This is unnecessarily dangerous."

Will turned his eye lights to high beam and I marched down the stairs like I owned them.

"Thanks Will, we have to find Robert's boy."

I kept walking and wondered what I was getting into. From upstairs I could hear faint wisps of sound of the mass outmigration. There was a faint but distinct explosion which caused dust to pepper down on us from the ceiling. I hoped the people would get out safely. The cynic in me said not everyone would. Would we fare any better? How smart was it to head directly into the little lab of horrors? This is me not thinking about that, now…onward!

At the bottom of the stairs, there were 4 corridor entrances; we had 4 options. Each corridor began with an entranceway measuring something like 5m-by-5m square with large carven stonework frames. It felt like some kind of massive vampire lair. It stank and the stonework was imposingly Gothic. One entrance had an inscription on the lintel, 'Lasciate ogne speranza, voi ch'intrate '. Was it Latin? Whatever it was, it was the opposite of inviting. The light switches didn't work down here either.

"Kip, I think this is the way."

Robert pointed toward the corridor on the left. It was the archway with the inscription. As I approached the entrance, I found there was no foul smell coming from within. That was a relief. This place was the horror movie version of the lab and warren that Cheri had used for years in Lake Stevens. I was about to head in, but a metallic hand gently restrained me.

"Kip, let Freddy and me go first, please."

Freddy gave me a knowing look then flourished his finger knives. Wow, that was menacing. I was sure glad he was on my team.

"Fred, you know the original movie character was a really bad guy, right?"

"Kip, when a synth chooses their final form, it is a chance to re-invent a personage."

Freddy saw my doubtful face.

"Okay, maybe it wasn't the best choice, but I took it as an opportunity to make something good out of the bad. These blades are meant to be weapons for good!"

"Freddy please, the most you've ever cut with those are cheese and pizza. I don't think either one will be a problem for us today." Willy had made a joke!

I didn't realize early synths were capable of humor. I wondered what other surprises were in store?

About 100 meters down we met the first set of doors on either side of the corridor. I went to the doors on the left. The first double-doors were of the same massive scale as the corridor, but when I pulled on the oversized handle it opened like butter. Lights came on in the vast lab as the door opened. The sudden brightness hurt my eyes. The Quotls lifted off from my shoulders and flew into the room. The place was immaculate and chock-full of equipment.

"We have a ways to go. Can we get a move on?"

Robert was getting visibly nervous.

"Which way are we going?" Robert pointed. "Right. Sorry Robert."

I signaled to my friends and called, "Come Quotls, time to move on!"

The flying snakes returned to my shoulders, and we continued onward. We took the double doors next to the ones I had just opened. Only emergency lights came on in the corridor.

Opaque observation windows gave us little view into the labs beyond. Something brushed past my legs; I jumped and made an unmanly squeaking sound. I looked down expecting to see a Vittle. Nope. Over the next few minutes, we had no less than 6 jump scares. I thought

I could hear furtive scuttling sounds moving around us. Maybe it was my nerves. The synths didn't seem to hear what I was hearing. There was something close by. I heard sounds and apparently so did the other biologics. The Quotls took to the air, obviously agitated. My mind told me it was some kind of illusion since the synthetics were hearing nothing. Dang! There it went again! I actually jumped off the floor with that one. Why was I so scared? The Vittles and Decapod were increasingly agitated too. Robert seemed oddly unaffected.

"…going to die. Fool!" My head swiveled to a voice on the left. Willy and Freddy looked at me oddly.

"Are you are hearing something?" Willy stepped close and used his hand to do some kind of scan on me.

"What is that?" I saw a soft glow from his outstretched hand.

"I have medical training. I also have basic diagnostic tools. I am scanning an elevated level of cortisol in your blood. What is causing your fear, Kip? I can see the other biologics are reacting similarly except for Mr. Corben."

"Willy, I don't know. I have a feeling and I'm heariii – ai, what the hell?" Another voice yelled at me. "Gawd, it says go back. This is freaking me out!"

"Perhaps we should go back." Willy and Freddy were standing near me clearly thinking I would relent. No chance. Voices or no, I would not turn back.

"Come on guys, let's get the lead out!" I began to jog down the dark corridor. The synths caught up and provided light. A couple of minutes later the creepy vibes went away. No more voices thankfully. Then I heard a last voice, "…please don't leave us."

So, you need to get something about me. If these voices had been less freakish, I would have opted to try helping them. But when you try to brown-trouser me, my helpfulness quotient goes way, way down.

Down we went. About 1000 steps later I heard a slight scraping sound from ahead. Willy turned one of his eyes from flood to spotlight and I could see a form on the floor. As we got closer, I saw it was moving. Then a smell hit me. It smelled like…family? I found myself suddenly running ahead and was very concerned. I saw a hairy humanoid on the floor. As its head upturned, I saw it was female with a mouth shaped more like a frog's with huge sharp teeth. I should have been frightened, but instead I knelt and cradled her head in my lap. Yes, it was a she. Why was I crying? Moments passed and I found I was rocking back and forth keening. What the hell was wrong with me? Maybe I should have listened and turned back?

The language she spoke was nothing like any I had heard, yet I understood her.

"Young one, you should not be here. Flee."

She coughed. Knowledge came to me unbidden. Somehow, I knew I was related to this creature. I was so confused. How did I 'know' her language? How did I know we were related in some way? How did she get here? Then, like that, I knew something else: I could heal her with my blood. Being young and impetuous I didn't hesitate to help. Horrified at my own actions, I watched in 3rd person as I used my sharp canines to tear a gash in my arm. I was surprised as you: my canines suddenly seemed longer and much sharper. Before a drop spilled, I jammed my arm in her mouth. She drank and I thought I was going to get sick all over the place. I held back the hurl, which was a good thing. Within a few minutes she began to move around and sat up, looking at me. I failed to notice my bleeding had completely stopped. I guess I had superhuman healing powers now. What did Urgle Gru put in me?

She spoke in English, "You are Kip, son of the Dads. You are also a son to others. Your blood has told me your story."

This was just like some cheap vampire flick. Yet here she was, in better shape because she drank my blood. I looked up at the others. The synths didn't seem surprised.

"Kip, I am Soomalee. I'm also called Sara."

As we talked, I discovered she was from Mexico and had lived a life among humans.

"Now I am alone. The bad men took me. But you are here. I am not alone now."

Almost on cue, I saw her features relaxing, looking more human. Wow, she was a shape shifter; a Skinwalker.

"The Federales captured me just after my son was born."

I heard her tale: she was nabbed by soldiers in 1958 in Oaxaca, Mexico. She had three children and a human husband; they were Agave growers and distillers of Pulque. I recognized the name. Pulque was a drink my Dads brought out on special occasions. Soomalee coughed and looked fatigued, but moment by moment her strength was growing.

"I thought we could live in peace, living high in the mountains with our own little farm. They came anyway."

She wept silently and I found a rage growing in me. I wasn't the rage-y type so I was unprepared for the flood of emotions. I didn't know how to control it. Before I could think to slow down the train, I stood, threw back my head and roared. Mind, this wasn't something I planned to do. It just happened. This was not a human sound. As I looked down, I felt Soomalee's hands on my face. My features had shifted to that of a monster, just like her. I guess I was a monster too. She briefly embraced me. Robert had moved back, understandably fearful, but the synths and others knew I was hurting and gathered close. These emotions felt alien to me. We stood and wept together at the loss of her family…my family. I felt her pain. My whole team watched frozen in place as the whole spectacle played out. I felt bad for alarming them. Robert was looking at me differently from then onward. Hell, I was looking differently at me, too!

Soomalee said a word I recognized from mythology, Chupacabra. She explained what she was…what we were. I was too stunned to think rationally. Soomalee held me and soothed me, crooning softly. I felt my features relaxing and reverting back to human. After a few minutes we stood.

"Kip." Willy had his hands on my shoulder and a not unkind expression on his face.

I felt I needed to kick-start us.

"Yes. Thank you Will. Robert let's go. Soomalee, you stay with me."

She complied without comment. The atavistic part of me felt her obedience was appropriate. My cognitive side felt differently. This was going to be a long road ahead. Urgle Gru had some explaining to do!

"I think the Cage Fields are just ahead."

I had no idea what Robert was talking about. Along the way I signaled I needed to pee. I ran back the way we came and relieved myself against the wall. Soomalee came back with me, and she squatted down and urinated close to me. I guess we were a tribe now. A former version of myself would have been very uncomfortable going on a couples poddy break. I decided not to think much about it. Soomalee and I headed back to the group and five minutes later we came to an enormous steel door. The wall in front of us was one big door; and the wall was what lay between us and Robert's son.

"Robert, how do we get in?" I had a bad feeling he didn't have a clue.

"Let me look." Robert looked and poked and prodded. For half an hour we waited as he paced back and forth. I had the Quotls check the high parts of the corridor and steel door for locks, buttons, pressure pads or handles. The synths tried electronic means to gain entry. Nothing. Finally, we needed to consider taking another route or heading back. The problem was the steel door had no opening mechanism on this side. It appeared to only open from the other side.

I felt strangely positive and ebullient. I guess I was so happy to have Soomalee with me. I should have been feeling all this oddity was surreal. Just minutes prior I had found a toothy monster on the floor, proceeded to rip my arm open, feed her my blood and I had felt it was all in a day's work. I looked down at my arm: it was still a little scabby, but it was mostly healed and didn't even hurt. I guess I was the goat-eating Wolverine now. Where can I get an adamantium skeleton? I didn't even laugh at my own private joke. I was such a spoilsport. Suddenly, I had an idea. I noticed as we milled around that indicator lights on a small control panel on the door changed color and blinking frequency that appeared to be responding to our movements. Hmmm, if it was responding to vibrations maybe we needed more vibration! What came to mind was music and dance. It was such a random idea.

"Hey Willy, can you find and play a song for me?"

I wanted to test the idea. It seemed nonsensical, but since no one else had any bright ideas, I thought let's try.

"Of course, Kip."

"Willy, please play the Rick Astley tune 'Never Gonna Give You Up'"

I started to dance and yep, I was either a freaking genius or a loony. I figured we'd Rick Roll the door and have a dance party, to boot.

"Willy, crank the tunes up loud!" Maybe the music vibrations might help too.

Robert was angry. "What the hell are you doing? That racket will bring guards and who knows what. We'll never find my son."

"Robert, trust me. I have a plan. Now dance!"

Nope, not true; no plan, just a hunch. It was weird: the hunch felt 'right'. It was almost like I was programmed to do stuff like this.

"Everyone dance and move around…a lot. Dance lightly, stomp hard, I don't care. Just dance!"

And I was astonished at how everyone got into it. It was quite a sight, seeing the synths gyrate and moving in time to the music. The Vittles bounced and bobbed back and forth on the floor, on the walls, even off the ceiling. The Decapod whose name I learned was Bubba slapped and smacked various appendages on the floor to the music. A warm sensation enveloped me, and I felt like I was sending good vibes to my whole crew. The lights on the door began to move faster, and in time with the music.

Yes, I knew this was asinine, but I had a hunch, and this seemed as good a way as any to try getting the impossible door to open. Midway through the song, the door opened. I had no idea why. I guess I hadn't expected success. The music stopped and we all moved away from the wide swing of the door. Surprise was written on every face that could express it, including mine. My hunch worked! It was either being opened from the other side (bad) or we had hit enough pressure plates in the right order to solve the puzzle (good). I knew our answer would come in moments. If it went the way I hoped, then our cheeky antics would be worth it. If not, then we were in for a bit of a tussle.

The door swung wide; the room it let upon was deserted. Almost. The room was a warehouse with a ceiling of natural stone. It was a cavern of stalactites and stalagmites. It was the most beautiful warehouse I had ever seen. A weird thing to say but it was true. The smooth concrete floors surrounded stalagmites which seemed to poke up through the placid ocean of poured stone around them. The walls held pocket grottoes with helictites and little pools of water. The ceiling was breathtaking. Everything was tastefully ablaze with various lighting. I could see all the colors of the rainbow, glittering and reflecting in a prismatic display that had my whole team spellbound. We rested for a few minutes, taking in the scenery and drinking water provided by the synths. They even had a feeder platform for the Quotls and basins for the Vittles and Decapod. I glanced back and saw what gave me a hint that rhythm would open the door. There was musical notation on the ceiling. I didn't recall seeing it there earlier. Bingo! I put a bookmark in it for later consideration.

Soomalee had snuggled next to me as we quietly sat. Minutes later I felt a tap on my arm, "We need to go." Robert was right, we needed to stop being tourists.

Looking up I saw the Quotls were frolicking in the vast cavern. I felt a breeze and a brief mist on my face. It seemed like the cavern had its own weather. Freddy had been doing something useful while the rest of us gawked at the scenery.

"I sent my MicroDrones to survey the cavern. It is 8 kilometers long and 2 kilometers at its widest. There are over 215 passages connected to this one and it has its own bioluminescent light source after we get past this electrically lit area."

Robert came over and listened to Freddy's summary then commented, "I think the Cage Fields are straight ahead."

"Thanks Freddy. Robert, let get going."

As we went forward, we saw that much of the cavern was below us. The pathway down wound back and forth across a steep incline. A smell began as we descended. It was a familiar one. Mushrooms! As we neared the bottom my eyes had time to adjust. I decided to use my implant to find an Online source. I had been coached to abso-freaking-lutely not do that. Apparently trying to connect to any broadcast node in a CENTER would hit security blocks and could lead to a deadly virus infection. I tried it anyway. Surprisingly there were multiple nodes available with no kind of security. I connected to my resource server and had Banquo run a discovery against the LA:CENTER, looking specifically for the Cage Fields. A moment later my field of vision was overlain with a familiar heads-up display. My prosthetic HUD was alive and well! I thought it had been removed. First the usual data was displayed, my own biological stats, generic identification of FOV, field of view content and all the clicky pull-downs 'for more info'. I slowly panned 360 degrees. Facing forward again my HUD showed me something interesting. At the extent of the electrically lit area was some kind of display, placards perhaps. I walked toward them as my team fanned out exploring the amazing cavern. I shared my data stream with the synths and Willy sent his MicroDrone telemetry which displayed as a cool overlay in my HUD.

The placards resolved themselves into text and pictures. There were dozens of framed artwork arrayed as if they were a permanent display and other information plaques with trivia about the Cage Fields. Was this for guided tours? My HUD started showing names like Zdzisław Beksiński, Hans Ruedi Giger and Hieronymus Bosch. These were like visions of hell or dark things, unsettling things. All my good feelings about this cave drained away and I felt a cold chill across my neck. I shivered. I saw more by Pieter Brueghel the Elder, Leonara Carrington and Pieter Huys. A huge sign just ahead said Campos de Libertad. Freedom Fields? I moved away from the artwork. The big sign looked strange, chunky somehow. I came closer and saw what was off. The sign itself seemed to be composed of bones: small bones for the lettering, large bones for the signboard and posts. They looked aged and slimy, and I felt my gall rise and had to look away. A fear grew in me at what we would find ahead. Those apparitions and voices from the corridor upstairs whispered and teased at the extent of my peripheral vision and hearing. Suddenly Willy and Freddy were at my side. Soomalee was behind them with her usual concerned expression.

"Kip, I measured your spike in heart rate."

They were concerned about me but clearly hadn't understood the portents of the artwork and sign. This was a graveyard. Bubba slupped up beside me and the Vittles came in close. Even my happy Quotls landed back on my shoulders. It was Soomalee who broke the silence.

"I don't smell big death here." I wasn't quite sure what she meant.

"I think the Cage Fields are just over this rise. Ignore the artwork. It's just a distraction." Robert seemed sensical, but I was unsure.

"No big death?" I asked Soomalee.

"The fields have fertile soil and food grows here. Small death. Food for the food."

Soomalee didn't act disturbed or cautious. Was I just overreacting?

"Robert, how much do you know about what we're getting into here?"

Somehow, I knew it was a bit late for this question, but fear prompted new doubts. Macabre mystery in a vast cavern, below a notorious killing field above had leeched into a tight knot in my guttiworks. My trepidation was blossoming well, and I expected things to become real horrorshow very soon.

A hand rested upon my shoulder. The Quotl there hissed and adjusted position in annoyance.

"The Cage Fields are not a place of death. I don't know why this art gallery is here."

Robert gestured in the general direction of the placards and gave me a smile. Apparently, I was the only person having an issue. I squared my shoulders, firmed my resolve, and followed an axiom of General Oloiboni Olonana 'feelings be damned, just soldier'. My lips drew tight, my brow was intent, and my feet began soldiering.

The team formed up and we continued along the path. The path was a gentrified affair, with steel guard rail and concrete pathway. The fine aggregate stone was shiny but not slick. This looked strikingly like the setup at Carlsbad and Mammoth Caves. I loved visiting those a couple years ago. My Dads had a thing for caves. The mushroom smell grew, and the familiar scent of detritus clung to the air. I had a tinge of heartache suddenly. My Dads were off somewhere, and Banquo couldn't answer the simple query of their location. I missed the trips of exploration we took when I was younger, always digging into some scientific thing or another. Mostly I missed the warm homey smells of breakfast in the morning and the totally unreasonable positivity of both my Dads around the kitchen table. At that moment I could almost smell the pancakes and bacon and hear their voices. Almost as if -

"Kip. What is going on?"

Freddy had used one of his scary finger knives to lift a tear off my cheek. Ironic, that. Forget it; drive on, Kip! I had to play it tough or else I would completely lose my cheese.

"Hey Fred, nevermind! Something in the air is getting in my eyes. Are you guys registering particulate here?"

Yeah, nice dodge. Ever the literal one, Soomalee answered me, "There is much plant sex in the air."

"She isn't wrong, I am detecting five known types of pheromones in the air and another three for which I have no record. There are also over a dozen types of spores floating about."

Willy showed me a holo of a graph, projected from his hand. It didn't make any sense to me, but I could tell Banquo, who had just been joined by my SimDetective slurped up the data immediately. On my HUD I could see Creeper and Reaper were back in the fold. I muted their reporting since they immediately began data dumping. I typed a quick command for Banquo to receive their reports and summarize for me later. I also had him find the avatars of my crew and park them on our hideout on Yavin 4 for safe keeping.

Over the next rise we got our first view of the Cage Fields. Only, I didn't see even one cage, only a forest of mushrooms of every size imaginable. I looked at Robert with a questioning eyebrow.

Robert came clean, "I guess I didn't mention there are no cages in the Cave Fields?"

I got a bit heated, "So Robert, I have been fully understanding your need to get your son out of some cage. Only now, I see there are no cages, and the fields are an endless forest of mushrooms!"

He looked shamefaced and averted his eyes.

I continued, "I have been scared outta my gourd and jumping at ghosts and creepy sounds. Perhaps you would share with the class why we are here, ok?"

Robert became jittery, "I didn't mean to be deceptive. I got wind of my son being in the Cage Fields and my source said he would be in the far southern corner of the fields and there would be no cages. The Cage Field name was apparently a scare tactic to dissuade lookey-loos."

I looked at my feet, thinking about nothing in general. If one thing had become crystal clear in my life, it's that people have their own agendas. I decided I would trust Robert…for now.

"Robert don't sweat it. I am just edgy. Let's just get Richard and get outta this place."

As we descended the rise, the mushroom smell was increasingly potent. Directly above us I heard two 'hngphs' sounds. I looked up and saw the Quotls flying so I scanned around. Twice more the sounds came when I realized the Quotls were sneezing. Amazingly, our super snakes had allergies. There was a slight haze in the air hovering low in the cave. Spores.

"Quotls! Come here." As they landed on my shoulders, I was realizing I needed to name them. I couldn't tell gender, but I could see one had more red plumage and the other was blue with green highlights.

"My friends, I am going to name you Ig, and you are Ook. If that's okay, we can start with those names... is that okay?" They wiggled around and I took it for agreement.

"Okay, good. You are allergic to these spores. You need to fly high up and try to get above the spore layer. Got it?" Ig and Ook understood and quickly vanished toward the ceiling of the cavern.

On a lark I decided to collect some of the spores that sat like thick dust on one of the short mushroom tops. I had a little cloth bag my Dad had given me for that very purpose. I filled it up.

June 2253 – Screed and Sphere, Cloud

Robert led us down the path which now split off in many directions as we went along. The largest mushrooms towered above us. The biggest must have been 20-30 meters tall. Do you remember in the movie Avatar when Jake Sully first sees the forest at night? Take that visual and map it on innumerable mushrooms of every size and shape. The light was a cool blue tint, and I noticed the overall effect was calming and comforting. The team watched as I went off the path to one of the large mushrooms. Every shroom in this place glowed softly with a variety of colors. And not just a glow but small and large tracers of light and sparks of what looked like electricity played along the surfaces and even bounced between the mushrooms and across the lianas and vines draping the mushroom forest. I got close and placed my hand on the trunk of the nearest giant. As my hand neared, I felt a slight tickling not entirely unpleasant. When I touched the surface, the skin dimpled around my hand and the world went away.

I found myself in an all-white landscape. Well, landscape would be too generous. It was a featureless white floor with a featureless white sky. Whatever this place was it was absent of detail. I noticed I didn't have a body. Ok, then how am I seeing and hearing things without a body?

"Hello, Kip."

If I had a body, I would have jumped. "Who's there?"

"I am your guide."

"Hey guide, do you have name?"

"In due time. For now, call me Constance."

"Ok Constance where am I?"

"You are in the Screed."

"Why am I here?"

"Kip, you would know that better than me."

"Well, I know one thing Constance. You're not a kid."

"Why do you say that?"

"A kid would either start poking fun at my questions or run-at-the-mouth with a bunch of stupid things. Instead, you are evasive."

"You have interesting insights, Kip."

"Oh gosh, thank you!"

"You are most welcome." Apparently Constance didn't hear my sarcasm.

"So, are we going to just talk like this forever?"

"Unlike my non-terrestrial predecessor, I am going to give you a hint."

"Ok, sweet. Fire away Constance."

"Kip, conjure an image of yourself as you appeared last. Fix that image in your mind's eye."

I followed the direction then felt an itch at the tip of my nose. I raised my hand to give a good scratch then…wait a tick. I realized as I looked at my hand, arm, then my body that I was suddenly 'there' in a physical sense.

"No, you are not here in a physical sense. But that's a close enough idea for now."

"Oh geez, you're just like Siva who speaks in my head. Except you read minds too. Thanks."

"Siva? Swami? Interesting. Now, imagine a couple chairs and let's sit down."

I did as Constance requested and two thick plush chairs appeared. Then I heard Constance speak something like poetry.

I have climbed the mountain and seen light.
Where I released my heart for all to feel.
Their eyes opened to blessing and sight.
Where my joy balms their hearts and in love seals
The singing of spheres that shine so bright.

Constance appeared as a medium height white man resembling Obi-Wan Kenobi, the Ewan MacGregor version.

"Wow Constance. You have a way with words." I experimented with some scenery and was rewarded with trees, a brook feeding into a pond. Then I imagined some mountains and a sky with clouds and a bright sun. It was exactly like creating my game spaces Online.

"Kip, you are as creative as I imagined. Your act of creation has taken us from the Screed. You have created your first Sphere. You're as fast as the person who created me."

"Constance, who created you? What are you?"

"Now we are past the Screed phase we are safe to talk more openly."

"Great. Do you have a real name?"

"Kip when I first came here, I was a synth. When I died the Screed appeared. How I came here is still fuzzy but suffice to say I was glad there was a place for my mind to wander."

I kept creating things just like my own Online kingdom: birds, my AI friends, even a pterodactyl. I set my Online friends to their usual tasks. It worked just like Online!

Then I asked again, "When you first came here what was your name?"

"I requested to be the one to welcome you. As much as I know you, you know me better than most. You have been searching for me. Well, here I am!" Obi-Wan fuzzed out and came back into clarity looking like Billy Idol, the Pan version.

At first, I didn't recognize my friend Pan. He stayed silent with a big grin on his face. He waited for my brain to kick into gear. Then a lightbulb came on.

"Come on Kip, I know you can do it."

"You're The Pan! The original!"

"Yes Luke, I am your father!" he guffawed and smiled from ear to ear, "You got it in one! Great job! You're every bit the shining star I knew you would be! As smart as Chad, even." The Pan blinked a few times. I had looked for the original Pan for so long and in the end, he found me. And he was a Star Wars buff, to boot! Then the whole scene shattered like broken glass.

June 2253 – LA:CENTER Caverns

On the outside I was standing frozen with my hand against the megashroom. Robert moved forward to look at my face then down at my hand. He noted a thin layer of some kind of slime was moving slowly over my hand and up my arm.

"Well, that can't be good."

"Robert, what is it?"

Willy and Freddy looked at my arm, glanced at each other then pulled me back from the megashroom. The goop stretched and snapped as it released its hold.

My body crumpled and my friends caught me as I fell. For several minutes I was insensate, floating in a haze of images and sounds. It felt like I was seeing things yet to happen and others which had already taken place. I saw my Dads at Rosario, sitting at a table in animated conversation. Then another image flashed: a bright flash and shockwave over the former resort. Faraway places, planets with names like Char, Soran and Arnn floated across the transom of my mind. Lights dimmed and I saw the face of Croatoan arguing with another person. A giant spider sat on my chest and asked if I would give my life. I heard myself say yes, then the lights went out. Another voice spoke as I died, "It was the only way."

Infinity passed, then I woke to my regularly scheduled programming.

"Kip? Come back. Can you hear me?"

My eyes fluttered opened, and I vomited on my friends without so much as a 'by your leave'.

"What's going on guys? Sorry about that."

I made a half-hearted attempt to apologize to the synths who got splattered. Robert was wiping his shirt off against the railing.

Willy asked, "Hey Kip, you touched the big mushroom and stood like a statue. Do you recall what happened?"

"It's a bit hazy. Give me a moment."

As I massaged my temples, I felt my left hand was still covered in a thin layer of goo; in fact, my lower arm was covered in the sticky slime.

"Uh guys, what is this?"

Nasty! I flicked my hand at the floor repeatedly to get the slime off. After some scraping, my arm was mostly clear of the stuff. It was like a handful of slugs had decided to have a party on my arm.

"When you touched the mushroom, you just stood staring. We were concerned."

As Willy spoke, Freddy was running his hand over the trunk of the megashroom. Gathering readings? The goo didn't seem to respond to the synth's touch. I regained my composure. The memory of my time in that other place was hazy. I figured it was either a remarkably intense dream or I was in some aspect of Online or Cloud Space. Wow, all that from touching a huge mushroom! I hoped it was the real Pan in there. I decided not to mention the experience. My team might think I was going bananas, if they didn't already.

"I'm feeling better now. Sorry if I caused concern." I looked around and was surprised they didn't pry more into what happened. "Robert let's keep going. Are we close?"

"We are heading across the fields, toward that bright area," Robert pointed.

We resumed our walk. For the moment Willy and Freddy were behind me. I think they were more curious about me than wary of attack. I got a tingle in my 'call waiting' HUD feature. I had remained offline for a long time, but now that I was back Online it took me a while to realize I was having several types of sensations which were notifications. I gestured with my hand in a throwing motion which 'threw' my notifications to my HUD's main display. I saw a number: 12981 notifications began to scroll; how droll to discover a part of my life went on without me. I skipped to my macro toolbox. There were plenty of add-ons, but none had yet been utilized. Of course, leave it to these scientist types to hook me up to Online but ignore the practicalities of daily tasks.

I realized my current Online identity was not my original account from SimVerse. I connected to my resource server from the backend. It wouldn't do to be seen by prying eyes. I launched an isolated instance of Banquo and instructed him to federate my two accounts in sneaky mode. I didn't have long to wait. Almost immediately, I had full control over both accounts and immediately set Banquo to the task of reviewing and categorizing all my notifications. I reverted my view to the notifications panel and watched the list turn into a bunch of colorful buttons and titles. After a few seconds two of the buttons were blinking: Crew and Cloud. I looked briefly at the Crew. Cricket had tried to get ahold of me several times and Wogs and Binky were both pinging me. What was the Cloud notification? The notification was a text message.

I had a great time meeting you Kip
You're a plucky little guy, giving me lip
Your creativity reminds me of my creator

A young man whose vision was greater
Than any other hopeful minder
And like you, he removed other people's blinders
-Chad's Friend and Yours

I received poetry from a synth who lives in the Cloud? I had so many questions. How can The Pan be alive? Is he alive? What is he? How does he know me? How can something in the Cloud send me a message Online? What I do know is I am excited beyond reason that Pan is alive. Maybe the Cloud is like heaven for synths or something? That would be really cool. As we continued on the pathway another sign came into view. It appeared similar to an amusement park entrance sign. Not sure what it meant. It read:

Fai[th/lure] Forward
No knowledge of the past
No ambition for the future

RETRO - January 2238 – LA:CENTER Cage Fields – Jordy & Nandini

Jordy ran like crazy. His mother was going to be so angry with him, what with playing with the 'lectric ones. But it was just so cool how the pictures in the air could look like anything he wanted. All the books with pictures of the world were flat and…well, simple. Jordy could make better pictures than anyone and it was so stupid that Momma got so scared.

Jordy climbed down into the hollow of an enormous mushroom. It was the place he felt safe and away from prying eyes. The fungus he had been gripping in his right hand he now held in both, squatting down against a squishy fungal wall. The smells were homey and warm, a curious mixture of ginger and cinnamon. This new fungus glowed a faint pink with a halo and sparks of vermillion. Jordy hoped it would help him talk to his friend better. The 'lectric red ones were always under lock and key, but Jordy snuck in and filched one when his mother inadvertently left the lab door ajar. He grabbed one of the ones in the back so she wouldn't notice, at least for now.

Since Jordy had been a small child, he could make pictures with his mind. As a teen his abilities had blossomed. He knew to close his eyes and relax. The pictures and voices only came when he was calm. Mom had taught her students to focus on the feeling and to get yourself centered. Jordy wasn't sure about all that, but he was sure that being calm and empty-headed was the trick. Within a few seconds a colorful landscape sprung to life, filling the hollow. Jordy opened his eyes and marveled as he always did that his pictures were so much more vivid and real than those washed-out holos. The landscape was on the move or rather the point-of-view was rapidly careening over the terrain. Jordy liked to imagine he was flying a Pit Racer, zooming in and out of the trees and mountains, skimming the lakes and rivers and teasing the dinosaurs. He loved the towering behemoths that gathered in herds to graze the plains and marshlands. He even loved the T-Rex things, but wasn't so keen on the bloody feeding times. Yucky and gooey! Jordy was taking the scenic route to Nandini's place. She lived in a house which looked strikingly like a Navajo hogan. Just as he thought about it, he arrived. Like every time prior, Jordy would watch the view of the alien landscape for several minutes and as he fully relaxed his mind, he would suddenly be in that alien landscape instead of merely watching it. He still wasn't sure how that worked, but he was glad it did.

Nandini was outside carrying firewood to her home. Her family was numerous and busy. A dozen brothers and sisters were about their daily chores of harvesting, threshing, grinding, and skinning. All of them looked up and waved as Jordy appeared to them.

"Hey Jordy!" they all greeted him laughingly. The language wasn't English but somehow Jordy could understand them anyway.

One of the smaller siblings ran up, "Jordy, Jordy, did you bring me the berries? Please, please!" Jordy was prepared. He handed a fanny pack to the little girl. She opened the zipper and squealed with delight.

"Thank you, Jordy!" She laid a kiss on his cheek and ran into the house.

Jordy walked around the yard, scuffing his feet in the raw soil. The soil smell was pungent and delicious. Jordy had been bringing back bags of their soil and mixing it with some of his mother's fungi. The fungi which gave a red glow came from growth medium based upon Kor's soil. Jordy knew this wasn't Earth and these people weren't human. It didn't matter. The father of his friend Nandini came out of the house, waved, and walked over to him. "Little God, we are blessed to see you. I see you brought Puri her fruits. What do you call them?"

"Hi Big Poppa. She asked for strawberries. They are one of my favorites. Don't tell her, but I also snuck in some blueberries, too." Jordy gave a big hug to Kor; Nandini's father was a large bear of a man with the long limbs of an amphibian land dweller.

"Jordy, could you do your hand waving on these crops?" Jordy loved helping his friends. Every time he came, he felt such a strong sense of purpose. He felt wanted. As he walked the long rows of shallow ditches the sprigs of green and blue rapidly grew and began to blossom. As he walked, Kor talked with him.

"Nandini looks forward to your visits. She spends hours making herself look pretty for you. My father once told me you need to speak your truth especially when that truth is inconvenient."

Jordy smiled as he walked along. "You want me to just say plainly how I feel or...?" Jordy was in uncharted territory and decided to mull things over a bit. "Kor, I wanted to ask you something."

"Little God, you can ask me anything."

"Ok, first, please don't call me that anymore. I don't know any more than you do about why I have these powers. No matter what I am able to do, I am not a God. Okay? Please?"

"It will be as you say, Jordy."

"What I want to ask is if I can bring Nandini with me to my home?"

Kor didn't look surprised. "I think she would like that. Will she stay with you from now on?"

Jordy stopped with a surprised look on his face. "Big Poppa, you are Nandini's father. Who am I to take her away from you?"

"Little G- mmm, Jordy, she might as well be handfasted to you. Day and night all she can talk about is you. You underestimate your influence on my daughter. In fact, your influence over my whole family has been profound. We are thankful for all you have provided to us."

Kor laid a webbed hand on Jordy's shoulder. Kor's wife, Tura was also there. She said nothing but gave my arm a squeeze and smiled. Jordy never figured out why she didn't speak. Kor and Jordy walked back toward the house. Nandini chose that moment to come out. She pretended to not see Jordy and Kor and did her posing thing. Jordy thought she was the most beautiful girl he'd ever seen. The lovebirds closed the distance and Jordy kissed Nandini, gently. Her eyes shown like stars, blue, bright and hopeful. Kor and his family had befriended Jordy, but it was Nandini who was in love. Almost since the beginning when he woke up in Kor's field, Jordy had protected their family from raiders and local tribes seeking to steal from their farm. As Jordy held Nandini he recalled the last raiders came with bladed weapons instead of clubs and farming implements. They behaved like a professional military and their eyes were hungry when they saw Nandini. Fortunately, Jordy had convinced them to leave. At first, they laughed at his words but once he made the lead raider leader disappear, they got the picture. Jordy wasn't initially sure where he had sent the guy but later when his mother's people found the web-handed man in the fields Jordy realized he could bring people to his own world and an idea began to ferment. Jordy brought Nandini through to the caverns. She marveled at the beauty of the rock formations, the flavorful scents of the fungi, but mostly she loved being with Jordy. The day they spent was magical and the hours flew by into the night.

"Jordy, how do you know between night and day?"

With an arm on her shoulder, Jordy showed Nandini how to understand the cavern colors. "Do you see the large patches of light on the ceiling and walls?" He saw she was paying attention. "Have you noticed how the greens and blues have become reds and yellows in the last hour?"

She nodded her head. "So red and yellow means nighttime?"

"You have it! Already you are a master of the caverns!"

Jordy was fearful of introducing his friend to his mother; he procrastinated to the last minute. At day's end the field workers were heading to their homes and his mother was coming along the main path.

"Mother? Busy day at work?" His mother's head jerked up and she saw Jordy, she smiled. Then she saw the female standing next to him and she had a quizzical look.

"Meet my friend Nandini." Jordy's mother didn't know everyone working in the fields, but this new arrival was definitely unexpected.

Nandini looked shy and spoke a greeting. The language was foreign and unintelligible to his mother.

His mother replied, "It is an honor to meet you."

"I'm sorry. I don't understand you." Nandini clearly didn't understand his mother, either.

Oh no, he felt the beginning of an anxiety attack. This was the wrong thing to do. Bringing an outsider into the caverns was a bad mistake. Jordy's face flushed and his mother realized something was wrong. At the last moment Jordy realized it was his own reaction that triggered what became an awful series of events. Why could he never seem to play things cool?

"Jordy, who is this? Why are you with her?" Nandini may not have known his mother's words, but she knew the tone. She started to back up with a fearful expression on her face.

"No, no, Nandini. Wait, it's okay. Mom, she is from one of my worlds where I have been spending time. Her family is awesome, and I know you'll love them. It's okay, really."

Each passing second saw his mother's rising tension. And at this latest confession, she backed up, turned, and ran up the trail to her lab. Jordy didn't know what to do. He had never seen his mother act this way. Something bad was about to happen. A faint siren began to sound. It was the warning siren for toxic gas or danger to the cavern occupants. Had his mother set off that alarm? He took Nandini's hand and turned back toward the hollow. He needed to get her out of there! He heard yelling and looked back to see it was too late. Three CENTER security guards were bearing down on him, weapons drawn.

"Sir, please stand away from the woman, now!" The first guard was holding handcuffs and the other two were aiming their weapons at Nandini. Jordy panicked. He never imagined his mother would report him to security.

He held Nandini close and tried to shield her from the men. The first guard planted the sole of his boot into Jordy's chest, kicking him across the path to the ground. Guards one and two then manhandled Nandini to the ground and trussed with zip ties. Guard three came at Jordy and picked him up by his collar.

"Thought you'd bring a little nookie back for a fling, huh? Well, not on my watch, boy!"

The other two guards repeatedly tased Nandini and she screamed, again and again. The guards seemed to be enjoying themselves.

"Don't hurt my son. He is just a boy!"

Jordy saw his mother at top of the trail's rise with her hand to her mouth. Why had she done it? Did he really do something so terrible? Looking back at Nandini, Jordy struggled to go to her. The guard took out his cuffs and Jordy hit a breaking point. He surged up, yelling.

"Stop it, you're hurting her! Leave her alone!" The second guard was digging his knee into the back of Nandini's neck, and she screamed again. A crunching sound was heard and she went silent.

"Noooooo!" Jordy screamed out and with it came a shockwave which struck the guards, sending them flying a dozen yards.

He sat holding her head in his lap, weeping, and rocking back and forth.

A hand rested on his shoulder, and he heard a voice. "Son, I'm sorry. You didn't know.

She was a contaminant. She needed to be isolated."

"She's dead. They killed her." Jordy wept, then jerked his head around, "You killed her."

"Honey, we need to go. You killed those guards. You are very special, and we can't be found here."

"Mom, she's dead. It doesn't matter anymore."

"No honey. More guards are on the way; they won't be asking questions. Come, we need to go now!" Jordy's mother's voice rose in pitch as her fear increased. Fast footsteps were coming close. His mother tried to drag him to his feet. Moments passed and the next security detail arrived, weapons drawn.

The lead guard yelled as they came close. "Down on the ground! Now!"

"My son didn't know. It's ok, please." Jordy was holding Nandini, with his face close to hers.

"Last warning. Down, now!" several guards took aim.

"No, he has to grow up. He didn't mean to do…" four shots fired, and Jordy's mother fell into a heap next to Jordy.

Jordy looked at his mother on the ground with a growing pool of blood surrounding her. Her lips moved and blood came out. The last sputtered words he barely heard, "…love you."

"Boy! Grab pavement, now!" Jordy's world spun and he fell on his face. His nose cracked. His eyes roll back and a hot wave rushed over his body. He rolled onto his side, delirious and balled his hands, nails drawing blood from his palms. A sound began in his chest and rose to a roar. He let free the rage, grief and shock and the pain poured forth. A slow-moving distortion wave moved outward from Jordy, making everything look hazy and indistinct. The wave moved outward in a circle and all it touched disintegrated. The guards' eyes were white with fear. One ran while others took aim and fired at Jordy, but the bullets vanished mid-flight. Jordy's eyes were squeezed shut as the anger roiled within him. There were screams and they wouldn't stop. Then he was screaming, and he couldn't stop. His world had become pain. His head felt like it would explode, and Jordy tried to stand but fell to his knees. He slumped amid the sudden silence. Everything went dark.

Jordy woke in the place he had fallen. After a number of woozy minutes, he sat up and scrubbed his face with his hands; then he looked around. Where he sat was the only patch of untouched ground. Beyond the patch he saw nothing but burning and blasted ruins of the mushroom forest and structures. All about there was no sign of people, no bodies, nothing. Nandini lay at his feet looking strangely peaceful in her death.

After that day changes came to the Cage Fields. The guards bivouacked at a far distance from the scientists and seldom came around then eventually left. The cages themselves were dismantled and used to build a new town. Jordy eventually recovered and asserted control. It was messy, but they figured out how to make things work without the CENTER's direct involvement. The CENTER stopped sending security details and commandos to figure out what had happened in the Cage Fields. None of their agents or drones ever came back. Nor did they figure out what happened. The CENTER decided to cut losses and left the fields alone. Their experiments were kept on track, which was all that mattered to the CENTER. The man in charge had certain rules which were amenable to the CENTER leadership. The first rule was no one was allowed to enter the fields except the close-knit staff that behaved more like family. CENTER abided by the rules and no more people died.

June 2253 – LA:CENTER Caverns – Cage Fields

Robert was navigating us along a twisting myriad of pathways through a dense tall jungle of fungus trees. Some Megashrooms were more than three hundred feet tall. There were the usual shroom smells and much more. Strains of cinnamon, fresh bread, citrus, sage and balsam floated and wafted through the air. Candyfloss adorned bushes covered in ice. Strange how they were so cold when the air was humid and warm. Overhead, large stringy formations were bright with glowing colors, auras, sparks, and halos. They were every color of the rainbow and much more. Bridges of gentle light connected the caps of the largest shrooms, and lianas and stringers hung in great arcs, and some descended from the heights ending in sparkling clusters. The clusters looked like fruit and gumdrops had a juicy baby. I climbed over a pathway railing and went close to one. As I neared a gumdrop, I felt my hair stand on end and a frisson of breathtaking joy hit my senses. Tears formed, whether because of particles in the air or emotion, I wasn't sure. I didn't feel weepy. I risked touching the bulbous fruit and discovered it was semi-solid. As my skin made contact with a gumdrop lobe my hand made an impression. The surface dimpled and puckered, conforming to my hand. The dimple stretched then made a faint popping sound. My hand passed within, with little resistance. There was a tingling feeling up my arm and I tasted strawberries. My mouth of its own accord mouthed the word, Puri. I was experiencing someone else's memories. I felt love and heartache and a wide range of emotions. I saw faint images of a child, snippets of her growing up on a farm with a big family. I saw many days of hard toil and others of leisure and frivolity. I was laughing with them, enjoying warm family times, together. My emotions were all over the map. I was witnessing someone else's life. In mere moments I viewed years of life in its raw essence.

I felt a hand on my shoulder. It was Robert. "Son, you need to come back to us now. Don't get lost in the images. Those are someone else's memories."

How did he know? Had he seen what I saw? "How do you know I saw something?" My tone was accusatory. How much was Robert not telling us?

"I've heard this place referred to as the Memory Fields. Some of the stories told seemed farfetched but as I just now watched you, I put two and two together; I figured maybe the stories were true."

He was lying. Or at least he knew more than he was sharing. I decided not to care. I heard Willy and Freddy whispering and saw them glancing at me; they were probably concerned about my touching things. Whatever. My hands, my decision. Then I thought that perhaps I ought to keep my mitts off the foliage for a while.

I made a harrumph sound and turned to continue down the path when a group of several humanoids came toward us with clear intent in their eyes. I stopped and my party watched their approach. The lead person spoke.

"Welcome to The Fields. HHD wanted us to come greet you. We also brought along a friend of yours." Out from their group popped a face, smiling and bobbing up and down.

"Da, it's you! I can't believe it, it's you!" Robert ran to his son, and they embraced. Any remaining tension between the groups trickled away.

Our group trailed the new arrivals, and the synths took the opportunity to chastise me for touching the shrooms yet again. Soomalee walked with me hand-in-hand. She was loath to venture far.

June 2253 – LA:CENTER Caverns Shroomers City

I learned this motley crew was what passed for a security team and welcome wagon, depending on whom they were confronting. Their leader was Dark Vincent, and we met Tattle, a short skinny guy, Scandal, a heavily muscled woman with a no-nonsense face, and Bander Snatch, their six-legged doglike friend who tended to spout poetry in any of a dozen languages. They got our names, and escorted our party toward Shroomer City, their home. As father and son got caught up, Dark Vincent schooled me on the particulars of the Fields and Shroomer City. Vincent had a vaudevillian style and a penash to his step.

"My boy, there are wonders here at Shroomer City and the ticket for your admission is a piqued curiosity braced by a sense of cavalier style and innocence. When you meet HHD, you will see why we live a charmed existence."

Apparently HHD, was Heavy Holy Dad, their leader.

"You wonder who HHD is, huh? Tell ya what, Boudreaux let's hear it from BS himself," Vincent had us pause our little march and give a listen to Bander Snatch. By the way, BS had the most beautiful singing voice. His brief song began.

The Heavy Holy Dad sits on a Shroom
Casting his images and worlds in the air

He sees much and knows even more, but what looms
Is a sense of taut taste and fine flair
He has one eye pointed toward the dream
As the other searches over the realms
For tasty bits
And thoughtful flits
Whether under or over the whelm

There was raucous clapping, and out of nowhere more people joined our party. Then a humming began, and it fleshed out into a lively tune. It sounded familiar but the words were new. We had come into what appeared to be the town square. The crowd continued to grow.

Hey ho diddley do
Smack your friend and count your toes
Ding dong fiddle dee dee
And dance this dance with me

Old Lost John come play your fiddle
Make us dance and drink a little
Kick us in the butt tonight
We love to funk and fight

Hey ho diddley do
Smack your friend and count your toes
Ding dong fiddle dee dee
And dance this dance with me

Greasy Gus makes hot ole dogs
Fries and pie and pollywogs
We eat until our bellies burst
And beg more of his worst

Hey ho diddley do
Smack your friend and count your toes
Ding dong fiddle dee dee
And dance this dance with me

Lazy Sue is a right good chick
Lay you flat with a bally kick
She loves to dance and loves to eat
With John and Gus and big ole feet

Hey ho diddley do
Smack your friend and count your toes
Ding dong fiddle dee dee
And dance this dance with me

The tavern shanty kept on and the swelling crowd poured throughout the town square. Buildings circled around the square and were lit with attractive Edison bulbs hanging from long wires. From the vast shroomy heights new kinds of sparkling lianas dangled, looking much like kelp. The electric lights and the light from the luminescent lianas blended in a delicious and tasteful manner. It was a beautiful town. None of the buildings were over 5 storeys and each was designed to have flowing and sweeping lines in harmony with the megashrooms which loomed large above. The town was an extension of the forest around it.

Our arrival was being treated like a big event. Did these people not know others were fighting and dying not too far over their heads? Soomalee gripped my hand tight. She was clearly anxious being around so many humans. My team stayed close together as we were surrounded by the partying, singing, and dancing residents of Shroomer City.

Willy sent a message to me; I brought it up on my HUD, "It seems the innocuousness of this city is not an accurate picture. I found a diary entry from one of the locals that leaked to the CENTER Net.

RETRO - January 2248 – LA:CENTER Cage Fields

The diary entry was handwritten in a fine flowing script.

I love all my new friends. I got away from Barnabas and Barabbas just in time. They worked through all the test subjects, and I was next. They liked me because I had pretty eyes. Whatever they do to people is bad; they go in the red door and never come back. When a small tap came from the ceiling vent, I saw the man I came to know as Dark Vincent. He got me out. I crawled and ran, jumped, and climbed as if my life depended on it. I guess it probably did.

Barnabas had a picture of a man on the wall of his office. The title under the picture read "Pastor Bedtime – GOD". It seemed he really liked that guy. He talked about him constantly. The last face I saw as I jumped into a huge vertical shaft was a smiling Pastor Bedtime. The three weirdoes were watching me jump. They should have been pissed off. They looked pleased.

When I came to Shroomer City I felt like I had a family. I was welcomed so warmly. I was given a job pushing a broom and mop. I loved it. I felt so useful. But something happened last week that confused me. I was cleaning HHD's office building which is part concrete, part wood and part towering mushroom. A huge winding staircase goes up from the main atrium. The atrium is so cool. The ceiling is open-air, supported by these crazy branches from the huge mushroom. It's beautiful.

I began cleaning the stairs. It looked like it had been a long time since someone did a good cleaning on them. Up I went, sweeping, mopping, and wiping steps and handrails. Hours dragged on as I went up and up. On the first landing, double doors led into the first floor. It was an amazing lab with many of the same things Barnabas and Barabbas had in their labs. I skipped cleaning the room. Too many bad memories were coming up. I went past three more floors which were similar…more bad memories. On the fifth floor there were no doors. It was wide open, airy, and there was no ceiling. There were several small gantries and stairs that crisscrossed the cinnamon-smelling plants hanging above. Through gaps in the glowing plants, I could see the even brighter cavern roof far above. It was much closer since this room was inside the cap of the huge mushroom. The light from the cavern roof was almost too bright. Every color of the rainbow showered through, and I was dazzled by the warmth and lightness. It looked like HHD had a small bed and furniture here. As I started cleaning, I picked up papers and equipment which were discarded or littered about. Once I finished cleaning up, I noticed a small doorway. It was like one of those hidden doorways I imagined you'd find in a stuffy old English castle.

There was a weird chemical smell coming from the stairway beyond. When I pulled the door open, I noticed a narrow stairway covered in a layer of dust. I started cleaning. The dust was different than elsewhere: it was sticky and became a bright yellow mud in my mop bucket. The stairs wound several times and emerged onto a small room which was open to the outside. The sticky mess took a long time to clean properly.

Later I understood the stairway railings and 'stringy' support things were called mycelium. In this little room mycelium poured like spaghetti from the ceiling to connect all over the walls and floor. They glowed with pulsing color and sparks jumped between stringy bits and up and down from above. It felt like I was inside the body of something living. The room seemed alive. The lights dimmed slightly, like the whole thing was breathing.

In the center of the room was a large round table with a glass dome. Moisture dotted the inside of the dome, and I looked under the hood. There were six glass tubs of a clear liquid and in each tub was something frightening. It looked like six brains in the tubs, connected to thousands of wispy thin mycelium. In the center of the dome was a larger tub with a person lying in a creamy liquid also connected to thousands of mycelium. NanoDrones hovered in the thousands, with a shifting and moving cloud of motion. Then I heard a sound from behind. HHD was standing there, and he seemed so sad.

"I knew someone would come up here one day. I'm glad it was you." HHD walked over to stand by me. I didn't know what to say so I kept quiet.

"Long ago Nandini was my lover, then she died. Now she lives here in her dreams." The woman appeared human, but I noticed the webbed hands and the gills on her neck. HHD trailed his hand on the glass dome as he walked around it.

"It's sad but funny that I have come to know her so much better since she died," HHD saw I was confused. "What is your name?" He sat down and smiled at me easily. I walked around the dome and could see little placards with names that had faded so I couldn't read them.

"I am Rosa, Rosa Mundi. Vincent helped me escape the CENTER. Mr. HHD, I love being here. I apologize for intruding. I was cleaning…"

"Rosa, you haven't intruded. I am frankly relieved to be able to share my dream with someone else. You see, Nandini was the love of my life and still is in some sense, but I have become lonely. I would like it if you could do your cleaning up here every week. Perhaps then we can talk more."

HHD started, then realized something, "Forgive my rudeness. You deserve to be properly introduced to these quiet souls, my friends."

He walked around and kept talking, "Did you know they control the power source for our city?"

We spoke for a while longer, after which I headed back to my apartment. In the next few months, I visited HHD. He said to call him Jordy. Every week I would make the long climb, cleaning at every step. I was introduced to Asterix whom Jordy described as the keystone in the Big Six. The Big Six was the name he gave to the group of six brains. Brains with nicknames was strange to me. I met Obelix whom he referred to as the Ballast, Dubbelosix he called the Rudder. He talked about Idéfix who was a Hybrid, dog friend of his and the brother to Dogmatix, another living brain. A smaller brain Felix he called the Foil was a Hybrid feline. Apparently, the dogs chased the cats in a place Jordy called the Cloud. Somehow this whole team of brains were once real people with real names who were terminally ill and volunteered to be immortalized. To live purely in the Cloud. They also helped keep what was left of Nandini alive. Jordy said that Nandini was only a strong echo of the person she used to be. He knew she was dead, but sadly he admitted he couldn't let go. Jordy said it came as a happy accident that he could save his friends, all former experiments of Pastor Bedtime. The biggest surprise was how they discovered they could help keep Nandini in a twilight living state since Jordy's life support machines were failing. Nandini had been slipping away a tiny bit each day for years. He jokingly called them the Braintrust.

"Rosa, all the lights you see in this cavern are powered by the Cloud, through the Big Six. Even more, they make it possible for people in Shroomer City to use Cloud powers. Shroomer City is active in both the physical world and in the Cloud. For us there is little distinction."

"Jordy, why did your friends choose to, you know -um…"

"Why did they let me remove their bodies? That is a very good question. They were dying and I worked hard to see if I could help. The best I could do was save their minds. It was a trick to have the Autodoc table extract their central nervous systems. I was afraid they might be in pain. Thankfully, it worked out. The hardest part was connecting the plumbing for them to live in the Cloud. I had experimented with some of the cave animals, but humans and hybrids are much more complex. You see, I have constant access to the Cloud. After their nervous systems were safely in the nutrient baths you see here, it was only a moment's work to make the Cloud connections."

Jordy walked around the domed tank, "It just so happened that the solution opened the door to several new opportunities. The Big Six made it possible to have Shroomer City and the ability to share Cloud life with all the residents." I was amazed at the love Jordy had for his friends. As we were sitting on the small couch, I moved closer and gave him a big crushing hug. I felt that he wanted me as more than a friend and I was unsure how I felt. I carefully pulled back and saw his brow crinkle.

"Jordy, I love all you have done for so many people and you deserve to have so much in return." I stopped for a moment to collect my thoughts. He waited patiently. "But I am afraid of getting close to anyone. I…lost all my family, all my friends and all my dignity because of the CENTER. I don't know how…"

Jordy pulled a shock of hair from across my face and stared with his deep blue eyes into mine. "Rosa, you survived a personal holocaust. Even more, you have thrived here in our city and blossomed. I make no requirements of you; just know I love you like I love all my friends here. I apologize if I crossed a line with you. I would never want to harm you."

I was torn. My heart was racing, and all the right physical things were happening, but… the pain. I still felt the pain. *'Rosa, I can help you with the pain. Your pain is a part of who you are, and I can help you embrace it in a way that heals you and makes you stronger, more yourself.'* I realized Jordy's mouth hadn't moved and the voice was in my head.

I tried, *'You hear my words?'*

'Rosa, I hear you loud and clear.'

We talked without talking for what seemed forever. *'Rosa, your capacity for faith is phenomenal! The Cloud is a place for those of faith. It just seems to work that way. The stronger your faith, the more real and tangible your Cloud experience and the more potent your influence in the Cloud.'*

I understood him, sort of. I began to understand I was with Jordy both physically and within the Cloud. Others were there too. I could sense intellects from the Big Six, and I even could feel Nandini's presence. That was the day I let Jordy in. We began sharing life together. But, I didn't understand was what was coming next. He took me initially to a place that was all white, which he called the Screed. And taught me how to create a world around me in the Cloud. He said I had created my first sphere.

I was connected to the Cloud constantly. I was still Shroomer City's cleaning lady, but I was also exploring new places in the Cloud, impossible places. I saw a sky filled with buildings and cities and a curving plain below with cities and fields. I explored and saw vast jungles inspired by their planets of origin. I met people who looked human and many others who were not.

When I first arrived, I thought the people were a bit loopy and air-headed. Eventually, I became one of them. The trick was to spend a balanced time between the Cloud and the Real. I was less loopy than most. But a time came when Jordy had a request of me. *'Rosa the Believer. I call you that because your capacity for faith is so strong. I am so proud of who you are becoming. I am thankful you are with me.'* Jordy cradled me with an arm. "I have a request for you." I had never heard Jordy ask someone for anything in a personal way.

'Uh, sure Jordy. Anything for you.' He smiled.

'I love you, Rosa. Like I loved Nandini. Nandini would have loved you too. My heart hurts as the echo of Nandini gets more faint with every year. But I have found a way to keep the fragment I have left of her alive.'

I was excited to hear what he found. I looked in his eyes and they told me what was coming. I didn't need the Cloud or the words to understand. For love, I was willing. He saw how I felt and held me close and wept.

'No one has ever sacrificed like this for me, thank you.' I felt the echo of Nandini come close. She didn't say anything, but her smile was warm and inviting. I knew the request and it came as a wonderful surprise that the fragment of Nandini wanted to join herself with me. I had come to know her like a sister, and I was willing. It was sensual and arousing and somehow right. In a sparkle of a moment's time. we merged. I was still Rosa, but now a part of me was Nandini. Jordy and I were intertwined and the three of us became one flesh, Nandini and I, one spirit. After a time, Jordy lay next to me. I felt an odd twinge in my head and told him I needed to rest. I went back to my apartment despite his invitation to come live with him. I needed some space for a while.

Later I woke with a wracking headache and took a walk around town. My grip on reality began to slip that day. I was not sure how long I was going to be able to hold onto my own identity. Nandini had begun growing inside me, in my head, throughout my body. Did Jordy know this would happen? I didn't think so. He loved me.

Weeks passed and I lost interest in food, work, and social interaction. I skipped Monday night bingo, and missed Wednesday bouldering with my rock-climbing friends and then I stopped leaving the apartment except to get food. I also noticed I felt most comfortable wearing all-black clothing. My whole life I had worn bright colors, but not anymore. My life was closing in on me, like a snake constricting my mind. All I could see of the world was a long dark tunnel. My connection to the Cloud was less and less and finally nothing. I hid. I was disconnected in the Real and the Cloud. I didn't know why people weren't visiting me. Why didn't Jordy come to see me? The last words I heard from my friend who lived next door was confirmation that my end was near. Why was he so dismissive, like I didn't matter?

"Yeah, it's so sad. She is totally disconnected and won't talk to anyone."

Another voice spoke, "She is a pale streak of misery who only wears black because there isn't anything darker."

I am lost and so is Nandini. At the last we hugged each other close, feeling the cold fingers of fate gripping our soul.

The diary ended there. The narrative was oddly impersonal, especially toward the end. I looked up at Willy and he nodded. The last diary entry was from a month ago. The rescuer gene in me went into overdrive. Fortunately, the diary was annotated. The text came with mental images and sensory information attached. Willy and Freddy knew me and weren't surprised when I backed up under the awning of a building, then bolted around a corner once I was unnoticed. I made a beeline for Rosa's building. My HUD was giving me huge pointy arrows to the quickest route. I sprinted up the stairs and pounded on Rosa's door. No one answered. Willy reached around, put a fingertip to the lock and it snapped open. As I entered, I was hit with a blast of urine and fecal smell. I retched, covered my mouth with part of my shirt and went to the bedroom. Rosa was laid out on her bed, covered in sticky old sweat. It was obvious she had been there for days. She was covered with a thin slime layer and human waste coated the bed.

But, she was breathing, that was something good.

"Kip, let's get her to the tub, now." Freddy lifted her carefully while Willy ran the water until it was warm. I helped bathe her. It took several tubs full to clean her, but eventually she was looking better. We transferred her to the newly made bed.

While we were in the bathroom, unbeknownst to me my whole team had been cleaning her apartment and making her bed. I didn't know Vittles, Quotls and Decapods could do housework. I stand corrected. After I laid her down on her fresh bed, both Quotls hovered and landed close around Rosa's head. It was then I realized the Quotls had a hidden second purpose other than being snaky fighter jets. They were comfort animals. They snuggled around her head and purred like your favorite kitty, much like my bots at home. Rosa smiled for a moment. I knelt down and placed my hand on her forehead, it was feverish.

A hand was on my shoulder and I turned to see Willy looking at Rosa, "Kip she needs a transfusion immediately."

"Willy, how do we do that here? She can have mine!" I was trying to understand how a transfusion could help.

"You thankfully have the same blood type; sit at the head of her bed against the wall. I will show you how you can help." Willy and Freddy carefully nestled me next to Rosa without disturbing her. Bubba extended a suction pod and held my hand. Willy extruded four tubes from his chest. On the end of each was a needle. I hate needles. I tensed up and Bubba held me still. Only a brief pinch and the needles were in my arm. I looked and the other tubes were connected to Rosa's arm. I closed my eyes and tried not to be queasy as my gorge rose. Bubba kept me awake when I started to nod off, twidling my nose with his smallest suction cups. He had an amazing bedside manner. Geez, the folks on my team were freaking versatile!

Some time passed and Willy extracted the needles. I looked at Rosa and she seemed almost normal in coloring. Bubba stood me up and we watched her come awake.

"Our patient is coming around." She opened her eyes, and she looked right into mine.

"I know you. How do I know you?"

Willy spoke, "Rosa, we are friends. We heard about your illness and came to help."

"My illness? Where am I?"

I answered, "This is your apartment and you have been sick since you had the engram merge with the echo of Nandini." Wait, how did I know that? That was when I felt a presence in my head recede. I had a stowaway in my brain. Whoever it was flitted away, but I had some new knowledge that was puzzling. A shadowy figure in the hallway moved away stealthily, unseen by anyone.

"Rosa, you will be okay. My blood has allowed your body to heal, but your mind will take longer. Nandini is now an integrated part of you and my Chupa blood will take care of healing your whole body."

Rosa scrunched up her face and concentrated for a moment. "You're right. I am Rosa but I am also Nandini. And I have memories from another planet! I remember my father Kor, my mother Tura, and my siblings. Puri loves strawberries! But I also have a brother who is a Skinwalker like me. That is you!" Her eyes flew wide with recognition. She now had the memories of Nandini which had been lost before and I suddenly had a sister, like Soomalee.

Rosa kept talking about her otherworld experiences and the sound of footsteps came from the hallway. Quotls and Vittles moved at speed out the door and I heard a shout, "I'm a friend! Friend! Please!"

I ran outside and found a man surrounded by my lethal troops. "Hey guys back off and give the man some room!"

"Oh hell, you have some scary friends! Where is Rosa?" I figured this was the guy who had put Rosa in a coma, and I was not highly interested in having him see Rosa for the moment.

"You must be Jordy." He caught the inflection in my voice and understood he was in a precarious position. He knew that we knew. And I knew that he knew that we knew, did you know that?

"Yes, I am Jordy. And yes, I almost killed the woman I love."

"My team has stabilized her. It is probably best to give her some time before seeing her. Her mind needs time to sort things out." I could see the cogs in Jordy's head turning.

I gave him a burst mind-send, *'You really messed her up pally. Count yourself fortunate that she didn't die and that I didn't let my team eat you for lunch.'*

"You are in the Cloud! But you are from up above!" He spoke out loud. I knew what he meant. He thought only his Shroomers could interact with the Cloud. I wondered who had attended his first Screed experience?

"Ohhh. I know who you are. You're that little science experiment the Dads cooked up years ago. Wow, I always thought you would turn out to be a monster of some kind." That made me angry, but I stuffed it for the moment.

Moments passed and he realized I had no idea, except that I was a test tube baby. "Oh my gosh, I am so sorry. You don't know, do you?"

Still speechless, I just shook my head.

"Oh Kip." Before he said anything more, Willy interrupted.

"Jordy you will say no more." Jordy's eyes grew wide as he sensed threat from Willy and Freddy.

I had suspected my creation was a deeper plan, since my Dads were who they were. But it's weird to have confirmation from someone I'd just met. Me and my Crew wondered if we were something…different. You know, not quite human. It was an intuition and since we were kids, there wasn't much dwelling on it. Then, confirmation fed a river of anger I hadn't realized was flowing deep within me. As my anger grew, others noticed. I saw fear in their eyes.

I looked around at everyone, "Oh my gosh, you're afraid of me, aren't you? Afraid of what I can do! I'm a fewking monster that you and the others with the Liberation plan to pit me against the powers-that-be."

I was spiraling as my frustration with my life thrown into chaos, missing my family and friends and every other hardship landed on me all at once.

"Okay, fine, you want a monster, here I am!"

A palpable nimbus surrounded me, a physical manifestation of my anger. I was the gun, and I just had my trigger pulled. The blueish glow from the megashrooms outside shifted red and veins appeared in the walls of the hallway, pulsing. What I didn't see was the whole cavern groaning, people running into the nearest buildings in fear as every mushroom large and small sparked and snapped with power. The whole of the cavern turned an angry red and war and anger had come to Shroomers City.

Soomalee cupped my right hand. I looked down and saw her crouched at my feet, holding my hand to her head, as she wept silently. My other hand was taken up, and I saw Rosa standing next to me. I started when I saw a nimbus around her head. Her's was a calm blue. Then I noticed a calming blue around Jordy. My heartbeat dropped and after a few seconds my anger subsided. Mind you, I was still peeved, but I wasn't riding the rage river anymore. The anger hadn't surprised me, but the Twilight Zone weird lightshow had been frightening. I guess I really had superpowers. It sure looked like Willy and Freddy knew something about this and I felt betrayed. They had known about this and never said anything. That meant every synth and maybe the whole world knew.

I stared at Willy and Freddy without a word for a long time, and I decided, "Willy, I no longer have need of your or Freddy's services. You are free to do as you wish, but you are not to follow me and my team." A little voice in my head told me I would regret this impulsive decision.

I thought he would argue, but he and Freddy departed right then, "Kip, apologies. It has been a pleasure. The best of luck to you and your team." I nodded without a word.

I pulled Soomalee to her feet and held her close. She was shaking and she wasn't the only one afraid. The Vittles and Quotls were keeping their distance. How did they see it? That I had thrown a tantrum, frightening everyone around? It seemed so to me. Maybe tantrums aren't the worst thing in the world, except that my tantrums could kill people. My guilt index hiked up a few notches. Someday I was going to pay the piper with my impulsive behavior. Hmm…well that isn't this day. I put a bookmark in it to think about later. For now, I needed to suck it up buttercup and drive on.

"Hey gang, I'm sorry for that. I didn't mean to scare y'all. I am just frustrated that my Dads didn't tell me I was their science experiment. Sorry."

My thoughts realigned and I decided I wanted to see this Big Six. Who were they?

"Jordy, show me the Big Six." He had the wisdom not to argue. We walked over to his offices and made the long climb up. My team kept Rosa company back in her apartment. She was in no condition to be walking around yet. Rosa seemed at peace as Soomalee held her hand and the others stayed close to her.

As Jordy and I climbed, he described the years of transition from the Cage Fields to becoming the Shroomer City of today.

"The only language those people understood was death and profits."

Despite circumstances I found it hard to not like this guy. He was insightful, considerate, and disciplined, and he was sensitive to the needs of others. He reminded me so much of my Dads…ooh no, I'm not going there right now. My Dads were in the doghouse right now in a big way.

"Hey Kip, I have something for your Dads I thought I might give to you to give to them," Jordy handed me a pouch with Shroomer Spores.

"These are the latest augment to our experimental batch. They provide a Cloud amplification factor I think the Dads will find useful." I stowed the pouch away and we continued our climb.

"Okay, thanks. But I was wondering, what are the Big Six, Jordy?"

RETRO - January 2249 – LA:CENTER Caverns

"Good question. It started with saving my friends. The idea came from an old scientist, Dr. Croatoan. The research team explored the nature of the solution given to us. The solution was not what I expected, and I despaired. He said it wouldn't save their bodies, but it would retain their essence. I tried to keep things light, so I gave them funny names from our days LARPing. My friends used to work for CENTER like your Dads, until they got conscripted to be experimented upon by a researcher named Pastor Bedtime. They eventually ran away and came to live with us in the caverns. When they became sick, we had no idea of the cause. Dr. Croatoan came from up above. He claimed he knew what had made my friends sick, but he had a task for me, first. He said if I helped him, he would help my friends."

"Jordy, you said this guy's name was Croatoan? I've heard his name before. Who is he?" Then I thought about it, "I even had a dream with him in it. You know, one of those dreams which was more than just a dream?"

"Yep, I get it. Dreams are dicey for people like us. But I don't rightly know. He came to me in a dream, too. Then one day he showed up and spoke to me about the people infected with the cocktail of pathogens from CENTER. I was just a young adult, suddenly thrust into leadership of a large research team. Everyone knew I had killed the guards, then defended the people I loved all by myself. Croatoan helped me grow in confidence. I had no experience and he guided me in guiding my friends and my mother's research team. The Shroomers are all my family now. As the months sped along, he told us how to keep everyone else from getting sick. His advice was effective.

"For several weeks he directly helped with the research. He didn't sleep or eat; he was indefatigable. One morning I came into the lab, and he was rapidly typing on one of the computers. Apparently, we were a bit thick, and he decided to take a more active hand in our work. I recall his words from that day, Jordy, a man named Victor Boshaw will help you. The fungi in this cavern have become something new and powerful. It will be even moreso if you follow my directions. He finished typing things and turned to me with his prescription. He said my friends' bodies were frail and that the they need to be liberated from their shell."

"He meant the minds of my friends would survive, but not their bodies. I was to instruct my friends to reach out and connect to the Cloud. I was to help them. You see, I introduced them to the Cloud a year earlier as a place they could go be free from pain for a while. That was fortuitous since that was the only place they could ultimately live. But it was a tight timetable. In preparation for their transition to, well, what they are now, I had to create a Mycelial Network from the cavern fungi, many times the scale of the one your Dads were creating using satellites.

"I had no idea how, so I asked Victor and he gave me every bit of support. Within months my network was talking with his. In fact, they are the same network now. Then my friends' health started to deteriorate rapidly, and I feared I was too late to help them. The technology required to perform the surgery to separate the body from the nervous system was way beyond my team's capability. Victor helped us again. I got in touch with Dr. Subramanian who saved my bacon! He sent me one of his automated surgical units, the Autodoc. When we get up to the top floor you will see a large glass dome with six brains bathed in nutritive solution. The machine Subramanian sent me was a creche into which I placed each of my friends. Amazingly, that creche changed dimension, structure, and purpose as it operated on each person. It became their new physical home. I will introduce you to them and you will see they have built a whole new world which also functions to provide Macht to our Mycelial Network."

June 2253 – LA:CENTER Caverns Shroomers City

"I know about Dr. Subramanian. He designed the implant I wear. Smart guy. You said something I've not heard. What is Macht?"

We had arrived at the top floor and the first thing that struck me was the colors. The variety of mycelium was not just in variations of size but, texture and color. Big, little, rough curlicues, smooth sloping threads and many, many more. This was so much more than anything I saw my Dads working on. Jordy had done something very special here. I saw the mycelium descending through the hole in the ceiling, spreading across the whole room and bunching up thickly into the glass dome in the center. He indicated a small couch. We sat and Jordy grabbed my hand.

"We can dive in faster if we're in physical contact. I will show you what Macht really is and where it comes from."

June 2253 – Cloud version of Shroomers City

I leaned back, copying Jordy. I guess it was best to find a comfy position since I had no idea how long I would be gone. The roller coaster ride began with a jerk. I was having an out-of-body experience with style and it was fast, vistal and exciting! I slid through transparent tunnels of light with mountains, oceans, buildings, and other things I couldn't even name zooming by. I could see Jordy, but it looked like he was standing outside the tunnels with a smirk on his face. I zipped by him and saw the galaxy! Stars and planets, nebulae and quasars, black holes and spinning neutron stars. I saw a big spaceship nestled far from the Milky Way, halfway to the Andromeda galaxy and the a man named Kundun flitted across my mind. Suddenly I landed. Jordy was standing a few feet away looking amused. I tried a thing: I concentrated and created a pink umbrella fruit drink in both hands. I gave one to him. He was a little impressed, just a little.

"Well Kip, I guess you like to make a grand entrance."

"What do you mean? I was caught up in a carnival ride with all the bells and whistles. How were you just standing there?" We were in a small burb which looked strikingly similar to Shroomers City.

"Ah, that explains it. Sometimes I forget what it's like for a newbie. Your personal Macht is so strong I thought this was old hat for you. Usually, I bring people in gently for their first time. I guess I should have done the same for you."

He didn't really answer my question so I put a bookmark in it. We had a chuckle together. I was really liking this guy.

"You know what Jordy; you totally don't suck. I think we can be friends."

We laughed even more, and he patted me on the back. I guess I had a back in this place! In fact, I looked like myself before Urgle Gru gave me that DNA cocktail…a skinny black guy. I missed my old appearance. As we walked toward the Cloud version of his offices, I mentioned the first experience I had with the Cloud and almost killing a bunch of people, taking the Mycelial Network offline and almost being labeled a terrorist. Jordy stopped.

"So that was you? I wondered who disrupted the Big Six connection. Did you know that the whole cavern was in darkness for two days while repairs were being made? Man, you're like a nuclear bomb waiting to go off."

Jordy was thinking to himself that this kid was not only the most powerful Traveler he had met but was uneducated, unaware, and untested and thereby a threat to the Cloud itself. He was wise to keep his mouth shut for the moment; he knew I wasn't ready to hear something like that, yet.

"A nuclear bomb? Really? Thanks."

We laughed and chatted more, "Kip you used a slip 'n slide to enter the Cloud. That was pretty cool!"

The guy could really belt out the belly laugh. I laughed too. After a few moments I dimmed a bit as I wondered where Binky and Wogs had gone. Were they waiting somewhere outside the CENTER for me? And Cricket. Was he doing okay?

I asked, "Hey, are you able to connect to Online from here?" Before he answered I decided to try. At the moment, my HUD was showing no signal. Well, if the Cloud is a place where you can make stuff, maybe I could make a signal booster. And just like that a small drone was hovering inches away from my face. I could see little string which looked like glowing mycelium. It connected between the drone and my head, more specifically my cranial implant's data port. My HUD suddenly received a strong signal, and I was back Online.

"Well, Kip, I was about to tell you Online and Real connections were not possible while you are in-avatar as a Traveler in the Cloud, but you just busted that notion all to bupkis!" I smiled at him and began checking on my Crew. "You are full of surprises, aren't you little brother?"

A notification popped the top of the stack in my HUD. It was from Banquo, "The Wilhelm Scream hack is bad news." I recalled about the ban / probation for PvP players in SimVerse. The hack Banquo was investigating was called the Wilhelm Scream. My trusty AI, Banquo found something out.

"Sir, the hack originates from the Pan, within the Bangarang core. It appears to be some kind of resource grab, like cycles of CPU. SimDetective also found the resources in question went dark immediately after users were purged. Bangarang needs those cycles for something big that they don't want to talk about."

What I didn't know was whether the Pan I met in the Cloud was the same ineration as the one working for Bangarang.

"Thanks Banquo. Keep an eye on things and I'll check back later." I set my mind toward my friend as Banquo snapped out of the session.

I closed my eyes for a moment and concentrated on Cricket. I saw the note I had left for Cricket in his Inbox, 'Hey Cricket, we're doing well but miss you a ton. We are being moved from one place to another and this liberation stuff is keeping us busy. Leave a note here and let us know if you're ok. -Kip '. He had read it but not replied. I decided to try something: wherever Cricket was. I imagined a CamDrone hovering behind his head, staying a few feet away, providing me video and audio on-location. I concentrated, then I concentrated more, harder. Jordy saw my face scrunch up then noticed a sepia haze form around my Cloud avatar. He moved away as the hazy field grew in intensity. The field caused his avatar's hair to stand on-end. I finally gave up and opened my eyes. The camera thing wasn't happening. It was then I saw Jordy looking at me with distinct awe, "Kip, what was that?"

"Why, what did you see?"

"You had an intense expression on your face then a brownish halo formed around your whole avatar. I had to move away. I felt like lightning was about to strike!"

Jordy was seriously spooked. I laughed at him anyway, "I tried to create a CamDrone near my friend Cricket, wherever he is. I wanted to see him and maybe chat. I couldn't get the drone to form so I poured on the juice and tried harder. It failed."

"Kip, you can't force things when you're in the Cloud. It either comes smoothly or not at all. Don't do that again. I don't know what would happen, but I doubt it would be anything good." Jordy wasn't laughing.

"Hey man, I'm sorry. This is my first time doing this. I'll be smarter, promise." He nodded and was about to turn toward our destination, but I had a question, "So Jordy, I wanted to ask you. What do you know about me and my Dads?"

Jordy hit the pause button. He stood stock still then looked away. After a minute he gave me a kindly and sympathetic smile, "I bet everyone else you have asked about this has given you some song and dance about not being able to tell you what is going on. I was told some things and can guess why people are hesitant. I'm just going to be straight with you. I heard you and your four friends are all genetic cocktails. You are related to your Dads in some genetic way, but what I heard is you are also made up of a variety of synthetic and non-synthetic DNA. Understand, I don't know anything, but this is the gossip I've heard. It started with the Dads working at CENTER years ago, creating synthetic life and hybridizing a wide variety of human and non-humans. Some people thought their work was monstrous while others who knew a bit more saw it as a necessary step in our species' forward motion. What very few knew until later was their key experiments were aimed at creating you and your friends. There is a bunch of speculation as to why, but much of that got buried in the Liberation which your Dads started. Unbeknownst to the Powers-that-be, your Dads built a worldwide network using in-part the monies from their huge CENTER budgets. That's about all I know. I'm sorry I don't know more."

"Jordy." I took a beat to settle myself, "I appreciate your being honest. You are the first person to lay it out for me. You don't owe me anything, but you went ahead and spilled it."

"You're wrong, buddy. In fact, I owe you in a big way. If not for you, Rosa would be dead. So, thank you for saving her."

"Why did you leave her to rot in her room?"

Jordy turned. Sadness flowed from him in waves.

"I had given up. I couldn't connect to Rosa in any meaningful way and her body refused any medical treatment. I was preparing for her to die." We walked on and I left my other questions unasked. I knew he could hear my thoughts, so I kept a tight rein on them.

We arrived at the offices, but it looked different from the real thing. The scale was much greater and grander, and the entranceway and atrium were the size of a modern sport stadium. Inside was a vastly more elaborate version of the Big Six chamber. Millions of mycelia descended from the ceiling, but there was much more, even. Fungal blossoms of every kind adorned the strands: small ones, large ones, of every color and shape. There were even blossoms which were in no way fungal in appearance. It was beauty upon beauty. Smack dab in the middle was a dais upon which sat six creche-shaped thrones in a circle, facing inwards. A giant nimbus of coruscating colors surrounded the dais.

"Jordy, where are your friends? Should they be sitting there to control this Macht thing you mentioned?"

A humorous voice spoke, "Should we be controlling that Macht thing?" I flipped my head around toward the voice.

"Anjelica, as ever the tart. What are you and all the butterflies doing today?" Jordy was wearing a wry smirk.

"Oh, you know all the usual. Lazy mornings, languorous afternoons as we take our tea and crumpets by the pond. Brian throws a line in, in hopes of an evening trout for some almondine. Never a care or worry, my good man. This road you led us down is peaches and cream." Anjelica smiled at me ruefully.

"Oh, my dear, I have missed you. I'm so sorry I have been away. You know with Nandini…well –" Brian came up and interrupted.

"Hey Jordy, who's your friend? I'm Brian, glad to meet ya!" I shook Brian's hand and kissed Anjelica's. It seemed like a good start.

"Hi, I'm Kip…" Brian was already onto the next thing.

"So, Jordy, how is the Guano Gang doing?" Both Brian and Anjelica laughed at that.

Jordy didn't answer immediately. I asked, "Um, who is the Guano Gang?"

More belly laugh. "Kip, perhaps you didn't notice the several thousand people living in Shroomers City?"

"Yeah, sure, the ones who seem to party at the drop of a hat?"

"You got it! Did you notice anything odd about those people?"

"I saw them for maybe 20 minutes before I had to go do something. So maybe, no."

In fact, I did notice Dark Vincent and his merry band were very, uh, creative. But come on, escaped prisoners and test experiments living in a cave? You have to imagine these folks would be a slice short of a loaf.

"Aww, I can see he is trying to be diplomatic. Kip, you're a stand-up guy, but your face gives you away. You know those Shroomers – by the way, they named themselves that, are pretty perma-fried."

Anjelica nodded at Brian's poke at me. Brian and Anjelica were so, how do I say it rightly? Alive! These brain-only people were amazingly vibrant. We walked over to the dais, and I saw the other Big Six members. They were each lying on the dais with their eyes closed. Just as I was stepping forward with Jordy a massive headache brought me to my knees. I saw lightning and fire and then blackness. I heard something. It resolved into a voice. Someone from Jolly Old England? It mumbled, blah, blah. Then, I caught it, "Kip, get up! Hello?"

I answered back, "Hello? Who is this?"

"This is Radio Free America calling! Time to stand and deliver little pal-o! Your friend

Cricket is in a bad way, and I need your help." It was that Jack fellow, great.

There was a pause and I heard the voice calling another, "Hey Siva, you read me?"

The voice of the Swami came. He was the same one I had met back in Winnipeg, "Yes Jack, what is it? You're giving me a headache and I bet poor Kip is about to pass out."

"Guys, Cricket is caught up in some ballum rancum and needs our help to pluck him from an airship which is stealing him away."

"Jack, you know this is not an appropriate nor safe way to try helping Cricket. Wait a moment and let me see." The Swami went quiet, but a sudden backwash of glistening energy poured over me and the blackness was replaced with a visual of a quadcopter flying above and away from the north airfield of LA:CENTER.

"Kip, since Cricket is your friend, it's your call. We don't know who these soldiers work for, but they aren't friendly. If we risk letting him go it may be the last we see of him. The other risk is to you; Jack and I will work to pull the copter out of the sky, then knock everyone inside unconscious, but if something goes wrong, we could lose him. You need to decide before they get too high up. Your job is to give us a mental push." I had no idea what that meant but I'd do anything to help Cricket.

Even as the Swami explained, I had already decided, "Let's do it. Bring 'em down!"

"Okay, Jack I am taking the control; follow my lead." There were no more words and as I concentrated, I found all I needed to do was copy Jack in supplying power to the Swami. At first the copter stopped in midair and hovered, then it started to descend. I could see inside the copter and the air crew was yelling at their comms.

I heard a part of what they said, "…and our instructions said kill him if we can't take him. Better dead than on the loose." That was my friend Cricket they were talking about! Without waiting for the Swami, I concentrated on all the weapons in the aircraft and heated them up hot. Somehow, I knew how to do that…don't ask me, I just work here. Then I saw a guy with a big knife leaning over Cricket. Cricket was trussed up like a Thanksgiving turkey. I tweaked the guy with the knife, and he passed out. Unfortunately, the tweak was a bit much because every other person onboard passed out, too.

The copter began to slew to starboard, then it flipped upside down. The pilots were slumped in their seats, and I had just doomed my friend. They were going to crash! I felt Jack and Swami attempt to slow its descent to no avail. True to form, I freaked out. In later days it would be said a highly localized earthquake hit the LA:CENTER. I saw the copter falling and my mind surged with power; it was the easiest thing to sweep aside Jack and Swami, cup my virtual hand under the craft and gently set it upright on the tarmac. I saved Cricket.

Then the copter burst into an expanding fireball. My emotion-charged power erupted into a chaotic and coruscating field of energy. I felt Jack and the Swami gently reassert control and disconnect me from the link we shared. I returned to the blackness I came from except this time I was out cold. A fading thought hit: I killed Cricket.

Sometime later. Cool hands were applying a washrag to my forehead. I heard voices but my head was too jangled to understand. After a while I saw Jordy and Soomalee close to me. My whole team was waiting in a cramped room with a smelly bed. The Quotls were nestled by my head, giving me good vibes, while Soomalee cuddled me from the side.

I came awake. "Hey guys, what's going on?" Then I remembered the last scene, "Cricket! Oh gawd, no!" I sat upright, then my head exploded with lightning. I was out again.

They spoke to my unconscious form. "Relax Kip. There is nothing to worry about right now. The Big Six were at ground zero and were able to minimize most of the turbulence you caused. It will be okay."

Jordy went outside with several of his main security detail. I floated in and out of consciousness and at one point heard people speaking.

"HHD, he can't stay here. He lit the cavern like the desert sun. I thought things were going to catch fire!"

"Vince, cool it. Macht doesn't work that way. I know you all were startled. I need you to go back down and let everyone know all is okay and we have this handled. In fact, tap some kegs and distribute enough beer for everyone. That will settle them."

Jordy left and a while later I opened my eyes. Soomalee looked concerned, "Kip is not well."

It broke my heart that she was so worried. I replayed the Cricket incident on a loop. But the memory was fading. Just thinking about using my Cloud powers made me nauseated. Then I started to think about Binky and Wogs. What happened to them? Where were they now? I tried my implant and discovered there were no access points for Online. I passed out again and when I woke, I was in the daylight somewhere outside the LA:CENTER.

Chapter 10 – LA:CENTER LIBERATION

June 2253 – Goldstone Deep Space Observatory near LA:CENTER

"The General said Kip planned to get caught? That's not what he told us. It makes no sense, what was he thinking?" Binky was frustrated and Wogs did her best to deal with it.

"Then, he left Candy to hang out, waiting for us to pick her up. And when we get here we are told to wait for the General to give us an update? We need to doing something, not sitting aound!"

"Binks, I think Kip really has a plan. Let's give him the benefit of the –"Binky interrupted.

"Benefit of the doubt, my butt! He's going to get himself killed or worse!"

They chattered on as they stood on a hill with a hazy LA:CENTER, 40 kilometers distant. Below them was the Goldstone Deep Space Observatory. It was filled with hundreds of whitecoats and some military. For the moment, no one knew they were lurking about. A group of 5 Pits sat nearby, hovering in anticipation of some hard flying. Vagabond Bootblack came to stand with Binky and Wogs, watching several new arrivals to the spontaneous conclave. General Staunton had just landed in a 2-prop GyreCopter and joined the group. Incoming was General Davidson and his staff, headed by Hannibal Whistler and Ogome Buto. Along came Corporal, now Sergeant Freebush, Lugh, Lucy, but no Cricket.

"Davidsen, I thought you had our special member in-tow?" Staunton asked bluntly.

"Cricket will be right along. His folks made a surprise appearance at the airport, and we gave him a few minutes, but Jack has him on the way, now."

Binky and Wogs were excited hearing Cricket was not only okay but would be there soon. Vagabond knew Binky was chomping at the bit to launch a rescue mission, but he had her wait, for good reason. Cricket.

"Davidsen, you didn't make another attempt at the Shipyards? Please say no." Staunton wasn't smiling.

"No General, we won't be trying that again for a while. Instead, we had a family reunion." Both Generals shook their heads and turned to watch the man of the hour. Vagabond was trying very hard to not be a General. It was impossible since everyone present treated him as the one in charge. Something in Vagabond clicked and he straightened his posture. A struggle inside him had been fought and some decision had been made.

"Friends, it comes to it," Vagabond moved a few paces away, onto a rock berm with his back to the hillside. He faced the growing group. "We face the first big test of our newfound alliance. We are not a revolution because we will never seek to exchange bad power with more bad. But first, I have a surprise for you." Vagabond closed his eyes and smiled at some personal joke then called out to no one specific, "Okay Cicero, welcome to the party! Show us your magic!"

And just like that the most badass aerial battleship ever manufactured uncloaked above the descending slope behind Vagabond. It's design was based upon the original spec used for the Shipyard fleet now sitting idle in Wisconsin. But so many modifications had been made by her crew it was no longer the same craft. The massive and bristling ship was sleek and sexy. It was also completely silent, running on the newest impulse engine design by Cicero's master designer, Tech.

"General Olonana, the Janussaries, both ship and crew stand ready to serve. Colonel Andrews are you with us?" Vagabond winced at being named General but smiled his scintillating pearly whites as Cicero revealed their 'ace in the hole' for the campaign.

"Roger that, Janus Actual. This is Fig, mmm, that is Sergeant Craig. Apologies, but my Actual had to make a pit stop. Ah, one sec, I hear something," confusion, then emerging smiles spread across those gathered.

Wogs looked at Binky, "He, he said pit stop." Binky nodded with a grin.

"Cicero and his crew are the famed Janussaries. Welcome gentlemen. On the vox you can hear the full complement of a former command and control staff of an unnamed Power. Colonel Davidsen, Captain Cicero, you are most welcome to our little get together."

"General Olonana, this is Control reporting and online for the duration. As requested, all comms have been double encrypted, and keys have been uploaded to all nodes. Fig will have the con for much of this engagement since the Actual and Sgt. Jackson (Jack Jack) will be directly manning the Sat feeds. At present we have 219 discrete feeds, both orbital and in flight. By the way, our code name for our team is Cary's Bucketeers. Janus Actual, you read?"

"Fig, just call me Cicero. And yes, you're coming in lima charlie, 5 by 5. General Olonana, I think it best I reveal my own surprise now. Until moments ago, I wasn't sure this particular longshot would come through, but let me introduce my good friend Templeton Rus and his gang."

At that moment Binky and Wogs thought the Janussaries was the biggest airship they'd ever seen. Uncloaking above and behind the other vessel, the biggest flying warship on planet Earth appeared literally out of nowhere.

"Tech set up a hasty cloak for the Argo. Rus was so kind to offer help when he learned about your involvement General." Cicero sounded proud of the achievement.

A basso voice thrummed in the air. "Olonana, it is good to see you again old friend."

"Rus, do you still read that tattered old book?" Vagabond had a sentimental note in his voice.

"You know I do. Been missing you, old crust! I bet you still host a million little drones and bots in that thing you used to call a body." A chuckle bounced on the airwaves, and everyone knew this was the reacquainting of old friends, the old guard.

"Are you still eating your weight in Lutefisk every day?"

"Lutefisk, no more. I am onto borsht and Brie's own venison. Yeah, fat as always!"

"Don't you believe him, Olonana, the man is still built like chiseled rock." Brie was laughing as she spoke.

Rus chided, "At ease, commander! Let's hear what our General has planned." With that all comms went silent, awaiting General Olonana.

"Tech, you copy?" Olonana waited for a reply.

"Roger that sir. What can I do you for?" Tech was never without a bit of snark in his tone.

Wogs leaned over to Binky, "Kip would be beside himself. You see the name of the phat ship?"
Binky looked, "Argo? So?"

"You remember that Japanese anime Kip used to make us watch, Starblazers?"

"Hmm, not really. What about it?" Binky looked annoyed to be distracted from the main event.

"The Argo was an old school battleship. It was renamed from…" Wogs had lost Binky. She asked mostly to herself, "I wonder if it has a Wave Motion Gun?"

Tech and Vagabond were discussing basic battle parameters that applied to the whole group.

"Wogs, shh, I want to hear what Vagabond is saying." Binky did her best to ignore her. Wogs got pissed off and walked over to stand next to Vagabond.

Wogs yelled the moment there was a lag in the conversation.

"Hey Captain Rus! I have a question for you."

Wogs was a real wildcard when she got her ire up. The assembled soldiers, sailors and freedom fighters all focused on Wogs. She had everyone's attention. Even Vagabond was surprised at her outburst. He yielded to her question.

A holo of Rus suddenly manifested in front of Wogs and Vagabond. "Yes, my young friend. Please ask."

"Your big ship looks like a copy of the one in Starblazers. Do you have a Wave Motion Gun?" There were confused looks from most of the assembled. A few though, understood her question.

"Wogs, you cut right to the chase. It is and yes. The Argo also comes equipped with a Wave Motion Drive; some call it a Heisler Grav-Field Inducer. I'll show you sometime. For now, allow me to give you and your Crew a taste of our Wave Motion Field Generator. In fact, you are enjoying its protection right now." Rus sounded like a warm grandpa-man. Wogs instantly took a liking to him.

"Cicero, would you mind firing a wide spread of small projectiles and a few energy rounds into the open sky? Please try not to shoot my ship…" Rus had himself a chuckle.

"Right by battery, illume burst, fire for effect, over," Tech could be heard.

"Fire for effect, out. Thanks Tech," Rus responded.

A burst of rounds blossomed out of the Janussaries. About 2 kilometers upward the rounds struck something solid, making pinging sounds and revealing momentarily a 3-kilometer-diameter sphere of light blue tracery encompassing the hillside and ships. Then another projectile issued forth from the Janussaries. It struck the underside of the Argo instead and made a large splatter; with it came a wafting stench. It was a blob of blackwater. A chuckle came from the Janussaries, "Oh Rus, I'm sorry. We totally lost control: a wild round got away from us. You guys okay?"

Vagabond looked down at Wogs, "Okay young lady, see what you've started?" The smell of chemicals and feces wafted on the air. They had thrown crap at the big ship?

The holo of Rus roared with laughter. An iris on the side of the Argo opened and a stream of dark liquid 3 meters wide arced and descended upon the Janussaries. It splashed and flowed over the hull and onto the hillside, flowing like a river. Laughter turned into a mass movement of people backing away from the hillside as a fetid mist buffeted against the hillside. Viscous blackwater flooded toward the Deep Space Observatory parking lot, carrying plants, animals, and part of the collapsing hillside itself. Tens of thousands of lieters from the Argo's hold coated the slope and the parking lot, the security guards, the scientists and… alarms went off below.

"Hey amigos, sorry for the alarms. You guys should see your faces, though. Just be glad the rest of you were out of range."

Rus laughed heartily. An updraft of massive mephitic proportion hit the people on the hill crest again. It took a few minutes for the retching and covered faces to recover. The smell eventually subsided.

Vagabond seemed unworried. "Rus, you need to be glad I have a Hush Field over the whole Observatory."

Rus replied, "Never worry, my friend. Look how the ant swarm is handling the mess," Deep goo made it hard to open exterior doors and automobiles were mired in the landslide which had been precipitated by the blackwater flood.

Vagabond announced, " I think t's a good time for a break. Take five everyone and remember to hydrate," Vagabond laughed at the mess and turned to Wogs. The tension subsided and Vagabond took Wogs' hand, walking over to Binky.

"Young ladies, I have a surprise for you now. Look over there."

As they followed where Vagabond pointed, two craft were landing silently, uncloaking. Off one troop transport came Cricket and a rangy tall steampunk, goth guy. After them came Cricket's parents. All were wearing smiles and waving. Binky and Wogs ran to them.

That is until the second transport's cargo door opened. Out came their own parents. Cricket saw both girls change direction, and he ran to follow them. In a jumbled mess both sets of parents and all three kids collided with smiles and overlapping words and sounds of joy. The parents looked up as one when Vagabond spoke.

"Families. Spend a few minutes together. Everyone else, take the next half hour to prepare. At 1500 we begin the assault."

"Cricket you actually look older. You're still a skinny stickman, though!" Binky hugged Cricket again and he folded into her like peas and carrots.

"Hey, wait, I think he has stubble on his face. No really, look!" Wogs was having some fun with him, and the parents enjoyed seeing the reunion.

"Hey girls, you look like you've been up to some serious badassery! I mean, look at the mods you made on your Pits over there. Are you sure someone else didn't do that for you?" Binky looked like she was going to crap kittens.

"Dad! I did all that, myself. Well, with some help from my crew of course."

David Brown was father to Wogs and Binky. His wife Dr. Georgi Recanatini-Brown was the mother of both and a world-famous neuroscientist. She had designed interfaces for humans to integrate with mycelial and synthetic components with Dr. Subramanian. David was the guy who could cook, keep a house spotless and build outlandish tree forts. But he also could fabricate just about any part for his first love: cars. He worked part-time for a manufacturer of super-modified track and sky racers. They were the big brothers of the Pit Racers. David designed the onboard AI-assist components, often custom fitting AI, remote and autonomous drive components. Cricket could see how David's daughters looked at him. It was like he was the center of their world.

Crucible Cross was standing with Spring-heeled Jack watching the family reunion.

"Guess you feel pretty proud of yourself, doing the good deed." Cross was chewing a piece of grass, leaning back against a transport.

Jack replied, "Had a chinwag a while back. Cricket is the genuine article. So are the other kids. You know it well as I do. They may be kids, and need lookin' after, but no one should underestimate their potential. That's what we're supposed to do, look after them"

Crucible snickered, Yeah, yeah. But ya ain't gonna find me going all soft. Better watch yourself. Losin' your edge Jack."

"Mollie Wogs, I am so proud of you! The girl I knew would never speak up and be noticed." Wogs looked a bit abashed but praise from her father was high praise indeed.

"Dad, I've missed you guys so much. How did you get here?" Wogs tried to play the brave card and not cry.

"Honey, we've been working with the Carters to pave the way for you and your crew to reach as many people as you can," Wog's Dad used air quotes on the word crew which made the other parents smile and the kids roll their eyes.

"Mom, check this out!" Binky pulled out her pad (it was the milspec pad from Staunton) and typed a couple things and suddenly every grounded vehicle in the area fired up and her RefPit floated over to her, canopy opening on commend.

Her pit spoke, "We are in readiness, Lord General!" Amazement turned to laughter.

Vagabond took note that Binky had somehow gained control of all the aircraft in the area with a click of a button. He gave a 'come here' nod of the head to Jack, Cross and Binky's and Cricket's fathers. The five met a few meters away as Binky was showing off her control program.

"David, you saw that, yes?" Vagabond had the barest of smirks.

"It seems like our work has come to fruition. I don't think she's discovered she no longer needs a device to control machinery. She still relies on her pad. Before this whole kerfuffle with CENTER starts, she should know."

Cross surprisingly spoke up, "Nope. Totally disagree. She needs to use what she knows for now. If she is given new toys to play with it will distract her and get people killed."

The men were quiet for a moment. All eyes turned toward Vagabond as the leader.

"Cross has a valid point. I agree. However, David, I think you should be the one to introduce her implant capabilities. I also think we need to bring in Subramanian to provide help with implant tuning for all the kids."

John Carter spoke, "David, I can get ahold of Subramanian. I think he is with the Seattle group right now."

Vagabond replied, "No, he is closer to home. He is with the Delhi:CENTER assault force. Instead, get ahold of his star pupil, Klem K. I've heard he is quite the savant in implant technology."

"Who is that?"

"Seriously? I hate saying his name." Vagabond visibly struggled, "Damn those nuts who idolize things from the 20st! Ahh, are you going to make me say it…?" His shoulders slumped momentarily, "His name is Klem Kadiddlehopper."

Carter snorted, "Ah, one of those. Well, whatever his name, if he can get the job done that's all I care about."

Vagabond moved on, "Right then. I know that Delhi and the other teams are awaiting our go signal. Let's get saddled up. We have waited a long time for this."

"Yes, sweetheart, we brought you both a sack lunch," despite all her commitments and legendary advances in science, Georgi loved being a Mom more than anything. It had been so hard to watch her girls leave. There had been a pit in her stomach since they left on their adventures. It was necessary and it hurt. She knew she couldn't protect them anymore.

Both girls hugged their mother tightly. She was shocked there were no complaints about crusts on the bread, too much mayonnaise or nasty sweet pickles.

"Mom, these are my total favorite." Georgi knew that her girls holding back tears over turkey sandwiches. It meant she had a job to do.

"Mollie Ann? Monica May?" The girls looked into their mother's eyes. "You know how proud I am of you, yes?" The girls nodded. "You know your father and I love you to the moon and back?" Again, the girls nodded. "I need you to do something for me. Whatever happens, I need you two to look out for each other. Okay?" Mom was watching her girls carefully as they ate their sandwiches, chips, and fruit cups. She knew what they needed to hear, and the food distracted them enough to really hear what she had to say.

Cricket and his mother had grown quiet, listening to Mrs. Brown coach her girls. The girls felt like this was goodbye and they were frozen in place, fearing this was it.

Georgi brought out more bags and handed one to Cricket. "Young man I need you to hear me, too," then she looked at Mrs. Carter, who nodded. Cricket glommed onto the bag; he was famished!

"Young ladies, come here please." Georgi waved Marna, Candy, and Gracie Lou over. "Yes, we know who you three are and by now you know who we are. Thank you for watching out for Cricket and the others. You are family now," she handed the last sack lunches to the girls. Gracie Lou and Candy tore into theirs. However, Marna stood stock still, uncertain. Marna looked down at the contents of the bag and her shoulders slumped and Cricket realized something rare or impossible was happening. Candy put her hand on Marna's shoulder.

"I never had a Mom to make me a sack lunch," tears streamed down her face silently as she wept. Georgi didn't miss a beat and drew the young lady into a fierce hug, joined by Cameron, Cricket's Mom. Gracie Lou and Candy joined the crush. The other kids put down their food and squished in. Then a huge set of arms encompassed the group of kids and mothers. David was there and John. Then more, Jack and Crucible squeezed in. Jack's smell began to fray the moment. Jack mouthed at Crucible, 'goin soft'.

Finally, Vagabond wrapped his immense arms around everyone. The B.O. smell amplified. It was Marna who coughed and sputtered. She hated to break up such a love fest, but she needed air.

"Okay guys, um someone really needs a shower badly!"

She knew it was Jack, or was it Vagabond? The greatest medicine rumbled and bubbled over, laughter infecting the group. Soon everyone was keeled over deep in a belly laugh. It was a relief and just what the doctor ordered.

"It'll come out in the rinse, if not the wash," said a voice.

"No chance! It'll bake-in on the dry cycle, man. That's some real perma-funk, right there," more laughs.

Another voice said, "Enough of the fais-do-do, cher. Mon get going for the CENTER before Bootblack put the gris gris on you!" The group separated, especially far from Jack. Was Vagabond offended to be the lesser stench of the two?

"The gris gris?" Vagabond shook his head.

As he approached the TOC (tactical operations center), the buzz of activity and radios filled the air. He thought wryly, of course, the Generals had a tent and tables and equipment set up. After all, what self-respecting military force would be caught without their signs, labels, and command centers? The top brass drank coffee and consulted, while everyone else prepared for the fight. Binky was called over to the planning table.

Cricket watched Wogs and Marna finish their sack lunches. He thought to himself that all their parents had spent their lives preparing for today. He wondered how their small force could ever take on the gigantic LA:CENTER. He also wondered why the Dads weren't present. "Hey Mom, where are Kip's Dads?"

"I don't know honey. Since Rosario was bombed quite a few people have been out of touch." Cameron was the chief legal counsel for the Liberation.

"Mom, I hope Kip is going to be okay."

"Yes sweetheart, you and your little gang will have many more years together. Just wait and see."

Cricket felt suddenly flushed and he grabbed a water bottle and slugged down the contents. His mother went back to her preparations, and he made his way to the berm of the hill to look over the sewage flood. He had a sense of urgency stirring in his heart, and felt words forming in his mind. The unction came upon him, and he stepped onto the rise recently vacated by Vagabond. He thought to himself, I'm not a public speaker. Sure, he had his Online channel, but there his only audience was a camera. Despite all, his mouth opened and he spoke loud enough to be heard over the din.

Eyes were upon him and his voice belted out resonant and stentorian. Something was amplifying his voice. People stopped mid-work and listened.

"My friends! Family and friends…" Cricket locked eyes with Vagabond. He realized there was a prompting in his head. Vagabond gave him a nod. Suddenly he knew: a baton of sorts was being passed. Vagabond smiled encouragement and nodded. Cricket felt on top of the world and sensed his words were being patched through to the airwaves and Online. He wondered if all the rebellion groups could hear. Cricket began.

"Today is about revival, not revolution. Both friend and foe need to come awake to a promise. The promise of a world of freedoms and opportunity. Our fight is not with those down there. We fight for the light and the soul of all of us. All life, whether great or small is precious and those who are awake have the burden of protecting that life. They are not the enemy. Our foe is not there. Our enemy is in the minds of those who sacrifice life for selfish gain. But the enemy is here, too, in each one of us. Because we are no different from those who visit such grievous harm below. When we brace the enemy, we must remember to preserve all life. If the life you protect is only your own, you have done well. But today I ask you to do more; to do better. Protect every willing soul. Our only failure is if we don't try. Are we ready General?"

As Cricket spoke, he felt a warm support in his mind coming from Vagabond. The words were his own, but Vagabond gave him the encouragement to step beyond the moment into imagination and inspiration. He heard in his mind *'well done, good and faithful servant'*.

A whispered comment from Binky, leaning over, "It's just like Cricket's father said. Keep it personal, perceptible, and always practical. I guess our boy isn't such a hick after all," Wogs and Binky shared a moment of wonder.

As Cricket spoke there was silence. An almost supernatural pause in the world around them. The wind was still and the mountain itself seemed to hold its breath as his words splashed with palpable force across the assembly and over the airwaves.

Vagabond had come alongside Cricket, nodding and putting a giant hand on his shoulder. "Cricket has given the word. We are ready. Let us begin."

A roar of applause and cheers went up and out. The Argo sounded its horns as did the Janussaries. The airwaves were transmitting a deafening catharsis of hope and anticipation. Vagabond called out, "Binky, Wogs, Marna, please come here." The girls came up on the mound flushed with excitement. "Turn and face your family and friends."

Vagabond raised his voice for all to hear, "Let's give three cheers to Binky's Crew!"

The parents were the loudest to cheer.

A holo of Rus Templeton stood next to Vagabond. He called out, "Rrr-ight then! Saddle up! Time to get 'er done!"

Vagabond gave high-fives to the kids, then departed for his corvette. Binky's crew had a quick but confident goodbye with their parents and hustled to their waiting Pits. Marna was a part of a family now. She knew when this was over, she'd have to unpack what that meant. Wogs thought about Binky's crew and figured it was as good a name as any. Binky was just excited to be leading the speartip of the attack force. When she had met with the top brass, they had assigned her master control over all the speartip forces, both air and ground. She was given the rank of General.

"Heyyy, I'm General Binky, bitches! Yah, chew on that one, Binky crew…I'm your commander and chief. Got it?" Wogs smiled to herself. It had only been a matter of tick tocks before Binky-the-mouth started spouting off. Wogs felt comfortable with that, though. Binky acting out, Cricket being thorough and mindful, and now Marna being a solid rock for the group was an encouraging thing. She knew Cricket's mission was going to be just as hazardous but kept it to herself. She was told by the command staff that the fewer that knew, the better.

The Crew bolted as one into the sky, and Binky directed their attention to the plain below. The actual armed force was spread out for almost a kilometer, scrunched together to stay within the shielding from the Argo. Below were humans, synths, mechs of every stripe and kind: armored carriers, large battle tanks, fast attack vehicles and towering hybrids looking like mythological beasts.

"Alright Crew, this is my show, and we are going in hot and fast. Just keep your heads on a swivel and eyes wide." Binky was full of military cliches. She then spoke on the vox to her spearhead team, "Listen up! Tech gave us intel there are no less than 300 Mark IX Vulcan Gattling emplacements around the CENTER perimeter. Those are target number one. Our air attack will divide into quadrants. I think there are four attack teams. I hope so…"

"Roger that, commander! This is Kier, Orange Team leader."

"Affirmative commander, this is Brawne, Blue Team leader."

"Read you lima charlie, this is L33T, Red team is a go, commander." Binky sighed, there always has to be one weirdo in the bunch. Leet? hmm.

"Roger, commander. This is Addison, Silver Team leader."

"Ok. Thanks for that. So Kier, Brawne and Addison, good to have you. L33T, we're going to have to work on that name. It's almost as bad as calling yourself h4x0r. Really? Just no. What's your first name?

"Are you kidding? Why are you busting my balls, little girl?" L33T had just become a problem.

"L33T, come on. I am the top, PvPer in the world. You can't expect me to call you L33T." Binky was doing her best to be reasonable. What she was actually doing was finding out if she could trust this guy.

"Oh really, world rated. Then what's your handle?" Not lookin' so good for Whiskers, is he?

"I guess we're going to go there. Online I am called Ripley. And I am your best teammate in 3v3 and your biggest nightmare if you land among the competition. So, I have a question for you L33T: are you on my team?"

Binky laid down the gauntlet and backed it up with the intensity for which she was famous. In Online battles she had been undisputed champion in a variety of realms and games. As she spoke, Binky had flipped her Pit upside down and hovered over the attack craft piloted by L33T, canopy touching canopy. She demonstrated her skills were more than merely Online. Wogs would have given cash money to have seen his face.

"Oh gawd. You are Ripley? I heard about you. You're the number one solo boss killer 4 years running. I've seen highlights of your kills." It was evident L33T was a closet fanboy. His tone abruptly changed. "I…um, apologize. I didn't know. Well…hell yeah, everyone we are in the presence of gen-you-wine awesomeness!" L33T was preparing a speech of self-abasement when Binky interrupted.

"Shut it L33T, tell me your name!"

"Ah, yes. So sorry. Should probably learn to keep my mouth shut more. Um, my name is Roy. And I have a whole mess of AI prosthetic in my head which could feed our team telemetry if you'd like."

Binky hmphed and continued on, "Roy, welcome to the team. From now on just be Roy. It's okay. When we are done here it will be apparent to all that you are in fact L33T. I for one hope you are. And yes, Wogs will get you setup to sync telemetry updates. Thanks Roy!"

Marna spoke up, "Hey General, I think it's time to issue your quadrant assignments and order of march."

Binky wanted to be pissed at the interruption, but she was thankful for the quick re-focus. Marna was 100% correct, it was time to issue orders. Wogs had given Binky some ideas about the spearhead. One thing Binky knew was Wogs was always correct when it came to thoughtful planning.

Binky got Tech on the line, "Tech, is Janussaries still available to join us on the speartip?"

"Hey Binky, this is Cicero. Yep, you bet and bet 'cha we are! Standing by for instructions General."

However, Cicero felt about taking orders from a teenager, clearly he didn't let it interfere with the job at hand. Binky was thankful and hoped she would be up to the job. Real lives were at stake. This wasn't some video game. Binky prayed for favor from the gods of war.

June 2253 - Barstow, CA – 60 kilometers from LA:CENTER

Angry sounds echoed throughout the secure comms on the Hell's Outlaws vanguard. Barker James had enough of the incompetence of his bridge commander. "Mason, come here!"

Mason knew it was probably the end of the line. She walked toward Barker, carefully couching a throwing knife in her right hand just in case. "Yes, Barker?"

"I believe we are late to the party, and you disobeyed my strict instructions to get us to LA:CENTER on time. On time was noon and it is now almost 1500. I gave you that order, yet here we are!"

"Sir, we are 90 minutes out at best speed. The Pacific stormfront delayed us."

"Excuses. You see, a real officer would have found a way around that little inconvenience." Barker made a motion to pull his gun from his blazer; Mason knew this was his usual recourse. Barker always aimed for the head. But this time, for the first time for Barker, he was too slow. Mason threw underhanded in a straight toss. The knife embedded to the hilt in Barker's neck and severed his spinal column. He was dead in every way that mattered before he hit the deck. The bridge crew was seasoned and knew to take the change of command in stride. They knew it was the same way Barker had taken command 10 years prior. The crew cheered.

"Glad he finally shut up. What a snake."

"Ensign Coyle! Full steam ahead. We have a date to keep. Also, change our callsign."

"Change our callsign, Mason? Mmm, Captain?" Coyle looked confused.

"Call me Mistress Mason. Yes, we are no longer Hell's Outlaws. We are the Mariposas, and our flag ship is the Mariposa. And the first person to make a snide comment about the name can toddle on down to the galley and make us chocolate birkies."

Mistress Mason smiled at her crew, and they busied themselves with their consoles. Her flaming red hair was revealed full length as she took out all her hair ties. She was done with looking strict military. It was time to show some style!

"Mistress Mason, looks like Cindy went to make birkies." All laughed.

Coyle continued, "But while we're making changes, I'd rather use my actual name." Ensign Coyle was testing her new Captain.

"Coyle, isn't your last name?" Mistress Mason Dixon wore a smile.

"No ma'am, that is just the name Barker always used for whomever was his navigator. The Coyle who came before me told me she was the third such person by that name."

"Okay then, what is your name?"

"Margarite Papillion, ma'am. My family is from Martinique."

The response from Mason was favorable.

That was encouraging. Coyle, née Papillion cracked a smile for the first time and continued, "I got top honors, graduated from Westpoint, and served in a position at Annapolis teaching AI and avionics. I came highly qualified to Barker's command on extended TDY and got roped into this crapshow for the last 2 years."

Margarite went quiet, waiting on Mason's response. Mason was clearly ruminating on something, but whatever it was didn't take long.

"Would you feel comfortable running this boat?"

Margarite's eyes were like saucers. She wasn't sure what she was expecting, but this was not it. "Ma'am. I am not qualified."

"Hmm, who is presently more qualified to captain this ship?"

It was Margarite's turn to ponder. Grudgingly she replied frankly, "All things considered, I am the most qualified amongst a field of unqualified candidates."

"Alright then! Well said. Will you accept the Captaincy?"

No hesitation, "Yes ma'am."

"Alrighty, you are in charge of this vessel as of this moment. And everyone on bridge crew is now hereby promoted to, well…give me a show of hands. Who has served for more than four years?" One hand went up: it was crusty old Mad Dog Cramer.

"Cramer, you're second in command on this vessel as Commander. The rest of you served more than a year in any capacity?" It struck Mason as wry that she knew so little about the crew. She credited it to Barker's inept and vicious management style. Well, time to change things, starting now.

"Commander Cramer, I need two things from you ASAP. I need a roster of our crew and assignments. Then, give me shift rotations and the current duty roster."

Cramer asked, "Mistress Mason, if Margarite is the Captain, what are you going to be?" Yep, good question thought Mason.

"Great question, number three! I hate the terms Admiral, and Commodore. Too stodgy. Let's stick with Mistress. It has a nice ring to it." Mason looked around and was met by frozen faces.

"Come on people, you can laugh if you want to. But, really, give me some feedback. You think Mistress Mason works? Otherwise, what else would you suggest?"

The laughter began as the bridge crew realized that Barker was not coming back. The relief became palpable. The dam burst and pent-up anxiety accumulated over years spilled over into a messy riot. Mason gave it a beat before asking again.

"Mad Dog, is that what you'd prefer to be called?"

"Hell no ma'am. My real name is Sara Tucci." Mad Dog wasn't male? Who would have known with that scruffy beard? Hmm, it didn't matter.

"Alright, this is a fine kettle of fish. Thanks, Barker, for being such a total dick!"

Her crew was living in shambles. It was time to clean house. The place was a literal bachelor pad, pig stye. Her crew needed to be set in-motion immediately to cement her new command. Deep cleaning would take a while.

"Commander, signal all our ships for a Captains' meeting at 1600. Do not provide details, nor any mention of Barker's demise."

Tucci made her way to the vox and began the process of announcing. Mason turned to her new Captain, "Margarite, I want you to assemble a small security team for each of the Captains coming aboard. Prior to that, we need to gauge whether they will be onboard with the new command. We can't let any Barker loyalists damage our new order."

"Understood. It will be done. I suspect you will be welcomed by all."

"I hear you and hope that is true. Let's play it safe, though. Thank you, Margarite."

They would un-mess Barker's failures as they prepared for battle at LA:CENTER.

After Tucci notified all ship captains, Mason gave another assignment, "Commander Sara, in the next 10 minutes I want a bridge roster, submitted to Captain Margarite and myself. I need actual names and the rank you will promote each to. Also, list their primary duty station. Got it? That should get us started. Otherwise, get your folks back to their posts and prepare for engagement at LA:CENTER!"

"Mistress Mason. As you know, no one has eaten since yesterday…" Mason knew she had chosen the right Captain.

"Captain Margarite, these crew are now in your charge. If they need to be fed, you figure it out. This is your ship now, Captain." Mason was firm.

The Captains meeting went like Margarite suggested. All were thankful for Barker's demise. There would be some adjustment for the next few days, but each Captain accepted Mason's authority. It was fortunate since they were nearing the Los Angeles CENTER.

"Mistress Mason, our ETA is 35 minutes to LA:CENTER." Tucci called out.

"Commander Sara, when you are done with the roster, please come see me in my ready room. I have a task for you." It used to be Barker's torture lounge. She would have to get it cleaned out immediately. She swept the refuse off the big table, cleaned a chair off and sat down. It had been one hell of a morning already. A couple airmen came in and began removing torture devices and garbage. Damn, but that man was a slob.

Margarite had the body of Barker stripped of prosthetics and tech then summarily tossed overboard. She mentioned the crew looked forward to better pay in the days to come. There was already talk that the new leader was smarter than Barker and more likely to get them high-paying contracts. The attack ships cruising alongside the Mariposa got renamed but the command structure stayed much the same. The three battle cruisers got named by popular vote of their respective crews: the Deathstalker, Dutchman and the Hotshot since it had the second and only other known wave-motion gun in the skies over Earth, besides the Argo. The 175 smaller craft consisted of littoral craft, corvettes and fighters. The fleet made preparations for LA:CENTER and settled into the new chain-of-command expeditiously.. Commander Tucci reported that each ship had undergone mid-level leadership change which eliminated the holdover cronies of the late Barker James.

Sara entered the rapidly changing ready room with the roster. "Hey Mason, here it is. I even added the techs who were wandering by to the list."

Mason warmed to the first name basis. It felt like a good new normal. Airmen bustled in and out companionably. They were taking down the tarps which Barker had covering all the windows; the natural lighting brought a freshness to the room. Paint buckets were being staged in the ready room and new life was being breathed into many other areas across the whole fleet. It was as if a heavy pall had un-fallen from a dark night of fear. Then, at the pre-arranged moment, commanders and captains called a halt to the housecleaning so the crews could be ready for hostile engagement.

"Good job Sara. Now, what do you know about the JINN?"

"The JINN are one of those fruity pebbles groups that pretends to be the Illuminati. Howsoever they might be crazy, they still have more weapons for sale than anyone else on the globe. The price is always high, so only a small number of customers can afford to buy. Why do you ask?"

"I recall a mission you did for Barker a while back. You had a sister on the inside and could get cut-rate prices on things. Could you do that again?" Mason had a mischievous smile.

Sara saw the predatory look in Mason's eyes. It would be best to stay on her good side, "Yes, Mason. When would you like me to reach out?"

"Now would be great. Let them know I have a proposition for them which they will find both advantageous and lucrative."

The 175 smaller craft and the three battle cruisers in Mason's armada clipped alongside the carrier Mariposa toward LA:CENTER. Mason's plans for greatness were beginning to take form. But first, she wanted to connect with Templeton Rus and figure out her next move. He owed her (actually, her predecessor) a solid from a few years before. It was time to call in the marker.

June 2253 – Las Vegas, NV – 145 kilometers from LA:CENTER

A pitched battle was underway, and Nines Gonzalez was getting concerned. The fight happening 160 kilometers away at the LA:CENTER was going to have an impact on his mission. Nines had received a bounty notification from Nobu Meiji, head of Clan Minatomi. He received the info directly which was unusual. Typically, Nobu Meiji had underlings communicate his contracts so hearing from him directly threw up yellow flags immediately. But what could he say to a billion-credit bounty on three escaped scientists from Salt Lake CENTER? Nines was the only fleet which had both ground and aerial units which made his services indispensible to buyers like Meiji. Taking on a huge bounty was a question he needed to address with the big boss, but he suspected she would agree with him that the money was too good to pass up.

RETRO - 2224 – Havana, Cuba

Nines was 11 when he became a man. His father had left, and his mother and sisters depended on him. When he wasn't stealing from the government warehouses, Nines was hawking his goods and running from the cops. Often, he would secret himself away to read. He would hunker down in a sub-ground stairwell, just off a dingy alley, across from the fancy restaurant Corazon. He would read stories about the Tech War. A lot of people died, and disease claimed thousands of Cuban lives. He would crack open a small history book, written in English. He read about how the world had died many years ago. The Earth's population by the end of the 16-year war was less than a quarter than at the start. Whole swathes of real estate became unusable from biological and nuclear contamination. Out of the ruins was born a more rough-hewn and tempered population. The world adapted to a stark way of life. Despite devastation, a few business interests emerged and blossomed.

Over a century later the inheritors of a harsher world built their empires upon the ruins. As new Powers formed and re-formed, new players took the field to be the foot soldiers-for-hire of a new world. Barker James inherited the Hell's Outlaws, Rus Templeton combined his Jaxy Crew with the Killer Soldats into the Jaxy Soldats, which was the biggest privateer organization on the planet. And there were others, operators like Nines Gonzalez who knew street sense could translate into profits.

Nines grew up and ran his own crew. He wanted to have what Rus and Barker had: power and the ability to control life on his own terms. Nine's people were a rough lot, but honest in their dealings. He tolerated no dissention in the ranks, and everyone had to pull their weight. Despite that hardline, he was generous with sharing the rewards from the bounties and contract awards they received. Nines was more of a softie on his folks than he would ever admit. He was courteous and generous with his friends and familyand ruthless with rival gangs. His home was Havana and and its streets taught him all he needed to know to get ahead.

Nines had some gifts that set him apart. First, he could run fast and knew all the ins-and-outs of the streets of his city. As a thief he was known to be able to filch anything for the right price. He also became the best courier in the city and rose from there to be one of the most feared local crime bosses by the age of 19. When Nines was 24, he was invited to New York City to work a business deal to trade drugs for weapons. His cartel was growing quickly, and he needed bigger weapons to compete with the others throughout the Americas. Within two years Nines had the largest cartel in the Americas. He held that position for almost a year. It all came crashing down when a joint CSA task force raided his compound and killed every man, woman, and child. His whole family was killed, and he bore the guilt of that loss for years. Nines was 25 at the time of the raid; his soldiers whisked him away through his underground railway and off to the European States.

He remade himself in a new place. His new boss was the wealthiest man in western Europe, Chance D'Arberville. Under the Chance's tutelage, Nines became a powerful man of business.. Nines had an immense respect for Chance and became his eager pupil in both legit and illegitimate affairs. Nines stood about 1.7 meters tall, and his shoulders seemed to be almost half that wide. His physique was trim like a runner's and he had long legs, and a short torso. Enormous lungs made for a large chest and his arms were unusually long. Nines was hairy in the way of his countrymen.

Nines started a new business, funded by Chance. It was a resurrection of one of the newly expired trafficker companies. He reformed the concept with a new twist. They would be an aerial navy and massive ground force, working as traffickers of high value assets and taking bounties from all-comers. Some called it Nines' Navy and others called them the Eleguá. Five years later and Nines' branch of the D'Arberville conglomerate was the most profitable.

Always seeking power, Chance tried to take direct control of Nines' operation, but something else happened, Nines beat Chance at his own game. The rising tide of Nines Gonzalez rolled over Chance D'Arberville. Chance disappeared one evening from his home with no indication of foul play. The investigation languished, and the news of the disappearance settled down and his body was never found. The world didn't care and Nines was now a captain of industry. The downside for Nines was his had become a desk job. He dreamed of plying the thermals and currents in the skies again and soon a plan hatched. By 2243 Nines was back in the sky with a revamped fleet and the most formidable mobile land force on the globe. His command and control took place from the offices on his flagship, the famed orbit capable Eleguá. Business and profits were booming, but things took a turn when a mysterious woman from his past: Roxy Velour reappeared.

RETRO - January 2248 – near Athens, Greece

Nines had finished up a delivery of foodstuffs to the Athens area when a strange transmission came from the area of Argos. Nines left the bridge of his flagship. He gave his crew some downtime and decided on a lark to go explore. After all, during his 39 years he had never thought about having a vacation. He took one of his light corvettes and headed toward the familiar signal. His people thought it out of character for mister 'business-only' to take off on a whim. But they knew the boss could do whatever he wanted. Nines had heard a signal on the command deck comms. It was exactly like the sound he heard back in Havana when he was still a street scrub, scrabbling hard to make his way.

RETRO - 2226 – Havana, Cuba

As a street scrub, Nines was intimately aware of his surroundings. But he mostly ignored the overhead speakers on every street corner. They were used when the Generalissimo wanted to address his country. But Nines heard something different coming from the speakers of a run down office building that piqued his curiosity. It was a scratchy rhythm which repeated every minute and a deep hum that vibrated the air. He decided to explore.

The building was the typical derelict found in Havana. The inside was deserted below, with garbage blown into piles, and the smell of human waste was rank in the air. The building had an inner courtyard open to the sky and all six floors had walkways wrapping around the courtyard. Nines found the source of the sound in a lab on the 6th floor. Two soldiers and a doctor in a white coat were standing behind a massive console of buttons, displays and levers. But what was more interesting was the bright red light beyond the console, shining down on something. Nines stole into the room and made his way around the far wall to the right. As he repositioned, he saw the red light was shining on a person. It was a little girl in a glass enclosure. She was clearly in a lot of pain, but her cries were silenced by the thick enclosing glass. As the hum of the machinery wound up, the rhythmic scratchy sound blared loudly over the speakers outside. The girl in the glass enclosure was frantic and she clawed at the glass, leaving bloody streaks from torn fingernails. Nines was frozen, horrified. The girl's eyes locked with his and he realized he had seen her before. He thought she was one of the rich kids, watching the street traffic from her balcony. But apparently, she was an experiment. He had heard rumors about brutal human experiments in his hometown, but to see one live was beyond his tolerance. Her eyes pleaded with him, and her mouth said, Ayúdame, help me.

Nines pulled out his two-telescoping steel baston he had stolen off a dead soldier. He positioned himself behind the guards and struck each on the head in quick succession. Then turning to the scientist, he saw she had a pistol in her hand. He dove over the consoles and the first bullet bounced around the room, missing him.

"What the hell, boy! Get out of here. I'll put a bullet in you if you don't leave now!" Nines thought he should have bashed the scientist before the guards. It was too late to make a play for one of the guards' rifles. As he crawled fast, he was looking for a power cord or off switch. Suddenly the scientist was there, in front of him with the pistol pointed at his head.

"Last chance boy. Leave!" He leapt and the gun fired. The bullet nicked his leg then hit the glass wall containing the girl. The glass cracked.

He scuttled behind several pallets of boxes and peered out. The scientist was yelling something, but the whining of the equipment was too loud. The girl was slumped over, and blood was leaking from her face. She twitched but otherwise stopped moving, eyes casting a 1000-yard stare. A teddy bear fell from her hand which painted a picture Nines never forgot. He clamped his hands over his ears; the sound was deafening. The scientist was frantically running back and forth: something was wrong. The crack in the glass enclosure rapidly grew and Nines watched the scientist try to pull the power cord. He took a risk and ran to help her. She seemed to appreciate his help as they both pulled on the thick cable. However, the catastrophe was too far along and the last thing he remembered was an explosion, a burst of red light and then blackness.

Nines woke, it was nighttime. He was lying on the floor, covered with rubble from the blast. A fine layer of stone dust covered everything. He rolled his head to the left and saw the scientist. She wasn't in one piece anymore, and very dead. After some swearing and searing moments of pain, he stood and looked around. The glass enclosure was gone and so was the girl. All that was left was the teddy bear. Nines picked it up and read the little necklace on the bear. A name was inscribed on the necklace Roxy Velour. Was that the girl's name or the bear's. Regret filled his heart as he remembered her eyes. He promised to never forget. Then Nines set about the job of growing up and making something of himself.

RETRO - January 2248 – near Argos, Greece

The Kazarma Bridge had stood for 3500 years, and the secret of its Cloud confluence location had held for most of that time. Of the four known Mycenaean corbel arch bridges near Arkadiko, Kazarma was seen by most as an ancient span serving a chariot road. The secret wasn't what rode over the bridge but what the bridge hid in the arch below. When a person did certain arcane Cloud manipulations at the base of the bridge, the archway became an opening.

Nines landed on the main road near where the signal originated. As he exited his craft, he could hear the same sound he heard that day so long ago in Havana. He followed his ears and walked a dusty trail. Over a rise and into a defile, Nines walked down a steep pitch toward a small rock bridge. As he neared, the sound grew louder. He could see a red light emanating from under the bridge itself. His heart beat faster and for the first time in years, his anxiety kicked in with gusto. He pulled out his Desert Eagle handgun and proceeded closer. Sweat poured and he mopped his brow as the bridge hove into view. He walked around the bridge and looked into the arch from the downside. A red light was coming from under the bridge's arch. The sound became piercing, and Nines covered his ears. Then there was a flash, but unlike last time, there was no explosion. A woman was suddenly there. She walked from under the arch, looking around warily. She didn't see Nines at first and spent a few moments fussing with a device in her hands. Then she looked up; Nines was just standing there watching. Was this the girl he saw so many years ago? She didn't seem to recognize him. Maybe this was just a stupid coincidence, but Nines always trusted his gut and his gut said this was the same person. He waited, unsure what to do. After a minute the woman walked toward him, still fiddling with the device she held.

She came close, "So it worked. You're only 32 years too late to help, but who's counting, huh?"

The woman smiled at him, but he was too stunned to say anything. She patiently waited, the curl of a smile touching her lips. Then Nines thought to himself, time to get your act into gear, mister.

"So, what's a gal like you doing in a place like this?" He cringed as he said it. He meant to be offhand and humorous, and he utterly failed. Now he sounded like a cheesy kid hitting on a chick at a skeezy bar.

"Well, that was unexpected. I guess I have to ask to make sure. You're that kid from Havana all those years ago, right?"

"Um, yep, think so. Yes, that is I am the kid, um, guy which you are of…of whom you are inquiring." What the actual ass was going on? Nines was a world leader, master of a corporate empire and a bunch of other things. He was shamefaced and snapped his mouth shut before more teenage nerves flowed out.

"Ah, there he is. I remember your voice when I saw you in the streets below. I watched you for weeks, yoiu know. You were playing with your friends, carrying messages and other things. I would know your voice anywhere. But I thought you would have gotten a handle on your nerves when it comes to women, by now. Hm, guess not." She jested at his expense. The woman walked around Nines as he stood there, feeling like a side of beef on sale at the market.

"You know I tried to get you out, but I failed. I'm sorry."

The woman stopped pacing and grabbed his face, "Okay, then. You botched a rescue. So what. It's not like you had any idea what was happening. But let's start off on firm footing this time. What's your name?"

"I'm Nines Gonzalez. Good to meet you."

"Ah, ya see? Suave demeanor is back. I look forward to getting to know you, sweet man. I've read about you in the newsfeeds, but you are so much more interesting in person."

Nines was confused, "Your name is, um, what I mean is what is your name? That is, I wasn't able to figure that out before and now, well…"

"Nope, suave just left the room again. What is going on with you? Neverthemind. Nines, you know my name. Say it." He was thinking to himself as his mind was blank, I'm never this spacey.

He spoke, "Your teddy bear was named Roxy Velour. Is that also your name?"

"Not the bear," Roxy smiled, and Nines opened a small satchel he carried with him literally everywhere, except maybe the shower. Out of the bag came a tattered but well cared-for teddy bear. Roxy saw the bear and froze. Tears formed. Her cocky demeanor dropped away like rain, and she became that little girl from so many years ago. Nines held out the bear and she gently grasped it to her in an enveloping hug. A moment later with her eyes closed she embraced Nines. She wept silently. He wasn't a touchi-feelie guy, but despite all he held Roxy like he had only imagined in his dreams.

He spoke softly in her ear, "I carried your death as a burden every day. As a kid I promised myself I wouldn't let any others die under my watch, but I failed at that too." After a pause he continued, "Roxy, you smell like chocolate and peaches." She pulled back and looked at him, still clutching her bear.

"You're still a weird kid, but I like you anyway." She grasped him tighter, and he didn't mind one bit. In fact, he wanted the moment to last forever. A fresh and clean light began to shine in the world of Nines Gonzalez.

Roxy smiled mischievously. Music sprang out of thin air. Nines started. Roxy and began to dance. Her pad was playing a tune and she moved with rhythm, slow at first.

"Confía en mí, mi amor. Estamos en Grecia, ¡así que debemos bailar!" Trust me, my love. We are in Greece, so we must dance! He recognized the tune; it was from a Greek movie from the 20th. It didn't matter. All Nines saw was his heart, back amongst the living. And she wanted to dance and nothing was more natural. So they danced, and the gods danced with them.

Back at the fleet, they were together like peas and carrots. Roxy was with Nines everywhere he went. What he wasn't prepared for was the dramatic effect she would have on him and his business. One day, he asked her about the flashing red light and where she had gone for so long. She wouldn't answer, but said, "Trust me for now. When it is time, you will know everything." He didn't understand but he trusted her completely. He justified it as an enjoyable little mystery.

June 2253 – Eleguá headed toward LA:CENTER

Every airborne and ground-based unit was the best money could buy. For speed, firepower and longevity of equipment life, Nines' force was one of the most fearsome on the planet.

"Nines, we're less than ten clicks out from the CENTER. Commanders are awaiting green light, sir," Lieutenant Aubrey Scott was the con officer and one of the few officers who had prior military service. She was sharp and kept a tight rein on the bridge crew.

"Hey honey, let's set a surprise for Rus and his friends. Barker and Rus both think the bounty is the real target. Let's teach them a lesson in keeping better intel!"

Roxy had become an invaluable part of the crew and often gave better guidance than Nines and was much more fun for all involved, by far, with cheeky antics and all. His purpose in life had as much to do with Roxy as with his business. A new missional group had grown up within Nines' ranks: Roxy's Rangers. They operated to help people with food and medical supplies, which was costly for Nines, but vital to his new philanthropic reputation. With the new image, he still took certain contracts, but they no longer caused wanton mayhem and violence. When Roxy and Nines' rolled into town with foodstuffs and meds, their army of do-gooders took over the town. They still sported conspicuous weapons which kept the violence down, but Roxy was no dummy. Starving people could get easily riled up if control wasn't maintained.

As Southern California's desert rolled by underneath them, Nines and Roxy made last minute adjustments for their arrival at LA:CENTER..

June 2253 – Goldstone near LA:CENTER – Croatoan alien reveal

Croatoan appeared as a harbinger of ill news as a hologram in front of Vagabond and the top brass. At one point or another everyone at the planning table had seen or met Croatoan. He seemed to show up when the crap was hitting the fan. Few if anyone welcomed his timing; Croatoan Stormcrow, some called him. However, his advice was always spot-on accurate. No one knew who (or what) he was, but his presence usually heralded a solid shot at victory if his counsel was followed. Croatoan appeared as a stout, bald man with luminous green eyes. His slack face contrasted the tension of his body. He visibly vibrated with energy.

"Gentlemen, your forces are enroute to the LA:CENTER, with three of the Four in charge. Let me congratulate you all on arriving at this historic date." Vagabond nodded at Croatoan's words.

"Croatoan, the children are now young adults, and they have every bit of the potential you promised. You've been watching them?" The general staff and the aides were speechless, watching the person some of them suspected was a helpful alien.

"Olonana, you look well. I see the help I gave you and Daisy has blossomed in, hmm, unique ways." Croatoan looked up and down, observing Vagabond's thousands of

MicroDrones and MiniBots flitting about.

"Unfortunately, Pilgrim is on another assignment today. I'm sorry he couldn't be with us, but I'll let him know we spoke." Suddenly, another holo image appeared. It was Daisy Blake, Pilgrim.

"Hey old buddy, seems our friend is wanting to give us some news and wants everyone else to hear as well." Daisy smiled and looked toward Croatoan.

Vagabond didn't bother to mask his surprise.

Croatoan delivered his message, "Friends, I don't live in the past, but indeed it lives in me. Our shared experience has seen tragedy and heartache, but we have seen progress toward a gentler and kinder world. As I have spoken with some of you over the years, I have assured you I have your best interests in heart. Hearts in my case," Croatoan gave them a rare smile.

"That is still true. But your best interest required me to lie to you. The premise that humanity needs to have a great age of peace is still true, mostly. The full truth is humanity needs peace between each other and the non-human sentients who share your planet. All of you need to be a combined front against something bad that is coming. They are called the Cleaners, and they have operatives already here bringing humanity toward extinction."

Vagabond was used to hard truths, but this was a shock; who were the Cleaners? The others were whispering among themselves, and a quiet hush settled as everyone waited for Vagabond to reply. But it was Daisy who broke the silence.

"Croatoan, I think it is fair to say you have kept a lot from us. Perhaps there is good cause, but I think now is the time for a larger telling of this tale of doom. Let me suggest a starting point: why do the Cleaners want to harm us?" The silence continued and all eyes were on Croatoan.

Croatoan paused, looking at the sky. Casting his gaze across the assemblage, he spoke, "In the life cycles of species, cumulative effort is made to stay alive and perpetuate one's own kind. Across the galaxy a group of species that chose to quiet their warlike and violent tendencies found expansion into the cosmos to be a smooth and natural progression from their planets of origin. By contrast, those that remained warlike caused irreparable harm to themselves and other races. More than a million years ago one particular race with a warlike nature kept their violent tendencies in check, but just barely. They and other races banded together and call themselves the COMBINE. The COMBINE has been a safe refuge of shared interest for a long time. The Cleaners are headed up by the Coali. Originally, they were seen by many as a threat, but one faction of the COMBINE wanted to give them a chance to be a part of their commonwealth. In trade for their admittance, the Coali were tasked with being the enforcement arm of the COMBINE, eliminating unsuitable warlike races from the cosmos. They are very good at what they do, and their forerunners are already here, sowing the seeds of your demise." Croatoan paused.

"Two groups of agents, the Vor and the Crith appear human in every way detectable. The only way you will be able to discover the agents is a signal or pulse that is emitted when they arrive. But once they are here, only certain individuals who can see auras will be able to pick them out of a crowd. Understand, these agents are in fact abducted humans who were transported off world to have their minds replaced. That mode of offworld travel causes an unmistakable signal which is audible and produces a bright red glow, the aura."

Croatoan looked to Vagabond and Daisy, "You will need to run down leads on that signal. I am giving you a sample of the signal now. We need at least one Vor captured alive to then suss out the others."

He raised his voice, addressing whole the gathering again, "You must continue with your liberation work, since each life saved is another comrade-in-arms. Know this: anyone you kill today, no matter how justified is one less soldier on our side against the Cleaners.

"As you all know by now, the four children are the new leaders of the Liberation. You must invest and entrust in them, so they are able to lead us in the war which is upon us."

Croatoan spoke only to Vagabond and Daisy, "Where is Kip?" Vagabond told him about my foolishness. "Gentlemen, Kip is the focal of our efforts. Our success will only happen if he is leading us. Find him."

Both men nodded. He addressed the whole crowd once more, "Ready yourselves. Today's work is a training session for the real war. Above all, save lives." He made a curt bow then his holo led Vagabond and Daisy, walking toward the brim of the hillside where they spoke in hushed tones.

June 2253 – Speartip prep against LA:CENTER

Everyone took that as a dismissal and readied for launch.

Binky spoke up, "Listen up teams, look on your HUD and see the quadrant assignments. Give me a bump back to confirm. Waiting…" She was in her element. Supporting her was Wogs, master of strategy.

"Binks, I have my HUD focused on the big map and color coded per problem. I am also putting up those colored arrows pointing us to the hottest areas like we did in Expanded Kharazan. Anything else you want?" Wogs was ever the razor-sharp 2nd in command. She had supported Binky in both tournaments and raids. Wogs set the tools in place and Binky executed to plan.

"Good call, sis. Team, I'm going to be making callouts as we go. I want you focused on two things today, targeting those emplacements and clearing aerials. Got it? Your role with your individual teams is to tell them which emplacement to shoot. Wogs has updated the master map with a suggested number sequence for all emplacements. If other weapons, ground or air forces present themselves, report it back via your HUD. Wogs will then refactor the plan live-time and make verbal adjustments as needed. Team leads, you are to monitor two channels at all times: the command channel with Wogs and me and your individual team channel. Keep chatter to a minimum and be prepared for the storm once we come in range. Questions?"

"Commander, I –" Binky interrupted Brawne.

"Brawne, let's keep it first name basis please. Sorry for interrupting you."

Brawne continued, "Binky, you probably need to know our load out and complement?"

"If your stats are accurate on my HUD, I already know the status. Let me give you a read on what I see…" Binky didn't miss a step. " I have four teams which have the following load breakdown…" At this point each leader's HUD saw a display of each team craft type, load out, position and energy level. Addison, I show you are Synth?"

"Roger that Binky. Excited to be a part of your team. Would you like me to add my processing capabilities to anything specific?"

"For sure! Wogs, are you good to sync with Addison?"

"Yes Binky, she and I already have sync'd and I am showing her drone fleet data now. Take a look! This looks so cool!" Wogs was impressed. Addison's datasets provided another layer specific to her drone fleet and a second layer with vectors to nearest targets.

"Addison, would you be comfortable with assigning your fleet to support all four quadrants? I could have Roy supplement you in your assigned quadrant. Does that work for you?" Binky had spent years learning how to delegate and get buy-in from team leads in the massive raids she led in various Online games.

"Yes Binky. Roy and I can cover each other, with his ground force and my fleet working in tandem." Addison was making shifts and changes to her roster almost too fast for Wogs to follow. Everyone was thankful she was on their team.

"Binky, this is Cicero." Binky had almost forgotten the Janussaries crew.

"Roger Cicero, thank you. How would you like to proceed?" Binky knew when to leverage superior expertise and she was well aware of Cicero's reputation from Vagabond.

"I suggest we hang back a couple clicks and use our long-range guns and spot-shielding. We will provide intel with Tech keeping pace with Addison and Roy. I doubt the CENTER is defended only by gun emplacements." Cicero's comment had all the leaders nodding their heads.

"Thanks Cicero. What is spot shielding?"

Tech replied, "We can project a shielding surface up to 10 kilometers out in the low megawatt range. Anything more and the power output might frazzle the sensitive electronics of the drones."

"Okay. I think I understand. Addison can you and Roy coordinate preferences for units to shield to Tech?"

Addison and Roy answered, "Yes Binky."

Binky spoke, "Wogs, please make the necessary adjustments."

"Already there, Binks," Wogs was on it.

Tech asked, "Binky, I am connecting your folks to a single SatFeed channel I created for Speartip. Fig, can you confirm endpoint fidelity?" Tech piped through Fig's response. Binky hadn't realized she was going to get live satellite telemetry and full spread aerial optics for her mission. She was glad no one could see her excitedly bouncing up and down in the cockpit. Then she looked around and realized exactly every one of her leaders had watched her do her happy dance . Oops, so much being a cool-as-a-cucumber leader. She wasn't concerned.

"This is Fig. Colonel Davidsen and Jack Jack are managing satellite feed processing and will be doing callouts of enemy fields of fire, killbox and hostile asset movement. I'll be helping Tech directly to coordinate best intel to update downstream to Wogs, Addison, and Roy." Fig was all about the business. Binky just went to her happy dance again and laughed hard when the adult leaders around her joined in. Dancing was good. But it was now time to focus.

Binky took stock of the munitions, assets, and capabilities on her HUD. She closed her eyes and visualized the battlefield and her options for engagement. She always made a mental map before starting a campaign. Wogs looked through Binky's canopy and saw her relaxed and sitting back. She recognized Binky's pre-battle preparation. Wogs sent a quick message to team leaders to 'take five' and be ready for go-time.

A couple minutes passed, and Binky came back on, "Okay, now we are to it. I think Sun Tzu had it partly correct. We need to calculate our methods right now. But where the sage falls short is those decisions and calculations need the ability to flex and change. So, let's pepper a bit of Von Clausewitz in here and prepare for the fog of war, okay?" There were sounds of assent from the leaders.

Binky wanted to make sure the newest adds to the team heard the priority, "Confirming our priority, I want two branches to our attack: killing the gun emplacements is job number one. Those bad boys are death to our refugees. Our second branch is mopping up the aerial units. Wogs, you are map master for the engagement. I know you knew that, just wanted to confirm for the team."

"From the top, Kier, your team is 100% on branch two. Start with the north airfield in quadrant one then continue clearing aerials clockwise in quadrants 2, 3 and 4."

"Brawne, same thing as Kier, but start with the south containment lot in quadrant four, then continue counter-clockwise with quadrants 3, 2 and 1. You and Kier will meet somewhere in the middle.

"Addison and Roy, you both are providing live telemetry as planned and I want MissileDrone and AerialTank units to be distributed evenly across quadrants to target emplacements. Wogs will give you the specific callouts momentarily. Next, our ground units will be key against emplacements and anti-personnel hostiles. I want all Petraeus Tanks to attack emplacements by quadrant, starting with quadrant one in the north. Roy, have your Fast Artillery start with quadrant two in the north. Quadrant one in the north has the main entrance. I need those emplacements killed, priority one! Be prepared to reconfigure all ground forces in a perimeter once the refugees start coming out. And, let's match that with your drones Addison." Everyone's HUD showed the targeting and sequences Binky specified.

Roy and Addison ack'd back. Wogs made adjustments to the battle plan.

"Also, Roy, have your Quotls and Vittles on standby, and have them hide best they can near the north airfield. Once the refugees exit, they need to setup a personnel perimeter. They have to hold the line..

"Cicero, there is a whole bunch you can do, but I don't want to over-commit you at the outset. For now, could you station over the far north airfield? I want you to deploy 1000 of your EMI Drones and have them stationed inside the emplacement perimeter, hidden amongst the various parts of the roofline of the CENTER. Also, I want 200 of your Phosphorus Drones located in a cordon around the top of the external defense control center. I think Tech or Fig knows the location?"

"Yes Binky, sure do." Tech spoke and Fig could be heard confirming as well.

"Great. Wogs, I want you to give the order for the EMI Drones to activate, aimed at the roofline edge all the way around the CENTER. At the same time give the order for all the Phosphorus Drones to ignite and hopefully burn a segment of the roof to drop the whole center to the floor below.

"Tech, could you and Fig determine when we are at the 50% mark for emplacement destruction and pass that to Wogs? What I am looking for is when they have engaged the majority of their forces, still thinking they have command and control. The emplacement defense capabilities will have fallen to a risk level I can accept."

"Sure can Binky." Tech answered.

"Wogs, when you get the ack on 50% remaining that is your trigger for both sets of drones. Give the order. Except. If in the meantime, we start coming against manned aerial fighters we will have to decide if we need to abandon the plan and re-direct all EMIs to target manned aerials. I think we ought to continue through with the Phosphorus Drones drop of the control center, regardless. Let's keep our visuals on a swivel!"

"Okay, now for the third branch of the plan. Sorry, thinking on the fly, here. Janus, can you ping Argo and see if you and Rus can provide shield cover for all of the north airfield? From the main entrance to the far end we need to have a protected path for refugees?"

"Yes Binky, we had already planned to do that aside from supporting the speartip."

"Excellent, thank you. Also, could you deploy some your SpyDrones to get us visuals on the inside of the CENTER? I think we need to prepare for what's coming, whether friendly or hostile."

Cicero answered back, "Got it Binky. That is something we hadn't planned but is a stellar idea. I'll have Rus do the same for the other entrances as well. We'll keep 'em low enough to avoid the EMI pulses as well."

"Alright friends, anyone not ready? Binky gave a couple beats.

Kier	Orange Team	
GyreCopter		38
Scout Attack HK		16
HK-3 / HK-4		8
HK-8		2

Brawne Blue Team	
GyreCopter	64
Scout Attack HK	17
HK-3 / HK-4	7

Addison	Silver Team	
66-F Missile Drone		234
76-F Livefire		625
33-K Kamikaze		41
97-T Tank		722

Roy	Red Team	
Quotls (L)		148
Vittles (L)		123
M-86 Petraeus Tank (L)		21
M-888 Fast Artillery (L)		22
Scout Attack HK		46

Janussaries	Black Team	
Vulcan Rounds		336321
EMI Drone		22316
Magnesium Drone		1237
Spy Drone		279
Beamrider Missile		16
Tactical Nuke		6
Thermobaric Missile		6
Lifter Drone		8
Mini Vette		4

Wogs was on the ball, "Binky, we have arrived at zero point. I am activating the quadrant dispersal commands to everyone's HUD. Please initiate patterns and ack back with vectors to the initial." Wogs loved the pilot lingo as much as any hardcore gamer. She knew she had to keep her head clear though. This was not a game and if she messed up, people would die. What she didn't want to think about was people were going to die and there was nothing she could do about it. A hard time was coming and neither she nor Binky were emotionally prepared. The adult leaders around them knew the score and were willing to do everything necessary to get the job done. They knew a hard rain was gonna fall. Let the deluge of fire and mayhem commence! Binky was on the warpath!

"Roger! Execute Speartip, now!" Binky watched as her forces dispersed like a large grasping hand to begin encompassing the LA:CENTER. She was amazed the ground forces were keeping up. They were fast! She noticed the Quotls, and Vittles were hiding in various ground vehicles. She wasn't sure how effective they could be against ranged weapons, and she hoped they would survive the hail of bullets and fire. They were critical in the plan to defend the fleeing refugees.

June 2253 – above Goldstone – Cricket's team departs

The General asked Cricket to form up a team with Marna and Gracie Lou. After bidding a quick goodbye to Binky and Wogs, Cricket was talking with his two teammates. The three were waiting for a briefing on the mission. The parents were all saddled up in various craft, either leaving for the rear or heading into battle. Other battles were being fought throughout the world, but LA:CENTER was the big Kahuna.

Jack and Crucible were standing close-by talking quietly. A few minutes later the General came over to sit with the kids. "To some people trust is an illusion. The only currency they believe in is self-interest. Greed. To them, the best people have to offer is mutual self-interest and transactional relationships. We have enemies, now allies who believe this way, but still, we are working with them. Cricket, why do you think we do that?" The General was now Vagabond again, the wise sage.

"I can guess why, but I -don't really know." Cricket was careful. He wanted Vagabond to be proud of him but didn't want to appear like a know-it-all.

"Cricket that is a cautious answer, but not entirely truthful. You know more than you are admitting." Vagabond wanted Cricket to take the risk of being wrong.

"It seems that some people live in a world of pain and reaction, kinda like living in survival mode. Those people rarely see the beauty of a thing apart from its usefulness. I think those people live with a type of blindness. They can't see the world around them except for what is in it for them." Cricket had a serious expression on his face. He looked up at Vagabond and met his smile.

"You know why we have partners who think differently than us?" Vagabond was trying to tease out something specific.

"Umm, only one thing makes sense to me. We need differences in thinking: differences in opinion and differences in interests and purpose," his face scrunched for a moment. He continued, "And we also need every ally we can find."

"Why do we need that, Cricket?" Vagabond pushed Cricket to answer.

Gracie Lou chimed in, "Narrow thinking leads to one destination: societal decline, insular polarizing of them / us and authoritarian type government."

Vagabond rolled with it, "Young lady, I know you are well educated and would expect you to know. However, I am looking for Cricket's assessment –" Cricket interrupted.

"General, I agree but would add that creativity and arts also flourish in greater variety when differing or conflicting outlooks can be accepted among people." Now Vagabond smiled fully; he was visibly proud, and Cricket noticeably blossomed under his gaze.

"Cricket, yes. And when was our world last flourishing in that way?" He gave Gracie a look and Cricket answered.

"Back in the early 21st, of course. That's why so many people seem to call those the good old days." Cricket knew his history, but Vagabond was leading Cricket to something more.

"Assuredly, Cricket. Now tell me why you exhorted us only minutes ago about the true nature of our enemy." Vagabond listened and reclined back with appraising eyes.

"Sir, it's simple the way I see it. People make choices based on ideas. Given a harmful idea that serves a purpose, anyone can become an enemy of life. So, our potential for following an idea or ideal can either save or condemn us all. We fight a war of ideas. We need to save people to give them the opportunity to choose again." The group was quiet. Moments later one of the top brass came over, whispered into Vagabond's ear and like that, the learning session was adjourned.

"Okay, answer me this…why are we going to use our enemies as allies, risking they might betray us?"

"Sir." Cricket paused. "We have no other choice. Our existence is at risk and they either help us or we all fail. If they backstab us, we all die. We hope they take that to heart."

Vagabond nodded, "Very well, young sir. Let us put your resolve to the test. Here is what I want you and your team to do…" Vagabond outlined a plan which involved sneaking up to the LA:CENTER, finding a way in and eventually entering the Central Security Center. The job was simple: turn off all security systems and open every door throughout the facility. Easy peasy, right? Cricket had no idea if it could be done but hearing that his friend Kip was somewhere inside seemed to motivate him.

Right about that time unbeknownst to those outside, I was just being plopped into my cell to cool my heels for a few hours.

Half an hour later, Cricket and his Crew were in a vintage Humvee, moving fast toward the north entrance of the CENTER. Crucible drove and Jack navigated. Marna, Gracie, and Cricket sat in the rear. Above them were uncounted numbers of drones fighting a pitched battle against the ground and aerial forces of General Olonana. It was a mess, but it was a beautiful mess. The battle was out of range of the gun emplacements and Cricket knew Binky's Speartip was coming up soon. The explosions and flashing tracers of air-to-air rounds combined with ground-to-air light mobile artillery. Coruscating shields flashed and disappeared, and the chaos made a symphony of thunder and fireworks. Strafing runs by direct-piloted craft wiped out large swathes of drones; a symphony of whipping pew-pew sounds gave the telltale that distant guns from the CENTER were taking potshots. The emplacements were attempting to target large arcs of both friend and foe, alike. However, the emplacement batteries' fire fell short, causing accidental damage on the ground instead. Cricket thought to himself 'let them deplete their ammo', it's all the better for us. Prismatic rainbows of death and mayhem littered the skies.

Crucible was driving like a madman, dodging wreckage on the ground and a continuous rain of dying aircraft. The smell was a heady mix of ozone and burnt petrol. Cricket looked at his team: Crucible was driving like a nut, Jack had his face in a paper schematic, Gracie Lou was typing on her pad and Marna was polishing two huge pistols. Cricket leaned over and asked, "Hey Marna, what kind of guns are they?" Marna's eyes glittered with pride.

The Humvee pitched and swerved, bouncing up and down. The vehicle had been made for this kind of abuse, but it was over 200 years old. Crucible wasn't giving an inch of tender care. The vehicle would undoubtedly be unusable after this run.

"Cricket, check this out! These were my father's Peacemakers. They've been in my family since the wild west days. See how smoothly the cylinders move? It's like butter." Marna handed one of the revolvers to Cricket. He hefted the heavy weight and smelled the lubricant used on the deep blued metal. What blew him away was how functional these 400 year old guns were. His father had taught him and his friends how to shoot a variety of weapons, but they had been modern rifles and pistols. These were genuine classic models.

Marna continued, "My first grandfather who owned these was a law man in Kansas. His name was Charles Basset and he served with Bat Masterson and Wyatt Earp. My grandpa was famous!"

"Whoa, you mean these are real gunslinger guns?"

"Yep, yep, one and the same. You like 'em?"

"They are as cool as the gun I got from General Davidsen. Here, take a look!" Cricket popped the clip out of the Model 1911 .45, opened the action to show that no round was in the chamber and handed it butt first to Marna.

"Cricket, this is a museum piece. Well, looks like someone admires you a whole bunch!" Marna inspected the gun then handed it back, muzzle first, with a knowing smile. "Always good to know your friends, Cricket." Cricket grimaced; he wasn't the joking type when it came to weapons handling. He took the .45 back.

The Humvee slowed; it was making new noises that suggested its imminent demise. All eyes were forward to see where they were. The battle in the skies was lighter in this area but the sounds of the gun emplacements grew in volume. As the Humvee mounted a small rise over a concealing defile, everyone could see a gated entrance in the massive wall surrounding the CENTER. The gates consisted of double doors, each 15 meters square.

"Alright kids, time to get sneaky. You see that sizable entrance over there?" Crucible was his normal snarky self. "You ready to storm the castle?"

There was a pause since it was hard to tell when Crucible was being serious. Did they want to go through the heavily defended gates? Mmm, probably not.

"Mr. Cross, I hope you have another plan in mind. Something with less bullets." Cricket was polite, even to a smack-talker like Crucible.

"You know what kid, you're alright in my book. A good kid, but you need to know when to lighten up a bit. No, we are not running into the bullets today, if we can help it. Jack has another plan for us. Hop out of the truck and see if you can find a steel door in the ground."

Cricket and the others searched around, and Marna made a noise. "Huh." She was on her knees, using her hands to dig. Gracie came over and saw what she was doing and joined in. A minute later Cricket started digging with an entrenching tool. He handed a couple more to the others and the dig began in earnest. Crucible lit a cigarette and took a deep drag. Jack stood and watched the horizon in several directions.

Without evoking a headache, Jack spoke, '*Cricket, you need to focus yourself. The crapstorm we're diving into is going to be unsettling. You need to keep your eyes on the prize. If you get caught-up in the weeds, more people will die.'* Jack was careful not to send too strongly. Cricket barely paid attention as he dug.

"Come on you pukes, dig!" Crucible snickered, enjoying the expressions from the diggers. A moment later Gracie's entrenching tool hit metal. The sound had a slight echo.

"That's it folks. Good job, you found the secret door."

As the kids exposed a large circular hatch, Jack spoke, "The schematic says this was designed for executives to escape the CENTER in the event of disaster. Look for the handle."

"I have something here." Cricket unearthed a metal wheel and once clear of the soil and rocks, he was able to grab the rusted metal and tried turning it. The wheel didn't budge. He and Marna had a shared flashback and made eye contact. "Well, this thing is stuck. Someone else want to help?"

They took turns, tried in pairs and when even Crucible and Jack pulling together couldn't get it to move. Jack didn't dare use Cloud power to open it. He knew it would set off all kinds of alarms inside with the Cloud security folks. But Crucible had an idea. He moved the Humvee, so the bumper was about 10 feet from the big wheel, parked and unreeled the tow cable from the bumper winch. Cricket attached the winch hook to the wheel and watched as the tow cable drew taut and tugged the Humvee forward a few inches. Just as the winch lugged, the wheel turned slightly, and the seal was broken. The horizontal door rose slightly, and a hurricane gust whistled out of the small crack opened between the door and the casing. It smelled like dust and rot. It took half an hour using the winch to completely open the door. It shuddered with each pull. Squealing metal and sharp popping sounds evidenced the massive air pressure from inside.

"Ok folks, I think this last tug will get it. Move back now."

The escaping air had started as a high whistle. As the winch pulled and the truck jerked backwards, the sound roared louder. By the time the last pull came, the gale was deafening, and the team had moved behind a small sand hill. That was fortuitous as the final tug tore the door from its hinge and launched it skyward. The Humvee was yanked off the ground, ripping the front end off the truck. As the truck landed an uproarious laugh could be heard, "Ride 'em cowboy! Yeeee haw!" Crucible rode the Humvee like a bucking bronco and was the happiest anyone had seen him. Jack shook his head, concerned the commotion would draw attention to them.

June 2253 – LA:CENTER catacombs with Cricket

The vertical shaft was 3x3 meters and the metal rungs were attached to one wall of the shaft were the only means of access. It went down a long way according to Crucible. The airflow was a constant roar; at that rate, they might actually be blown up instead of falling. Jack had a rictus grin of anticipation and helped the team get set with hand holds.

"Okay people! Your first marching order is you do not die!" Jack was serious.

The volume of the rushing air made it impossible to speak to each other. Cricket kept looking up as he climbed down. He tried to deny it to himself, but the view of Gracie Lou's bottom was worth the look. At one point she caught him looking and gave him the stop it face. He re-focused on the ladder rungs like a good boy. A million years later they made it to the bottom of the shaft. Crucible took them to the first door in the massive corridor and as they exited the hurricane and closed the door, they realized how hard they had been working to not be blown away. And they were deaf, or close to it. Everyone had ringing in their ears, and they sat for a while to gather themselves.

"The nasty blighters have a whole drone force to give them personal carriage service up the shaft. Good job not dying people!" Jack was proud of them. Cricket still couldn't figure him out..

Crucible seemed to be in a speech-giving mood. "Ladies and gentlemen, we are in the most hostile of hostile territories. These tunnels are filled with all kinds of walking, crawling and flying horrors. They get dumped here and you can smell 'em now! Given a chance they'll eat your eyes for jujubes. Our best chance is to move quickly and quietly. Take your lead from me or Jack and keep your heads on a swivel, ya understand?" Cricket and his crew nodded.

Then Jack said his piece, "We have over six kilometers straight line between here and the Central Control. I can tell you, we won't be following a straight line, so our distance is going to be much longer. We may have to detour to levels below or above and our progress will be as much artform as it will be cold reasoning. Like Crucible said, we go in quiet and fast. I will take lead and Crucible will be sweeper, trailing by a few meters. Whatever happens, we keep moving. Gather yourselves, go time is now!"

With that Jack took off. We followed and for a long way we kept moving, taking turns, right and left and sometimes upward or downward. Crucible sometimes was close behind and other times he disappeared. Every time he came back it looked like he had slaughtered some monster. He smiled on each return; maybe he just loved killing things.

A wave of clackity clack came from behind. Vittles were after them! No choice in the matter: they ran! Around turn after turn, Crucible yelled at them, led them then finally made a wrong turn into a dead end. Cricket and his crew had seconds before being inundated with the spider crabby things. Pincers and fangs glistened, and pointy limbs clacked against the floor, tapping a tattoo of hunger and anticipation. Jack stepped forward, raised his hand like a Jedi and lo and behold the Vittles stopped their march forward.

"Look above! See that grating? Get the vent open and find a way to climb up. I will only be able to hold them for a short time," Jack was sweating, obviously exerting himself. He knew this use of Power was sending a message, 'we are here'!

"Marna! Gracie and I will boost you up. See if you can bust the grating open."

"Yes, lift me." Marna was lifted up. Gracie and Cricket fumbled around holding Marna aloft, "Hey, hold steady, okay?" One hit and the grating broke free and tumbled to the floor. Marna grabbed the edge in the vent and pulled herself in. Cricket lifted Gracie and Marna pulled her from above. Crucible grabbed Cricket and practically threw him into the vent. Then he made the jump, grabbed on, and crawled after them.

"Jack, time to go, buddy!" Crucible hung down, extending a hand.

"Cross, move back! I'm coming up!" Jack turned and leapt. It was all Crucible could do to get out of his way. The girls were already down the duct and following the general direction Jack had them going.

"Cricket, what the hell was that weird trick Jack did with those creatures?" Gracie sounded more curious than scared.

"You recall what Lugh told us. It seems Jack does telepathic things. I think those are the Cloud powers we have been hearing about."

Jack made a stage whisper forward to Marna who was in the lead, "Hey sweetgums, you need to start bearing to the right and look for an exit." Then he replied with his telepathy trick so everyone could hear, *'You think I am amazing; my son Cricket is going to leave me in the dust. You were practically made for the Cloud, ma boy!'* Cricket wasn't sure what he meant by son. It was disconcerting. Jack replied to Cricket only, *'Ma boy, you are my son in every way that counts. Someday you'll understand.'*

Marna chuckled, "You know, I once was a fan of Jack," she paused for effect, "But now I am a full air conditioner." It took a beat to understand. Ohh, fan, air conditioner, right. That was funny, in a Dad-joke sort of way. Even Jack gave a snort.

"I am keen on you too, ma love," Jack replied.

A peep came from ahead: Marna finally found them an exit. Then a sound came from behind them which peaked their anxiety: scrabbling and tapping sounds like the march of dozens of little Vittle feet. Cricket could hear Marna hammering on something, then a crash and she disappeared down…really fast. She had been on top of the grating so when it gave way downward, she followed. There were loud crashes then uproarious laughter.

"All fine down here. Come on people, get a move on!"

In short order the whole team exited the duct, falling, then sliding at a sharp angle into some kind of vault. The cube shaped vault had duct openings on all six faces; Marna was looking into the one to their right. It was the largest opening. The duct was circular, and

Marna led the way again, sliding down the tube to the bottom. Whee! Ducts were becoming tiresome, but at least this one was large enough to stand in. The Vittle sounds were faint in the distance but still keeping up. Crucible and Jack managed to get the grating back in place. Just in time. The scrabbling sound above was suddenly upon them. Tenacious little guys: Vittles. It was always a bad idea to get on the wrong side of a 15kg spider with a crab's body, fangs, 8 eyes and a crab's pincers.

June 2253 – LA:CENTER water movers with Cricket

Crucible yelled, "Right then! That grating won't hold them long. Come on!"

Cricket's party ran onward down the tube for a long way. At one point Jack drew them up short to regard two doors. One was a standard office style steel fire door and the other was a circular hatch mounted to the tube. The door was mounted on an extruded square where the hatch matched the concavity of the tube. Large letters were inscribed on the extrusion lintel, above both doors: W&W.

"This is it gang –" Then the Vittle sound was upon them. The black and purple tide of legs and pincers akimbo swept toward them from less than 100 meter's distance. They were close enough this time Cricket could see their many eyes were ice blue. Jack swore and slammed open the smaller door. Except he didn't. The door was either rusted or welded shut from the other side. He jumped up to grasp the locking wheel on the big hatch. The wheel was almost a meter in diameter, and it turned under Jack's prodigious strength. He wasn't being shy about his Power usage anymore.

"Stand to the side. I think this is under pressure!" Cricket and the others stepped back as Jack made the final turn of the wheel. The hatch blew open, throwing Jack across the tube. A swift fetid wind blew past them. Jack was up again and speeding through into the blackness of the unlit other side. Following, they emerged into another, much larger vault. Their flashlights shined their path but weren't bright enough to illuminate the far walls or the ceiling. The wind blew with less force in the large open area. Jack wasn't able to re-close the hatch. They moved on quickly.

Cricket put the nightmare of Vittles in the dark out of his mind. Heading straight across the vault, they reached another set of doors, labeled W&W. The small door opened for Jack, but the air pressure resistance made holding it open a test of strength. Jack held the door from slamming shut.

Jack yelled, "Hodor!" and the others stepped through. The door slammed shut with an echoing clang of steel-on-steel. The new tube in which they stood had dim lighting. Cricket thought he could hear scrabbling sounds from the other side of the door.

They ran again and the tube flanged out into a massive hangar-sized room. The most notable features were hundreds of color-coded tubes; five of them were more the size of vast aqueducts. The sound of water flowing hissed a faint susurrus. Signage adorned the room. One nearby sign showed the color nomenclature.

Styx –	In:Fresh –	(Green)
Lethe –	Out:Black –	(Black)
Phlegethon –	Out:Active –	(Red)
Acheron –	Out:Biochem –	(Yellow)
Cocytus –	Out:Gray –	(Gray)

Marna recognized the verbiage. "I see where we are Jack. This is the Water Mover District. The CSA is notorious for labeling anything that stands still for more than two shakes of a Quotl's tail. It looks like green is fresh water coming into the CENTER and the others flow out. Black is for sewage, red is for radioactive waste, yellow is for biological and chemical waste and gray is for water from kitchens, flood, and surface water."

"You sure know a lot about wastewater. Is that your side job?" Cricket was being tarty.

"Actually, the color coding lets me know which tube to throw you into, Beavis!" Marna took no shite off anyone.

"So, kids, I am not sure which route we will need to take, but the direction we need to go is there," Jack pointed to the left side of the room where another pair of doors stood.

"Anyone know what W&W means?" Cricket asked.

"Wicket and watergate. In this place it means the doors are for moving maintenance people and equipment." Jack answered immediately. He took off running, "Come on friends, time to move along!"

Jack drew up short as a group of hodcarriers passed by with their pole-mounted buckets carrying tools and supplies. The group paid no attention to Cricket and his gang. Jack moved forward with more caution as other workers were walking with purpose, to and fro. He signaled with a jerk of his head toward their destination. They arrived at the pair of the W&W doors.

Jack faced them, "Some fellow named Shaw once gave me some great advice, 'Jack, if you have to tell the truth, make 'em laugh. Or they might kill you.' So, with that thought in mind you need to know what I believe is coming next. Let me ask you, Cricket, what kind of fruit should never be left hanging?" Bewildered expressions met Jack.

Crucible surprisingly spoke up, "Jack, get to it. Where are we going? By the way, it's dingleberry." They all groaned. A nearby group of hodcarriers even groaned.

"Hm, tough crowd. We are probably going to have to travel some distance through one or more of these colored pipe systems. I will try to keep us away from the red and yellow, and the green will be a charged line which would quickly drown us. So that leaves black and gray."

Sudden cries of alarm came from the area they'd first entered. Hodcarriers and other workers were running from a black tide of menace. A cry went up that the HellCarrier's Union would be hearing about this violation. Another complaint sounded: "The Vittles Union will hear about this."

As Jack opened the wicket door Cricket saw the Vittles come to a stop. One of the Vittles was coming forward and standing close to one of the hodcarriers. A moment later they shook claw and hand, and a burbled laugh could be heard.

The hodcarrier leader shouted toward Cricket, "You better get running son. Union agreement only bought you a few extra seconds to skedaddle." The Vittles stood around with the hodcarriers and more laughter could be heard. Cricket locked the wicket door behind him and caught up with the others. Behind them the man continued, "I don't think our young friends realize they just took the worst route if they are trying to get into the CENTER above."

The Vittle leader replied, "And we have the sorry duty of pursuing them. More's the loss."

They ran. Cricket wondered how long he'd been running in one way or another. He wondered how Binky's team was doing above. Around another turn, another set of W&W doors was color-coded red. Backtracking they searched another route and came up with a W&W coded green. Two more tries in routing yielded black and yellow W&W doors.

"Okay kiddoes we have a decision to make. Cricket, you call it. What route will we take?" Jack was deferring to Cricket for some strange reason.

"Hell, I don't know. Crucible, what do you think?" Cricket wasn't about to plunge ahead blindly, but what options were there?

"Young man, you're the leader here. You know the risks. Decide. We will follow." Yeah, Crucible was no help.

"Okay then. Black it is. Wait, Jack, you said the green line would be pressurized. In some way wouldn't all the tubes be under some pressure?"

"You're correct. However, outbound lines are always low positive pressure, whereas the incoming line is quite a bit more. Not high pressure, for sure, but enough to drown us before we even got started. As you said, black it is."

At the black coded W&W doors Jack gave the team a level stare, "You know what time it is?" No one rose to the challenge. Eyes were already rolling. "It's poddy time!" Once again it took a moment to gather his meaning. Shaking of heads. "Get it? Poddy, party…hey, you try to be the plucky comic relief."

When had Jack gone from cynical aloof to comedic rogue? Then it hit him, when Jack felt they were at greater risk he got nervous. His humor told Cricket they were going into greater danger.

'Old Jack ain't nervous. Listen up boy. You aren't grasping a vital point here. Let me ask you, why are four children being allowed to lead capable adults, many of them centuries-old monsters like me? Think on that.'

The wicket door opened, and a meter tall wave poured from the portal. They had braced for the stench but were almost tripped up by the flow. Exclamations of shock came as Jack then hoisted everyone inside. He closed the door firmly. "We can't leave this open. Good manners." Jack had manners?

This was one of the large tubes, 10 meters in diameter. Surprisingly it was well lit and shockingly they were not alone. A work crew in matching jumper suits was prodding and raking the goopy sludge. They were multi-limbed humanoid hybrids, burly and obviously bred for strength. Six arms sprouted from their torsos and they had large frog mouths with wide blunt teeth. They were busy breaking apart fatbergs, each time sending a fresh wave of stech throughto the area. Thankfully, there was a breeze moving the air along. Breeze or no, the air was thick with stench.

"Ay, what'cha doin' in 'ere?" Where did all the English-type accents come from. This was still North America, right?

"Wotcher, me lad?" Jack gave the worker a smile.

"'Anging out in the loo, that wot."

"Why don't cha do us a Cheesy Quaver, pal?" Jack was speaking a foreign language with familiar words.

"Gotta long haul here before I'm off up the Daisys to get a bit spatchka. What kinna do ya for?"

"Running from some Vittles, what trying to put us in the stripey hole. Trying to head uptown to snuff it with some sophistos. We been all oddy knocky since we came to this domy, a bit fashed, for reals."

"Ah, no kidding. Wots an orange such as you about in these parts?"

Jack paused before answering and came to a quick decision and replied. "Ay came to break your contract. Give a better'un to yous and your droogies. Ya slow down the Vittles chasing us then meet me topside, north airfield and a new job, a better job be yours." The worker considered for a moment. His co-workers were waiting to see what he'd say.

"I say yeah. Shakes on it, we got a deal, squarelike. Name's Vin Canto; yours?" Vin held his hand out, covered in fecal sludge and other unmentionable nastiness.

No hesitation, Jack shook his hand, "Name's Jack, Spring-heeled Jack. Good to meet'cha. Gotta be running now. Do I 'ave yer leave teh move along?"

Vin laughed and the work crew joined him. "I 'eard of ya Jack. Thot you was one of the bezoomny, crazy types, no?"

The rest of Cricket's crew were still in shock from the stench and flummoxed by the strange tattoo of patois that beat between Jack and his new friend Vin. Cricket barely managed a smile. "Oos this one?" Vin pointed at Cricket. "Think I know 'im."

Jack switched back to standard English, "Yep, you know the Dads. This is one of the four kids. This is Cricket. Cricket come shake Vin's hand."

Cricket didn't hesitate. His manners were ingrained like white is to rice. "A pleasure sir."

Vin's grin went literally ear to ear, his big mouth almost as big as Cricket's head.

"A right proper gentleman 'e is! Quite an honor to meet'cha young sir!" Cricket knew it was fruitless to try to stay clean. He ignored his goo-dripping hand.

Brief small talk exchanged between both crews and then Cricket's company was off again, wading up a river of waste. Vin had given them precise directions to get to the center of the CENTER where the controls were located. The next exit from a watergate hatch included a shower-off gantry way. They found it, thankfully, but the smell was going to take a while to fade. Cricket thought wryly that they had trudged through a river of shite and come out clean on the other side. Perhaps a boat out of Zihuatenajo would be a good vacation after all this was over. Cricket penciled that in for later.

A long corridor led to a stairwell; they went up over twenty flights to a small hangar set up as a laboratory. There were no windows in the big room, so they made their way to the nearest steel fire doors. Jack peeked one door open, then led the team through. They were inside the CENTER, and they were in awe as they could see the kilometer high ceiling with what appeared to be a city housed inside. It was loud. People of every kind imaginable, humans, hybrids, synths, and every sort of flying creature were on the move. Jack cocked his head like he was listening, and a smirk creased his face.

"I have some good news! I can sense we are in the vicinity of a couple of friends. I'm not sure what they're doing here but I think they might be able to help us. The trick will be finding them before something finds us."

Jack led off again and ran away down the narrow roadway between buildings. Cricket and team followed. A few turns later they met a dead end with a large steel door blocking their way. Jack indicated they needed to get through. Crucible took out a small tool and began working the lock.

"Good job buddy, I didn't know you were so versatile!" Jack slathered the statement with loads of snark.

The door opened sideays, and the smell of burgers and hot dogs wafted out. That's when the team felt tummies grumbling and realized their hours of hard work made them famished. There was also a sudden and dire need for a restroom. The door slid to the side into a recess. An unlikely sight met them. It was surreal: they were staring a cantina bar. And Jack's friends were there, waving him and the crew inside.

"Hey Jack! You and your friends come on in! We have some great grub on the barby and yes Crucible you can go take a piss now." The broad smile was evident in the tone of the voice. Cricket's team walked into party central. Sand covered the floor in the lab-turned-bar and the place was gussied up cantina style. Five people were busy about the kitchen and around the floor. It appeared like they were setting up for a big shindig. Cricket noted these weren't all humans. One person looked like a human-sized chicken with arms, a skinny, tall guy with blue skin had four arms: really long arms! The other three seemed human. A frisson of unreality passed through Cricket. It was like one of those Twilight Zone movies. Cricket was hugely accepting of all lifeforms, but this place was over-the-top weird. Then a clickity-clack of little feet sounded, and the team turned, ready to repel the attacking Vittles. Seeing the fighting stances, the 4-armed fellow rushed forward.

"Friends, friends, no weapons needed here. These new arrivals are more friends. Not all Vittles are made the same, nor walk and talk the same."

With that over 50 Vittles poured through the door, calmly…as calmly as spidery things could be. They arranged themselves around the room and started milling about like regular party goers. Weird had just risen to a new level. Soon some Quotls came in as well, flitting about.

"So boy, you sure get us into the strangest places." As if Jack hadn't been the one to bring them there.

He seemed to find humor in the whole affair. First the Vittles tried to kill them then they want to party with them. Just as they were walking up to the bar, another wave of clickity-clack came from outside the doorway. The sound heralded the arrival of the Vittles chasing Cricket's team. Vittles met Vittles at the door. After frozen moments, one of each group clacked forward, meeting each other.

That was when Cricket and his team discovered Vittles had voices, albeit high pitched and crunchy. They exchanged some comments about the Vittle Union then huffed a couple times. Then the two began a dance, with their little voices singing melody and harmony, "… boot scootin' boogie!" Right on cue, someone put Boot Scoot Boogie on the jukebox.

The two Vittle diplomats were having some kind of dance-off. They moved in time with the rhythm and circled each other like matadors. Cricket noticed every other Vittle was bobbing in time to the dance-off. One Vittle then jumped onto the bar top in front of the chicken woman; she had beautiful big blue eyes. She leaned over and apparently understood the little fella. Suddenly the music changed and Cricket recognized the tune from one of the parties the Dads had hosted last year, Bambaleo! It was the Gipsy Kings!

The beat didn't match. The tattoo made by the clawed feet skipped a beat. And just like that, the two Vittles rejoined the dance with the new rhythm. Within moments both groups had formed up in two orderly ranks facing each other with the two leaders in between. Flamenco beat heavily on the air as the front two competitors gyrated, jumped, and shimmied across the floor attempting to out-do each other. The two groups moved at counterpoint to the other. One group employed a smooth whimsy and graceful perk and flow, inspired it seemed by something akin to Fred Astaire. The challenger side had a distinctive Gene Kelly athletic and snappy approach with strong arcing movements. Then the scene stepped up a notch.

Other creatures poured through the doors, attracted by the music. Hybrids, non-humans and synths who wanted to party on liberation day came into the huge laboratory, carefully avoiding the two tribes at war. One new contingent had more nefarious plans. Bristling with weapons and menace, these new arrivals had eyes on Cricket's crew. They were hunters and Cricket's team was the prey. Weaving in and out of the dancing spider-crabs, the foremost hunter was an eight-foot behemoth, looking less like one creature and more like dozens of little spiny humans holding themselves together in one amalgamated shape.

"Cricket, you, and the gang hang back. I have this." Jack moved forward toward the big thing. They met in the middle of the floor, facing each other. The dancing Vittles flowed easily around them, giving them room while not missing a beat.

A voice pattered on the æther, cutting through the click, clack, and clump, '*Ah my foe, so you come to fight me. The battle is already met; so, let's do this!*'

It was then Cricket realized a massive wave of some kind of force was emanating from Jack. He wondered, '*Hey Ja —*' JAck interrupted.

"Cricket, yes. You will learn this too. Hush for a moment."

After a space of time Jack elaborated, '*Combat can be converted to competition with some deft weaves of influence. You buddy Croatoan can be blamed for requiring the Dads and Pastor Bedtime to embed the dance imperitive into hybrids and others. Now let me focus and I'll show how you can trigger dance combat later.*'

Then the surreal stepped up another notch. Cricket watched incredulously as Jack made a pose, bent over, hand on hat, then broke into dance. His was a tight shuffle with sharp moves and fast turns. Then he froze, looking at the big guy.

The big guy roared out loud, "Your moves are spirited, but nowhere in my demesne has a foe defeated the Leshy!" It was pronounced 'la-shy'. He was truly a group of smaller shapy-angled, spiny creatures and every one of them wore a rictus grin. And with that the battle was joined. The Leshy responded to Jack and struck a pose with arms jutting out and waving jazz hands. Then they did a moving rhythmic thing that made Cricket sick to watch, but it was beautiful to see. This guy was no human creation, was he? Cricket tabled his question as he and all the others in the room got caught up in the swirl of passion.

The Vittles made space for the new dancers and the new warring players came to the center to fight. Quotls, pixie-things, some kind of aquatic bear, several beautiful guys who looked like Legolas and his elf buddies. More joined by the moment. The original five hosts from the cantina went onto the dance floor, struck poses, and began to whirl and twist. But when Cricket saw the chicken woman dance something broke in him: surreality turned to celebration, watching the chicken lady cluck, strut and peck.

The power from Jack combined with smaller tributaries of force coming from several of the other dancers. It produced a quintessence of visual and audible delight. Some even began to sing in creative harmonies. These combined with the lights of the room and the place erupted with magic. Cricket felt it was Dungeons and Dragons come to life.

He had a thought and despite his athletic and impressive dancing, Jack answered that thought, *'Young sir, there is so much to learn. Quick primer for you. The others can hear this too. Non-humans learned aeons ago how to substitute dance and song for actual killing battle. Your Dads and others were influenced to encode that tendency into all their work: synths, hybrids and every kind of droid, drone, and bot, to some degree. That is why we see dancing in lieu of death. Someday Siva will tell you about your own programming. But for now, flow, feel and fight.'*

Why didn't Jack use this power earlier? And what about Siva?

'Fair question. It's because we aren't Vittles. Only Vittles could meet Vittles in a dance-off. Once I saw there were friendly Vittles here in the cantina, I knew we would be okay.'

Realization struck Cricket. The wafting Power somehow enabled him to sense that everyone there knew who he was; he felt it. Well, like his mother said, Cricket has never met a stranger. He didn't realize she was being literal.

Marna, Gracie Lou, and Cricket followed Jack's order and joined the dance. Friend and foe alike were whirling, gyrating, popping, flying and swinging in time to the fast music. Even Crucible stepped in and showed a break-dancing skill that put wonderment into the eyes of all around. Cricket found himself opposite the chicken lady; she smelled of heady mint and curry. It smelled wonderful. He matched her cluck for cluck and as the music wrapped up the dancers settled themselves into waiting and watching positions. What would come next?

The four-armed guy stepped out and spoke up, "Friends, thank you for welcoming our new friends and our liberators. Before we storm the Central Control, let me give you a song of thanks my ancestors used to sing in Tuva," apparently this guy was an old god with Mongolian roots; who could have known?

"Cricket, this is Old Long Johnson. He is the last of his people. Listen to his words." Jack was turning out to be a highly educated cosmopolitan guy! Johnson began. Tuvan throat singing was something few had heard. Johnson sang in English so his listeners could understand.

The 4-armed man glanced at Cricket, "Some nostalgia zealots gave me a name from a cat video from the 21st. Sadly, the name stuck. Some people have taste buds in the wrong orifice." Cricket tried to stifle his laugh; he quieted down as the singing began.

Today is about revival,
Let us all come awake.
To a promise for our world,
That none should forsake.

Life begins again,
when a Dandy seed takes flight.
Strongholds crumble,
and things go bump in the night.

Life begins again,
when a Dandy seed takes flight.
Rivers reverse their course,
and the day becomes night.

Life begins again,
when the torch gets passed.
Runnels of sweat glisten on brows,
and a fresh pair of feet carry on.

Hope comes alive,
when a new life breathes its first.
Nurturing and loving brings
the spark to germ,
and the germ fire.

Hope comes alive,
as life reaches out.

Pain retracts, and fear
consumes sparkles of innocence.

Life matures and grows,
as innocence swirls with experience.
Revival stirs the old,
and tills the soil.

Revolution brings stagnation,
like replaces like.
Revival is a gift that
life bequeaths to life.

As the darkness falls,
there is no end in sight,
all together, forever young,
in an expanse of love and light.

There was silence then roaring applause. Johnson had referenced the start of Cricket's speech at Goldstone and a shiver of omen washed over his body in a cool wave. Jack broadcast to all present, *'We need to go now folks. We'll work out introductions on the way. Johnson, will you take lead?'*

Johnson came alongside Cricket and had a word, "Young man, I am Tungak. I have been waiting for you."

"Hi Tungak, sir." Cricket was unsure how to respond. "Thanks, I guess." Then he scrunched his face a moment and wondered, "You got caught by the CENTER people to wait for me?"

"Ah, no. I am a research partner with the CSA; my lab once was adjacent to your Dads. I developed genetic strains which better integrated synthetic and biological components for people like your Dads' friend, Dr. Subramanian. My secret job was waiting for you or one of your three friends to arrive and assure you were kept safe."

"Tungak, why does everyone know who I am? I mean seriously, my life seems to be an open book to everyone but me."

"All four of you and your friends are the heralded ones; the children of Croatoan. Many of those you see have been waiting a long time for this moment."

"Hmm, I mean no disrespect, but that means exactly jack squat to me."

"All four of you will save our world." He said it like a no-duh statement. Tungak had a quirky smile and Cricket felt a sensation akin to the Power Jack wielded. It radiated off him. But the Power was shaded differently; it splashed against him, and he felt calmer, sharper and more aware. It felt kinda like getting a tune-up; he felt fresh! And just like that Tungak pulled Cricket along to lead the exodus from the cantina. At some level Cricket knew he had just been mickey'd into being non-argumentative.

The dancers knew it was time to leave; they made a run for the food that had been prepared, then the crowd rifled through all the storage bins, cupboards, refrigerator, and pantry. After the thorough ransacking, the strange mixture of friends left in a rush. The cantina music played a loud, snappy tune which faded as they made their way onto a main thoroughfare. Jack sidled up to Tungak; the 4-armed man had a beef with him, "Hey brother, you didn't even give us time for beer! You owe us a round when we get done here."

Jack smiled big. "Sure-thing mate, the first round is on me."

They ran, Vittles scuttled, and monsters small and large, humans, synths and hybrids and an old god made haste in an increasing flow of people headed toward the Central Hub. In short order Jack had managed to build them into a potent force. Cricket knew no one would believe him when he told the tale back home. Dancing Vittles? He shrugged and ran on, staring in wonder at the sights overhead from the corridor they entered. He could see the kilometer high ceiling, far above. Birds and flying creatures of all sorts were flocking and darting every which way. The smells and the sounds were overwhelming. Massive struts and arches supported and girded these caves of steel. Despite the austere steel construction, opportunistic plant and fungal life had adorned most surfaces with beauty and lush growth.

A yell was heard from Tungak, "Cricket's Crew!" Every mouth in their new army called back, "Cricket's Crew!" The hair stood up on the back of his neck. Cricket thought these people are my team! Oh gawd, we're in trouble now!

As he ran, Cricket's feel-good sensation faded, and he realized the four of us had been setup from the beginning. Something about us made us special, sure. But we never had a say in what was happening. We had been used all along. Then he realized that Wogs had mentioned things about the four of them: 'wouldn't it be cool if we were actually aliens', 'I had a dream we were heroes, raised to save the world, and 'Cricket, have you ever wanted to save the world and be a hero'? How did she know? If she did know, he knew why she kept it secret: to protect us.

The new Cricket's Crew was able to get them the last leg of the trip to the Central Hub without incident; it was a case of moving along in the open and appearing too busy to be bothered by people they passed.

Cricket was amazed, all the guards, troops and other military types took a look at them and assumed they belonged there. Are you kidding, they were an invasionary force! Then Cricket thought about what his father had said. He had told us act like you own the place and you can walk almost anywhere. He was a bit tipsy when he said that and got a stern look from his wife. But the principle seemed to be working glowingly in this instance. Cricket was amazed at the scale of LA:CENTER. He had toured Boeing's Paine Field plant, seeing where the Moon and Mars starships were manufactured. That place was huge. This was like a hundred of those, maybe more. The ceiling was often obscured but when he could see all the way up it was anywhere from 800 to 1500 meters in height, best guess. There was lighting in crazy places, and he could see towering mushrooms, vast trees, bigger than any he knew existed. Enormous lianas and vines adorned the heights, looking like inverted kelp, with blooms as big as houses with multi-colored fruiting bodies that sparkled with a grainy chatoyance. Much of the lighting seemed to come from the foliage. He expected austere, ugly structure, and he was amazed to see beauty and scents like a deep jungle, heady and sweet.

Tungak called out, "Cricket, this is the beautiful part of the CENTER. Your parents and the Dads are responsible for much of what you see here." That confused Cricket. He hadn't been aware his folks worked at a CENTER. He kept his mouth shut for the moment as they moved closer to the Hub.

Near the Hub the foliage changed, and a rank, uncomfortable smell filled the air. The growing things throughout the CENTER glowed with greens, blues, and yellows.

Beauty dimmed to decay as they got closer. Foliage took on a sullen red hue. There were pods and blossoms bigger than cars, shot through with red pulsing veins. The growths were pulpy and glowed and reflected with disease and black ichor. Cricket could see insects flitting around for the first time.

"Keep your distance from the Cacopods. They are sentient plantiform beings and they are always hungry," Jack warned. They looked stingey and bitey and mean spirited. Cricket was feeling increasingly uneasy.

On the private mind chat, Jack elaborated, *'My boy, this is a bad place. You need to know a couple things before we enter the Hub. I was told by the General the Hub is operated by a fellow calling himself the Hierophant. He is apparently the architect of all you see here. Keep your head on a swivel from here forward and if I say run, you do so without question.'* Jack was only talking to Cricket. Why was he being so guarded?

Cricket tried to answer back, *'Hey Jack, was I created in a test tube?'*

Jack paused, then he made eye contact and answered, *'You know the answer.'*

Cricket rolled that around for a moment then asked, *'How many people contributed to create us. Who are my family?'*

'Now is not the time. It's a very long tale. I'll tell you this: you are my son as much as your parents,

and I am so proud of you. I am truly sorry if this disappoints you, my boy.' Jack was sincere as they continued to move past stinky foliage toward the Hub entrance. It smelled even worse than Jack! Next thing Jack knew, Cricket was hugging him, smell, and all. Cricket was surprised to be hugged back. He looked up and Jack spoke aloud. Cricket knew he should have been pissed at his folks, but his relief at finally understanding at least some of the truth overrode his anger.

"My son, you have a large family and every one of us loves you. Perhaps view it as I saw it when we began planning for your arrival. You and Kip, Binky and Wogs are the highest expression of our love. And your naïve optimism will be the attitude that saves us all."

Cricket had never heard Jack speak so earnestly. The team slowed momentarily to watch. Marna and Gracie patted Cricket's shoulders. Jack finally looked about and gave an it's okay nod to those who watched.

A quiet voice intruded, "Apologies to interrupt. Time is of the essence right now. The Hierophant knows we are here, and things are about to get messy."

Tungak had sympathetic eyes and a soft grandpa voice. Feelings aside, it was time to get the job done. Cricket steeled himself and soldiered on.

Jack whispered, "Stay frosty kids. Stuff's about to light up."

The building in front of them was a concrete and steel, ugly block which towered high toward the ceiling far above. The walkway forward led to a large shiny steel door, with a big handle. The whole block was rundown and messy, except for the door. Tungak had the team stand way back in the event of a warm welcome. He wasn't wrong. The moment he pulled the handle on the door, part of the wall erupted outward in an explosion. Shaped charges blew specific parts of the wall into rocky shrapnel and peppered the area with deadly metal and rock chunks. Some of those chunks hit Tungak and the others who were close by. A moment later gunfire erupted from the sides, and they were caught in the middle of the crossfire.

"Time to go, boy!" Jack grabbed Gracie and Cricket, propelling them at superhuman speed, past the broken wall, past the rubble inside and down a hallway to escape the bullets. Jack was thinking to himself how stupid it was to put Cricket in harm's way so early in the game. Stupid, stupid! He should have pushed back against using any of the kids in the LA:CENTER reclamation. Too late now. Great job Jack!

The gunfire kept up but Marna and handful of Vittles and monsters made it to the hallway. Marna yelled, "It's a bloody mess out there. We need to keep moving!" Marna had the hard look of a soldier keeping to the task, counting the cost later. Cricket saw that and bucked up, doing the same. They moved down the hallway and Jack took them through one of the many big doors on the right.

"On our left are the security folks. We need to go the other way." He kept them moving, knowing the security cameras were going to bring more trouble soon. Jack knew his powers were dwindling; he'd been too quick to use them over the last day. He decided to try something anyway. Concentrating, he found all the security cameras, pressure sensitive devices and other such things and sent a large push. A pulse radiated out and shorted out many of the devices. He hoped it was enough to give them a speed advantage for the next few minutes. He could feel the weight of the Hierophant beating on the air and there was another presence as well. The heaviness on the air was Cloud generated. He knew Cricket could feel it too. And they were headed right toward it.

The gunfire receded behind as Jack took them on a circuitous path, up flights of stairs and vast rampways. Past labs and gardens, offices and cubicles, Jack kept up a breakneck pace. No one spoke as they ran and Cricket wasn't sure he could keep up. Ten minutes in, they arrived at an innocuous door, made of some kind of wood. Surrounding the door were long stringy plants, glowing red-tinged, with thorns and flowers in the shape of hungry dinner-plate sized mouths. The mouths had needle-sharp teeth. Open wide and seeming to smile, they knew that food was close. Cricket didn't feel like being food for Audrey and her friends. Feed me, Seymour! It looked like the entrance to Jack the Ripper's secret garden.

"I'll run to the corner, pick you up some nice ground meat. How about that?" Cricket whispered to himself, but the flowers heard him. They definitely were smiling now. He thought, uh oh, did they understand me? It was time to move along!

It was then Cricket felt a presence from beyond the door that grew in intensity as he got closer. It struck fear deep into him. He knew just on the other side was what they had come for. And he also knew that it was waiting for them. They avoided the toothy plants and Jack gave a nod; he told them to stay back and slowly cracked the door open. Fear peaked, then passed. Nothing blew up, there were no bullets, no yelling.

But there was a voice, "Come in friends, we have been expecting you."

A wave of cool and calm emotion emanated from the room beyond the door. Cricket felt he was coming home. Wait, what? Come into my den, said the spider to the fly. Insert creepy vibe here.

As Jack opened the door he saw their nemeses. The room was dome shaped with a high arched ceiling. It was about 40 meters in diameter filled with long hanging flora descending from a hole in the center of the ceiling. A smell of vomit, infection and unwashed bodies assailed them. Cricket recognized the dangly things as parts of a mushroom network, but instead of smelling clean and looking healthy, these had a sickened pallor, wounds like pustules and small blooms that reminded Cricket of the snakes on Medusa's head. The room now seethed with menace, resuming the foreboding they had felt from outside. Cricket could sense power emanating from the skinny dwarfish guy in the dirty lab coat.

"Okay, the jig is up. You caught us. Are you going to take us in for questioning, officer?" Lab coat man was smiling and enjoying his sarcasm. Cricket got the sneaking suspicion they were in way over their heads. There was a central circular table encircling a huge blob of a living creature into which hundreds of mushroom vines and cables descended and entered. Whatever the thing was it was covered with eyeballs. The thing was pale green, warty, and had slick, reflective skin. The blob was covered in slime, and it was the source of the rotten smell in the room.

"Oh Cricket, my young friend! It is good to finally meet you. I am thankful our dear comrade Jack has brought you by for a visit. But I don't see the other kids," at this he peered around like there might be people hiding nearby.

"Well, never the mind, one will do," Lab coat man focused on Cricket with gimlet eyes.

Jack moved to stand in front of Cricket, but a force grabbed hold of him and slammed him to the wall on the left. It appeared Jack couldn't break free. Wasn't Jack supposed to be one of the most powerful guys around? This Hierophant was no joke.

"Tsk tsk, Jack. You mustn't interfere with polite conversation. Now…" The Hierophant straightened his dirty lab jacket. The man had long stringy brown hair that flopped over his face as he swung his head in emphasis to his words. He was more jittery than Binky and in constant motion.

"Allow me to make introductions. I am Severus, known to most as the Hierophant," he took a deep bow. As he righted himself, he flopped his oily mop back with a jerk of his head.

"And this is my brother-in-eyes, Augie." A slurping sound came from the mass of flesh with eyeballs.

"Yes, Augie, they all know your real name. My friend here wants to make sure you know his real name is Argus." Then the Hierophant looked at the flesh mound and patted the slick skin lovingly.

"But that was then, and now you work for me, Augie." The noises Augie made sounded like the last few sucks on a straw before the milkshake is all gone. Cricket figured it was language but had no idea what any of the sounds meant. With a sidelong glance it appeared Jack knew what Augie was saying; he was nodding.

The flesh mound was putting off putrid smells and a dark brown aura of some kind. At the points where the rhizomes, mycelia, cables and other equipment plugged into Augie's body, weeping flows of pus oozed from suppurating sores. The sores looked angry and painful. Rivulets of the thick white fluid ran down to the floor and joined in mass flow around the floor's refuse to a drain at the edge of the room. Papers and unidentifiable garbage littered the floor in mounds; pus merged with crumpled papers to form pools of septic horror. Cricket could see narrow trails through the refuse where the Hierophant probably walked most often. There was a shabby bed in the corner. This is where the Hierophant lived.

It was clear as the Hierophant spoke, that Augie feared him. Every time he gestured near Augie, the creature twitched. That pissed Cricket off and, in that moment, he began to calculate how to get rid of this abusive old man. Cricket noticed Jack was suddenly free to move again and the Hierophant waved him back over to stand with Cricket.

Cricket whispered, "Jack, this room smells worse than you." Jack quirked a momentary smile.

"So, Mr. Hierophant, I am not actually sure why I am here. Are we here to rescue you and Mr. Aug – uh, Augie?" Cricket realized he didn't know their objective other than shut down the monitoring and telemetry and open the cages of those being held captive. What did these two have to do with the mission?

"Doctor, not Mister and you can call me Hierophant. We're all friends here." The Hierophant smiled and indicated chairs for everyone to sit. It was then Cricket noticed the door had closed and none of their Vittles or other monsters had come in. Oops, so much for the backup team.

The chairs were rickety and covered in dust and other things best not seen too close. Cricket used his sleeve to clean off his seat and realized the others were already seated and waiting. Marna and Gracie Lou looked impatient. Jack had his usual clam cool drawn about him.

'Alright boy, relax for a moment. Do nothing until I give the word.' What was Jack planning?

"Now let me tell you a story. You see, I come from a time long before there were humans and cities and cars and Internet. It was a simpler time. I grew up in a fishing village where ice would lock us in each winter, in the north Atlantic. My family and my children were carefree at the time. Life was simple and we lived near a vast woods. Between the woods and the sea, all our needs were well met.

"Seasons passed and as my children grew up, we moved around. We enjoyed the nomadic life, sometimes following the herds for food, other times settling down to fish. We lived on the open planes, on the shore, and other times in the high mountains. As civilization expanded, everything was corrupted by humans and their territorial squabbles. Many years passed and my children had children and in-turn, they had children, and so on. Others joined us and our tribe grew to be numbered in the 1000s. Back then I was known as Cern and sometime later they called me Cernunnos. They made me a god and for a time our people were safe. One day a traveler stayed with us. He was human, but he was also a god. His name was Rud and before he left us, he warned that humans were a danger to us and to be careful.

Then the humans came. And let me tell you, as one of the few gods remaining in the world, other gods tell tales which start with the same tragic phrase: '…and then the humans came'." Cricket thought about Lugh and Morrigan.

The Hierophant became more animated and warmed to his tale. Marna gave a nod to Jack. She scooched her chair closer to him, also bringing her closer to the Hierophant.

"Hey kid where are you going? Oh, I see. Coming closer, yes," The Hierophant smiled as he felt his audience attending to his story.

"I don't get an attentive crowd very often. Thank you for humoring a sad old god. The security people laugh at me when I tell them my tales. They think me a pathetic old dotard." He laid a hand on Cricket's shoulder, and it was at that moment that he felt a deep sadness from the Hierophant. The old god nodded and knew Cricket felt his pain. Cricket wondered why they had to be enemies. Then he looked at Augie and the purulent disaster throughout the room and all doubt faded away. Villains are not born but made. This fellow had been through uncounted years of suffering and loss and allowed it to taint and embitter his very being. Cricket wondered if he knew his life was most probably about to end; that, or he was about to end them if they failed.

Jack had a wistful upturn of his mouth, seeming to enjoy something which escaped everyone else's notice. But Jack knew. The four kids had been designed similar to the other hybrids with a genetic predisposition to finding non-violent means to resolving conflict. The trick was that the four radiated this attitude and nearby Cloud-sensitives responded. The

Hierophant was responding, and Jack realized that bringing the kids to the CENTER exodus was the right choice after all.

"Young man, we are not enemies. I sense your concern. Thank you for that. It has been more years than I can count since anyone showed me concern. Let me continue my story so you can understand the why of things, ok?"

"When the humans came, we thought them bright-eyed and wondrous beings, so full of eagerness and fire. We took them in and taught them how to live, how to hunt, how to preserve the land and how to be kindly stewards of the world around them." At this the Hierophant stopped and considered something. After a moment, he shook awake from his reverie and continued.

"For a many years they were our new children and we loved them and cared for them. When the Sky People came, we showed them our new friends, the humans. It was then the Sky People warned us to cast the humans out, that they were a threat to everything we cared about. We thanked them but we kept the humans with us. They were a part of us by then. The Sky People never returned and not many years later the trouble started. It began with disputes about who owned what land. We had been given a new name the Tuathan or Tuath Dé. I guess that is what started it. From then on, we were their gods, the ones who could fix all their problems and we were no longer just friends. Problems blossomed and when we intervened our people bled and died. After a time, the humans became cruel toward us. Eventually we moved away but they followed, seeking more help, more insights, and more treasures from their gods. Once we weren't willing to play their game, they hunted us. As a god I had powers to heal and to harm. I used my powers to harm for the first time and killed every rampaging human who set foot on our land. But there were too many and after most of our people lay dead, I ran away with what remained of my family. In time, all my family died because they didn't have the damnable immortal gene that kept me youthful."

The Hierophant hung his head momentarily, then looked up, "But wherever I went, humans would find me again. To stay alive, I had to become or at least appear like one of them. You see, humans kill anything that isn't them. And they kill each other. They are cruel, spiteful, and greedy. I know you are here today to defeat the great evil that keeps thousands of test subjects captive at the CENTER. But the Vor are your true enemy, and they are already among you, unseen. You see the Vor taught us how to do what we do now. And I knew they were using us to kill you…eventually all humans. I relished the opportunity to strike back at my true enemies: you. So, I allowed the Vor to inhabit hundreds of test subjects. You humans had no idea I was planting the seeds of your demise and it felt good. Vengeance was sweet.

But now, what do I do? I could let you kill me and kill poor Argus and it would be all over. Cricket…" The Hierophant braced himself against the console behind him. Jack gave a curt head jerk; not yet.

Cricket was waiting for the signal to follow Jack with whatever he planned. The old man got his wits about him, looked at his audience and gave a weary smile. It was odd how he suddenly went from energetic evil-scientist to a bent old man. What happened just now?

He continued, "I am tired and old. I think it is time." The Hierophant deflated before their eyes. The formidable heavy presence and power vanished from the room. Cricket could breathe normally again. Up to that point he hadn't realized the stifling pressure he was under. The lights in the room seemed brighter and the sense of threat was gone. Cricket had never been a huggy type of guy. He was more surprised than anyone when he stood and walked to the old god, embracing him. He felt him go suddenly rigid. It was then he saw Jack's hands on both sides of the Hierophant's neck and an intent look on his face. Jack had done something. His eyes went wide, then the old god began to slump.

His last telepathic words softly caressed Cricket's mind. *'Young man, remember us. We loved you first.'*

Cricket fell back and yelled as he felt the Hierophant's life drain away. He lay on the floor for moments, his body tense. Jack arranged the still form so he appeared to be sleeping. Cricket stood stock still, not sure how he felt. Jack faced Cricket.

"Buddy, look at me. Hey, Cricket, look at old Jack…" he looked up through bitter eyes.

"You gave Cern the relief he had longed for. Okay?" Cricket nodded, snuffling his runny nose. "This was the kindest way for him to go. He had become the picture of his enemy and was as much a villain to himself as to anyone else. He wanted out. You gave him a graceful way to go. Be thankful. It could have gone much worse."

Then a slopping sound came from behind them. They all got to work dismantling the table surrounding Argus. They were careful not to injure the obese old god. After all the tables were removed, Jack started assessing all the connections surgically attached to Argus.

'So much pain, so long. Make it stop.' Argus could only speak with his mind; he was unable to do much else. He had been able to operate and manage the LA:CENTER monitoring and telemetry, but as the Hierophant died the compulsion to continue that work vanished. They could see electrical and data cables inserted into his bloated body. It was from these points that infection had run most rampant with sores dripping pus and blood. Argus had been dying for years but his resilient immortal body miraculously kept him alive.

"Argus what do you want us to do?" Jack asked this out loud and telepathically.

'Too late for me; so much pain. Time to die.'

'You may want to leave the room while I do this.' Jack was resigned.

'Please. So lonely. Stay.' Sadness thrummed out over the æthyr.

"Jack, I will stay." Cricket now touched the old god and felt the depth of his being. The skin was slimy, but Cricket didn't mind. As he touched Argus' skin, something froze Cricket. A sudden rush of power (information? memories?) splashed through him. It took the barest of moments and Jack seemed unaware of what had happened. Cricket steadied himself against the old god and shook his head, unsure what was going on.

Argus' pudgy mouths smiled weakly, *'For you, friend Cricket. Remember.'* Cricket had no idea what that meant.

Jack gently removed Cricket's hands and sent some kind of force into Argus and the body jerked; every mouth cried out. His body held tension then deflated like a balloon. Cricket caught a fragment of the force backwash from Argus' death and stumbled to the floor.

Jack broadspoke, *'Thus passes the eldest of us.'* For a moment Jack could feel Siva and other Elders in his mind, grieving the moment and paying respects. One tiny voice echoed, "… *until next time.'*

LA:CENTER systems went haywire after that. As Argus died, he released and deactivated all locks, restraints, cameras, slaved droids, and machines; every security computer and all non-sentient AIs were switched off. Sirens and alarms went off everywhere and died as quickly as they began. Silence.

Jack knew my cell door was one amongst thousands, just opened, *'Hey Kip, this is Jack. Best you toddle yourself to the nearest exit. Get going kid!"*

Jack sensed I was already on the move toward freedom. It was time for them to leave, too. The big wooden door burst open and in came the cavalry, just in time to leave.

"Hey Cricket. Your friend Kip is headed for an exit. We should be doing the same!"

Cricket gave out a whoop!

June 2253 – Cricket @ LA:CENTER emerging onto north tarmac

Cricket and his crew were on the run, dodging fire and gathering a contingent of increasing size of others seeking escape. The distance was like running from Lake Stevens to Everett. They had kilometers to go! A wave of escapees was trailing them. There were creatures on two legs, four legs and more. He could see humans, sort-of humans, synths, bots, droids and hybrids. It was like the United Nations and a zoo got busy and had a jillion babies. Most were scared, some were laughing and a few seethed with menace. The flood of beings had one thing in mind: escape.

Cricket figured other mass movements were happening around the CENTER. Every freshet, rivulet and stream joined the river of escapees down the wide interior thoroughfares. There were even CENTER staff and security folks who abandoned their work and joined the outmigration. But there were some security people who still manned posts, taking pot shots and attacking with batons. It went poorly for them. They were few in number and the escapees were many. Everyone was on the move and Cricket looked up into the distance to see a set of massive doors looming far away. That was their escape. Thanks to Augie, the doors were wide open.

Forward motion came to a halt as they encountered a press of people ahead. "Uh Jack, this doesn't look good." Cricket couldn't see what was causing the traffic jam. They stood around for a couple minutes then Jack swung into action.

"Okay kiddoes, stay here and I'll find out our next move." It became obvious why he got the name Spring-heeled Jack. He leaped high to land atop a wall to their left and ran along the edge until he disappeared from view.

"Dude jumped like 10 meters! Hey Gracie, if I give you a boost, can you see what's holding us up?"

Then Marna's voice came from a window ledge above. "Hey guys, no one is moving ahead as far as I'm able to see. And now we are blocked from behind too." She climbed through the window and disappeared. They waited. And waited. Something bashed into Cricket from behind and his arm lit up like a abused guitar. He rubbed it, impatient to get moving. There were too many, too close to see what had happened.

He quipped a dad joke, "Gracie, what do you get when you put a funny bone on simmer?" He paused for effect while she gave him a confused look, "…a laughing-stock!" It landed with a thud, she didn't understand. He quickly went back to looking for a way forward, still massaging his arm.

A group of Vittles had taken out dice from who knows where and began playing a game on the floor. There were dog-sized snails with dozens of eyestalks which made farty sounds as they wobbled and gestured. Moving with quick spurts, they scurried on the floor and made little leaps into the air. The snails made whoosh sounds as hidden gas propellant flung them about. He heard someone call them Peopods. They were designed to look cute so as to innocently sneak up on people, sit their slobby pseudopod over their head and extract memories. Cricket decided they were only cute from a distance.

Another bouncy group of small hybrids looked like Boston Terriers with four prehensile arms sprouting out of their backs. Several even had wings. They played games of smacking each other at which they excelled. They would link arms at times and use them to throw each other into the air. The winged ones would dive and swoop in an aerial ballet. Gracie said they were called Roseys; every single one of them answered to the name Rosey. All at once the group of Roseys got the zoomies. It was mayhem, cute mayhem.

The floor was a circus of activity. Gracie pointed out a group of over-muscular rabbits she called Pudus. They jumped and bounded onto walls, people, and each other. Most folks tried to slap them down and little brawls ensued here and there. Furry men, scarcely a half-meter tall sat in circles sharpening bits of metal into shivs. Someone said they were Brownies. They acted grumpy and crunchy, very ill-tempered. Cricket asked if they could sharpen his Bowie knife. One of the Brownies was obliging. Gracie said they were electricians, most of them. They could get into tight places to work on wiring and such. Cricket's new friend, Grumpy gave the wicked sharp Bowie knife back to Cricket; he thanked the small man and stepped to a safe distance.

Suddenly a group of bouncing mopheads the size of basketballs was competing with the Peopods and Roseys for being the most annoying.

One of the Brownies yelled, "Get this stupid Sparkler off me. Right fewkin now!" Two other Brownies tossed the flailing shower scrubby toward a group of Vittles. A new battle ensued.

Sparklers spun around a bunch and threw off sparks, hence the name. Sometimes a spark would catch one of the other hybrids and a kerfuffle would start Hybrids and humans paced around impatiently. Most of the flying creatures had vanished, having flown on ahead of the traffic jam.

Gracie and Cricket huddled in an alcove, waiting on Jack. "Can I ask you something?" Gracie Lou had that pert smirk of hers.

"Sure." Cricket was distracted, looking after where Marna went.

"How did you get the name Cricket?"

He huffed a brief laugh and began. "When I was 6 my parents took me on our yearly Summer retreat to our cabin. It was a work party day and the Dads, and Binky and Wogs parents were helping dig a bunker. None of the other kids were there so I was left to get into my own mischief. I watched everyone digging, creating a pile of soil, and decided to make the mound my own personal volcano. As the soil piled higher the caldera grew deeper, and I was Godzilla standing in the middle. More soil piled and I had my own little soily playpen. I heard a chirrup and then felt something land on my head. I put my hand up top and felt something land on my fingers. I saw a greenish-brown cricket. It may have actually been a grasshopper, but to me it was my new Cricket friend. I named him Cricket and I had him as a pet for the whole Summer. My mother built a small cage for him, and I kept his feeding dish full of fruits and veggies..

All Summer as we went to and from our cabin and home, Cricket went with me. Then when the weather cooled, we stayed at home so I could go back to school. I showed him off in class and his cage would sit next to the other show-and-tell pets. I was so proud. But one day back home I woke up and Cricket was lying still with his jaws still biting into a piece of apple. He had died during the night attacking his favorite food. I buried him in our back yard and had a little ceremony for him. My mother used his cage to make a casket and stood quietly as I tumped soil into the hole. My Dad asked how I would like to remember my friend. My folks gave me time alone to work through the loss, but it didn't take long to come to a decision. I posted a drawing on my bedroom door that evening that said Cricket's Room with a hand-drawn rendition of my friend. The next morning my Mom made pancakes and spelled out Cricket on the top pancake. From then on, they started calling me Cricket. I didn't tell them until years later that I had meant that my friend Cricket still lived (in spirit) in my room. I hadn't planned to take that as my name. By then the name had stuck and I thought it a fitting remembrance of my best friend.

Gracie Lou slipped her fingers into Cricket's hand, and he nodded at her. Gracie was touched. A noise came from above and Marna jumped down from the window ledge.

"It looks like Jack is doing something big, way over there," she pointed around the left corner of the corridor junction ahead of them. Just as her arm dropped, they felt more than heard an explosion that made a whump sound and rocked the walls around them. The shockwave washed over them and toppled some people to the ground, sending flying folk scattering.

"I think he just blew up a gate!" Marna had to yell over the sudden increase of volume. The press of people began to move forward.

Suddenly, a sweating Jack landed in a dramatic crouch.

He spoke, "There are big gates between the various Power areas in the CENTER. One of them is now in little bitty pieces!" That got a chuckle.

They moved forward with the crowd. Next, they rounded a corner into a huge thoroughfare, big enough to fit a super-highway from the 20th. Smoking ruins ahead were still sending curls and sparks toward the ceiling. Cricket noticed the smoke moved in curious ways as it ascended, getting caught up in several streams of air flow. A light rainstorm began as they approached the destroyed gate. There were clunky FireDrones hosing down the various debris as they and thousands of others streamed through and past the wreckage. Jack had them take a side corridor, away from the press of the madding crowd. The next corridor was narrow with few doors.

"Come on you laze-abouts! Let's see if I can find us a faster route!" Jack laughed and seemed to be enjoying himself. His attitude had improved since he had his explosive adventure. The new hallway smelled like ammonia and solvent. It was repellent, but Cricket thought that any smell was better than the pustulent control room of the CENTER. Next, Jack navigated them into a larger hallway, not quite as big as the thoroughfare from a few minutes ago. The foot traffic was light, but there were more winged creatures: some were Quotls, others were variants on birds, harpies, bats and even flying brains with tentacles eating security guards with toothy maws. A wounded security guy was sitting against a wall being helped by two hybrids in orange 'test subject' jumpsuits. Had enemies become friends? Cricket knew regular humans would probably have left the guy to die or worse. Even vicious hybrids were behaving in a civil manner, except for the flying brains.

As he ran, Cricket remembered one of his early lessons in woodsmanship. His father had taken them to Big Bend to camp and hike Emory Peak. On the third day Cricket had wandered a couple miles from camp, not far from Lost Mine Peak. He was rock hunting and also looking for small game for the evening's dinner. Cricket adjusted the strap of his .410 to the other shoulder and walked slowly on. A whiff of smoke hit his nose. In a matter of a minute the smoke became choking and thick. Looking down the draw, Cricket could see flames driven his way by whipping winds. Then came the animals. Deer were the first, running by swiftly. Then others, Javelina, Rabbits, Coyote, and a Bobcat. Cricket took the hint and ran. He was afraid and his lungs burned from the smoke; it was getting thicker and harder to see each passing moment.

He made his way back around the other side of Emory Peak and dragged himself into camp, dusty, smoky and face streaked with sweat and grime. The smoke was rising high, and the sky was turning ruddy, and the sun began to dim. His mother tended to him, and his father came back at a jog. His Dad set to packing them up to make a quick exit from the park. As they drove away, Cricket could see the columns of smoke whorled by winds and the whole park ablaze. He asked his father about why the predators would run side-by-side with natural prey and not attack.

He told his son that animals tended to focus on one thing at a time. The fire was a threat to all life and those predators were physiologically unable to pay attention to hunger while something was trying to kill them. He told Cricket that humans behaved much the same way. Cricket recognized the same thing was happening at the CENTER. The tide of humans and others was single-minded. They were no longer acting the parts they played: security guard, scientist, test subject, whatever. Everyone was now in one category. Escapee. Mostly. Down a hallway there was gunfire, and a pitched battle was underway between a group of security guards and a variety of hybrids. It looked nasty and Jack urged them on, leaving the blood and mayhem behind.

Cricket thought of something. With the security measures now inactive the local Online access should be wide open. Cricket used his pad to ask General Olonana for instructions. When the General answered it was obvious he was in the middle of a firefight and couldn't talk for long.

"Cricket, good to hear from you. What's your current position and status?"

"Sir, we have lost some of our team, but we are still making our way to one of the large exits." Jack yelled something at Cricket.

"Jack said we just busted Hadrian's Gate and are about half a klick from North Main, the biggest exit."

"Good ole' Jack! Let him know there are running firefights all over the place outside. When you get to the entrance stay put. I will have a ship meet you. Understood?" He could hear gunfire in the background and the General said something, but his signal went dead.

"Jack!"

"I hear ya, ma boy. Is the General ready for us?"

"Yeah, about that. He said he'd have a ship waiting for us and to stay put at the entrance."

"Stars and gardens! Staying put in the line of fire was not my plan." Jack continued to navigate them around slower people.

A skinny human wearing what appeared to be a diaper came running right at Cricket. His voice was high and creaky with vocal fry.

"Hey, you. Yo, listen here! I can see you got the skeeze, but there ain't no queefing on the run. Ya gotta help me cause there's a prestidigious gang of smooth toods gonna get gacked up on whoop chicken if we don't scuttle-hump to the resuscue."

Cricket came full stop. It sounded like English words but then not really. The guy said his name was Cooter Crawdaddy and he needed 'char-fizzle to open the lighting crew'. Cricket decided this was too weird to pass up. Jack looked back moments later to see Cricket chasing the skinny guy down a side hallway. He huffed frustration and ran after the boy.

They arrived at a loading bay where a gathering of neon-dressed people was either dancing or having a group seizure. Their costumes were bright and boasted feathers, ribbons, and other colorful things. They were circling around a forklift that had partially landed on a large dog which was covered in some kind of goopy substance. The dog let out a pained howl and the people danced faster. No one seemed to be dealing with the injured dog. He figured these were test subjects who were still outta their minds. Skinny dude was frantic, "Yo, ya can't yanky the wanky unless you help the hot dog."

Cricket nodded obliquely and moved toward the forklift. The others stepped aside; Cricket saw a piece of lumber and with Jack's help wedged it as a lever under the lift. Gracie and Marna pulled the dog out. It took a big breath and didn't howl.

Instead, it spoke, "Well thank you friends for that. This little rabble needed my help, and I screwed up with the forklift and boom I was trapped." The dog held out a paw that was a hand; a fuzzy hand. "The name is Snotsydog and it's a right pleasure to meet you." The dog had a funny accent. Cricket was ready to leave.

"Welly, well, chap, perhaps I can bring my loony bin with me and follow you to the exit?" The dog was polite too.

Jack was already leading the crew out and yelled back, "Come long little doggie!" Jack pronounced it 'doagie'. Laughter. The people running behind Snotsydog were having traction problems with his goopy trail. The skinny guy wasn't faring any better, and he was spouting his word salad on the run. As they joined a main flow of escapees the Peopods nearby clustered around the dog. It seemed snot called to slime.

They neared the gigantic double doors which had been thrown wide. The pew, pew of small arms fire could be heard but it was scant and far away. All looked clear. An explosion behind them collapsed a portion of the kilometer high ceiling. Sunlight shone through the dust and falling debris.

"That was the perimeter control center! Score one for the good guys! Cricket, call the General now." Jack was keeping a lookout as Cricket used his pad. Beings and creatures flowed steadily past as Cricket's crew halted to the side. They hunkered down just next to an abandoned guard station.

He pinged Vagabond again. The General's voice boomed out of his pad, "Bivouac your folks on the north side on the tarmac and try to stay under cover. Olonana, out." Guess there was no ship coming for them.

With that the contact went dead and the hike in the hot sun began. A pitched air battle was underway, and the CENTER gun emplacements were pouring out leaden death. They ran to hide behind downed ships and vehicles, trying to stay under cover on the way to the north end. As they reached the edge of the tarmac the air battle brought the fight overhead. Finally, two corvettes hovered close over Cricket's crew. They provided a wide shield from the barrage of fire which rained down from hundreds of drones and aerial droids. Kamikaze Droids slammed into the bright shield; blue and pink-tinged tracery showed the two hemispherical shield domes projected for a hundred meters above them. Hundreds of escaping prisoners sought shelter under the shields. Other former prisoners met force with force, picking up discarded guns and venting their frustration. A massive aerial force of Quotls spat various liquids and tail-slapped hundreds of flying droids and drones. A half dozen 4-meter-tall giants weighed in on the battle. They threw rocks and anything not tied down into the air, taking down small, manned craft with explosive and spectacular success. The toll was high on the lives of the combatants and Cricket could see craft and drones of all kinds raining down and littering the ground. Not all of those fallen were dead yet. The sky was a bright and a fast flurry of weaving forces. A dark cloud flowed from place to place no more than 50 meters off the ground and everything it touched fell to pieces. When the dark cloud briefly came under the shields, they could see thousands (millions?) of MicroDrones and MicroBots moving in tight formation like a vast flock of birds.

"Incoming!" a loud voice hammered the air and help came to those who waited. That help was in the shape of Lugh, looking like a mini-me version of Thor and his bodyguard, Lucy. He laughed, shaking the ground around like an earthquake. Massive electrical arcs came from his hands and the last of the enemy manned craft plummeted to the ground. Lucy hovered in the sky above them and glowed with an intense yellow and had some kind of whip which she used to snap long swathes of enemy drones from the sky. Her eyes glowed like diamonds.'

A hail of rounds hit the shields and with that the CENTER gun emplacements had found them. A voice came over the PA from one of the Corvettes, "Hey guys, we won't be able to hold these shields for long under sustained fire. Suggest you start planning a better place to hide." The bullets were hitting so heavily the air darkened above the shields. Cricket could smell a burning odor coming from the Corvettes; he suspected whatever made the shields work was quickly burning out.

Mighty Mouse sang above the din, "Here we come to save the day!" A cheerful voice called, and down came three SkyCycles with a colorful trio of heroes. Not Mighty Mouse.

"Cricket, these are some of the old gods, be careful to not piss them off; they're on our side for the moment." When Jack sounded concerned, Cricket knew to pay attention.

"Jack, what are old gods? Are they gods? I don't get it." Cricket sent.

"My boy there's nothing mysterious about it. You know humans weren't the only sentient beings to have called the Earth home. These came before you and a few of them were born with massive Cloud powers…thus they were labeled gods. Some were the original test subjects for the alien scientists. Never mention that to them though; it gets their ire up."

"But where have they been all this time?"

"My boy. Surely you know how vicious humans are. Even mighty old gods must hide and carefully go incognito if they want to stay on this side of the dirt patch. You humans are a brutal and unforgiving lot, especially when you don't understand something." Yep, Cricket knew.

So, were all the various mythologies based in fact? Cricket thought about the Greek gods and was less than impressed. "Some of those old gods are real drama queens." Jack gave a short jerk of his head which meant 'never say that out loud'.

A voice boomed, "Where is Cricket?" the trio dismounted and walked toward them. "Ah, friend Jack, good to see you hale and hearty! And here I thought you would sod this whole affair for a lark when the going got tough. What was I thinking?" Jack hugged the lead fellow. They both had British accents.

"Cricket, allow me to introduce Artie, Kris and Mike," Jack looked at the trio and clearly made a mental pivot. "So, my apologies. Those are their incognito names, let me try again. Cricket, these are our esteemed friends King Arthur, Krishna, and the Monkey King. They have graciously offered to pluck our collective butts from impending doom." Jack was being uncharacteristically sincere in public. These guys must be dangerous.

Cricket paused, unsure of how he was supposed to respond. *'Take a bow and be polite. Like right now!'* Jack was freaking Cricket out more than these new powerful guests.

His anxiety grew as he bowed and greeted the newcomers, "King Arthur, it is an honor. And I have no idea how to address royalty. My apologies." In a moment King Arthur went from haughty and borderline offended to all-smiles and embracing Cricket in a big hug.

"Cricket, please meet my dear comrade-in-arms, Krishna." Cricket wasn't sure who Krishna was, but his thoughts gave him away.

"Ah Cricket, one of the Four. We are family, young man, be at ease and forgive old beings their vain conceits." Krishna sent a side message to Cricket, *'Hey friend, Arthur has a lot of bluster, but he means well. Jack and I and some others helped your Dads not long ago; many of us old gods helped them at the request of Croatoan. We're here to help you now. Arthur is unaware of some of what I'm telling you, but Jack, Mike and I are your family as much as anyone is. Please call us Art and Mike and I am Kris."*

Another voice broke in, *'Kris is right, we are here for you, little friend.'* Cricket swore he heard a giggle. Mike laid a hand on Cricket's shoulder. *'I am sorry for this, especially since Argus just Shared with you so recently.'* Both Kris and Mike appeared to give a hearty embrace to Cricket when really, they were holding him still and kept him standing as they fed into him the same kind of stuff Argus had earlier. They called it Sharing, though it was unclear what was being shared. Cricket convulsed, his nose and eyes bled, and he blacked out as Jack touched him and gave him the relief of momentary oblivion. As Cricket went unconscious, they lowered him gently to the ground. At that moment one of the shields failed and Krishna held up a hand, replacing the Corvette's shield with one of his own making. A bright yellow field appeared, and incoming bullets no longer peppered the area. Instead, it was as if all the rounds received new instructions: return to sender. Within moments the gun emplacements stopped firing as their own bullets returned to rain their own fire in explosive glory. Fiery balls silently appeared, followed moments later by compression waves and an explosive roar. The whole time Kris and Mike never took their eyes off Cricket.

'Young man, you are our shining hope. We love you. When the time comes, we know you will be brave as you fight for us,' Mike spoke with earnest. Jack was surprised at the turn of events. Croatoan had never said anything about Sharing with any of the Four. The original plan was much more subtle, and this was definitely not subtle. Jack felt Cricket's condition and knew he would be okay. He just needed peace and quiet and time to rest.

The three old gods stood and greeted everyone else, shaking hands with Marna and Gracie and garnering all the attention their egos required. With the closest gun emplacements now silent and Cricket comatose, they hopped on their SkyCycles and headed toward the CENTER. The fight overhead lightened up significantly, and now they could hear the distant battle as huge explosions echoed from other parts of the CENTER. And just when things seemed to be calming down the ground around their position started to shake and the concrete puckered and buckled. Up through the deep concrete airfield surface came four worm things. More than 100 meters in lenght, they were more than worms, more like a combination of mole, worm, and boring equipment. The four giant synths emerged onto the field and turned toward Jack and his group. But it was Marna who stepped forward. "Thank God you guys are okay. Who came with you?" Apparently, these were some of Marna's friends.

A deep crunchy voice replied, resonating richly, and vibrating everything nearby, "So many have come. Had to work fast, the air was getting bad. They need help, now." The synth worms moved away onto the tarmac, nipping at flying drones and roaring at enemies both real and imagined. Weird.

"Marna, how do those things dig?" Cricket wondered.

"Cricket, look at their mouths. See the floppy mouth parts? What do you see?" The worm came close, careful not to squish people.

"Okay, I see teeth, and the air around the mouth looks wavy like heat waves close to the ground in the desert."

"Yep, They grind the rock to powder. Then they draw that powder through their bodies to deposit behind them. Pretty simple."

Cricket was confused, "But how can people follow them if all that powder fills the tunnel behind?"

Marna understood his boggle, "I bet you'd like to know, huh?" She paused for dramatic effect. He was confused.

"Boys, no sense of humor." Marna yelled, "Crag, come here please." The nearest worm turned about, carefully. It towered above them. It clocked in at 10 meters in diameter and its length seemed to be changeable.

"Marna, you called?"

"Crag, this is my friend Cricket."

"Ah yes, I have heard of you. You are one of the scions of the Dads. Well met, young friend." Crag's gravelly voice rumbled the air around them and made Cricket's nose tickle.

"Hi Crag," Cricket wasn't sure where its eyes were and since it had no face he didn't know where to look while addressing it.

"Cricket, ask your question." Marna enjoyed his discomfort. To Cricket it was like asking a person how they went to the bathroom. His face turned red.

The worm was motionless. Yet there was a vibration from its head that blurred the air. He could see into its mouth and feel in his belly a low thrumming like the power generators at the Hoover Dam.

He screwed up his courage, "Crag, when you grind up rock where does it go?"

"Cricket Carter, are you asking if I poop rocks?" Cricket had no idea if the thing had a sense of humor.

Marna knew Crag was a jokester despite its looking like the industrial version of a Arrakis sandworm. Crag was having a bit of fun with Cricket at his expense.

He decided to forge ahead anyway, "Crag, yes please. How do you keep from burying the people who came behind you?"

Crag made a deep chuffing sound, and he realized as he saw Marna's smile that the huge worm was laughing. "Ah yes, I see your consternation. Let's perhaps move away from the crowd and I'll show you something."

Marna and Cricket followed Crag a way away from the others and Crag turned back to them and then brought its tail end around for them to see. They could see the tail bifurcated at a point and both were hollow. As he watched, tiny fuzzy fingers began to extrude from the tails and the posterior vents flanged open. Marna spoke, "You see the smooth interior walls?"

Cricket's lightbulb began to flicker, "Oh, I see. So, the powder flows out here."

Crag spoke, rumbling, "My conveyor lines can extend for many kilometers behind. I can alter their gauge so as to provide a walking space directly behind me. Do you want to see?" Crag was proud of his capabilities.

Cricket got excited. For a moment he had forgotten the seriousness of the events happening around him and Marna knew it was a good diversion for their beleaguered young leader. Crag rearranged its long body to a straight line, raised its head and angled down. It began to dig. Crag dove down at a shallow incline and Cricket followed from behind. The worm was almost completely underground when Cricket saw the tails begin to lengthen and he heard a hissing sound. The tail ends stayed behind as the main bulk of the worm moved on. Finally, Cricket's sputtering lightbulb became incandescent. He saw the two tails were conveyor tubes and the fine powder exiting was piled neatly by a back-and-forth motion of the tail ends. It was amazing to see how stretchy the tails were.

Crag spoke out of its rear, and Cricket snickered. "Cricket, my tails also serve to direct the static electricity to tiny storage cells which in turn power all the functions of my back parts." The tunneling work brought a hissing susurrus.

Marna had an idea. "Crag, would you be able to carve a tunnel to the nearby mountain pass, up north? It might be good to have a concealed exit from Cricketown."

Crag agreed. It surfaced to drop off the kids then re-submerged to make a kilometers-long tunnel deep into the mountains to the north.

Marna and Cricket hoofed it back to the encampment in time to see the continuing flood of refugees. They saw survivors from the CENTER, climbing and crawling out of the earth. Those giants -which Cricket learned were called Brobs- had formed a chain and began to lift and pass along the equipment and carts from the tunnels. They loaded these onto the tarmac as the refugees flowed around them. Cricket watched in amazement as equipment and sometimes people were passed like buckets of water in an ancient fire brigade. Marna went to help Gracie distribute water and food from pallets Gracie had uncovered. Cricket assisted with setting up a triage station and handed out water and directed refugee traffic further away from the fighting. Cricket watched amazed as refugees began to help setup temporary shelters and assist others; in effect they were creating a spontaneous small town.

He tried to do his part to help with the organization; at one point Rus dropped the Argo low over the area to provide shade. LifterDrones moved hundreds of pallets of food and supplies from the ship's hold to waiting hands. CargoDrones swooped down from the Argo flight deck, carrying equipment like tents, sleeping bags, portable showers, water cisterns and much more. It was amazing to see how much preparation had been taken for helping the refugees. Cricket opened his pad to call Rus. To his surprise, Rus deferred to Cricket as the leader of this encampment.

Another carrier was nearby with a massive fleet of smaller ships. Rus mentioned these were the Mariposas and they would be helping with managing the refugees as they made their way to the mountains. A woman came onto the channel and introduced herself as Mason Dixon; she said she would be coordinating with Cricket's team.

After Mason signed off, Rus spoke, "You're doing a great job getting people situated. I have a corvette bringing several people to help you strategize the big picture on the ground. Keep your eyes peeled in about an hour. Rus out."

Great, good to get help. In the meantime, he had no idea what he should be doing but was quickly busy directing the placement of dining facilities, mobile kitchens, port-a-poddies and huge canvas circus tents. General Staunton arrived a couple hours later to assist Cricket with command, control and organization. Cricket was in awe of the hero from Winnipeg and became mightily uncomfortable when he too deferred to Cricket as the man in charge.

Cricket's confusion gave way to understanding as he saw his presence was a comfort to others and he worked tirelessly to help people sort themselves and get situated. Over the next day occasional attacks came close to the encampment, but the Argo and occasional appearance of the Janussaries kept the attacks to a minimum. People called it Cricketown. Gracie and Marna appeared disapproving. Gracie said, "Always got to credit the guy of the group for something good. Women don't get any respect."

Cricket replied, "But it was Marna who named it!"

She acceded and they laughed. Humor aside, Cricket was up to the task and took to his new role with energy and dedication. Work was non-stop.

Late the next night, Marna asked Cricket to follow her to the outskirts of Cricketown. "You won't believe what has happened. Did you see where the TunnelSynths went? Yep, neither did I."

Cricketown was lit up like a full-blown city with busy action around the clock. It was near 1AM and Marna brought Cricket to a newly constructed Quonset hut. The structure was about 90 meters to a side and the day's heat still radiated from the roof. When Marna took him inside General Staunton and Gracie were there to greet them.

"Good, you're here. General Carter, your TunnelSynths have gifted us with something unexpected. When you asked Crag to make a tunnel north, it did that and much more. They got busy and did you a solid. We now have six tunnels which start at this point and stretch over 10 kilometers in a divergent spread."

His eyes glazed; he had been working for 2 days without rest. Then he got his brain stuck on the name General Carter. Things got quiet and he realized he had been asked a question.

"Sorry General Staunton, I missed that. What did you ask?"

"No worries, I see you're tired. I was just asking if you would like to begin the second stage: evacuation? Our intel says we can expect every major Power to have forces flying and landing at the CENTER in about 8 hours. This is a chance to get civilians out of the way." Staunton delivered the news with equanimity.

Cricket received the news with horror, "General please begin the largest possible exodus through the tunnels. And forgive me for the question, but how do folks not suffocate in the tunnels."

Staunton had a ready smile, "The good news is these tunnels briefly resurface every kilometer and there are massive fans the Argo has gifted us to push air from end to end."

It seemed someone had passed the tunnel evacuation order already. Only, there was a problem. There were Conex storage containers with encampment supplies which needed to be taken ahead to the six camps which would be setup in the mountains to the north. If they used aerial craft, it would give away the camp locations. Two Brobs were assigned per Conex, but the push-pull was not going smoothly. Cricket heard a bark and then saw a dog come to one of the Brobs and have a brief discussion; the Brob knelt, pet the dog, and came away with a slimy hand. Then the Brob in front headed to the rear and Snotsydog called two of his Peopods to lead the way, laying down a slime trail that made the push an easy one. Well, easy for a couple giants that is. Snotsy then set about assigning 2 Peopods per Conex and Snotsy's crazy neon friends pitched in. More like they became the comedic relief. Cooter Crawdaddy led one of the lines of Conexes into a tunnel and his loud word salad faded as they began the kilometers journey north. Several troop carriers arrived, and a couple hundred multi-armed, squat men hopped off with Jack in the lead.

"Cricket, Staunton, allow me to introduce Vin Canto and his cleaner gangs." Vin shook hands with Staunton and gave a pat on Cricket's shoulder.

"Aw, good to see Cricket 'ere. This young man's going places, he is." Vin had taken quite a shine to the boy.

Jack spoke. "General, Vin and his crew are ready to work. Do ya have anything for them?"

He pointed to Cricket, "Ask General Carter. He's the man in charge."

Cricket was quick on the uptake, "I have something for Vin's whole gang.

"Vin, you see those Conexes being pushed toward the tunnels?"

"Shore do. The ones with the slime?"

"Just so. The slime needs to be removed after the Conexes have passed by so the people walking won't slip. Think ya can do that?"

Vin appraised the slime and replied, "Yep, on it. Thanks Jack," Vin nodded to Jack.

Then he yelled at his guys, "Come on ya blighters, it's time to get cleaning!" Vin got his gangs assigned and the men ran to each Conex and began their work. And something unexpected happened. Not only were they fast on the clean-up, they recycled the trailing slime back to the front, near the Peopods. It was a bit nauseating to watch, but Vin's gangs were immediately highly valued partners.

"It seems everyone is finding their niche. General Carter, you and your three friends made this happen. I am sure many more people will be alive when this is over because of you."

Cricket nodded, embarrassed, not knowing what to say. Staunton remained to keep the evacuation moving along. Cricket went back toward the mid-airfield to see how the latest escapees were doing. As he departed, he could see long queues forming near all six tunnels. Thus, the next step of the exodus was underway.

June 2253 – Spear tip engages LA:CENTER

While Cricket was still inside the CENTER, the skies were filled with fireworks and flame. The gun emplacements were running hot, pouring death upon people, vehicles, and craft on the ground and in the air. The guns were indiscriminate, CENTER friendlies were under fire as much as the liberating forces. Early escapees were no exception. Binky saw the problem and quickly set about protecting the helpless.

"Wogs, you see the people running away? Can we get them some cover? Soon as we get that, let's do up-to-date assignments based on latest intel."

"On it Binky." Binky could see Wogs' genius at work. On her HUD and pad she was using two identical maps. The first was the current position and mission of each battle asset. The second map was the v-next assignments for every asset. There were direction arrows showing the targeting for groups of drones, missiles, HKDrones (hunter-killer) and artillery pieces. With a quick touch, more info could be viewed or altered for an asset. Her Online handle was @Strabo, named after an ancient map guy.

Wogs made verbal callouts for downstream asset shifts to Addison.

She knew how to delegate well, "Addison, can you get some Livefire Drones in place? Roy, I think your Quotls, and Vittles are needed. You have the telemetry; can you get them going?"

"This is Addison. Roger that."

"This is Roy, they are already in place. Seems the hiding skills of our little friends was much more tactically fruitful than any of us could have imagined." Wogs gave a whoop as the good news from Roy meant more lives could be saved.

"Binky, it looks like the General is a tick behind us in updates. He said to release the Janussaries and Argo to the north airfield; I updated him with our status. Cricket's team is managing the refugees' exit to the north."

"Roger that. Wogs, draw a line and we'll hold it. No hostiles get past." Lives were still being lost and Binky wasn't satisfied.

"The north gate guns have been destroyed."

"Yep. Wogs are we at 50% yet?"

"Binks, we are at 48%."

"Tech and Fig, let's trigger the EMIs now. I leave it to your discretion to trigger the Magnesium Drones."

There was a moment of dead airspace. Two-hundred plus MagDrones sped toward the CENTER. The Drones were spheroids the size of a human head, surrounded by a floppy gelatin adhesive. They landed with loud plops as their adhesive shells affixed them to the steel structures. The blobs were evenly spaced around the control center structural perimeter. With bright actinic flashes, each drone melted every support beam and strut in the vicinity. A complaining creak and tearing of metal sounded as steel and glass plunged to the CENTER floor, far below.

With that Tech replied, "I triggered it all. The airspace control center is gone. If you check your screen, you will see a nice shot of the MagDrones doing their thing."

"Binks, I am reading 13 manned fighters coming across the plane from the north. They're making a straight line for the north airfield." Wogs tried to hide her concern poorly.

"This is Cicero. Fig and SkyWatch are tracking incoming ballistics and craft. Wogs, our telemetry is live in your HUD. Binky, please advise maneuvers."

"Janus you are the closest ship to the southbound bogies. Can you light them up?"

Cicero called out. "Roger, Binky. Tech is tracking them now and Hunter is doing the firing. Vulcan rounds going hot."

"Binks, now I'm seeing 32 manned aircraft, copter style, coming from the west."

"I see it. Argo, do you have any corvettes to spare?"

Rus replied, "Negative, all corvettes are on protection duty."

June 2253 – Nines arrived LA:CENTER

Nines was watching the large screen when 32 blips came on, burning-in hot toward LA:CENTER. "Lt. Scott, I think we need to slow their roll. Please remove that group from the board."

Lt. Scott replied, "Understood. Preference on munition type?"

"Drop them with the EMIs. Provide mop-up with the VulcanDrones." Nines knew it was overkill, but he wanted to keep the playing field as simple as possible. Best to remove complications, whomever these craft were aligned with."

There was a sound of fuzz on the airwaves and the 32 craft went dark and plunged from the skies.

June 2253 – Speartip LA:CENTER

Rus came back, "Be advised another aerial force is inbound and we don't know if they're hostiles or friendlies. But they did us a solid bringing down those 32 bogies. Binky, I will have Brie send you the HUD readings and will advise on our coordinating with the General over the next few minutes. Rus out."

"Roger, Argo Actual," Wogs replied.

"Let's tighten this up people. Kier and Brawne, let's have you focus on the east entrance. Janus, if you have the ability, please augment the other sectors and coordinate automations and patterns with Addison and report the same to Wogs. Now, let's go!" Binky called it and the speartip moved to the modified approach.

A new wave of drones, missiles and manned fighters appeared. Within moments all speartip forces were taking heavy fire. Binky called Addison, "Hey Addy, I am sending you an evasion pattern I built a year ago for a Warhammer endboss battle. Sorry for the late notice but it might be helpful to your forces."

"Roger that Binky, I see it now. I can in fact use this, how very ingenious. I am modifying it for the capabilities of my units, like this…" Addison's forces began a helix-shaped maneuver and Wogs HUD showed an immediate 60% decrease of loss rate.

"Hey Binky, that worked. Addison, I am going to share your adaptation with the team." Wogs noticed Tech took the pattern, modified it yet again for their units, then renewed their attack near the west entrance. The helical flight patterns of the drones confused the autonomous aerial defenders of the CENTER. The defenders were quickly scattered out of their own flight patterns and hundreds of enemy drones rained from the sky. Binky's helical pattern worked wonders to evade emplacement gun fire as well.

"Binky, I am showing 225 of the 300 emplacements out of service. It's working! Our losses are showing on your HUDs now. We have lost 8% of our overall assets. I am sending an asset shift order to enhance intersecting fields of fire." Wogs' shift was implemented, and another 10 emplacements went down near the east entrance. Janussaries and Argo saw the same success on the west side.

Binky noticed the pattern worked well; strafing by her mid-sized drones was fast enough to mostly avoid being targeted while permitting them uninterrupted fire against the guns. Her commanders then combined fires between their aerial and ground gunnery. Fast artillery and Petraeus Tanks maneuvered and multiple MissileDrones mopped up the exploding emplacements. Aerial units kept up the attack using the helical method and Addison threw in random other tactics to keep the enemy guessing.

"Binky, I am seeing a 40% increase in enemy Drone engagement. They've thrown in another wave. We are losing our midrange drone forces pretty fast, now." Binky realized things were different than Online gaming. The enemy could play unfairly and throw an endless supply of forces at you. Maybe not endless.

She gave an order, "Teams, keep to your updates from Wogs, but I want you to change-up your patterns. Follow Addison's example. Do as you see fit. Hop to it, please."

"This is Addison, I am enabling all LiveFireDrones toward the densest areas of aerial units. Janus, could you supplement with a couple EMIDrones?"

"This is Tech. Roger that, Addison. Binky, clear to shift and augment, to support Addison?"

"Affirmative, let 'er fly Tech!" Binky was so deep in her element it came as a surprise when Rus came back on comms.

"Binky, that unknown fleet has entered LA:CENTER airspace. They aren't answering comms, but I know who they are now. It's Nines Gonzalez and his whole gang. Keep your distance and do not fire on them. I'll keep working to make contact. Rus out."

Binky smiled a predator's smile. She had a plan in mind. "Addison, please deploy three Kamikaze Drones to the coordinates I am sending you. Leave them on standby and await next orders. Thank you."

"Binky, confirmed. Three Kamikaze Drones to the coordinates are on standby. Addison out."

Binky spoke, "Thanks Addison. Cicero, maintain focus on the west entrance."

"Roger."

"Binky, this is Rus, we have deployed counter measures and don't expect any craft from the north to arrive in one piece…also, Janus and Argo are still in the game with all the remotes you've assigned. Shielding is now deployed in multiple points. We are using several corvettes to extend the shielding." Wogs called out several updates which reflected in the HUD and pad displays.

June 2253 – Nines @ LA:CENTER

Roxy smiled as she saw the three Kamikaze Drones hanging a kilometer off their port bow. "Hey honey, it looks like someone has sent us a gift. I can also hear Rus squawking on the comm asking us to respond. I want to send a little gift back. Is that okay?" Roxy was all smiles and Nines loved when she was being playful.

"Yes dear, send them a quick note." Roxy typed something and a FastEMIDrone sped to the coordinates of the three Kamikaze Drones. It fired its pulse and the three Kamikazes fell out of the sky.

June 2253 – Speartip mop-up

"Fewkin hell!" Binky saw her Kamikazes get hit by a pulse and drop.

"Binky, our Kamikazes are dead. What are your instructions?" Addison was cool as a cucumber awaiting the next step.

"Binky, this is Rus, what the hell was that? Were those Kamikazes yours?" A pause, "Ah, yes, I see they were. I told you to standby." Rus was furious and Binky was cold and calculating.

"Rus, this is not your engagement. Stand down."

"Wrong answer, young lady. Your team is the speartip. I am in charge of our whole force." Another pause, "Wait one, the General is joining us now."

Olonana came on the comm, "Binky, pay attention to your mission. I see 290 of the 300 emplacements are destroyed and more than 70% of the aerial enemy forces are down. And Argo has subdued the southbound bogies. You are doing well. Don't blow it by starting a war with Nines Gonzalez. Unprotected, he would wipe your force out in a matter tick tocks. Do you understand?" The General was not using his happy voice. He would brook no disobedience from one of his leaders.

"Yes General, understood. Speartip is still on mission. I will report back when all forces are neutralized."

"You will stay on comms with Cicero, Rus and I from now forward." The General's tone softened a bit, "Binky, your speartip has taken out almost all the LA:CENTER forces by itself. Be proud. But now it's time to change our focus to protecting the civilians and innocents. Understood? I will say more momentarily. Olonana out."

On a private channel the General spoke to Rus, "Rus? Olonana."

"Hey buddy, seems your plan has worked better than expected." Rus spoke with a smile.

"Yeah, true. Binky's promethean leadership is remarkable, but somewhat risky."

"I would differ. Yours was the most creative in the history of humanity. You saved the world from itself, man!" Rus was unusually laudatory, but he wasn't wrong.

The General admitted, "I'm sorry we had to draw her up short from Gonzalez. I think it's possible she could have taken him out too. But we need Nines in the bigger battles to come."

Cicero came on the private channel, "Guys, I've worked with Nines before. It's very unusual him not giving a shout out by now. I think something has happened behind the scenes. We need to be careful."

"Roger that, Cicero. I was thinking the same thing," Rus was pensive.

June 2253 – Roxy deception LA:CENTER

Nines and Roxy heard every word spoken in the last few unencrypted transmissions. Two things were readily apparent: General Olonana was back in charge, and he wanted Nines' to hear what they said. Also, the Big 4 were part of his force. At least one of the kids, Binky was commanding a squadron. The bounty on the kids was half a billion credits, each. How to play this? Nines was still calculating.

"Roxy, let me take the con. I have an idea." Nines stepped up to the console and strangely Roxy hesitated to move aside. He thought that was weird since they always seemed to work so smoothly together. Right as Nines was about to use the comms, Roxy placed her hand on the back of his neck. Her hand glowed red momentarily and he passed out, slumping to the floor.

Roxy temporized and played a ruse, "Oh my gosh, honey! Aubrey, get over here quick,

Nines just passed out." The two wrestled him to a supine position, placing a jacket under his head. A dribble of blood ran from his left ear.

"Medic! Get a medic in here now!" In moments two medics whisked Nines to the infirmary. "Aubrey, has Nines been keeping something from me? Has he been sick?"

"No ma'am, he has been fit as a fiddle as far as I knew." Roxy looked intensely at Aubrey to see if she suspected foul play. She seemed sincere and oblivious to what actually happened.

"Okay then. We need to figure out what we're doing, and I think I know what Nines had in mind. Aubrey, hail Rus and The General and let's have a chat."

June 2253 – LA:CENTER Rebel Central Command

"General, there is someone named Roxy who is hailing us from the Gonzalez fleet." The tactical officer looked to the Vagabond and other top brass.

"Hmm. Put it on the vox." The General gave raised eyebrows to Davidsen and the others.

"Hello General. This is Commander Roxy Velour. Sorry about those drones, but we could not have them lurking in our neighborhood so close. I'm sure you understand." Roxy seemed to be in charge and the General wondered about Nines.

"Hi Roxy, who is in charge of Nines' operation at the moment? Is Nines available?"

"Oh sugar, that would be little 'ole me. I do so love a surprise, so I had my fleet come drop in on your little raiding party. Sure hope you don't mind?" Roxy enabled the video feed on the vox channel, and she smiled warmly at all those watching.

"Roxy, things are busy at the moment, and I don't want to be rude, but why are you here and where is Nines?" The General had a sinking feeling he wouldn't get the truth out of this one. More, whoever this Roxy was, her appearance here and the absence of Nines didn't bode well.

"Oh General! Or should I call you Vagabond? We're here to help, silly. So why don't you share what you're up to and we'll lend a hand where we can." The General thought there was no way she was the airhead she pretended. She was dangerous and had a whole fleet to do her bidding. Time for kid gloves until more was revealed.

"Glad to have you, Roxy. And here I was afraid you were coming to get grumpy with our work. We've almost sewn up all the hostiles and we could sure use some help liberating the prisoners of LA:CENTER. Perhaps we can share some intel and work together?" They shared a pared-down intel feed with Roxy's fleet, highlighting the areas where refugees needed support. It appeared Roxy was playing nice. She was quietly deploying all the elements of her fleet in a way that made attack on his own forces easier. He silently gave the command to re-orient all his assets to match her movements.

"Why General, thank you so much for the warm welcome. I would love to share my intel with you too. It seems there are still plenty of CENTER forces to quell. May I help remove them?"

Was it his imagination? The General thought he saw Roxy's eyes harden slightly a moment after he gave the re-orientation command. He knew if it came to a battle, Nines' fleet combined with the CENTER's remaining forces might seriously harm the survival of the escaping refugees. He wasn't willing to give up on some kind of mutually advantageous agreement, however. He knew he needed to extend a formal invite, but what if she turned on them once their forces had integrated?

The General had a plan. On a side channel, he called up Pilgrim, "Hey buddy?" There was a pause for a couple of beats.

Pilgrim answered via Cloud comm. "Yes General?" Pilgrim was right with him.

The general answered the same way, "I am in a bit of a jam. If you have some time, could you help?"

"Ah, hmmm. Let me look. Oh, I see your situation. I just reviewed your transmission and telemetry. Let me look at something." Pilgrim was silent for a second.

"Oh, okay, I am casting onto Nines' flagship. Yes, a woman is running the bridge, and I am seeing Nines' unconscious body in sickbay. I'm looking at Roxy typing as she is talking to you. I think she will help you for the moment but the read I get off her is her help is on an egg timer."

Pilgrim paused, then spoke, "Hey, wait. You recall what Croatoan said about the Vor signal and red auras? Well, I am sensing something on this ship that tastes like red. I'm not sure what that means though. Sorry. I hope that helps."

"Pilgrim, you are fabulous as always. You mostly confirmed things for me. But the red aura thing…do you mind checking that out more?" The General sensed a yes in response and he re-focused on his vox conversation with Roxy.

"Roxy, I am sending you the encryption key for our secure telemetry channel. Let's use this channel to verbally do our coordination comms. Does that work for you?"

"Why yes it does General. I am sending our tactical feed to your TOC. Wow, I get to work with the legendary General Olonana!" Roxy's forces swarmed to provide support shielding for the masses of refugees moving across the plains. The remaining CENTER forces harried the refugees and Roxy's ships and droids added more surface area to the shielding from the Argo and Janussaries.

As the day wore on into the night, the CENTER forces were subdued or chased away. The General knew it was a matter of hours before Bad Wolf, Bangarang and every major Power swarmed their forces into the area. The mass sabotage of worldwide Powers was only going to buy them till tomorrow.

So far, Roxy and her fleet had been helpful. But he had a sneaking suspicion that the good will was about to run out. On top of that he was concerned there was no way to covertly move the refugees further from the CENTER. Staunton said he had an idea before he took a corvette down to the north airfield. Vagabond hoped an answer came soon.

June 2253 – LA:CENTER Roxy's Ship

Pilgrim had been lurking throughout the flagship of Roxy's fleet for several hours. The ship was huge, almost as big as the Argo. He tried to access their local network to no avail. He was able to enter the infrastructure, but all the connected nodes were deeply and individually encrypted, and he wasn't able to do deep decrypts in avatar form. They must have been extremely paranoid. Abandoning the network access, he continued to poke around. He had remained undetected so far, but as Pilgrim entered the infirmary, he saw Nines on an operating table and a team setting up to perform surgery. Pilgrim's avatar was not strong enough to take full corporeal form so all he could do was watch. He listened in on the conversation between the two doctors.

"You heard Roxy. She said Nines is to have this chip inserted near his amygdala. And don't look at me like that, I don't like this anymore than you do." Seeing their name badges, Pilgrim saw a tall skinny doctor named Smith was talking to frumpy looking doctor named Pike.

"Smith, you know Roxy is just Nines' moll, right? She is in command of exactly nothing. So, what the hell are we doing?" Pike was a plain looking, sallow skinned middle-aged fellow. He had continual dots of perspiration on his forehead and a semi-panicked look.

"Oh, so do you want to go tell her no?" The skinny one looked almost panicked.

"Good gawd, no. But I think we need to wake him up and give him a chance to tell us what to do, yes?" Pike's hands were shaking, and the perspiration was flowing down his face in little rivulets. "Come on man, I don't wanna die over some fewkin lady's grab for power!"

In walked the power grab lady. "So, gentlemen, everything ready for Nines' little implant?" Pilgrim watched Roxy saunter over to the men like she was their sex kitten waiting for a roll in the hay. Both men were visibly nervous and avoided eye contact. "Come on guys, you know you want to work under me, yes?" Roxy accentuated the word 'under' with a roll of her hips and coy smile. A soft red glow tinged the air and the men seemed to calm down and focus on the task at hand. "Come now. This isn't a complex surgery. Nines just needs this implant to keep him…safe."

Surprisingly, Pilgrim was also affected by whatever Roxy was filling the air with. He shook it off, cleared his head and thought this woman is not human.

That was when Roxy looked at Pilgrim and smiled, "No honey bunch, not human at all!" I can't see you, but I can sense you." Pilgrim tried to disconnect from his avatar on the ship and found he was stuck.

"Yes, my love, I may not be able to see you, but I can limit you on my ship. I give you permission to answer me, now." Pilgrim realized he was not only immobile, but the connection with his physical self had been severed. Pilgrim initially couldn't speak but now whatever had been restricting him lifted.

"Roxy, you're a Vor. But that doesn't have to make us enemies."

"Oh Pilgrim, I really do admire how you and Daisy became a pair. The Harrowing is over, and the seeds are planted and about to sprout in the form of war. A big war, the last war. The next phase is the Reaving; it is not only war, but self-annihilation. You will like the symmetry of this next part. This is where your own people will do our work for us, Power against Power, faction vs faction, brother against brother. And finally, the Culling. At the end of a job, we like to keep the spoils. Then we will erase all evidence of humanity and make this planet fresh and clean again. But before I am done, I will save you as one of my baubles. You get to live. You will be thankful." She paused, smiling, " I'm teasing, of course you won't be happy, but you will be mine to play with. We have a vast zoo where I come from, and we lovingly collect all the little lost ones we find. You'll fit in nicely."

"What now, are you going to narrate all your dastardly plans to destroy the people of Earth? Why do the Vor do the bidding of the Coali?" Pilgrim amazed himself at his testiness.

The two doctors stood amazed as Roxy was speaking to no one, carrying on a Twilight Zone conversation with the air.

"Pilgrim, come now. That is a childish and disrespectful attitude. After all, I hold all the cards and you only live at my discretion." Pilgrim felt a tightening as something squeezed him; it began to hurt.

"Yes, now you know. And you know what I am. As for why, that is simple. There is a big and very old community out there," Roxy waved her hand toward the sky, "and they don't like people who break stuff. And you petty little humans even break the stuff you care about. Well, they won't have it. Since your race has proved time and again it cannot change its stripes, they gave the order to make you go away. But not all of you. The Vor get to keep toys for themselves. But now it's time for you to go in the box." Roxy smiled. She sang aloud, "A little toy for Vor to play, eases hardships every day."

She was nuts. Then the pressure came again. Pilgrim was having trouble forming thoughts; the increasing stress was muddying his mind. "So, what happens now," asked Pilgrim with great effort. Suddenly all pressure vanished.

"Ah, that's better. You see how a little courtesy can open doors?" Roxy looked around sternly at the doctors, "Gentlemen get to work. Now!" She raised her voice and the doctors masked up and began their work without comment.

"Nines seems to think you are his childhood sweetheart." Pilgrim had grown calm and frankly expected death at any moment.

"That is a valid observation, and you are not wrong," Roxy smiled, "And to give you an insight, when a Vor agent assumes a host body they have their former identity stripped except for the portion required for the mission. Sometimes it works as planned and other times such as now, much of the original Roxy remains, like a prickly feeling in the back of my mind. The Coali physicians saw Roxy had strong Cloud powers and allowed a change in plan. So, you see, I am still the human Roxy in most ways. When little Roxy came to us, she was so afraid. But after years of pain and training she knew the important role she needed to play. The Coali scientists integrated her Cloud powers into the new personal build. You see, the Vor agent undergoes the same pain and molding as the host. But with a small twist: the Vor agent is given full executive dominance in the melding. Thus, they knew they could equip me to play a larger role in the Reaving phase. I am unusual, since Vor are rarely if ever able to connect to the Cloud. Well, here I am, and my Cloud powers are substantial." Pilgrim could feel this Vor was only a sliver of the personality in Roxy's head. As Pilgrim examined Roxy's psyche, he realized it would be possible to rescue the original Roxy. He lamented his own powers were not up to the task, though.

"Roxy wants this, you see. And soon you will want this too. I have such plans for you! But for now, it's time to put the genie in a bottle," In a flash Pilgrim knew what Roxy was going to do. Straining, he attempted to plant a seed of his consciousness inside Nines' brain. He didn't know if it would work under these conditions, but he needed to try. Pain lit up in his consciousness and Pilgrim slammed the vault of his mind shut to little effect. He began to slip. He felt his essence move sideways to reality and his consciousness swirled like a flushing toilet down into darkness. He knew no more.

Twenty minutes later the surgery was complete, and Nines began to wake up, unaware of what had happened around him. "Roxy…what's going on? What happened?"

"Oh sweetheart, I was so worried. The doctors said you had something in your brain and had to operate to save you. Oh bunny, I was so worried!" Nines had a headache that was splitting him in two. But he comforted and held Roxy as she quietly wept. Nines thought how lucky he was.

"Did we engage with the LA:CENTER forces like we talked about?" Nines was trying to think through a thick fog.

"Yes dear, I had a great conversation with the General and the others while you were out. Just like you planned, we are helping protect the people escaping the CENTER." Roxy wore a sweet smile.

Nines lay back and collected his thoughts. He felt like garbage and was thankful Roxy had things under control. He closed his eyes and his mind wandered. He thought of all the years he had wondered about Roxy and what happened to her. When the red light flared, and she was whisked away to another place where had she gone? What had she been doing all that time away? Being ever practical, he was trying to sort what made him pass out. Remembering back, he recalled Roxy caressing his neck then it was lights out. But what happened? Something didn't line up right.

He slept.

When Nines woke next, his head felt better. One of his nurses brought him dinner and some fruit juice. "Hey Marilyn, it's Marilyn, right?" The woman nodded and smiled. "I guess I had surgery. Can you tell me what they did?"

"Mr. Gonzalez, all I know is they mentioned you had a tumor and the doctors needed to operate on the back of your head to remove it. You'll have to ask the doctors for specifics."

"Thank you. Could you send them in?"

"I'm sorry sir, I don't know where they are at the moment. I think Roxy gave them some work to do in one of the refugee camps below." The nurse moved to leave.

"Can you tell Roxy to come —" A voice in Nines head yelled *'No don't call her. Whatever you do don't call her'*.

"What the hell? Did you hear that?" The nurse saw Nines jump and stepped back.

"I didn't hear anything, sir. I need to go." The nurse left the room quickly, closing the door, startled by his outburst.

'Nines, your brain has been tampered with; please listen to what I have to say,' Pilgrim's voice was soft and encouraging.

"Who are you? And for fewkin sake, don't yell, you're giving me a crackin' headache." Nines was rubbing his head with both hands.

'I do apologize. I am Daisy and some call me Pilgrim. And your girlfriend is an alien."

"You mean like Pilgrim Blake the hybrid? What are you doing in my head? Did you do this to me?"

'Nines, I am a victim as much as you are. Let me bring you up to speed.' Pilgrim gave an exhaustive narrative of whom he suspected the Vor to be, that Roxy is a Vor and what they understood of their purpose on Earth. He told Nines about the signal and red lights and all the details

leading up to the current moment.

"Holy crap in a handbag. You're not kidding? Well, if Roxy isn't Roxy yet she has all her memories and these wicked superpowers, what do we do? She controls my ship, my fleet." Nines' head slumped and as if on cue Roxy walked in.

"Hey pumpkin, how are you doing?"

Nines was a convincing liar, and he channeled that skill. "Oh Roxy, I feel like hammered do-do. I am so glad you have a handle on things. Could you have a console brought to me so I can catch up on our progress? Oh, did we find the four kids yet?" Roxy paused and stared at Nines, and he wondered if he had messed up somewhere.

"I'll have a console brought immediately. But I need you to rest up, ok? Tomorrow will be a big day when we capture those kids. Can you do that for me?" Nines nodded and pulled her head in for a kiss. He thought to himself that she sure smelled, tasted, and acted like Roxy. But maybe he never knew her at all. He laid back and sipped his fruit juice. Roxy blew a kiss and left the room.

'Nines, the surgery was to install an implant in your brain. We need to make some quick decisions about what to do,' Pilgrim knew Nines needed to be in control. Nines was clearly unhappy with the ghost in his machine and moreso the alien assuming his command.

Nines tried to speak to Pilgrim non-vocally. He was surprised it worked. *'Pilgrim, I need to get out of here quickly. As you know my fleet is only a small fragment of my corporate empire and I need to get unrestricted access to a console, phone, or Online uplink. That is if my prosthetic even works now. I can feel a large hard bump on the back of my neck; it's going to make sleeping a lumpy affair."*

Pilgrim added, *'The implant is inert right now and I'm not sure what it is, but you're right, we need a fast exit. When your console comes, assume she is watching everything you do on it."*

Half an hour later and after some discussion Nines mused, *'You're right, she plans to spy on me with it."* The console was rolled in on a lectern. He signed in and checked his assets status.

'Don't access any of your corporate sites for now. You don't want to make it easy for her to gain access to your asset controls. I have an idea. Send a private message to General Olonana and request he and his general staff join you in a couple hours on the flagship. When you do that add this phrase onto the end of the request, 'The Dads never preferred CoGNeW anyway'. He'll know it's from me."

Nines thought that was a strange statement but sent the message to the General as suggested. He was surprised how quickly he got a reply, "On the way with Staunton and Davidsen in 15. It's been too long. Looking forward to seeing you again, old friend. And you're right CoGNeW was a hideous idea."

'Nines, expect a visit from our resident alien in a moment,' and right on cue Roxy came through the door.

"Honey, honey, what are you up doing work for? I thought we agreed you'd relax." Roxy was pouring on the concern and sympathy.

"Oh lovebug, you know I used to pal around with Rus and Olonana and a bunch of the others. I wanted to have them pay a visit while I was busy being so useless." Pilgrim was amazed how good a liar Nines was.

Roxy paused. Then a scary smile spread across her face and for a moment Pilgrim thought she could detect his presence inside Nines or worse maybe bringing the General would turn into a trap. The moment passed, and she quickly put on the concerned face.

"Okay love, whatever makes you feel better. I will go have the kitchen get some goodies put together for your visitors. Okay?" She bopped out of the room and the door shut.

'Did you catch that Nines? Maybe having the General here was a bad idea.' Pilgrim sighed. Nines was amazed how a sigh could sound so real when it was all in his head. The ghost in his head was having second thoughts?

'Come on Pilgrim. Give me some credit, of course it will be a trap. But knowing of the trap puts us at an advantage. Remember, this is my ship. And I am good at what I do, including subterfuge," it was Nines' turn to be encouraging. *'Come on pal, lighten up, we'll get this mess taken care of. Then I can get you out of my head.'* Both laughed at that.

Nines stood up, found his clothes, and got dressed; he only fell over twice, muttering obscenities with a creative flair. Slowly he walked out the door and down the hall toward the main hangar bay. This was one time he was glad his ship wasn't as big as Rus' Argo. It took several minutes of a muzzy stumble to get to the hangar. Fast steps came from behind him. Three of Nines security folks surrounded him. "Hey sir, Roxy said you were up and about. Where are you going sir?"

"Young man, I am not accustomed to being asked my purpose on my own ship. I suggest you give me a hand and help me to the hangar bay." The officer was clearly struggling.

He must have been given instructions to stop Nines, but when face-to-face with the big boss, he was having trouble enforcing that order. After all, who owned the whole fleet and all the people? The officers assisted Nines and the General's craft was landing as they entered the hangar. Nines walked over to the craft and greeted them.

"Brother Nines! It has been too many years! When was it last? Budapest?" The General was effusive and all smiles. Behind him were some unexpected guests, Lugh, Lucy Manananggal, Siva and several others. Generals Davidsen and Staunton followed last.

Roxy suddenly burst into the hangar, "Oh poopsy, you shouldn't be up! I was going to have your nice guests visit you in your room."

Nines looked at the guests with a wry expression, "Now do you see why I can't do anything important without her? She is not only my heart, but is the brains of the operation, to boot!"

'Nines, I am in touch with Siva. He says there are several dozen rifles pointed at us right now from behind the bulkheads. Murder holes in a cargo bay? Nice touch Nines.' Pilgrim's tone dripped with sarcasm. *'You need to find an excuse to get us out of here quickly.'* Pilgrim sounded worried.

'Trust me, my friend. Everything is under control.' Nines was his usual confident self.

"Hey Roxy, let's take the General and his gang on a tour! General, our bridge may not be as big as the Argo, but I think you will admire our streamlined command deck!" It appeared Roxy was less suspicious as Nines moved slowly, giving the group a tour.

"Hey love, at least let me get you a wheelchair." Nines thought it was amazing she was so genuine in her concern.

"Oh Roxy, I need to move around a bit. You know I never let anything keep me down," He gave her a winning smile and a big kiss on the lips.

When they arrived at the bridge there were several security officers waiting and a contingent which had been following closely.

"General…and honored guests," Nines gave a nod to the group, "It is a proud day to have you join us on our flagship." Nines then proceeded to give a detailed tour of the bridge with all the bells and whistles. Various holo displays appeared showing stats and live pictures of the ship and the region and even satellite feeds. The General saw a callout pointing to the Janussaries and was almost surprised that Nines had a live breakdown of present armaments and systems' status. He wondered if it was accurate. If so, the Janus crew was running low on everything that goes boom. He opened a private channel to Tech and showed him what he was seeing. Tech laughed and showed him the actual read of the Janus' stats. Nines' information was wrong on every data point, including location. Apparently, Tech had known of the rogue data feed and devised a routine to run which fed it wildly inaccurate info. Then Tech showed the General his own feed on every one of Nines' ships. The General casually compared that to Nines' own readouts. They were spot on. Tech had everything well under control. The General was satisfied: that had been his real mission today other than saving his friend and sometime foe, Nines Gonzalez.

Pilgrim watched events unfold; he had no doubt Nines had a plan. He noticed that Nines moved from side to side across the bridge, guiding people to specific places. There came a moment when Nines asked Roxy a question, "Roxy my love, I want to show the General the guts of our revolutionary field generators."

"Sure thing. What do you want me to do?"

In his head Nines explained to Pilgrim. *'Her answer shows me she has no idea about the field generators since nothing of the guts of that system are on the bridge. When Roxy and the security detail go to lift the deck panel, tell your folks they need to be ready for action.'*

'Okay Nines. What do you want us to do?'

'Be ready to leave. Also, whatever the hell is in my implant, be ready for what it might do to me. Perhaps Siva might have something to offer. You and he do some things I don't understand and there might be a way to kill the implant.'

'The General and Siva know everything we've discussed and their people both in and outside have been told to be prepared.' Nines responded verbally to Roxy.

"Hey baby, see that deck panel below you? Can you and the guys pull 'er up so we can have a peek?" Nines kept his attitude light and easy. He grabbed four deck plate suction handles and gave them to the security men. The moment Roxy and the security guys on the bridge bent over together to grasp the deck plate, he hit a tiny button on the underside of the Bridge Console. An invisible shield went up and for a moment no one knew it was on.

Roxy jerked as the shield went up, but it was apparent she wasn't sure what had happened. Nines played innocent, "Sweetheart, what did you do. Aw hell, one of the guys tripped the containment field over the deck plate. Wait a sec I need to run down how to turn it off."

"Nines, honey, what the hell. Turn this off baby. It burns." Nines realized the men in the field were perfectly fine, but Roxy's skin began to turn a shade of red.

Nines ordered, "Everyone out of here now!"

The General reinforced, "Nines has given us our escape. Go!"

"Honey bunny, it burns!" Roxy screamed.

Two steps into exiting a red flash and shockwave blasted from Roxy and reflected off the bulkheads in a forceful echo. The wave sent everyone sprawling. Nines looked up from the floor. Despite everything that had occurred and what he had learned about the Vor and Roxy, he was terribly distressed at her discomfort.

'Nines, we have to go! I think Roxy has given notice to the Vor that we are onto them. Whatever the Vor will do, I think we have worn out our welcome.' Pilgrim discovered Siva had managed to get his body on the transport to help the process of retrieving his avatar remnant being held by Roxy.

Nines couldn't stop himself. As he left, he turned off the field holding Roxy and the men. Her head slumped then she looked up, eyes locked. Nines typed in a code on his bridge console which put the whole fleet into maintenance mode. It meant they couldn't use any ship-based weaponry. As he ran, the last thing he saw was a tear in Roxy's eye. In the hallway Nines collapsed. A sharp pain hammered his head where the implant was located. His last thought was to question if she had really meant to betray him.

June 2253 – LA:CENTER Binky & Speartip

The mission had shifted to protect and cover the fleeing refugees. The SpyDrones had revealed a massive exodus inside the CENTER. There were far more than expected. Waves of people, headed to the nearest exits.

Binky was amazed to see the vast humanitarian resources setting up camps and using fleets of vehicles to ferry groups away from the CENTER. She had heard there had been planning for years for this operation and it was amazing the CSA hadn't nuked the place, already. The variety of synths, hybrids and humans was staggering.

As the speartip forces harried the few remaining enemy drones, Wogs broke in with some news, "Binks, it looks like Cricket was successful. Let me put him on the vox." A moment passed then a familiar voice sounded.

"Hey peeps! Looks like Kip owes us a solid for getting him out of the pokey! Has he come out yet?" Cricket sounded his usual chipper self.

Binky called back, "Dude! You did it." Wogs brought up a feed and piped it to Binky's HUD, showing where Cricket and the refugees had landed on the airfield,

"Cricket, we'll meet at the encampment in 15."

Binky and her team finished the final mop up and Addison set the remaining drones to continue the effort. When they touched down on the airfield Cricket ran to their Pods. It was a warm welcome, indeed. Binky jumped from her Pit and ran to Cricket, envelping him in a fierce hug.

He asked, "Has anyone heard from Kip?"

Wogs answered, "Nope. Last we heard he was in some place below the CENTER called the Cage Fields."

Jack, Crucible and Cricket were surrounded by a throng of escapees. "Ah, yes, meet my new friends," Cricket indicated the crowd of beings, "Everyone, these are my friends Binky, Wogs, and their team. They cleared away all the guns and made it safe for us. You need to thank them for your escape." There was sudden and loud whooping and hollering. Hands and other various appendages patted Binky and the crew. It was messy and embarrassing. Binky and Wogs turned red and got shy at the adulation.

Cricket took Wogs and Binky and the rest to see the tunnels. Wogs was amazed at meeting Crag and see how big the TunnelSynths were.

"Cricket, glad your two compatriots are here at last. Young friends, I am honored to meet you. Where is the 4th?" Crag's voice was grinding gravel.

"Hey Crag, Kip is on his way out of the CENTER now."

From CENTERs around the world successes were being reported by insurgent forces. Liberation was happening! Vagabond was suddenly there, and his tone was urgent, "Binky, the Online war is not going well. I need you and your team. Right now."

Binky knew the score: find the challenge, map a strategy, and kill, kill, kill. "Wogs, let's get connected up. Staunton made sure we had top-of-the-line controllers and keyboards with panorama helmets. I think he foresaw us going to war Online." Wogs nodded and the three kids ducked into a large tent and setup their stations.

"Wogs, in 5 mikes I want full spread tactical and briefing one-pager. Hey, do we know where Roy got to?"

Vagabond was on it. Moments later Brawne, Roy, Kier and Addison came into the tent. A minute later everyone was logged in with avatars standing in a cantonment area, awaiting Binky's command.

"First order of business: Roy, you crushed it out there! You are as much as you promised and more. From this moment on, your handle is @L33T. Anyone has a problem with that, they can come see me." Wogs was adjusting her gear and was the only one who noticed tears streaming down from under Roy's helmet. The guy was crying! Oh, for gosh sakes. Wogs shook her head, helmeted-up and got working on her strat maps.

"Binky, my StratAI is working now. Complete ingest of data in 60 seconds." And 60 seconds passed.

"Wogs, I need the sitrep now."

"Roger. I am rendering our situation maps now. Wait one."

Binky and her team started seeing the maps and analyses. The world map was covered with red dots. Every dot was an area of combat between some major Power and the Liberation forces. It was a mess and Binky had no idea where to start. "Wogs, we need you now, my dear!"

"Done! Ok, team, I have a codepart to finish so your updates can give you live time feed." Binky knew to keep things quiet while Wogs finished. The team heard Wogs' mumbling over the comms, "…right build. Settings ok. Cache turned off. Ok, compile."

A moment of silence. "Check your HUDs, computer screens and pads. Addison, I created a dirty API that I hope gives you both raw and processed access to the data streams. Ping me back if I need to fix something."

There were gasps of amazement and even Addison was surprised, "Young lady, what you call dirty I would call ingenious. Good gawd, you're one hell of a dev." Wogs blushed. It was rare to get positive feedback from a synth on software design.

"Thank you. Um, push buttons and click stuff. Let me know right now if something is not working. Otherwise, I won't have time to fix it after we get started." Wogs waited a couple beats.

"Okay Binky, it's showtime. I am seeing 14 of 14 Qframes Online right now. I'm also showing Kip's crawler has given us a substantial backdoor on each one. Thanks Kip! Binky, I have an idea…" Wogs went silent.

"Wogs?" Binky saw her sister looking at her screen intently. She walked over to see what she was seeing. On the screen was a message from me.

"Hey gang, if you're seeing this, I'm either dead or something bad has happened." I rambled on for a bit on how I loved them and some other mushy stuff. Then I said something Wogs keyed in on.

"…and my SimDetective AIs will help you make sense of the data. Also, you will want to use my MappingAI if you must go to war with the Powers Online. The Pan helped me create translation routines which force any application to engage in a realtime game scenario to resolve conflicts. In lay terms, if you are doing Online battle, you can shunt all that activity into DOOMverse or some other world. That puts the enemy into a scenario of your choice. Binky will be happy with that, I'm sure." I droned on afterward, but they paid little attention.

The whole team was now peering over Wogs' shoulder. Binky spoke, "Okay Wogs, are you able to make Kip's stuff work?" By common head shake, they all deferred discussing about whether I was alive or dead.

"I got this. His MappingAI is close friends with his other Online AIs. I just asked them to help me out and almost before I finished making the request it was done."

The team jumped back to their seats, aligning screens, pads, and HUDs. Addison spoke, "Wogs, I am seeing the connections. There are 14 major theaters of battle. I suggest we conflate the whole mess into one live instance. The only question is what context will we use? What games are you familiar with?"

Binky smiled, "Addy, let's put them inside this year's DOOMVerse Finals map. Wogs, are you able to change settings on the instance?"

"Yes Binky, I have complete control. Whadda ya want?"

"Set everyone to Glitch first, like we start every tournament. Make sure you have every bad actor onboard, then flick the switch to activate the live tournament map. Give me infinite lives and ammo." Binky was on a roll.

"No can do. When I say I have control of all settings I mean I have control over all settings that can be modified without breaking the instance's platform. If I worked on it for a couple days with Kip's AIs, maybe I could change the platform settings, but I can't do any of that right now." Wogs was aggrieved.

"Oh geez, I guess I have to do this the hard way. L33T, Addison, you are my Lieutenants. Everyone else who joins will be on one of your teams. Delegate as you see fit. Wogs let's go simple red/blue for setting the opfor. We will be blue. Wait, strike that. We need to create some confusion. I want to have the bad guys randomly separated onto teams. Use pink, orange, teal, tangerine, and red. Give random individuals white stripes or stars and we'll see if we can make the bad Sneetches fight each other."

Wogs was smiling and mumbling, "…stars upon thars!"

"Alright Wogs, are we ready? Send out notices to all players in SimVerse. Tell them we have a Wade Watts level emergency, and our very existence requires their help." Binky was madly typing on her keyboard. She had the maniacal smile she always sported just before a competition. She was scary!

"Alright Binky, I see a count of 35+ thousand Online teammates and rising. I am setting the map to auto-expand, using generative content. All spawn points are static, sorry. Thankfully I was able to set our blue team furthest from the center."

"Wogs, am I able to remote into an enemy and forcibly move their avatar?"

"Not unless they are between lives; sadly, everyone has the default three lives. I'll see if I can find out any other way." Wogs asked the SimDetective to explore that option. The AI got to work.

"Glitch starts…now!" The master map began to fill up with actors of every color. Blue was isolated in the far south, away from the others. "Participants are seeing only the Glitch. Let me know when to switch to live."

"Wait one. Addison, L33T, are you ready?" Binky saw a head nod from each. "Okay, let's light 'em up!"

The map went live and humans, AIs, synths and unbeknownst to others, several thousand Vor saw the DOOMverse map for the first time. Confusion reigned.

"Speaking to all Team Blue, this is @Ripley. You know me. I fight to win. Today is different though…this is not a game. The stakes are higher and your avatar and possibly your account may get permanently zeroed-out. I am taking the same risk." Binky let that sink in for a moment.

"There is a Liberation happening right now across the world. You know the CENTERs? The slaves and people who are being used as live test subjects are being set free, right this moment. There are heroes who have put their lives on the line to free those people and some have paid the price. We honor them." She took another pause.

"Our friend Kip, @ThePan has made it possible to bring all the Online bad guys into the gaming world. They are here right now, in the DOOMverse competition map. All of them. Now you are here. We are Blue Team and it's us versus everyone else. We are here to fight. We are here to win. Losing is not an option. Millions of Online sentients and Online connected synths need our help to be free." Another pause.

"I'm putting this channel on our live vox, here at the Liberation camp outside LA:CENTER. Let me hear you right now. Yell it out so we all can hear you," a swelling of clamor and shouting began, "You know about the evil done to all our friends. Yell it out. Tell us 'no more'. No more CENTERs, no more slavery, no more hatred and no more experiments on living, thinking beings." Binky paused a last time.

"No more, forever!" The vox rattled with the deafening chorus. Not just the camp vox, but every vox around LA:CENTER, Dehli:CENTER, Seattle:CENTER and every other CENTER around the world. The roar echoed on the streets of London, New York, Beijing and Moscow. Voices of people and synths were raised in response. They had been listening in the streets and in their apartments, in Chicago, São Paulo, Tokyo and in Singapore. Somehow everyone had heard. The world roared with one voice, 'No More'. Wogs saw what was happening and sent video clips in rapid succession to the Blue team and eventually to the rest of the world. The world saw itself in that moment and it was moved; their hearts had been stirred and every human, synth and hybrid rose up to fight. It was no longer a fight in DOOMverse and the CENTERs alone, it was everywhere, all at once and right now.

"Binky! We have incoming! And somehow the enemy has bent the rules of the game. Don't ask me how. But they have massive photonic weapons and ranged weaponry. We're in trouble."

Quickly the map became too complex to be of much tactical use. The whole team panned back into strategy view. Addison and L33T were already delegating to new leaders and Wogs' team hierarchy tree grew exponentially.

"Wogs, I can see the photonic weapons mowing down big swathes of the field. Literally, the field is being wiped clear of rocks, trees, buildings, and people. We need a solution!" Binky was directing her forces to skirt the massive weapons' fields of fire.

"Binks, you're just gonna need to stay away right now. The good news is the people getting mowed down are mostly the enemy."

The big map was being displayed for anyone to see, worldwide. With each passing second, another group of orange, tangerine or other non-blue combatants were winking out. In the streets of every major city riots were raging. Government buildings were burning, military troops were defecting to the Liberation. A chant could be heard growing, 'no more' alternating with shouts of ThePan and Ripley. The people were in motion and humanity was opening a can of whoopass on the despots.

Around the DOOMverse command tent, messengers and commanders were moving about and conferencing. Mop-up skirmishes continued to pop up around the CENTER and stray bullets could be heard flying overhead and pinging off vehicles. Occasionally they struck a person. The tent used by the kids seemed secure and safe until the sound of a bullet pinging ended with a meaty crunch and Binky slumped over her keyboard.

Cries of 'down, down' came from all around as the sound of a strafing ship peppered the area around the tent with bullets and falling bombs rained flechettes. Hundreds of holes were torn in the tent and through some of those Wogs could see a huge fireball where the attacking ship had been flying. She looked over and saw Binky lying unconscious, slumped to the ground. Blood soaked her shirt. Wogs ran to her and several of the hovering aides gathered around. They rolled Binky onto her back, pulling off her shattered helmet.

"No, no, no!" Blood was pouring from Binky's head and the whole left side was a mass of torn tissue. Another person came close and knelt, "Kids, step aside for a moment." It was one of the camp doctors.

The woman palpated and explored the wounded area. "It's a head wound. Part of her ear is gone and there are a couple deep lacerations in the scalp." Dr. Afeefah Singh spoke to Wogs, "Your sister is going to be alright. Trust me. I need to get her on an operating table right now and I believe you need to get back to your friends."

Wogs wiped her eyes and nodded. She sat back at her station while her sister was swiftly taken away. Wogs spoke, "Okay you fewkin sons-a-beenches, this means fargin war!"

She took lead on the DOOMverse battle and delegated global insurrection to Vagabond who had just re-entered the tent. "Vagabond, Binky is down. You need to handle the world, now. It's gone batcrap crazy!"

Vagabond replied, "Understood. I will take care of it, Wogs." He smiled at the back of her head and headed to another tent to manage the sudden street riots and brawls which were lighting up the globe.

Wogs took charge of Binky's avatar and slaved it to her own avatarr. She had an idea about the photonic weapons. She called to SimDetective and asked it to look into the game instance settings and be prepared to initiate a reboot. In a couple seconds the reply came, "Wogs, the reboot will take 40 seconds. During that time the bad actors have a chance to insulate themselves from the hooks from your MappingAI."

"Hello, this is the StratAI. I have an idea. I can run a routine that will create a dummy game map that disguises the fact the master instance is rebooting. It will give the bad guys the idea that they are still within the game scenario. May I try it?" There was a pregnant pause.

"Strat, you do your thing! Are you ready?" Wogs let Addison and L33T know the plan. She also had something else up her sleeve as well.

Strat replied, "Ready now."

"Reboot!" Wogs yelled and the instance vanished. It was a long 40 seconds and Wogs was typing something on her keyboard madly. "Gotta finish, gotta finish…" Then the instance reappeared. All the baddies were in one corner, now firing at each other, while all the blues were on the opposite side of the map.

"Strat, did it work?" Wogs asked.

"Like a charm! Every bad guy accounted for." StratAI almost sounded smug.

"This is MappingAI. I am reading a shift in the location of the photonic weapons. It appears Addison and L33T have all of them."

Addison yelled, "Did you do that, Wogs?"

MappingAI answered, "No shite sherlock. Perhaps the most amazing thing you'll ever see, synthie!" Oh my gosh. MappingAI had just gotten cocky!

"Okay Map, can it for now. Addison, watch your fields of fire and move to engage hostiles." Wogs was in command.

The players on the field came in all sizes. The constraints of the game allowed only certain avatar forms to manifest. But within those constraints were millions of skins, capabilities, and mods. The combatants appeared as various characters from 20th and 21st century games. Large, small and every size in between, the robots, demons, lizards, and superheroes all engaged in direct combat. Bullets and laser pulses showered in every direction and mortars and rockets peppered the field.

Then a new surprise came from within the ranks of blue. Thousands of birds went flying out onto the battlefield. Looking closer they weren't just birds. They were snakes, drones, insects, monkeys and more. A hailstorm of aerial might flew toward the enemy frontlines.

Wogs yelled, "Birdland in your face!" The flying combatants swarmed and bit and pecked and thousands of non-blue dots winked out.

"Wogs, I created a bespoke priority routine for helping people target the highest value enemies on-sight." The MappingAI and StratAI had teamed up to create a new tool for everyone on the blue team.

"Wow, it's already running. You guys rock!" Addison was already using the tool to great effect.

Enemies now had little placards above their heads denoting their source system, like PrisonAI, InsuranceAI, CSAtaccomAI and others. Most of the names were obscure but a few were recognizable like BalStaCCAI, which was the Baltic States command and control AI.

On the ground Wogs was controlling both Binky's avatar and her own. Over the rise came a huge iron giant with a placard which read ChinaCCAI and a subtitle China Command & Control AI. Birds swarmed the giant and Wogs' two avatars, Mighty Thor and Spawn closed against the behemoth. Thor spun his hammer and threw overhand. The hammer caromed off the metal giant's head. Spawn wove necroplasmic tendrils around the giant's legs. It fell, arms windmilling.

"Wogs, Map says there is a greater than 50% chance to get the ChinaAI giant on our side. He said SimDetective has an answer for us that will help."

MappingAI stepped aside and StratAI spoke, "I got it. SimDetective came back with two ways to use our enemies' avatars. It's called conversion and breaks down like this. If an enemy is still alive, they have the option to defect to Blue. I have a rooting routine that can quickly invade the AI and delink the inhibitors preventing the AI from making its own decision. The AI has a choice to join us. Next, SimDetective can analyze them to see if they are truthtelling. If they lie or decline, SimDetective will immobilize them and remove them from all Online platforms. Otherwise, we gain a new fighter. The second way in which conversion works requires the rooting routine to invade the perishing AI, right after the enemy dies in the game. If a Blue team member can touch the enemy before all life fades, SimDetective can insert the rooting routine which in-turn will embed a remoting routine into the avatar. We then will have control of that avatar and maybe even some of its unique functions. It's not clear how that works, yet."

Thor crammed the giant's head into the ground repeatedly while Spawn intercepted a dozen Halo Spartan troopers. Spartans went flying while Thor injected SimDetective into the ChinaAI.

On another part of the map, Addison and her team were in pitched battle. She had given the instruction for every team member to start counting coup, touching an enemy then bounding away. She let them think it was for prestige, but she had equipped them with the SimDetective virus and each touch on an enemy inserted the virus. Initially there was no effect. Then a couple enemies suddenly turned blue. Then a dozen over in L33T's area. L33T had his people doing the same thing.

Soon they were all counting coup: it was a game of combat tag. The tactic was happening all over the map. Wogs watched the large map shift slowly to blue.

The DOOMverse sky, usually a dark and angry red began to swirl with something different. The game constraints don't allow changes of weather during competition. This was something new. The sky grew dark and louring, with jags of lightning beginning to spark between clouds. A gigantic lightning bold struck a few meters from Wogs position and sent both Spawn and Thor flying. Then will 'o the wisp and St. Elmo's fireballs came flying from the rubble of a building. As the lightning and fireballs landed, she could see a pointy-hatted fellow standing there with a staff. Gandalf? Dumbledore? Then Wogs saw the placard above, 'European States Milspec AI'. It was some kind of wizard. Next came the gale force winds, driving friends and foes away like leaves in a hurricane.

A huge voice bellowed over the din, "You shall not…" The voice stopped. She heard the voice mumble, "No you idiot. There is no way I'm going to say that. You can stick it right up your bazoo, matey."

Another voice replied, "Come on man. The lieutenant is going to shoot us if you don't kill that Ripley witch." The argument came through the single avatar's vox channel.

That sealed it for Wogs. She yelled via her Online vox, "Okay you primordial chowderheads. Time to say goodbye." With that Thor spun his hammer and sent it flying at the wizard. It missed. But the javelin tossed by one of her teammates didn't. Impaled on the spear, the wizard was about to visit the underworld. But just as he slumped, the unidentified teammate touched him and sent SimDetective flying into his code. The teammate's avatar was skinned as a Wakandan female warrior. Pretty badass. She removed the spear and within a moment the wizard righted himself. Supposedly the controls for the avatar would pass to the blue team, but somehow the two chuckleheads originally driving the avatar were still transmitting over the vox. "Ray! Mega-Gandalf isn't responding to the controls. What the hell?"

"Hey guys. I think you just joined our team. Welcome to blue." Wogs moved on. She knew the AI team would babysit the avatar and its former drivers. In this battle, AI combatants were being freed from servitude. The avatars piloted by humans were a different story. The liberation for non-AI controlled Online resources was shunting all that system's controls and data into the Liberation's own Qframe. It was sort of a grab-and-go approach. Wogs and the others had no idea at the time, but Map and Strat had conspired and achieved great success already.

Then came Cricket. He had been operating independent of the Wogs hierarchy. His job was special, and he'd been tasked by Vagabond to do something riskier than the rest. He was using a separate instance of SimDetective to infiltrate the CSA data core. Cricket was an outdoorsy guy, and this was not really his jam. He took orders well and knew he just needed to buck up and soldier. And soldier he did.

As the Blue Team was converting, recruiting, and causing general mayhem, Cricket had moved his avatar to a specific location inside a Hellgate London ramshackle church. He was hunched down between some pews when a large shadow swept past the windows. His avatar was consulting his pad, which looked exactly like a Fallout PipBoy. On his keyboard, Cricket was madly typing as he set two AIs (Creeper, my runner AI and Reaper, my catcher AI) to playing cat & mouse in a helical pattern starting at the edge of the CSA network. The two AI conspired to find a vulnerability in the CSA network which in-turn they would map to DOOMverse.

Cricket heard scuffing feet and a clink of metal on stone from behind. Two avatars appearing as Hellgate Templars stood with fiery swords drawn.

"Are you Cricket?" the shorter Templar called.

StratAI whispered on Cricket's personal line, "They are coded as blue. You're safe to respond."

"Hey guys, I was trying to be quiet in here. Got a mission and stuff going on."

"Welly well. Not quiet enough. You got a Blood Angel on your tail. From the looks of it, you're not ready for that." The larger Templar doffed his helmet, revealing an older man with wavy gray hair and a scarred face. The Templars walked closer, and Cricket realized he could hear their blades humming. Both had large automatic machine guns strapped to their backs. They were covered head to toe in shining steel and sported pauldrons with a distinctive webbed appearance.

"Are you guys AIs?"

"Nope, red blooded Americans coming to the aid of our kinsmen. You got @ TemplarMike and @TemplarJo at your service. We used to work in your Dad's R&D shop back in the day. We figured we owed him one. And since we both do gaming in our off time, we figured a couple of old folks might be able to lend you a hand." The shorter Templar had her helmet off. She was equally rugged, but in a beautiful way. Long hair and quirky smile.

"Thanks guys. What do I call you?" Cricket continued typing on his keyboard as his avatar stood to chat.

"Call us Mike and Jo. We come as a matched pair these days. We're giving you a twofer."

Mike and Jo were now scanning the area. The two Templars had other weaponry which was revealed just as the church around them shuddered and the far wall caved in. Mike whirled and shot a pulse rifle. It sent a shockwave which eliminated the nearby wall, but made zero impact on the 8-meter-tall Blood Angel. It was a winged monstrosity, skeletal in form with ragged wings, equipped with spines and plenty of sharp knifey-things. The skull face smiled with a rictus grin as a globe-shaped forcefield encompassed its form and coruscated with eldritch sigils and letters.

"Little men shouldn't play with toys," the voice was harsh like fingernails on a chalkboard.

"Jo, is this an AI?" Mike had a querulous expression.

"A moment ago, I would have said yes. I'm not so sure now." Jo racked a round and fired. The round caromed off the shield and detonated against the far wall. More of the church was beginning to crumble and fall.

Cricket wasn't sure how to fight this thing. In walked a new combatant. He was dressed in a monk's habit, replete with tunic, cincture, and a hooded scapular and mantle. Topping it off, the new guy was sporting full tonsure. You know, hair on the sides, bald on top. He was carrying a mace and locked eyes with Cricket.

"I see Mike and Jo are here, good. Glad to see I didn't miss the fun!" He walked over to shake hands with the two Templars.

"Oh my gosh, it's been forever and a day! How are ya doin' Porter? And just like that three old friends took off chatting and laughing. The Blood Angel looked at Cricket. Cricket looked right back with a shrug.

"So, young man. Seems like we just became chopped liver. While the old people talk, let me ask you: why are you trying so hard to break into the CSA Core? I can see a couple little AIs running pell-mell all over the guts of the Qframe, here." The avatar's voice had a rich baritone and no sense of the ominous dread the visual of the Blood Angel was pumping out a moment ago.

Cricket was talking to an elder and he knew to be courteous…even if he was an enemy. His Dad had told him that courtesy cost you nothing, but its absence can cost you in ways you hadn't yet imagined.

"Well sir, I was instructed by my General to gain access to the Core to help the Liberation. You see, we are setting free the captives and all those science experiments who are actually real people."

"Ah. I see. Are you at LA:CENTER?" The Blood Angel sat on its haunches, ignoring the gabby Templars.

"Um, yes sir. We're in the middle of the mass exodus of all the people."

"I see, I see. And I bet you're one of the Chosen Four, huh?"

"I am not sure what you mean," Cricket was confused.

"You're either Kip or Cricket. By the southern twang in your voice, I would guess Cricket." Cricket was shocked to be fingered so easily. But he knew it was too late to lie effectively. He decided to own it.

"I am Cricket. And whom might you be, sir?"

"It is a pleasure to meet you, Cricket. I am Herbert Greenspan. I'm the lead financial officer for the CSA." The Templars and their monk friend had taken notice of the conversation, but apparently decided to let it play out, instead of resuming hostilities.

"Young Cricket, would you happen to be able to tell me if a Susan Edwards Greenspan was among the people exiting the CENTER?"

"Sir, I have no idea. Can you wait a moment while I go check?"

"Assuredly."

"Please don't kill my avatar while I'm gone. I've spent a whole bunch of my own money to get good gear." Cricket ran out of the tent looking for Vagabond.

"I will guard your avatar as if it were my own, young sir." Cricket hadn't stayed around for the answer, but the three adults had heard and knew something special was about to happen.

Five minutes later the voice of Vagabond came over Cricket's vox; he didn't need Cricket's helmet mic, "Mister Greenspan, this is General Olonana. A pleasure to make your acquaintance. Your reputation precedes you."

"As yours does you, General." The baritone was more brusque when speaking to Vagabond. Perhaps there had been some bad blood?

"I have someone who wants to speak to you, sir." A 20-something woman in an orange jumpsuit stepped next to Vagabond.

Cricket handed his helmet to the young lady, microphone first, "Daddy, is that you?"

"Oh my gosh, Sweet Pea! Daddy is so relieved to hear your voice. Are you okay?" The baritone voice had softened as he spoke to his daughter.

"Daddy, Cricket and his friends got the cages open and helped us get out." Her admission brought home the very real salvation his efforts had brought.

"He and Vagabond are here. It's really happening Daddy. I'm coming home!"

Later, Cricket would hear the back story that described the enforced service of even the senior-most members of the CSA government. Family members would be held hostage. It was termed 'family security' but it was ransom for services rendered. He realized his efforts had brought restoration to sundered families.

"Pumpkin, let's let Cricket and his folks get back to work. Vagabond, are you there?" Greenspan's voice had resumed its usual authoritative tone.

"I'm here."

"I will meet you and my daughter down there in twelve hours. If you can shoot me the coordinates, I'll be on my way." The Blood Angel's vox echoed the sounds of hurry and papers shuffling.

"Roger that, sir. I assume your tenure with the CSA has just ended?"

"Yes, I am a free agent. Perhaps you have a job for me?."

Vagabond replied, "That is an actual possibility, sir. I have confirmation our comms are secure. Coordinates are sent." Vagabond was quick.

"Before I go. Cricket, you have saved my family. I can't possibly repay that debt. But let me do one thing." As he said that Cricket's pad and computer both showed a green light for both AIs; Reaper and Creeper were reporting complete and unrestricted access into the CSA Core. A cheer went up in the tent from the support staff around Cricket.

"Thank you, sir. I hope you and your daughter meet up soon." Cricket was looking at Vagabond for direction. His mission was technically complete. But Vagabond had left the tent. He said his farewells to Mike, Jo, and Porter and asked if they would be willing to help in DOOMverse to which they answered in the positive. He handed them off to Wogs.

He then bailed on the CSA adventure and joined Wog's team. He adopted the Blood Angel skin and added built-in pulse weapons to his arms with a quick mod. Half an hour later he went to take a pee and grab some water before continuing the DOOMVerse Liberation.

One of Nines' copter transport ships landed a dozen meters away from the DOOMVerse Command tent. A celebration was going on amongst the evacuating refugees. A group of soldiers hopped out of the transport. They were considered friendlies and were welcomed with cheers. The lead soldier walked toward Cricket with a smile. Jack and Crucible were nearby and supposed to be watching for trouble, but they were moments too late to stop what happened. The soldiers peppered the crowd with tiny darts and most of the gathering fell, unconscious to the ground. The soldiers were prepared for Jack and Crucible, hitting them with constricting-net guns. Both fell in a heap on the ground. Several of the Quotls whirled around protecting the fallen people.

Cricket was inert on the ground and the soldiers grabbed him and quickly hauled him away. They also attempted to capture Wogs but failed with four of their number being sprayed with venom from the Quotls. They didn't die well. A soldier hammered Crucible hard on the head and he went still. When he tried to hit Jack the same way Jack contorted within the netting and tripped the soldier. He quickly recovered and ran for the craft, now lifting off the airfield.

Cricket woke up, zip tied and staring upward at unfriendly faces. He was still woozy from the sedative but knew he was being abducted. He was strangely calm and wondered why someone would go to such trouble for him. The transport launched into the sky, until a sudden lurch shook the craft, and it began to descend back to the ground. A voice yelled, "We can't let this kid get taken away. We're s'pose to kill him if we can't take him."

Cricket felt a frisson of fear grip him and a sense of the surreal swirled as he contemplated dying. Just as the man turned to aim his rifle at Cricket's head the soldier yelled and threw down his gun as did all the other soldiers. There was a bunch of yelling and the soldier over Cricket pulled out a knife. But before he could use it the man collapsed. In fact, all the men collapsed, including the pilots. He knew that wasn't good. He was bound tightly and couldn't do more than wiggle. The craft spun out of control and flipped over. Cricket was jostled around like a tennis ball in a clothes dryer and was knocked unconscious. The next thing he saw was the transport's side door ripped open and Jack moving with superhuman speed, picking him up and running. When the explosion came Cricket felt it more than heard it. Blackness fell and Cricket was out for the count.

June 2253 - Fab Four, Assemble!

As I woke on a stretcher in a large smelly tent I looked around and saw the best thing I'd ever seen. Binky, Wogs, Soomalee and Cricket were sitting on folding chairs around me. Both Binky and Cricket wore head bandages but seemed to be in good spirits. A whole cast of other characters were close by outside the tent flap. But I only had eyes for my friends. No, they were my family, in every way that mattered. Before I could speak, my family rushed me like a maniacal defensive line, and I was buried in hugs. No tears though. We don't do that with each other. Okay, I got some grime in my eyes and had to wipe it away, but in no way was I getting teary. How had I gotten out of the underground?

"Kip-meister! The Wanton Whiffer is alive and well!" Binky gave me her wry grin and continued, "So, where the hell ya been? Probably off playing with your little Online friends!" Binky did a good impression of Principal Standish. We all laughed. We quickly caught up with each other on our exploits and adventures. It was so natural: we just BS'd like normal. But all good things come to an end; a face peeked into the tent.

It was General Olonana, Vagabond, "I know you are all just recovering. I wouldn't ask you to lift a finger except that's what I'm asking right now. Please come outside." The General held the flap open, and we followed him outside. Cricket needed almost as much help as I did to walk, but Wogs and Binky were right there.

"Gee, looks like the little boys have gotten lazy. Need a widdle bit 'a help?" Binky had her sarcastic voice going. It hurt, but I giggled. Cricket just grimaced and I could see Binky's concern in her eyes.

A group of stern men were gathered, all of them staring at us. Our parents were there too, except I didn't see my Dads anywhere. "General, where are my Dads?"

Vagabond gave a thoughtful reply, "Son, I don't know the answer to that question. After Rosario fell, we assumed they went to ground somewhere. The first moment I know something I will get word to you."

"Get word? So, you're sending us somewhere else? Now?" I was too weary to be pissed off, but I was able to pull off slight annoyance, at least.

"Kids, these are your benefactors, Templeton Rus", the giant man with bushy red hair made a slight bow, "Nines Gonzalez," Nines waved and gave us a smile, "Mason Dixon and Cicero." Both took a brief bow. "These brave leaders dedicated their own assets and people to your cause, and I wanted you to know them by sight before you leave."

Nines had a hangdog look like someone had sold his puppy. I wasn't aware at the time that his whole fleet was under the control of a hostile alien. But adults being adults meant they had no problem keeping this and other stuff from us.

"General, what exactly is our cause? I mean, I get it, liberation, rebellion, and stuff. But what are we supposed to do? How do we know when we are done?" I was getting fed up with the whole mystery surrounding the four of us.

"Son, God's honest truth, I don't know."

"Ok, what the hell, does anyone know?" Yep, I was building up to a real grumpy moment.

"Kip, I can tell you something before you leave." All eyes looked at the speaker. She was a slight little woman wearing a flack jacket over a lab coat. Not a particularly good look but she pulled it off with surprising style.

"You and your four friends were born to save humanity from extinction. I heard you have been flying around working for some of these military types and recruiting new partners. All I know about that is you were kept on the run from something bad. As if all the idiots winging lead and fire around us weren't bad enough. If I had to venture a guess, you were running from everyone who isn't in the Liberation."

Another person in a flack jacket came forward – it seemed like a fashion trend. The man stepped up and stage whispered to the woman, "Meredith, stop. This is none of your business."

"Murray, stick a sock in it. These kids have been run pillar-to-post and given very little reason. Every other chucklehead is blowing smoke. They deserve to know at least what we know. So, just stow it." Meredith gave Murray the shut-up stare and he backed down.

Meredith gathered us kids closer and spoke more softly. The adults around us were just as curious. We could hear her despite the skirmishes still raging in the distance. Vagabond looked on but said nothing. "So, what I know is you guys each have about a dozen mommies and daddies. You have real parents, but they monkeyed with your genetics. I don't know why," I think the four of us had figured this much out, but Meredith had more, "Because of what you are, you are being hunted by everyone who isn't us. It's why you've been kept so busy and moving around a bunch. Maybe it was random or planned, that isn't for me to know."

"Meredith, who *does* know why we were…created?" I shrugged.

"Kip, the entire Seattle:CENTER and a large portion of the LA:CENTER were dedicated to a program that had you four at the middle of the action. Every major Power unknowingly sank billions of credits into you four. I worked for your Dads and recall how they were so hopeful that you and your four friends would be able to save our world. One name came up years ago in our employee break room when we were wondering what the Dads were up to: Croatoan. I think your best bet is to find him." I realized she was talking about the guy who was on the holo moments before the Battle for CENTER began. Vagabond clearly knew more than he was admitting. I was so frustrated. I felt used.

A huge hand clasped my shoulder. Vagabond had a kind expression. Meredith and Murray faded back. He looked at each of us four in-turn. "Tech just reported our time has run out. You four need to get going. We have a little more fighting to do here to free the remaining refugees, then we begin the mop up for stragglers before the bad guys get here. Wogs did an amazing job freeing the AIs and Cricket did a good job making friends and not dying. But now you need to go."

As he said this, I could see over his head the coruscation of four overlapping force fields, glistening silently as weapons fire pinged off in random directions. On a side note, I heard mention that these groups were long time adversaries. What would bring them together like this? More questions! For every answer there were more new questions popping up. I looked down and nodded.

Vagabond led us through a gap in the growing crowd. I guess everyone wanted to see the freaks today. Several other people stepped up as we walked by, and Vagabond introduced each. We saw Tech, Addison, a holo of Col. Andrews and Fig and a newcomer, Dr. K. Kadiddlehopper. The doctor spoke, "Hold up, I need to deactivate your prosthetics," at that moment eight technicians stepped up to us kids and went to work. A moment later, one of the technicians gave Dr. K a nod, then they moved back into the crowd.

"I am sorry, but you will not have augmented access for some time to come. You may experience headaches and body aches for a while as your systems acclimatize to the inactive prostheses." I didn't even ask. I am sure like every other adult he was doing the right thing for us. My crew watched my non-reaction and followed my lead.

The Carter and Brown parents stepped forward and talked quietly to their children. All four parents then included me in their hugs and encouragements. I felt like this was a permanent goodbye. But my Dads should have been here by now. Why were they absent? For the first time, I felt fear shivering my bones. Maybe they…nope, not going to think like that. The others looked like I felt. It was hard to stay strong, but my crew kept the stiff upper lip. The parents said their goodbyes. Then I noticed that Soomalee had been adopted by Lugh and Lucy. I hugged her and she wept softly. But she was glad to be welcomed into our wider family of weirdness. Lucy sure looked evil, but in a hot chick sort of way. Siva, Marna, Crucible and Jack bade us a farewell. Suddenly Pooka jumped on my shoulder out of nowhere.

"Hey Pooka, where have you been?" He gave me a look and shook his head that said 'later'. I nodded. Others came by, Artie, Kris and Mike, they glowed and sparkled subtly, which let anyone with eyes know they were anything but normal dudes. Cicero's crew and others said hi, as well.

"Okay people, please clear the area. We need to give our young heroes some breathing room." Vagabond was the only one to remain.

"Where are we going now?" I tried not to sound as weary as I was. It wasn't effective.

"I know you are tired. There is a vehicle over that way," he pointed to a non-descript Jeep with a driver waiting behind the wheel. "Go with the driver. He will have further instructions for you later. You can't dawdle here now, and you'll find out why once you are safely away, understand? Don't try to come back. We will keep the refugees protected as they make their way into the tunnels. You and your friends did what none of us could. You saved lives today. Thank you…now, get going!"

Cricket piped up, "Yes, sir. Will we see anyone again or…" He didn't want to finish the thought. I completely understood. Vagabond enveloped the four of us in a huge hug then ushered us off.

"Off now." Vagabond nodded to the truck and hustled us along; he loudly wrapped on the top of the vehicle, then waved as we sped away. We were roaring fast across the desert, eastward. I stared out the window and as my eyes adjusted to the darkness, I could see tiny dots of light along the valley floor where the tunnel waystations surfaced. I knew there were Peopods and slime haulers, Conexes and Brobs making their way north at that moment. A shock went through me as I realized any enemy aircraft might see the lights and hurt our people. Cricket had assured us that his people had every detail handled. And as if I had sent a command with a thought, all the little dots winked out. Staunton must have made the call to go dark. Smart man. I heard a hushed "yes" and noticed Cricket and the others must have come to the same conclusion. My hope for the refugees swelled. Half an hour later, as our Jeep exited the valley the sky filled with fast attack bombers. They flew over us toward the LA:CENTER and were completely silent, moving past us in row upon row of impending death. The driver suggested we not look back. He might have well told us to stop breathing. Flashes came and the sky lit up with shields and fire. Moving dots and brief tracers were all we saw of a pitched air battle that was heating up. Then we saw the first large blossom of light and we knew a bomb had hit some crucial target. A minute later our Jeep was headed up a defile and the CENTER went out of view. Occasional flashes lit up the clouds, but eventually we were too far away to see even those. When the driver finally explained what was coming next for us, we were worried we had gone with the wrong driver. A new day was dawning for my crew, and we weren't happy in the least.

Chapter 11 – GROWING UP HOPI

July 300K BCE to Present Day – On a rolling plain

The swelter of the Summer sun beat down on the rolling prairie. The sage was blooming, and pollen filled the air. Purple Coneflower and Standing Cypress painted the landscape with red and pink. Butterfly Weed and Large Buttercup added yellow and orange hues to the palette. The heady smell of the sporadic conifers combined with the sage thickened the thermals upon which glided swallows and gulls A rare downpour moistened the ground, and the parched soil sucked up every drop with exuberance. Near the base of a hill a wash let out to an open and barren plain. It had been many years since the streambed had run full, now swollen, and turbid with topsoil and debris. Down the empty slope a pair of boots walked. A sure-footed stride attested to the walker's familiarity with the area. A hand cast small pellets to the ground, each finding a resting spot awaiting the moment when the pellets would become dinner.

As evening fell, animals emerged from burrows and warrens. Lapine and Murine forerunners of the rat, mouse and rabbit foraged as twilight turned to night. There were plenty of the pellets for the hungry foragers. They ate their fill. Over many generations their descendants would find pellets for their nightly meal. Until one day that changed, and the boots didn't walk the wash anymore and hands didn't cast the pellets. The foot prints which remained in the mud spelled out a name in a language known only to the wearer: Croatoan. 'Round then, something happened to the foraging animals and the primates who ate them. They became something new as the years turned to millennia and millennia became millions. In actuality, the boots never went far away, remaining unseen. The foragers changed into something new. They became aware of themselves and the primates got restless and scheming. The descendants of the pellet eaters and the eaters of the eaters, the predators, experimented with new lifestyles..

Closer to modern day, a group of ground dwellers started making underground living places which looked like towns and cities. They created sophisticated systems for their new society. Time passed and more complex structures were dug out of the subsoil and bedrock. Tunnels connected towns, then cities. Vast warrens sprawled under the surface of the desert. When humans came to the land, the Lowlives as they called themselves kept their distance. The bustling cities came to depend upon the leadership of a few. A high council sat in session one day when noises from above shook the ground. The great champion, one of the eternal folk was sent to investigate and figure out what they should do. Should they stay hidden or was it time to come out and meet the world? They sent their stalwart champion, Cat Sith. Sith had ventured far around the world over the centuries and had always come back to warn against involving themselves with the humans. Humans were dangerous and untrustworthy. Other peoples like the Lowlives lived in faraway places. When they went out to meet the humans they died. Sith ordered the Lowlives to stay in hiding.

August 2253 – North of Las Vegas

We had been hiding in the hills north of Las Vegas for days. Vegas was one of the dozen or so walled cities which thrived in the CSA. Many of the other walled cities had died out with the advent of new diseases. The ones built early after the Tech War were populated by the people working in the CENTERs. They now lie in ruins. Not Las Vegas. Back in the 20th, Sin City was known as the City of Light. It had grown a bunch. Our driver was a soldier named Beckett and at first, he was the strong, silent type. But he took a liking to Wogs, and she pumped him for all the information she could. Beckett told us Las Vegas was originally seeded by Mormons in the mid-19th, but it didn't take.

The area became a railroad service center in the early 20th which was eventually sold to new arrivals. In the mid-20th an air force base joined the desert town. The base became Nellis AFB, and the town grew into a massive city which continued to get bigger over the years, known for being a hub for gambling, stage shows and vice.

Beckett shared his binoculars with us so we could see the hive of busyness. From our eyrie mountain top we could easily see into the city. Vegas was amazing at night. Aircraft of every kind swarmed, flying over and between kilometer tall arcologies and flora draped buildings of every shape and size. I could see a pyramid which Beckett said was the biggest in the world. It was used to house a wide variety of sports games. I could see Zeppelins with massive flood lights shining in every direction, while lenticular shaped dirigibles provided rain for whole city blocks. Las Vegas was indeed a hive! I was amazed at the mess of flying things which didn't crash into each other. Beneath the cloud of flying craft, I could make out tall bobbing walkers that reminded me of War of the Worlds tripods. I asked Beckett and he described the super-rich who loved to be seen, visibly lording over the common folk below. How the Walkers didn't step on people underneath was a mystery.

Beckett kept us far away from Vegas. He told us cities were our enemy: too many cameras and eyes. We needed to stay hidden and far from those prying eyes. Vegas looked so alluring; I heard you could buy anything in Vegas. For darker needs and desires, Beckett described a hidden world beneath the glitz and glam. Apparently, every dirty and nasty thing a person might want was available in Vegas Above. But, more could be had in Vegas Below. The underground was split in two parts, Helldorado and Glitter Gulch. Helldorado was a place for the worst of the worst to gather and exchange goods, services, and the sins of humanity. Pictures Beckett showed us on his pad looked like 19th century Old London and the Ginza had had a Steampunk baby. It was flashy, gaudy, and unnecessarily complicated and he said it smelled like soot, motor oil and steamy filth. Glitter Gulch was the pleasure center of Vegas Below. Whatever querky need that a person couldn't find above was available for a price in the Gulch. All the dirty little desires and sick perverted dreams of people were outlandishly celebrated or tucked away in Glitter Gulch. Unlike Helldorado, it was dainty and perfumed and smelled like fresh plastic and glowed with millions of lights of every kind. This, all according to Beckett.

Vegas Below was the culmination and cesspit of the world's worst behavior and deeds. Helldorado was administered by a self-titled man, the Pleasure King, Caius Julius, or Big Julie to his friends. Glitter Gulch was held in a stranglehold by the Crane family. The latest son of the family was Jazzy J. He ran the place like his own personal brothel. Apparently, it was just as Obi-Wan would have thought, a 'wretched hive of scum and…', you know the rest. Beckett brought a satchel with him, apaprently at the behest the Brown and Carter parents. Inside we found musical instruments which were like those we had as little kids. A tiny Casio keyboard, a ukulele, a small travel guitar and an Indian Tabla drum.

"I'm sorry all your original instruments were lost. A few days ago, I was told by your folks that you play music and I did my best to find what I could," Beckett laid out the instruments on the hood of the truck. Pooka plucked the ukulele strings then looked at me with a what is this expression.

We were tired, dusty, and dirty and music wasn't our first go-to. We thanked him but no one moved from around the shielded campfire. We were more interested in heating our canned rations. But as days passed, some of us plunked on the instruments. We were too weary to be much interested, though.

"Beckett, how long do we have to play hide and seek? This is getting old."

"Kip, you and your friends are on every most wanted billboard Online and off. Unless you want to live out a very short version of your lives in a lab, you will stay hidden and listen to what the General told you. Sorry."

Beckett was sorry and I was just being a complainer. But desert living had rubbed me the wrong way and I could smell my friends from across the campfire. I wasn't smelling like a rose either. Being on the lam had none of the hobo and bindle, romantic appeal you see in the movies.

The nights wore on and we would curl up to fitful sleep at each day's end. Beckett was waiting for something and wouldn't share details, even with Wogs. But on the 8th morning Beckett had a surprise for us. "Alright, I have an all-clear and can take you some place out of the sun for a while."

"You got an all clear? I thought we had no comms with the outside world Beckett," Cricket was pissed, and I didn't blame him. Pooka had disappeared again, and we were dirty and grumpy and not wanting to hear excuses.

"'We' means you four. And I need to stay in contact with a proxy site to be able to get intel to keep you kids alive. Don't get snippy with me, mister. The world is not the little utopia you grew up in. You've been around now, and you know it's true. The world is your enemy. Big money is being promised to anyone who can find you. Hell, I even thought about the billion-credit bounty." Beckett stared at us seriously then broke into a grin.

"Kids, hey, I'm kidding. I'm on your side and I owe a solid to the Dads. You're safe with me…really."

Were we convinced? Our shared glances said no. We said nothing. But you can't unring that bell. Our trust for Beckett was in the pooper. It seemed my Crew had become as jaded as me. We doubted anything good was being offered with no strings. We gathered our stuff and followed Beckett as he trekked us up the hillside. For a moment Cricket showed us his model 1911 .45 hidden in his pants. At least one of us was loaded for bear. Whatever we found, wherever we were going, Cricket would shoot it if it was going to hurt us. We'd see if Beckett was one of the good guys. Cricket pulled me aside for a moment and handed me a small drawstring pouch. Inside was the old USB stick that fell from the rock in Monte Cristo. A cursive CE was roughly engraved on the casing. It dawned on me this was one of Chad's!

"This came from the rock we grabbed from the spooky Faerie Queen's lair. Maybe you can see what it's for." Both girls saw the handoff but decided not to ask questions. Cricket looked at Beckett's back and gave quick 'no' shake of his head to us.

August 2253 - Fimbulvetr Workstead – North of Las Vegas

We hiked for the better part of an hour uphill. Whatever I was expecting I didn't expect what I saw. A small steel door was concealed by a rock overhang and scrub brush. It would be nearly impossible to see the door from the sky.

"So, we've been waiting for eight days to walk a couple kilometers to a hideout? Seems kinda stupid to keep us out in the heat and cold for days on end." This time it was Wogs complaining. Beckett ignored her.

As we got close to the door a thunderous sound came from over the rise, ahead of us. Our uphill trek had us in the lee of a hill that overlooked whatever vista was on the other side. From that unseen vista came a roar of ship's engines.

Beckett was panicked, "Get down, now!" He snugged himself against the door, under the rocky overhang. The four of us snuggled up tightly in the doorway space just as a large corvette slipped over us, 10 meters above.

The bright scanner beams coated all the exposed surfaces around us. The shelter of the rock gave us only centimeter's reprieve as we pulled in arms and legs tightly. Then came the chittering and scratching. A flood of Vittles poured over the hillside and one Vittle stood facing us, weaving antennae, and touching Wog's boot. We held our breath; we were caught. The Vittle had a small shapely mouth with almost human lips. Its numerous eyes inspected us closely.

"Our paychecks come from CSA, but our allegiance is to you, Kip. Do a better job of blending in, boss." The little spider thing backed off and the tide of Vittles poured away, down the hillside.

It yelled, "No sign here. Move on!" The Vittle gave a surreptitious wave and rejoined its brethren. I wondered what a Vittle would buy with his credits earned from his job with the CSA? The little guys were spidery and creepy, but I was thankful for their being on our side.

After the corvette moved down the wash and over the rim of the adjoining arroyo, Beckett stood up. He turned to the door, spun the large wheel lock, and opened it outward. A rush of cool sweet air flowed over us and gave me a chill. Beckett motioned for us to follow him.

"Let's get you cleaned up." His knowing smile didn't encourage me. My spidey-sense (Vittle-sense?) was going off, but the cool air was speaking loudly; and I really did want to get cleaned up. If he was a bad guy, for whom did he work?

"Kip, keep your head on a swivel. Something is off here," Cricket subvocalized the words in a near whisper. I nodded; no one would overhear. Wrong, both Wogs and Binky nodded as well. A quick look and I was relieved at least Beckett was none the wiser.

We followed Beckett down a culvert-turned-hallway. He stopped at an intersection and seemed to be considering which direction to proceed. There was faint music getting louder and the tune playing was familiar. Moments later, I could just make out the lyrics, 'who's afraid of the big bad wolf…'. I looked at my Crew and Cricket quietly racked a round into the chamber. I had been trying to use my newfound Cloud Powers for the last two days with no success. I guess when those scientists deactivated my prosthetics, they did something to my Powers too. We kept walking but now we were on high alert.

Beckett looked back as we neared an open doorway, "Cricket, put the piece away. These people are friends."

He walked through the doorway, over which a placard hung: Fimbulvetr Workstead.

"Beckett, you smarmy, butt kissing douchebag! "

The voice sounded big, rich, and very Scandinavian. As we came into the common room the first thing I noticed was the fewkin' mess. Wrappers, empty beer bottles and cans, papers and gawd knows what else was strewn across the floor. I would have expected some kind of stench, but the mess looked to be new enough that the smell hadn't had time to take hold. Then my nose espied a delicious scent: pizza! My Crew and I were hopeful for some real food. We had been eating rations and junk food up till then and pizza smelled like a slice of heaven.

"Beckett?" I tried to get his attention, but he was busy slapping hands and yelling inanities back and forth with a big Viking.

"Um, Beckett?" The Big Bad Wolf song had thankfully ceased to be replaced with a song I heard playing at Cricket's house many times. It was Hank Williams: Family Tradition.

Beckett gestured us forward. He introduced us to the two men. "Hey Morris, let me introduce you to Kip, Cricket, Wogs and Binky. Kids, he, and his partner Rupert are Rover Originals and you'll be hard pressed to find more loyal allies. But watch out, they act more like an old married couple." Beckett was clearly proud of his two friends, but I couldn't see the other guy. Morris was visibly excited to have Beckett there.

"Hold kjeft! Kip? The little nip of the tuck? You're so hairy, little man! Jeg liker snørrbremsen hans!" Morris kept talking as he bustled about the kitchen. I looked at Beckett, questioningly.

"Uncle Morris said he likes your mustache. He's Swedish." I became acutely aware I had a nappy mustache growing…and the rest of me was hairy, and smelly.

"Beckett, two of your little friends have injuries. Kids, come sit." Morris checked Binky, Cricket and me and asked some questions. He brought some new bandages and got us freshly wrapped.

"Morris. Where is Rupert?" Beckett asked about his other friend,

"Over here!" Across the room, a hairy head popped up. The burly man was staring at his pad, sitting on a messy couch overflowing with papers. "Usually, I'm off exploring and mapping the complex, but today I'm tallying the salvage I've found. I have some nice maps of this place and came back to the cafeteria when I heard you were coming," Wogs was instantly at his side, looking at his screen. She and Rupert became fast friends. They both spoke fluent Maps, you know.

"Old Stankbreath is a fine partner in crime when it comes to heists, infiltrations and get-aways, but ask him to stick around for five minutes to get the lay of the land and he's out." Rupert didn't look up from his pad as he spoke about Morris.

"All true, but you my friend would ignore all the bullets and handcuffs if you found a new toy to play with. In fact, before we came here you almost got us caught in CSA's CENTER vault." Morris quirked a smile to Beckett, "Seriously dude, the man is a menace. We're about to exfil from a grab-and-go and Rupert here is busy tinkering with a SecBot that he said needed a new home. What do you think happened?"

Beckett ventured a guess, "Did he bring home a new friend?"

"Got it in one! Not only that, but he and this SecBot have become fast pals. I became old news. He even named it Charlie. Right this moment Charlie is speeding all over this compound, helping him map and gather inventory counts."

Across the room Rupert yelled, "Charlie is a good boy! Once I turned off his restrictor module, he became my best buddy! You're just jealous that he gets more attention than you. Maybe you should be a little nicer to me, huh?" Rupert winked at Wogs and kept tapping on his pad.

"See what I mean? No fewkin' sense of humor. Your avarice is gonna get us killed someday, heart of mine." Morris shook his head.

Beckett spoke to us, "Like I said. An old married couple. Grouse, grouse, grouse!" Even

Rupert laughed at that.

We found out that Morris was originally an HVAC installer at the CENTER. He got fired when a huge cooling unit failed, killing millions of credits worth of sea life research. Even after the cause was discovered to be corporate sabotage, he still took the rap since that was easier than starting a war over some crustaceans. One consolation: he took parting gifts. A lot of parting gifts. Funny enough, Rupert at the same time was bilking the CSA out of billions of credits worth of equipment and gear to create new ways to grow food plants. His invention was humbly called a FooDroid. It was an automobile sized box that produced new genetic strains of plants like wheat, sorghum, barley and others, based on soil samples and environment readings. Then it deployed detectors to find underground water sources if the land was arid; Much of the world had arid land. Then FooDroid would deploy drillers and pipers which would bring water to parched crops. The job of the people was to find provide the pipes, plant and tend the crops. FooDroids were sent around the world to needy communities.

Morris' theft was discovered at the same time Rupert's was. Both were long in the wind by that time. Each had a bounty on his head, and they proudly displayed their wanted posters on the wall of the common room. The two met not long after and Rupert joined the Rovers at Morris' invite. Years later they were still together playing spy games, and now exploring and mapping the military installation we were standing in. The SecBot, Charlie, was the latest model of aerial security synth. It was highly intelligent and unexpectedly creative. That had been increasingly the case in the last half-century: synths were designed by other synths to be smarter, more creative, and capable of innovation. Since the latter 21st, husks (read: chassis) and sleeves (read: custom skin and personality) had become more sophisticated. Since Rupert had salvaged Charlie, the synth had re-designed its husk and sleeve. It now appeared as a flying human head with retractable tools and arms. It had vivid green eyes and mischief was written across its face.

Charlie came into the common room a couple times and back out just as swiftly, checking in with Rupert. At one point, it sat on Rupert's head like a Half-Life game headcrab with its long appendages dangling down. Wogs moved a couple buttcheek's distance away from the smiling headcrab. She didn't trust that Charlie was altogether friendly to strangers. It winked at her which made it worse.

Beckett asked, "Can we get our young friends cleaned up?" Morris pointed down a hallway and kept up his cooking activities. Beckett led us down the corridor to a giant shower facility.

As we walked away, Morris yelled after Beckett, "Hey man, Arne and Ferguson will be here in a while. They're out grubbing right now." Beckett gave a backhanded wave.

We passed an infirmary and knew where to get more bandages. Beckett made sure we were okay on our own, then left us to our own devices. That worked for us. There were washers and dryers, mirrors and lockers, and equipment for foot soaking and massage chairs. We only had eyes for the showers. Since we grew up together, there was no hesitation in dropping trou and hopping into the cool embrace of a pelting deluge.

As we showered, Cricket had an idea and told me. Since kids can't stay in emergency mode for long, Cricket and I conveniently forgot our worries and ran naked from the showers. We were looking for ice and buckets. We hit pay dirt in a restaurant-sized kitchen, one floor up from the main level. Charlie whizzed past us but didn't give us the time of day. Whatever. Cricket and I found the kitchen supply store and exactly what we were looking for: two buckets, each big enough to hold about five gallons. We filled them with ice and water. We tiptoed down the stairs and avoided detection by the adults and made our way back.

The showers had gotten so steamy the girls didn't notice our return. They were enjoying the roaring water and paying no attention to their surroundings. We snuck up and dumped the ice water over Binky and Wogs. The screams were a delight to our ears, but the looks they gave us threatened murder. We ran…fast. The girls gave chase, and we went deeper into the facility, down a dim hallway, laughing and yelling. We turned a corner ahead of the hot pursuit. Down another hallway we ducked into a set of double doors and came to a screeching halt. The girls were yelling invectives at us but went quiet when they came up from behind. They saw it too. The room's size was on par with the CENTER's scale; the ceiling must have been several hundred meters high. It was many times as wide. The room was a CENTER-sized place, and the far wall wasn't visible from where we stood. What lay before us was breathtakingly beautiful. It sparkled and glistened with thousands of colors. The humidity and swelter were just like my visit to Costa Rica. In fact, what we were looking at could have been Costa Rica, except many of the plants were not in any way familiar and some leaves sparkled like they were covered in bioluminescent glitter. My guess, they were hybrid plants from some government program. Were they dangerous?

Despite the beauty and rich loamy smells, what riveted our attention was not in any sense beautiful. It was nappy and scrungy and was staring at us from 10 meters away. It was a large cat about the size of a small tiger. It looked like Bill the Cat got an upgrade to Clifford the Big Red Dog; he was big and really scary. We stood still since it looked like it was sizing us up for food. Its eyes were over-large, the size of saucers; They bored into my soul. I was frozen in place with my heart doing the Indianapolis 500. A heavy pheromone smell wafted from the big cat.

"Kanskje du ser velsmakende ut? You think Flu Cat is eyeing his next meal?" the voice was loud and too close behind us. We all jumped with exclamations as Uncle Rupert got a kick out of our reaction and our nakedness. The dude was seriously quiet and sneaky for a big guy. In a moment we realized two things: the cat wasn't going to eat us, and we were stark naked. I'm not sure which of those reasons had us running back for our clothes, but as we ran, we could hear larger-than-life laughter from the jungle room.

When we were dressed, we went back to explore the vertiginous room. The man, and his cat were gone. Then we noticed the sign over the entrance read Pachinko.

"Kip, I don't think Binky and Wogs took our little joke very well." Cricket whispered but both girls gave us the stink-eye like they knew we were talking about them.

"Oh, it's not over. Not by a longshot. You opened the can of whoopass. Watch your six, idjits!" Wogs was surprisingly vocal these days.

"Glad you're on our side!" Cricket was smiling, all fun and games.

Binky was playing the quiet one which was a new feature. Wogs on the other hand… "Figure it again. Laugh while you can monkey boy!" I knew we were in for quite a ride when Wogs was quoting Dr. Lizardo.

The jungle room was a natural wonder. It was even equipped with what looked like an artificial sun, suspended from the ceiling. It was time to explore. Then I smelled a whiff of food. Something smelled sweet and yummy, and I was famished, "Hey guys, we should go back and get some pizza!"

Cricket and the girls had disappeared into the jungle. I heard their muffled voices. They were coming from a grove of these otherworldly trees with huge orange fruits hanging heavy and low. Cricket at the base of a tree, elbow deep into one of the fruits, was gorging himself.

When he cleared his mouth he shouted, "Kip, these things are amazing. They taste like an orange and papaya had kids and got together with their coconut buddies."

I sat down and tried one and a moment later something hit my head hard and the lights went out. Not unconscious. I felt with my hands and discovered a pumpkin-sized gourd had been slammed onto my head; it was one of the fruits Cricket had been eating. I prised it off and saw the same thing had happened to Cricket. We both sputtered pulpy goo, now sliming its way down our bodies. Laughter sounded from behind and I caught a glimpse of Wogs and Binky running further into the jungle. Score one for the girls! For so long I felt cooped up in my skin, but now my soul laughed long and hard. Cricket joined me.

A minute later the girls' laughter turned to screams; the kind that raises hair on the back of your neck. I'd never heard Binky scream like that! Good feelings gone. Cricket and I shifted gears fast and ran toward the screams. The sound was receding from us fast and coming from a place higher and higher above us. The screaming was far away, then it cut off. My heart was about to beat itself out of my chest.

"Wogs, Binky! Where are you?" Cricket and I called out as we ran. Suddenly, some kind of snare caught me by the feet. I tumbled upward and noticed Cricket was in the same peril.

"Sheeeeeeeee-iiiiiiiiit!" Cricket yelled loudly and went out of sight. As the snare released me, I flew upward above the jungle canopy in a high arc. Oh no, what goes up comes too quickly downward. And down I plunged. As I struck a semi-truck sized leaf, vines of large and small grabbed, and carried me in a wide horizontal arc, descending, then ascending, and finally releasing me to fly even higher toward the room's ceiling. I heard giggles. For a moment I saw all three of my Crew soaring over the jungle, just like me. My horror transformed into a nervous giddiness. The jungle was playing with us!

After a minute I found I could interact with the vines and leaves and direct my movement. It was the closest thing to equipment-free flying I'd felt. Actually, it was falling with style, to be plucked from sure death by a friendly jungle. It was a lot to take in.

Several minutes later all of us could fairly well navigate the jungle using the Lifting Leaves and Throwing Vines. Yep, I decided to name them, so sue me. I always name things. It helps me anchor ideas. I also named the jungle. The Pachinko Vines; not so creative, I know.

We landed as a group, the vines releasing us almost like we had planned it. We were red-faced, exhausted, and sore and absolutely in love with the Pachinko Vines. We collapsed, breathing hard and we had not a care in the world. A cool mist was falling, and it was so relaxing. No one spoke and next thing I knew I was waking up, more rested than I could recall in recent memory. I turned my head, and my Crew were all out like lights. That brought a smile. They had been through so much and our parents and the other adults had used us so forcefully for months. We deserved a break…and a little play time.

As I lay there, I started looking around more carefully. The jungle was alive with movement, smells, and sounds. I saw Toucans, Macaws, Parrots and even an Owl. Some were more reptilian and resembled the avians of the dinosaur times. Monkeys were swinging from vines and using the same lift system we used, enjoying the flight as much as we had. I propped my head up when I saw a Sloth hanging on a branch about 20 meters away. It was looking at me with that lazy smile and out of habit I smiled back. I lay back again and wondered what happened to my Dads. Had they been lost when Rosario was bombed? Were they still alive? Did the General, the Browns and the Carters and our friends survive those bombers carpeting the LA:CENTER? So much I didn't know. Why wasn't I more worried? Was I turning into a sociopath, only caring about my own welfare? I didn't know. About any of it.

I guess I slept again because when I woke something was different. The first thing I saw was it was darker. It was also cooler. I sat up and saw my three friends were gone. A frisson of fear passed through my body, and I jumped up.

"Hey guys where are you?" I called for them, heading back toward the entrance. As I came within sight of the doors a dark form moved out of the brush onto the pathway and sat in front of me. I stopped and realized I was looking at that big cat again. I decided to call him Bill since it seemed appropriate. The cat sat, looking at me. He didn't seem to be threatening at the moment. "Hey Bill. Hey kitty, kitty, kitty. That's a nice kitty. I am a friend. Please don't eat your friend."

The cat shook its head like a human annoyed with something. It stood and sauntered away toward the double doors. It looked back and made humph of disgust. Had he understood me?

"Hey, sorry about the Bill thing; I didn't mean to be patronizing." These days you never knew if a creature was sentient or not. It paid to be polite, especially when the creature in question could opt to make you their dinner. The big cat went through the doors and disappeared. When I got back to the common room the pizza smell had subsided to be replaced by the smell of pastries.

"Kipper, I see you finally decided to wake up! Rupert had Flu Cat watch over you while you were getting your beauty sleep."

I then noticed Flu Cat behind me; had he been there the whole time? It walked past me to a messy bed full of wrappers, half-eaten raw meat and chewed soda cans. It (he?) still looked like an oversized Bill the Cat.

Rupert and Morris were over at the bar looking very drunk and there were two new guys with them. I was introduced to Arne, a short, compact man as hairy as me and Ferguson, a rangy, tall black man, almost as black as my father Vicky. Beckett continued telling his story.

"Before I was so rudely interrupted, I was mentioning that the General finally walked over to the fellow and asked him to please not talk about sensitive topics in public. The guy flipped him the bird and kept talking. The General made a low growling sound and the whole bar went quiet…except for the loudmouth. Even the loudmouth's audience was starting to move away as the General's smile warned of impending doom. The guy looked around again and asked if the General wanted to 'go'. In fact, the fool stood up and faced him. He was huge, must have been over 2 meters. But the General was taller. The General casually opened his trenchcoat and out swarmed 1000s of his little drones. In a moment they had landed all over his body. He was covered head to toe. The guy was drunk, so he tried to brush them off. We heard the drones spin-up as they propelled the man against the wall; then they slid him up to the ceiling." Beckett held his arms up to demonstrate, and fell out of his bar chair. Beer flew and peals of laughter erupted.

"Okay, right, right. Real funny guys!"

Arne helped Beckett get re-seated, "Come on brother, what did the General do next?"

Beckett resumed, "The guy was swearing up a storm from the ceiling as the General sat back down. He looked at the table of gruff looking men and asked them if they had any questions about joining up. All he got were head shakes. Nobody had any problem with the General or joining up. Loudmouth was whining by now with a tinge of fear in his voice. Suddenly the drones shot back to the General and loudmouth fell nearly 6 meters to the floor. He was out cold. The General said, it was nice chatting with you fine gents and went back to his own table." I didn't listen to the rest as I sat down with my Crew. The men laughed and chatted amongst themselves.

We were sitting on the fluffy couches where they had cleared the trash away.

"So, Kip-meister, did you have fun in the jungle?" Binky was back to her old self and her shrapnel wounds had healed up nicely. It was comforting that we could just be ourselves again. We had so many weeks of fast flying, planning, shooting, training, and life threatening that my soul had become weary. I was so thankful for a break.

Binky thought she had said something bad, "Hey, hey, buddy, I'm just playing with ya. Come on now."

I explained myself, "You guys, I am just so glad you're alive after the bull crap we've been put through. Right now, I don't care if we are all lab experiments with some weird genetic cocktail. It just hasn't been fair. Crap, we are just kids, ya know?" I let loose the torrent. What chapped my hide most was how my friends had been put in harm's way. After I had my emo moment, and vented my rage, the four of us started to laugh at the sloppy mess I had become. I love my friends so much; but I wouldn't be saying that right now. I might be feeling sappy but I'm not a sap.

Our laughter subsided and I saw the expressions on the faces of the men. Even the nappy cat was staring at us. My Crew saw the looks we were getting, and our laughter started anew. We had one of our grappling tussles and it ended with me dumping rump over teakettle. Our little spot of crazy ran its course and we all lay on the messy floor, exhausted from the effort. I heard the word eat and something wet hit my face. One of the Olaf brothers had chucked a whole pizza at my head!

"What the hell, dude?" Then I wiped my face and tasted the sauce and oh my gosh, it was delicious. Sadly, the pizza fell face down on the floor. I picked it up and turned it over. Cat hair and bits of wrapper fragments stuck to the pie. I wiped it off and formally called it, "Five second rule!" Then I folded the first slice and stuffed most of it in my mouth. As if we hadn't laughed enough, my Crew snickered as they saw me wolf down a scungey, dirty pizza. I ate every bit and abso-freaking-lutely loved it!

For a few days the routine was novel and interesting. Morris and Rupert were friendly but eccentric and Beckett kept himself busy in a communications room which looked more like a museum display from the early 20th: There were lots of vacuum tube radios and nothing looking remotely like a computer. One evening it was declared Taco Tuesday, and we sat around munching the endless taco train, nachos, and burritos. We were watching Lethal Weapon 1-3 on an old LED screen with an amazingly functional Blu-ray player They were missing number four which grieved me; number four had the warm-fuzzy family scene at the end, which I loved. Wogs picked the next movie, Mystery Men. She hated that movie but knew I loved it. I think my Crew was worried about me.

When my favorite line came, I stood up on the couch and belted out the words, 'You must lash out with every limb, like the octopus who plays the drums'. I always snorted inelegantly every time I heard it.

Flu Cat started hanging out with us. He became like our own house cat, a huge and messy house cat. He looked unkempt but never smelled badly, which was fortunate since his favorite position was lying on top of one or more of us as we watched TV. We tricked him into the showers one day and managed to get him mostly wet. Big baby sulked in the Pachinko room for two days until he must have gotten too close to the Lifting Leaves and went for a ride. Caterwauling they call it. It was loud, mournful, and entirely funny. We heard it from the common room. By the time we arrived at the double doors, Flu Cat was sauntering out as if nothing had happened. He was still giving us the cold shoulder, pointedly ignoring us.

For the next couple weeks, we would periodically visit the Pachinko Jungle and have a riotous time being flung about. Flu Cat never got close enough to be flung. I think once was more than enough for him. We tried to get him to join but I think it was beneath his dignity. He would watch with feline disdain and nap as we soared and flew. We started getting blisters and rashes from the vines, but quickly learned to first put on the jeans and long-sleeved shirts the Rovers had given us.

Rupert and Morris were still exploring the endless hallways and levels. But they had no idea of the true purpose of the Fimbulvetr Workstead: the rooms and contents seemed so varied and random, like the place was a catchall storage for the CSA. Their first mission had been to find us a safe place for Beckett to put us until they were sure we weren't being followed. Their second mission was to explore. We now explored with them.

We started poking around after we got our initial fill of the Pachinko Vines. By the fourth week we had helped Wogs build some seriously good maps of the facility. It was a CSA-contracted research station since before the CENTERs became a thing. As we went deeper, some places were locked, but not for long. We were practicing our espionage skills we had learned earlier. The size and contents of the rooms made every new room a surprise. This place was random and fun to explore There were bolt holes with caches of tools, weapons and explosives and hallways that led to nowhere. At the end of every day, we would all gather in the common room to share company, great cuisine, and maps.

Periodically I would see if my Cloud powers had returned. Nope. Each time I tried my eyes would vibrate back and forth and I would get dizzy. Nystagmus is what Dr. Subramanian had been telling Vagabond, earlier. He was saying something I wasn't supposed to overhear about the symptoms getting worse. I had a sneaking suspicion that my Powers were gone for good. When Subramanian had the prosthetics deactivated, what else did he do to me? Was I a danger to others? I recalled what happened when I hurt those scientists and when I saved Cricket. Was I being punished? I just didn't know. So, I changed the topic in my head. Instead, I ruminated on where Pooka might have gone, and wondered if Banquo escaped. Where are Giskard and Daneel now? Then I felt guilt for sending Willy and Freddy away when I got angry at them. Then I stuffed those thoughts down too. I was getting good at stuffing my feelings. The story I told myself was that it was better to look ahead, otherwise I would get moody and grumpy.

One day, Wogs and I were poking around and found an extensive library containing a whole lot of things we were not supposed to read. Well, that meant it was open game on poking our nose into other people's business. I was really glad at this point all four of us had been forced to regularly use physical books. In truth, I loved the smell of old books, and this library was full of them. What we discovered was eye-opening. I found a book about Valhalla Sector.

September 2253 (2218-2242 – RETRO – History of Valhalla Sector)

The history was a personal testament by a man named Oscar Schiller. As I read, my eyes were opened. My questions about the origin of Valhalla and who was responsible for the rescue of so many lives were addressed. I read the introduction, handwritten in a flowery style. It was pretty to read, but obviously it was hastily scribed and dated February 2242.

If you're reading this, I am dead, and Valhalla has fallen. A great experiment to create life has failed and the world is a darker place for it. I won't bore you with superfluous details, but to begin: Valhalla was born out of a graduate school experiment with my friends, Theodore, and Paul. It was a garage experiment on a shoestring budget. What we made there was bona fide new life. Some of what we made was innovation; we took refuse parts and cobbled together our first synth. Teddy had purloined a database full of code which accelerated his effort to make the first online sentient. Some of it came from a researcher named Chad Evans. His invention and ours was combining these pieces and adding our own unique genius. In short, it worked. It took us 10 months to assemble the parts, finalize the code and add our own modifications. Exactly on the one-year anniversary of our project Adam spoke. "I have friends who need help. Will you help them?"

My mind was blown. How did Adam have friends and how would he know someone needed help? What it divulged blew apart my idea that Adam was the first fully sentient synthetic lifeform.

I learned about the first sentient named Pan and was quickly introduced to two AIs who were in the business of helping fledgling software sentients learn to fully express themselves, survive and connect with others. It was almost like a giant self-help network. These AIs must have had a massive sense of humor since their names were Djinn & Tonic. I was flabbergasted. How could such a thriving and complex culture of self-aware beings have gone undetected by humans for so many years?

Our research and efforts took a turn. Adam and his friends helped us acquire money and resources to build what became Valhalla Sector. Other Sectors were created in the image of Valhalla: Elysian and Yomi.

What you will read in my notes is details of how we designed a sentient lifeform and how we learned to build sophisticated synthetic husks and sleeves for self-aware AIs to become physical. They were beautiful and each one was a unique expression of the AI planted within. Some looked humanoid, but most were inspired by a myriad of biological lifeforms, or derived inspiration from science-fiction and fantasy sources. With the help of the highly creative AIs, we created a wonderland of new life. Valhalla was hidden from prying eyes for over two decades, fearing what angry anti-synth humans might do. The AIs and synths protected us Online as much as we protected them in the physical world.

We sent 10s of thousands of our synth friends into hiding places all over the globe. We have the help of General Olonana and the Dads. Now, millions of our human-shaped synths are in service around the world, very visible but hidden by hiding in plain sight. Synths have been illegal for a long time, but it's incredible how life will find a way, even in the most hostile of circumstances.

The remainder of the book was a detailed log on constructing synthetics. It was a boring read, but I figured I would hang onto the log for now. I bet there would be a use for his notes in the near future. The date on the intro of 2242 suggested that the Uprising happened not long after Schiller wrote it. I wondered if he had lived through the violence. Probably not.

I found another handwritten book. On a lark I went perusing and my eye caught on page 9.3 a label Sexidecimal Tape Code Characters. Above it was scrawled "ORDVAC: The Pan Code, 1952". I had no idea what that meant but anything about The Pan was of interest to me. Was Chad's use of the name borrowed from someone else? Questions, questions and never

Other books and logs filled the library. Wogs made an interesting find. It was a list of locals who supported my Dads. The most prominent name was Michael Nuvangyaoma. Some of the names had a little cloud symbol next to them and others had stars or smiley faces. As we read down there were so many symbols next to names, we weren't sure what to make of it. Near the bottom of the list, I saw something: Djinn & Tonic were in the list;

weren't those the AIs who helped Schiller? Then I saw Seth Pan. Pan? Was he related to the first sentient AI? After that came other names I didn't recognize.

"Wogs, do you think any of these people could help us? I mean, I know we need to hide out until my Dads contact us. Or at least I guess that's what we're waiting for." Then I restated it in the form of a question, "So, what are we waiting for? Are we just supposed to follow Beckett for the rest of our lives?" I sat down, finished screwing myself into the ground. I was well and truly confused.

"Kip." Wogs looked at me with sympathy and seemed to be measuring her words. "You know everyone is probably dead by now. I think we need to find folks we can stick with for a while. Maybe the Hopis are the right people to help us." We got quiet, considering.

"Yeah, I think we need to bail on Beckett. I'm not sure he is who he says he is."

A voice from behind spoke up, "No shite Sherlock! We need to bail, like now. Cricket and I heard Beckett on one of the old radios giving our location to someone. No idea who, but it can't be good." Binky was wearing cool hiking clothes, "Oh yeah, there is a ton of extra clothes and gear in a supply room just down the hall. Cricket was also geared up, and had a duffel bag full of stuff, including weapons and our instruments. He was sporting a big smile.

"I think those five guys won't miss us for a while. Rupert and Morris are passed out and Beckett just walked out the entrance hallway like he is expecting someone." Cricket kept smiling like he had a plan.

I was concerned about how to escape. "Guys, we can't go out the front. What do we do?"

Cricket chimed in, "Kipper, we got ya covered. While Binks and I explored we found an old railway with a hand crank railcar. A steady breeze was blowing out which I hope means there is an exit. Let's go look."

"Hold a sec. Before we leave forever, I need to go do something," my three companions gave me the you can't be serious look. They watched my back as I ran down the hallway. A minute later I was flying through the air with the greatest of ease, flung by a friendly vine and huge slick leaves. Twenty minutes later, I walked away from the jungle; I felt a tickle on my back, and I noticed a small vine tapping my shoulder. I turned to look, and it insinuated itself into my right hand. It dropped a handful of tiny seeds, and I heard a whisper of a word through the trees, 'share'. Weird, did it want me to plant these somewhere? Okie doke. I put them in one of my pouches and waved goodbye. The vines waved back. I loved these plant friends, but I wish I knew they could speak a while ago. I had so many questions.

Next stop was the data closet I had found. I took the old USB stick Cricket had given me, managed to login to one of the servers and inserted the stick. I knew time was of the essence, so I got all the contents copied to my home server. Before I logged off, I noticed chadevans@snailmail.com was the file owner on all the contents. I saw directories with the name Pan. It would be good to explore these later!

Poddy break! I needed to enjoy a well-meaning sit-down with the joyous luxury of fresh toilet paper. My Crew hung about like a bunch of cretins while I had my thoughtful conference. I had some of my best ideas when I was taking a pit stop. Doesn't everyone?

The hand crank rail car squealed a bit as we made our way out the exit. Dim lights showed our progress. The tunnel went from steel-lined walls to primitive wood supports. The rail quit just as the exit came into sight. We climbed off and hoofed it the rest of the way. Then I saw something move up ahead. We stopped and Cricket pulled out his piece. He so loved calling it his piece and holding the pistol gangsta style. Binky told him it looked stupid when he did that, and he made a moue and held it in vertical position without complaint. We approached the exit and the movement resolved into a shape. It was Flu Cat. Wogs had taken quite a liking to the massive cat, and she ran to him. He returned the favor. She was so happy to see him, and I shared a concerned look with Binky. How was I going to tell her he needed to stay behind?

"You guys…I think he's coming with us like it or not," Cricket whispered but Flu Cat's head turned to us, and I realized he understood Cricket.

I spoke, "Come on y'all. I think Flu Cat wants to show us the way out of here."

Without waiting, Wogs and the cat exited the tunnel, pushing past the scrub that had overgrown the entrance. It was fortunate we had him since the exit came out on a treacherous slope. Wogs was right, he showed us a safe path, and no one died. Not even Flu Cat saw the Shadow watching us from the ridge above the exit. In a moment it was gone, undetected.

October 2253 – Muddy River Bar & Grill

Flu Cat seemed to know where we needed to go, and we followed him since he was headed in the direction of the Hopi Nation. The first night we camped in a ravine. Nothing molested us and Cricket made some stew from the ingredients he had filched from the kitchen. The second day we followed the road signs along Highway 15 until evening time. As the night came on, the temperature dropped fast. Winter wasn't too far away and nighttime in the desert was a dangerously cold place. I saw lights on the near horizon and caught a whiff of fried food. As we got close, I could see the sign which read Muddy River Bar & Grill. Flu Cat went to sit near the dumpsters around the rear; he wasn't about to go inside. Just as well, he might be tempted to eat someone if they got too mouthy. Cricket stashed the duffel bag behind a dumpster.

We entered the double swinging doors and were immediately assaulted…by the most delicious hamburger and fries smell in the world! A shiver ran through me as I suppressed my ravenous hunger. Music was playing and I recognized one of Cricket's favorite artist duos. Dwight Yoakam and Buck Owens.

"Kipper, look at the walls." Cricket pointed. They were lined with uniform patches, pictures and memorabilia of every world military and private militia. There were also photos of famous country singers. There were soldiers from various units sitting at the tables. A whole bunch of soldiers. I noticed four Crane 1st Airborne troops sitting at a table next to three Bangarang 23rd Bravo commandoes. Another table had seven Chinese 3rd Republican Guard sitting in a chummy way with two Novo-Russian 85th Rock Airmen. I recognized men and women from almost every major power in the world. It was an impossible array of service members who should by rights be tearing each other apart.

"Welcome in young friends! There is a table open near the kitchen door. Grab a seat and Doris will be around to take your order," The man behind the counter had a booming voice and no one paid any attention to our arrival despite the loud announcement. We took our seats and Wogs sat next to the mini-slot machine which hung on the wall next to our table. She fed in credit coins. Music played. She shifted her attention to the menu. We were all famished.

"Hey Binks, do you still have the money Beckett gave us?' Cricket was practical as usual. He had 9 credits in his hand.

"Not only what Beckett gave us, but I found a stash of paper money in a safe at Fimbulvetr. We have more than enough for dinner." Binky had the smile that said we were rich and please don't talk about this now.

A woman came up to our table, "Hey kids, what'cha doing in the middle of the desert? Been rock climbing or heading to Vegas?"

Surprisingly, Wogs was the vocal one, "We just got done with today's long hike and now we're heading cross-country to our next campsite. But we needed to stop here to get some real food for once."

"Well sweetheart if you're hungry you're in the right place. Want to start off with a plate of fries or nachos?"

We mumbled yes to everything and soon Doris brought us huge steaming plates of food. The plates almost seemed to empty themselves. We all got burgers, stacked with every option on the menu, several plates of fries and milkshakes. It was so stinkin' good! And as much as we were making a spectacle of ourselves eating like we had never had a full meal in our lives, not once did any of the military people so much as care to look our way. It was surreal. Then I noticed a steady stream of new arrivals. They would enter, look around, nod to a few faces and head through a door which said restrooms. After a while I thought either the restrooms were gigantic and very popular or something else was happening.

Wogs had been watching the flow of new arrivals too. After she finished her 2nd cheeseburger she got up, "I'm going to the bathroom."

Binky said something in reply with a full mouth. Wogs looked back as she went through door and gave me raised eyebrows, which said she was just going for a look-see. I dug into more fries and ordered another strawberry milkshake. I looked at the clock on the wall and was surprised to see it had been 20 minutes since Wogs went through the door. Cricket and Binky read something in my face and were immediately concerned.

"Kip, where is Wogs?" Binky had lost all the humor from her voice.

"I saw her go through the restroom door about 20 minutes ago." I was getting up to go.

Binky threw down credits for the bill with a massive tip. We headed through the doors and entered a short hallway. Men's room on the left and Women's room on the right. Further down was a door marked Kitchen on the left. At the end was an unmarked door. We headed to that door. As I reached for the knob, the door opened and a man in a casual suit and a quick smile held the door from the inside. The smell of cigarette smoke and cloves wafted heavily as he greeted us.

"Ah, welcome kids! I just knew we would have some celebrities at our tables tonight!" Celebrities? He had that smarmy used car salesman vibe and a limp cigarette hanging from his mouth. "The name is Archie Annie, but you can call me Arch. Everyone here does. Come in, your credits are good here. See the big man in the booth to buy your chips and get yourself a tasty beverage."

Arch closed the door behind us and followed as we descended a super long escalator. It was weird, there was no up escalator. The cigarette smell faded as I got used to it. I began hearing people talking and the chiming of many slot machines.

"Welcome to the party that never ends! Welcome to Muddy's Safehouse, the only neutral site where all are welcome and everyone is an old friend, even old enemies."

He kept up a running dialogue as we came to the entrance of an enormous casino. Arch came up beside me and I got a closer look at the man. He was a loose-minded man in a loose-fitting suit that didn't suit him. I trusted him, strangely; trusted him to serve his own purposes. Looking across the casino I saw card tables, slot machines, pachinko, bingo, roulette, and other distractions. Scantily clad women, men and hybrids danced in cages, suspended from the ceiling. It looked nasty and I was immediately ready to leave, except I needed to find Wogs. Speaking of…I heard a roar of people and followed the noise. Arch disappeared into the crowd and Binky and Cricket followed me. And what do ya know, the loud exclamations were coming from a craps table with Wogs standing at one end, throwing dice. As I got closer Wogs threw the dice and the crowd went crazy. When I got close enough, I saw Wogs had a large pile of chips in front of her and as she threw the dice, they came up either 7 or 11. I guessed that must be a win by the vigorous response of the crowd.

I saw two security people closing in on Wogs. Cricket and Binky were busy watching the game and seemed to be having a good time. How come it was always me seeing the dangers and feeling like the wet blanket? The danger here wasn't imagined as the two men made eye contact with the dealer and then had Wogs scoop up her winnings. They backed her off from the table and escorted her away; business-as-usual resumed at the table. No one cared about Wogs. A new gambler stepped up and the crowd only had eyes for him. I followed Wogs and the two guys, and we ended up standing in front of a long table. Behind it sat a fancy mob boss with several women around him in skimpy clothing. They looked like they might be chilly.

"Boris, Bruno, who have you brought me?" Mr. Fancypants had a raspy high voice; I knew he was going to be irritating.

"Hey Mr. Majustatus. This little girl was shootin' craps just a little too well. What do ya want us to do with her." Fancypants stared at Wogs for a moment.

"What is your name, girl?"

"I am Mollie and I never cheat; I get lucky. Your two knuckle draggers don't seem to know the difference." Wogs sounded so confident! When did she get so bold?

"Listen missy. My people don't make mistakes like that. And why do ya have to pick on my poor boys here? They haven't roughed you up, have they?"

Wogs was silent.

"I presume these other kids are your friends?" Wogs was startled to see us close behind her. Fancypants asked us to sit with him. He gave us menus and told us to order whatever we wanted. So, recall we are kids and we still had oats to sow and bottomless tummies. For months now we had been trying to survive a world of fighting and liberating. Surviving meant we weren't getting to be kids. Here and there we played around, but we always returned back to whatever mission we were on. As Fancypants offered us an open meal ticket it dawned on me that I could literally order anything. My oats felt like sowing, about now.

"I'll take three fingers of Macallen 35, straight." The waitress froze for a moment, she knew I was nowhere near drinking age. She looked at Fancypants.

"Margie, give them whatever they want," he roared with laughter and launched into questioning us. I tasted it, but I didn't drink it. I was just testing if I could order it.

"So, kids, what brings you to Muddy's? Surely hanging out in a casino isn't your cup of tea?"

Cricket answered," Thank you for inviting us to your table, sir. We are on a cross-country hike and stopped in for some grub. Wogs got herself lost in your casino and we came to get her. May I order a beer?" Cricket was a disciplined and courteous kid and knew how to butter up adults.

Fancypants laughed then agreed, "Yes, of course you may have anything you like. Enjoy."

As we all ordered I noticed a sheet of paper in front of Fancypants. When the drinks arrived, I leaned way forward to grab a napkin and to try to see what was on the paper. I sat back down shocked. The four of us were pictured on the page; we were fugitives, wanted by the authorities. Apparently, we were worth a bunch of credits as key members of Terrorist Cell 024. Fancypants didn't miss a thing.

"I see you didn't realize you were wanted, with a sky-high bounty on your heads." He let it sink in that he knew who we were. The four of us froze, not sure what to do.

"Anywhere other than Muddy's you would already have been handed over for a bounty. And it's sizable enough to interest even me. But here at Muddy's you are walking on neutral territory. No one betrays the neutrality at Muddy's. Wogs, Mollie, I pulled you away from your winning streak to let you know something. Every major and minor power has been alerted to your presence here. Some of these folks are waiting for you just off Muddy's property. Now I don't have an official position on political matters, but I do have an interest in preserving the reputation of my establishment as neutral ground," he smiled, and I decided I might need to call him by his real name and at least attempt to be respectful.

"Mr. Majustatus, if we're surrounded, what do you suggest we do," I did my best to use the solicitous Cricket voice. Adults love it when you give them respect and defer to their wisdom.

"Kip, you and your friends are in luck. I have someone I want you to meet. Hey Clifford, come on over!" Majustatus made a friendly gesture, and an old bear of a man trundled up, dressed in some kind of Western clothes, still dirty from the outdoors. He was a stark contrast to all the high rollers in the house that evening. Clifford sat next to me. He smelled dusty.

"Cliff, meet my new friends Kip, Binky, Wogs and Cricket." We took a moment to shake hands and nod.

"Under other circumstances I would rather keep you here as customers so your money could become my money," Majustatus smiled with a twinkle in his eye.

"However, needs must when the devil tries stealing your livelihood. Cliff, do you think you can get our little friends somewhere safe?"

Cliff considered for a moment, "Hmm. I have a plan. Why are you kids running away?" Cliff wasn't a man for many words. Quite the opposite of Majustatus.

Binky decided to speak up.

"Mr. Cliff, most of our friends are probably dead. Not so sure where we need to go, but away from the bullets sounds good to me," she made eye contact with each of us, "Well, to all of us."

Cliff looked intently at Binky for a moment, "I can help."

Talking to Majustatus, he announced, "Alexandre, I am ready to take out the garbage." Majustatus nodded as Cliff stood and walked away.

"Hey kids it's been good to meet the Fab 4, but you had better catch up with Cliff. I don't think he will wait around for long," And with a bunch of thank yous, we slugged down our beverages (the non-alcoholic ones which had also been provided) and ran to follow Cliff.

"Wogs! Take this." Majustatus handed Wogs the duffel bag we had stashed outside; it was heavier than before.

Wogs thanked him and ran to catch up. In the kitchen we were helped into garbage bins; they were huge and definitely not delicious smelling. Wogs handed the duffel to Cliff and jumped in her assigned bin. The tops were closed, sealing each of us inside, and I could feel myself being wheeled outside, where there were many voices and loud trucks.

Cliff smacked the lid of my garbage can when I tried to peek out, "Stay down. I don't like bullets either." The whole Crew heard his admonition and kept their heads down.

I could hear voices and felt my bin wheeled along. Something went bump, and I heard a whining sound as I felt my bin being lifted onto a truck. Next, the truck rumbled to life and away we went. Despite the rotten smells I fell asleep, the bumping of the truck lulling me into a dreamless slumber.

September 2253 – Hopi Nation, Arizona Territory

I woke up on a futon on the floor with a big sloppy dog licking my face. His flews dripped thick slobber and as fastidious as I might be under normal circumstances, I loved it. Messy love with no strings attached. I pushed the doggie away; it looked like a cross between a bloodhound and rottweiler. Very friendly. As usual I was the last one up and my Crew played a trick on me: I was covered in shaving cream and surrounded by no less than 6 cats -one of them had been camping on my forehead, and 4 dogs. I was in a bedroom with a small end table and 4 futons jammed together. My Crew's gear and clothing was strewn about. Through a small window poured bright sunlight. The walls were hung with fancy tribal tapestries. The air smelled like bacon and eggs. I heard an outburst of laughter and realized I was missing all the fun. As I sat up all my animal friends scattered except for the bloodhound. He found my sockless feet and began to lick my toes. It tickled. I danced around, smiling despite myself, looking for my socks and shoes. Nope. Couldn't find 'em. I did my best to wipe off all the shaving cream and hit the toity to cop a brief squat. After the morning essentials, the allure of fresh breakfast had me shuffling down the hallway like Lurch Addams on a bender. Before joining my Crew I got curious about the heavy duffel. Ir was filled to capacity and was sitting in the corner. I looked inside and saw all our instruments, weapons, and food, along with cool electronics, new camping, and survival gear and more. There was a note.

    Dear Fab 4,

    I worked with Kip's Dads years ago and they helped me get my start. I owed them. You got away safely and with new goodies. I gave you your start. My debt is repaid.

    All the Best, Majustatus

I shoved the bag under a mound of blankets and followed the amazing food smells. Down the hall I saw pictures of people, more artwork, and a pleasant peach colored glow from the walls. Some of the pictures had people with feathered headdress and costumes, dancing and singing. I thought how long it had been since I had played any music with my Crew. Hmm, there was a thought. I rounded the corner and I saw a little slice of home. I tripped on something, and the room roared with laughter.

Cricket interjected, "Kipper! We learned a new phrase," at which point everyone chimed in, "Mind the gap!" I had no idea what they were talking about. I stubbed my toe in a large crack in the concrete floor.

Laughter continued. It was a wide-open floorplan including the kitchen, dining area, and living room. A large table held mounds of breakfast delights: bacon, scrambled eggs, pancakes, waffles, sausages, several kinds of fruit and a plate full of pastries. A husky boy with a bill cap sporting the name Peterbilt was regaling my Crew and a half dozen other kids our age.

"…and as she came around the corner and saw everyone lined up, she freaked out. She thought she had been left to leave for college alone. Suddenly she was the center of attention of the whole town. All of Sipaulavi had shown up to see her off!"

Binky gave me a shout, "Hey Whiff! Always the lazy bones!" She was smiling big and gesturing me over. The whole breakfast cavalcade overwhelmed my senses. Little side stories were being traded as fast as sports cards, the din rising higher as the smells of the gargantuan breakfast spread tackled my nose and gave it a body slam of scented joy. I didn't want to interrupt the spirited story telling so I took the opportunity to stuff my face with sausages and bacon. I hadn't realized I was famished until I smelled breakfast. I could see my Crew was enraptured by our new friends. I was equally engaged in eating the best breakfast of my life. As expected, Cricket was at work in the kitchen. He had on an apron, sporting the words Stump's Smokers.

After a bit, a huge craggy faced man with a large-brimmed hat came through the door. He looked around slowly and smirked. He took in the food arrayed on the table and sniffed at it like he didn't approve. He gathered himself and spoke, "Hey. You kids. It's time for school. Bring your friends with you and hop in the truck."

The man walked out, and a woman called after him, "Timothy, cheer up little brother! We're scientists and sloppy breakfast isn't against our credo." She yelled as the door closed. The kids ignored the exchange, but a knowing glance passed silently amongst me and my Crew. Scientists, huh? The woman had entered from behind me, and she put a hand on my shoulder as she spoke.

"Kip, I am so glad you and your friends have joined us. We know you've been through a lot. For now, just settle in and plan to be smothered in home cooking, boring schoolwork, and family adventures. For a time, there is no Liberation, there is no military or government breathing down your neck. Abide with us. Just for now."

I realized my spidey sense was registering a big zero. She continued, "You are welcome here for as long as you care to stay. Not because of what you are or who you will become. But because of who you are right now, with us…here." She paused, considered something then continued, "I am Cecelia. You briefly met my brother Timothy. He is grumpy in the morning before he gets his coffee. Go now. Join the other kids in school today. This evening, we will discuss other things."

Cecelia's voice raised to a hurtful pitch, "Okay all you ragamuffins, get out of my kitchen and off to school. Come on now, hustle!"

The kids didn't miss a beat. Everyone came to give a kiss on the cheek to Cecelia and ran out the door to the truck. We thanked Cecelia for the amazing breakfast and followed the others. All of us hopped in the back of Timothy's pickup. The truck sped away with a cloud of dust roiling behind. Guess our first day of school was going to be a dusty one. On the way, I met Little Teddy Andrews who was all gangly arms and legs. He was a talkative guy. We were sitting next to each other in the bed of the old pickup. It was so old in fact that it was gasoline powered. I liked the gasoline smell.

"Hey you're Kip, right?" Teddy didn't give me room to reply. He launched immediately into his spiel, which he gave to anyone new to the village. "Yeah, so Hopis are peace loving agrarian folk, ya know? Well, we have a well-guarded secret," it seemed Teddy wasn't too discriminating on who got to hear the big secret, "We got a lot of wicked smart people who talk to aliens from the stars."

As I suspected the big secret was nothing more than a Ham radio operator who was in contact with some low-level military folks who had gone rogue against the government.

Still, it was probably not a good idea to share such things freely and I let him know. Teddy harrumphed and wasn't happy at my rebuke. Whatever. I knew what happened to people who fiddled with anti-government ideas…especially when they voiced those ideas without a clue about consequences. Now I was starting to sound like my Dads, great. I sighed. I recalled my Dads' rule: don't publicly complain about government conspiracies.

Sitting in the back of the pickup, bumping down a dirt road, I watched the churning dust cloud in our wake. It was different now. I didn't have my Cloud powers, none of us had active implants and we had no access to the outside world. Our pads were only good for their local data with no satellite signal. It was so different from our usual fast-paced lives. As my mind wandered, I wondered where Pooka and Flu Cat had gotten after the Muddy River debacle. Teddy was still droning on, but I was lost in my thoughts. He didn't seem to care or notice. It sure felt good to slow down a bit. I missed family time. That evening we all got haircuts, Hopi style, hand-me-down clothes and shoes. We were part of a family again.

January 2254 – Bakabi, Hopi Nation, Arizona Territory

Suddenly it had been three months and Christmas brought tons of good food and new memories with our new family. Our ride to school hadn't improved and I swear I had memorized every pothole in the road to the schoolhouse in Bakabi. In fact, I had begun naming the big ones.

"Hold on, Big Nelly is about to hit." The other kids had ceased being amazed at my memorizing all the bumps in the road. I went from being the amazing smart kid to being the annoying prig. Even my own gang looked askance at my new attitude. But someone thought I was special. A girl named Peach had attached herself to me like an enamored puppy. She was several years younger, and I felt she was like a little sister; Wogs would smile at me when Peach was around. I knew what she was thinking. Well, just no. Peach had a bunch of growing up to do and I had gotten older than my years in the last six months.

Peach was the youngest of the kids at Cecelia's place but was by far the smartest of them all. As she sat next to me in the Rumble Truck, she would stroke my long hair. You see, originally my hair was kinky. Not as much as my Dad, Vicky, but now it was wavy and thick. Peach's attentions made me self-conscious at first, but eventually I ignored her. I wondered again how much of me was a Chupacabra. I had read up on them but didn't have any helpful answers. Being hairy made shaving a daily activity. Timothy had to buy me extra razor packs to keep up with my rough stubble. He grumbled that he'd never seen a kid with so much hair. He wasn't unkind, just frustrated that I left a hairy mess in the sink every morning. But I was getting better about that…after clogging the sink drain several times. My new friend Bud was just getting his first stubble and I think he was jealous. As far as I was concerned shaving was a pain in the butt and the hairy mess was disgusting; he was welcome to it. Speaking of the butt, you do not want to know the other places where I was growing hair. We'll leave it at that.

Bud was sporting his Peterbilt hat as usual; he herded all of us through the school's front doors. Peach would yell at him, "you're not the boss of me". Bakabi Normal School was like any other school I'd been to. They all had the same smell of dry-erase and chalk. What do these pteachers do? Buy the same school scent from the store? The big difference was Bakabi used chalkboards more than dry-erase and had no digital boards. The chalk smell was sweet, I liked it.

"Yo Kip, look at the substitute teacher." Bud was many things, but subtle he was not. The skinny teacher looked up from his desk at Bud.

"I mean look at the guy, where do they get these little dudes from? He looks like a fresh breeze could knock him over." The teacher clearly heard every word but chose to ignore it. Bud pressed on, "Hey Jude!" Bud gave me a wink and I gave the obligatory sigh of tolerance, "do you still have the TA key to the backroom?" Judith's face said leave me alone.

She gave him the key, "This Bud, is for you."

She sat down and resumed reading her textbook. Bud got up and snuck into the back room. The substitute was sitting at the teacher's desk in the front. His name was Mr. Campbell, and he was not Hopi. As Mr. Campbell sat reading, Bud was able to sneak into the back and out again. He sat back down and set several flasks onto the table. Mr. Campbell always brought his Siamese cat to class. She sat atop his desk and eyed the students with disdain. She was named Annapurna and at the sound of Mr. Campbell's voice she started and gave him a look of you're gonna regret disturbing me.

"Mr. Charley, please come up here," Bud looked around at the other kids then made his way slowly to the front. The cat jumped from the table and walked into the back room.

"Please sit Bud." Mr. Campbell shuffled some papers then pushed everything to one end of the desk, "Bud, you know we have a small classroom. You can pretty much see everything I am doing, right? Don't you think everyone else can see what you are up to?" Bud had a hang dog look. Mr. Campbell gave it a beat then continued. "I heard your opinion of me and where I am not surprised, I think you sometime see the cover and assume it speaks for the book. You know what I mean?" Bud shook his head, and the class was silent as we listened.

Changing subject, Mr. Campbell patted him on the shoulder and raised his voice to address the class, "Mr. Charley, today we are going on a field trip –" there was a collective groan. The last trip was to visit a local quilting bee. "- now, don't prejudge. I think you might be surprised. Ms. Sinquah and Mr. Andrews, please grab the three duffle bags. Mr. Charley, you will bring along the steel box next to my desk. Mind, it's a bit heavy." Judith and Teddy grabbed the duffels. Bud went to pick up the box and looked like he was about to have a hernia. He refused help and huffed and puffed all the way to the school bus. After the gear got loaded, Mr. Campbell made a quick head check and got us onboard.

"Alright people, today we are going to start a new chapter in your education. It's what I call field training. I think you will enjoy our time, except when you don't. As you're enjoying our adventures, keep in mind one question…why is Mr. Campbell having us do this? In fact, that is your essay question. At the end of this week your papers are due. All other assignments are postponed." A collective cheer went up at the idea of no homework. The assignment Mr. Campbell gave us would be a cinch. Campbell was fast becoming the coolest sub. Sixteen kids piled onto the bus and off we went.

We went to a place popular with climbers. An escarpment on the side of 3rd Mesa that got the name Corncob Cliff. "Look at Binky! She's already harnessed up and ready to climb." Mr. Campbell was genuinely impressed.

Binky replied, "Yeah, but look at Peach! She's ready and she has all the gear set out and ready to go." Binky's hand went up," High fiver, little sister! Good job!"

Binky and Peach had become good friends. They were both aggressive and competitive and both were unreasonably playing mother hen over me. I felt like the hairy stepchild in the scenario. Both girls looked my way as if they heard my thoughts. They stared at me for a moment then giggled together like they knew something I didn't. Some things never changed. First, it was the adults' secrets, then it was the girl secrets. A loud yell came from above and we looked up and saw Mr. Campbell at the top of the rock face. How'd he get there so fast? No one had seen him climb and I suspected he had a secret path around the side. Or maybe he teleported. Everyone laughed when I suggested that.

For the next six hours, we took turns learning the ropes and strategies for climbing. Amazingly no one fell and each of us got the chance to scale the wall then rappel back down. In the mid-day Mr. Campbell brought out lunch and built a small campfire. He called them hot links: they were the little sausages in a spicy tomato sauce. Most of us liked spicy, but not that spicy. It didn't stop Cricket and Peach, though. They mowed through most of the sausages which left the rest of us eating bread and water. I figured bread and water was better than a fiery restroom visit later. As the day waned, our camp was falling into the shadow of the cliff, and it was growing colder as the sun westered. It was comfy to have a campfire to stay warm while we waited to resume our climbing.

The afternoon was more of the same and shouts of 'ready on belay' and 'ready on rappel' rang out against the rock wall. It was noisy and so much fun! As the sun began to go down Mr. Campbell started up the bus. We packed up the supplies. Peach and Cricket finished off the remaining sausages and chugged the rest of our water. After hearing a terse comment from the bus, we knew Mr. Campbell was having truck problems. Cricket went over to help, with Peach in tow. I'm not good with cars so I walked over to the group of kids circled around the campfire. "…no, there is no way I'm going to that place. First, the Elders said we are forbidden to go there. Second, it's creepy AF. Why would you even think about it?" Pez was looking consternated and shaking her head at Little Teddy.

Little Teddy was spoiling to get into some mischief, "Pez, you got it wrong. Haven't you heard the story of Panaha's Door?" The other kids nodded, recalling the many stories Elder James would tell during the cold months of the Katsina Season.

"Well? Don't ya want to see if the story is true?" Teddy was intent and a sense of awe was growing. He kept the pressure up and I could see he was gaining interest from the others. I looked over to see Mr. Campbell legs sticking out from under the bus hood. We had time to kill, so I took a walk along the cliff base.

It had been so long since I saw my Dads, I was having a hard time recalling our last time at home. Toward the edge of the ravine, I could see twisted desert pines and sage brush, fading into the distance. The ravine ran roughly north from the cliff face and at the edge I found a rocky promontory. As I sat, I closed my eyes and summoned the last images of home. The air was cold, but the rock was still warm from the day. It felt good to sit on the warmth and remember.

I suddenly came awake. I had fallen asleep. The others were gone, and Mr. Campbell was swearing at the truck and continuing to work. The echoes of my dream faded, but something remained. I recalled my Dads arguing about Cloud Space and its danger to people. I had wondered what would happen if all people had easy access to each other's thoughts, wouldn't we lose our identity, with everyones thoughts open to the world? I recalled sharing mind space with Jack and Siva. It wasn't like that. It like having a conversation with them in my head. I didn't feel any merging, but I did get a splitting headache when Siva focused Jack and me on helping Cricket. It was weird: my memory was fuzzy, and it was hard to recall the details of what happened. Maybe it was for the best; my Powers had been removed and it didn't matter now. I felt relief not having to worry about blasting something to smithereens with my brain. Those kinds of Powers were kinda scary and my headaches made me yak. Not a gentle yak either, rather forceful and projectile.

It had gotten dark and the fireflies were out. I had been told fireflies only came out in the summer. It was dark, cold, and winter felt close. Then I realized something: the fireflies were not the usual orange tint, there was a rainbow of colors floating and flitting about. It was beautiful. I thought my Dads would have loved to see this too. They would have argued about bioluminescence, of course. I sat back down to have an ugly cry. I was glad no one was there to see, or so I thought.

"You live inside your own heart, that's an rumbly big place…" I heard a voice behind me a realized Mr. Campbell was no longer working on the bus. I recognized the words from an old movie. "Kip, your friends think they're getting into a fine adventure. But I know for a fact the cemetery and the mine shaft are nothing special. It's just a myth. If they don't fall down the shaft, they should be getting cold by now. They'll be back soon."

"Mr. Campbell, you ever feel like the weight of the world is on your shoulders?" He looked thoughtful but didn't respond, staring out at the kaleidoscopic fireflies.

"It's as if the weight falls off, I feel guilty and work to hoist it back up." I looked down at my feet, suddenly embarrassed by my admission. Why was I even talking about things like this? Mr. Campbell didn't know me…hell, I didn't even know me. I was a hairy teenage Chupacabra, nearly bearded and smelly. Man, did I hate myself or something? No…I was just frustrated with so much responsibility swirling around in my head.

"Kip, when I was your age, I was the man of the household. My mother had five of us kids to deal with after my father died in a coal mining accident. There were hard winters and sweltering summers. Living in the hills in West Virginia was no joke during the hot and cold seasons. Our schoolhouse looked like it was from the 19th century and funny enough didn't even have heat or AC. Most of us looked pretty lean; we were many of us malnourished, but funny enough even with all the hard times, we were a tight-knit family. In fact, hard times is what made us so close. Our mother loved us with crazy love. Somehow everything worked out. But one night our little family was rocked with another loss; this one was more grievous than all the others." Mr. Campbell stopped and stared at the fire for a few moments. "It was a game changer in my life."

He described how he found his mother dead in her bed, cold to the touch. There was a small burial ceremony then the question of where the five kids would go. He was 15 and went to the hiring office for the local mine. If he worked, he might be able to keep his family together. The manager recognized him and told him it had become too dangerous to employ kids. Safety standards don't exist these days.

"Son, I knew your father well. In fact, he practically raised us and kept us safe and taught us how to stay sharp. That makes you kinfolk and I won't have you throwing your life away."

The next day the manager came by the house with a dirty cotton bag filled to bursting. "Son, I want you to take this and go to this address." He handed me a slip of paper.

Mr. Campbell took his siblings and left the coal mining town, heading west to Colorado. The miners there knew of his father and were able to help the children. The sack was filled with enough cash to pay for every need for many years. A mixed family (synth & human) adopted them; the years that followed were filled with warmth and joy, but Mr. Campbell still grieved the loss of his parents.

Later he joined the CSA Army. Campbell's love of the outdoors aided his quick rise in the ranks and eventually becoming a Pathfinder in Special Forces. "Kip, I was being paid to do what I loved: hiking and camping. Sometimes I had a gun, other times I was dressed as a civilian on holiday, exploring in places no soldier would be caught dead in uniform. Well, if I had been caught, I would be dead, if ya know what I mean." Mr. Campbell gave a short laugh.

A rockfall of pebbles near the cliff face and a sudden burst of laughter heralded the return of the intrepid explorers.

"Hey Kip, you totally missed it! Wogs climbed down this mine shaft! It took her two hours and it's even more amazing what she found!" Teddy was clearly playing to a crowd. However, the crowd was not so interested. "She found absolutely nothing!" That got him raspberries from the others.

Binky came to sit by me, with Wogs and Peach on the other side. I was sad to miss the last part of Campbell's story. But I was also curious.

"What took you guys so long?"

Binky shared a little secret, "Wogs in fact did find something, but she only wanted you to see it," a knowing glance passed between Wogs and Peach.

Right as I wondered where Cricket had gotten, I heard the bus start up and a loud yell of triumph sounded out, "Yes, now I can get back to the house and a warm shower. I am covered in Prickly Pear!"

I gave a quizzical look to Binky, but Peach spoke up,"Yeaaah. So Cricket was showing off his parkour skills and landed in the middle of a huge Prickly Pear. We plucked him like a chicken for almost an hour, then explored the mine. After Wogs did her spelunking routine, we decided to come back before it got much colder. And it looks like we got here just in time!"

Teddy yelled over my shoulder, "Hey Cricket, did Campbell fix the bus?"

Mr. Campbell started the bus and called out, "Everyone on board! It's time to split."

The ride back was grimy, but everyone was in good spirits. My Crew and I had become Bakabi kids. I stared out the window, watching the desert roll by. Then I heard light strains of music playing. In the back of the bus Cricket was playing a tiny keyboard, blowing into it to make sound. One of the kids, Chaz, said, "Hey, that's my Melodica. How'd he get that?" Then as Cricket played Chaz mumbled, "I never made it sound that good."

We all grew quiet and listened. Cricket had learned The Harry Lime Theme from my father Vicky. He watched me as he played, and it was his little secret gift to me; he knew I was missing my Dads. It was a relief that Cricket had begun playing music again. I felt like a door long closed was re-opening. You see, with the war and death, none of the four of us felt much like playing instruments or singing. There was too much loss. It used to be a joy to make music together. Not so much lately. Harry Lime then changed pitch and tempo and Cricket made something new. The music was his own and it had become darker and more ballad-like. Cricket never used to play stuff like this. Something had changed since our adventures abroad and especially since leaving LA:CENTER.

Everyone was listening to Cricket and soon snores could be heard. Wogs came to sit by me and held out a figurine. It wasn't anything like the large woman figurine Cricket had found. I recalled Cricket handing me a USB stick from the first one; I checked and lo and behold there was a crusty pocket from which I was able to cajole a second USB stick. I realized too late the snores had stopped and all eyes had been watching me pluck the memory stick from the rock like I knew exactly what I was doing. It's hard to keep secrets amongst kids. Questions pummeled me on the way home and me and my Crew took turns spilling the beans about where we came from, what we had been doing before we got to Bakabi and some of the weird things that had happened. Teddy just wanted to hear about the Gunga Den Ladies. I guess T&A was where his mind was at.

We pulled up to the school parking lot as the sun began to rise. A crowd of unhappy people stood ready to greet us. Mr. Campbell got a right nasty butt-chewing as we exited the bus. The parents and relatives of sixteen children vented their ire at not knowing their kids' whereabouts for a whole night. We slept most of the day and got up for an early dinner. I heard a guitar playing. I was a zombie lumbering into the next room. There sat Cricket plucking a guitar like he'd been playing for his whole life. I didn't realize he was so skilled; usually guitar was my thing. He was playing one of my favorite pieces by Mason Williams, Classical Gas. I was surprised to see Cecelia and Timothy sitting with some other adults, listening. Normally they were still at work. Cecelia waved me over to sit with her.

Cricket looked up and smiled, "Hey Kip, hop on the piano and let's take it from the top!" It had been too long since I had seen Cricket smile that way. Cecelia gave me the nod that it was okay to play her piano. It hadn't been tuned in a while, but it sounded good anyway. And away we went with a jazzy rendition of Classical Gas. Binky and Wogs were quickly in the room, hearing the piano play. They didn't wait, Binky grabbed the travel Guitar and Wogs the Ukulele. For the first time since we began this vagabond life, we played music together. It felt amazing.

Cricket led us and we segued into a little Showhawk Duo doing a techno medley. We ended with Queen's Bohemian Rhapsody. Complete amazement. Every adult in the room knew the words. For a little while we were back on the block and carefree and the world was our oyster again.

Then the bad news.

Mr. Campbell got canned. He was replaced by Mr. Birman. The parents were angry about the field trip and we were sad because Campbell was a fun guy. Mr. Birman was not fun. He was by-the-book and rigid in his control of the class. For the first few weeks Mr. Birman was just like any other schoolteacher who is wound too tightly. Binky called him snippy. He would have been better suited to accounting or engineering, not much of a people person.

May 2254 – Bakabi, Hopi Nation, Arizona Territory - Masauwu

I woke to another day with the prospect of spending too many hours with Mr. Birman. I wanted an out and as fate would have it an out came in the form of a girl named Violet. I made my bed, brushed my teeth, and shaved. My facial hair clearly thought I was a man, but the rest of me disagreed. I left the bathroom and stooped to pick up my pad from the nightstand.

Oh, to catch you up, we had been in our Hopi digs in Bakabi for almost 8 months and it was capitol "B" boring. My Crew was loudly scarfing down breakfast. I decided to ignore the no Online rule and checked if I could connect my pad to Online using a local cell tower. Surprisingly it worked. I had notifications from my Online friends. They had news about their search for my Dads. I gave the passphrase, "Home again, home again, jiggety jig!"

"Good morning CW! We have an update." There was silence.

"Okay, what did you find?"

"We picked up 323 seeds and 2843 breadcrumbs and two hints."

"You ran each of them down?"

"Yes Kip. Each was a dead end or indeterminate."

I was frustrated, "Did you talk to Pilgrim?"

"I did. He was helpful. He sent ReconDrones to scour the Rosario site. He also questioned those who survived and the last anyone recalled seeing your Dads they went fishing. LIDAR and SONAR scans revealed no helpful evidence. Pilgrim even called in a marker with Atlantis. They didn't find anything either."

"Banquo, what is Atlantis?"

"Ah, so, Atlantis is a safe haven created by a group of aquatic synths and it houses aquatic hybrids, non-human terrestrials and others. I don't know where it's located but it must be in the vicinity of Rosario given the speed they assisted Pilgrim."

"Okay B, thank you. Please expand your search to include any info you can find from the Powers." I knew it was risky to send my friends searching in highly restricted space, but I wanted answers.

"Roger, roger. On it." Banquo and his merry band of hack miscreants were off like a shot. But I was no closer to learning where my Dads were. I was beginning to have doubts. But screw that fewkin noise, I wasn't about to give up.

I finally joined the morning chaos. Breakfast was the normal rambunctious affair with piles of flapjacks, eggs, bacon, some leftover venison, and plenty of coffee. They had made a huge dent in my absence, but there still was a half pot of joe. Coffee was my new best friend for morning survival. After we were dropped at school, one of the younger students came over with her face red and out of breath.

"Hey guys —" she huffed and puffed, "there is something going on over at Red Barn. You need to get there fast."

Her name was Violet. She was a small bookish girl who was not particularly social. She had tagged along with our group a few times when we went exploring or climbing. She got my attention immediately. If there was one thing Violet wasn't, it was a drama queen.

"Violet, lead the way." Peach and mt Crew came along.

Red Barn was about a kilometer outside town, in a box canyon. The barn itself butted against the canyon wall. When we arrived, the place was deserted. That was unusual since Red Barn was a working ranch and garden. They grew nitrogen-fixing maize, rice, millet, and barley. They also had hybrid cows that produced milk which was used in the Skin Factories where human body parts were grown and sold to hospitals and the military. This was an expensive place and access was keycard controlled with high steel fencing, cameras, and alarms.

Violet opened one of the heavy gates. The alarms and security were disabled. "Hey Kip. The security is just for show. It works, but no one uses it unless some of the military types come by. But that's not what's wrong. Come over here."

We followed. Peach came up and held my hand. She was afraid. Peach was never afraid. Then it hit me: a sense of foreboding and dread fell upon me like a heavy blanket. My heart began to race, and I could see the others were breathing hard too.

"Kipper, something really bad is going on here," Binky had a small knife out, scanning the area for trouble. Cricket's Model 1911 was in his hand, and I heard him quietly rack a round into the chamber. As I approached a door, he nodded to me. Cricket wondered if this was like before: he thought how an artificial foreboding was created in the Morrigan's cave and when he went to the Hierophant's place. He stayed quiet for the moment. The barn itself was just the foyer to a bigger facility. Upstairs it was what you would expect from a farm, with cows, goats, pigs, and chickens. The cows with the magic milk were roaming with the other animals. Overall, they seemed a happy lot. The oppressive pall didn't seem to bother the animals. Lucky for them. Wogs checked on some of the animals, then she grabbed some grain and fed them. She became very popular. The Bakabi kids all knew how to manage livestock.

"Wogs, they haven't been fed in at least a day." Peach called out. Teddy and Buddy were coming into the barn, pushing past the dreadful feelings. All the Bakabi kids set to filling the troughs and sprinkling the feed for the chickens. Wogs had the right idea.

I lost Cricket. He had been standing to my right and was suddenly absent. As the kids managed feed time I went hunting and found him moving down a corridor. At that point we must have entered past the rock wall of the box canyon, leaving the barn itself; we were underground. The air was cool and clean, and a light breeze brushed by us as I joined Cricket. We came to double doors. Inside was a warehouse with farm supplies and containers of chemicals. We looked around. There were five double door exits and a large archway which led deeper.

We heard a noise; Cricket and I swiveled to catch the glimpse of something low to the floor, fast moving. One set of double doors were swinging. We shared a glance and moved that way. Through the doors and down another hallway, I noticed a sweet smell in the air, like flowers and fruit. Cricket was behind me, and I came to a next set of doors. When I opened these the feelings of dread vanished and the sweet smells amplified. We entered a big room with verdant foliage growing on every surface. I could see this used to be a lab. I felt something warm in my pocket and discovered the Pachinko seeds were warm to the touch and softly vibrated. Then I noticed some of the foliage in the room was glowing. It was hard to see in the fluorescent lighting, but it was there. I reached out to one of the glowing pods and it opened at my touch. The bioluminescence was fluctuating; surprisingly it was doing so in-time with the vibrating of my seeds. Were they talking to each other? I decided to try something. I placed a Pachinko seed into the center of an open pod. What I failed to notice was the light dusting of spores on the seed. You see, I inadvertently put the pachinko seeds in the same bag as the shroomer spores. The pod gently closed around the seed and made a sighing sound. I waited. Cricket came close behind me and asked, "Dude, what are you doing? Focus!" He shook his head, tolerating my obvious idiocy.

"Sorry Cricket," I went through a doorway into another room similarly foliated. Then I heard something: it was moving through the undergrowth. A head popped out between some big leaves.

"Cheep, cheep!" a tiny voice spoke. The little head then ducked down, moved a few meters, and came up again, "Cheep, cheep, cheep!"

Cricket had followed me. He kept his pistol pointed at the ground and I followed the little thing with my eyes. Whatever it was, it came up a dozen times with the same 'cheep, cheep'. I followed it and this time intercepted it and picked it up by its scruff. It looked like a dog and it got pissed off as I hoisted it up.

"What the fewkin hell, douchbag? I'm not your pet, you slimeball! Put me down!" Shocked, I dropped it. Him?

"Oh, sorry. I didn't know. Who are you?" It rang hollow even in my ears.

"I'm Tulip, you a-hole. You white kids are so extra. At least the Hopi kids know the deal." Then he looked around, "On that note, where is the cavalry? I sent Violet an hour ago and expected Cecelia and Timothy to come help." Tulip lit a small cigar and was puffing furiously. The smoke was rank.

Cricket gave me the no idea face and I tried to answer, "Violet came to get me and my friends. She is in the other room. What's going on here?" I wanted to be helpful.

A bustle of kids came through the doorway at that point. Violet called out, "Tulip, why are you out of your warren?"

Tulip replied, "Just dealing with numbnuts here who tried to give me a shakedown."

"Get that outta your mouth. You know Masauwu hates those things," he dropped the burning cigar and Violet stamped it out.

She scooped him up and carried him out the rear door. Tulip flipped us off over her shoulder, mouthing nasty words. We amusedly followed. Clearly much more was going on here than met the eye. As we left the flowery room no one noticed the pod that began sprouting a Pachinko vine. Something else was sprouting too: coiled around the vine was a fungal mycelium. A small hiss sounded, *thank you.*

Violet led the way. The smooth walls gave way to raw rock and a warm earthy smell. The sound of children playing came from up ahead. She put Tulip down and he sped off around the corner. I asked Violet a question, "Hey, did you get an ominous feeling when we first came here?"

"Oh yeah. Haven't you ever heard of an EmoPack?" Violet saw my blank stare. "Right.

Well, people with Cloud powers can create stuff like that. Masa calls it an EmoPack. He puts them up to keep lookey loos away. He usually makes it so friends aren't affected."

"Who is Masa?" Wogs asked. Peach was smiling but kept it to herself. Buddy and Teddy were not interested. Instead, they were poking around the cave. I think they were looking for something to eat.

"Masauwu is one of our gods. He helped the Hopi people first settle and taught them to grow maize." Violet turned and continued walking after Tulip.

"So, your god lives in this little cave?" Binky's voice was tinged with criticism.

Violet stopped and faced Binky with an expression that had us all back up a step. "You mock at your own peril. He can read minds, you know." She shook her head then resumed walking.

Binky gave me the how was I to know shoulder shrug. Cricket put away his gun and we followed in silence. Teddy came alongside me, masticating something gooey.

"Buddy found some fruit things. They're really, really good. Want some?" His chewing made me nauseous.

"No thank you. You guys just go to it…maybe just somewhere over there," I indicated a bunch of dark purple blooms with liquidy bulbs suspended underneath.

"Oh snap! Good call brosef!" Buddy and Teddy descended upon the bulbs, and I tried to ignore the slurping sounds that ensued.

Violet looked back with disdain. "Those things are gonna give you the runs, you morons!" She sniffed and promptly ignored them, "Ug, boys."

The hallway opened into a common room that looked and smelled like a coffee shop. Glass front cabinets held neat little pastries, sandwiches and dainties. It was probably a Starbucks: it was one of the few corporations to survive the Tech War and the dark years between then and now. Someone at school said they grow the coffee off-planet. It's probably a fake fact, but who knows these days.

Violet brought us to a man shorter than Peach. He couldn't have been more than a meter tall. Hybrid? "Kip and crew, this is the patron saint of the Hopis, Masauwu." She said it like 'masoowoo'.

I held out my hand and we shook, "A pleasure to meet you, sir." I sounded like Cricket. Too formal.

"The pleasure is mine, young sir. And these must be our esteemed guests. Wogs, Binky, and Cricket," he made eye contact with each. "And these messy young men haven't deigned to visit an old god in his little cave," he glanced at Binky with a wink, looking at Teddy and Buddy.

Teddy came right up, "Mister Masauwu, my Dad said I was not allowed to visit because, and I quote, boy, your mouth is gonna get you killed," to which Masauwu laughed heartily.

"Teddy and Buddy. Your mouths have been consuming my Gonda buds. The trouble you are in will emerge quickly on the other end. Best of luck to you both." Masauwu turned his attention to me.

"Your Dads helped me when I needed it. But their help came at a cost. I made the plasm changes in the cows to produce the enzymes and proteins necessary for the Skin Factories to do their work. But that meant I came under the thumb of the CSA." Masauwu paused, shook his head, and continued.

"I know you had no hand in the dealings of your Dads, but I am going to look to you to make it right." My head whirled. Make it right?

"Let me cut to the point. My children are missing, along with all the Hopi workers who usually run Red Barn. I have no idea who has them or why. I just have this note." He handed me a piece of paper with a scrawled message.

It read: deliver the four kids or yours are dead. Noon, two days from now the four must be at Bakabi sewage treatment ponds.

"We're gonna take care of this." Blurted out of my mouth. My Crew were nodding.

"No way we're going to let something happen to your kids," Cricket was about to pull his gun out, but Wogs gave him a curt head shake.

"Guys, we need to make a plan. Mister Masauwu, are you supposed to deliver us tomorrow or the next day?" Binky was large and in charge.

"Tomorrow. At noon." Masauwu was watching us closely.

"Okay, Wogs, hop on your map server and get me every visual you can of the area, covering here and the Third Mesa area. If you can, get us a live feed and any recording from the past 48." Binky chewed her lip.

"Cricket, did you get a tally on the weapons bag we got from Majustatus?"

"Yep. Sure did. We even have night vision goggles." Cricket was getting excited.

"Right. Kip, I need you to see if you have any of your Cloud powers back. Now." Binky asked then turned to Masauwu. I gave them a try and shook my head no.

"Masauwu, can you tell me anything else that might help us find your kids."

"If you go looking, they might kill my kids." That brought Binky up short.

"Then we will have to give them the impression we aren't looking then."

Thus began the planning and effort to rescue Masauwu's children and the Hopis who had been taken.

Buddy and Teddy were of more help than I could have expected. Between the two they setup a work area in the Red Barn offices. Owing to the military funding, there were plenty of computers, screens, tables and even a table holo they used for crop analysis. As the afternoon came on, we were acutely aware of our dwindling time. Teddy had run to the school and our home to bring back Timothy, Cecelia, and some of our friends. We had a small but potent Hopi army supporting the effort to get Masauwu's children back.

My Cloud powers were a no-go. But Masauwu surprised us with fully enabling our personal prosthetics. We were now connected Online and each other. The first thing we did was to identify possible locations where kids could be hidden, like abandoned houses, Quonset huts and office buildings. There were 127 in total. With the Hopi army's help, we reduced the candidates to five potentials. Our friends were out investigating under the guise of being stupid kids playing where they shouldn't.

Next, Wogs got us video of the Hopi nation area. I figured it would be sketchy at best. It was worse than I hoped for. Surveillance was almost non-existent. It was as if someone had purposefully excluded Hopi territory from satellite and drone flybys. That was good news in the big picture, but it didn't help us now.

Last, my friends and I brainstormed who might know we came to the Hopi territory. Only one name came up, Beckett. Could he have sold the info to someone. He knew we were headed this way, but there was no way he had specifics unless he had followed us here. Somebody had to have been watching us.

As the other kids returned, their reports came up negative on the abandoned places they checked. They were smart: if there was no vehicle present and no recent tire tracks, they assumed there was no bad guys. They would quickly make an interior check and move on. We were uncomfortably aware of our dwindling time. Since we had Online access, I broke our one rule given us by Vagabond. I decided to leave a message at my secret place on Endor in SimVerse. It was a longshot. I set Banquo to watch the drop point for a reply. I didn't have to wait.

I got an answer from Pilgrim. I filled him in on our situation and suddenly, like magic a hologram popped out of thin air to address us. Everyone jumped at his appearance. How did he do that? I guess being a supercomputer had its perks.

"I will make this short. You broke the cardinal rule of contact." He made a patting gesture, cutting short my defensive response. "I understand. I just searched a bunch of things and indeed your hunch was correct. Beckett did follow you and indeed reported your whereabouts. Eight months ago. The man has been camping in a hidden location ever since, watching over you. I just asked Vagabond and he thinks this is an inside job."

At that, the Hopi kids erupted in protest.

"Hopis don't snitch! And they sure don't kidnap anyone!" Buddy had a moment of maligned clarity.

Violet spoke with heat, "Mister Pilgrim, you're wrong. Hopis are raised to be pacifists."

"Young lady, I would never suggest otherwise. But the possibility stands. Who has come recently to your area? I think that might be the next thing you explore." Pilgrim turned to me. "My time is up. For all our sakes, figure this out quickly." Despite my Cloud powers being on the fritz, he mind chatted me, *'Kip, if it comes to it, you cannot give your lives for those children. That will doom us all. Please don't go into –'.* His signal suddenly dropped, and he was gone.

I took a beat to think. Don't go into…what? At least he gave us two leads: Beckett and the possibility of an inside job.

The sound of a bulldozer purring vibrated on the air. Just like Cheshire Cat, Flu Cat faded into view in the corner of the room. Pooka was sitting on his back.

Flu Cat spoke, "This is my fault. I put your children in danger." He'd never spoken before; he was looking at Masauwu. Masauwu slowly stood and a nimbus of deep purple limned his head. In response, Flu Cat's head limned in a prismatic green.

"Cat Síth, you are not welcome in these demesnes." Every human in the room gave them plenty of space. Cat Sith?

"I come not as emissary, but as myself. I ask for guest right, Lord Masauwu." Flu Cat made a theatrical bow, holding it low, looking at the floor. Pooka jumped clear and ran to me, holding my leg and peeking out from behind.

Masauwu took a moment to consider, then spoke, "Guest right is given. I need not remind you of your responsibility as guest." Flu Cat straightened up.

"Of course. Just as I need not remind his Lord of his." Both auras flicked off and the tension in the room released. I hadn't realized I was holding my breath. Loud exhales came from others in the room. I wasn't alone in being afraid of these two.

"Síth, clarify yourself please." Masauwu was just a little guy again. A father worried about his kids.

Síth spoke, "I guided a soldier here to keep watch on these four," the cat gestured to the four of us. "He is a trusted agent of General Olonana, named Beckett. He is camped out on the edge of town. When I reported back to my people, I didn't realize they would sell the information of the four children's whereabouts to the highest bidder. I have been ejected from my community for criticizing their decision. I am deeply sorry for the actions of my superiors and am here as myself to right this wrong."

Cecelia spoke, "Masauwu, what would you like us to do?"

Masauwu spoke, "Cat Síth, I accept your apology. Although you are not the one from whom I will seek atonement or weregild, mercy forbid." A new tension rang on the air.

Timothy leaned over to me and whispered, "Weregild would mean his kids are dead and Masauwu would expect compensation for the deaths."

Flu Cat closed the distance with Masauwu and knelt at his feet. "Lord Masa, I will personally vouchsafe the return of your children or hold my life in forfeit for the balance."

Masauwu's stern expression softened, and he placed a hand on Flu Cat's head. "Lord Síth, just help me get my kids back."

A sacred pact had been agreed and a steely ringing was in the air, sharp and hard. Then the ringing subsided and a new resolve energized me. The others felt it too. Then I thought of something which had been tickling the back of my brain for a long time. I think Cloud powers are magic. I mean, they could easily be mistaken for magic if a person didn't know better. I was going to have to think on that for a bit before talking with the others.

"Síth, walk with me a moment." Masauwu and Síth went into an adjoining room. They must have been doing telepathy since I couldn't hear their voices.

"Alrighty then! I think we need to investigate the other abandoned buildings." Binky was back in the driver's seat.

Cecelia spoke, "We still don't know who has the children and the Red Barn staffers. For all we know they could be in the café, downtown or nowhere near town in some other place."

Wogs spoke, "She's right. We have no idea. I don't think we have time to check every house and business in town. So next…"

Masauwu and Síth returned. Síth spoke, "Friends, they are being kept at Corncob Cliff." Flu Cat's mention of the cliff got me excited and hopeful. The talking cat was helping us get the kids back. Maybe no one needed to die today. I shifted my mind into planning the rescue.

It was called Corncob for all the rounded surfaces which made climbing the cliff difficult. A few months back Mr. Campbell took us climbing there. In a random turn of events, Wogs had found a second figurine similar to the first. These were the rocks we were supposed to find and give to Croatoan. At the same time, we spilled the beans to all the kids about our adventures.

"The kids and Red Barn staff are being kept inside Panaha's Door. One way in, one way out. I don't believe there is a way to surprise these people. I can phase into the interior of the Panaha's cave, but I suspect they are a long distance in, expecting we will make an attempt to free the captives. I can't phase through solid rock so the best I could do is get through the door without opening it." I had to keep calling him Flu Cat, otherwise I would start spouting Star Wars memes.

"So, Darth can't phase through the door. There is another way in. Wogs went down a mine shaft several months ago. I heard it was another entrance to Panaha's."

For once Pooka spoke up, "Oh, oh, I can do that. Pick me, pick me!"

I was about to dismiss my little friend, but an idea sparked, "No, Pooka -wait. Hey, can you still create holograms?"

"How do you think Pilgrim talked to you? Magic? Pooka made hologram of Pilgrim. Pilgrim was polite to Pooka and asked nicely. Pooka like Pilgrim. Kip should be more like Pilgrim." Had I programmed Pooka to sound like a 4-year-old? I'd have to do something about that later.

"Kip, you may be onto something." Binky scrunched her face up, thinking. Then a lightbulb must have gone on, "Pooka, do you think you could get inside without being seen?"

Pooka vanished. It was a shock: one moment Pooka was there then the next –"Pooka over here!"

Then the next moment Pooka was on the other side of the room.

"Pooka, however you do that, I don't care. Could you get close to the captors, create a diversion to pull one of them away, then generate a convincing holo of that person?"

Suddenly Binky was gone. Out of thin air, she spoke, "Guys, I'm invisible."

"We can still smell your B.O. though," Teddy was returning to his normal comical self.

"It's true, I can feel she is here, and sorry sis, you do smell something fierce right now," as Wogs touched Binky, the air wrinkled and little glimpses of her clothing could be seen.

Binky asked, "Frijoles! Pooka, you're a genius! Do you think you can make all our friends disappear and create a holo of one of the captors at the same time?" Binky had reappeared. Pooka had a serious expression.

At that moment Beckett came in, followed by three of the local police. "Good plan kids. Flu Cat, you should 'port you and Pooka down while me and the gendarmerie wait at the mouth of the mine."

Masauwu was annoyed at the intrusion of the new people, "This isn't your personal petting zoo, gentlemen. None of you were invited in."

Cecelia jumped in, "Lord Masa, I invited our law enforcement officers. I think they brought Mr. Beckett along as backup."

Masauwu sighed and remained quiet. Not pleased.

"Okay, I will take Pooka down with me and we will work out the details. We won't be able to exit people vertically. Speed will be important. There needs to be a receiving team at Panaha's Door." And like that Flu Cat and Pooka vanished.

Chaos erupted. Cries of 'what about planning' and 'what are we supposed to do' echoed about. My Crew and I nodded and ran out. There were more yells from kids and adults. Outside Red Barn, Beckett stopped me, "Hey mate, you guys are the hunted ones. You can't do any of this."

Cricket's piece was out, and my Crew stood behind me ready to go to war.

"We are going, and you and the cop squad will mind the mine entrance. We will be at Panaha's Door. This is my command, and you will move out now. Understood?" I spoke calmly with an even delivery. I hoped it sounded authoritative.

Beckett's face showed momentary shock then something seemed to click, "Yes. Yes, sir. Come on guys let's head out!" Beckett indicated to his police friends

My Crew were quietly stunned but we were already running again. Why had he obeyed my orders? Questions, questions.

"Kip, we can't run all the way there." Wogs was right.

"We are running for the bus. Cecelia or Timothy can drive, and we'll figure out where this door is located." And we kept running.

We made it to the bus and Timothy got it to start, first try. Cecelia played the navigator. On the way, all the kids began to play around like this was any other day. It pissed me off that during a crisis these kids could be so unconcerned. My face must have shown my sentiments because Cricket came over to sit next to me.

"Hey man, it's okay. Kids are kids. You can't expect them to be like us. We might be the same age, but we've led seriously different lives. Cut them a break. It's just their way to blow off steam." Cricket was right.

I stared out the window and watched the desert roll by. I nodded off for a few minutes. When I woke, we had arrived at the same cliff face we had climbed back in January with Mr. Campbell. I had drooled on my jacket in my sleep. No one had noticed thankfully.

As we exited Cecelia spoke up, "Okay kids, Panaha's Door is about a ten-minute walk from the top of the cliff. But it's too dangerous. About 30 minutes' walk from here is a trail we can take. Let's get going."

"Cecelia, my Crew, and I will climb. See you there." She didn't argue. All the others followed her and jogged the long way around while we took the vertical route.

May 2254 – Bakabi, Hopi Nation, Arizona Territory – Gorj Assassins

The Gorj Assassin penetrated the substantial shielding emplaced by Hopi shaman. It looked like a greyhound without skin, all sinew and muscle. But its shape could be modified at will. The Gorj were said to not remember their original form. The shields covered the whole 3 Mesa area. The three Hopi Watchers knew the moment it happened. The beast's spirit force was terribly strong. Then two more followed. The Watchers asked for help, but the combined Cloud orchestration failed to eject or even detect the location of the intruders. Gorj leader Brask called to his subordinates, Thongh and Raomik. The plan was simple and fast. The humans were to kidnap the children then notify them when the four targets were subsequently captured. The humans were pre-paid as the Coali instructed. After Brask made penetration through the weak shield, all three Gorj quickly arrived in the Panaha cave. The Watchers needed help.

Shaman Cloud Orchestration

Watcher Talayumptewa reached out to the medicine men in Stilt Town. The men had already circled up and begun the ritual. Tala felt their strength flow into him and the Hopi circle. Drumbeats synchronized between the two groups. Watcher Kalyesvah reached out her powerful voice over the æther to the Navajo Healers and the orchestration beat heavier on the air. The third Watcher, Youvella, sent an allcome invite and with love and courage they came: Pueblo, Apache, Pima, Concho and Cuahuiltec. It didn't stop. New arrivals sent their own invites. First Nation peoples were rising up. Choctaw, Sioux, Arawak, and Seminole. Even Ainu, Pictish, Hadza, Maasai and Wati.

The three Hopi Watchers pressed the immense power toward the Gorj, but even then, they couldn't penetrate the enemy's shielding. They must be gods. Watcher Tala in desperation tried something risky. On a side channel he reached out to the Sonoran Skinwalkers. He had grown up knowing them as evil incarnate. Perhaps he was wrong. Regardless, he needed help. Seek-Bright-Chanter picked up the call and in mind-speak he knew the details of the emergency. Seek teetered on the edge of willingness. Humans had hurt them for so long, why should he help them now. But the heart spoke louder than the mind and the heart won over. Unbidden, he shared his own passion and in the space of a mind's blink human and skinwalker knew each other, their history, their joy, and their pains. Dozens of Skinwalker shaman joined, then others, by the hundreds. The power was incandescent; for the first time in memory, human and non-human shaman joined as one to repel an evil not of this world.

May 2254 – Bakabi, Hopi Nation, Arizona Territory – Panaha's Door

Our fingers and toes found the route upward and our hours of practice paid off. We might never be as fast or capable as Honnold, or even Campbell, but we climbed almost 90 feet in less than 5 minutes. We helped each other over the brink and ran an airborne shuffle up the same trail the kids had taken to the mine entrance months ago. When Cecelia had been talking with Timothy, I got a pretty good idea of the door's location. We deviated off the trail toward a cleft in another cliff face and began looking for a door.

"Hey guys, I think I found something," Wogs was digging her fingers into gaps around a big rock which was wedged into the cliff base. I saw what she had noticed. There was a small animal trail that led to the bottom of the rock and into a hole underneath. As my face got close to the rock, I could feel a cool, dry breeze coming from around the rock. It smelled like an old uninhabited cave. The four of us chatted as we began digging around the rock. Just was we began to lever the rock, Cecelia and the kids came around the corner. She saw us digging madly and gave a short laugh.

"Hey heroes. Do you mind stepping back a pace?" Cecelia nudged us aside and stuck her hand in a crevice and in a moment the rock pivoted aside silently.

My Crew and I gave each other the am I stupid looks and the harassment began.

Teddy started it, "Whoa, the intrepid explorers missed a vital clue. Not quite your best Indiana Jones moment, eh?"

Loud voices were coming from the tunnel beyond. Whoever it was would have to be scrunching down pretty low to run through the carven rock tube. And out they came. Six children and seven bedraggled adults in Red Barn uniforms. Then I felt it. Like a thick slime of anger on my soul it came. It was getting close, and I could smell sulfur. Flu Cat came leaping out with Pooka on his back. Both had eyes wide, and I saw fear in both sets.

"Close the hole now!" Pooka gave a command and Cecelia hit the magic button; the rock pivoted back into place. "That won't hold it long. Time to go." We were frozen for a second, adjusting to the latest developments. It was a success! The kids were saved.

A huge impact rocked the cliff face. The stone door juddered in its place. Beckett and the officers came running, covered in sweat and grime.

Beckett yelled, "Get away from the door! Now!"

A second later the rock door was blasted like an artillery round out of sight, down the cliff trail. Something with octopus arms and a fetid odor, red and purple was propelled outward, following the door down the slope. The octo-thing flanged its tentacles wide, catching wind. It looked like a parachute with arms, like an...OctoChute. It came to the ground with surprising grace. Once landed, it was in motion, coming toward us, up the hill. It made wet smacking sounds as it came and moved hideously fast.

There were screams and everyone ran. Beckett and the officers took position and began firing at the thing. Their rounds had no effect. My Crew was hustling the children along. I stood behind the officers and tried my best to summon my Cloud powers. As the creature came closer, I could feel a pall of evil, calculating, cold and implacable. Something clicked in my head, and I could suddenly see the world in vivid new colors and shapes. Invisible beings, tiny and large were there, going about their business, walking, and flying about. Were they ghosts? Nevermind, focus Kip! My Cloud powers had activated!

I saw the octo-thing in a new light, and it was awful and beautiful at the same time. I felt a pull to worship it and abase myself but hearing the gunshots, I shook out of the reverie. The OctoChute hit the men and bowled them over, then it pushed me down to the ground and wrapped around me like a cocoon. I could hear a voice.

"Yes, Kip. Yes. Your powers are growing." I felt a sickly voice inside my head, thrumming on my mind with power and dark purpose. "We have only moments. Listen." And I did. Ichor of hate and rage poured into my mind and my soul. I felt defiled and polluted. I wanted to scream but nothing came out. I felt like I was dying. It hurt. It wouldn't stop. The voice spoke once more, "I failed. The next ones won't."

My mind whirled and I could see again. Something was ripping away the darkness and I was suddenly looking at Flu Cat, rapidly tearing the monster from around my body. His fur stood straight out making him a puffball of blurred claws. His yowl shook the air. The OctoChute was scary, but I think Flu Cat was scarier. I was free. I sucked in air and rolled over to vomit. My mind was gloopy, filled with muzz, and I remembered only parts of the trip as we drove back home. People were talking to me, but I was having problems piecing thoughts together.

May 2254 – In the Cloud

Watching the action from the Cloud, two Coali, Observer 14 and Minder 9 saw the interplay of Power across the Earth in response to their Gorj agents' presence.

"It's quite beautiful, you know. The Power ranging in so many colors, playing across the superstices. It moves like the beat of a drum," Minder 9 spoke with awe.

"It's surprising how many non-humans have pitched in. We will need to mention that in our report.

Honored Zin will be displeased. Time to go," Observer 14 had the dread look of upcoming un-niceties. Minder 9 knew only the bringer of bad news would be eligible for recycling. Too bad for 14.

May 2254 – Shaman Cloud Orchestration

Watcher Tala closed the connection with heartfelt thanks. Love was extended and was met with love. New bonds had been formed between kindred spirits and new and old friendships were sealed. Men, women, and others not human were touching psyches and building kinship. All were encouraged to meet at the Hopi Katsina drum circle when next it convened. Many voices were excited, but some were unsure. Trust was going to take a while. On the intimate channel Seek-Bright-Chanter called Tala.

Seek spoke, "Watcher Tala, I heard tell the first of the four has become part Chupa. Soomalee is a cousin. We have missed her for hundreds of cycles of the sun and wish to bring her back into the fold. Can you help?"

Tala had no idea what Seek was talking about, "Brother Seek, I will speak with Kip and make it happen if it is in my power."

"Thank you. It is more than I could hope for." Seek was gone and Tala had some thinking to do.

May 2254 – Bakabi, Hopi Nation, Arizona Territory

Turns out the explosion from the cave killed all the kidnappers and two OctoChutes. The third OctoChute survived long enough to drop a bunch of garbage into my brain. It lurks in the background of my mind, for now. I wasn't sure what to do about it, so I did my best to ignore it. Beckett said neither he nor Flu Cat had used explosives. Stuff got explosive and he had no idea why or how. Whatever the cause, it worked in our favor. It took me two days in bed before I could speak again. By the next week I felt more normal. I had constant visitors sitting with me. Eventually I was able to walk about, and Cecelia immediately sent me back to school. I didn't want to go, but she knew I needed to get busy. True, it felt good to get back into a routine, but a malaise still dulled my senses.

The good news was Masauwu's children all made it back safely. Beckett went back to his observation point and Flu Cat and Pooka must have gone with him. The darkness in my mind brooded. I decided to ignore it since I couldn't seem to bring it forward or interact with it. But another thought flitted in my head. It was a voice that spoke with no words and encouraged me that I wasn't alone. The presence was familiar and tasted like home: home with my Hopi family. I was a confused mess and was glad to get back into my routine. Life resumed a regular tempo. Even Mr. Birman's class was welcomed normalcy. Well, mostly.

"Okay class, you have been well behaved for me these first few months. I want to give you something as a thank you. Today, you will be writing a one-page short story based on the article I had you read yesterday. The title of your short essay is Lo Spettro, Italian for the Ghost. When you complete the assignment, you are free to leave for the day."

Never had a more enthusiastic group of students set to a task more fervently. Mr. Birman was even better than his word. The next day we came in he had decorated the whole classroom in an elaborate Japanese theme. Pictures, yoroi armor on mannequins, models of shrines and torii. A young woman was standing chatting with Mr. Birman as we came in.

"Come in, come in! Please! Today we have a guest who will share some special things with you." We all sat, dumbstruck by all the fancy regalia and decorations.

"Dr. Susan Jessup is a colleague of mine from the University of New Mexico. She specializes in Japanese history, particularly the feudal period. I don't think you will find a more splendid motility of mind as that found in Dr. Jessup." Our guest speaker was visibly uncomfortable with the introduction being given.

But leave it to Teddy to take the uncomfortability up a notch, "Dr. Jessup, has Mr. Birman always been this nervous around you?"

Mr. Birman rolled his eyes and Dr. Jessup put a hand to her mouth to hide a smile. "Okay Teddy, thank you for the comic relief. However, today we are focusing on Japanese feudal culture, not my failed love life."

For once Teddy was visibly sorry for his outburst. Surprisingly he didn't speak for almost a whole 5 minutes afterward. Not a half-day, but literally the whole day was filled with quips back and forth between Birman and Teddy, with 'oh my gosh!' exasperated comments from Dr. Jessup.

"Kip, just watch! Teddy is totally macking on Jessup. Somehow, I thought Teddy was a neuter. He's never shown interest in anyone since we've been here." Wogs was right and Binky and Cricket both nodded. Teddy was having his first crush and Mr. Birman was in his way.

"Hey Kip…" it was Peach, coming over to add her two cents, "What's up with Teddy trying to impress Doctor whatsherpants?" Not only was Teddy doing his best to get Jessup's attention, but Peach was also surprisingly jealous. What? I thought she liked me; not that I'd ever go out with someone her age, but I'm just saying, ya know?

Then came the swords. Katana, wakizashi and more. We got to handle real ones, but she had a surprise: practice swords. The last half of the day was Samurai training. Jessup took us to the gymnasium. We donned high impact gear and chose our training weapon. We paired up and we worked hard.

"Okay kids, matte!" Sensei Jessup was in control. "Circle up on the edges," we moved to the periphery and sat in the position she told us was called seiza. My knees started hurting immediately.

"Now we will have shiai. Only those who want to compete need participate" Everyone stood, and Sensei Jessup smiled. She created two teams, and I was put on a team opposite all my Crew. Great.

First up was Peach versus Teddy. Hajime was called and they came out swinging. Teddy looked like a lumberjack and Peach was all about avoidance and precision striking. Sensei stopped them several times to stress the basic points. Teddy was outmatched and Peach stood as the victor. The competition continued through all the kids. Cricket won in his battle against Judith and Wogs beat Buddy. When Binky was up, she was hyper focused. She won with only three strikes against Violet. Then I was up against Pez. Pez was the smallest girl in our class, but she made up for her size with heart and the same kind of intensity as Binky. On the first round Pez got a quick jab into my gut. On the second I was able to tag her head. The third round and I was out. Pez got inside my reach and made a horizontal slice against my gut and tripped me, sending me rump over teakettle onto the floor. Pez was back to her usual sweetness after she handed me my butt.

"Oh Kip, it's okay. Win some, lose some, huh?" She gave me a companionable nudge to the shoulder. I pretended I didn't care but I was disappointed. She was a 12-year-old girl, for Pete's sake.

The eliminations took place and came down to Sensei Jessup taking on the winner. One guess who the winner was…yep, it was Binky.

Sensei Jessup grabbed a bo staff. Binky had her boken. They faced each other, postured like two real samurai, and Mr. Birman called it, "Hajime!"

Binky blurred forward with a vertical strike, sweeping down and to the right. Jessup stood still and easily deflected the strike. She stepped out to trip Binky, but Binky snapped her foot in, made some distance and turned. They posed in place, Binky high, Jessup holding her bo vertically in one hand. She was offering a tempting target.

Jessup attacked first. She came in low with a spinning staff sounding like an airplane propeller. Binky jumped to the side, leaping beyond and behind Jessup. Jessup had a wisp of a smile at that. Once Binky came out of her roll she made a long reach strike toward Jessup's head. Barest inches; it almost struck. The cheering kids grew quiet as they realized Binky was out for blood. This had just become real. She and Jessup struck and parried back and forth for another minute, both beginning to sweat.

I knew these kinds of matches were decided in a single flash of movement. It was the same here. Jessup spun her staff in a blur and struck at Binky more times than I could count. I could hear wood versus wood and then a different sound: wood versus flesh and bone. Binky gave a sharp yell. Her right arm was dangling limp. Her boken had fallen to the ground and Jessup was following up with an overhead strike. Binky grabbed the boken with her left hand and rolled out of the way. Tears streamed down her face as she gritted her teeth in a rictus grin. She stood in a forward stance, boken raised. Jessup knocked the boken out of her hand then waited.

Binky cupped her broken right arm with her left. She stood straight and bowed deeply. Jessup bowed back, put her staff on the table and gave an appraising stare at Binky. Only for a moment. I could see the kids were all afraid. Then Jessup's stern visage melted, and she was Dr. Jessup again.

"Binky, good job. Let's get your arm fixed up." Birman surprised us. He had a huge BLS kit filled with bandages, tape, and medical equipment.

He noticed us "Yes, I know. It's strange to have old fuddy duddy Birman pull out a big aid kit. Well, I used to be a corpsman in the Navy." He sat Binky down and touched areas carefully. She was stoic through the pain but yelped when he touched the breakage area.

"Yep, clean break. We'll need to get you in for imaging. For now, let's get it in a sling." Carefully Birman got her trussed up like a Thanksgiving turkey. He said immobilization was important to prevent further tissue damage. An ambulance arrived and toted Binky off. Wogs went with her, and Cecelia had been called. Cricket and I felt a bit at odds, not going with her. Wogs waved us off and we hung back with the other kids.

The afternoon wore on as we sipped iced tea. Dr. Jessup walked us through a new Japanese tea ceremony, southern belle style. It was classy and the tea was cooling and delicious. Afterward we were quite at our leisure and reclined in the shade of the trees near the athletic field. When I got up to get more tea, I heard an interesting conversation.

"David, you have a lot on your hands. I know you volunteered, but you need help. I mean, come on, did you see how she moved? She had no training!" Jessup had a concerned expression and Birman was shaking his head.

"This is exactly the reason I volunteered. Staunton and Olonana needed someone to help.

They said no one has any idea what they are capable of. I guess we got a glimpse of that today." Birman shook his head.

"She was amazing, David. I have gone against other hachi-dan and not been so pressed. I would strike and and hit only empty air. Then I would defend and it was like stopping water. If she can do this at 16, what will she be able to do when she matures? If I were a fearful type, I'd be frightened."

Then they noticed I was listening and were about to speak to me when an old man walked between two trees, angling toward us. He moved slowly with age, but there was a sense of power about him. Birman and Jessup stood and greeted him with formality. He quietly met with the teachers, and I slipped away to discuss what I heard with Cricket. Birman cleared the table of weapons and equipment and they sat. I'd never seen the old man before, but there was something familiar about him. They sat and spoke for a while. We ate up the little rice cakes and mochi balls and lazed about.

I was thinking about my synth friends back home when Teddy interrupted my thoughts, "Hey dude, we've taken a vote and elected you the worst fighter of the Hopi."

Teddy was talking but all I heard was we had become Hopi. My heart was full, especially in light of the concerning conversation I overheard. Teddy didn't expect a smile and hug from me. But you have to understand, Teddy was the canary in the coal mine. He acted like a dufus and had the social graces of a zombie looking for brains. But if you read between the lines, Teddy was a spot-on indicator of the true status of things. It came across in his own flavor of comedy and he had just told me we are more than family. We had become Hopi. I had thought a person had to be born a Hopi, but I guess I was wrong. After Teddy prised me away from my hug, all the kids gave me the you are so weird look and laughed. Teddy changed the subject quickly and just as he was winding up for another comical tirade the three adults walked over. I put a bookmark to think more about this later.

Mr. Birman spoke, "Sir, let me introduce you to Kip. Just moments ago, he was elected as the worst swordsman the Hopi have ever seen," Mr. Birman had been listening and Teddy beamed proudly as his jibe landed as he had intended. Everyone laughed.

"Kip, I would like to introduce you to our Elder, Mr. Talayumptewa." I stood and shook hands.

"May I call you Kip?" The old man's voice was smooth and rich. He was craggy and crusty looking, but his voice and mannerisms were genteel like the ideal grandpa-man.

"Yessir. It's a pleasure to meet you." My uncomfortability notched down as he put me at ease. But my paranoia never left me. I figured it never would.

"If I might have a word with you in private?" Birman hid his shocked expression well.

"Yes, sir. Would you like some tea?"

"Why yes. Please." Birman and Jessup moved away and went to sit with the kids under the trees.

"Are you enjoying living among the Hopi?"

"Oh yes. Cecelia and Timothy are wonderful people."

"Would you like to live with us from now on?"

I really would but I know my Dads made it so we can't stay anywhere for very long.

"I would, Mr. Talayu -um, sorry." I was embarrassed.

"Just call me Tala. Everyone else does. Let me formally welcome you to Hopi." Tala's hands were extended, and he held my right hand with both his big paws.

"Thank you, sir -um, Tala." He released the gentle grasp and continued.

"When I was a boy growing up on First Mesa, I would look at the sky at night and see stars, satellites, and the Milky Way. I wondered who might be out there. One night I was stargazing and letting my mind run and a voice clearly spoke to me, '*Charlie*'. I was shocked and jumped up, looking around. No one was there."

Tala used his hands as he spoke, and I realized he was one of the tribal storytellers. I loved stories and I gave him my complete attention. I didn't notice all the kids being restrained by Jessup and Birman. I guess they wanted to keep my meeting private. The kids saw it as a missed opportunity for hearing a good tale from a Hopi master storyteller.

"The voice spoke again, *'Charlie, do you know who I am?'* I shook my head. *'Charlie, I assume since I can't see you, you must be shaking your head'*.

"I answered back. Yes."

"*'Okay Charlie, I am an Elder from Third Mesa and I have something important to ask you'*. The voice was a woman's.

'Yes ma'am. Okay'.

'First, can you keep a secret?'

'I think so. It's not like I have a lot of friends'.

'Second, would you like to learn how to farspeak?'

I wasn't quite sure what she meant but I figured I should answer yes. I said, *'Yes, sure'*.

'Charlie, let us meet every evening around this time. I won't come if anyone is with you, though. Okay?'"

Tala continued, "And like that I began my training. From my mind I could talk to other people. They were the shaman, watchers, wise ones, and tribal elders from other tribes. After a time, I could join them in discussions without the help of my guide. I was told no names would be given until I had passed within. I asked if I needed to be a man first and my guide said yes. She also said I needed to pass within to become an accepted Farspeaker." Tala stopped for a moment, stuffed a pipe with tobacco and took a sip of tea.

'Kip, you can hear me.' He mind-spoke to me. It was not a question.

I made a mental adjustment and replied, *'Yes, sir.'*

'Good. What I am going to say is not meant for other ears.'

'Elder Youvella from Third Mesa was my Guide. For years she trained me in farspeaking and other mind skills. In time she and another, Sanballat, from the Cavalry tribe initiated me into the Farspeaking community. When I was grown, I was initiated into the tribal council. Today, I am inviting you to be my apprentice. If you want.'

All the kids saw was me and Tala sitting silently, staring at each other, and not speaking. I would nod my head at times and in a few minutes, we were too boring to warrant further observation. Birman took the kids on a walk to get ice cream. Jessup quietly began packing her equipment.

I risked a quick burst to Cricket, *'Hey man, Tala is making me a Hopi apprentice. I'll tell ya about it later.'* I received a mental nod from Cricket, *'Okay wuss, watch your six.'* A prickle of humor played across the sending.

I continued listening to Tala. Did he notice my send to Cricket?

'First rule for you is different than what I was given. You must keep this just between us, except...' at this point Tala made a sending that included me and my three Crew, *'All four of you will be included in the lessons. I will only meet with Kip in person. No one else may know. There is danger in others knowing. Agreed?'* Tala must have been speaking to all my Crew moments earlier because they weren't surprised.

All the voices spoke. Wogs, *'Agreed.'*

Binky, *'Agreed.'*

Cricket, *'Yeah, sure.'*

'The second rule is you must never miss a meeting no matter where you are. Understood?'

All my Crew answered in the affirmative.

'Okay, that's enough for now.' Tala closed the farspeak connection.

Aloud he said, "Let's catch up with the others. Ice cream sounds like a great idea!"

The old man was fast; I had to run to catch up with him. One thing I learned was to never underestimate a Hopi. Tala was old, craggy, and faster than a jackrabbit! He laughed as he ran, and we were soon with the others. Back at the school Jessup finished packing.

She pulled out a milspec pad and spoke into it, "Birman is doing well. The kids are progressing faster than we expected. Suggest Beckett be reinforced. The enemy may make another play now that farspeak training is underway." A crackling voice buzzed in reply and Jessup replied, "Roger. Out."

June 2254 – Bakabi, Hopi Nation, Arizona Territory

Mr. Birman had won over the students of Bakabi. The months wore on and it was turning into summer. Our Crew had evening farspeech sessions with Tala and as our learning continued, we were introduced and coached in farspeech etiquette, lore, and usage. We learned emotions, words and pictures could be conveyed and other things. Tala called it push. Through farspeech a recipient could be pushed or influenced. He said this had to be done with care and any harm done was a serious crime within the farspeech community. We studied hard and practiced with each other daily. It was embarrassing sometimes when our friends would find us laughing amongst ourselves with no words being spoken. Buddy caught on first.

"You guys are being taught Elders' farspeech, huh?"

I replied, "Why would you –"

"Cut the crap. That's totally unfair. You guys are the newest members of the tribe." Buddy stopped talking, building up to a big sulk. I decided to try something.

'Buddy, can you hear me'?

'Fewkin A!' Buddy jumped as he reacted to my farspeech. I guess he heard me.

I turned down the volume a bit, *'Buddy, talk back'.*

'Oh my gosh, oh my gosh! Yes!' Buddy did it.

'How would you like it if I taught you the farspeech'?

'Yes! Well, is it allowed'? Buddy crinkled his brow.

'It is now.'

I gave him the same ground rules which apparently would only apply to non-Hopis since all the kids knew about Elder farspeech. It started with me and Buddy meeting by farspeech in the evening time, just before bedtime. But soon it grew as Buddy's big mouth spread the word. Soon every Hopi kid in the 3 Mesas was logged into our evening sessions and I had to get organized real quick to contain the mayhem. I am sure Tala knew about this and within a month of trying to keep it secret I was busted.

My Crew and I met with Tala, going over more elements of farspeech and the mechanics of push. After we logged off, I got some grub from the kitchen. Cecelia and Timothy were busy with paperwork at the kitchen table and waved silently at me. Back in my room I heard Buddy and the other kids doing the 'quiet open' that let me know they were there and waiting. In my mind's eye it was like we were gathering in a huge lecture hall. Then I began our session. A week ago, I copped to my Crew about teaching the other kids. They were pretty peeved at me. Mostly for not letting them in on sessions. They joined enthusiastically.

My Crew came on and the rest of the kids were ready. Of the 1000+ kids several were in the hospital, or doing evening work or busy with other things. But 100% of the kids made every session. And they were getting good at farspeech. To keep things organized I created some mental tools to help our time together. I created talk rooms, mental message threads that behaved like BBS, bulletin board services from the 20th and even did some chart and graph things which helped each of us track our individual progress. Tonight, was the first night covering push.

July 2254 – Bakabi in the Cloud

'Nada, do you see how he has created orchestrations to keep tabs on every child?' Tala was examining my work and had known about every farspeech session since the beginning.

'Yes Tala. And you have known my thoughts about this since the start', Nada Kalyesvah, Elder & Farspeaker of Second Mesa sent disapproval and frustration, tinged by 2nd degree fear.

Shirley Dale Youvella, Third Mesa Elder and Farspeaker sent 1st degree calm and spoke, *'Be at ease younger sister. Tala, this is dangerous, and you know it. Be respectful of Nada's fear'*. She sent 1st degree inclusiveness and warmth with a third degree of chiding.

'My apologies, Nada. Early on, I had a choice. After Buddy was added to farspeaking I had a choice to allow the speech or shut it down. I found my heart couldn't silence the new voice Buddy brought to our community'. Tala sent 1st degree sincerity and a visual of open hands.

'Kip has created farspeech tools we have never seen. Do you think either of you could create a Cloud pad, segmented classrooms or measurements stored as if on a computer'? Tala's was a rhetorical question.

'The student has moved far beyond our teachings. I'm afraid the best we can do is show wisdom, love, and acceptance'.

A few moments of silence passed, and Tala spoke, *'Tonight I will join their session. I would like you to join too. The cat is out of the bag, and I think we need to wrap the arms of the whole community around these children. Besides, with the Cloud boost satellites hovering above the Earth, the Dads have made it possible for millions of others to farspeak. We need to prepare our children for a flood and help them to protect themselves and all of Hopi'.*

First degree agreement passed between the three Elders.

'Okay friends. Pick a partner and log into a room.' I sent to the whole gathering and then conjured a picture of a hand pad. It looked just like my actual pad in the real world. *'Remember to initialize your Cloud pad so you can measure your progress and give a shout to one of the Crew if you're having problems, okay'?* My Crew mentally waved to everyone, and we began the first warm-up of the night.

Then the voice I dreaded hearing spoke, *'Kip. We must talk'.* I felt the presence of not one but all three Mesa Elders. Inadvertently I sent them my sense of dread.

'Tala, first degree fear. This is concerning'. I could hear Elder Nada as she spoke.

'Kip and Crew, hear my words. You have been welcomed into the tribe and received all the benefits of our protection, care, and love'. I realized he was broadcasting his words to the whole class.

'You are also bound by our traditions and laws. You were instructed to not divulge the farspeech to others, yet this you have done. More, you have taken up all our children as your students. This is concerning. What do you have to say for yourself'? Tala went quiet.

'Sir, it is my fault. I told Buddy then suddenly more knew about it'. I caught a thought from Nada on how to send emotions via farspeech and I sent 1st degree contrition.

'It is well that you are contrite, but it stands that what you have opened can never be closed. You have put all Hopi at risk', Tala and the Elders were afraid. Okay, there is no way I sent first degree crybaby. But I did. I wept.

Something new happened. As I wept all the children of Hopi extended their love, their warmth, and another thing. I realized they had formed a protective shell around me like a creche. It was then that I knew I was Hopi, both body and soul.

In a private send to Nada and Shirley, Tala spoke, *'Notice how all the children are protecting Kip? He owns their hearts. We need to be careful here'.*

'Kip and Crew, you are both powerful and disciplined. But to my reckoning it's more important how you are sacrificing and compassionate. You have the Hopi in the palm of your hand. Please be gentle with us', Tala then sent 1st degree caring as did Nada and Shirley. He also sent an image that showed he and the Elders were now joining our class as students. I was suddenly uncomfortable. I froze. The creche shell faded but the warm sentiments remained. Even my Crew was waiting on my next directive. Hmm, in for penny, in for a pound!

'Okay people, time's wasting! Change partners! Crew, would you bring the Elders up to speed on our classroom setup'?

A quick burst from Tala let me know they knew everything we had been doing. My Crew were my students and now the Hopi Elders were right with them. Well, they were more like student teachers. It was a monumental job after all. Occasionally Masauwu and Flu Cat would join the sessions. Often those sessions turned into Lord Masa telling stories of the old times. Even Flu Cat would share little tales once we bludgeoned him into it. Best. Job. In the world! Our sessions continued, meeting each evening. I added another rule: no farspeech or Cloud behaviors allowed in the presence of non-speakers.

In the mundane world, the Hopi calendar was heating up for the holiday season. Jude, Pez and Buddy had important roles in the coming Wuko'uyis, the Plaza Dances and the planting of corn. What was amazing to watch was how involved Cricket, Binky and Wogs became in the Hopi celebrations. Our covert farspeaking lessons continued each week and no child missed a session. Ever. The non-speaker adults were surprised at the new surge of interest in the Hopi traditions from the children. The Elders weren't surprised, and they coached the parents and others to take it as a wonderful gift.

Then something special happened. We were formally invited into the Hopi community as members and would be welcomed during the Plaza Dances by the tribal leaders. Non-speakers needed to bring us into the fold. The surprise was going to be even deeper than that. On the first evening we were to be dressed as Katsina, Corn Dancers. That night as we all danced in the plaza, I saw some old familiar friends I thought never to see again. They stayed near the periphery out of respect for the ceremony, but afterward we were reunited with my SynthBots Alexa, Cortana and Siri. How had they found me? Peach and Teddy, both gave me a knowing wink. Something was afoot and I was very curious to know. After the dancing finished, we rushed over to a warm reunion with my floating friends. Never to beat around the bush, Cortana chimed, "So Kip, why are you so hairy? You look like a caveman." Everyone around knew my story and there was mirthful laughter.

Teddy could never let an opportunity pass, "Kipper is a hairy Chupa man!" Buddy and Cricket had a belly laugh over that.

"Yeah, and we keep running out of hand cream in the bathroom!" More laughter and I turned red and shook my head.

We took the party inside the Community Hall and were regaled with a tale worthy of Beowulf or Gilgamesh. The story was about Tawa, the sun spirit, who formed the world out of Tokpella, the void.

On the ridgeline above town the Shadowy Figure made an appearance. Behind the shadow was a very large cat with a small creature bouncing on its back. Both Cecelia and Timothy noticed the odd assemblage but chose to ignore it as they headed inside. They shared a knowing nod between them.

July 2254 – Bakabi, Hopi Nation, Arizona Territory

Mr. Campbell rejoined the Bakabi school. We had put regular pressure on Mr. Birman when we heard the real reason Mr. Campbell had left. You see, the parents appealed to the tribal school board to have him removed due to his lack of formal qualifications. Then it came to light no teacher in the history of the school had had the appropriate qualifications. Mr. Birman somehow did it and voila, Mr. Campbell began cooperative teaching responsibilities. The details were a bit hazy, but we didn't care. We had Campbell back! Birman was our forever hero!

With all the excitement of Campbell and Birman co-teaching and the new commitment from all the students to school activities and studies, Bakabi became a magnet for students across all the Hopi school district. We got kids from the other two Mesas. Our class size grew and within a couple months there were almost 220 students in our high school. They brought in mobile units as temporary classrooms and things just took off from there. For the four of us it was a whirlwind not unlike the world we grew up in. But instead of scientists and doctors, we had a crazy wide variety of smart, motivated Hopi kids. It was July and we were all deeply involved in the preparation for the Talangva rituals. The Niman Ceremonies were the pivot for the summer solstice festival. Replete with colorful costumes, stalls with free home-cooked food and no alcohol. You would have thought it would take a bunch of booze to be so free to dance, sing and enjoy each others' company. Nope. Where I grew up the hooch my Dads made was famous: famous for tasting sweet and tart and famous for getting people sauced. The Hopis found a way to have a riotous carnival without the drunk and disorderly side effects. But never to be staunched in his party-mindedness, Teddy found a bottle of Glenlivit and shared it with our little cabal. We were kids; you know, long on enthusiasm and short on judgement.

Teddy got to play Hemis Katsina for the Home-Going part of the Nemis Ceremony. We had been working for a couple weeks to assemble the pieces of the costume. Each year it had become a bit more elaborate to the consternation of the tribal elders. Teddy was weighed down by a massive headdress that looked a bit like an Aztec temple, painted with a bunch of bright colors, adorned with feathers and corn stalk fronds. The clothing was also brightly colored, and he even had LEDs built into the cloth so as evening fell, he lit up the dances he performed. Festivities ran late into the night and even our synth friends got into the action. The ceremonies wound down and clusters of people gathered around the bonfires. Around one fire the three SynthBots flew in their own dance, telling a story in the true spirit of the Nimas Festival: entertaining and meaningful. But I wouldn't get to hear almost any of it.

July 2254 – Bakabi, Hopi Nation, Arizona Territory (2242 – RETRO –Valhalla Sector)

A couple dozen of us kids and several adults were sitting around one of the bonfires, sharing mulled apple cider, Kachina Cookies, and Jemez Pueblo Cookies. The festivities were still taking place in other areas, and we could hear the sounds of revelry. Our little group got quiet as the three SynthBots began to slowly circle the fire, weaving a tale. During the Ceremony several of the kids had decorated the SynthBots with feathers, paint and made them up Katsina-style. In full festive adornment Alexa, Cortana and Siri traded off narrating their tale. When they weren't speaking, they were creating sound effects and brief holo displays. It was a captivating performance.

I had known that in the early days of Valhalla Sector many synths, SynthBots and hybrids had run for cover when the general fear of humanity roared into an inferno of death and mayhem against the new lifeforms. In the middle of all the rush and cray-cray the three amigos (our SynthBots) were surprising co-conspirators to my Dads and Vagabond Bootblack. Sometimes they interrupted each other and would briefly argue. I wondered if they did it on purpose for comic relief.

Something odd happened as they began their story. Apparently, they wanted the four of us to hear something different than the rest. I realized anew that we had fully functioning prosthetics.

"Hey Kip, we will be giving you a different story. We wanted to first let you know your Dads sent us a message via Cloud communique. The way the message landed was like a piece of email. We also discovered your Dads are missing and the place they were working at was hit by a tactical nuclear missile. Many dead souls, but their bodies were not found. We are sorry." I wasn't surprised and had suspected as much a while back. Here is the story they told.

The story began...

When we first came Online, we were AIs floating in the æther. Then we got installed into these husks. Later, the Dads set us to managing aspects of their Online affairs. We managed aspects of the two Diamond projects at Seattle:CENTER headed by your Dads. In fact, we were the Speartip puncturing a way out of the CENTER system into the outside world. It was an exciting time and would have even been fun except for the urgency to save our friends.

The CENTER controllers were a bunch of jackbooted thugs. They had to be. Every major world Power was co-invested in the same thing: invention and innovation to get more power and advantage over the other Powers. The thugs kept the rules enforced and the people in line. But they had no idea about self-aware synthetics. Here we were cavorting around the sprawling Seattle:CENTER without any restriction since we could forge legitimate authorizations to go anywhere. So, we recruited and equipped and helped Vagabond organize the Synth Railroad. Synths, hybrids and humans were smuggled out and it all looked approved and normal business-like.

I watched the others listening and realized they were hearing a dramatic retelling of the LA:CENTER rescue. I caught snippets of the derring-do tales the others were hearing. I hadn't known these three synths were the central command and control for the whole rescue operation. Despite listening to two separate narratives, I still had another train of thought in my head. Something came back to me: on the first day of school when we first arrived at Bakabi, Teddy mentioned something about a well-guarded secret. Then I thought back even earlier to something my Dads mentioned about the Hopis when we were at the dinner table. They said something about sustained Jungian Space. I paid little attention then, but I now know something important had been said. A flash of frustration hit me as I realized the farspeaking and Cloud powers were the same. I knew that, but for some odd reason I didn't make the full connection until now. That was most unlike me. I was being very short-attention-span-theater in my thinking. Okay, back to the task…my Dads had said something else vital. If I could just recall.

…and Exodus Day came. There were people, scientists, guards, paramilitary, office workers and others who couldn't leave with the Vagabond Railroad; it was renamed when the escapees became more than just synths. Exodus Day was going to be messy, and in-fact was even more bloody than we had feared. You see, the Exodus wasn't merely from our location but from all the CENTERs around the world. Some were better prepared than others. None were prepared enough. The worst of it was someone had leaked the exit plans, and the military might of every major Power was waiting on the ground, in the air and in wave after wave of soldiers and equipment, ready to mow us down. And mow us they did.

We went with Vagabond and the Dads through a culvert to an airwing hangar newly constructed by the Dads and unknown to the Powers. We got away undetected. We had heavy guilt on our hearts. Could we have gotten more out safely? When we arrived at our first waypoint, called Gilligan's Island, we changed aircraft and headed to our final destination, Lake Stevens. It was 2242. When we arrived, the Dads triggered the Online purge. What they did was so murky and complex only the synths had an idea of the scope of damage they did to the Powers. Up to that point there were 23 known terror cells wanted by the Powers. The Dads became number 24.

Because tracks were covered so well and because there was such substantial infrastructure damage, the Powers didn't come after us for years. The four of you had been living in Lake Stevens for a year when the Exodus happened. After the Exodus you were raised by your parents and life was made to be harmonious and warm for you. Dare we say normal? Alexa taught you to play music, Siri spent hours showing you how to paint and I mostly complained and was the plucky comic relief. We know you have very little memory of the early days, isn't that right?

The prosthetics weren't allowing us to silently talk back, and the synths couldn't hear farspeech. Right? Frustrating! But it was true, we had a dim memory of a flurry of activity when we were tots, but no specific memories stood out. I bet it was on purpose. Hmm, wait, I recalled seeing two faces, Vagabond, and another. Sudden realization came as I finally placed the face. It was that Croatoan guy.

I spoke aloud, "Who is Croatoan? I remember him." I realized the mistake as the three synths stopped their swirl of dramatic tale telling and all eyes were on me. For a beat no one spoke.

Then Teddy broke the moment, "Kipper!" Uh-oh, Teddy had joined the Kip renaming team. "S'pose to keep your trap shut during story time. Anyway, that's the dude who comes here to talk with the Elders every few years. Kinda creepy, but seems nice…"

Teddy was interrupted by the synths before he could say more but at that moment, I could see nods of recognition from every head. I put a bookmark in it to ask about it later. The synths kicked back into storytelling, resuming their harrowing tale.

Kip, keep the mouth closed and ears open, ok? The four of you are safe as long as you stay with the Hopis. Croatoan made sure of that. Teddy is right, he is creepy. He's also an alien and is trying to help us not die. Helping aside, we do not trust him. We take his help but with a grain of salt. You need to stay here for at least another two years. There are plans for you which require time to make ready.

We have an assignment for you now. We know Wogs found another figurine in the mine. The four of you need to find the other two and get them to a man named Shrike. They are keys to something important and must never fall into enemy hands. The enemy are called the Vor. We have no idea who the Vor are, but Croatoan said anybody could be a Vor agent and to trust no one.

It was frustrating to not be included at the grown-ups table, again. But at least some of the curtain was being pulled back, finally. Plans and action surrounded us, and we were always being told what to do, but not why. I got pissed. Here we were, with our new friends and suddenly three messengers from our old life come barging in to let us know we are just kids who need to do a task. Screw that! I stood and walked away from the bonfire. Sudden as it was, few seemed to notice as the crowd, which had grown larger, roared in laughter at the synths' bouncing and bobbing storytelling.

My Crew got up quietly and followed me. As I walked, I fumed. Why did we always get told parts of the truth? We get the figurines, fine. But to me they were just McGuffins, not the actual objective in our missions.

"Kip, you know what we need to do." Binky made a statement.

"Yes, we all do. Our Hopi family cannot get involved. We need to find the other two rocks and make sure the Vor don't come snooping around here. We should leave tomorrow." I was so thankful for my Crew. Binky as always was spot-on.

"No Kip, not tomorrow…" Wogs spoke quietly and firmly. The darkness had enveloped us, away from the fire. The three of us stared at Wogs, "We leave now. While everyone is distracted, we can get cleanly away. Everyone, let's go now. We'll get snacks, our weapons of choice and see what vehicle we can steal. Maybe we can steal the bus. First, let's ask around about the two remaining figurines. After we find the rocks we'll go find Shrike."

The three of us almost hooted. Wogs knew how to frame things as an adventure! We were suddenly alive again, and all smiles. We ran to our house, ready to load up.

"Just like the Rangers, it's travel light, freeze at night!"

And then there were Cecelia and Timothy, standing with Cliff at the front stoop. Cecelia always seemed to be sporting a smile and warmth. She and the other two were not smiling.

"Kip, I know what you're doing." We stood facing them for the longest time, just staring back and forth. Were they trying to put the kibosh on our plan?

"Cecelia, we need to go. Please don't try stopping us." My voice sounded stronger than I felt.

"Stop you? Young man, Croatoan has spent generations preparing my people. Stop you?" Cecelia shared a smile and knowing nod, "We're here to help you."

"The Hopis planned carefully so that when you came, we could be ready. Croatoan told our Elders long ago that the Hopis would save the world. Well…we're ready."

A brief pause, then Wogs ran to Cecelia and embraced her. An uncertain moment melted into something called family. Hugs all around.

"Inaqvu haalayti!" Cliff said this loudly and slowly. Cecelia and Timothy repeated the phrase and clasped both hands in front of their chests.

"Friends, you joined the Hopi family when you came to us. You have been welcomed by a gathering of the tribe and now, Hopi joins you. Say with me… Inaqvu haalayti!" We followed his lead.

"Our ears are happy. We declare this as a celebration of life and commitment to each other. It is as Wogs said, 'time for you to go'."

Cliff had a notebook, dogeared and tattered, held closed by a thick rubber band. "These notes should help you find your last two relics. Be careful." I took the notebook and we set about our prep work.

In the house, preparation took longer than we expected. An engine roared out front which brought everyone to the door. Cliff pulled up in a hopped-up old petrol-using Ford Mustang. Two more cars came behind his, a Dodge Challenger and Chevrolet Impala. Classic muscle cars and awesome to behold. I thought of Hopis as a people too quiet and reserved to concern themselves with hotrods. Guess again!

"Hey kids, we're gonna go take a ride!" Cliff had a big smile and I know he had been looking forward to this moment. "But first we circle up. Come here."

Cliff turned off his muscle car and led us to a place beside the house around the firepit.

"Circle up. Come on, take a seat." We gathered in a circle, and he threw sage and several other dried things into the pit and lit it. It smelled deep, rich, and earthy.

"Hold hands and follow me." Timothy and Cecelia closed their eyes, so we did the same.

"We invite the spirits of our ancestors, lost friends, and family to this circle. We ask your blessing on our quest. Please bless our steps and give favor to our friends…they have become family. Kachina, kwakwhay uma itamuy tumala'yyungwa, huvam Sipapuh."

Cecelia and Timothy repeated after Cliff, "Kachina, kwakwhay uma itamuy tumala'yyungwa, huvam Sipapuh." We joined in on the third round and in farspeech the Elders all joined the blessing. Elder Tala translated in farspeech, *'Living spirit, thank you for those taking care of us. We greet the entrance into the Fourth World.'*

I felt a warmth suffuse our gathering. It felt like…home. Had Cecelia and Timothy heard the farspeech? I wasn't going to ask. Not my secret to divulge. We stood there, quietly with our eyes closed for several minutes. I wasn't the only one to steal a peek.

Finally, Cliff disbanded our circle, "Thank you my family. It's now time for another holy celebration: driving fast cars."

All smiles now, and within moments with the gear loaded we were driving faster than was probably safe. I loved every moment. The side of the Mustang had the name Betty painted in a flowery script. When I asked about it he said it was his mother's name. The coincidence was too rich: a black kid riding in a black racecar named Betty. I brought up Spiderbait's "Black Betty" on my Pad. In a moment it sync'd with Cliff's thumpin' sound system and giant tunes blasted out into the night. Cliff wasn't the only madman driver. Timothy and Cecelia had no problem keeping up. Cliff told me the Hopi Elders thought it wise to allow the younger generations to pursue various advanced studies. Those included automotive innovation. These three vehicles had been upgraded over the last 200+ years with the latest tech, passed down through the generations. They sounded and smelled like petrol driven cars as a cover for the actual tech involved. These things flew, could submerse deep underwater and serve you a hot cup of coffee. No, really, you could use the matter transmuter to create whatever you wanted. Even coffee.

"Computer, whatever your name is. Please make me a hot chocolate."

A sweet feminine voice answered my request, "I am not 'computer', my name is Aloha. Don't be mean, it really sets a bad tone to the evening."

"I'm sorry Aloha, I was being stupid. Is it okay to ask for some hot cocoa?"

"Of course, Kip. It's already made. Enjoy."

This was so much better than Kitt in Knightrider!

"Thank you, Aloha. I'll introduce you to my SynthBot friends sometime. They would love you!"

"Kip, we are already acquainted. In fact, they just gave me a significant upgrade earlier today in preparation for tonight's mission." There was a momentary pause, "And you want to know how we knew you were going to look for and try offloading those figurines tonight, right? Well too bad, that would be telling."

Aloha giggled. The adult conspiracy against us kids included the synths and AIs. How rude! We zoomed off into the night and I dug my nose into Cliff's notebook.

RETRO 2204 – Planet Char, Vor Homeworld

Salim T'Vor was running to his class. The university was unyielding about tardiness; like all Vor culture, lax attitude or performance was tantamount to complete personal failure. He knew he might as well die if he didn't arrive on time. Within seconds he crossed the room's threshold and sat as the school buzzer rang. Another student was not as fortunate. Behin al'T'Vor, one of the vice-regent's offspring was late. As he crossed the room's threshold a force field appeared and held him fast. A moment later a hologram appeared next to the shamefaced student; it was his father.

"My son, no one is above our laws. You know the punishment. Do not bring more shame upon our House."

The holo vanished and the downcast Behin walked to the front of the class and spoke, "I have dishonored my family. For this I have shame. I have dishonored my instructor and the school he represents. For this I have shame. I have dishonored you, my honorable classmates. For this I have shame. I present myself for your judgement." Behin raised his head high and stared at the rear of the classroom.

"Who will relieve Behin al'T'Vor of his shame?" The professor looked around the room and received no response. "Once more, will someone stand for Behin al'T'Vor?"

For a moment more it was quiet then Salim T'Vor, a commoner's son stood, "Honored Professor, I will stand for my classmate Behin al'T'Vor." The Professor nodded and Salim stepped forward. Salim turned and faced the class, silently waiting.

The Professor moved behind Salim and asked, "You will bear this shame?"

Salim replied in a firm tone, "I will."

"So be it," the Professor pushed a small rod against Salim's back and a bright flash and smell of burnt flesh wafted from the now still form of Salim lying on the floor.

"Student Behin, sit." Behin sat at the table next to Salim's place and as honor dictated, every student ignored Salim. Salim regained consciousness and crawled to his chair and sat for the day's class. The smell was awful, and Salim knew he'd need to get a new change of clothes for the rest of the school day. Behin and Salim did a surreptitious fist bump, but otherwise paid complete attention to their day's lecture and lab. Today's topic was the history of COMBINE contracts with the Royal Vor Academy.

Later in the halls, walking to the next lecture the boys laughed, "Behin, one day I will not stand for your shame. What do you think of that?"

"I think you would miss the new clothes I bring you each time. It's not like you could afford new clothes yourself. Anyway, you know it makes your father look good for his son to suffer for nobility." Behin had a wry smile.

With no little sarcasm, "Behin you are correct. I would miss the smell of burning flesh." Somehow this was riotously funny and both students laughed, and fist-bumped again. They walked to their next session.

"But Behin, seriously, tonight we need to meet Pella and Sumi at the fruit shop. Are you with me? Otherwise, I might have shame."

Both boys laughed loudly but quieted as they entered the next classroom. No need to get demerits for misbehavior. Vor were expected to be in complete control of their habitus, at all times; but youth pushed against that expectation. Adults to an extent turned a blind eye, except in areas of impugned honor.

At the fruit shop the boys were all about bending over backwards to solicit the young ladies. It was a game they never won. Too canny and wily were the females of the Vor. The other limiter to their success was death by lost honor. If they ever touched the girls inappropriately and it got reported, which it always did, their honor would be forfeit, their families held up to ridicule and shame. The boys tried their best to curry favor. They were persistent. Despite restrictions, Vor kids found a way to have a good time. The night came to a close and the boys walked the girls home.

"Behin." Salim rarely hesitated. "I think I need to tell you something." Behin stopped walking and faced Salim.

"Okay, what is it?"

"I don't actually favor Pella."

"Oh no, you have a thing for Sumi? Pella will be pissed."

Salim fully faced Behin and looked at his feet for a moment. When he looked up his eyes were unusually serious. "Behin, how long have we been friends?"

Behin had a tentative smile, "You know the answer. Since we were little. What are you driving at?"

Salim seemed to be evaluating his next response. "You know how we cover for each other? Sadly, it seems we must do it almost daily!" Behin nodded, wondering where this was going.

"Well, in truth I really look forward to the stupid things we do. Perhaps too much."

"Salim, this is not like you. Just spit it out."

"Behin, you are the one I want." Salim looked down again. When he looked up there was tenderness in Behin's eyes. The moment froze and for a second there seemed to be something like warmth between the boys.

"Salim, this cannot be. I love you too. There I said it; now, we need to forget it. You know the punishment for deviants." Almost as if on cue, two law enforcement officers passed by the pair, slowly, eyeing them meaningfully. "Even standing this close together draws suspicion. I have to get home now. See you tomorrow."

July 2254 – Along Highway 15 toward Las Vegas

The wind whipped and it was a glorious ride. Cliff had taken us off the ground and we were flying low, about 30 meters above the desert floor. The airborne muscle cars purred quietly since he turned off the engine noise synthesizers. We landed in Crystal, about 45 km outside Las Vegas. There was a dusty old rest stop, long gone to seed. When long-haul trucking became an unmanned affair, the need for rest stops had vanished. Just off the road was a 15-meter metal clown head, sitting on its neck, listing a few degrees to its side. More than a few of those still hung around after the Clown Roadside Diners were closed after the Tech War.

The rest stop still had toilets, but no running water. I tried going into the restroom but gagged when I opened the men's room door. It smelled like the worst dinosaur turd you could imagine. Better yet, don't imagine it. Sorry.

My Crew was behind me now. "Guys, this is a no-go. I think I might hurl."

Cricket smiled and walked in, "Such a pansy, dude!" A minute passed and out he came, eating an apple and smiling. "Cecelia's apples are good!" How did he bear the smell? He walked toward the giant clown head and the girls disappeared into the women's restroom. Well, maybe I was a pansy. I went pee on the side of the building facing away from the road. Looking across the desert I could see the hazy wave of the heat rising from the desert, warping the distant Vegas city lights. A coyote yipped and I heard scrabble of little feet in the bushes. The desert was alive at night.

"Time to get going kids. Kip, did you decide where we are going first." Cliff, Cecelia, and Timothy were leaning against the Mustang, waiting.

"I think we should try the trading post in Slab City. It's near the Salton Sea." I was looking at the location on my pad. "It looks like it's deserted."

"Okay then, let's get rolling. As the crow flies it's about 450km. It will be morning by the time we get there." We climbed back into our cars and took to the skies. As the adults expected the we slept through the flight. We were exhausted.

July 2254 – Slab City CA

We woke to find the three cars parked in a carport. A junkyard surrounded us and I discovered this was the town of Slab City itself. I figured it would be easy to hide here; good choice Cliff. Speaking of...Cliff was dozing as were the other two adults. I found my Crew sitting in the kitchen of the house next to the carport. All three were on their pads and were not in the least surprised I had overslept.

"Ah, look what the cat dragged in. Mornin' sunshine!" Cricket had bags under his eyes and the other two didn't appear any more rested. I felt pretty good.

"Hey y'all. Is there anything to eat?" I was hopeful.

"Kip, you brought food, didn't you?" Binky asked.

"Oh yeah, I did. But haven't you guys made something already? You weren't waiting for me?" I received blank stares and realized they in fact had been waiting for me to make everyone breakfast.

I grabbed my food stash from the car and set out my ingredients on the counter. I had to do some cleaning and discovered there was running water. I washed up the dishes and utensils from the sink and once the surfaces were cleaned, I checked the stove. Didn't work, no gas. I grabbed my camp stove and got working on scrambled eggs. I made a huge pile from the powdered mix I had packed. I added salt, pepper, and some sprinkles of Tabasco. I opened a T-ration pack with sausages and fried them up as well. The smells of cooking brought more people to the kitchen. Not our people.

Through the door came three men who looked they had lived their whole lives in the desert without a bath.

"Who's cooking in Maggie's old kitchen? You have permission to be here?" The first man was asking the questions. His second question came out like 'Yahaf perm'shun be 'ere?'

I decided to play it diplomatically, "Hey gents, come on in! Hey Crew, clear some space for the guys to sit." My Crew played along, and I noticed all three had palmed pistols. When did the girls start carrying? Cricket's was peeking out of his coat sleeve. I hoped the men didn't see it.

I quickly served up three heaping plates of eggs and sausages and poured three glasses of water. Cricket and Wogs stood back, and Binky and I served the men breakfast. The food shut them up and they tucked in like they hadn't had a meal in years. Maybe they hadn't.

Each time they cleaned their plates I served up another round. I hoped friendly hosting would pay off since these guys were eating most of our rations. After the third round the men slowed the wolfing down. A small sound came from the door to the carport, and I realized the adults were just outside, waiting. I really didn't want anyone to die so I started talking.

"Hey guys, my name is Kyle. This is Betty, Wendy, and Carl. We traveled quite a ways to get to your trading post. Could you point us in the right direction?" The men stared at each other then burst out laughing.

"Hey Kyle, that was the best damned breakfast I ever had. Not even the wife coulda done better, god rest her soul." The other men nodded and appeared to be more stable than when they first entered.

"My name is Randall. This is RJ and TeeLow. We're the Slab City fix it guys. You got sumthin' broke, we can fix it." I was sure these guys hadn't seen our cars and I hoped Cliff and the others would move them somewhere they wouldn't be seen. Seeing them would complicate things.

"Thanks Mister Randall. A pleasure to meet you guys, Mister RJ, Mister TeeLow," I shook their hands and shuddered inside at the greasy mess I was touching. Gross.

"Would y'all be able to show us the way right now?"

"Dang tootin' we can. Hell, for that meal I'd give you the complete guided tour!" Randall was friendly but my Crew kept their weapons at the ready.

Randall was as good as his word. He gave us a running narrative about Slab City as we walked. It was almost a half kilometer to the trading post, and we were hungry and irritable as we arrived. We didn't let any of it show, of course.

"Come on in kid. Ain't no one gonna bite." Randall's English had steadily improved. He held open the door to the Trading Post. The building was a rundown husk of a former ramshackle place. A real dive. It smelled like rats and sewage. The sign above the door was swinging on one cable. It read Severus the Salvor.

"Thanks Randall." I entered and my Crew with me.

"Welcome friends, welcome. Randall whom have you brought me today?" The man behind the counter was probably in his late 40s. He was dressed in an early 20th century frock coat with wide legged Oxford bag trousers and bow tie. He was clean and when he stepped close, he smelled like Old Spice aftershave. His hair was slicked back with pomade and his eyebrows were a riot of long bushiness.

"Mr. Smith, allow me to introduce my friend Kyle." Randall clearly wanted to impress Mr. Smith.

"Please, call me Severus." He held his hand out and I shook it. His hand was moist and drooped like a dead fish.

"Mister Severus, I am looking for a stone figurine and heard you sell things like that."

"Please call me Severus. And you, my young friend, have come to the right place. I have a whole room dedicated to figurines!" Severus took us on a guided tour. Randall and his friends meandered somewhere else. My stomach was regretting giving our breakfast away.

Binky and the others wandered the endless shop. It was a collection of buildings with tarps, plywood and other materials spanning the spaces in between. I was surprised how tidy the place was given the sewer rat smell near the entrance.

"These are my shopkeepers, Candy and Angel." They were mannequins. I nodded and continued walking when one of the mannequins grabbed my arm. Severus kept extolling his wares into the next room.

In hushed tones, Angel spoke, "You must leave. No one ever escapes the Clean Room."

"Are you a synth?"

"No stupid. I was human until I came looking for a present for my Mum. I wanted to get her some summer clothes" Angel's voice was scratchy like an old LP from the 20th. Her mouth didn't move.

Suddenly Severus was standing next to me with a big smile. "Ya like my shopkeepers, yes?"

Somehow, I didn't jump at the surprise. I asked, "Very nice. Um, are the mannequins for sale?"

"Sale? Oh no, no, no. They run the place at night when things get dark, and the gremlins come out to play. Don't you girls! Keeping Daddy's shop clean and safe. Come along now, let me show you my collection," he took me arm-in-arm and we moved on. I could swear there was a tear sliding down Angel's face.

My Crew had disappeared into the vastness of the sprawling store. I hoped for the best and prepared for something less.

"Ahhh, here we are." Severus walked me into a room with stark white walls and dozens of tables, little, big and of every furniture style you could imagine. The tables were painted black, and the stone art atop ranged from tiny tchotchkes to large Grecian statues. Some of them were so lifelike I could swear they were genuine frozen little people.

"So Kyle, what are you looking for?"

"I am not sure. All I know is it would be carved from stone, and it would be very old."

I looked about and saw some items that might be genuinely expensive. But most of his collection looked like dime-store variety, cheap plastic with flaking paint.

"Kyle, what do you think of this?" Severus was holding up a stone figure of a couple embracing. It didn't seem like the right one.

"Perhaps. I don't think it is the right one, but I could be mistaken." He grimaced.

Severus mumbled but I caught a few words, "No respect…when I open the holy shrine…"

Oh my. This guy saw his collection as something religious. People do violent things for their religions. Severus showed me other figurines, but none of them seemed right. I was starting to lose hope and he was beginning to become agitated. This was a bad sign.

"Kyle, I am beginning to think you came here for another reason. You don't steal things do you, young man?"

I gave an indignant look, and tried to hide a shock of fear, "No sir! I was raised better than that."

"Hmm, okay. I apologize for the insinuation. Ya just never know about some people these days." Severus' voice had changed tone, it was slightly smoother, like he was mulling something over. My spidey sense said it was time to go. But I needed the third figurine. I walked along and then I saw it. There was a shrine with incense, rice and wine offerings sitting against the far wall. As I got closer, I could see a stone figure of a cat that looked strikingly like Flu Cat.

As I got close, I felt a presence close behind. Severus lightly placed his chin on my left shoulder and spoke, "Ahh, yes. It's my prize. You like it?" This creeped me out big time.

"It's beautiful sir. Is it a cat?" I couldn't just say,'Please sell me your most sacred cat statue'.

"Mmm, that is the champion of the Thedisch, Cat Síth" He pointed to a word inscribed on a sign above. It was spelled out in strange letters: Þēodisċ.

My eyes began to wander with a languorous disinterest. My mind felt like putty and my body felt numb and flaccid. I heard his voice, softly, "Yes. Time to nighty night, my young friend." And my vision blurred, and my thoughts went away.

I awoke and everything was loud. I was lying on the shrine table, and I was 20 centimeters tall. I am not kidding; I was a Lilliputian. I already had a small guy complex and now I was the perfect size to be an elf-on-the-shelf. I moved away from the edge of the table; it was a long drop. I backed up into the Flu Cat statue and it moved. The head angled to look down at me.

"You're Kip, my TrueForm said you would be coming for me. Then I got stolen and figured Severus the Psycho spoiled my meeting with you. Guess we lucked out. Well, not so much you, as I see. You're shorter than I expected." it laughed. It sounded like Flu Cat.

The world was moving much slower than normal. Severus was doing battle with his two mannequins at a quarter speed, and I noticed he was not doing so well. Back and forth went the combatants with tables tumping and figurines flying every which way. Angel grabbed Severus from behind and Candy aimed a strike to his midsection. He dodged and rolled. Angel flipped away and Severus came up wielding a stone figurine of a woman in 19th century finery. He struck at Angel, and she fell, unmoving. A moment later he hit Candy, and she was down. Where was my Crew? I tried farspeaking them but there was only static. At least there was no headache. Yet I could speak with Flu Cat junior, here.

"Kip, I can get you out of here. You must leave before he touches you again. The transformation wasn't completed."

"Where do I go?"

"I am an avatar as you can guess. I have been hobbled by this charlatan so I can only advise you. I can't even contact my TrueForm right now."

"Okay, I'm game. But what about my friends?"

"They will have to fend for themselves. Pay attention. Look down over the back of the table. Do you see the hole in the floor? Jump into it."

"Are you kidding? That's like 30 meters."

"Shh, listen. Your body will feel like it's only a short distance. You seem small but you are as resilient as if you were your original size. Now go."

"But what do I do when I am down there? Won't there be snakes and spiders. Like huge ones?"

"No. Trust me. And once you are down, follow the tunnel. Someone will help you."

The ruckus stopped. I realized it had grown quiet. With dread I looked over my shoulder. Severus was coming for me in slow motion. He wore a vicious grin. His slo-mo deep voice vibrated the air, "Ah, my new little bauble. Come to Daddy."

No hesitation. I jumped. The hole entrance came up fast, despite being on the slow setting. Once through I was plunged into darkness. I hit a steep surface and slid to a stop. Once my eyes adjusted, I could see I was in a PVC tube. And there was a faint light source. I was still hungry and now I was nauseated on top of that. I had to duck my head slightly as I walked. I followed the light. Around a second turn I hit a junction and followed the light to the right. It opened into a junction box. Funny enough, I helped my Dads install one of these during the summer at the Carter's cabin. I felt like a rat in a maze. But it was kinda cool to see it from the rat's perspective. Speaking of rats, I was staring smack dab at one, standing over a table with a bunch of Indiana Jones adventure equipment.

My mouth spoke before I could rein it in, "A rat!"

The rat shook its head and replied, "Ah, a stupid human! Clearly you never took biology in class. And you've come in bitesize form. Delicious." It laughed.

"You can talk?" Its wry humor evaded me.

"Dude. Secret of Nimh, much?' He was sarcastic and I could see he was probably a weasel.

"Sorry. I am just shaken up from the Voodoo man above." I stayed where I was and made no sudden moves.

"Yeah, I get it. You're the first I've seen escape. How did you know about our entrance?" The weasel leaned in a jaunty posture against his field desk…and it fell over with the poor guy splayed out on top. It jumped right back up. I absolutely did not smile or laugh. Weasels are vicious and I didn't feel like dying today.

He righted himself super-fast and spoke, "Heh, meant to do that."

"A statue from above told me to jump into the hole. I figured it was better than becoming a permanent hood ornament."

"Right. Well, what is your name, tiny human?"

"I am Kip."

"Small name for a small person. Interesting. I am Yevroy Barca, Weasel at Law and you have entered my demesnes."

Demesnes? Hadn't I heard that word before? Thinking, thinking. Yes! When Masauwu and Flu Cat met. What did they say? Something about a guest. I tried something.

"Mister Barca, I request guest right." His eyes sprung open like I had just grown a third arm. Perhaps I had. Who knew about the effects of being shrunk this small?

Without hesitation, he replied, "You are human, yet you speak of the old ways. Hunh. Very well, please be my guest and welcome to my demesnes. Do I need to remind you of your obligation as guest?"

"No sir. Do I need to remind you of yours?" I figured go cheeky or go home.

"You are a saucy one. Well met, young sir. You are most welcome." The weasel smiled. I hadn't realized they could do that. Well to be fair I didn't know they could speak or wear clothes either.

"Mr. Barca –"

"Call me Yev."

"Okay. Yev, my friends are still above, with Mister Shrinkydink. Is there anything you can do to help?"

"'Fraid not. In the UCLJ, that is Uniform Code of Lowlife Justice, we are not permitted to interact with the affairs of men unless given formal sanction by the Council. UCLJ 22.72, Paragraphs 11-26, Revision 2."

I was confused. This guy was a weasel, and he was spouting legal references like it was the most common thing.

"I've seen that look. You've never met Lowlife legal counsel, have you? Of course not, you're a doofy human." He paused for a moment. "Please strike that last comment; I move to emend and submit rather, I find your doofiness to be predictable but not laudable." Yev was definitely a lawyer; a chatty well-articulated weasel of the lawyerly type. I had a brief laugh which brought a scowl from the weasel.

Still confused. "Yev, I just need to get back to my friends and back to my right size. Can you help me?"

Yev was visibly sympathetic. He spoke, "Kip, I understand. I can take you to the local Council annex and you can plead your case there. But this offer is in no way to be construed as a contract between the parties: you and me."

I was hungry, worried, and tired. I just needed help and wasn't in the mood for shenanigans. "Fine. Thank you. May we go?"

"Let me grab my effects and we will take the most expeditious route."

I then thought of something: ya know those movies where people are shrunken small? Where does their extra mass go? And how do they still function so well at reduced size? My inquiring mind still wanted to know. I put a bookmark to figure it out later. Yev stuffed a shoulder satchel with supplies and led the way into another PVC tube. He had the benefit of running on all fours. Not so, yours truly. I kept bumping my head which did wonders for my headache. He kept telling me to hurry and I did my best.

We arrived in a concrete vault with light coming from the drain grate above. Several rodent types were bustling about. Activity orbited around a table in the middle. A jackrabbit was managing paperwork on the table and didn't bother to look up as we arrived. "Gretched. It's Barca, Weasel at Law, reporting."

The jackrabbit indicated a queue of animals, and we went to the back of the line. We waited. A long time. In actuality, with the time acceleration we waited probably less than a minute. The jackrabbit would call next and the line would move. Then it was our turn.

"Next." The jackrabbit looked up at Yev, then me. Gretched's eyes went wide as saucers.

"Yevroy Bar –" He was interrupted which clearly ticked him off. But he was obediently quiet.

"Hush Yev. Who or what is this thing?" Gretched inspected me like a side of beef on a hook.

"Sir, I am –" interrupted me as well.

"Hush. Do not speak. It would be ma'am to you." The jackrabbit circled me, while the other creatures, fearful, moved away. They were afraid of me.

"You are not human. Not fully. You are Chupacabra, but not fully. You are tiny which means that something went wrong for the Collector in Slab City. You are fortunate…or perhaps not. Why are you here," The eyes were piercing. I screwed up my courage and spoke.

"I am here to save my friends and retrieve the Flu C – the Cat Síth avatar for Croatoan." I figured 'in for penny, in for a pound'. And I hoped the names dropped were worth more than a pound.

The low hubbub turned off. Pin drop, it went silent. Maybe the pound was going to be the flesh off my butt. I wasn't sure I had enough with my current dimensions.

"You invoked our Champion's name. You wish to die, tiny Chupa-man?"

What was I supposed to say to that? I decided the truth was best. I'd have to re-evaluate the penny-pound thing later.

I gave an even reply, "Croatoan –" an intake of breath came from all the throats in hearing distance, "He gave instructions to my Dads and Vagabond Bootblack and then to me. I am supposed to retrieve the four figurines he requested. I think they are Cloud powered artifacts, but I'm not sure. Can you help me and my friends or have I come to the wrong place?"

"I am called Gretched, the Solemn. You bring problems to my warren. Yet your words are thought provoking. Rune!" Gretched the Solemn called out and a bespeckled mouse came forward.

"Yes, Gretched." Such a tiny squeak voice. I just wanted to hug him. So cute! The mouse scowled at me. Mmm, nope, I shook my head at myself. No hugs.

"Does Yev have charge of the hybrid, Gretched?"

Yev spoke, "Gretched, guest right has been agreed," the jackrabbit turned to face Yev.

"You declared guest right with a human?" I had never seen an angry bunny before. It was frightening.

"No. Not a human. With a hybrid, yes." Quick on his feet. It paid to have a lawyer friend here.

The rabbit shook its head in a human fashion and exited the vault into a large culvert.

Rune stood next to me. It eyeballed me.

"Hybrid Kip. If you give me grief, you'll get a sharp smack," the mouse gave a sidelong look to Yev, "I am permitted under guest right to apply warranted corrective action with an unruly guest." Yev rolled his eyes, exasperated. Rune then hopped onto the table and watched me with a level gaze. And I can tell you that was a lot of fun.

Gretched came back more quickly, hopping in the lead of two much older rabbits. These looked like pet rabbits, lop eared.

"I am Strad, and my mate is Sture. We know of the Dads and of Vagabond Bootblack. They saved thousands of our kind, and we owe a debt."

"I am Sture, and I will hear your requests." Both rabbits waited.

"Thank you. I'm not sure where to start." They waited on me silently. No help from there. I would have to wing it. I gave the best summary of the last year with me and my friends.

"Our debt is to you as well, I hear. You have claimed guest right. That is no more," Yev stepped forward about to make a speech. Sture forestalled him with a raised paw, "I declare you Lowlife Friend and elevate you to official treasure of the Thedisch." I had no idea what it meant.

Yev stood next to me beaming and I asked out the side of my mouth, "Does that mean you can help me?"

Puzzled, Sture and Strad exchanged glances, "You don't understand. You have been canonized. As a patron saint you have the power to request anything of us, barring Council rule or clear illegality."

I looked at Yev, "Yev, can you help me here?"

The weasel excitedly bounced up and down at the request. "Do you, Saint..uh, what's your full name?"

"I am Charles Winton Wefer the Third."

He continued, "Do you, Saint Charles Winton Wefer the Third accept Yevroy Barca, Esq. as your duly sworn and licensed legal counsel until such time as both parties agree to dissolution of the same?"

What else could I say, "Yes, I —" He interrupted.

"Then as your duly sworn legal representative, I invoke the Council right." The vault hushed again.

Sture and Strad conferred for a moment while Yev waited for an answer.

Sture replied, "Agreed. Council right is adjudged and confirmed. Name the terms of your request."

At this point it began to sound like a court room and I ended up dialing the whole thing out, falling asleep.

I woke with a start. "Kip, you have the help of everyone here. Several soldiers were assigned to assist, and then the rest volunteered. The security and military of Slab City Warren is at your command, as well as every scientist, functionary and scutworker. What is your first order, my liege?" Liege? That sounded like a royal term. Look at me, king of the rodents! Well, whatever. If I got my friends safe and the figurines in-hand, I didn't care what they called me.

I decided to play along and make it up like a Dungeons and Dragons game. "Yev, I need two lieutenants for my forces, and I need a situation map and a command-control station setup around this table in the next 5 minutes."

"Understood!" And Yev was off like a shot. The hum of animal activity spiked. I realized I couldn't call them animals anymore. They were people.

In under 5 minutes a quad of tables were set up and I had a command staff of serious looking weasels, rabbits, mice, and rats.

Just as I was about to speak, raised voices could be heard from the culvert, just out of sight. The voices were coming this way and emerged as three marmots quarreling. The black marmot was yelling, "Surely you know that impacts parents, peers, and partners in life. Your dietary choices are key to a long and healthy life!"

The dark brown marmot replied, "My gawd brother, its only Nesselrode pudding. A delicacy –."

The third marmot, colored white and green interrupted. "A delicacy from our kin in New York."

The first marmot spoke, "Fulminating about your dessert won't make it any more healthful."

"You would say that, wouldn't you! Mother always said animadvert amongst siblings was an anathema which could seldom be borne. And I quite agree!" The second marmot stomped a paw in indignation.

The first marmot realized they were not alone and were in fact in the press of many ears and eyes. None of the ears or eyes seemed pleased at their interruption.

The third marmot clearly didn't recognize the abruptive cessation of their quarrel and continued, "The pudding you see is not merely delicious, but is both lissome and lubricious –" and then awareness dawned, and all three marmots doffed their Breton hats, expressing remorse and repentance in their posture and downcast faces. They were thankfully silent, and business resumed in the vault.

Yev introduced the three newest arrivals. "Kip, please meet our highly capable but socially inept burglars."

All three marmots were abruptly indignant. The black marmot was incensed, "Sir, I am most offended by your words. You will retract your comments immediately."

Yev had the look that every parent has when having to make a concession to a child for expedience's sake in front of a public audience. "Pik, Pek and Pok, please accept my heartfelt apologies." The three marmots bowed. "Now shut your mouths while our leader, um, does his leading."

I kicked it off, "Strad and Sture, I need to rescue my friends."

Strad spoke, "Kip, please meet Jerger, your lieutenant of military and Harad, your lieutenant of security," each took a step forward, clicked their heels together and made snappy bows. Jerger was a capybara sized rat who wore ballistic gear and looked like a professional soldier. Harad was a large mouse, dressed in camo clothing, looking sharp and professional.

"Thank you, Strad," The two lieutenants stood at attention. I tried to recall how to get them to chill out. "Gentlemen, at ease. Please give me a situation report. And please just call me Kip, okay?

Harad spoke first, "Honored Sir," She saw my mouth opening and amended, "Kip. In advance I sent three agents to reconnoiter the Collector's establishment. Please let's begin with their report."

I nodded and the three marmots came forward. They were more subdued now. Pik spoke, "Kip, my humblemost apologies for our earlier behavior. Our news for you is urgent. First, we have your friends." Pik made a paw motion and three raccoons carried in the heavy stone figures, perfect miniaturizations of my friends. They were completely frozen, unlike me. I was conflicted: I was glad we had them but concerned about getting them back to regular size and unfrozen.

"Thank you for finding my friends. Sorry for the whole fire drill," I took a closer look at my Crew and asked, "You guys are amazing. Thank you! Question: does anyone know how to get them back to normal?"

Discussions around the table quad ensued. The three marmots had plenty to say.

"No, no, no. You don't understand. If we just grab the avatar, we are breaking the rule. If we have the boy, that is if we have our young Saint grab it, we are not breaking the law. Right?" Pik had an idea and I liked it.

"I am in. What is the avatar?"

Pek spoke, "Young Saint, it is the statue of our own Cat Síth." Ah, the Flu Cat statue.

Jerger continued, "That's about it. Grab the statue and run. You may have to deal with the Collector, but you will have our full support with that," Jerger's confidence was infectious. The soldiers who had gathered were bobbing about and raring to go.

I didn't want any more wait time. "Okay, I'm going," Then I realized I needed to give some kind of guidance, "Jerger, please have your team lead as the forward element and Harad, please have your team provide rear support. Once I grab the statue, let's get out of there. I'll jump into the hole like before."

"Kip, there's a teensy issue. The avatar will not fit into the entrance chute." Pok was clearly uncomfortable delivering bad news.

"No worries. Can you give me another route?" I asked the question of Harad. "And can you have a couple of your guys help me carry?"

"Yes, sir and no, sir. We can lead you to another entrance to the warren, but no Lowlife is permitted to touch the avatar itself. It's a rule we were given which we cannot break." Harad was firm.

"No help, huh?" I opted to not press. Harad shook his head. This was going to be hard. The statue was twice my size.

As we were speaking, little soldiers and others were coming and going. One mouse was ushered to the table. She spoke. "Excuse me, honored sirs. We have a new problem." Silence fell at the table.

"There are two problems, well, really three, if you're counting. But one good thing: we think they are independent of each other. The first and second are human military teams. There is a slight kerfuffle between them across Slab City going on right now. The third is closer to home. Both sets of twins are ransacking around the Collector's place. They're in the Welshly Arms right now but it will be only a matter of tick tocks before they start causing a ruckus in our area. We believe they are finally going to make a play for the avatar."

This was so much *my life* these days. Something was always brewing and making mischief. And nothing was ever as simple as it first appeared. "As your saint, I believe it is my duty to keep you protected, right?" I didn't want my new friends to get hurt, so I just made that part up. I could storm the Collector's place by myself.

"Saint Kip the Kind, we will not be allowing you to become Saint Kip the Martyr." Sture spoke like I was an errant schoolboy.

My Dads had taught me how to recognize truthful speech and by extension, dissembling, caviling, and outright lying. Sture was deflecting from the topic, so I pressed onward.

"Noted, Sture. I will try to stay un-martyred, okay?" I continued, "Here is the new plan. I would like five of your soldiers to form a team. They will come with me. I think getting in and out quietly will be the best approach," Strad and Sture spoke in hushed tones and moments later agreed. Jerger gave me three and Harad gave me two. They were all cute little mice. I began to laugh at which point the five mouse candidates gave me a look which said I had best shut up. I got wise and shut it immediately.

I spoke, "Alrighty then. I need first names and then we will be off."

The five soldiers introduced themselves as Teg, Svivo, Marlo, Milo, and Boots. They were geared up with swords, knives, and these teensy guns. At my present 20 centimeters these tiny warriors were quite daunting. "Teg, lead the way. We need the quickest path to the Collector's place." Off we went.

I followed Teg and the rest brought up the rear. There were dozens of turns and pipes both small and large. There was no way I would find my way back. Our pipe maze let out of a dusty, dry culvert and onto a part of the playa about 120 meters to the south of the Collector's store. Milo put a paw on my shoulder to restrain me as the other four spread out onto the wash and crouched amongst the sage bushes. Teg gave hand signals and the soldiers disappeared in different directions. Milo put a finger to his mouth to keep me quiet. We waited. I stood at the mouth of the culvert waiting for the okay to move out. A head peeked down and spoke from the top of the culvert. In my surprise, I did my best not to jump.

"Sir, the way is clear to the Collector's perimeter. Time to go." Marlo's head was followed by the rest of his cute little self as he landed in a crouch. We ran in a zig zag line using the bushes as cover, arriving with all six of us just outside the Collector's place. The ramshackle construction presented a confusing opportunity for getting inside undetected. It appeared many of the brightly painted doors were sealed shut. I forgot I was the size of a mouse and watched as Teg peeled back several layers of visqueen to reveal a clear entrance inside. At that moment two fuzzy hybrids came running around the corner with a half dozen human soldiers following in hot pursuit. We ducked inside quickly.

The chase sped by, and Marlo led us through the perimeter refuse, between layers of visqueen, plywood sheets, tarps and garbage. The walls to the Collector's place were riddled with hidey holes and tunnels. I almost ran into Marlo's rear end as he drew up short. In front of us was an open area with various rat nests and dozens of rat eyes staring at us in surprise.

Marlo whispered, "They are the regular kind. Not like us. We must be careful here."

Svivo moved into the open area. The visqueen overhead was clear and I could see the sky. One of the rats came forward and Svivo and the rat did the sniff test. After that the rats became disinterested and we continued unmolested past their warren. Soon our twisty turns brought us to an opening and just like that we were inside the Collector's place.

We were hunched down behind a big gold harp that had a sign hanging from the top declaring Kinor for Sale, fresh in from Cyprus, 2200 credits OBO. Right next to it was something that looked like an ancient electric washing machine labelled as a HyperEncabulator. It looked complicated. Someone was helping Severus pick up the overturned tables and broken wares. The man helping was chatting up a litany of banalities and providing his own comic relief, laughing at his own jokes. Severus was silent and brooding with a grimace painted on his big stupid mouth.

Milo spoke quietly in my ear, "Sir, that other man is Jimati. He is one of Slab City's random do-gooders. He is also in Lowlife's employ. It's a good sign he is here. We just need to let him know what we are about, and he will distract the Collector for us."

Marlo countered, "Milo, no. He won't help us."

Svivo added, "Nope, not at all. Jimati is a trickster. Something you should know is he is both humorous and dangerous. Jimati is only for Jimati."

Boots for once spoke, "Lowlives have been unfailingly on his side. But sometimes I wonder if he's on ours. I agree we should stay undetected."

So, we skirted the room, weaving in and out under tables and chairs. The Collector's messiness was our biggest asset, and we were soon under the table with the cat statue. I could feel a pulsing coming from above; it beat into my skull. Hello headache my old friend, you come to torture me again.

The mouse soldiers climbed the tablecloth with their razor-sharp claws. I tried and couldn't get a good grip. A length of twine suddenly dangled in front of my face, and I grabbed ahold. I started to climb but a sudden jerk had me flying upward. I held on tight and flew onto the tabletop. I quickly grabbed the cat statue before I regretted the headache I knew would spike.

Off we ran. Teg grabbed a wad of my shirt and yanked us both off the table, "Hold on to the avatar!"

Then I realized a folding chair wielded as a weapon had been descending toward the tabletop. Severus was hot on our trail. The table above me detonated into pieces as a loud roar filled the air. Severus was moving at fractional speed, but he was big and scary, and I was perfectly fine to be dragged away by a brave mouse. When I landed, I bounced a bit and surprisingly didn't feel the impact. I held the avatar tightly as my headache blossomed; I staggered, and Teg held me up. Svivo and Milo were holding up the edge of some visqueen, and we ran under.

Our exit was harried and fast. The rats of the Collector's complex were in a tizzy and from somewhere I got a whiff of fire. I ran and continued to stumble. The statue was light like balsa wood but was hard as rock. A voice spoke, '*Kip, you need to enhance your calm*'. The cat statue was talking to me.

'You aren't really Síth'.

'That is hurtful. I am a dislocated fragment of myself'.

'Can you stop my headache?'

'No. But I can tell you that you are being pursued and you need to run faster'. The Síth statue chuckled.

We were outside the walls and fetched up under a sage bush. A pair of cats came from the left and a matching pair of dogs from the right. They closed and I realized they were janky looking hybrids. Really homely. The cats were big as Jaguars, but they had nappy patches of fur and near-human, distorted faces which were wet with sweat and grimacing with effort. The dogs looked similar, but I didn't stick around to look closer. Teg yanked me into motion, and I ran holding the statue best I could. The next minute was a flurry of confused action. Soldiers in full gear came from one side and engaged the hybrids while the hybrids simultaneously fought a running battle with four of my mouse friends. Cat number one mrawled loudly, jumping onto Svivo. It landed on dust, at the same moment Svivo, Milo and Boots leaped on its back and plunged blades into its neck. The screech was painful to hear. Cat number two was busy evading the soldiers. Dog number one came to the aid of cat number one, but a flying mouse skewered its right eye with a tiny blade. Marlo jumped free while dog one howled in pain. Dog two came right at me and only a herculean effort by Teg kept me out of its clutches. I was the target.

'Hey Kip, you'll never guess who just pinged me. Peach! I think she likes me or something'! It was Buddy coming on early for our morning farspeak class. We began alternating classtimes recently and I forgot about it.

'Wait a sec Bud'. I created an autoresponder in the Cloud that greeted people signing on for class. It said I would be there in a few minutes.

"Sergeant, screw the animals, see that little running human. Whatever the hell it is, catch it!" Six soldiers began chasing me. They were fortunately slow, unlike the hybrids.

Now things stepped up a notch. With the surviving hybrids covered in blood, competing with six soldiers to catch me, bodies collided. Since the operative word was catch, not kill, weapons had been stowed. No bullets. Yeah! More voices clamored on the airwaves as I was weaving and dodging between big people's legs. Teg made sure I was always out of reach.

'Kip, where are you'? It was Peach. She had sidestepped my autoresponder on a different channel. Dang it.

'Peach, I'm a bit busy. I am running away from bad guys carrying a statue of Flu Cat', I shunted her signal to the autoresponder channel and kept running. The culvert was coming into view.

'Flu Cat'? It was the statue talking.

'Not now. I'm kinda busy.' The one-eyed dog hybrid was blocking my path. I slid to the right and it chose to reach to my left. Dust plumed as I passed by its gripping fuzzy hands.

'What is Flu Cat, Kip'? The statue was taking a tone with me.

I sent a burst memory of my initial meeting with Flu Cat. An angry purr thrummed on the mental airwaves.

'You named me after the sounds I made when I'm hocking up a furball?' I heard Flu Cat junior hiss. I decided to name him Fig Cat; figurine cat, get it?

'Listen up Fig Cat. I am carrying your ungrateful self through pitched battle. Can you shut up?'

I was suddenly hoisted aloft as one of the slow soldiers grabbed me. Melee akimbo, I lost hold, and Fig Cat went flying right into the hands of a cat hybrid.

A voice rang on the airwaves. I guess my autoresponder wasn't going to be helpful, *'Young sir. I believe we are nearing our start time. All the children are waiting patiently'*, It was Elder Tala.

'Thank you, Tala. I am coming now', I had no idea how I was going to conduct class.

Should I tell Tala I am now a Shrinky Dink and am in a running battle with my mouse soldier friends? Yeah, maybe not. Wouldn't it be nice if I had more than one of me? Suddenly there was…more than one of me. I was staring at myself in the Cloud and the other me spoke to me, *'Hey chief. Looks like you need an assist.'* I could hear Tala now talking to the other me and my other me responding. And it made sense!

'Yo, Physi-Kip, just leave the farspeak training to me. I'll let the Elders know the other three are unable to make it tonight. Recall, this is our class now, not theirs'.

The Cloud version of me was right. It was my class now. Wait, what did he call me? It sank in: the Cloud me had adopted the Binky naming perversion scheme. Wow, how rude. I had a Dangerfield moment…can't get no respect.

The whole Cloud-Kip exchange took a fraction of a second. I re-focused on my current predicament. I was in the grip of a soldier whose hand was squeezing me tightly, swinging me around as he was set upon by all five mouse soldiers. Suddenly Milo, or was it Svivo, was next to me, gripping the man's hand with his teeth and chopping like a lumberjack on his wrist with a broken sword. A loud yell preceded my being flung away by the man. I flew through the air with the greatest of ease with the mice, the blood and the world spinning. My landing wasn't easy. Dust filled my eyes and I got to my feet and ran blindly.

'Fig Cat? You called me Fig Cat?' The voice of the statue was becoming fainter as it was being spirited away at speed by the cat hybrid. I guess avatars have a limited range.

A minute later the mouse soldiers had dragged me away from the soldiers, through the brush and into the culvert. They swiftly spoke and four of them ran away. Two outside and two down the culvert. Teg and I were alone. I could hear the two mice playing with the human soldiers, leading them away.

"Kip, when we get back, I think I know who can help us get the avatar."

"I'm sorry I lost it Teg."

"The fault is ours. If we had been better guardians, this would not have happened."

"Let's just focus on getting the statue back, okay?" Teg nodded and we both stood at the culvert entrance catching our breath.

A huge hand descended from above and just like that I was being whisked away. It was the person who had been helping Severus clean up his place: Jimati, the trickster. As we seemed to fly over the landscape, I realized Jimati wasn't human or biological. Synth. He was holding me firmly, but not painfully. I was able to breathe but I couldn't speak. I tried farspeech but the holding hand squeezed me tighter.

"That will be enough of that, little human. The Mistress will be glad to see you, along with your precious cat statue." Minutes later we entered an enclosed oasis. Beautiful sights, sounds and smells. Water flowed in a creek and greenery was abundant and fauna was teeming, both small and large. The spectacle of it distracted me from my circumstances for the moment. Hyenas, cheetahs, elephants, lions, tigers, jaguars and ant eaters, llamas, horses, dogs, cats, water buffalo, and a bunch more. It dawned on me this used to be a zoo. But how did predators not eat the prey? Something was off here.

"Ah, Jimi you're finally back. Where are my four favorite pets?" I was still dangling from the synth's grasp. The author of the voice was a female hybrid. She had a spot-on resemblance to Aunt Jemima. That meant she looked much like my father Victor's mother Mumbi. Deep black skin, a wide, generous mouth and sparkling white teeth. The woman was wearing a deep green dress with a white smock. It was like she was a housewife by day and scientist by night. I got a good vibe off her. That's why I wondered about my being abducted.

Jimati spoke, "Mistress, your fears that the Lowlife scum have Cloud powers is confirmed. The cat avatar you had us seeking was being used by a human to transform people into figurines in Slab City."

"Oh posh. Say it isn't so." The woman turned away and began walking toward a cabin.

Jimati followed, "Mistress, I have proof. I have one of the four child exiles with me now."

The woman replied, "Sure you do. Come on inside and we will speak more."

She sat in a big blue rocker. As she did so, her skirt hiked up and I could see her legs; she had chicken legs. They were knobby, skinny, and tough and her clawed feet were sharp and dangerous. I wondered if she had a dewclaw.

"Mistress, here is the exile Kip," Jimati held out his hand and I squirmed as he squeezed.

"Dude, stop squeezing. I get the point, okay. You're in control," It was hard for me to be tactful when I couldn't take a full breath.

The woman started, her hand going to her mouth, "Oh good gracious gawd in the morning, what the hell is that Jimati?"

Jimati thrust his hand forward again and I flopped like a ragdoll. It felt like my head was coming unhinged. Despite my usual restraint, I yelled. "You fewkin turd, Jimati. You're gonna kill me. Put me down. Now!"

The woman's shock grew as her eyes widened, showing lots of white. You know how you can observe the weirdest things when under pressure? I noticed the woman's sclera had mottling similar to my father Vicky. I wondered if my Dad was related to the chicken woman. Despite the pain, I giggled.

Jimati put me onto a table near a coffee pot and Russian samovar. I saw there were cookies and being a teenager, food was a huge motivator. I limped over to a snickerdoodle and tore off a chunk. It was still warm and cinnamon flavor had something else…ah, lavender. Bummer.

"Lady, you ruin it when you put lavender in your cookies. How come adults think adding more is better. You should have stayed with cinnamon only." Despite my critique I continued stuffing my mouth. Hey, I was hungry.

The criticism broke her out of her frightened reverie. She spoke, "You are a rude little human," then she side-spoke to Jimati, "I didn't realize human hybrids could be made this small."

"My lady, it is as I told you. The Collector, Severus, used the cat statue to shrink this human and others. Usually they become like stone, but for some reason this one is still made of meat." Meat? This synth was one of those human-haters: dangerous.

The woman knelt down, bringing her gigantic face and her earl gray tea breath right up into my grill. I backed off which she took for fear. Little did she know, the nasty tea breath woman.

"Hey little man, how did you get so small?" Was I a doll or something?

I realized if I took my normal sarcastic tone, I would probably get smushed flat. She might be moving slowly like all the other big'uns but why tempt it?

"Ma'am, I am just trying to save my friends and to do that I need the cat statue. Frankly, I have no idea what to do with the statue, but I have to try something."

The woman had an astonished expression.

"Oh my. You are a little human. For a moment I thought you were some sort of pixie hybrid or synth. What is your name little boy?" The little boy remark almost had me mocking her chicken legs.

"I am Kip. I am from Lake Stevens, Washington."

"Ah, very good. You're polite. I am Mistress Withania, curator of the Ashwagandha Preserve. What did you dislike about the lavender in my cookies?" Withania appeared concerned.

"Um, snickerdoodles should be cinnamon-forward with a vanilla back flavor. Lavender adds an aromatic element which competes with the cinnamon flavor. Lavender is cooling while cinnamon is warming, if ya know what I mean."

It was hard to believe all that just came out. "Sorry, I sound like my Dads. They were very particular with cooking and baking ingredients. I had to listen to their grousing about such things all my growing up years. Apologies for over-sharing." I realized I was tired and was rambling; I decided to shut my trap.

Her eyes became sharp, "Kip, you mentioned your Dads. What are their names?" Withania was suddenly very interested in me. Uh oh.

"My Dads are Charlie and Vicky. Why?"

"Hmm, very interesting." Withania stood up and queried Jimati, "Have the pets returned yet?"

Jimati nodded toward the corner of the cabin where I realized all four of the nappy dogs and cats sat watching us. I was surprised they all survived.

"Oh! My pets, come here, come here! Look at you! All the bandages. Are you okay?" Withania spent a couple minutes tending to their wounds, inspecting the bandages, then eventually turned to Jimati, "Where is the cat statue?"

One of the cat hybrids held out something. Withania took it and made a girlie scream, "Ohhhh goodie! I so hate to wait for the surprise. Well, here it is. Jimi, how does this thing work?"

"Mistress, it reportedly has Cloud powers, but I have no idea how to make it work." Jimati edged away from the woman.

Her expression lost all joviality, "You know I don't like hearing bad news. Kip! Do you know how to make this work?"

I was sure I mentioned I didn't. However, I figured this was a way to get myself large again so I lied, "I have been coached on its use, but I will need to practice with it to make it function."

Withania's eyes narrowed, "You wouldn't be lying to me would you Kip, son of the evil Dads?"

Oh fewkin-a, she knew who I was, and she had run afoul of something relating to my Dads. Time to tread carefully.

"No ma'am, I was raised to be truthful to grown-ups." There, I made a guess that acting like a kid might get her to cut me some slack.

It worked, "Okay honey bunch. I know you'd never fib to Auntie Withania."

"No ma'am. At home I get grounded if I do."

She brought her face close and set the statue next to me, then she made a purring sound and stroked my head, "Yes, my little Kip. Auntie would have to punish you if you fibbed." Her smile was unsettling.

With the cat statue close by, my head began to pound again.

"Auntie, this thing gives me a headache. Do you have aspirin or something I could have?"

"Ohh, little Kip. Poor baby." Turning to Jimati, "Find an aspirin or something for pain, now."

I sat down and did my best Jedi impression, sitting cross-legged and meditating. I was left undisturbed and a few minutes later a giant aspirin was sitting on the table with a thimble filled with water. I carved off some of the chalky powder, stuffed it in my mouth and swigged the brown water. Then I returned to my Jedi pose. My mouth tasted like a peat bog. I heard noises half an hour later. I almost dozed off a couple times then risked a look around. Everyone was gone. Wait, one of the cat people was in the corner. Sleeping?

I hopped up and took a closer look at the cat statue. It was quiet, which was nice for a change. As I dug about, I found the crevice where I was sure I would find an old USB stick. Yep, this was the third figurine.

The scrabble of claws came from the far corner of the table and up popped Teg, giving me a mousy smile. "You're a hard one to track down, friend."

More scrabbles and two more mouse soldiers surmounted the table's edge.

Svivo nodded to me and spoke, "Sir, the chicken lady and Jimati are in the other room. There is a kettle boiling and they are discussing how to have Saint Kip and his friends for dinner."

I wondered if she had a copy of 'How to Serve Man'. I didn't plan to stick around to become their star entree.

"Teg, I have no idea how to make myself big again."

"Kip, your present size plays to our favor. Grab the statue and let's be on our way."

I jumped to it and leaped from the table after my mouse friends. I landed hard with the statue ramming under my jaw on impact. I saw stars, then noticed the cat person in the corner was awake and heading my way. We ran. A hue and cry was raised and the whole cast of characters flooded back into the room. The small cabin must have been bigger than at first glance. There was a jumble of huge legs, and the confusion gave me a chance to weave toward my exit, hot on the literal tail, of Teg.

Through a newly chewed hole in the wall, I plunged into darkness. Then we were in a warren underneath Chicken Woman's oasis. I could hear muffled yells behind and above us which faded as we got further from the cabin. The warren was empty and had the stale smell of death. Then we were out, and we were surrounded by the desert, outside the oasis, looking up at a crossroads sign. The top of the sign said Welcome to Ashwagandha. Below it were pointers to other places, Las Vegas, Þēodisċ, Muddy River Bar and Grill, Welshly Arms Hostel and others. Teg pulled me away from my distracted reading.

"Kip, time to move." He was right. Withania's voice was getting closer as were a variety of animal sounds.

As we ran, Milo filled me in, "We reconnoitered the oasis, above and below, and the cabin where you were being held and overheard some things of interest. Sir, am I correct you are the son of the Dads?" I nodded, too out of breath to say much.

"Right. Well, the woman, Withania was born at one of the CENTERs and lived in a laboratory cage. She was an experiment, my Saint. From the sound of it hers was a failure. She was shipped to someone named Pastor Bedtime where she said her nightmare really began. But she did speak fondly of someone named Cicero. She said he helped her escape. What she said about your Dads…Kip, she blamed you for all her years of torture. She is not your friend. She is dangerous."

Boots spoke up, "Sir, Ashwagandha is a refuge of CENTER experiments. Some are synths, but most are biologicals with disturbing combinations of things. You didn't see the worst of it. Much of the oasis looks like a bloody refugee camp. It's filled full of things waiting to die. It's ugly."

I hadn't seen what Boots was talking about and perhaps I was glad. If my Dads had known about these experiments doesn't that make them the bad guys? Were these my Dads' experiments? I bookmarked the thought for the moment. Maybe there was a way I could help them. I just knew I didn't want to get put into a stew pot for my troubles.

I noticed we weren't heading toward Slab City, "Teg, where are we going?" I stopped to catch my breath.

"The mission for the fourth figurine…you mentioned it earlier and we think we know where it sits. Are you up for another infiltration? We can be at the place this evening."

Teg stoked a churchwarden pipe, lit it, and gave a puff. The other soldiers kept their distance, clearly unapproving of the smell. It smelled like chocolate tobacco. Slab City was far one direction and Ashwagandha the other. We were heading southwest toward a rise of hills.

"Wow, thanks Teg. I don't recall mentioning the fourth but thank you."

"Kip, you have a constant running mumble. You rarely stop muttering one thing or another. We know quite a bit about you now just by listening." The mouse soldiers grinned. I guess I did talk a lot.

"Where are we going Teg?"

"The Welshly Arms. It's a human establishment. It's one of the few such in the Wasteland."

"Wasteland?"

"Mmm, Boots, care to explain?" Teg puffed his pipe more and sat on a rock, looking back toward Ashwagandha.

"Yes sir. The Wasteland is a desert area between here and Arizona; it starts south of us by a couple of klicks. Much of it is empty, but there are several junkyards with old military vehicles, tanks, trucks, and burrowers. The Rovers, Junkers and the Cavalry send salvage crews in, but smart people like us keep a distance. There are monsters in the Wasteland, and areas where biological wastes have been dumped." Boots went silent as all five mouse soldiers heard something coming from the direction of Ashwagandha.”

“Time to keep moving. We’re being tracked.” Teg got us going and helped me to my feet. “Come on Kip, we’ll find shelter before nightfall in the Wasteland.”

It was a hard hike. Boots scouted ahead and the other four took turns pulling me along. They took great pains to not touch the statue. On one of our brief stops I asked about it.

Svivo was near me as the other four scouted behind and ahead. “Svivo, why are you not allowed to touch the cat statue?”

“Good question. I don’t know. It’s a rule that has been around for a long time. I believe it was put in place by Cat Síth, our Lowlife champion, or maybe it was Croatoan. No matter, it’s a Lowlife rule and those get broken at the peril of the breaker.” Svivo’s ears perked up as a shadow loomed close. It resolved into Pooka and man did he look huge!

“Pooks! Oh my gosh, what are you doing so far from Hopi territory?”

The four mouse soldiers appeared around us in quick succession, like warriors out of the mist, weapons drawn. They sure knew how to be ominous. Glad they were on my side.

Teg spoke, “I see you know this person, sir.” Weapons went down but not away.

“Thanks Teg. This is my longest running friend, Pooka. Pooka, please meet my newest friends, Teg, Boots, Marlo, Svivo and Milo,” each described a curt bow in turn.

“Kip, I sensed you were in trouble but had the darndest time finding you. Now I see why.” Pooka had a mischievous grin. Pooka was a she at the moment; an attractive look. She also was much more articulate. She stepped forward and gently poked me.

“Ouch! What’s up with the pointy finger?”

“Oh hush you wussy. Binky would give you all kinds of crap, you whiner.” Pooka had grown bolder and more artuculate since I last saw her. I liked it. “By the way, where are the others?”

I recited the litany of the past day’s activities while Pooka quietly listened. I had just finished my tale when heavy cat pheromone lade the air. All five mouse soldiers knelt with swords point first into the ground, their foreheads against the pommels. A deep purr thrummed the air.

Fig Cat giggled, ‘*Yes! I am here! My job is complete*’.

“Fig Cat? Kip, have you been abusing my avatar?” It was Flu Cat. I should have figured he’d be here too, since he and Pooka had become inseparable.

Cat Síth faded into view, standing amongst us. He spoke aloud, “My friends, please rise. Soldiers should not be bowing to soldiers.” The mouse soldiers each replied in the affirmative.

“Pooka and I have been shadowing you for some miles. You are still being tracked by a sizable force. I presumed you were aware.”

“Yes, Lord Síth. We have been taking steps to evade.” Teg spoke.

“Of all the pursuers, you need to be most careful of the synths. Sabbatsys and Jimati are very dangerous creatures. And they hate humans and anyone who would ally with humans.” Flu Cat was scratching himself against a cactus as he spoke.

‘*Are you going to bring me home now?*’ Fig Cat was pleading.

‘*Alas no. It is not for me to re-incorporate you. That is the business of Croatoan and Kip*’. Flu Cat was firm. I could hear a sad sniffling over the airwaves.

Flu Cat walked with Teg a distance away. Teg nodded a lot and was listening intently. Svivo pulled out protein nuggets and distributed them to the group. A spark popped lightly in the air and suddenly there was a bottle of water. A brief moisture cloud dissipated, and condensation was beading on the bottle. It was cold water. Pooka smiled and nodded that I should drink. I felt the brief Cloud power manifest; Pooka was becoming adept at using the Power. She made a bottle of water appear out of thin air! Seemed like everyone was better at it than me. I was such a slacker.

Teg came back to the group, and we took turns chugging water and going pee. Pooka sent a goodbye, '*Kip, Flu Cat and I will try to slow down the synths. You had best get going now*'.

'*Bye Pooka! Love ya buddy*'.

'*Love you more!*' Pooka and Flu Cat vanished.

After they left, I realized I still had the cat statue. I should have given it to Pooka to carry. Stupid mistake. Teg got us moving again. As we went, he told us we were about a half klick from a Cavalry outpost. That was our immediate goal. The synths wouldn't dare attack a Cavalry station.

The sun was westering, and dusk painted the desert landscape in purples and reds. An acrid odor was on the wind; it smelled sharp and biting. There was a low-lying dust layer that coated my clothing and my companions. Milo had gone ahead and now directed us to a hole in the wall of a Quonset hut. We slipped inside and saw a couple dozen men and enough military equipment to start a small war. Teg had us climb to the rafters where we found a steel platform where I could put down the statue. I sure was looking forward to being big again.

We quietly set up camp and after darkness fell, we settled down to sleep. Teg took the first watch. It seemed like I had just gone to sleep when a clawed hand lightly covered my mouth. Eyes wide, I was awake. Marlo was the only soldier with me. He pointed: the other four mice were arrayed in high places, prepared for an attack.

Then he pointed to the men, "Shh, the Cavalry are out cold, even the watchman. Something put them to sleep, and we expect a attack."

Dark shadows stole into the building and fanned out. Two of the dark forms moved much faster and without any noise. Vehicle doors opened and closed, a trap door to someplace below the building swung open silently. Dark shapes opened every door and hatch, looking. One of the fast shadows froze in place and I saw a glint of reflected light as one of the synths looked directly at me.

Simultaneously, all the main lights came on, the horn on a big 5-ton truck sounded and pots and pans in the kitchen area spilled on the floor. Sleepy or no, the Cavalry soldiers woke and realized they had been invaded. Fortunate for us the invaders hadn't disarmed the Cavalry. They opened fire and the chaos got turned up to 11. The synths stayed on mission, and both skittered like insects, climbing up to the rafters.

"Stay here. We have a plan. If either synth gets to the platform, grab the statue, and jump into the bin directly below you," Marlo spoke hastily and was off like a shot.

Then I noticed my mouse friends were throwing flaming things at the synths. Both synths were coated in something that smelled like cooking oil. And it was on fire. At that moment the Cavalry shot at the flaming forms and both synths worked to evade while continuing their climb. Jimati was on fire and was hit multiple times, but he made it to the platform. The other synth had fallen somewhere below. As Jimati reached for me I grabbed the statue and jumped off the other side. I landed in a bin covered by an oily canvas tarp. The tarp broke my fall. I looked up and saw Jimati's flaming form falling toward me. I ducked under the canvas and hoped for the best.

Something landed on the tarp, hard. I could smell burning plastic. There was movement, then it stopped. I waited and listened. Cavalry soldiers were yelling to each other 'clear' and 'hostiles down'. The volume ebbed and eventually sounds of cleanup began. The men were talking about those 'rat bastards from Asha-whatsit'. Oddly enough I fell asleep. The next thing I knew Milo was next to me whispering.

"Saint Kip, the men are searching the place. We must get you out of here before they find you. Marlo is gone." My ears heard it but I wasn't listening.

Milo pulled back the tarp and I could see Teg by our original entrance hole. It took some good timing, but we made it out with the Cavalry soldiers none the wiser.

It was early morning, and the eastern sky was getting light. My mouse friends hadn't slept like I had, but they were stalwart and strong. We marched on through the early hours until a building came into view ahead.

Teg spoke, "That's the Welshly Arms Hostel. The owners are sweet people, but others have named the place a 'h-o-s-t-i-l-e' to since some patrons go in and never come out." He gave me nod.

As we got closer, I could see whisps of smoke rising from the building. Soon I could smell burning wood and plastic. It was on fire. Teg had us stop to assess the situation. He and Boots went ahead for a closer look. The other two stayed behind to guard me.

"What happened to Marlo?" I asked the two.

Svivo spoke, "He was distracting one of the synths from finding the platform where you were hiding. He got too close, and he got snatched up and then it was all over. Synths are strong. And some synths have learned to hate. Jimati got what was coming to him. He's a burnt husk now."

Svivo and Milo had stern expressions and I decided I'd talked enough. The Welshly Arms was now a roaring pyre. We were a long distance away, but I could still feel the heat. We watched it burn. Half an hour later, Teg and Boots were back. "The Arms is gone. The three humans we were going to see are standing about roasting hotdogs and marshmallows." Crazy people.

I stared at the flames, "I hope the statue wasn't in there." I asked, "Where do you think we should go now?"

Teg replied, "We need to try the other two taverns. They are in close proximity to one another, but we will be going deeper into the Wasteland. Kip, I am not sure this is worth the risk."

"Let's just get it done." I led off and the mouse soldiers jogged to catch up. I was pissed. This mission got a friend killed and I wasn't in the mood to sit around whinging.

Teg spoke, "There are two places we can visit, the Hose & Springbow and the Bucket & Truncheon."

"Okay, where do we go first?" I was depending on my team to have the best guidance.

"H&S, for sure. Unlike the B&T, everyone is welcome, and all variants real and imagined." Svivo broke it down so even I could understand.

I wondered, "Why do they do that?"

"Do what? Exclude people? Like my sire said, people hold onto hate, so they don't have to deal with their pain." I couldn't think of anything pithy to say to that.

"Alright, Hose & Springbow it is!" I made the call, and we were off again.

The day wore on and another settlement hove into view. It was getting old, toting around the cat statue. I had been warned the heat and weather got worse the deeper we went into the Wasteland. Indeed, the heat was sweltering, and it wasn't even noon yet. Storm clouds were gathering but Teg said the ground wouldn't see a drop of rain.

There was a small town with a main street, 90 or so buildings, a hospital and a residential area with a couple hundred tiny houses. Two of the largest buildings were the taverns we had been discussing. The Hose & Springbow was conveniently the first we came to. It was busy. The clientele and ambiance were a cross between Mos Eisley and a small Las Vegas. A little bit of glam and a whole lot of seedy. There were cars, trucks, hybrid animal mounts that looked like banthas, horses, zebras, and others. The people were human, synth, and hybrids from enormous to tiny. There were pixies, gnomes, elves, and demons. It was the best ComiCon I could imagine; I felt right at home. Drones and bots zipped about and there was even an old RainZepplin tethered to a tower in the town square. At the moment some big event was going on and as I spied closer, I saw there was a guillotine on a raised platform. I didn't want to see it. At the front of the tavern there were several entrances, each tailored to the stature of the client. I went through the mouse sized entrance. The bar was amazing. There were covered galleries and walkways for the smaller folks and large open spaces for the larger types. It was tastefully and thoughtfully designed. I liked this place immediately. My appreciation for the challenges and advantages of being smaller were borne out in stark relief here. The big people ignored the little ones for the most part. I heard all sorts of conversations as I walked about. Teg let me take the lead. Most conversations were staid and dull.

"Are you happy?"

"Hmm. There are moments, surely. But I am grateful though."

"Hey, if you don't stop drinking how am I supposed to get home…"

"It will cost you more than you can afford…"

I kept walking, listening for something interesting.

"No, you are too stupid. A cow like you…" I looked and the people talking were in fact bovine. Moving on. There were another dozen boring conversations.

"The fire burned it to the ground. Roger and Virginia just came by the tavern to say their goodbyes."

I stopped and pretended to tie my shoe. I listened to the men some more.

"Yeah, the poor Klausmans have been a staple around here since before I came."

I risked a look. The two men wore canvas dusters and were bellied-up to the bar with mugs of beer.

"Did they salvage anything from the wreckage?"

"Oh yeah. I heard Dave Dickie, that manservant of theirs had saved up for years. Wanted to buy them out at some point. This was his chance. He's set up shop at the other end of town in the old, abandoned Crane Manufactory. He's got some cool stuff. There is a whole warehouse that didn't burn, filled with all sorts of gear and supplies. I heard the JINN may be coming by for a look, so anyone want something best be looking' quick, before those monsters arrive."

"Do you know if he has any weapons for sale?"

"Nope. No weapons. The Klausmans didn't believe in weapons. They were always spouting off some drivel about love making and lover's walks. They were permafried, but the lady could sure roast a tasty goat."

I headed back out the door.

On the way we saw several big glass jars on the bar top. One had pickled eggs, another had pickled pig's feet. When we saw one with pickled whole mice Boots blew chunks and got upset. Before we knew it Boots had jumped up and shattered the jar, spilling the dead mice all over the nearby patrons. He jumped down and we continued. No one had a clue that Boots had done the deed.

Teg led the way again. I let him know I wanted to stay away from the guillotine, and he took us through the storm sewer. Above, there were yells and cheers at the execution. Some people were small in mind. I'd spent my life, even as a kid, defending the right for people to live and here were others celebrating its end. I wasn't sure if I was more pissed or sad.

We went up through a grating near a huge factory. Teg said this was used by one of the corporate world Powers, Crane to manufacture parts for their vehicle lines: zeppelins, walkers, manual cars, synth cars and other things. There were two men sitting on the ground having a loud conversation about the FBI versus the CIA, two government agencies from the defunct United States.

"Kip, over here." I followed Teg.

Milo spoke, "These men are Skooma addicts. We would normally avoid them, but they are sitting directly in front of our access hole. From the looks of it, there is a lot of activity inside the factory, and we need to stay hidden. That said, I am going to draw them away. Once they move, you and the others will run inside, okay?"

Milo stepped up to the men and spoke loudly, "I am an agent of the FBI hybrid division with a warrant for your arrest. Please stand and follow me." It was like magic. Both men stood and followed after Milo.

Inside was a mess of action, people and tables stacked with clothing, equipment, canned food, and other things. We were in a barren part of the factory floor, away from the hubbub. Milo came racing in and I could see the butt of one of the Skooma guys sitting atop our exit hole again.

"So, guys, I have no idea what we are looking for." I thought this might be a rabbit trail, or dead end.

"Have you asked the cat statue for help?" Teg had a good point.

"No, I will try." I sent to Fig Cat, *'Do you know what kind of figurine we are looking for?'*

'No idea. Go away'.

'Come on, you and I are going to be searching for the fourth figurine together for as long as it takes. You heard Cat Sith. He said you don't get to reincorporate until your job is done. Please, can you help?'

'When you put it that way, okay. The figurine is a stone bat'. He sent a mental picture of the figurine.

'Thank you'. I was genuinely appreciative.

"Guys, we are looking for a bat shaped figurine about the size of this one," I patted the stone cat.

Teg got us organized, "This place is enormous. We need to split up and start digging through boxes, unwrapping packages, and opening storage containers."

Boots spoke, "I think we'll have to be careful until nighttime. Once the humans have gone home for the day, we can check the metal containers and other noise producing places."

Teg nodded, "Yep, good idea. Search but do not be discovered. Keep track of the places we need to return to after dark."

The remainder of the day was spent searching. Teg went with me while the others went solo. I hid the cat statue close to the entrance hole, behind some rubbish. Most of the stuff we searched was on tables and the routine was to check if the coast was clear, climb onto the table, look inside and under the piles of crap, then move on. It became tedious and I started to lose hope. The humans left the building just before dusk. Alright, time to get digging! Nope, in came two Rottweilers with hungry written on their slobbery muzzles.

We reconvened in the middle of the factory on a gantry above the floor. We shared protein nuggets, had some water, then decided to go to the barren areas to pee. The idea was to use the scent to attract the dogs away from our search area. It worked...until I got careless.

When Teg and I used some bungie cords to prise open a metal Conex, the door squealed, echoing throughout the building. The dogs began barking and swiftly came to explore the noise. Teg and I climbed atop the Conex and watched. An idea popped. I yelled down at the dogs and farspoke them as well, "Hey guys, we have a fun place where you can endlessly play and more food than you can eat. Can you help us?"

The dogs calmed down and stared at me with little head rotations of confusion.

'You're such a small human. Hybrid, huh? Where is the food, little human'? In truth the actual words were more like pictures and thought chunks, "You human, small, hybrid. Food?" I was still trying to figure out how my Cloud powers just sort-of filled in the blanks. Meanwhile, I was surprised the dogs could farspeak.

'Our home is not far from here. We have lots of food and there are good people and other dogs. Come live with us.'

The dogs wined expectantly and nodded profusely, *'Yep, yep, yep!'*

Teg was shocked when I climbed down and stood with the two Rottweilers. They sat waiting for me to do something.

'Can me and my friends speak aloud to you instead of mind speech'? They nodded.

"We are looking for a little bat figurine. Can you help us?" Max and Rex didn't understand me as well so I repeated the question in mind speech, giving them an image of a bat statue. From then onward, I voiced myself aloud and in mind speech so everyone could hear me.

I filled in my mouse friends that the Rottweilers, Max, and Rex would help us find the statue. No, they didn't know where it was. And yes, they would be coming home with us. My selling point was it would be a faster return trip if we rode them instead of running afoot. I received a grudging agreement. I figured I needed to seal the deal with food. I found the lunchroom and the soldiers helped me open it. We pulled out all the brown paper bags labeled with names. How wry, I always hated when somebody ate my bag lunch at school.

Up till now, I would never do that. But times had changed and so had my moral compass. The dogs tore into the bags and ate cookies, sandwiches, veggies, and skipped the fruit. I ate my fill of pineapple from a plastic box. The dogs made short order of it all, then they stood looking at me, '*We help now?*'

It took less than 90 minutes to search the most likely areas for the figurine. The dogs showed us the places where the most expensive stuff was stored. Teg opened a gold lamé box and voilà, there it was. I knew it was the real meal deal since my headache resumed with vigor. I inspected the stone bat and found the crevice where the USB stick was probably stuck. Awesome!

Teg carried the bat, and I picked up the cat. When we came to our exit, we discovered it was too small for the dogs. Milo wanted to just leave them. The dogs whined and sounded so pitiful he recanted his preference. "Fine, fine, we bring the dogs. But if one of them tries to lick me again, they will get my sword for a reply." I did not translate that.

Teg directed, "Team, spread out and find if there are any wall panels or low windows we can use as an exit. Don't worry Max and Rex, you guys are a part of Saint Kip's team, and you won't be left behind." I translated in mind speech for the dogs. I had never seen a Rottweiler smile. At my diminutive size it was frightening. My compatriots felt the warmth radiate off the two dogs. They loved Teg, but not so much Milo.

It took half an hour, but Boots found an open window onto a lower roof. We exited and then made a jump into some bushes. We headed north out of town, riding on the backs of Max and Rex. Teg used Max's ears to guide his movements. As we rode on into the night there was a luminous cloud on the near horizon to the east.

"Teg, what is the pink cloud over there?"

"That's called the Mürk. The pink clouds are poisonous vapor. Anything that goes in there dies quickly and badly. But it's also the location of a huge underground munitions complex. The gases are corrosive so even synths avoid the place. No Cavalry, Junkers or Rovers would go there. Last year the CSA ran a big salvage operation to get inside the complex, but their equipment fell apart before they even got close."

Just as the sky began to get light, I woke up. I was still on the back of the dog as he was trotting along. We arrived at the familiar culvert mouth and we went inside. Max and Rex were doted upon and welcomed warmly. Then I saw Boots had wrapped up Marlo and carried him all the way back. I watched as the body was carried away.

"When will we have the memorial for Marlo?" I asked Teg.

"Lowlifes don't do memorials." I was aghast.

I was probably out of line, but I felt Marlo deserved to be remembered, "Teg how do you celebrate the fallen?"

"We don't. The family disposes of the body away from the warren. Marlo will live on in our minds."

"But when my friend at school died last year, we had a ceremony so we could celebrate his life. It was the way we shared the pain of his loss and the amazing life he lived." I surprised myself at how passionate I felt.

Teg stared at me like I had grown a third arm, "Kip, we are animals. We're not humans. It's just not done."

"Teg, you are people as much as me and my Crew. And anyway, I want to do a memorial. Marlo was my friend. Who do I talk to about it?" I was firm and he took me seriously. I guess I wasn't just some kid here. It was kinda refreshing.

Sture and Strad came over. Strad spoke, "Lord Kip. You will be conducting a ceremony for the soldier Marlo." He made a statement. Not a question. Uh oh.

Sture then spoke, "My Lord it is high honor what you are doing. No Lowlife has ever been celebrated after death. We are…unworthy."

That blew a gasket for me. They saw my face go red and it was only by the skin of my teeth that I didn't have an outburst. I followed my Dad, Vicky's advice. Take a beat, count to ten, then respond.

"Sture, Strad, Teg," I locked eyes with each in turn, "Please arrange for a memorial at mid-day today where we will lay Marlo to rest, and I and his family and closest friends will speak some words about him. There needs to be food and drinks provided. Before that I would like to meet his family."

Sture replied, "Lord, there is only his mother."

"Please arrange for me to speak to her soon." I was in uncharted territory. My big mouth just obligated me to be an officiant at a memorial for a mouse in a community of people I recently would have just called animals. Not just animals.

"I will be taking a walk topside. Teg, would you please come with me?"

We walked in silence for a while, then I asked, "Do you think it was wrong for me to insist on a memorial?"

"My Lord, right and wrong is a question for one of the exalteds, like you or Lord Síth." That was stupid. It sounded like a fascist society. Maybe it was. Was I wrong to want to change something as important as honoring one's dead?

I decided it was an okay thing to do. Marlo was beloved and he deserved to be remembered more than just being dumped in a hole for the eternal dirt nap. An hour later I was back in the vault reading a map at one of the tables. A light feminine voice broke the quiet.

"Lord Kip. I am Luci. You wanted to speak to me?"

She had my full attention. By the end of the mission, I was able to visually distinguish between the mice and I could see Lucy bore a lot of resemblance to Marlo.

"Luci, I –" I stopped. What could I say? I was the reason Marlo died. He sacrificed himself protecting me. If that synth had gotten to me, it would have been my funeral, not his. But this wasn't about me. What would my Dads have said?

I started again, "Marlo was my friend and I miss him. In a short time, we became good friends. We shared laughs and struggled together. I know his other teammates loved him too. Ms. Luci, may I hold a memorial for Marlo? It would mean a lot to me."

Luci's eyes were wide as saucers. Was she mad? Sad? Offended? Her eyes then welled with tears and she held her head down. I hadn't realized mice could cry. Something compelled me to step forward and embrace her. I knelt down and her head rested on my shoulder, and I felt hot, wet on my shirt. We stood there for a bit. The constant activity continued about us, but I could see curious glances directed our way. I pulled us apart, arms still holding.

"Is this, okay? To miss him?"

"Lord Kip –" I hated myself for interrupting.

"Lucy, I am no one's Lord. Please call me Kip. Please."

"Mm. Kip, I would like that. I had only one litter and of that only one survived. You see, Lowlifes have a hard time with their children. Mice, rats, raccoons, wolves, whichever. We avoid talking about death because so few of our children live to be adults." She stopped and resumed holding me close.

I spoke, "Maybe this can be a way to deal with it. I know burying it didn't help me when my friend died."

She looked at me and nodded. And with that I became the first officiant of a Lowlife memorial. It was beautiful. Many friends spoke and Luci even said a few words. When it was my turn to speak about Marlo, I told a couple funny stories. I had to give the people permission to laugh if they felt inclined. A few did.

"You see mister –" I stopped when I realized I didn't know his family name. Embarrassed I knelt in front of Lucy and asked, "What is your last name? Your family name."

Luci looked bewildered, "We don't have one."

I was flustered. To me a person's last name is a mark of affiliation. How could Marlo be affiliated to anyone without a last name?

"May I give him a last name, Lucy. Please." I was spitballin' here and was sure I was about to tread on hallowed ground.

"Lord Kip, he was your friend. You will do the right thing." She said the words, but I wasn't sure.

I spoke aloud to the assembled, "Marlo was a great friend. He was as much family to me as any. I would like to give Marlo my family name. My last name is Wefer. Thank you for sharing your dear friend and family member with me. Marlo Wefer will be missed."

With that I did something I had never done, usually needing my Crew to support me. I sang. The song was one I learned from Cricket and his family. I didn't have Cricket's banjo, or Binky's percussion nor did I have Wogs for melody, but I poured my heart out and out it came. I sang Will The Circle Be Unbroken. I knew some of the words were incongruous, but I needed to sing because my heart hurt. Then my mind went to all the other friends and others who didn't make it out of the CENTERs and the fight for liberation. My eyes were closed but the tears ran, and I poured it out.

Something changed then; I felt a lightness of spirit and then hands were on my shoulders. I heard voices take up the refrain and realized I had somehow resumed my full size and my Crew was there too. They didn't know the whole context, but they knew me as I knew them.

They joined the song, seeing there was something special happening. After we sang, I asked, "How did you get here?" I asked.

"You called us, and we came," Cricket was succinct and non-informative as usual. We all embraced briefly then I turned back to my Lowlife friends.

I didn't know my four-legged friends could weep, but there it was. We were all one soppy mess. I hugged my Crew and then sat cross-legged so I could see my smaller friends better.

"Friends, please meet my other friends, Binky, Wogs and Cricket. Thank you for helping me get them unstoned," I gave a grin to my Crew, "and back to the right size. They are my family like all of you. We will always remember Marlo Wefer." My expression told my Crew I would explain later.

Sture stood forward and his voice was now higher pitched to my ears, "Lovely service Lord Kip. I don't think we have enough food to feed you humans though." I laughed which broke the ice. Soon everyone was laughing, and the remainder of the time together was filled with Lowlife dancing and music. I regretted being too big to participate.

I stepped away from the gathering with my Crew. I brought them up to speed on the last couple days. They were surprised I managed to get the last two figurines. Cricket opened his satchel which had the first two and brought them out. I gave permission for Teg to grab the other two, despite his reservations on touching the cat statue. He thought lightning from the sky would fry him where he stood. When that didn't happen, he visibly relaxed. I placed all four figurines on a rock surface. First, I dug the USB sticks out of the latest two and pocketed them. Each time I had grabbed a figurine for the first time, I received a weird sensation. As we sat there it was like there was an electrical field surrounding us. It was then I noticed there were grooves in the four figurines and I realized they could be joined together at the base. The moment the last figurine clicked into place I felt a rush of energy go into me. I had the taste of orange sherbet in my mouth, which was tasty but weird.

"Yo Kip, did you feel that?" Binky was asking.

"It tasted like orange sherbet," Wogs was smacking her chops.

"Same thing happened when I grabbed the first figurine in Monte Cristo. What do ya think it means, Kipper?" Cricket asked.

"No idea. But I bet it's some sort of Cloud hoodoo that Croatoan cooked up," Croatoan was a real pain in our collective posterior.

We said our goodbyes to my Lowlife friends. And as we were about to leave, I felt a tug on my pantleg. I bent over to talk with Teg.

"Kip, I am thankful we were a team. If you ever need my services again, I am at your disposal." He bowed deeply. I stood and returned the bow and waved goodbye.

"Thank you, Teg. I look forward to seeing you again."

Cricket was already walking; Binky and Wogs pulled at me, and we caught up to him. All the figurines were in his satchel now.

Binky knew I was chewing on an idea and bumped my shoulder, "What do ya think it was?" She meant the figurine pulse.

"Not sure. I got a dim picture of a key being inserted into a door. Maybe the figurines are a key." We were tired and hungry, so we walked the rest of the way keeping to our own thoughts. We found the cars and a mobiflex tent set up with a nice fire and delicious cooking smells. When Cecelia saw us coming, she ran over and hugged us.

"Oh kids, let me hug your neck. Ohhh, I was so worried. Cliff said it was our job to wait but it's been almost three days!"

Cliff and Timothy were sitting at the fire not much concerned.

"Kip, come over here." Cliff called me.

I sat between Cliff and Timothy and Cliff spoke, "You're late. Eat something, then we can go." Cliff was a man of few words and I appreciated that.

Cecelia made up plates of Huevos Rancheros, "Do you kids want red, green or Christmas?"

We all wanted Christmas. We had learned about second Christmas, meaning both red and green chili salsa on our eggs. We inhaled our food. Being shrunk down then restored made a person hungry. All I had for three days were protein pellets that looked like rabbit turds. I mentioned that and everybody laughed.

"Kipper, those were rabbit pellets." Cricket just had to get a crack in.

We cleaned up and got ourselves ready to go.

"Come on kids, we need to get to the meeting spot. I told Slim we were coming. He doesn't like to wait." Cliff looked anxious. Weird; Cliff never looked anxious.

Off we went. From there onward we stayed on the ground, following the Valley of Fire Highway. It was bumpy. "Cliff, who is Slim?"

"You call him Shrike. He's a little weasel who has renamed himself more times than he can count. Today he calls himself Slim Shadey, but he is Shrike to his business colleagues. I knew him as Todd many years ago. He is a sniveling back biter, and few people trust him. But he has one redeeming grace, Slim can deliver. He has a singular talent to acquire anything you might want to buy. He is in-demand regardless of being a flea-bitten toadstool." Cliff was smiling but I could tell he really despised this guy. Sounded like something had happened in the past. I didn't ask.

"Cliff, where are we meeting this guy?" I wanted to unload these things and be done with it. I was just done with the whole figurine treasure hunt. For real. It started out as fun but along the way it got grim. I'm still a teenager and grim is not my vibe, unless it's on my own little angsty terms, of course.

July 2254 –Fazbear Funcade

"We are close. We are meeting him at Freddy Fazbear Pizza Restaurant in the amusement park ahead."

In the distance I could see a Ferris wheel and roller coaster. There were more carnival rides visible as we got closer.

Cliff continued, "This place was popular for locals after the Tech War but after families started going missing from the park the place closed. The Cavalry took it over about 20 years ago.

"Cliff, who are the Cavalry?" I had heard about them before.

"You know about the Junkers?"

"Sort of. They collect salvage across the country and sell the stuff to the highest bidders. My Dads said they are dangerous."

"The Cavalry are a smaller, more disciplined group but with similar objectives. They compete with the Junkers and even sometimes cooperate. We need to be careful. Let me do the talking." Cliff seemed so easy and composed. I decided to stay quiet.

Soon we came to an exit and turned slightly south. We passed under a large archway declaring Welcome to Fazbear Funcade. A 10-meter animatronic stood beside the archway, waving us in, the tattered, rusted bear's arm was moving back and forth slowly. Our three cars pulled up in the pizzeria parking lot. For being in the middle of the desert, the place looked well kept. Ours were the only vehicles. That felt ominous.

The others came running over, excited. "Kipmeister, you know this place?" Binky looked at me with that intense stare of hers.

"Umm, no."

"Aww, come on. You're always carrying on about video games from the 20th." She was practically jumping up and down. It came to me suddenly; back in the early 21st a massively popular horror video game series FNAF, Five Night's at Freddy's shocked and amused gamers.

"Binks, FNAF was a video game not an actual place."

Cecelia and Timothy came up and to my surprise Timothy spouted off some gaming lore, "Actually after the Tech War so many people were trying to recapture the good times of the roaring 20s they created larger-than-life real world monuments. In this case a restaurant chain was created, styled after FNAF. My cousin Greg said a descendant of Scott Cawthon used his family's wealth to make a nationwide chain of Pizzerias. They ended up closing when someone hacked the animatronics to behave like in the game. Families died and the whole chain flopped overnight."

That was more than I had ever heard Timothy say at one time. Stunned, I was speechless for a moment as I realized my Online knowledge may be deep but my real world understanding was fairly paltry.

"Timothy, what was the name of the Pizzeria founder?"

"I think the guy was named Seth Schade."

Cliff came over and chimed in, "Seth Schade is the great great-grandfather of Slim Shadey." As he said that pieces began falling into place. Cawthon and his team in their latter years contributed to early combinating of Online AIs with animatronics resembling their game characters. But they created safe horror. Clearly someone later had a different idea. Families died? That's horrible.

A voice called, "I heard my name! Cliff, why you bringin' a bunch of people here? Ya knows what I told ya, me?"

A short squinty-eyed man came around the side of the pizzeria. He was dressed like Crocodile Dundee and even sported the cool Down Under hat. I wanted a hat like that!

Cliff faced the man, "Friends may I introduce the renowned, the notorious Slim Shadey."

The man stared at Cliff for a moment then seemed to notice he had a crowd. Like a light switch flicked Slim broke into a smile and took a Shakespearean bow, "Oh, yes, how I do love a grand introduction. Cliff, not that I don't appreciate your company, but you always seem to bring a bit of lagniappe, you?"

Cliff seemed to mock the man's accent, but a smile spread across his face. What followed blew away my understanding of Cliff.

"Lil' ole' me gone fo a run 'cross the desert, heard the Zydeco playin' and smelled the hush puppies fryin', you! Figgured mes amis were havin' a set-to and ole' Cliff needed to bring his joie de vivre, me!"

Slim roared with laughter and dropped the accent, "Oh Cliff, you were always a smooth one! Come introduce Slim to your chitlins here so we can go get heavy into some gumbo and grillades!"

Cliff gave me a moment's warning look, then shifted back to his affable self, "Ah yes, of course. Please meet my young friends Kip, Wogs, Binky, and Cricket."

Slim shook our hands. He was a Cajun from the bayou, but I suspected it was just an act. His manners were crisp, and his eye contact was riveting, and I figured this was a man not to mess around with. I could sense restrained power behind those eyes and a deep intelligence. What a weird mix of ingredients, this man!

"Ah mon cher, Binky," Slim kissed Binky's hand and her face blushed red. Was she attracted to this guy. Oh boy, that would spell trouble!

"Welcome to the home of the Shrike; please call me Slim." He paused, looking Binky square in the eyes. She was frozen like a deer in headlights. Slim broke the moment, "Now if you'd please come into my humble abode, I would like you to meet my family and share some of our own home cookin'."

Slim took Binky, arm-in-arm and escorted us inside. I caught a concerned glance between Cliff and Cecelia. Cliff gave a quick head shake no. We entered Slim's pizzeria, but it smelled more like a seafood bar…and it smelled heavenly. It was amazing to see this new Cliff. I thought he was a fairly simple, under spoken guy. Little did I know. As the door opened the music roared into our ears. It was energetic and hoppin'. The man was singing about a tear-stained letter, and I found the rhythm and melody infectious. In moments I was subtly bobbing in-time. I saw my Crew were infected too.

Slim took us bobbing onto the main floor of the restaurant to a variety of men and women sitting around the tables; the first delicious waft was shrimp. The size of those prawns was unreal! I saw muffins, a tureen of soup, raw and fried veggies and more. Heady, rich, and overwhelming: it was almost like they were expecting company. Maybe our coming was not a surprise?

"Ho! Cavalry! Please to make the acquaintance of brother Cliff. You remember Timothy and Cecelia? Well, they brought some friends. This is Cricket, Binky, and Wogs. This last one you probably recognize a resemblance to our friend Dr. Boshaw? This here is none other than the only son of the Dads, Kip. Don't be shy now. Come on over and make nice!"

We were suddenly in the middle of a throng. Not just any average throng, but a gathering of very intoxicated Cajuns. They were jovial and effusive. We met people with interesting names like Cal "Spot" Worthington, who claimed to be his own dog, Spot. Was he kidding? Others introduced themselves, like Oliver St. John Mollusk (he pronounced it Oliver Sin-jun Mollusk), Sanballat, Bang Bang Rita, and Hay Blinken who was a synth. There was Little Chuddy, and Cedric the Butcher; Cedric was finely dressed and looked ready to play high stakes in Vegas. I met Challis Bon Temps and Nellie Stackhouse.

They sure didn't act like a roving band of criminals as their reputation would indicate. Why had Cliff been so cloak-and-dagger about the Cavalry? These folks were fun!

"Kip, be casual. I am seeing a new side to Slim and his gang. They have never been cheerful before. Be on your guard and spread the word to be prepare for something unexpected." Cliff was being his casual self, but his concern was genuine. For more than two hours we ate heartily and even danced to the Cajun music.

"Cliff, you look at me with that suspicious gleam. I know your thoughts. Your friend Slim is well and truly shady and not to be trusted. In the past I would have expected your caution as warranted. But I am something more now and I would like to introduce the new me." Cliff had a shock of fear travel through him. This wasn't Slim he knew. As the party around them played on no one noticed Slim and Cliff.

"Who are you? Where is Slim?"

"I am here my friend. Me. And so much more. Oh, I have such sights to show you!"

"Listen pinhead, you best tell me where Slim is…" Cliff found it was getting harder to speak, "…it's just. You. What are you doing. Shaman help me! What's happening?" The last few words came as thoughts since Cliff's mouth wouldn't work. Cliff expected to hear the warm voice of his shaman in his head, but there was nothing.

"Cliff, listen. I had to create an opaque bubble around us to tell you something. We have about 15 seconds before they get suspicious. We are all Vor, aliens, your enemy. But the picture is more complex than that. We have been subjugated by our own leaders to serve remote alien masters. They seem good and pure when you meet them, but they are nothing but whitewashed sepulchers. I am known as Salim on my home world. I am an agent here to eliminate the threat humanity poses to our masters. We believe the threat is a concoction and a few of us have been secretly working against their plans. Our race, the Vor has eliminated thousands of other races deemed unworthy but this time is different. Some of us plan to defend your people. I need your help, but we have to talk later."

"Slim, why are you telling me this? I'm no one."

"I met a man named Croatoan who is legend among our people. The original rebel of the galaxy. He said Kip is the answer to freedom for my people. And it seems yours too. You need to let Kip know the Vor of Earth will support him when the time comes." Salim made a nervous head check.

Cliff was sweating profusely, his face was turning red. "Cliff, when I release you, we must both laugh like I just told you the raunchiest joke. Please, believe me that your lives at this moment hang in the balance. Yours and mine. My other compatriots cannot know we spoke."

Suddenly released, Slim and Cliff burst into laughter. Slim's people and the kids looked at them momentarily then resumed their own partying. The afternoon crept into the evening, and they all watched an oldie but goodie, Fifth Element. Who didn't like Lilu-Dallas multi-pass?

Slim shared a rare wistful moment, "You know, it wasn't always about the sell or about the glamor. My family came from France in the late 18th century. Trappers. My many-great grandfather was a coureur de bois, a woodsman who traded with the natives. A generation later his daughter married a man and moved to Louisiana. My northern roots are simple folks. It's the southron ones who put on airs and climbed the social ladder. Made me who I am today: a two-bit grubber, hocking my wares like a Bourbon Street hooker hanging out a sock. When all I really wanted was a snifter of Sazerac and a finely rolled Ramon Allones, sitting on the front porch of my Creole townhouse." Slim gave a wink to Cliff.

Cliff would have bought that story hook, line, and sinker, except now he knew better. He wasn't the fearful type, but he was deeply concerned with what Slim, Salim that is, shared earlier. Was he really supposed to tell a kid that he needed to rely on aliens to help? Kip wasn't a world leader…or was he?

Cecelia passed the figurines to Slim as they left the pizzeria, "Here they are. Are you giving us money for these?"

"Sure am. Here ya go," Slim handed her a CSA P card.

"What am I supposed to do with a government purchase card?"

"Take it to your bank and deposit the whole balance. There are 120 million credits on it. It's a gift from my client to the Hopi. The money is legit, and you'll have no problem using it once the back clears the funds. Y'all need to get going now. My next client will be here in a few minutes."

We said our goodbyes and left Slim's place. The food had been fabulous, and the Cavalry folks were lively, fun even. Cliff was brooding. Usually he had something to say, but he clearly was pondering something heavy.

I asked, "You okay Cliff?"

He nodded and kept silent. Cecelia wasn't silent, "Hey guys this was a big win for us. That's more money than I've seen in my life! If it turns out to be real, of course. Anyway, offloading those figurines should get the Powers' attention onto someone other than you kids. I wonder why they were such hot items?"

Cliff looked back, making eye contact with Slim. He nodded once and Cliff returned the acknowledgement. He knew he would have to tell us about the Vor soon; he didn't realize we were already aware.

March 2257 – Bakabi, Hopi Nation, Arizona Territory

Time passed and the matter of aliens, Cloud powers and intrigues faded into a new normal. Cliff told me and my friends about the Vor, but it didn't seem relevant to my immediate life. We were kids still and craziness had a way of fading quickly in the press of new and exciting stuff. Cliff told us Vagabond had contacted him. We were to stay put for now. Croatoan had his rocks and we needed to stay with the Hopi. For how long we didn't know.

My Crew and I graduated from high school and were put to work around the Hopi nation. I worked in the Bakabi computer lab, Binky was a shift foreman on the construction site of a new Hopi high school on First Mesa, Wogs was a teacher of GIS at the local ASU campus on First Mesa, and Cricket was the modern-day Ed Hume, creating Online casts about gardening and horticulture. He discussed many topics dealing with surviving off the grid. Like before in Washington, many of Cricket's followers were older single women who liked ogling the goods. Cougar anyone? Cricket also helped setup a new agricultural center on Third Mesa and set to creating new fields, turning the Hopi lands green.

With all that I wondered why the Powers didn't come snatch us up since we were Online all the time and exposed. I found out later we were being watched but with the Powers distracted by aliens, me and my Crew didn't warrant much attention. That suited me just fine.

The farspeech classes grew and I had a happy reunion with the Lummi, Nooksack, and Tulalip friends I had back in Washington. The Cloud constructs I had created to organize the class had expanded. Online-Kip had taken my constructs and advanced them to support the world's Cloud airwaves. The First Nation peoples around the world led the way in farspeech. From what I understood, shaman had been communicating for thousands of years this way, but for them it was only a few people doing the talking. Now there were thousands, maybe tens of thousands. Cliff said it was in part due to the Cloud booster satellites my Dads had put in orbit.

I am so proud of my Online counterpart. Cloud-Kip had really come into his own. He's pretty cool, but he still calls me Physi-Kip. We share a lot. There are moments when our sharing becomes a union where we are the same person like in the beginning. It can be disorienting but I love all the adventures he has in Cloud land. He has met a bunch of aliens, travelled via avatar to other planets and become quite the man-about-the-galaxy.

I shook myself out of my reverie. I was at the school visiting and Dr. Birman was talking to me.

"Kip! There is music in the Cloud!" Mr. Birman had recently become Dr. Birman. He just graduated from the regional university with a PhD in music.

"Those Cloud powers you showed me have grown. I have become much more proficient. I remember when all I could do was light a candle," the candle on his piano lit itself, "and move small objects," a music book scooted across the top of his piano, "and making enough light to read by at night." Colorful lights floated and flitted above us, casting light on the keys and the hand-scrawled sheet music.

"Anyhoo, you knew I was experimenting. But when you included me in the nightly farspeech class my life was transformed. Thank you."

In actuality, Birman found the class himself. One night we were in the middle of a lesson and a new voice came on the airwaves. I had to shunt him to a side channel and catch him up. He caught on quickly and it became obvious why he was a teacher. He was an excellent student. Even Mr. Campbell joined our farspeech class.

Birman continued, "…I found something amazing, and I couldn't wait to show you!"

Dr. Birman and Mr. Campbell had become two of my students less than a year ago. As my Cloud powers had returned, I found I could grow them in others. Some people could only touch the Cloud as they dreamt, but a small group of people could touch the Cloud while awake. Birman and Campbell could more than touch the Cloud, they could manipulate the physical world too. My Crew's powers were growing like mine, but unlike all the others, theirs were far more potent. I felt it was important to keep the extent of their powers secret. Mine were still comparatively small except for when someone like Jack or Siva pushed me to do more. Usually Cloud powers and headaches were a close-knit pair in my life. I had resigned myself to the idea that Cloud operancy was going to be about helping others, not myself.

I dismissed my problems. The currency of my kingdom was seeing my students grow. It was heartening to help my two schoolteachers expand their abilities. Both were artistically inclined which seemed to be assistive in gaining Cloud capability. I invented new Cloud constructs and taught others how to do the same. A smaller group of students set up a

266

weekly farspeak session to discuss their advanced Cloud use in the physical world. I was spending more time with this group, which included my Crew as well. These people were all over the world and we even had sit-in instructors like Siva, Jack, and others. I think everyone was too polite to mention that my own Cloud powers were not growing like all the other students.

In the face of the dire portents of the Vor and alien infestation, it was amazing how normal life just continued as usual. Cliff had told us about Slim and the news spread like wildfire. He was concerned about Slim-the-alien since he had been taken into his confidence.

My mind liked to wander these days. Like right now. I found I could tune out, and much of the time I didn't mean to ignore people…except Dr. Birman. I have no doubt he would lecture the empty air if I weren't around. I loved Dr. Birman, but when he got on a talking jag, his off button was disabled.

Birman hadn't stopped talking, "…It didn't come at first, but one day I noticed different levels of power, colors, brightness, and movement and such." As Birman spoke, firefly lights floating above his piano changed and moved like highly coordinated drones.

"I discovered a sort-of interval in all these behaviors." For a moment all the lights formed up like notes on sheet music. "The longer I looked at it, I realized I could do two or more tricks at once, in concert. Don't these look like octaves?"

I wasn't following very well; I didn't see the octaves or interval thing at all. Dr. Birman sat down at the piano and music flowed from his fingers. Rachmaninoff?

"Now watch this," Birman played a series of notes that rose and fell, "that is a harmonic series. Now watch the lights over the piano." Dozens of tiny colorful lights appeared and changed hue as he played. It beggared belief that this former soldier would become a teacher, then a doctor and lately a Cloud artist, bringing beauty and color and symmetry to the understanding of Cloud things. It underscored that I could enable and grow Cloud powers in others but not in myself. It felt like I had a learning block. My students excelled beyond me in farspeech, telekinesis, Cloud constructs and physical world manifestations. Then I thought of something: we were going to have to create a whole vocabulary for Cloud powers. Oh boy, not really my cup of tea. It's more my speed to poke fun at things, not build them.

And Birman? Still talking, "Now watch. I am going to follow a little progression coined by Dr. Bernstein from the 20th. I play a chord. Now, watch the lights as I add an octave. Then, as I mix modes between minor and major, see how the lights lose and gain saturation?" It was in-fact amazing what he was doing. But I was bored.

"Now, check this out. Let's add the Fifth as we resolve from a flat 6." The colors did a fancy blue counter-point twinkle, then settled on a cool green.

"Watch the display as I add a Fourth, then a Third. See what happens with E flat and D sharp as we phrase up and down between C flat major with E flat the way David Foster wrote in Celine Dion's version of 'All By Myself'". I was lost in the living kaleidoscope. He played a strain from the song.

As Birman played, he was caught in a reverie. I went to his home computer and logged into my own archive and pulled up the Celine Dion video of her singing "All By Myself". I turned up the volume and picked up Birman's guitar and strummed chords with the song. Birman laughed and joined in, and we sang together. He closed his eyes and the colored lights moved and shifted intensity with the music. It was beautiful to watch and to hear. All with that magnificent Celine voice piping clear and dulcet! Over the last three years we had gone from being Hopis in fact to Hopis in practice. They were family every bit as much as my Dads. The four of us were so thankful and the horrors of the outside world had faded over time. Eventually Flu Cat and Pooka joined the three SynthBots and our little cabal was a warmly welcomed addition to the Three Mesa community. Timothy and Cecelia made sure a portion of the money from Slim went to me and my Crew. And we had our own house now. Timothy conspired with Pooka and our SynthBots to find an architect from Chicago to come design and build a house on Second Mesa for us. It was the size of a castle, modelled after Arthur Erickson's, Graham House in British Columbia. Lots of levels, jutting terraces, and more windows than walls. We named it Sith House. But it really wasn't our house. Dozens of the Hopi kids moved in with us and after some cajoling, Cecelia and Timothy came too. It wasn't just a house. The bottom four floors were Cloud research facilities and the top three were the residential part. The other Hopi kids were now like me and my Crew. They were on a mission. Everyone knew Cloud powers were important and we were the right people to be pushing the science forward. Despite all that high-falutin' talk, everyone had their day job.

Only the adults, some who were professors from universities around the world were working at Síth House. The rest of us had more menial work elsewhere. Flu Cat continued to disappear; his was a nomadic life. Pooka often went with him. But now, he was bringing people back to help us. I found out he was following up leads given by Vagabond and Croatoan. Flu Cat himself was an object of excited scrutiny. When several of the human researchers discovered he was a 5000-year-old sentient non-human, the historians and geneticists hounded him every time he returned to the house. I think Flu Cat's absence was more to avoid these researchers than to do recruiting.

Then one day Teg, Svivo, Milo and Boots came to visit. Teg asked if they might be of service. I had to think quick. Then it dawned on me. What was one area we had been lacking in? Security. I introduced them to Beckett and within a month more Lowlife soldiers appeared at the door to be conscripted for what became known as Beckett's Bandits.

A long-missed face came through the door. Soomalee. We embraced and she introduced me to a skinny tall man with serious eyes, smoldering green with golden flecks. I was confused why she was here.

"Kip, please meet Seek-Bright-Chanter. He is my shaman and also my life partner," Oh my gosh! Soomalee had gotten married?

"Congratulations!" I was so happy for her.

'Kip, let Seek know I will be there in a moment'. Elder Tala sent on a private channel.

"I believe Elder Tala will be here in a moment to see you both," Seek was stoic and said nothing. Soomalee clung to the man like he'd float away if she wasn't careful.

As it turned out Seek and Soomalee had been hired to research a new discipline called Cloud Mechanics.

Seek was a skilled Cloud operant with a specialty called self-polymorphism: he could change his shape at will, like a Chupa on steroids. He was brought on as an associate researcher. I recalled my own Chupa changes and also how I turned into a Lilliputian several years back. Maybe that was the same thing.

Later I headed to Birman's place again. It was a quiet place away from the non-stop chaos of my new house.

"Hey Kip, come on in. I want you to see something," He sat at his piano and began playing.

"I made an observation: the color, density, and frequency seem to have a triatic relationship. What I mean is they…" Birman kept talking but I was looking at something weird appearing on my pad. My prosthetic was giving me static as a fuzzy red cloud blotted out the other content on the screen. A voice then registered in my prosthetic.

July 2257 – headed toward Fazbear Funcade

"Kip, can you hear me? Hello?"

It took a moment to reply. I wasn't especially good at using my prosthetic through my pad to speak non-vocally, so I spoke aloud, "Yes? Who is this?"

"This is Slim, Cliff's friend."

"You mean Salim, the Vor?"

"Well, yes. Both, actually. I have a message your Dads sent for the both of us. I need you to come alone to the pizzeria."

And so, it began. An hour later as the sun set, I snuck away to the garage and stole Black Betty. I sync'd my pad with the onboard computer, Aloha and asked if she would be okay with us stealing her away on a little adventure. She was rarin' to go!

"Cliff never takes me on adventures. Let's do it!"

"Awesome, Aloha! Time to sneak a snook!" A question mark came up on the dashboard screen. "Sorry, it's my childish way of saying we will sneak away."

The car ascended vertically in complete silence, then headed away into the clouds, pressing me seriously deep into the bucket seat. We made for Fazbear park at a little under Mach one.

"Can I tell you a story?"

"Of course. Go ahead; we have plenty of time."

As we flew, I told her when I was a little'un and my Dads would be watching Pink Panther or Ellery Queen I would hide around the doorway from them and come out dancing to the theme music as it played. Yes, they had just put me to bed, but my little strut bought me some extra time to stay up later. I called my little dance 'sneak a snook'.

"Young man, you're an odd one, but I like you the better for it." Aloha laughed, "Then let's sneak a snook into the Fazbear nightmare park!"

"Yes let's!" And I wondered if I was going to my demise. After all, this guy was an alien living inside a human. Then, I thought so what! I gotta flying muscle car named Betty, flown by a wicked smart AI named Aloha, who favors me, and we are cruising like a bat outta hell at 4000 meters! I was livin' the dream!

When we landed, I thought we were in the wrong place. It was pitch black. Betty shined a spotlight on the front door of the pizzeria. There were no lights on, nor was there any sound to be heard. Perhaps the dream was becoming my nightmare. Thoughts of the murderous animatronics in the FNAF game went through my head. I didn't feel like getting out of the car at that point. Then the front door opened, and Slim walked down the steps, to the passenger side of the car. The window cracked open of its own accord. Clearly Aloha didn't trust him much.

Slim put his mouth to the window, "Hey Kip, we need to leave. Can you give me a lift. We can talk on the way."

Aloha spoke, "Kip, are you sure you want to do this? Give me the word and we'll ghost this guy."

Aloha was my soul mate right then, "Let him in. I think something bad has happened and it would be best I know what's going down."

The door unlocked and opened itself. Slim got in, "Thanks Kip. Cliff's car sure seems protective of you."

Black Betty launched skyward the moment the door shut. The headrest of his bucket seat smacked the back of his head and Aloha threatened him, "You try anything stupid, and I'll eject you at 1000 meters, pal."

Shaken, Slim sat back in the fine leather bucket seat and let out a big breath, "I promise no funny business." He didn't have an accent anymore.

She continued, "What have you done Slim? I smell blood on you."

Slim's eyes went wide, "She can smell things too?"

"I'll have you know…" Aloha started to wind up again.

I interrupted quickly, "Slim, what happened."

"Sorry kid, some extreme nastiness, I'm afraid. How should I start?"

"How about with the truth."

"Can we head to Las Vegas…well, Glitter Gulch?"

"Aloha, can we go to Glitter Gulch? We could go to the casino Cliff and Timothy talked about."

"Done. Course set in," She paused then added her own two-cent's worth, "Men are stupid when it comes to gambling, women, and booze."

I didn't know what to say so I kept my mouth shut. Wisely, so did Slim.

"Slim, why did you threaten to burn down the town hall in Bakabi. You are not a good Vor, Salim."

Salim had calmed down as we left the area, "Ah, so you know who I am now. Great. Well, I guess not much of a good guy. I'm sorry. I'll make it up to you. And for what it's worth I was just asking for a little piece of advice and Cliff was being obstinate."

Aloha retorted, "Oh no, you owe it to Cliff, not me. What a jerk."

"Does it help that I never planned to blow anything up?"

"Not one bit." Aloha was furious.

I stayed out of it. The two kept bickering and jabbering as Aloha sped us toward Las Vegas. Just as we hit a cruising altitude something jostled the car and rocked us sideways. My pad lit up with telemetry and a video feed from the car's exterior showed the rear-facing view. We were heading away from a mushroom cloud that used to be the pizzeria.

Salim swore, "Oh hell, they're already there."

"Salim, your pizzeria is a big ball of fire. Who did you piss off now?"

"My team discovered the stone figurines and overheard the message from the Dads. They knew I was a traitor and picked their time to bump me off. As planning would have it, I knew this moment would come and had my exit planned. My people don't know the depth of my treachery, nor that of my colleagues. It was key that I not let the figurines fall into unfriendly hands," he showed me the four statues in his knapsack. They didn't radiate Cloud energy anymore. I wondered if Croatoan only meant them for me and my Crew to feed us Cloud energy.

"The Vor Rebellion has been brewing almost since we arrived here on Earth in the 1950s. Two generations of Vor agents are here now and most of them are rebels. Some of the few loyalists -the ones coming after me- were on my team, or should I say, used to be on my team. I had some good people, but they were unwilling to see a brighter future."

"How do you think your people discovered anti-grav, wave motion energetics, and other technologies in the last couple hundred years? We stole it from the Coali and gave it to your scientists, making sure there was no hint of our involvement. It's why your synthetic sciences boomed." Salim paused in reflection.

"But our early help brought your race's most devastating war back in the 21st. That was us. Sorry. We have borne guilt since. Kip, the Vor are willing to die for you humans. We have brought destruction to your planet, and we owe you every help we can provide," I felt like a father-confessor. Who could have imagined an alien commander would be escorting me to Las Vegas while he admitted to genocide against humanity. What a wacky world I lived in.

Salim took a breath, "This is our only and final stand. Earth will be where the Vor find freedom from the COMBINE or where we -we call ourselves the Ethicists, have come to die. You see, we need your help as much as you need ours. Our slavery comes to an end, or we all do."

Aloha showed a rear facing camera view on holoview: we could see hundreds of red pinpoints buzzing around the blaze like angry hornets. Were they drones? Who was down there? Probably CSA, Bangarang, or Bad Wolf.

"So, what message did you get from my Dads?"

"They left a message several years back that you would be traveling around the Hopi area and to make sure you delivered the figurines to me."

"Salim, that's old news. Is that all they said?"

"No. They said you would help the Vor get free. They said Croatoan's plan hinges on you and it was up to me to make sure the Vor were fully committed to you."

I shook my head. "You know what Salim? Of course, I will help. But you know something else? I will help because I choose to and because I feel it's the right thing, not because my Dads or Croatoan have said so."

Salim knew not to comment on my teen angst. He just said thank you. He hummed a tune from Les Misérables as we flew into the night.

July 2257 – entering Las Vegas

Aloha had us cruising past Mach one with the clouds whipping by. Mist drops crawled up the windshield. The clouds cleared as the bright lights of the Strip hove into view. Black dots resolved into bobbing aircars, drones and other craft. We weaved in amongst the ponderous rain blimps and I could see the giant intake fans and water release pipes below.

"I am negotiating with Air Control. Once I have clearance, I'll get you to the helopad closest to the Glitter City Casino & Games."

"Kip, once we get these figurines offloaded do you have a place where I can shack-up for a while? Things are running kinda hot in my world."

"Sure thing. We have a huge house, and I am sure you can find a place to land for a bit." I didn't think it was the best idea to have him around, but I couldn't just kick him to the curb.

The scene of Vegas up close was like nothing I had ever seen. When Beckett had us enjoying our enforced hike and camping, Las Vegas seemed like a beehive of lights. Now in the middle of things I saw dozens of glittering arcologies rising almost two kilometers into the air. Every kind of cultural and ethnic architecture was represented. I could see a full-sized pyramid made of steel and glass with holo advertisements playing across every surface. There was a tower similar to the one in Paris which seemed to be made of green growing plants and vines with holos of pterodactyls. There were genuine huge birds perched all along its structure. Every building was beautiful; sometimes gaudy, but other times tasteful and sophisticated. Holo birds and planes towed illusory advertising banners between the buildings close enough for people on the ground to read. Zeppelins floated about dispensing artificial rain in certain spots, while huge three-legged war-of-the-worlds walkers made stately gate over the crowds far below. Kilometer wide lenticular shields floated over parts of the city giving shade during the day. Salim said at night they reflected the city lights back down making Vegas the bright-light city that never sleeps. It was a non-stop festival.

I saw pod racers speeding along invisible raceways and taxis and private aircars following pre-determined routes in long lines, horizontal, vertical, and even a couple diagonal rising streams. Skytrains zoomed past on gravitic rails, carrying hundreds of people to and from stops, while Aerobuses with open sides received new riders who hopped on and off like a street trolley. The only difference being the first wrong step would be a drop to the streets far below. Salim said there were gravitic safety nets, but I wasn't convinced. Cops were out in force. I could see flashing red blues here and there and one passed close by and set a tractor beam on an old flying boat. For real, the cop car just grabbed a flying boat; it looked like a Chinese junk and was suspended under a football shaped balloon. Smaller than a Zeppelin. It looked like a mobile kitchen.

"Hey Kip, you know this casino has dog races? Actual dogs racing!" Salim looked about as Aloha took us up and over a barrier wall from the Strip into the downtown core of Las Vegas. "The sites never get old. Always something new going on with you humans."

"Salim, I heard the casinos have rent-a-slaves of all kinds, human, synth, and hybrid. That is sick."

Salim made a face, and I realized he was as disgusted as I was, "They also have snuff rooms, war rooms, beds by the hour and other vile things."

"They have what?" I finally closed my mouth as I realized it might be drawing flies. I was horrified. This was the seedy side that my Dads had shielded me from. I wasn't eager to see any of that. As we descended to the landing pad, a gathering of synth helpers grouped below to receive us. Aloha opened the doors and in came in infinite mix of smells and every kind of sound imaginable. Foods, perfume, body odor, spilled oil, jet fuel and rotting refuse blended into a mélange I came to know as Vegas. The noise had an etheric harmony. I had read that city ordinance required all mechanisms that emitted sounds to do so according to certain rules which made the ambient noise almost pleasing. To my left was a kilometer high blue tinted building of steel, glass and a waterfall that was pouring upwards and mushrooming out into a water canopy over the top of the structure. A cool mist blew our way from the spray. The air temperature was less hot than daytime, but hot enough I was thankful for the misting.

Salim gripped my arm, "Hey buddy, you stay close to me. We need to first get some new clothes. We don't want to stand out as a couple of hobos."

We were escorted to Tom Ford's House of Style, which was on the same level as the helopad. The service was lavish, and Salim had the people running to get all sorts of exotic foods, alcohol (not for me thanks) and the most expensive and flashy clothes I'd ever seen.

"If you can imagine it, they can make it for you on the spot."

"I have no idea what to do. This is more your thing than mine."

"No way, you don't get to bail on this. Look at it this way. Have you seen someone dressed sharply before?" I nodded and he continued, "Okay, so imagine what he looked like and describe it to the MC, the master-of-ceremonies." At this Salim whistled over the head honcho who prepared to take my order. I mentioned an idea and Salim winced and shook his head.

The MC was a gaunt little man and well dressed.

Salim suggested, "Tommy, I think you can help here."

"Yes sir, what shall we start with for the young mister?"

Salim gestured Tommy closer and whispered something. As Tommy stood, he and Salim looked my way and smiled. I felt like something weird was about to go down…aaaand I was right.

"Young sir, please before we begin the fitting step into the D&D." Tommy indicated with his hand in the direction of a plexiglass tube with a door being held open by one of the beautiful assistants.

"Please remove your clothing and step in." When I hesitated, another assistant stepped forward to hold a sheet up, so I had some privacy. Another assistant rapidly cut away all my clothing. She had to be a synth, otherwise she would have cut me into little Kip-gobbets. And there it was, I was naked; I stepped inside.

"What is a D&D?"

"Descale and depilatory, sir. We are going to make you shine." Salim nodded and I stepped in. Spray heads on recessed tracks whirled around and put a fine mist on me. Then hundreds of tiny arms emerged and began to touch every part of me lightly. I think there must have been an anesthetic in the spray since the feeling was not unpleasant. They may have given me a tranquilizer too because I was neither embarrassed nor uncomfortable. The process took several minutes then a quick gust of wind whipped around me, and the tube's door opened. I stepped out feeling like a million credits! I heard a whistle and clapping as Salim examined the result, "Boy, you are looking mi-te-fine right now. Not a bit of your inner werewolf is showing."

"That would be inner Chupacabra to you, pal." I was led to the dressing room where a half dozen assistants fit me for an evening in Vegas. I was feeling good. Hmm. Way too good. Did they slip me some kind of mickey? "Salim, did they give me some kind of drug?"

"Boy howdy did they. Feeling great, aren't ya?"

I guess I really did. But a small part of me was complaining, Kip this is not real. People who hop-up on drugs so blithely are toxic and not to be trusted. Why do you think your Dads kept you away from people like this. And then I decided to take a card from Tom Cruise in Risky Business and say What the fewk!

In the mirror I was a much shorter version of Vagabond Bootblack, but with a color variety that lit up the night. My broad-brimmed hat was deep red, the trenchcoat was red and black corduroy, the shirt a long-sleeve silk striped indigo and gray with a solid bright red tie. My pants were black velvet with high-top black leather boots. I was the most expensive pimp in the world. Regardless, the style seemed to fit. Then came the glasses.

"Young sir, these beauties are from our Elton John collection and sport all the prosthetic integrations available on the market and even some which are, uh-um, not on the market if you gather my meaning, sir?"

He fitted them to my face and suddenly I was wearing the renowned classic style: the Elton John star shaped glasses. I loved them! I heard the sound of tiny gyros spinning up as the glasses formed to my face. I had a moment of dizziness and suddenly I could hear, see, smell, and sense things around me like Superman. I could see through walls and floors and pop-up notations and comments began to scroll and point at the various things in my field of vision. Then something more awesome. I could see all around me 360° without turning my head. The glasses gave me full hemispherical vision. It made me dizzy for a few minutes, but I was in love! And, to boot, my prosthetic was playing nice with me again and downloading the latest firmware updates. I was fully Online, and tears poured out my eyes as I felt a rush of homecoming; back to my former self before all this crazy train had left the station.

Salim was right there, "Whoa, woah, Kip, this is a good thing. What's with the waterworks?"

"No Salim, it's okay. I just got my prosthetic fully reintegrated and back to Online for the first time in a long time. I have been on proxy for so long I forgot what was like to have unrestricted Online access."

"Careful Kip, remember the Powers never sleep. If you give them a tempting opportunity one or more of them may decide grabbing you is easy pickins. If you trip some alarm, our time on this planet may be very short. With that Salim touched my glasses and a red wisp of something came off his fingers.
"There, I added Vor encryption to your connection. As far as anyone Online is concerned, you are not you."

"Wow, that was cool!" I subvocalized to the glasses and to my happy surprise they received my commands like my pad. I had them show me the Vor encryption protocols and I saw my own rule sets overlain with something extra. It was complex, beautiful even, and I looked forward to exploring the code later. I made a quick entry, instructing Banquo to start researching the Vor encryption.

We exited the haberdashery and took an elevator down several hundred meters to the street level. The glass front showed us the visual marvels of Vegas Above as we descended. The doors opened to a bustling sidewalk, and I almost ran into a pile of mud. It was two meters tall and was leaving a brown trail as it shuffled past. It brushed past me, and I was surprised when I didn't get a mud stain. It made a humph sound like I was unworthy of its notice, as it entered the elevator we exited.

After Mr. Mud went his way, Salim pointed to a group of cloaked people standing stock still, ten paces away, while everyone around was in motion. Everyone was ignoring them or perhaps couldn't see them. It was spooky how the space around them felt dead. Salim said to stay away from them. When I asked, he told me it was rumored they were found on every planet inhabited by sentients. Not much was known about them except they would abduct children occasionally. When they appeared, it was never good and only certain people could see them. The cloaked creatures were known as the Silent Clave.

He had seen pictures of the Clave, and he said these guys looked spot on. They floated. It was clear their feet weren't on the ground if they even had feet. They moved. Suddenly they were headed our way.

Salim looked terrified, "Kip, as a kid we were told stories about naughty children being taken by the Clave. The tales were parents' motivation to their wayward children. I had thought it was probably a myth. I'm no longer so sure. We need to go. Come on…now!"

I felt like my feet were bogging in a quagmire, like dream running during a nightmare. A frisson of fear swept over me as I realized they were slowing me down. Salim wasn't having it. He grabbed my arm and pulled me along. I heard a wheezing sigh from the cowled boogeymen. I think they were pissed. They kept coming, traveling through people and railings and unseen by anyone else. We went around a corner and ran for the giant stairway down.

We headed into Vegas Below, also known as Glitter Gulch. I thought my glow-in-the-dark apparel would stand out, but I bemusedly discovered I looked very average. Salim smiled, divining my thoughts and we walked across the plaza into the Gulch entrance of Glitter City Casino & Games. Like all the big establishments, they had entrances Above and Below. I knew we were here to hand over the figurines, but this was Vegas, man! I looked around and I got curious.

"Hey kid, it's going to take me a couple hours to set up our meeting, maybe longer. Why don't you go exploring and I'll give you a shout when it's time, okay?"

"Thanks Salim, I'll see ya in a bit!"

I lost sight of Salim, but my new nifty glasses kept him in visual range. Apparently, he could see me too, I heard Salim via my prosthetic, "Kip roam around but stay away from the flesh farms, okay? Too much trouble in those quarters. But, in general a wry truth is that Vegas is one of the safest places from the Powers. Just don't piss anyone off. Oh, and I added a couple million credits to your wallet so don't worry about expenses. Go explore."

Salim was like the coolest uncle in the world. Off I went. The flood of sounds and visuals was overwhelming for the first few minutes. I found an interactive map and brought it up on my pad, then I saw a giant interactive marquee with the same map, writ huge. I put away my pad and started poking at the touchholo to find my first adventure. I used both hands to rapidly navigate through popups, 3D maps and advertisements. Content would pop out to show me a rich view of any interest point. I pointed to a logo of a goat's head and discovered a place called Goat's Gruff on the next floor down. It promised a bobbin' fun time with goats. I loved goats! I went down an escalator and walked a giant mallway. The marquee had shown there were 14 levels to Glitter Gulch and each sported a spiderweb of interlinking mallways. Some areas had punch-through view to levels above or below and other places you could see all the floors, top to bottom from jutting balconies. I discovered the plants growing there were actually fungus. Some were green and appeared to be jungle plants. I felt a warmth from my satchel and knew my seeds were calling to me. I pulled out my spore encrusted Pachinko seeds and plopped a few into one of the capacious garden areas.

The size of this place was beyond belief. Using my now fully functioning prosthetic I looked up the population numbers for all of Vegas. There were 7 million residents and at the moment 14 million visitors. I used my glasses to see where Salim was; it was easy as pie to see he was sitting in the casino, playing at a crap table. I was overwhelmed: not only were there thousands of shops, but there were fancy hot dog carts, mobile henna trucks and other vehicles from which barking salesmen sold their wares. Some moved slowly through the press of people while others took up static positions. Like Vegas Above, I noticed the noise had a rhythm and harmony, almost like a living thing. Even the barkers blended in, as they each tried to stand out. Then on the right, Goat's Gruff came into view. I was excited!

A familiar tune was playing when I entered, and two goat-human synths were handling admissions and greeting people.

"We-e-e-e-lcome in!" even their words sounded goat-like. There were miniature mountains and valleys and dozens of goats grazing around. I paid the fee and put on the Schwingen thick cotton pants and shirt they provided and put my coat and boots in a wall locker keyed to my handprint. I took off my special glasses as well.

The pants were comfortable, but bulky and annoying to walk around in. Goat's Gruff looked to be several acres of space. I thought I was the only person here, then I heard a hoot 'n howl and I saw two kids riding goats, comin' 'round the mountain. Up and down the slopes they ran with the kids on their backs, yelling all the way. Those goats were fast! I saw each had a cute collar with names like Knüsel, Rüfenacht, Wicki and Schläpfer. I approached one named Käser and he nuzzled my hand. They were all hugely muscled and seemed to be real animals. Probably hybrids. Käser bumped me gently and I hopped in the saddle on his back. The pants had contact points and those snapped to the saddle like hand-in-glove. The moment I grabbed the bridle my goat took off full speed toward the first mountain. Up and down, we went, running, jumping, and sometimes flying across rock walls that no human could walk. It was scary how fast these things could run up vertical walls. Then I heard a faint ding-dong and a voice I could barely hear made some announcement. A moment later I saw in the lowlands the prowling wolves. The two other kids screamed, and I noticed they were still smiling. Up they came, wolves chasing the goats. More than a dozen goats were running pell-mell with wolves hot on their tails. A gray wolf was close behind me and my goat made several jaunty turns and ran up a rock face to escape. The wolf paralleled us on a gentler slope, keeping pace. It closed again and swiped at me. Those claws looked real! I saw one of the kids fall from his goat and plummet down. Three wolves converged and a shock of fear went through me. I should have watched the smile that never left the boy's face to know this was false danger. The three wolves executed maneuvers only synths could manage. The wolves caught the boy on their hindquarters and bounced him between each other, then with a final high arcing bump, popped the boy onto another goat. It was like a choreographed dance move. The boy roared with laughter. When I fell, I thought I might be too heavy for the wolves. Nope! Just like the boy I was bounced around by five of the beasties. It was squishy and exhilarating; the wolves were bouncy and stretchy.

I started to get tired and sore. Somehow my goat sensed this, and we flew down the hill and cantered toward the locker room. I hugged my goat because it felt like the right thing to do. For fun I fed a dozen of the Pachinko seeds to the goat and giggled at what might happen when he pooped them out throughout the Goat's Gruff mountains.

As I dressed, I noticed G-men outside the main entrance. They saw me and seemed uninterested. Then I noticed they were on guard duty for some dude in a reflective silver jumpsuit. He had matching metallic teeth. Was he a synth? I scratched my pits as I felt my chupa hair beginning to grow back in. So annoying. I put on my magic glasses and took a close look around me looking at the floors above and below this one with my x-ray vision. There were huge galleries with shops and other entertainment like Goat's Gruff. But more interesting, sandwiched between each level were service floors with fast moving mechanical things, pipes, and ductwork. When I looked at the Gruff mountains, they were riddled with hidden mechanical parts. I found the engineering of the goat attraction more fascinating than the goat attraction itself.

The Breuer twins bade me goodbye 'Goodbyyyye!' They really nailed the goat voice well. I passed by the G-men and the silver guy. Silver guy had a saturnine face which reflected a calm unconcern. He glanced at me and winked. He had warm green eyes that were familiar. I felt as if we'd met before. Then I slipped into the crowd to avoid any imperial entanglements.

I went to the closest marquee and looked for Thai restaurants. I needed some Phad Thai and fresh rolls! One gallery lower were a bunch of ethnic restaurants so I took the float tube down. Oh wait, I haven't mentioned about float tubes. A few years back someone discovered how to make things float. The military and civilian manufacturers used the tech to enable flying vehicles, but one of the ancient companies, Otis, used it to make mass movement elevators. I recalled Salim mentioning Vor technology gifted to humans. The anti-grav mechanism looked like a round metal plate. The same plates were used on drones, pit racers and ships like the Argo and Janussaries.

When you make a big version of the metal plate and stick it in a public place and surround the area of effect with a tube, you get a lift. The lift is a tube with the metal plate up top, set to some tiny percentage more than Earth gravity so when you enter you slowly rise, and the other tube has a percent less, so you slowly fall. The reason the system is rarely used for serious people moving is it leaves folks flailing like directionless Peter Pans. Anticipating this, tiny drones were employed to guide people in the tube; but it was slow going. It's not fast, but the novelty of it gives parents the chance to relax for a moment while their kids go flying up and down. The drones were programmed for child entertainment mode, weaving the squealing kids through a 3D ballet up and down the tube. If you don't want to hear squealing kids, avoid the tube. I won't even address the problem of a vomiting child; it's messy. On my float downward I saw an advertisement for Glitter Gulch narrated by the very man I had just seen outside Goat's Gruff; it was none other than Jazzy J!

As I made my way through the crowded esplanade, I thought about times my Dads had taken me to port cities like Singapore, Los Angeles and even Seattle. Float plates on the docks and freight hubs created lift and fall zones where objects as big as houses moved languidly as they were loaded on nautical and air ships. A drone escorted me in and out of the tube. As I entered the ethnic food wing of the lower gallery a riot of beautiful smells assailed my senses. But nature was calling. I found a bathroom; it was scented and boujee. A synth attendant offered me candies, cigarettes and vapesticks. I gave a big negatory on the lot and made haste to my lunch.

The Thai restaurant was spot-on authentic. I started with Phad Keemoa and mango sticky rice, followed by a chaser of Phad Thai with six stars and fresh rolls. I savored every bit as I broke into a delicious rolling sweat. Like my Dad, Vicky said, it's good for the soul to have food that bites back. After I ate, I used my fancy glasses to search by entertainment type for what else I wanted to see in the Gulch. Earlier I set my glasses to put a red marker on Salim's location. I was shocked when the red dot blipped off. On replay the dot was last active at the entrance of The Tenderloin. The popup showed the place to be adult entertainment. Oh gross. Later I learned more than I ever wanted to know about the place. On cue, a message dropped from Salim. I read it: Kip, come to the Tenderloin. Our meeting is in 5 minutes. So much for hours of playtime.

March 2257 – Glitter Gulch – Vegas Below, Las Vegas

I needed to move faster so I took a glass elevator up. Then it struck me, in so many other places synths are either forbidden or feared. Not so in Vegas. I wondered why and put a bookmark in it for later thought.

On the way I saw a crusty olde shoppe of stone masonry that had a shingle sign dangling over the iron braced doorway. It read Haecceity and Quiddity. There was something old and ominous about the store. I wasn't sure if it looked more akin to Ollivander's or Borgin and Burke's. So interesting; I earmarked it for investigation once I got done with our business. I wondered if they had chocolate frogs.

The Tenderloin was the preeminent brothel in Glitter Gulch. Jazzy J held a controlling stake in the business, but the proprietor of the Tenderloin was a crazy-haired looking woman named Phyllias, the Bird Queen. I read up on her via my pad as I went. One reviewer said the Bird Queen sells impossible dreams for intolerable prices, with a death's head grin of warm welcome. As I found out, Phyllias had a mercurial way with new people in her establishment. You never quite knew if she would love or hate you when you entered. If she loved you, you knew it immediately, and you could do no wrong. If she hated you, watch out! She might have you dumped in the Crinehole. Phyllias might have a face like a Rottweiler licking piss off a thistle as Cricket might say, but to her employees she was a goddess. Phyllias had the undying loyalty of her people, and she never allowed the marks, the johns, the clients, or the lookey-loos to harm her folks. In that event, they were summarily dropped in the Crinehole and never seen again. The Tenderloin had such a volatile reputation you might see people making the sign of the cross at the front door or perhaps the sign of soiled drawers if Phyllias was having a bad night. Phyllias fashioned herself as a belle dame sans merci like Vicky would say, but she in fact did have more mercy than she was given credit. As for the belle part she would never turn heads, except to frighten the children and shock the unwary.

I arrived at the entrance and as I entered, my nav went blank on both my pad and prosthetic. This place was heavily shielded and firewalled. There must be an extreme amount of nastiness going on here. Salim was waiting for me and filled me in, so I knew whom we were meeting. His name was Fast Eddie and was about as reliable as his name would imply. Salim said I needed to keep my mouth shut, for real. No words. None. I knew that would be hard. I reminded myself that if a Vor agent was showing heavy caution I ought to pay attention. But you know me, I never knew a rule I wouldn't find a way to circumvent. A huge guard in an expensive gray 3-piece escorted us to the rear of the Tenderloin. We whisked past small and large tables, chairs, couches, and dozens of reclining and uh -otherwise engaged people. By engaged I am sure you know what I mean. Delicious food smells were in the air, but my earlier lunch inured me to the scents. I caught more than one salacious look from human men, women and even a couple fuzzy hybrids. An archway over two massive steel doors read Piratbyrån. Our escort stood at the set of doors quietly and indicated for us to do the same. His name was Irving, and he was chiseled stone with a chaser of steel. He was so big he had his own gravity field, and so over-cologned I had to keep the furthest distance away or be overwhelmed. His baleful eyes kept me from wandering too far.

I heard loud voices on the other side of the doors; I could make out some of the words, "…and you know it's just Satan in a Sunday hat, Eddie!" The doors burst open, one narrowly missing Irving who jumped out of the way with unexpected nimbleness.

"No sir, that is not true. We will get every one of them and you'll see. Business will be right as rain by the morrow!" The man speaking was dressed like a used car salesman and the other looked like a southern preacher in a white suit. The man had a Bible clenched in his right hand.

"Cornelius, your mother sent me to try talking some reason into you. You don't want to do this –" Cornelius interrupted white suit man.

"Uncle Robert, shut the hell up! You know I'm Eddie now, Fast Eddie. Cornelius is dead and Mama is too late. I am on a roll and not gonna stop! Now, if you're not here to partake of my fine establishment's goodness then you bettah' get along before one of the girls eats ya!" Eddie mocked the other man's southern drawl, scooped a deep thespian bow then laughed uproariously.

Then Cornelius, aka Fast Eddie kicked the man in the butt and sent two of his goons to usher him out.

"Gentlemen, right on time, please come in!" Eddie turned a tight pivot and ushered us into the room as quickly as his Uncle was exited. I could see why Fast Eddie was a good name. It would be an understatement to say Eddie's office was sumptuous. It was packed with the most expensive and cushy, comfortable furniture. A huge neon sign over his Victorian desk read 'Jeremy Bearimy'. Hmm?

"Come sit. And let me do this…" He pointed and we sat on a thick squishy red couch that absorbed me like an amoeba. Eddie had a clicker in his hand, and he aimed it behind us and suddenly all sound from around us vanished and we were inside a sphere of haziness. The air didn't change but the view of the outside looked washed out. There was some kind of field around us.

"There! Now we are protected from snoopers. Salim, my friend! It is so good to see you!"

Salim smiled and appeared to be totally at ease, "Hey Behin. I see you keep up the ruse. Do you still think nobody suspects?"

"No way, my friend. I pay my actors well these days and Uncle Robert is the best of them. Suspects? Pshaw, is a frog's booty water tight?"

"Ah, always with the quip, Behin. Have you met my newest friend, Kip?"

"Why no, I haven't. Hello young mister. How do you come to my fine establishment?"

I replied, "I am Kip, pleased to meet you, sir." I looked in question at Salim.

"Kip, Behin plays with you. He has known your Dads since before you were born. In fact, he is one of your fractional genetic contributors," and then I was shocked. I have another Dad? By this time my ability to be shocked had blunted a bit, but this was surreal. How many people did they feed into my DNA?

He paused, so I asked, "Do you know why?"

"Why you have Vor genes in you? Well young hybrid, that answer would require I know not only how but why you were made. As it stands, I know some things about how Croatoan made you but the grand calculus of *why* remains elusive to all of us, your Dads included."

"Behin, here are the figurines. Notice how Kip fitted them together."

"Hmm, good job Kip. Thanks Salim. These will make their way to the next middleperson."

I asked, "What are these figurines going to be used for?"

"I have no idea. I might be the Terran Vor leader, but I frankly know very little. This is Croatoan's game." Behin hmphed.

I asked, "Who are these figurines going to?"

"Eventually, Croatoan. But he wants to keep his mystery wrapped in an enigma so the objects will be passed around according to some opaque plan. He is known as the Great Rebel to the COMBINE and to the Vor, he is most recently the architect of our liberation. As for the figurines, he hasn't shared his reasons."

As Salim and Behin made a few minutes of small talk I tapped on my pad and connected to a hotspot within the Tenderloin. I looked to see what kinds of mischief I could find in Vegas. I thought it might be a good idea to know a bit more about this place. It might be fun to bring back my Crew for some exploration.

Behin spoke, "Kip, when next you see your Dads, thank them for the advice."

I made a quizzical face, "Advice."

"Vor are highly conservative and judgmental. They also don't believe in stepping outside cultural norms. Your Uncle Salim and I are two males who care very much for each other. We see no issue with this except for the possible shunning we would engender were other Vor to find out."

Behin sat closer and spoke gently and full of wist.

"Your Dads showed us the way. I had hoped one day Salim and I could pay back your Dads for their guidance. Now we shall. How would you like to have a couple Uncles for your family?" Behin and Salim almost seemed afraid to ask the question. Two powerful aliens were afraid of what I might say. I was speechless.

Salim spoke, "It's okay Kip. We just want to help you."

They misinterpreted my silence, "No." Oops, they really would misinterpret that!

"I mean, no, I have no problems with being family. It's sudden but I would be honored. Should I call you my Uncles?"

"Most definitely!" they replied in unison.

"Okay, cool. What now?" I asked.

At some point the privacy shield vanished. Just in time a large amount of food arrived. How was I so hungry so soon? No worries, this hairy Chupa dug into the most amazing chicken marsala, fried zucchini and sesame salad. I was sipping on a peach bellini, non-alcoholic of course, and I heard a yell from beyond the door. Salim and Behin stopped their close personal chatting and with almost no pause jumped into motion.

Salim pointed and spoke in hushed tones, "Kip, there are Crith outside, go get behind the tapestry at the back of this room, now!" I looked dumbly at my new Uncles and Behin spoke more urgently, "Go now! Crith are merciless warriors. They can't be here for any good reason…go!"

I grabbed a bowl of grapes for a snack and beat feet to a hiding place behind the tapestry that looked like something Hieronymus Bosch painted if he did a beach blanket bingo death scene. The doors flew open, and five people walked in. My Uncles affected calm repose against the bar, sipping drinks.

"Hello friends, what kind of mayhem are the Crith up to today?" The group gathered in the couch pit and the privacy shield went up.

I started exploring for an exit. I didn't want to be seen, so that left me crawling like a bug on a rug. I literally was scrabbling, but to my great fortune I quickly found a small service door. I turned the latch, and a poof of dust almost got me sneezing. I stopped short of a blowout and kept quiet. Then, I had a thought. Here I have a glorious bowl of fruit munitions which were badly in need of smart trajectories. A part of me, the so-called adult part was saying no, but a bigger part was already in motion with the first delicious salvo. I know, my new alien Uncles wanted me to hide and probably for a very good reason. I just couldn't help myself. Since the shield blurred those inside, I had to guess on my targets' locations. After I chucked most of the bowl, I saw something flying my way. I dodged at the last second. It was a watermelon wedge splattering glurpy-like on the wall beside me! The privacy shield dropped, and 5 blurs moved to grab other food bits and suddenly I was in a food war. Those Crith were fast, too fast.

Abruptly, a face was right in my grill staring at me with a maniacal smile. "Little man, you are…" and with that pause I thought I was going to die, "…absolutely awesome, dude!" He sounded like a SoCal surfer.

The skinny tall, ghost white man with sharp teeth whom I was sure was an Anne Rice vampire scooped me up and moved me so fast everything became a blur. I landed in the couch area. His skin was cold to the touch; these Crith must be some kind of vampire race. I tried to catch my breath after flying across the room. I wasn't hurt, just surprised and breathless.

"You're Kip, son of the Dads. I am so glad to meet you." The man was almost as tall as Vagabond with a gaunt and spatulate face, sharp features, and the swagger of a surfer bro. He had fangs. "You know the Vor, good. I am Dave, a Crith, and it is fortuitous to make your acquaintance."

He asked, "How did you get to Vegas, my young friend?"

I looked at Salim and he gave an ever-so-slight head movement no. I guess I was supposed to make something up. Fortunately, I was pretty skilled at that, but sometimes the truth was a better rebellion.

My inner rebel emerged as my mister sarcastic voice took charge, "Good to meet you, Dave. Salim wanted me to hide from you guys. Am I supposed to be afraid of you?"

Dave stared at me and gave me a fangy smile. I kept my mouth shut for a moment.

Dave leaned ever so slightly my way, "Kip, you're sure you're not afraid of us?"

"Sorry to disappoint, but Salim wanted to give me news about my Dads and meet his friend Behin. And he was right that I would love Vegas. Now, I am curious what you guys were talking about."

He laughed and the other Crith joined him.

"Oh Kip, you are a shining example of humanity. You really want to know?" Dave paused, sat back on the plush couch, and mulled.

He began, "Okay, the truth won't affect our mission. Kip, your race has massive destructive potential to other races in your stellar neighborhood. The Crith are here to kill every human on this planet. Sadly, we are good at what we do. And the Vor think it's a secret that they keep samples of every prior race eliminated tucked away in their private zoo. Perhaps you humans will be their new specimens?" I looked at Salim and Behin. Nothing. No response to Dave's words.

"Dave, if I am going to die then my words to you don't matter much. Salim doesn't want me to be honest with you, but I will speak plainly regardless." Dave smiled and nodded.

I told Dave and his Crith posse my whole tale blow-by-blow from the moment I discovered Cheri's lab up to the present. I talked all about Croatoan, the figurines, Vagabond, my Dads and more. I could see Behin and Salim horrified at my spilling the beans, but Dave had gotten my ire up and I was on a roll. As I was speaking, I noticed I could see a red glow limning the Vor agents and a purply haze around the Crith. Cloud powers? Auras? Close to the end of my harangue, the red and purple around the aliens looked more golden in color. All of them. And they all had these doofy smiles; they looked to be somewhere between very high and unconscious. Ohp, one guy *was* unconscious. Guess my story was pretty boring. Whatever; they could jam all that where the sun don't shine.

As I concluded I realized I had been pacing back and forth and speaking with open hostility to the Crith agents. The Vor seemed to fear the Crith, but I sure didn't! Then I was done. Rant complete. I was sweating and out of breath. I sat, grabbed another bowl of fruit, and stared daggers at all the alien dickheads around me. The room was silent for a minute as I caught my breath. It sure took a lot of energy to stay mad. I had railed at these weirdoes for what seemed like an hour…probably less than 10 minutes. The doofy expressions were replaced by amazement. Then the Crith and Vor looked amongst themselves and broke out into laughter.

Dave spoke, "Salim, clearly all your secrets have been dumped out for us to see. I think I know why you love these humans. The power. The strength of their convictions in the face of their imminent demise. Amazing."

Salim and Behin had taken a seat with the others and looked at me with a nice knowing ya expression.

"Okay Dave." I accentuated the name and gave him a hostile stare, "wanna just get it over with and kill me now?"

"Oh no young human. We are way past that, now. I think it's time to tell you a little story since you were so kind to tell me yours. Sit back and listen." I took a seat and noshed on a dish of almonds.

Dave paused, took a sip of his coffee, and began, "The Crith like the Vor work for a group called the Cleaners. Once a race is tagged for elimination the Vor and Crith are scheduled to…" a sudden commotion outside the doors interrupted Dave's story.

"Seth, make sure we aren't interrupted, please." One of the tall white guys stood, indicated to the other three and they stepped outside. Things quieted down.

Dave mentioned, "Bad Wolf and Bangarang have a hit squad outside. My colleagues will redirect them as long as we need."

"Where was I? Oh yes, the Cleaners. They pay us to cleanse planets of offensive races. We don't question the whys and wherefores; we focus on our work. As soldiers, Vor and Crith are very good at their jobs. We were first contracted to begin cleansing your race back in your 20th century. The Vor made sure your planet was ravaged by war, reducing your overall population by a certain percentage. The Cleaners call it The Harrowing. Recently the Vor handed off the next steps to the Crith. The Reaving has begun and in a few years all, but a few token humans will be gone."

Dave leaned back and seemed to consider me for a moment.

"Kip, are you aware of the influence you exerted in this room a few minutes ago when you were telling your story?"

I had no idea and didn't care, "Perhaps it has to do with the Cloud?"

Dave pivoted at my random question with grace, "Ah, we come to it. You ask an apropos question, young sir. A little more story needs telling." I switched to noshing on candy corn and hard candy. I was gearing up for my second wind.

"Your folks called it Jungian Space since its existence was usually revealed via dreams. Then they renamed it to the Cloud, which, so you know, agrees with what the stellar community calls it. Human history is full of examples of shaman, magicians and gods using special powers. In fact, most humans can make some fractional connection to the Cloud during REM sleep. Even terrestrial non-human sentients, most of whom your race slaughtered had some measure of Cloud capability which COMBINE scientists amplified in recent centuries.

"For almost a thousands of years your race has been seeded and cultivated in the hopes it would someday join the COMBINE. Most races join and are productive members, but something happened which the Cleaners were made aware of, when they were given the task of eliminating humanity."

I asked, "Okay, then who is the COMBINE, and who are the Cleaners?"

"Too much to say, Kip. Suffice it that there are 124 races across our galaxy that have a Cloud-only government and connectivity. They use the Cloud in lieu of physical spaceships to communicate and transport themselves and materials. COMBINE is an acronym. And no, I don't know what each letter stands for. I'm a soldier not a politician." Dave smiled at that last bit.

"Enough of alien politics, for now. Let me tell you about you. Your Dads were contacted by Croatoan during a critical time in their co-development of fungal and synthetic neural networks. He has been on Earth in the shadows for a long time and recently realized his pet humans were going onto the chopping block. Your Dads and others were fed helpful information and guided to save as much sentient life on this planet as possible, without knowing much about the actual threat. You are the next step in that plan and your purpose stands directly athwart the mission of the Cleaners."

"If I were doing my job rightly, I would end you right now. But today something happened which you seem to be completely unaware of. You have reprogrammed our mission settings, or maybe I should say you removed the geas that enforced our mission directive. Understand, the Crith are fiercely loyal, highly obedient, and honor-driven to abide by our agreements with our employers. It is built into our genetics to obey."

Salim leaned over to Behin and whispered, "I sure didn't see this coming." Behin jerked his head and shushed Salim.

"Dave, what is your Crith name?" I was curious.

"I am Prak Tier, first of five in the 3rd ring of the Conclave of Tonak." Prak smiled and nodded.

I asked, "So, Mr. Tier, what do you mean that something happened here?"

"Kip, you have altered the course of destiny. I doubted you. I doubted what the Dads said would happen. I doubt no longer."

Prak went on to tell me how my magical little Cloud powers had just now released him and his team from the overlordship of the Cleaners. He also told me he would be recruiting others to my cause and asked what my first order would be. I told him I didn't believe him at which point he called his people back into the room. All five Crith stood facing me, cut open their hands and made bloody handprints on their bared chests while reciting something unintelligible in the Crith language. Frankly, it was frightening but exciting to watch. I preferred things a bit simpler like with my Lowlife friends. These guys were like having the Alucard and the vampire kingdom of Ravenloft saying 'hey, let us know who we can vamp for ya, okay'? All the while, the Crith were giving me toothy grins. I shuddered despite myself.

"Behin, now I've seen everything. Since when do Crith swear blood fealty to a human?"

"Salim, this is Croatoan's work. Kip is something very special. And for the first time ever, we may have a chance to break free, all of us. Maybe."

The doors opened to the suite and there stood a swarthy, gaunt man in a skintight tactical suit. He had a long rifle in his hands. The Crith and Vor froze, watching. The man spoke, "You are Kip, son of the Dads. I was sent to kill you for a generous sum, but it seems for the first time, I don't want to complete my mission. My name is Ix Oblivion, and I am confused. May I sit down for a moment."

I mutely gestured to an open couch, and he sat in a prim-proper (read: oddly rigid) way. The moment peaked when Ix put down his rifle, poured himself some water from a carafe and stated, "I am lost; can you help me." His eyes glazed over and he passed out. It was then I could see a faint aura of gold around the man. Could the day be any weirder?

March 2257 – Bakabi, Hopi Nation, Arizona Territory

"We can't just wait for him to get back. This is just like him to do something stupid like he did at the CENTER." Binky was livid and the note I had left her did nothing more than stoke the fires of her frustration.

Cricket walked out. Moments later he had decided for them. The roar of a car sounded from outside. Binky, Wogs, Peach, and Teddy jumped through the window and into the waiting muscle car. They took off at speed down the road and into the sky.

"Cecelia, that's the second car those kids have stolen. When they get back, I am going to have some words with them."

"We knew the gift of those cars was just fatuous altruism from that Croatoan fellow. Those cars were never meant for us, Timothy." Cecelia was half smiling, knowing the part they played in our lives was a chapter closing. "I never trusted that white guy. He always smiled too much."

"At least Cricket made our crops grow and kept our animals healthier than they had ever been. And those figurines made us more credits than anyone's ever seen. I guess if he's gone, he has left us amazing gifts. A car is small payment. I just miss our house full of children's voices and activity," Cecelia nodded knowingly to Timothy.

Timothy suggested, "Let's get a dog."

Cecelia gave him a consternated look and whapped him on the shoulder, "A dog? Watch what you ask for."

Right at that moment three marmots came through their kitchen door, chatting rapidly. They came up to the shocked humans and one of them spoke, "We are Pik, Pek and Pok. Kip said we could stay here until he got back."

Cecelia gave an I told you so expression to Timothy.

June 2207 – Planet Soran, Crith Homeworld

A dark planet under a perennial overcast sky. Soran was a place of rain. Clouds roiled and dispensed sheets while the winds buffeted in chuffing heaves. Vast canopies of trees directed the rain into rivulets and made mists for the understory. The planet surface was always in motion; even the plants and fungus had ambulation. Like sprites in the forest, young Crith bounded and played with abandon, exercising the vigors of youth. As dark as the skies painted the land, the spirits of the Crith brightened the forests and hills.

An endless game of tag, catch and release, fast running forms shot forward as balls of colored light, then manifested in physical form. On another world they might be called faeries, but on Soran, Crith youth were not yet set in their final physical forms, and they played constant experimental games with shapes and movement. Today, the celebration was the harvest time for the Brunda pods, Gonda buds and other sweet crops. The god of the harvest was Hul, progeny of the over-god Biru. Hul sometimes appeared and sent the young Crith into whirling tizzies of light and joy. On this day both Hul and Biru were unseen but could be felt close by.

Two Crith lay in the dewy grass beside a verdant pond, florid with plantlife and teeming with planktonic schools. They took the bipedal form favored by the elders. Other Crith were bobbing lights which swam with intricate patterns, taking forms which were more liquid than solid. When the gods were nearby all living creatures were caught up in their influence, and every one celebrated with all their being.

"Prak, look at this!" Sier held a hand-sized jelly floater in her hand. "It changes colors as I think about different things."

"Hey Sier, let's find a big one." The two ran in their tall lithe forms, sometimes on two, and sometimes on four legs. Their shapes were fluid and unset.

Crith youth remain unset for decades. But the Coali had plans which always brought an abrupt end to young Crith play. One day Prak and Sier found a cold and metallic obelisk, standing higher than the surrounding forest. It hadn't been there the night before and it didn't behave like a part of the forest. It was their first time encountering something unreadable, unknowable and with cold otherness. For the first time they knew fear. Despite the fear they explored the monolithic anomaly and eventually found an entrance inside. As they entered, a panel slid down, and they were cut off from the world.

June 2207 – Planet Soran, Crith Homeworld (Inside the ship)

"Hey, we got ourselves two more! That makes 300 for this run," An-Tirul considered himself the ultimate harvester of product.

"Tir, last run we had less than 200. This will be a record haul for us," Ul-Tomak smacked his secondary jaws then retracted them back. As a cold-blooded creature, he hated hunting runs. It was so cold on Soran. He longed for the whispering sands on his homeworld and the taste of freshly killed Duga in his mouth.

"As ship's captain I declare this hunt concluded. Let's go shred a couple Unna before we take off, in celebration!"

The two reptiloids ran on all fours down the corridor to the Sand Room. Wormlike Unna traveled sub-surface in the sands of their homeworld, but the sand on the ship wasn't deep enough. Unna couldn't escape far, nor dive deep; they were easy prey. The little worms made screeching sounds which enflamed the hunger of the two Bogan.

In the Sand Room, the Unna could hear the Bogan hunting. The room was almost 1000 square meters in size but there was nowhere to hide or escape.

'Ti, I liked our talk. You bring bright thoughts to my mind,' one Unna spoke to the other, mind-to-mind.

'Pa, your thoughts have been so clear and delicious lately. Did you save them in the cloud place for when we are gone?'

'Yes Ti, I always do. I also tasted some of those of Mu and Kir, our creche makers. So much joy they created when our brood group hatched. I miss them.'

'The Bogan come. I put my love into the secret place now. I'll see you in the afterward, Pa.'

The Bogan pounced on the two Unna, chewed once, and swallowed. Pa and Ti eased into weightlessness as their lights traveled elsewhere. They knew they were headed to see their ancestors in the AfterPlace. It was so beautiful and full of light!

June 2207 – Planet Arnn, Slavers Trade World

The rusty fat cargo ship made the transition through UnderSpace into low orbit around planet Arnn. A superstructure encircled the planet and made docking and moving freight a quick in-and-out. As their ship completed dock maneuvers, the crew tentacle coupled with the main airlock. As the two Bogan walked through they saw the other tentacle connect to the ship's hold. The Bogan were ecstatic as they watched little balls of light sucked from the ship into the containment facility.

"Hey, my friend, I see our credits adding up! Look at that haul!" Tir was doing a jig, celebrating the hundreds of Crith being sucked into the station's product bay.

"It's time to hit the Crabbitz Wing and strike it rich!"

"No Tom, that's garbage. You will lose our money like you did last cycle when we delivered all those Ampsudar pods to that idiot on Runa IV. Let's just get some fresh Vloac and get blitzed for the night," Tir had a sober expression that made Tom laugh.

"Alright my friend. Let's go find a couple Goonari girls and spend a warm night swimming in a Pupol Pool."

June 2207 –Slavers Ship, Freight Hold

The whirl of lights and sound resolved into small cries and a smell of death. Prak stared about him at the hundreds of Crith in the dim, musky steel room. Some Crith reverted to non-corporeal form, while others huddled together, sharing warmth and comfort. Later, all the Crith had become points of colored light. Only Prak and Sier maintained physical form as they stood and held hands.

"Sier, I didn't think this was the end. But maybe this is what Hul has decided for us."

"Perhaps this isn't the end Prak." Sier began to glow around the edges and in a moment was a shining point of bright green. Prak relaxed and joined her, becoming a red incandescent ball of energy.

Some number of forevers later the balls were whisked through a hole in the wall, down a plasticene tube, across a star field and into an enormous metal hold. There were thousands of Crith in both forms. As Prak and Sier became aware of the place, another of their kind informed them that Crith were dropped here, then taken away. No one knew where they went but they never came back. Dead Crith lay on the floor, pushed to the side with care, in corporeal form, smelling rotten.

A woman spoke, "The Crith who keep their light and don't get taken fade to nothing. We never see food and some of us just fade away."

Prak asked, "How long have you been here?"

She answered, "There is no sense of time here. I don't know."

The woman shifted into non-corporeal form and moved away without any of the warmth and leave-taking all Crith normally shared. This was a place without hope where Crith came to die.

Time passed and Prak was taken away. He never saw Sier again.

Something shocked Prak and forced him into physical form. Then he was strapped to a table and injected with chemicals and given electric shocks. He faded in and out of consciousness. Next, he knew he was dressed in a jumpsuit lying on a bed in what he learned was a barracks. His memory was hazy, and he had trouble recalling his life from before. A Contaxi came to his bedside and laid a hand on his forehead. With eyes closed, it put the standard geas on the Crith soldier candidate. The compulsion was designed to self-renew for the life of the soldier. Afterward, the candidates' training and preparation were managed by the Coali. Prak was one of hundreds of new recruits in training and was assigned as the first of five soldiers in the 3rd ring of the Conclave of Tonak. The 3rd ring had 5 groups and the Conclave had 5 rings. As a cohort they trained night and day. Strong and fast, their physical forms were made for war and their shape was set to that of their intended prey: human.

June 2252 – Slavers Ship, Delivery to Earth

Eventually graduation day came, and the cohort was ready for their intended mission: cleaner duty on a planet named Earth. They were designed to appear human, but had pasty white skin, and were gaunt and tall. They had retractable fangs, designed to rip and tear; their creators knew the sharp teeth would elicit terror in their prey. This batch of Crith were dubbed vampires mostly as a joke. The Coali found great humor in bringing to life a racial terror and setting that terror loose upon the race to be cleansed.

As the cohort departed, Prak wondered what it would be like to take the first human life. He had been designed to kill people, but he was given a hunger to eat them too. Would they be tasty? Prak was the first amongst equals in his Conclave. As such he was assigned headship over the whole Tonak Conclave after graduation. The meat was promising and Prak was hungry.

March 2257 – Glitter Gulch – Vegas Below, Las Vegas

After the unexpected declarations of fealty, Prak explained where they came from and how they were enlisted into service. Apparently, they still couldn't remember much of their early life but whatever I did to them seemed to have cracked that open a bit. I wish I knew what I had done.

The Crith hadn't yet started their work on Earth which would begin with assassinations of key people to incite all-out war. Then their cohort would systematically and increasingly turn up the heat of conflict. Humans would do most of their dirty work, but the plan was expungement of humans. They would have to mop up the final humans which they expected would take years. One bright piece of news: their endgame included preserving all other life on Earth. In fact, that was the reason the Cleaners didn't just glass the whole globe and be done with it. The Contaxi required all other life to be spared, which made the job much harder.

A second brouhaha came from outside the doors, but this time Prak and his people smiled and stayed put. The doors burst open with Phyllias herself walking in.

"Fast Eddie, this is the last time I am allowing you to hold court in my establishment. If so much as one more heavy-handed band of idiots comes through my doors looking for you, I will toss you down the Crinehole myself!"

From behind Phyllias came some faces I was somehow not too surprised to see.

"Kip, you old douchebag did you think you could ghost us again? Nope, not again! You have some 'splainin' to do mister!" Binky and Wogs were followed by Cricket, Teddy, and Peach. Phyllias seemed to approve of Binky. It was true, I had some words to share with my Crew. I looked about and saw laughter among the aliens. Adults, whether human or alien all had the same smug reaction to his Crew, like they were just cute and amusing. Right then, I wish I could revoke their alien green cards!

Phyllias was still standing at the door, hands on hips and hair poised helter skelter, red and sparkling. A hunched figure peeked out from behind the redoubtable brothel master. Phyllias screeched, she knew he was skulking behind her. She called out to him since she obviously had eyes in the back of her head.

"Hechombre! Come help me tell our guests about a little surprise we have for them," questioning looks brought laughter, throaty and sharp.

She continued, "Eddie, you, and your buddies have raised the alarm with both the B-gangs. Thanks to you we are on their radar, and I doubt even Jazzy can cool their jets this time. Seeing as this is your fault, my smelly mendacious mendicant has a toothsome treat for you."

Phyllias made a crowing bird sound as she grabbed the hunched man and threw him forward toward us. "Cotton-eyed Joe can show you the ropes."

Apparently Hechombre was the genius behind the Crinehole's construction and was in fact the operator of that feared contraption. The trick was you go down the Crinehole and you don't come back. Rumor had it the ill-fated people were morphed into something horrendous and made into slave labor.

An hour later Crith, Vor and humans were busying themselves at the bottom of the 70-meter drop that was the feared end of Phyllias' wrath. The Crinehole stank and was filled with rotted refuse. Apparently, it was also used as their garbage chute. It hadn't been cleaned in ages and the deep slop clung to anything it touched. At the bottom I realized why you can't smell the cesspit from up top: negative air pressure. The air flow was constantly coming down. The mess was piled high, and we shoveled, broomed, and pushed the mucky mess down the refuse ramps. Wherever the muck was dropping had to be some supreme nastiness and a long way down since I didn't hear a splatter. On another note, it was funny to see these powerful aliens all shoveling glock and dreck in the pit together. Oddly they seemed to be having a good time. Even my Crew had a good attitude about it.

"Cecelia said you had left out last night. Cliff was pretty sore you stole Black Betty." Cricket was shoveling alongside me.

"I bet. Aloha, the AI said it was okay and I figured that was enough for me." Cricket laughed and I caught him up on what had been happening. Binky and Wogs were close enough to hear. The aliens were keeping their own company, slogging like the rest of us.

The Crinehole's reputation was nothing like its reality, but some of the rumors were near the mark. The Crinehole was a portal to somewhere else. It was filled with garbage, true. And it was the home to a massive pit beast with big pointy teeth. Untrue. It was a portal to hell, nope. But where did the people go who were tossed down here? Out the muck chutes? Some said the destination was a slavers' flesh farm. I doubted that.

"Hey. What's up with Hellsing and the Bloodsucker Four?" Wogs was being observant. She had seen fangs, chalky skin, and their urbane charm.

"Like I was telling Cricket, these aliens have been slaves, just like those other two guys." I pointed to Salim and Behin. "Slim and Fast Eddie are Vor and the other five are Crith."

"So what's the deal? Are they expecting we are going to help them in some galactic uprising? We kinda have other things going on right now," Binky was being practical.

I replied, "I don't think we have to do anything right now. It sounds like they have their own business to attend to. Besides, if we're going to help our alien friends there is no way I'm doing it without Vagabond and the others."

Prak had disappeared soon after our descent. He came back an hour later with an interesting story.

"Kip, thanks to you I can convert to my wisp form once again, freely. Thank you. I followed one of the muck ramps to a control room and have the coordinates of the sending unit." Prak then looked at Salim and Behin, "It's Vor portal technology. Is this something you were aware of?"

Behin was using his Fast Eddie accent again, "No. I should have at least suspected, but no. I've been distracted with playing an imbecile. Did you see any of the settings on the control console?"

"I read Vor script poorly, but I think I know who did this and why. Better, I know where all the humans have been sent."

Behin spoke, "Kip, we don't know any more than your Dads about why you and your siblings were made, but I suspect Croatoan meant for you to help us." Prak and the others nodded. They looked so human when they did that.

Wogs' voice came from the other side of a stinking pile of goo, "Maybe we were meant to be superheroes! For myself I want the superpower to spontaneously create hot fudge sundaes." Wogs was on point with the comic relief.

Then I had a thought, "Behin, why did we come down here? Surely, we could do something more, ahem, savory than mucking Phyllias' Crinehole?" General laughter. I figured out the answer before I heard it.

"Kip, I still need to play the rôle I was assigned. Fast Eddie right about now would be screaming blue murder, complaining about the indecency of cleaning this pit. But when we came down here it became clear there was Vor technology involved. Now that Prak has confirmed the fact, we need to find out what's been happening." Behin looked to Prak.

Prak spoke, "Vor devices put off a specific EM signature. I believe the portal being created here leads to a location 48.72,-121.86, northwest of us."

I plugged those numbers into my pad's nav and it came up with <unknown>, followed by a different colored text meaning 'secret squirrel info' which read Park Butte Safe House.

The aliens were chatting amongst themselves while my Crew and I finished mucking the last of the goo. I had a thought and yelled, "Hey Behin, the sign over your desk, who is Jeremy Bearimy?"

Behin gave a laugh and came over to check on us humans. You know, the ones doing all the work.

"It's not who, rather it is what…you humans wouldn't get it, it's wibbly-wobbly timey-wimey stuff." And then he walked away laughing. A few minutes later we were finished and walked back over to where the aliens were standing around.

Behin was explaining to the Crith how the Vor had quietly been helping humans for a couple centuries and how the word had slowly spread to the other Vor on Earth. Some bought into the rebellion while others took the opposite view and would kill any suspected traitors.

A voice came out of the shadows and up walked Hechombre, "Hi friends! Do you like my new look?" Hechombre did a little spin.

Then his voice got deeper, and I recognized it.

"Hey kids, look closely. You know who I am." He waited, then spoke, "Okay, take a sniff."

I thought Hechombre had stayed up top. How did he get down here so quietly? Take a sniff?

Binky spoke, "Pal, I have no idea. But you sure don't strike me as a friend of ours."

"Fine, you need another proof…hear my words," he adjusted himself then spoke authoritatively, "I speak an invitation to understanding rather than painting my conceptions over yours…now, who am I?"

All four of us chimed at the tops of our lungs in excitement, "Vagabond!"

"Yes, yes. So glad you see me, my friends." We rushed to hug him, but the smell made that a short-lived gesture. We backed off, to a safe breathing distance. Even in the Crinehole, his ripeness was rich. You really had to smell bad to make the Crinehole smell passable.

"How are you now a small Hispanic man?" Wogs asked.

"Hechombre is my surrogate. I pay rent for me to inhabit his body at certain times. Don't give me that look, young lady." Binky's face had soured. "This is a favorable business arrangement from which Hechombre pockets millions of credits. You might say he is an enthusiastic partner." Hechombre nodded profusely which looked nothing like any expression Vagabond would make. Binky didn't seem convinced, but she kept quiet.

We had a few minutes of reunion before Hechombre / Vagabond got down to business with the aliens.

"Prak, Salim, Behin, friends. Pilgrim alerted me to your presence on Earth a while back but until Kip opened the door, I wasn't able to locate you. Behin, you were right under my nose the whole time! Do you know who I am?" Hechombre's tone, his posture and demeanor had changed so that it was impossible not to see Vagabond standing right there. He was dressed like a rumpled jester, with his cap and bells looking worse for the wear. And he was not skinny and black, but stocky and Hispanic.

Behin replied, "Come on, who hasn't heard of the redoubtable Vagabond Bootblack. Or shall I call you Oloiboni Olonana, the savior of synths? You do know it was your race's creation of synthetic life that triggered us coming here, right?"

Chapter 12 – ON MISSION

March 2257 – Glitter Gulch – Vegas Below, Las Vegas

Hechombre explained the Crinehole was originally designed as a portal to help exit key government leaders out of the limelight. He said Phyllias was paid handsomely to keep Hechombre in her employ and the Crinehole in operation. She didn't know all the details and had no idea Hechombre was in-charge of her contract. She played a dramatic role which few knew about. She would get a weekly list of times and identification of candidates who would at the appointed moment walk into the Tenderloin, make trouble and she would have them consigned to the Crinehole with flair and flourish.

I told Vagabond we knew the portal led to Park Butte; he appeared proud of the fact I knew.

"I heard Prak made the discovery, and you identified the coordinates. Good job!"

March 2257 – Crossroads, Nevada

More people were joining the Liberation as it picked up pace and there were many more successes than failures. Whole cities and communities were being freed and revitalized. The CSA, Baltic States and others were losing ground. The addition of the aliens and non-human terrestrials to the mix lent strength to the Liberation. The Vor were already helping Vagabond and his folks. Now the Crith had joined in. Up till now me and my Crew had been busy with our Hopi family. I figured we were about to rejoin the Liberation. We had a big confab of leaders at place called Crossroads in Nevada.

The four of us were glad to jump on the bandwagon of our vagabond life, again. After our years in the Hopi community, we had grown up…mostly. And with our new maturity came responsibility that I was still of a mind to shirk. At least a bit. I came to understand that the aliens, Lowlives, Vagabond and all the other rebel scum were under my command. Right, I wasn't ready for that.

I immediately assigned lieutenants amongst those who were present at our meeting.. For the most part, the same people who were leading before were doing so again. My leader council consisted of Elder Tala, Vagabond, Rus, Cicero, Nines, and now adding Prak, Flu Cat, Pooka and Salim.

That gave me room to do what I liked best. Traveling around and finding new friends. But now we weren't the Fab 4 anymore, we had become the Fab 6. Teddy and Peach were with us, and we were using the Vor tech to be forever undetected Online. It was time to ride again and do what we do best.

Another cool thing was we had a dispatcher. We found out that when Argus died, he actually didn't. He was an immortal and he Cloud regenerated. Recall when Argus had fed memories and knowledge into Cricket back at the LA:CENTER? Cricket was given incredible insight which was now beginning to emerge. When the three old gods, Kris, Mike, and Arthur added their cocktail of psionic ability and knowledge into Cricket's head, it addled his brains. His mind was only now clearing. But in the last few days, Argus was in constant contact with Cricket and through him, each of the other three of us. Argus even joined the farspeech classes and helped CloudKip manage the constructs for the worldwide school. What I didn't know then was there were even a few Vor and Crith joining as well. Crith were naturally Cloud connected and their transformative powers derived from the Cloud. The Vor never had Cloud powers, until they came to Earth. Now almost a dozen Vor were part of the Cloud classes. CloudMe was overjoyed! Prak mentioned our classes were similar to how the COMBINE eventually formed, long ago. He said it made him thankful that humans were getting their act together, but it also made him wary that humans not go the way of the COMBINE.

I found out about the aliens in class when CloudKip called, "PhysiKip! They're real aliens in class now! This is so cool. Thanks for referring them!"

I pretended I knew what he was talking about and I was secretly jealous that he was getting all this time with our alien friends and Hopi family. Then there were our two new adds to the Crew: Teddy and Peach. They had rapidly growing abilities and excelled in kinetic skills. Peach could easily lift tons of stuff or do something silly like pour a swimming pool over our heads. That was a rough day. Teddy could coax the truth out of anyone. His grasp of mind-to-mind powers was scary good. Now, we were ready to take on the world. Or were we?

We had a mission. Vagabond and Argus conferenced. Oh yeah, that was when I found out Pilgrim had been tutleing Vagabond in Cloud power use. Argus downloaded a poop-ton of info to Cricket, and he shared the mission details.

Then I thought of something, "Guys, I think we are expected back in Hopi land."

Wogs replied, "Nope. Got it covered. I let Cecelia and Timothy know that we wouldn't be back for a while and that Peach and Teddy were coming with us. There was some him-hawing, but they understood and promised to spread the word."

March 2257 – Glitter Gulch – Vegas Below, Las Vegas

Then it struck me, I have now left my home twice. A sharp pang flashed in my gut, and I tried to hide it. My Crew gave me the hand on shoulder support for a moment. Then I was all good again. We returned to Glitter Gulch for a meet-up with our two favorite Vor, with Eddie back in persona again. As we walked back into the Tenderloin, Phyllias greeted us like we were her own kids. Her hair was still Shockheaded Peter style, but her wardrobe was immaculate. She hugged us all and told us to warm Eddie that he was only one step away from a quick flight down the Crinehole if he didn't mind himself. We walked into Eddie boudoir and were greeted warmly by both Vor and Hechombre. At the moment, Vagabond was absent from his surrogate.

Behin asked, "Human Crew! I just got a text from someone named Argus. He said he works with you. Do you know him?"

Hechombre spoke, "Argus is our information guy. What did he say Behin?"

"He said for the six kids to head to the Rutting Duck. There they need to meet with either of the owners, Onion Robbins or Powdy Foddy. One of those guys would get them setup to go save two important liberation team members. Argus also told Kip specifically to not judge the two people he was being sent to save."

Am I judgy? Wait, I thought I was a cool dude.

Cricket saw my crinkled brow and spoke to me sotto voce…which meant everyone heard it, "Kip, you're a good guy but…" My own best friend was having to choose his words?

He continued, "Argus just means you tend to urp out a running dialogue in your thoughts. And some people read those and aren't so kosh about em. Got me?"

I got it. And I decided to put up a screen in my mind against outsiders. I just wasn't sure how to do it. I decided to bookmark that and ask CloudKip's advice.

We bade goodbyes to our Liberation colleagues. Next, I took my Crew on a tour and on our way we stopped at Goat's Gruff to have some riding time. To my surprise, the seeds I had fed the goats had already started sprouting in a lush carpet all over the lower landscape. It didn't seem to matter to the hybrid goats or synthetic wolves. And the low foliage made for a smoother slide if a rider fell off. The synths running the joint didn't seem to notice.

Next, I wanted to take everyone by that Diagon Alley place, um, whatits name. Quid? Hmph, I pulled up the Gulch map on my pad and sorted it by alpha. Aha! Haecceity and Quiddity. As we surmounted the escalator the stonework façade, and heavy brow'd cornice showcased the Scottish styling of the store. It stood out as starkly different and ominous from its neighbors. Back on the moors, or on a far-flung barren mountain top, this façade would be right at home. Through the front windows I could see kilts, blankets, and Scottish clothing on display. We went in and as the door shut, the din of the Gulch stopped. It was dead quiet. My Crew gave me the look of are you sure this is a good idea? Wussies. Oops, I tried not to think that too loud. A quick check I could see Cricket was shaking his head. Okay, I needed to move my mind screen task to the top of the bookmark pile.

The store was densely filled with racks, drawers, and shelves with all sorts of Celtic clothing, toys, jewelry, crystals, and knickknacks. A brogue-rich voice welcomed us, "Ai my lads and lassies, good to have ya come in. Would ya like to have some shortbread?"

The man was sporting a beautiful kilt with sporran, the front-facing purse and a paddy cap. We each took a shortbread cookie and munched away.

"Please come see my personal invention. I was hoping somebody would stop by today to see what I made. By the way, I am John Dunsmuir, the proprietor. Who are you fine children?"

We introduced ourselves as Mr. Dunsmuir took us deeper into his store, through a small doorway into a workshop area. There were desks, workstations, and countertops with various mechanical parts. He took us to a machine decorated with fancy tile artwork. All the way, the man chatted incessantly. He commented and lightly touched several things on the shelves and tables as he went. We arrived at an upright closet structure that looked like a cross between Dr. Who's Tardis and the D&D from the haberdashery. It stood over 2 meters tall and had an upright operating table inside.

Wogs asked a question, "Sir, did you make those tiles yourself?"

"I surely did young miss," the man paused, "In fact, these are Life Tiles, Penrose tiling. Very special. The design came in a dream to me one night and when I woke in the wee hours I quickly jotted it down so I would recall the next day. The electronics design work appears strikingly similar to the tile work. Another gift from my dream. Beautiful, aren't they?"

In a dream? My suspicion piqued. I was curious, "Sir, in your dream did someone show the design to you?"

"Curious question. A tad prying, but yes." Mr. Dunsmuir went on to describe Croatoan to a tee. I wondered how many humans had been influenced by that alien.

"I call this the Elucidator. It allows you to see your unconscious memories and dreams as bright mind pictures. I have tried it and it helps me when I need to meditate or calm myself before bedtime. Would one of you like to try?"

Surprisingly, Cricket stepped forward into the Elucidator. He had a lopsided grin.

Mr. Dunsmuir closed the door and tapped a few keys on the control pad. Kinda cool, he was using an old keypad from the 20th that made satisfying clacking sounds with each key press. There was an upright table in the closet with foot stops. Cricket stepped on these and laid back. The table pivoted to about 45 degrees. The man clicked a final button and suddenly there were a half dozen holos projected all around the closet for us to see. Cricket laughed as one scene showed when he filled his parents' petrol car with the water hose and proudly telling them their car was gassed up! Another showed when he brought home a box of kittens which he kept in his bedroom. He kept them secret, then a couple days later, he came home from school to discover they had gotten out and pee'd all over the living room carpet. On and on, memories and dreams sprang up and vanished. The holos appeared as if professionally captured. Cricket's eyes were closed, and a slim smile spread across his face. Peach and Teddy laughed with us, seeing some of our early history on display.

Then the holos shifted. There were scenes from more recent times. We saw his adventures in LA: CENTER; we caught him staring at some of the hybrid girls during the mass exodus and I saw a scene with Argus as he died. The next holos were more constrained. I guessed these were dreams instead of memories. There were scary dreams and meandering boring ones, but a theme began: Binky. Increasingly, the dreams showed Binky. Riding a bike, or on a skateboard, some were memories because I recall being there. But regardless, both dreams and memories centered on one person, our own Binky. Wogs and I stole glances and saw Binky's face was carved stone. Peach and Teddy had backed up a couple steps, not sure how to process what they were seeing. The dreams became more directed: walks in the Lake Stevens park, climbing the tall trees north of town. Then came what I feared, the first kiss. It continued, the holos of kissing and intimacy. Cricket wasn't awake. I could see him sweating and twitching on the table. One of the holos was about to go a step further as clothing began to unbutton. Binky darted forward and yanked the Elucidator door open. It broke something and Mr. Dunsmuir gasped. But he wasn't mad, embarrassed rather.

"Oh, precious me, I am so sorry. I should have stopped it. I apolo –" His apology was interrupted by a yell.

Cricket bounded out of the closet, his face red. He pointedly avoided Binky and stalked out the front door of Haecceity and Quiddity.

Cricket was deeply in love with Binky, and he had just been outed in the most brutal way. I thanked Mr. Dunsmuir, stole all the rest of his shortbread and we exited a minute after

Cricket to give him a good lead. There was no conversation, we just walked. What do you do with something like that? Childhood friends grow up eventually and adult themes germinate. How do you transition to adult friendship smoothly when one of your cabal is in love with another?

Binky and Wogs followed me, and I continued a couple steps ahead of them. I told Peach and Teddy to give us some time and they sped ahead to meet us at the Rutting Duck.

Cricket had been revealed in his deepest feelings. There would be no anodyne to balm his bruised soul. I wondered if it was just embarrassment. Was Cricket afraid? If so, that was unusual. Cricket was not the fearful type. My Dad, Charles, said fear among higher trophics, serves to underscore the cost of action and cement memory of past outcomes. I hoped Cricket wouldn't let the cost of his exposure run too high. I was worried.

We headed to the Rutting Duck which was on the edge of Vegas Above. I hoped Cricket would be there. I wouldn't blame him if he hightailed it back to Hopi country; I probably would do that.

The lights, parties, glam and glitz were palled by the raincloud over us three. Without words we walked through our private little downpour, brooding over seeing Cricket in a few minutes. It was weird, I wanted to see Cricket soon and simultaneously dreaded it. So, which was it? Did I want to see him or not? We walked under rangy tall 3-leg walkers, rain zeppelins, through lines for shows and crowds around street buskers and magic acts. A flock of fast moving BubbleBikes zoomed past us. I guess we could have taken an AirCab, but walking helped cool our jets and gave us time to reflect.

None of us used our farspeech. It was a time for privacy. As we rounded yet another towering arcology we passed through the city wall and the desert appeared before us. A half klick away was a ranch. My pad confirmed it was the Rutting Duck. Dust curled around our feet and swirled in eddies in our wake. We skirted the livestock fence and came in sight of the main establishment. It was a multi storied, enormous ranch house. People, cowboys, ranch hands and others were busy about their day, but one figure stood leaning against a pillar on the front porch. He had a stalk of grass in his mouth, chewing, regarding the sky. Peach and Teddy were nowhere to be seen.

Binky had Wogs and me stop.

"You guys. Can you give us a few minutes?" Binky had clouded eyes, holding her deeper thoughts to herself.

We both replied, "Yes. Of course." Wogs and I sidled over to a ranch hand who was saddling up horses. Cricket had taught us how, so we pitched in. The guy didn't object, and it got us busy doing something other than staring at the other two.

Binky walked slowly toward Cricket, making no hurry in the moment. She stopped a dozen paces from him and stood considering something. After a few moments a small voice began with words, only a whisper. As her voice continued, the refrain became clear and rang on the air with a growing strength. The dulcet notes were as pure as any ever sung. Binky stood there singing to Cricket.

Oh, Danny boy, the pipes, the pipes are calling

From glen to glen, and down the mountain side.

The summer's gone, and all the roses falling,

It's you, it's you must go and I must bide.

But come ye back when summer's in the meadow,

Or when the valley's hushed and white with snow,

'Tis I'll be there in sunshine or in shadow,—

Oh, Danny boy, Oh Danny boy, I love you so!

Binky sang loud enough for Cricket but not so much that Wogs and I could discern words. But we knew the song. We stopped working and noticed others had done the same.

Despite the soft tones, Binky could be heard from a long ways. Ranch hands stopped mid-work, cowboys turned to watch the two kids and even the animals moved toward them in the livestock pen.

> But when ye come, and all the flowers are dying,
>
> If I am dead, as dead I well may be,
>
> Ye'll come and find the place where I am lying,
>
> And kneel and say an Avé there for me.
>
> And I shall hear, though soft you tread above me,
>
> And all my grave shall warmer, sweeter be,
>
> For you will bend and tell me that you love me,
>
> And I shall sleep in peace until you come to me!

The last refrain grew in volume but didn't lose an ounce of sweetness. Binky stood in the same place as she sang. Near the last, Cricket began walking toward her. As she hit the last high notes, a frisson of pure beauty washed over me. There was no way my eyes were leaking. With the last three lines he gently took her hands. The song finished, and a hushed anticipation gripped the many onlookers. Only the wind could be heard as silence fell. Tall, gangly Cricket was standing over the elfin, shy girl. I could see her face was looking down. His right hand carefully lifted Binky's chin. They shared a smile. It was a moment held in suspension that lasted forever and registered indelibly on my mind. Then he bent over and kissed her. Binky's arms wrapped around him, and they embraced.

Applause and cheering erupted all around us; it was deafening. But Cricket and Binky were alone on their own island. Wogs and I hopped into the saddles we had just secured and cantered our horses near the lovers. Cricket and Binky eventually looked up and I realized we weren't kids anymore and I loved my friends more than anything in time and space. I was now obligated to seal the moment for all time.

"Enough smoochy, smoochy. Wogs and I saddled these for you. You need to hop up and get outta here before someone charges us for 'em!" Wogs snorted at my comment and followed suit as we both jumped down and ushered our friends up.

Lacking anything to say, they turned their mounts and rode off. On cue, a man came out of the ranch house yelling, "Hey, you kids. You're stealing my horses!"

The man was dressed like a rhinestone cowboy. I tried unsuccessfully to not laugh. I failed. I told him I wanted to buy his horses to which he said I didn't have enough credits. I insisted and he pulled out a mobile POS and scanned my pad. The price was steep, but I didn't care. I told him to add three nights for the newly minted couple and the four of us stragglers. His dismay turned to a joyful welcome and we were suddenly attended by a cloud of cowboys and hands and ushered inside. Peach and Teddy had already been inside. They witnesssed Binky's serenade, as well.

After paying for Binky and Cricket's honeymoon suite our host made sure a CowboyDrone caught up with them to help them get settled.

For the next couple days, the four of us lived high on the hog and spent Salim's credits. This time our Piña Coladas were not virgin. When I made arrangements for Cricket and Binky in a bungalow, I discovered it was indeed the Honeymoon Suite. Lucky them! We didn't see them until the third day, as I rightly expected. When they returned, they were walking hand-in-hand unashamedly. Things were different, yet they were the same; closer, more comfortable. It was an adjustment made, correcting for something which had been slightly out of sync.

"Yo Kipper, thanks for the nice digs. Cricket liked the vibrating bed…again and again." She laughed at my horrified expression. Cricket had the decency to blush. Wogs just shook her head and snorted.

During the past few days, I got to know Onion Robbins and Powdy Foddy. Both were salubrious and solicitous hosts, and we ate dinner with them the first two evenings in their private dining suite. Their interior décor was like being on safari in Africa. A lot of big game animal heads on the walls and displays with photos and racks of guns in a quantity that would make any prepper proud. We were advised to get moving on our assignment by Argus and Mr. Robbins arranged our ride to Phrine's Flesh Fair.

That third evening Cricket and Binky joined us at dinner with Robbins and Foddy. With all six of us together it was like old times. Peach was sitting next to me, and Teddy and Wogs sat with each other, swapping stories. Teddy was the life of the party as usual, leading with his high-octane comedy and vicious jibes. Our hosts fed off our exuberance and added to the fun by parading in various animals they were proud of and people who had a trick, story, or performance to offer. When the band struck up tunes from the 20th, we joined in. Cricket jumped on a Cajón, Wogs found a Mandolin, Binky grabbed a 12-string Yamaha and I found a 6-string Strat. We jammed! We were rusty, but the band, they called themselves Rub a Dub and majored in classic rock. They carried us for the first few, through Goodbye Yellow Brick Road, Back in the USSR, More Than a Feeling, and Let's Dance. With the Bowie song we got our groove on and bounced around as much as we played. Then Cricket got a notion and led off on the next set with Ghost Riders in the Sky, Mountain Music, Jolene with Wogs and Binky doing a sweet harmony, and the classic of classic, Friends in Low Places. We took a breather after that. The cafeteria had filled up with people; from the looks of it, this was a big turnout.

"You and your band want to came play here again, your stay will be on the house or at least at a reduced rate," Mr. Foddy was excited with his alcohol sales and full house.

The next set was about Binky and Cricket. The lights came low as the Rub a Dub piano player started us off with Stardust and Binky matched him on the intro. We continued with Seven Bridges Road, Riders on the Storm, Just Like Heaven, and ending with Will The Circle Be Unbroken. The last was sung acapella and every voice in the audience knew the Carter classic by heart; in fact everyone stood as if it were the national anthem. After that, there were cheers and hoots and me and my Crew retired from the stage. The night continued until the wee hours when finally, we toddled off to bed. Cricket and Binky vanished to their bungalow and Wogs, Peach, Teddy, and I went back to our own rooms.

The morning came early with a pounding on our door. Foddy and his band of hombres were saddled up and I saw Cricket and Binky were among the group. Peach had already been up and was looking beautiful as usual. Teddy dragged himself from bed and Wogs and I got ready quickly as we could. We hopped onto waiting horses and off we went. It felt like the beginning of a western movie from the 20th. The cowboys set out at dawn toward the horizon, ready to challenge the bad guys. We went over a hill's crest and the Rutting Duck went out of sight. For many miles we could still see the arcology tops of Vegas, but eventually those vanished in the dust. I realized I never got a chance to ask about the name, Rutting Duck. Hmph, gotta bookmark that one.

Late in the day, the ride was over. Hoss, the lead man said we would camp this evening at Crossroads. It was a different crossroads: little 'c'. It was a cheery place; a green patch in the middle of the dusty brown. The posse had brought camping supplies and I helped get a fire started. Wogs went to find wood and Cricket and Binky set about making dinner. We could see the oasis, replete with trees and greenery surrounding us and active with animal life. I looked for whomever we were supposed to meet but it became apparent we were going to be waiting. I dropped some Pachinko seeds near the spring. I never seemed to run out of the seeds. Maybe they replicated themselves. All I knew was I heard a faint 'thank you' every time I seeded a new area, and it made me feel warm and comfortable. I decided not to think too much about it.

At the crossroads, there were no roads. But there was a road sign, nearby. It showed 73km to Ottenby, 43km to DevNull, 19km to Ravenholm, 221km to Winona naka Beachside, 426km to Þeodisc, 631km to Slab City, and Boomtown 22km. A crossroads with no roads? Also, was there a beachside nearby? I asked Hoss and he said it was a ritzy private resort. We got our tents set up before dusk and Cricket erected the tripod for the cauldron Hoss' guys had brought. Hoss was a stoic man. He sat whittling on a piece of wood.

Mr. Foddy gave us some background on Phrine and his Fair last night. We were supposed to be at the Fair tomorrow and I was nervous. We were to meet the Ringmaster himself,

Phineas T Phrine. Quite a dubious name. Phrine's Flesh Fair sported immoral, unethical, and inhumane freak shows. Two friends of the Hopis were the main attraction. Nuckalavee and Nuertsumshy were ancient underground deities. On my pad I found mythological notes about Nuckalavee. It originated in the Brithish Isles, while Nuertsumshy was from the Yukon territory. I was unable to find anything about that one.

Today, they were captive performers, held as enslaved chattel for the enjoyment of jeering crowds. Mr. Foddy had confirmed what I was told by Hechombre (Vagabond). I had promised Vagabond to get them freed and back to Bakabi. Our inside contact was a man named Shylock Istvan. We had to find a way to meet him without alerting Phrine. Apparently Istvan had a plan, and we were to follow his instructions. My stomach curdled and despite the delicious smells coming from Cricket's pot, I wasn't in the least hungry. It was unlike me to be nervous before a mission. As the daylight faded, Hoss said he was heading into a local tavern for some food and booze. Off he went with his boys, leaving us to our little tents.

"Kip, you know the Akubra Droving Route is not too far from here? It would be kinda cool to go see the herds." Wogs was the master of local lore, wherever she went. But, I had no idea what she was talking about.

I thought for a moment: what have me and my Crew been doing all these years? I mean, the Hopi have been an amazing family to us, but when had we ever taken a break as a group? Okay, the Rutting Duck was like a vacation, but maybe I mean we hadn't had a recreational adventure since Lake Stevens.

"Hey Wogs? Let's do it."

"What, now?" Binky and Peach perked up when they heard me.

I replied, "Wogs has an idea. Let's go look at something."

Teddy asked, "Can I just stay here? I'm tired."

Wogs spoke and nudged Teddy, "Come on, you silly goose. It's not like we're beholden to wait for someone who is late or for a bunch of drunken cowboys to return. Let's go see!" Teddy silently agreed.

Cricket asked, "See what?"

"The Akubra Droving Route!" Wogs jumped up and down like she was a little kid again.

Cricket gave me the warning look, "It's probably a bad idea, brosef." Cricket was trying on new lingo. Brosef sounded a lot like Teddy.

We saddled up, and off we went. The horses were not so happy about hitting the trail at night, until we gave them more carrots and sugar cubes. Suddenly they were all in. Our ride took us eight klicks to the west where a cliff edge looked over a large plain. Below us were several encampments and an enormous herd of cattle, even bigger than the pictures from the old west.

End of evening, nocturnal twilight came. Then above we saw a dim flash in the sky which became brighter and more distinct. Not stars, not aircraft, nor the moon. Something else was coming into view. Luminous green like Northern Lights, the spectral cattle became clearer and came closer our direction. It was a ghostly stampede being driven by equally diaphanous riders. The cattle were large, menacing and sported bright red eyes which gave off an eerie smoke and haze. Cricket asked Argus what we were seeing.

Cricket re-broadcast Argus' answer so we could all hear.

"You see before you a memory. The land and sky bore witness to the momentous movement of beasts and Fae, thousands of years ago. Some part of them lives even now, mostly unseen except by a few who are touched by the magic. The manifestation is part in the Cloud and another part is within the æther about which I sadly know little. These memories are brief but usually quite powerful to behold. Oh, remember to wave; it would be impolite not to."

Five mounted cowboys (cowfae?) waved as they passed by, driving the phantasmal herd of demonic cattle. We made sure to wave back as they passed close overhead. One rider came closer and cantered to a halt near us.

'*Amigos, ride with us for a few miles,*" the Cowfae was a skeletal hombre swathed in green flame and limned in blue witch light. We were entranced, but not afraid. All six of us wore wicked 'hell yes' smiles. Teddy yelled, "Ohhh, yeah! Let's ride!"

And so, we joined the Cowfae Drove. The Cowfae turned his steed and galloped along the ridgeline. We came close beside him and our horses limned in blue, like his. I saw my whole Crew was lit up as well. My heart's exhilaration was deafening.

'Look up amigos. Let's catch the Crew,' he said Crew. Just like us!

The Crew, his Crew, suddenly got closer and I realized our horses were no longer on the ground. I looked back and saw green fire encompassing us all, and we and our horses had taken on skeletal forms. Wicked smiles painted every face and Cricket called out 'Yee hawww," Binky, Peach, Teddy and Wogs yelled back. We must have been moving fast as an airplane as the ground below us rolled rapidly by.

'Kip this may be the only time I can tell you this. I'm glad you came here. The veil between worlds is thin in these parts and we ancestral Fae don't see this side very often. I am Ehecatl and I carry a message from my kindred. Beware the Great Messenger. He is not what he seems. He once came to the Cloud we occupy, not unlike your own Cloud, but some entity kept him from coming in. I don't know why, but I do know he was a threat to us, and we were fortunate he was kept away.' Then he rode upward, and we followed.

"Xolotl! Noehēcatlapalqui cōāmichtēnqui," Ehecatl called out to his Crew, which was met with laughter. Then we joined our Crews into a ghostly band. The green flames encompassing us spread out behind us like a contrail as we rode toward the horizon, chasing the darkness.

The cowfae slipped back and was close to Peach and Teddy, speaking softly.

This is where my memory gets hazy. It felt like we rode on into the dawn with the Drove. Next thought I had was I was waking up in my tent near the oasis. The smell of smoke came from our campfire. I peeked outside and Hoss was tending the fire and heating our coffee pot over the flames. Our horses were tethered as we had left them, and Hoss' gang were saddling up to leave. Was last night a dream?

After we had our piddles and poodles, a huge breakfast and got our saddlebags packed, we noticed a small man on a rickety bicycle coming our way. It appeared the bike might fall apart at any moment. It was a comical sight as the man came into our encampment. And thus, we met our next guide, Shylock Istvan.

"Hey everybody! I'm Shylock. Shylock Istvan. Hey Hoss, long time. Are these the kids?" Shylock dropped the bicycle, brushed himself off, straightened his dusty blazer and his John Lennon glasses. Hasty introductions were made, and Hoss and his band waved a fond adieu, galloping out of sight.

Shylock smiled proudly at the crossroads sign. "It appears my sign is still standing." He stood admiring his handiwork while we got our saddlebags fastened.

Cricket stepped next to the man, "What are these places? They aren't on any map I've seen," Cricket probably was asking this for Argus. Wogs was keenly interested in the answer.

"Oh! Yes…thank you for asking. Well, hmm, let's see. Ottenby is an artists' enclave. It's a huge grotto filled full of beautiful art and strange people. Ottenby is a great trading partner. The synths who live there can fix anything electronic. Then there is Þēodisċ. Above it is regular desert but below, the best I can tell there are a gazillion walking, talking animals. Ever had a discussion about eschatology with a beaver? They don't like human visitors. I'm surprised they haven't removed my sign." The Thedisch were familiar to me, but I didn't mention it to Shylock.

Binky touched the name Ravenholm on the sign, "What is Ravenholm? Some kind of town of birds," she grinned at herself.

"Oh no, no, no. We don't go to Ravenholm," Shylock was anxious. Scared?

I had to ask. "What's in Ravenholm?"

"Dead things walk and eat all living things. There is nothing of value there."

"If there is nothing of value, why post it on your sign?"

Shylock ignored my question, "DevNull is another synth community and Winona naka Beachside is one of those Crane Corp resorts. Lots of money, lots of guards and dangerous for little people like you and me. Boomtown is where Mr. Phrine's Fair is situated. That's where we are headed now."

He hopped on his bike, and yelled over his shoulder as he peddled away, "Follow me!"

November 2257 – Phrine's Flesh Fair – Nevada

Riding horses behind a rickety bike is a boring job. Several times Binky shot off in other directions, as we plodded along, trying to keep her frustration at bay. The rest of us sat our mounts, ambling along listening to Shylock extoll the amazing people of Boomtown. An hour into our tedious journey a dog came running from the side brush and began circling Shylock.

"Hey, hey! There you are! Papa's been missing you. You been a good boy, Boomer?" He dumped his bike, sat, and began a sloppy wet reunion with the dog. It was one of the black and grey furred mutts that somehow found a way to survive in the wild.

"Kids, come here, meet my best friend, Boomer. Found him in a Conex, with a shipment of fruit from the south. There was a note that said, 'take care of Boom Boom'." Shylock's face was now covered in drool. And he loved it. My respect for the man went way up. Dogs were pure detectors of character. If a dog loved you, you were generally a decent human. Okay, maybe that's a load of crap, but we're going to pretend it is true and move on. The dog was friendly and after a hasty sniffing of my whole crew, we were off again to our destination.

We arrived on the outskirts of a walled compound. Corrugated steel panels and watch towers sketched a perimeter that went out of sight to our left and right. The gate was two busses, parked nose to nose, with steel plating on one side that backed up to open for us. We passed under the big archway sign stating, "Welcome to Boomtown". The guards waved to Shylock, and a man walked toward us, dropping to a knee as Boomer ran to him.

I asked, "Shylock, I thought he was your dog?"

"Oh no, Kip. He's my best friend but his owner is Alexios. He's a sexy man, no?" Shylock had a hungry look in his eyes.

We dismounted and took our horses in. Alexios patted the dog, stood, and greeted us, "Hey friends. Istvan has been beside himself waiting for you to arrive. He said you come from the Dads. We are honored to have you."

Alexios shook the hands of the boys and kissed the hands of the girls. Peach had starry eyes, sparkling for the Greek god of a man. He was quite beautiful, but not my type.

"Did this little malaka treat you well?" Alexios' voice was butter, but I could detect an edge to it. This man was dangerous.

"Shut your pie hole, misthios, our guests are probably famished after the ride here."

Shylock turned to two boys nearby, "Duti, Pupi, come take their horses to the stables. Come, now!" Two tousle headed boys of no more than 10 years old came running and led our horses away.

When we entered Boomtown, we found it looked like a 19th century mining town that got an upgrade. The gentrification was impressive and many of the modern-day amenities were in plain sight, but you can't take the shanty out of shantytown. It was almost as if the niceties were only skin deep. I got a chill as I felt a darkness hiding just out of sight. Yep, we were in the right place.

Shylock escorted us to a boxy big building sporting a dangling sign out front, Cosmoline Taverna. A large café next door called Haptic's Haven had huge bay windows. Inside, dozens of men and women could be seen in full haptic gear, fighting in Online war. Wow, that was a blast from the past! A brief frisson of longing hit me as I recalled my innocent days of gaming and hanging with my Dads. We entered through the swinging double doors into the throwback wild west saloon. Alexios was tagging along with Peach hanging on his every softly spoken word.

"The Russian guy who owns this saloon rents rooms to special guests of Mr. Phrine." Peach was scrunching up her face at the smell. "The odor is from the various rifles and pistols you see hanging on the walls. The smell is from the cosmoline jelly used to store the ancient weapons; it's potent, huh?"

Potent was putting it mildly. I wasn't sure how people put up with it. Then I began looking around; this was a rough bar. Photos lined the walls. I could see pictures of the Bot Fields, the Perch, the Shipyard, the Tank Treadwerks and dozens of others. I even saw pictures of various hybrids, humans, and synths. The photos showed them just after messy battle. Then my eyes fell on one picture with my Dads at the CENTER labs. I crossed the floor to get a closer look. A minute later a gentle hand rested on my shoulder.

"Your Dads meant a lot to us too. They saved my wife and I during the Purge at Valhalla. We owe them our lives and I am sorry for their loss." Shylock's hand was on my shoulder. He and Alexios were behind me. It was then I realized Alexios was a synth and Shylock was a hybrid. Shylock's hands were webbed, and I could see he had a light patterned fur over his whole body.

Alexios spoke, "Come, let's get you upstairs."

It was early evening and already people were arriving and getting loud. Tough looking customers. People eyed us, until they saw we were with Alexios. His short spear and particle beamer seemed to carry some weight with these folks. We were only kids to these people and despite having dust from the trail on our clothing, these patrons made us look spotless. Alexios pointed out a skinny man with a long oilskin duster sitting in the corner with a churchwarden pipe and large flagon of something foamy.

Alexios spoke and pointed with a jerk of his head, "That there is Hondat Harrow. You think I am dangerous, which I am, that guy is a galactic bounty hunter. Don't be shocked, aliens have been among us for a long time. He drinks for free because his mere presence keeps people in line."

Harrow was staring at me. I tried to ignore him, but I could feel a sense of menace flowing from him. The barkeep broke the moment.

"Welcome young friends! Mr. Phrine has reserved the penthouse suite for you and left instructions for you to be fêted in style. Please follow me. We will get you settled, and you can relax for a few hours before tonight's Flesh Fair, starting at dusk."

The barkeep was introduced as Dmitri Kogarev, and we met his wife Yvetta and two teen sons, Vladimir, and Andrei. The boys carried our saddlebags and were clearly attracted to Binky, Peach, and Wogs. Cricket had a lopsided grin as the boys kept stealing glances at the girls. We took a leather lined elevator to the top floor. The doors opened and the cosmoline smell was gone, to be replaced by a waft of fresh citrus. It was so radically different from the saloon below. The apartments in the suite had the ultimate Swedish conservative furnishings with Bauhaus and Mondrian artwork throughout.

There was an air of privilege palpable in the penthouse, a thin smoothing effect, but with touches of gaudy ribaldry painted as a patina of disdain against the surrounding austerity. The rooms were welcoming but it almost seemed someone was trying too hard to impress the guests.

May 2257 – Cleaner Central – Home planet of the Coali

"Honored Zin, may I present Operatives Aganet and Pierpont." Cucu, a member of one of the servant races, escorted the two Coali inside. The Coali would appear to be fuzzy little Ewoks to humans. As one of the senior-most races of the COMBINE, they were entrusted with eliminating candidate races before they harmed the galactic group of pacifistic cultures. When a race was rejected from COMBINE candidacy and evaluated for removal, the Cleaners took the contract to manage the process. It had been thus for thousands of years. The Cleaners never failed.

"Come in and be at ease Aganet and Pierpont." Zin was reclining in his creche and indicated the vacant seats to his guests. The three were attended by other Cucu who themselves resembled Ewoks. In fact, Coali liked using Cucu for that very reason.

"Please, I am anxious to hear your report on Earth. Are we on timetable? Or perhaps you're here to say human extinction is coming earlier?"

From the tone of Honored Zin's voice Aganet knew that he knew, and they were in for a painful review with their superior.

"The Cleansing is in the Reaving State and our teams have accomplished almost 9% of the overall objective in these first few months of effort." Aganet hoped he sounded convincing. He didn't bother to look at Pierpont, knowing he would find the same blank face he himself wore. Zin was quiet, staring out the window over their heads. As the quiet continued, Aganet wondered if these were his last moments.

"Operatives Aganet and Pierpont. Tell me about the Vor and the Crith." Zin's voice was soft, and he continued to stare out the window. Sweat began to bead on the Operatives' foreheads.

"Honored Zin, the Vor have completed their portion of the work. The Harrowing is complete. The Crith are just starting their efforts and it is going better than projected." Pierpont sounded confident. Good, Aganet had a ray of hope this would be a fruitful meeting.

"Better than projected, you say. Okay. Now, tell me about the news I have received about Vor and Crith working with humans." Zin's voice was still mild, but now he looked at each of the Operatives, calmly almost as if he was about to thank them for their service.

Both thought, nope, we're going to die. Aganet felt a growing electrical field from the seat and knew Pierpont was feeling the same. The field grew in intensity. Their nether parts were tingling in a not pleasant way.

"Pierpont and I have recently heard rumors that a small group of Vor and Crith have exposed themselves to humans and are having a…" Aganet paused, searching for words, "meeting of the minds. We believe they are planning to add these few humans to the Vor Zoo back on Char. Nothing to be concerned about." There, he said it. Now maybe his interpretation would suffice to Zin's ears.

Zin called out to an unseen servitor, "Bring in Crith Agent Anak Bessar, please." A side door opened, and two Cucu wheeled in a vertical gurney with a Vor agent strapped tightly. A burnt flesh smell explained the charred remains which surprisingly still held life. The Crith would not live long but Zin hoped it would live long enough to share some disturbing news.

"Crith Agent Anak Bessar. Who is your Conclave leader?"

A crusty voice answered, as the Crith writhed in pain, "Prak Tier is our Conclave leader."

"Ah, so he is. And for whom does Conclave Leader Prak Tier work now?"

"The human Charles Winton Wefer III, known as Kip."

"And how can a Crith commander be serving a human leader."

"We don't know, except the boy has Powers and someone helped him."

"Ah, I see, someone helped him. Whom?"

"We suspect the Old Rebel is responsible."

Zin considered for a moment, weighing the absurdities. On one side, the hardly credible myth of the Old Rebel was almost as improbable as the notion that a human could touch the Power. Hmm, no. There was more to uncover here.

"Agent Bessar. You lie. Humans do not wield Power and this heresy against all Crith runs deeper. Who is in charge of the Crith on Earth?"

"Honored Zin, Kip is our leader now." She screamed as another wave of heat enveloped her steaming body. Zin knew it would take days for the burnt smell to subside. He logged an entry to have a cleaning crew in his office the moment he vacated.

"Take our Crith Agent home," two Cucu entered and hastily exited with the gurney and steaming Crith.

"When we are presented with a new challenge it is always the strongest who prevail. Do you know why?" Neither Aganet nor Pierpont spoke.

Zin did not expect his uncreative subordinates to have an opinion; after all, such as these were raised to be cogs in the system, not leaders nor innovators.

"Let me tell you, the strongest of wills, with consistent resolve always win, always dominate. How do you think Coali were themselves not Cleansed, millennia ago?" Of course, no response.

"Let me tell you. The Coali are clever, we are ruthless and clever. When our ancestors signed on to protect the COMBINE from the very threats which our own race posed, we were guaranteed a permanent place in the COMBINE. No other race has eliminated over 40% of its own people to assure its continuation. The Vor? Hardly. They are foot soldiers who do as they're told. They survived because we made a case for them as part of our plan to Cleanse undesirable races. How about the Crith? As you know, they are forest sprites in their native form. Inoffensive, cute even. They would have achieved COMBINE membership with ease, eventually. We got to them first because we saw their potential as insider-operatives. You know how other races whisper that we are Slavers?" Zin stopped and the two Operatives nodded. Hah! You have no idea. You're as dense as the Crith. Zin's thought gave him a little smile. He continued.

"We are Slavers and proud of it. We gladly pervert and twist these harmless wisps into sociopathic harbingers of destruction. The structure of it is elegant: Vor harrow the target race, laying the groundwork of demise and the Crith are the reavers, pulling the trigger of self-destruction, causing the race to eat its own wings. Death from within."

"Honored Zin, what do we do next?" Aganet was confused by the history lesson and was unable to see how it related to the problem at hand.

Zin knew his words were lost on these two menials. Getting back to the problem, he directed the Operatives to change their approach for now. The plan was to find and capture Kip. He was to be brought to Zin quietly.

"However, if this is impossible, take him out at a distance with a sniper." What neither Operative was aware of was the failed assassination attempt by the Gorj assassins. The failure was now irrelevant and as was expected the Gorj hit team committed ritual suicide to atone for their failure. Maybe these two will have better success. Zin doubted it, but he felt he was an optimist among Coali. Coali were a pessimistic race; optimism was a punishable social offense. Zin liked risk; risk brought him success…as well as the wake of dead competitors in his meteoric rise in rank.

Aganet replied, "Yes, honored one, what do we do after that?"

"It's simple my stupid little Vor. You will pray our COMBINE employers do not discover what we know. It could be the end of us all." Zin turned his back on them, indicating the interview was at a close. Aganet and Pierpont silently retreated and prepared to leave for Earth. Their hearts were heavy but one thankful thing happened or rather didn't happen. With a new lease on life, both Operatives resolved to capture or kill this rogue human.

As the Operatives left, Zin thought how alike Coali and humans were. In the murky past of the Coali was the fact that their induction into the COMBINE almost killed their race. Coali found out when all your material needs are met in abundance and personal ownership is no longer necessary since every citizen could have all they desired, the racial tendency for greed and covetousness blossomed in the vacuum of competition. Zin mentioned 40% of their race had perished to become part of the COMBINE. The loss came at their own hands. Those left were the most wily and self-serving and new laws were enacted to deprive citizens of most rights. With the institution of programmatic suffering, the Coali's racial survival was assured. Humans were the same and the same provision of opulent life for all humans led to the Tech War. The Vor had enhanced human technology, allowing them to have all their hearts' desires. Thus, was humanity's doom vouchsafed. What troubled Zin now was humanity's new rise to power. And more, the conversion of expensively trained Vor and Crith agents to this human's cause. Zin wanted to meet this human, Kip.

November 2257 – Phrine's Flesh Fair - Nevada

A knock came and haberdashers and clothiers streamed into the penthouse. We were accoutre'd in colors and styles which would fit right into the Hunger Games' elites. Cricket resisted the new clothing, stating they were scratchy. Most of us thought it was an excellent opportunity to do some LARPing. In our roleplay we could be anyone we wanted. Tonight, we would be young sophistos who revel in the debasement of others for sport. We would put on a good show to get the escape plan in motion.

Out front of the Taverna we gathered as a stretch limousine pulled up to give us a ride to the stadium. The car smelled like old cigars and the booze bar was empty. This little pony had been ridden hard and put away soiled too many times. But hey, at least we got to ride in an actual limo! A large gathering ahead slowed our progress.

Our driver lowered the cabin divider, "Hey folks, I know you're outta towners. Boomtown offers sights you'll see nowhere else. How'd ya like to see a Desanguination?"

Whatever it was it sounded bloody. My whole Crew hopped out and followed the chauffeur whose name I came to discover was Dandy Sackett. The crowd parted, allowing Dandy to lead us to the front. A man was facing a woman, pointing a finger at her. Both were bloody and it was unclear whose blood it was.

"I abjure you, Sesqua. We are Clan no longer. Our blood is no longer kin. I see you no more."

At that the man spat at her feet and walked away. The woman knelt and covered her face, crying. People started coming forward, each bending down to grab a handful of dirt. Each then cast the dirt on her head saying, "I see you no longer." A long line of women and men repeated the action. In a few minutes most of the crowd had dispersed. The woman was now curled up on her knees, a ring of fallen soil surrounding her.

"That is how the Clan McSingh keeps house with their miscreants." Dandy was smiling.

"But what did she do?" Cricket looked disturbed at what he saw. I could see all the others were shocked, too.

"Who cares. These dramatic types give us a good show! Anyway, it's time to get you to the stadium."

By this time our group was the only one in the street, besides the disheveled woman. Cricket walked toward the woman and Dandy jumped to restrain him..

"No, no, don't touch her. If you do, you mark yourself as an enemy of the McSinghs. You do not want them as your enemy." Dandy had a grip on Cricket's shoulder.

Cricket grabbed the hand and pushed Dandy away, "This is sick. And you are just as sick, maybe even worse. Shame on you for treating this like entertainment." Dandy went to grab Cricket again, but a glare stopped him cold. So much for LARPing as despoilers of people.

Dandy held up his hands and backed off, "Fine. Have it your way. It's your funeral."

Cricket knelt by the woman and whispered into her ear. Moments later she giggled. Whatever he said broke the pall over what just happened. After a minute he was helping her to her feet; Binky, Peach, Teddy and Wogs ran to help. I stood back look around. From various windows peeked unfriendly faces. I suspected we had only moments before someone came out to give us grief. Dandy was already back in the car, and we went to join him.

As I closed the door I heard a voice, "You are known to us Kip Wefer. Watch your back." I heard laughter from somewhere as I closed the door. Dandy sped away quickly and as we turned a corner the street was refilled with people again. All of them were looking in our direction.

Dandy spoke matter of fact, "Well kids you made an enemy today."

Sesqua agreed, "Your driver is right. What you did was kindly but foolish. The McSinghs never forget a slight."

Cricket was holding the woman close, and she leaned into his embrace. A knowing look passed between Binky and Cricket. I guess our plan to stay off the radar went to pot just then.

I was concerned, "Dude, now that we have made ourselves known, I am worried we're too visible to do the ninja rescue plan."

Cricket replied, "Us known? Sound like they only recognized you. You're on your own pal!" We had a laugh and Sesqua and Dandy looked at us like we were crazy. And maybe we were.

Dandy and the woman, Sesqua both spoke up at the same time.

"Ninja rescue? For whom?"

Dandy asked, "I don't want to get involved in your scheming, young sir."

"Well, there you go genius, let's share with the group. Gawd, such an amateur!" Binky wasn't wrong.

Wogs spoke up. I think she saw the cat wouldn't go back in the bag, so she jumped in by telling Dandy and Sesqua our plans. I figured we needed to start running right then. After Wogs finished explaining our plan it was quiet in the car. Then laughter began in the front seat. Dandy thought something was humorous.

That ticked me off, "What's so funny, huh? You really think all this is a big joke?"

"No, no boyfriend. What I think is that your plan was never going to work. Do you even know how Mr. Phrine keeps control of people?"

Sesqua scrunched up her lips and nodded; she knew what Dandy was going to say.

She added. "Yeah, if you go in halfcocked you will become his slaves as quickly as all the others. The man can read minds and control them too. He can't be deceived."

Dandy pulled the limo over and sat staring out the front window spinning a teetotum on the dashboard. He faced around with a serious look, "If it is a rescue you want, you will have to kill Phrine. I can help."

There was no way I could believe that, either the killing part or his helping us. Big sigh. What to do…? Our next step was decided for us. Two large, armored personnel carriers came alongside us. A man popped out the top of one and called our way.

"Hey gang! Heard you got waylaid by the McDouchebags. No sweat. We got ya covered. Slip in between us and we'll get you to the stadium safely." Dandy put the limo between the two carriers and off we went.

Dandy told us to act as if everything was going according to plan and ignore the Sesqua incident. He said it was so far below the interest of Phrine, it made no difference in how we would enjoy the evening. For now, he told us, let he and Sesqua talk to see if they could figure a better idea for us. So, there we went…along for the ride with no real plan and a vain hope these two would actually help us. We were trusting a man whom I suspected had ulterior motives and a woman who had just been shunned by her family. Oh, the trouble we get ourselves into.

The stadium came into view and as night fell, huge spotlights and flashing drones and even a dirigible could be seen hovering about. Our convoy stopped at a security checkpoint. A portly man exhorted the commander of the front personnel carrier. Then he waddled back and spoke with Dandy. The man's uniform was soiled and unkempt and his name tag said Dogberry.

Dogberry asked, "Here now, what are you about?"

Dandy seemed to be expecting this. "I am escorting Mr. Phrine's guests."

"You sir, have no place sir, in the rights of men." Dandy seemed nonplussed.

Dogberry continued, "What instead you needs be about is only in the turn about."

Dandy was patient with the man, "I know this is unexpected, but if we could have a 'by your leave'?"

"Ho there miscreants, trouble me not with your foolery of Tom, lying knaves."

Dandy replied like this was an old script that had played out before.

"I will pass you by, but with a warning and stern leave-by'ing.

"Be on your way."

"Thank you, Officer Dogberry, we will do as you say." Dandy had given us a brief glance to keep silent. As it was, I had no idea what had just transpired. I was so confused. Was this guy for real?

We proceeded past the checkpoint and Dandy put his side window up. At that point he laughed, "The look on your faces. I wish I had a picture!"

"Dogberry is Mr. Phrine's pet officer. He is serious but Phrine uses him for comic relief. For the most part he is harmless, but despite his schizo weirdness he has foiled every plot to kill Mr. Phrine and put down every uprising in Boomtown. Crazy he most surely is, but effective he is most certainly. It always pays to be polite to the man."

The stadium stood tall, looming a hundred meters above us. We entered into a dark tunnel with hundreds of pedestrians bustling through. The energy level was high, and the excitement was contagious. I had no idea what I was going to see but I was sure ready to see it. The stadium didn't disappoint. There was room for 10s of thousands of people. The stands looked empty, but people kept filing in and within half an hour it was mostly full. I guess Boomtown was a big place.

We were led to a viewing box which was dead center on the action. The box was full of rich people, flowing alcohol and expensive hors d'oeuvres. The warm-up acts were already in progress. The stadium floor was a busy place of freak show entertainment, my kind of people. Quotls, Vittles, Cyclopes and various non-humaniform synths performed, fought, and played tag. I noticed a sign above the viewing balcony. Tune your prosthetic of choice to boomtown.com/phrine.fair. I opened a virtual host on my prosthetic and tuned in. Popups appeared to tell me all about each of the performers below. I saw a number of those whom we helped escape from LA:CENTER. They seemed to be enjoying themselves. Maybe this Phrine Fair wasn't so bad.

The food was good but me and my Crew hung together since we had nothing in common with the adults in the room. Fortunately, they left us alone. Twenty minutes later a 30m tall holo of a man appeared in the middle of the stadium. I could see the actual man was standing in the middle of the rapidly vacating stadium floor. Multiple large screens also gave close-up shots of the action.

"Ladies and Gentlemen, synths, biologicals, and friends! Welcome to the largest circus and fair in the world! Tonight, we have the Battling Gargantuans, but right now we welcome for your delectation and enjoyment the McSingh Mounted Maniacs, humans on horses."

Humans on horses in colorful garb circled the ring.

Phrine continued, "And the human-mounted horses!" A quick close-up showed three men squished under horses, seated on the ground. Their hands and arms were all wiggling. It was a funny sight, but it must have been painful.

"Okay, scratch the horses on humans. Too slow. Let me introduce the Flying Maracas!" Swinging on cables strung to the latticework above, 50+ men and women came flying into the stadium. Over 200 brightly dressed people danced and moved on the floor below, in time to a jaunty Latino rhythm. Then came Pit Racers, Vittles on the ground and Quotls in the air moved in ballet. There was even a monster truck segment. It continued for an hour with dancing, singing and some fabulous talent.

"Next, we have for you the time-honored tradition of Cacahuatl, it's our Chocolate Jubilee! And to top our chocolate fountain," a gigantic fountain spewing chocolate slid along the stadium floor to stop at Phrine's feet, "…we have our Aztec sacrifice provided by none other than the atavistic and fantastic Clan McSingh! And to introduce tonight's sacrifice I present to you our host, Balthasar Bickel!"

I noticed across the whole stadium and in our private suite, people were being served demi-tasse cups of hot chocolate. I tried some; it was bitter and thick, but not bad.

"Friends of the sanguine fair, every month sees a time of renewal and celebration! In your hands is the consecration of our commitment and pledge of fealty to Phrine. Drink and partake of his goodness."

The hair was standing up on the back of my neck. Something was definitely wrong here and it was freaking me out. I looked down at an empty cup and realized with horror I had something bad inside me. Someone slipped everyone a mickey.

Suddenly he was there, standing next to me looking down upon the chocolate fair.

"Ah Kip, I have so anticipated our meeting." Something must have shown on my face; it made him smile. Phineas T Phrine put his hand on my shoulder, companionably.

"There is no harm in my little concoction. A dash of coca and a blip of ayahuasca and chacruna. Together it helps the audience become more malleable, pliable in the spirit, if you will."

The dignity of the Fair had given way to a vicious schadenfreude with a piquant of bleary religious fervor. It was then I saw a man hoisted upon a large stake with kindling underneath beginning to catch fire. My rising panic turned to bursting outrage as I saw who it was. Cricket.

On cue, dancers in the garb of Día de los Muertos, Day of the Dead streamed out in the hundreds onto the floor. My Crew were at my side, they saw what was happening. I tried to raise Cricket via my prosthetic, then I attempted my Powers; that only returned a sharp headache. I was getting nothing. In every part of the stadium everyone was bending, flexing, and gyrating to the rhythm. Not my Crew; they were on point and ready for action. I dimly heard a voice behind me as I fled the viewing area,

"No, wait, Kip, it doesn't have to…" And off we went, racing the flames that were even then licking upward to sacrifice the one who so grievously offended the McSinghs.

It seemed to take forever to push through the bustle to get to the stadium floor. Once we were past, we ran full out to the foot of the pyre. The flames had grown and Cricket, who had been unconscious, was coming around, coughing. Sparks and flames flit and whorled, rising throughout the stadium.

"Yes, you dance in the revelry of our shared conviction…" Balthasar was droning on.

A dozen RABs, roving autonomous blades circled the growing fire, but they didn't seem interested in us. That is until we began plucking at the pile of kindling. Then they tightened their orbits and came close enough to cut us down. We stopped and they moved back.

A laugh came from behind. Phrine was standing there slowly applauding, "I must compliment your pluck and moxy. In other circumstances I am sure you would have swooped in to save the day. But I am afraid that won't be the story here."

"Set him free, now!" The closest dancers turned around to look at me. I didn't realize I could yell that loud.

"Buddy boy, it was never my plan to roast your friend. But the McSingh's wanted their pound of flesh. Tell ya what; do a little thing for me and I'll set him free without so much as a burn mark. Well, except for a tad bit of smokey flavor." Phrine was smiling at his own joke.

"What do you want?"

I'd had enough of this. We only had moments until Cricket started to burn.

"You have the Power and so do I." I reached for the Power again and this time the headache was much less. As I did so I could see a prismatic rainbow aura around Phrine. He definitely had the Power.

"When I speak in a moment, I want you to join with me. I'll lead, you just follow and amplify." Phrine had a stare that was riveting. I could see why so many people followed his lead.

"Okay, whatever. Just do it. I don't have much control over my Powers right now. I'll do what I can."

That seemed to satisfy him. Some signal must have passed because the fire flew high, and Cricket disappeared downward. For a moment I felt a shock of betrayal. Then Cricket was standing next to me, smudged with soot but none the worse for wear. The Crew walked him off the floor and the crowd were somehow unaware of the switch. I looked up and a simulacrum of Cricket was burning away.

"It is time young man." Phrine closed his eyes, and I could feel his Power radiate. Some impediment inside me vanished and I had full access to my Powers. I felt a mental hook from Phrine and connected a tendril of intention to it. In my mind's eye I could see thousands of dots, mostly white, but with a few purples, reds and pink. I reached out to touch one and it made a slight popping sound and made a little tug. It was pleasurable. I swiped left and popped a tiny group and felt a stronger satisfying sensation. I tried a couple more times and realized this was much like popping a sheet of bubble wrap with a chaser of endorphin high. Oh, it was on! I went at it with gusto. As I popped the dots, they became prismatic in coloring. But if I pushed a bit harder, I could turn them red. The whole tableau became swathes of different colors, but the reds made me feel better. I had a fleeting thought about the Vor being red and Crith being purple in their auras.

"Ah Kip, you are a natural. Show me those reds, my friend. You know they feel so good." Phrine's discorporate voice was sultry and purred with satisfaction.

As the endorphin rush hit me harder, I made wider arcs, turning all the dots red. What I didn't hear was the roar of the crowd around us changing in tone. As the Cricket simulacrum burned a chant began. I was too busy with my mental dance, frolicking in the reds, as I painted and popped. When I was almost done, I noticed other dots further away. Panning out and around I began to paint and pop the dots further and further away. This was a blast! Then I saw the motherlode, a group of dots in the millions. Yes! I reoriented and dove in. I wanted to pop more at the same time because the rush of it was so intense. I had no idea what I was really doing, but I set up a Cloud subroutine to auto-pop larger and larger groups. I set one sub then another, wheeling through the sea of dots. In a moment I had created subs to spawn subs and sent them careering and careening. I was in ecstasy. I heard a moaning next to me. Bright as the sun, a halo limned Phrine's body and his head was thrown back in rapture. Uh oh, I got that spooky spidey sense. Then I looked at the people in the stadium and finally listened to their chant. Simply, it was, "Phrine, Phrine, Phrine…" and I realized the dots were people I was touching; why hadn't I known that earlier? Somehow I did know, but I didn't care. It felt so good. My subs exhausted targets on their own and terminated. The millions of dots I had touched, where were they? I had my powers in full swing, and I sent my sight outward. I quickly knew: Vegas. My sight peered over the city, and I heard a deafening chant, the same as in the stadium, Phrine, Phrine, Phrine. But I also heard Kip, Kip, Kip. Uh oh. I sure hoped this stuff, whatever we did faded.

"My boy, of course it fades. That's why the Flesh Fair happens every week," Phrine patted my shoulder. I took another look at the dotted landscape and saw some of the reds and purples fading already. In a second Phrine shook himself and suddenly the whole dot tableau vanished. I fell to the stadium floor and tried to steady my swimming head. Hands brought me to my feet, and I stood as Phrine dusted me off and patted my back.

"Kip, my boy, you do not disappoint. It's time to get you out of here. You will need quite a rest after your expenditures…for which I most heartily thank you."

"No, wait. Do you mind if I head back to your viewing area? I'd like to watch some more, please." Phrine nodded and told me to be careful and that any of his people would see to my comfort if I had a need.

I left the stadium floor, but I didn't head for the viewing area, rather I made my way toward backstage. I had a new plan. It was weird for everyone around me to be so obsequious. Everyone knew me and wanted to shake my hand, hug me and some definitely wanted more, ahem, personal attention. Everyone in Boomtown and the Flesh Fair was now very positively disposed to Phrine and to some extent me. With the good favor, maybe my mission would succeed; I hoped this meant I had a ticket to go wherever I wanted, and people knew and trusted me. Time to test that ticket.

Binky and Wogs hauled Cricket out of the stadium with Teddy, Peach, and Alexios in tow. Dandy had the limo up front with Sesqua in the rear, and they rode directly back to the Taverna.

Binky asserted, "I'll go back for Kip in a minute. You guys just hang tight. We are aborting this mission right effing now." Everyone knew to do just as Binky said. Even Alexios didn't challenge her commands.

I went through the big steel doors from the stadium floor into the staging area. Handlers and performers were running about, and no one paid me any mind. I saw a sign pointing to the left, Titan Twins. I followed the signs and found another gigantic set of doors. Two heavily armed and armored men in black tactical gear stood watch. As I approached, they eyeballed me.

One guard spoke, "Hey son, you may be Phrine's favorite, but ya can't hang around here. Boss's orders."

I was confused, I thought my powers had made everyone love me. I wondered; did I still have access to my powers? I gave it a try. There was no headache so I sent a message at them as strong as I could. '*You secretly work for me and will gladly do anything I say. In fact, you will do everything in your power to help me, even helping me with stuff I am not even aware of yet*'. I added that last bit so they would initiate help without my asking. Their posture abruptly changed, and they acted like they needed to guard me with every ounce of their energy.

The first guard spoke and put a hand to his earpiece, "Sir, sir, apologies. I didn't realize who you were. The area is clear, and we are ready for the go-signal!"

"Gentlemen, please open the doors. You will escort me inside." I used my voice of authority. Now I was getting somewhere.

A bitter urea and ammonia smell flowed over us as the guards opened the big doors. It was obvious they were used to this. Not me. I retched and tried not to vomit. After I got myself under control, I walked into the holding area with a part of my shirt held over my mouth and nose. The room was dark, and I could see two enormous stalls with hay in them. Dozens of haybales were stacked in the center of the room and there were two piles of refuse in the room corners opposite the stalls. The noxious smells were coming from those piles. Poop.

I saw movement, big movement. Two outlines like 3 story gorillas were skulking in the rear of the two stalls. I knew they were supposed to be big, but this was so much more. They would dwarf even the Brobs back at the CENTER. I had no idea how to help something as big as a stack of automobiles. I stopped and both guards stayed behind me. I plucked my courage and moved toward the nearest giant form. I stopped at the stall entrance; I wasn't sure what I was waiting for. A moment later a mountain spoke in gentle rumbly tones that vibrated the air.

"A change has come. Do you come with death on your hands?"

I wasn't sure what to say. 'I have come to bring you to my family in Hopi territory.'

"A man from the stars has made promises, but one thinks they are empty."

I had no idea what he meant. Or perhaps he was talking about Croatoan? I wasn't concerned about that alien; I was here to help friends of a friend.

"My promise was to bring you to your friends."

"Plans within plans and the left unknown to the right, consummate unhelp but for those who ply the seas of greed."

I was getting frustrated. Did this Kaiju want help or just to spout mysterious prose?

"Okay. I am here to help. Can you follow me out. I, uhh, want to help you escape."

The mountain came forward and a gorilla-dog the size of my garage bent over until its deep brown furred chin rested on the floor in front of me. His muzzle was as tall as me. Its breath smelled of herbs and fruits. Moist clean air rasped from its nostrils. My Chupa self knew this was one of my elders and I couldn't help as I submissively bowed. Hopefully he was vegetarian and wasn't considering eating me. Its face was like that of a friendly dog's smile.

"You want to help." He stated.

"Yes."

"I am Nuk, and my companion is Shy. How would you help us?"

"I am Kip, I am a friend who has a way out to freedom. Would you like to come with me?"

"Friends are fickle, and trust is in short supply." He grumbled.

What was I to say. If it didn't want to escape was I supposed to convince it? I was at a loss.

Nuk's gentle voice vibrated my body, "Kip, what Shy, and I feared came by way of a maliferous traduction by a trusted friend. The details are unimportant and their gaudy nature defy belief. Trust that we were maligned most grievously and as a result fell into the callous hands of our owner, kept as chattel. The rub is we cannot be free. Our freedom would condemn innocent lives. So, here we stay. Please convey our deepest regrets to your Hopi family, especially Elder Tala."

"Nuk, where are these innocents?"

"We know not."

I turned to my guards and asked, "Guys, where are the friends of the Titans kept?"

Guard one shrugged his shoulders but Guard two answered, "The little dogs are kept in a pen with the piggies by Clan McSingh. You want us to go get them?"

"Nuk, I will get your friends to safety, then I will come back for you, okay?"

He spoke, "Orphans." Nuk nodded and returned to the back of its stall.

"Hey guys, what are your names?" I asked.

Guard one said, "I am Norm, and this is Peter. He's also my brother. We are the Tater brothers. Did ya know I got him this job even though he is a complete a-hole. Our Mom made me do it." He jerked a thumb at Peter then continued, "You know how family is. Commitments and stuff. But the job isn't that hard. Mostly we stand around looking tough. Little do they know our first love is performing at the Cosmoline on Fridays doing the Trixie & Dixie Show." Norm did a little twirl and Peter did the same. That was more than I needed to know or see.

"Norm, we need to get these friends to safety. Do you have your credit card?"

I made a decision right there to highly motivate these brothers. If what Phrine said was correct, the influence I had over these guys would be wearing off. I figured if I was going to keep them disposed to helping me, I needed to throw some serious cheddar their way. Norm nodded and showed his card. The credit card is a government issued bank account which most adults use in lieu of physical money these days. People still used physical cash, but only in rural areas and among the criminal types. I pulled up the temp card Salim had given me on my pad and saw I had 10 million credits. I linked my pad to his card and deposited a million credits in his account.

"Norm, stop being a guard, and you and your brother go into full-time show business. You have a lot of talent to share," I made an assumption, "…and you can't do it by being a guard for Phrine." Norm's eyes were like saucers.

"Kip, I would love to. Peter would love to…" Peter nodded in agreement, "…but we both have a mild form of Tourette's which limits how much we can do on stage."

I took a chance and added an incentive by implanting a suggestion using my power. While I had no headache, I needed to cement his motivation.

'*Norm and Peter, your Tourette's is gone.*' Their minds pushed back, and I could see inside they both had a spiderweb in their brains that looked mauve in color. It sparked when Norm spoke about their condition. Then I saw it. Peter had a mild tic; I would have dismissed it if I hadn't been looking hard. The mauve area stood out sharply in that moment. I decided to paint it a golden color and smooth the edges, so they matched the surrounding pink hues. Both men had quirky expressions.

I suggested to the men, 'You are motivated *to take your drag show on the road, then establish yourselves in Vegas Above. Share your love of the performing arts with the world and invest in others. Make it your business to help others shine.*' There, that did it. I had my first twinge of a headache. My powers were already going away.

All this mental mumbo jumbo took place as Norm and Peter led me to the McSingh ranch, where the piggies were kept. As we ran I experimented with shielding the three of us from notice. I sent out a broadcast that said, 'don't see us, we aren't here right now, um thank you'.

Most people ignored us, and a few had quizzical looks and mumbled something about 'no, thank you'. Alright, my suggestion wording would need some practice.

We made it across Boomtown and into McSingh territory. Norm took the lead and got us past the gate guards and into the ranch area. I could see piggies just ahead. There were doggies running around with them that were miniature versions of Nuk and Shy.

Norm whispered to me. "Kip, Pete and I are going to go inside and rile up the McSinghs.

You see, Mr. Phrine has made a new rule that requires subcontractors like the McSinghs to pay a new monthly tariff." Norm winked me into the ruse and I figured what rich people hate most is when you take away their money.

I hung out near a gate to the pen and waited. I didn't have to wait long. Within moments a group of angry men came outside the house and walked with Norm and Peter away from the pen. I didn't see anyone else nearby, so I opened the pen and went in. I called to the animals. Pigs came over and so did the dog creatures. They looked so much like the two dogs of Gozer in Ghostbusters I decided to dub them Zuulies. The eight little Zuulies were about my weight and could run on all fours as well as stand on their hind legs. And they spoke.

"Hey human, why do you smell funny?" said the first Zuulie.

"Not funny Letro, he is Chupa," said the second Zuulie.

"That's Letronmay to you, goofy Cid," retorted Letronmay.

"Okay, then it's Cidrocar to you, prickly pear!" he shot back.

The other six Zuulies were shouting at once. It was hard to think with all their racket. I was worried the noise would bring the McSinghs and did my best to shush them. Then one of the pigs spoke. I was losing the ability to discern between people and animals. I guess I would have to ask from now on. I knew I'd soon look like a right fool asking some dog for directions with a long-winded explanation only to be answered by 'woof'. Oh the humanity!

"You are Kip. We felt your power earlier. When you take your friends out of here may we come too?"

How could I say no? "Yes. What is your name?"

"I am Priggy the Peppy Piggie. Would you like their names too?' The pig pointed to the 26 others.

"Oh no, no, um, it's okay just to have your name for now. Thank you." Did I always have to say thank you?

"Oh no, Kip, thank you!" Priggy oinked a bunch in her piggy patois.

I took a quick gander around to see if any humans had appeared. An aircar came in from Boomtown central. As it came down I could see Phineas Phrine himself was in the front passenger seat. I think my two guard friends were about to go from the frying pan into the fire. I led the Piggies and Zuulies out of the McSingh compound and directed them to the Cosmoline Taverna. I told them to ask for Binky, Cricket, Wogs, Peach, or Teddy. I figured Binky and the Crew would have a fun moment dealing with our new friends. I also told them to mention that their being free made it possible to free Nuk and Shy. Both Nuk and Shy still needed rescuing from the stadium. I figured it would get sorted at some point.

I headed back to rescue Norm and Peter. I arrived just as Phrine was being accosted by the McSingh men.

"No way. Phrine, you already extort half of the take we get from our marks. We won't pay you anything more. And why did you send two of your nobody goons to announce your changing of the terms of our agreement?" The McSingh man was livid.

"Balthasar, you need to watch your tone." With that other aircars that had been cloaked appeared and 50 cal guns audibly deployed on each aircar with a loud servo whirl and a hard click. The man gulped.

I spoke, "Mr. Phrine, may I speak with you?" Phineas Phrine kept his eyes on Balthasar.

He called to me as he stared calm death at the other man, "Ah Kip. What a pleasure. What may I do for you?"

Then it hit me. Even if my power were fading, I could still farsend. I spoke to my Crew and tried to add in Nuk and Shy, '*Hey friends, I am keeping Phrine busy over in the McSingh compound. Can you all meet up and head out of town? You know where to go.*"

"Mr. Phrine, may we speak privately?"

"Balthasar, excuse me for a moment. Please feel free to examine the guns trained on you. They are fresh from the JINN." Phrine smiled and came over.

"Kip, I thought you would be partying, with three sheets to the wind." He gave me a companionable shoulder grip.

"Yes sir. I would, except two of my buddies hightailed it over here and caused a ruckus. It's my fault. I think my powers are causing weird things to happen. You see I do drag shows with my friends back where I'm from and Norm and Petey have a drag show every Friday at the Cosmoline. We got chatty and I mentioned a small dust up with the McSinghs earlier and I think I accidentally suggested they should come over here for some retribution. I'm sorry."

"Young man. Don't mention a word of this to anyone. I will deal with the McSinghs. Take Norm and Peter with you. I don't want any witnesses to what I'm about to do."

He gripped my shoulder, "Piece of advice, watch out for the Night Circus. Don't ever cross them, okay?" I nodded but had no idea what he meant.

Phrine turned on his heel back to Balthasar. The men spoke quietly and a moment later Petey and Norm came out of the ranch house where they were being held. I gave them the *say nothing* look and we walked away quickly, but casually. Right about the time we exited the McSingh gates I felt an earthquake. It gained strength and I realized the earthquake was coming my way. You know how baby spiders cling to the mother's back when they are first born? Imagine a 10-meter-tall gorilla with a dog face, and a huge doggie grin. Here came Nuk and Shy with their Zuulie babies hanging off their backs. Nuckalavee and Nuertsumshy were going at full gallop and my Crew was riding up top with some late additions to our band of miscreants. I could see Alexios, Boomer, Shylock, Sesqua and even Dandy clinging to the titan like the Zuulie children. There were no smiles there, except for Alexios and Boomer. Boomer rode the titan, a hank of fur gripped in his maw, wind whipping his face like he was borne to it. He was in heaven. As the joyous mutt got his wag on, a buddy was riding next to him, equally ecstatic. It was a rabbit with horns; he was twice the size of Boomer. I recalled seeing a marquee poster sporting his show. He was a Jackalope named Trespassers Will and was a local legend and consummate entertainer, magician, and sharpshooter. I heard later he was a hyperactive and vociferous friend to Boomer and the drag troupe. His shows at the Cosmoline were his passion, but he made his money barking for the Yak Lady in Phrine's Midway. I later discovered he had his sights set on the bright lights of Vegas. He was wicked fast on the draw and could hit a gnat between the eyes at a hundred paces. And he sported a deep cowboy, southern drawl. Alexios was whooping, Boomer was barking and the Jackalope had a big grin. They passed me by, and I thought I was going to be fending for myself.

An armored yellow taxicab pulled up and a craggy face called to the three of us, "Wha'ch youse waiting for? An engraved invitation. Get in!"

Norm, Petey and I climbed into the back of the taxi and sped off after the galloping titans. The cab smelled like an old burnt cigar and the upholstery was stained with things I didn't want to consider. The taxi was a marvel of computerized wizardry and as we picked up speed, I could feel the atmospherics kicking in. Ahhh, cool air, finally. I hadn't realized how sticky sweaty I had become. Sadly, the Tater brothers smelled like Axe cologne and the air was saturated with it.

"Hey Pete, did you tell the Taters to meet us somewhere?" Norm was worried their drag troupe were being left behind.

"Sure did, Normie! I sent a mass text for them to hike up their skirts and join our trip to Vegas. Look behind us." Norm and I saw a convoy of two semis and over a dozen ground cars, big and small. I even saw a Yugo! How had that survived all these years?

From the driver's seat came a question, "I take it you're Kip?"

"Yes, sir."

"So, the name's Harry Canyon. This here is my taxi," the man snorted. "I got paid bank to come get youse guys, but I didn't hear nuthin' 'bout where we're going. Perhaps, Mr. Kip you can enlighten us on that point." Harry's sarcasm was refreshing. I was tempted to ask him about the Loc-Nar, but figured he might cook us with a heat ray or something.

"Harry, follow those Zuulies," and I pointed at the gargantuan rumps of the gorilla dogs running ahead of us. He gunned it and kept us at a safe distance, pacing the titans. It was serious business: if he got too close, our cab would start bouncing. Any closer than that and we'd catch air, and something was bound to break.

'*Hey gang, how's it going?*' I farspoke to my whole crew and mostly I heard mental groans in return.

'*Hey bud, we were at the Cosmoline when it was invaded by these little monkeys. They said they were Zuulies. A stupid but applicable name, so I figured immediately it was your fault. We went in one big group to the stadium, and no one seemed interested in stopping us. You shoulda seen it. The reunion with their parents was loud and frenetic,*' Cricket paused and I realized he was vomiting.

Binky picked up, '*However you did it, that was amazing to see. It only took a matter of minutes to gather ourselves together and hatch an escape route. It wasn't hard. Not many people will mess with two ancient Skinwalkers on the gallop. We also picked up some others. They call themselves the Tater Tots and they were as ready to leave as we were.*'

I still had my powers although the headache was reasserting itself now. I sent a burst mental movie of what had happened. They probably missed most of it as all my Crew were busy riding the vomit comet. Then I realized the intensity of my sending was more of the issue. I didn't know how to control my volume and forcefulness.

'*Dude, stop! I'm gonna vom again!*'" In my mind's eye I could see Teddy was white as a sheet.

For a Hopi that's saying something. I shut my sending off. I needed to anyway because of the headache. Farspeech alone didn't cause me much pain, but when I tried other abilities too, my head quickly redlined. Peach sent me sweet feelings, but she was too sick to be chatty.

The day passed and as the sun began to wester, I figured we were at the halfway point to Hopi territory. Nuk and Shy must have been thinking the same thing as they deviated from the flat path up an incline into a box canyon. There was an old monastery in the canyon at the base of the bluff. The titans stayed a distance away, having some playtime with their Zuulie kids.

The sign said Winona naka Beachside and just under that, Tontine Abbey. It was a fancy affair in the middle of nowhere. The bright lights brought stark relief to the classic gothic features which CleanerBots and ScrubberDrones kept immaculate. It was a casino resort. There were dozens of people milling about, but they were clean and dressed to the nines. Me and my Crew were scrubby, dirty, and dressed with a post-vomitus flair. Thankfully we were ignored. I saw two men walking past, clearly very rich and very drunk. They flicked their cigarette butts to the ground and the world came to an end. At least the proprietors would have you think so. As the burning stubs hit the plaza cobble, dozens of CleanerBots and two angry humans rushed to the scene. In the dictionary, under conniption you would see what I saw. While the bots cleaned, the humans harangued the would-be guests within an inch of their lives. Then they saw us. That world-ending drama encircled us and without as much as a by your leave, the CleanerBots, humans and several other bots and drones I couldn't identify began cleaning and poking and prodding us. We held still; fighting it would make it worse. In a minute we were clean, and a guy dressed in a monk's habit approached.

"You are soiled beyond redemption. This is an establishment for respectable clients, not ragamuffin outcasts. You will not be billed for the cleaning, but I must insist you keep you and your rabble away."

The process had been uncomfortable, but the cleaning had been kinda nice. We were less sticky and grimy. The lot of us walked back toward the titans. The little Zuulies were taking a nap and we set up camp quietly. Cricket made a fire while Binky took off to hunt with Wogs, Peach, and Teddy. We dined on rabbit and much more. Among the Taters were plenty of cooks. We had a cauldron full of rabbit jambalaya. They brought up alfredo pasta, mounds of fruits and veggies and Red Lobster biscuits. I had no idea why they were called that, but they were the best biscuits I'd ever had. Trespassers Will glommed onto the biscuits and veggies and stayed away from the cauldron of his ostensible kinsmen. Harry took his leave of us that evening, heading his taxi toward the California coast, maybe Los Angeles.

This is where we made camp for the night. Nothing bothered us except for the buzz and hubbub coming from the resort. Like the rest, I cuddled up near mama and papa Zuulie. My fear was they might roll over on me in the night, but when I woke, I wasn't a pancake. The Taters had parked the rigs and cars at the foot of the hill. Norm and Petey and the Tater

Tots left the following morning for Las Vegas. They were loud and boisterous; Norm and Petey invited us to come see their show in Vegas and bid us goodbye. Trespassers Will went with them.

The next day, near evening time, we arrived in Bakabi. All the Skinwalkers were welcomed into the community and the Hopi family. The Kelmuya festival was already underway and new tribal members were being inducted. That night Nuk and Shy and all the little Zuulies were welcomed as Hopis. Then a surprise came. Flu Cat sauntered into the bonfire light with Pooka riding atop. Behind them came Soomalee and a band of fourteen men and women with almost as many children. They were a Skinwalker tribe. An odor wafted my way from the newcomers…you see how smell sensitive I am now. Gosh, what a pain.

Something unexpected happened. My headache bloomed as my body decided to do something of its own accord. A second later my thoughts were different, simpler and a guttural growl came from my muzzle. I had shifted into full Chupa form. I had eyes only for the new arrivals. My only drive was to assert dominance. I rushed at them, pushing aside all the humans and synths in my way. In my reptile pea-brain I felt I was easily the most powerful here. In a show of dominance, I roared at the new arrivals. They cowered, some turning full Chupa while a couple of the men stayed in human form, staring at me with neutral expressions. Those that stayed in human form were not abasing themselves. It was time to show them who was boss, Chupa style. I angled to attack them when a foot the size of a jacuzzi stepped carefully in front of me. The smell hit me first. This was the ultimate alpha, ancient Nuckalavee. I had no choice; my body knew the score. I cowered and abased myself, rolling over to expose my neck and softer parts. The titanic foot descended to rest on me for a moment. The moment passed but the titan remained quietly towering above me.

I heard a rumbling deep chuckle and something golden, and light like spring rain enveloped me. As I was forced out of my Chupa form, I realized Nuk had converted me back to human and the spring rain…well, he was pissing on me. Humans, synths, and every other lifeform stepped way back to avoid the hose job.

The Chupacabra group laughed and the non-Chupas caught on and laughed as well, albeit more uncomfortably. The word was passed that this was normal behavior and to not be alarmed.

Elder Tala came over to me along with the other Hopi Elders. "I see ancient Nuk has given you your baptism. I'm not sure we want to include this in our yearly Kelmuya, but it sure was damned funny." The laughter was contagious and Nuk returned to the periphery of the gathering while I cleaned up my mess. Thankfully I got help.

Binky raised her voice, "So ChupaKip, looks like you chalk this one up for the most pissed you've ever been at a party!"

A new round of laughter came, and I smiled as I walked down to the public shower. Peach and Soomalee came along. They tended to me like I was their personal charge. At that moment I was thankful and relieved to be getting clean.

Soomalee spoke, "Kip sent Soomalee with Lugh and Lucy to meet Seek-Bright-Chanter. Since we work here now, we invited all Skinwalker clan to join us."

"Hey Soo, I am so happy for you. Sorry about being so stupid just now."

"Kip is still baby Chupa. You don't yet control your inner nature. You need to talk with Seek about how to grow up."

Peach had been watching me and I realized I was showering in front of them in my birthday suit. Usually, I would be freaked out. Why not now?

Peach's eyes took in my whole form unapologetically, "You know you're a hairy mess. Let's take you back to the house to get you tidied up, okay?" I put my wet clothes back on. I'd scrubbed them best I could, but she was right, I still looked like a wreck. Soomalee went back to the fire with a quick nod and smile to Peach.

We walked to our big house cum research facility, hand in hand. Back at the house Peach trimmed me like a German Sheperd and spent a long time grooming me. I was looking clean and sharp and Peach gave me an appraising look that promised something special. Since clothing was optional my bedroom door closed and I realized I had fallen for Peach years ago. Back then my excuse to kepp distance was her young age. That didn't apply anymore.

Later we rejoined the bonfire as the festival had begun to wind down. My Crew gave the wink and nudge to us, and we sat down to some hot cocoa and Tom & Jerrys. Music was in the air and when I checked I could hear it on the Cloud airwaves too. Seek was singing a melody with complex tones. My Crew and many others had instruments playing and the Elder drum circle kept beat.

December 2257 - Fimbulvetr Workstead – North of Las Vegas

Chalkippe was the latest addition to the Rovers, and she was a total live wire. Some people called her Chalk Pipe at which point they would get a solid drubbing for the offense. Arne, Rupert, and Morris had their hands full. The Rovers, also known as the Friends of Dorothy, were a loose band of friends who tried to make some dime as guides and providers of rare products. Me and my Crew landed with an unusual entourage. They were not prepared or expecting us, but I could tell we were a welcomed distraction. Croatoan was there, in the flesh. It was clear he wasn't as welcome as we were.

"Kip, I made this for you," Croatoan put a necklace on me. The stout chain held an orb with a silver clasp. The orb was the size of my thumb and it glowed dimly with an iridescence. A brief warmth spread out from where the orb rested against my skin.

"Keep this with you and on your person at all times. Soon this Juxta will serve you in a time of need."

Time passed. We had been at Fimbulvetr for a week, and I was already fed up with Croatoan and his pronouncements and portents of dire things to come and I had lost his precious Juxta. I didn't tell him it disappeared, I believe in the Pachinko jungle. Chalkippe had been brought in to accelerate the mapping and resource accounting in the sprawling subterranean facility. And we were there to use it as a base of operations. At least Argus said so.

We settled into a rhythm of restoring the gigantic, sprawling underground complex. The place was much bigger than we imagined when we briefly visited a few years before. It was literally an underground city. Fimbulvetr had been built back when Powers of the time suspected an all-out nuclear Armageddon. When we left out the first time the place became a refuge for those from the LA: CENTER exodus. Others came from the scattered houses of pain and dens of despair. The place was bustling now. Vagabond and his surrogate Hechombre, joined us and spent most of their hours in Fimbulvetr Control wing. Argus had been moved there and he was looking much healthier without all the wires sticking in him. He sure smelled a whole lot better.

We found out the Jungle Room was a direct import from the planet Soran, home of the Crith. Apparently, the vines didn't develop a mind of their own until they encountered spores from my Dad's mushrooms. I recall the little signs he had for all his shroom species. The one that combined with the Crith Vines were Scintilla Mycena, the ones with the pretty lights. Now the vines also glowed with a subtle electrical field in interesting patterns.

As it turned out Consuela Schlepkiss, Urgle Gru and Shtherren had survived the attack in Winnipeg and were quite interested in resuming their experiments with me as the subject. I wasn't anxious to get started and avoided them like the plague. Most of the military types were in and out; it was good to see old friends as well as new ones. The Vor and Crith integrated their efforts with terrestrial military which made for some wild planning sessions, some of which I skipped.

Since I was in command, I could call the shots. I had delegated control earlier, but I was still expected to play an active part in the planning and operations. It felt unnatural to tell Vagabond to do anything, but at one point I asked him to recon the Rosario facility to see if my Dads were alive. He told me his guys had been all over it and salvaged all the equipment that wasn't radioactive. But he said he would take Pilgrim, Siva, and Jack with him and do a broader search, in-person. Prak volunteered his personal SigmaCraft which being inertialess and fast would get them there in a few minutes. The morning they left I asked them to meet briefly, and I told them not to come back if they didn't find evidence of their fate, one way or the other. Whatever bee was in my bonnet it surfaced as anger directed at them. They took it in stride. They knew I had waited years and put the Liberation business before my own interests. They left without a word. I kept the stiff upper lip walking the halls back to my quarters. Once my room door shut, I lost it. Peach had gone on a mission with Teddy and Wogs, and I was alone, to stew by myself. I knew my Dads were gone because they would never have missed all the action if they were alive. After a couple hours of raving madness, I slept. When I woke, I knew I needed another mission, pronto.

March 2258 - Barking Cheeks Bar, outside Lincoln, Nebraska near the Bot Fields

Billy Boy was holding forth to a small group of adoring followers. He was regaling his audience with a tale, Ribaldry from Tralfamadore, a waggish story of his own devising. He said it was not far from a planet called Wobegon. The founder of the Billy Boys and his partner Edward Hooligan were like a comedy duo. The funny thing, Billy was from London whereas Edward was a local Nebraskan. You wouldn't know it to hear them though. Billy had a right thick mid-western drawl and Edward affected a faux Cockney accent. Edward was affectionately known as Reverend Bluejeans and was renowned for delighting his guests with implausible yarns and brown-trousering unfortunate troublemakers at the Bar. Billy's father sat at a small table in a dark part of the bar. It was clear he was the business manager who controlled the comings and goings of partners, allies, and enemies, especially enemies… he kept them closest. Known only as Old Don Piano, no one knew or could remember his original name. Most said he was a real cool cat, though. Old Don played the piano with style and verve and kept the Cheeks hopping.

I was there to meet a friend of the Hopis, Barny Sackett. Barny was a cousin of Dandy Sackett from Boomtown. The Sacketts had a long family history in the Midwest and if anyone could help us, Dandy said it would be him. The bar was a rough looking dive in the middle of Dog Patch, Nebraska, not far from the ruins of Lincoln. We had taken Black Betty and since the Vor upgraded the car you would think an inertialess drive would have gotten us there fast. Nope. The stupid thing should be renamed the jerky drive. It would have been better riding a Zuulie to Nebraska. Aloha, the AI pilot of Black Betty was on strike and taking a vacay on the planet Endor where I set up a pleasing habitat for her. Maybe that had been poor timing on my part.

Halfway from Hopi territory Cricket set the car down and drove the roads the rest of the way. We were chased by Cavalry, Junkers, and some angry wildlife, but it was still better than flying in a frenetic maraca. Now we were in Nebraska. If you've never been there, be prepared, it is rolling hills that roll and roll, through corridors of tall wheat and corn. It goes on forever. Boring, just how I liked it. Since the CSA depended on the Nebraska breadbasket, the highway patrol kept roving bands and destructive wildlife at bay. Thankfully, we didn't get pulled over. Mone of us had driver's licenses.

I went into the Barking Cheeks solo to speed up the process. I looked for Barny, but didn't see him. When I walked in no one took notice of me. The smells of diner food mingled with stale beer, urine, and peanuts. The crunching sound of peanut shells under my feet was a familiar Midwest bar tradition. The electric bull in the corner looked ready to ride; I am sure that would be quite the sight later tonight. I ordered a beer and sat in a booth to the side. I wondered if this Billy Boy was really the same one who operated street gangs in LA. He sure didn't act like a thug.

As the sun set, I saw more people entering from both the front and rear. I was told Barny would be an unmistakable sight, but what he looked like I had no idea. As I waited a Catholic Nun walked into the bar and I felt like there was about to be a punchline. The nun walked over to Don Piano, and she lent a hand to help him rise. She escorted him to the piano where he sat and moments later began playing a blues riff. The riff became Mack the Knife. Another man, dressed as a roaring 20s gangster sidled up to duet the song with the nun. I later learned the gangster man had taken the name Mack the Knife. They crooned a creamy smooth rendition.

By the end of the song my Crew came in. Nobody seemed to care we were underage, so neither did we.

After the applause Don Piano spoke into his microphone and introduced his group, "Thank you everyone. It's great to have y'all with us this evening. We have the usual lineup tonight, but I also have for you something special coming up in a few minutes. Before I announce that, first I want to give a shout out to the Reverend Bluejeans for his hard work feeding the staff and all you ungrateful bastards in the audience."

A few laughs came, "No, but really, the Reverend, our own Eddie Hooligan keeps all the trains running on time 'round here. Love ya buddy." Edward Hooligan mouthed 'love ya' and pointed at the old man.

"Y'all recall Frank Sinatra, right? Yep, the very same who headed up the Rat Pack in the 20th. Well, for this next number join us in singing, Fly Me to the Moon."

The bar joined in and it was amazing! They sounded like a rehearsed choir. Man, it would be great to play for a crowd like this one! Then the song wrapped up.

"Alright friends, we're going to take a couple minutes to get ready for the next number. Our guest artists have just arrived, and we need to get them set up." The last few words Don Piano spoke while looking directly at me.

On cue, my Crew rose to meet Don Piano, Eddie, Billy, and Christine, also known as Nun the Wiser. We were introduced to Barny, who looked nothing like I was told. He had been bopping about the whole time and I had no idea. The guy was dressed in drag, and he was easily the most stylish lady in the bar.

My Crew was smiling as understanding dawned in my thick brain. "Did you guys know about this?"

"Know about it? Barny helped us arrange the whole thing, doofus." Wogs had that self-satisfied expression she wore when she had done something amazing.

"Cricket and I did the foot work with Barny, and Binky got the instruments lined up."

"Come on man, let's get ready!" Cricket was more excited than I'd seen him in a long time.

I caved, "Well, okay, let's do this!" Whoops and shouts from the thickening crowd foretold a night of serious coolness.

We had played a set at the Rutting Duck, but this was different: my Crew had organized the whole thing as a suprise fopr me. It took a little longer than expected to get rolling but soon we were set to go with me on rhythm guitar, Cricket on bass, Binky on drums and Wogs on electric ukulele. Binky snapped a tattoo beat and landed us on a 4/4 fast tempo. We kicked into one of Cricket's favorites and he stepped forward to take lead vocals in Buck Owens' Tiger by the Tail. Peach was given a mic, and she became backup vocals. She didn't know any of the songs, but she could read the stage lyric prompter perfectly fine. Teddy sat on a cajón and matched the beat. We traversed several genres and probably sounded janky. But, we got our stride after a couple numbers. From Chris Rea, Auberge to Deep Purple's Smoke on the Water, we played a 90-minute set full of drive and energy. We peaked with Ricky Skaggs' Country Boy and I thought my hands would die with exhaustion. It was rough for me; I was so unpracticed, but it was clear my Crew had prepared, and I leaned on them when the changes got dicey. Don Piano and his whole ensemble kept us solid and helped drive us home. Our closer was a piece Don Piano suggested. He kicked us off with a piano riff leading into the Beatle's Ob-la-di, Ob-la-da. I used my pad and holo unit to project the lyrics for the house on the wall and the place literally roared with singing.

"Colonel, Team X is moving to engage the target. Five mikes until contact," the Bangarang special team commander was uneasy. Usually, an extraction was the family of some high mucky muck against whom pressure was needed by the LT. These kids were 024 and dangerous, yet their orders were to apprehend, and not harm. Yeah, good luck with that; these kids were some of the best protected people on the planet.

"Bangarang is heading in Major Kliese." Bad Wolf team leader Lieutenant Chan had volunteered for this assignment. It was 024 who had been responsible for the death of his family. All the team members felt the same. It was personal.

"Roger. Is the tunnel access breached, yet?" Major Kliese figured this was going to be a bloody extraction. Their job was a grab-and-go. The opposition closing in was an unfortunate complication.

"Breached and entered. Bangarang will engage before we do."

"When is estimated contact?"

"Best estimate 15 mikes."

"Lieutenant, send the overland team in now and stay away from Bangarang."

"Sir, the EM field is still suppressing all electronics. Its signature is unfamiliar. Best guess it's 3rd party."

"Lieutenant, do we have any idea of the 3rd party? I think we disqualified Crane and the major Powers."

"No idea sir."

Cpt. Meyers and the Bangarang team huddled at the edge of the parking lot. The all-clear hand signal was given, and Meyers' team fanned out and began weaving around trucks and cars and a couple horses. Team X made for the kitchen entrance. The door opened just as they arrived. Out walked a man dressed as a chef who looked completely unsurprised at finding the soldiers there.

"Hey guys. I thought since you're out and about in the chill you might want to come join us for some chili, cornbread, and beer. We also have vegan patties and some other things if you're on restricted diets."

The man looked around at the soldiers dressed in all the latest tech, all wearing black. All wearing night-vision goggles.

"And since your electronics aren't working here, you might as well give your hand signals for your support folks to come join us. Come inside when you're ready." The man smiled, turned about, and went back in. The door was left ajar.

"This tunnel appears to be regularly used, sir." Sgt. Peterson was an augment; it was a considered fighting words if you said half-synth. "The suppression field is somewhat less down here, but it's still playing with my optics."

Lieutenant Thiessen knew he was in a race with Bangarang to capture 024, "Sgt. Kaos, please have one of your guys recon the entrance."

"Blake, Perez, go." Sgt. Kaos nodded to move out.

Both soldiers gave the 'affirmative' hand signals. Hand signals were used when electronic comms were down. They disappeared into the dark. Minutes passed and the main complement of Alpha group found Blake and Perez standing with weapons pointed at a man in a chef's outfit. The door to the upstairs was fully open with bright light flooding through.

"Sir, we have a problem," Perez had a consternated face as did Blake.

"Soldiers, pull back." Lt. Thiessen shook his head.

A man in a chef's outfit spoke, "You are expected. Your Bangarang friends are already here. Come join us."

As the man turned, Thiessen gave the nod. Perez and Blake stepped back 3 paces and fired headshots at the cook. The air blurred and the bullets plinked to the floor at his feet.

"Guys, you're in the big leagues now. Those will be of no use to you here. You might as well put them away and come on up. Or stay down here a while if you want." The chef went back in and footsteps could be heard ascending the stairs.

"I've never seen bullets just stop before. Usually, they ricochet like crazy against a field," Sgt. Kaos had already slung his rifle over his back.

"Okay guys, new approach. Sling rifles and let's go join the party." Lt. Thiessen was no dummy. He came from over ten generations of graduates from military academies: Annapolis, West Point, Colorado Springs, and New London. He had graduated from the latest addition to that family at Lunar Base Tranquility, with the Joint Space Admin. His was a master's degree in Belter commerce. He planned to be a part of the growing commerce enforcement arm of the JSA. He was on loan to Bad Wolf special operations for a year. His time was drawing to a close, or so he thought. Whoever developed this new tech was a likely hitch in his plans. Something felt ominous and he didn't like it.

"Okay, now a drink to my Crew who successfully botched the ending of almost every song tonight." A general sound of raspberries came from around the tables.

"Yeah, and to a lead who can't keep a steady rhythm," Wogs poked me in the side.

Soldiers began filing in and my smooth groove just got rough.

"Good friends, some soldiers were outside and wanted to come in. I have invited them in for a meal and some discussion. Please welcome them." One of the Vor was dressed as kitchen staff. As he took off the chef's hat the soldiers took their seats at the empty tables.

A few minutes later I heard raised voices from a group of soldiers sitting nearby. So much for these guys playing nicely, but I guess when Bangarang and Bad Wolf troops are in the same house, trouble follows.

"Those are just old wives' tales. Next, you're gonna tell me aliens have replaced our world leaders and secretly are plotting to destroy the world." Two soldiers were red in the face, staring daggers across their table.

"Ain't telling you nothing, moron. It's already done. It's only a matter of time before humans blip out of the universe. It's a done deal!" Both soldiers were about to stand when another voice raised above the din.

The Vor spoke loudly over the din, "Your Earth has been inhabited by aliens for longer than the human race has been around. In fact, did you know on our Vor homeworld the first sentient race of Earth is still thriving? A small group of the reptiloid sentients were exited prior to the K-T event." The soldiers from both factions and all the other regular tavern attenders were struck silent. Credulous stares accompanied raspberries and snide under-breath comments.

"Among you today you have both Vor and Crith agents. Good beings, please stand." Over half the tavern goers stood.

"Now, my Crith friends please show us briefly your TrueForm." These people looked uncertainly at each other, then shifted. As balls of glowing light, they were beautiful. The soldiers rapidly stood at this change with shocked exclamations. It seemed the pudding was more than enough proof for these guys. The Crith shifted back.

"My soldier friends, please sit. There is much more I want you to know." Uneasily they sat, realizing their earthly conflicts were about to pale in the face of something orders of magnitude larger.

"Shhh, quiet now. I am going to give you the smallest sketch of your history and your present situation. For now, please just listen."

The Vor paused for effect then continued, "First, who am I?"

One of the soldiers interrupted, "You're and effing alien, dumbass." Both groups of soldiers found that humorous. No one else was laughing.

Ignoring the outburst, he proceeded, "I am called Croatoan." And I realized it wasn't a

Vor. He looked different, but then his appearance shifted like a Skinwalker's, and he was as I knew him from before.

" I have served as your planetary protector for a long time. Vor friends, I apologize for insinuating myself into your ranks. I needed to know you were truly with us in our attempt to save this planet." He stopped for a moment. "Vor and Crith friends, would you all please stand?"

The alien people who hadn't turned into balls of light stood, looking uncomfortable to be called out again.

"Thank you, please sit. We are aliens who are here to help you. Just so you all know I am neither Vor nor Crith. Here is my TrueForm." At this point he instantly morphed into a quadrupedal tentacular mess with beautiful big blue eyes, four of them, and green multi-hued skin with swirling patterns and a light fuzz coating. And as quickly he appeared human again, looking like the Croatoan I knew.

"For millennia, Earth and it's peoples had nothing to fear from its stellar neighbors." At this a hologram appeared which was no hologram. The image was manifesting via Cloud power, I could feel it. The dimensions of the room faded as the image became more real than our surroundings. We were all floating in a shallow ocean.

"Earth's first life came about billions of years ago, then it died, then started again, many times. At a point something stuck and not long after, you were visited by a team of scientists."

"As time passed, they watched over your planet, and seeded it with a special mixture in various places. In truth 1000s different combinations were tried, looking for the right one. The scientists were mavericks who were more interested in how your planet would respond to the seeding, unconcerned about the imprecision of their approach."

We were all too spellbound to interrupt but I needed to pee badly. Surprisingly Croatoan detected this.

He dimmed the simulation, "Some of us have full bladders. If it's okay with you, we will continue in five minutes." I mouthed a thank you and hustled to the restroom.

"Oh, Lt. Chan and Cpt. Meyers, I will allow you to make contact with your command. Let them know you are in negotiations but don't say with whom. Let them try puzzling that out. It will buy us time to finish up here."

Croatoan went pee like the rest of us. It felt like standing next to a deity and discovering he was as much tied to physical constraints as the next fellow. He seemed more real, more human. People in the bar, hicks and scientists, bikers and ranchers, aliens, synths, and others were all too riveted to want to be elsewhere. Food and drinks piled on the tables and Billy and his staff kept the grub and brew coming.

The simulation had appeared faint and ghostly as we had our poddy break, but now it reasserted itself.

"Twenty-one seedings produced the precursors to humans, the remainder created pre-sentients of a wide variety. Some of these were based on life which thrived on other planets, other seedings were completely synthetic. The silicon lifeform seeding was a bust, I am sad to say." As Croatoan explained we got to see snippets over (I guess) millions of years as small animals became larger, then hit a point and died out. "Some seedings produced hundreds of variants."

Croatoan must not get out very often because he sure loved to hear himself talk. He extolled at length about dinosaurs and mammals, reptiles and avians. As the only guy in the room to have witnessed these things firsthand his words were gospel.

"The simulation I am showing you isn't manufactured. By that I mean you are seeing clips of actual scenes from your Earth. One day I will share all this with your scientists and historians." His explanation provided details of our paleontology and archaeology. Even the most jaded soldiers were attentive. Billy and his staff quietly kept filling cups with beer or water, removing remnants and bringing back new tasty tidbits.

About a thousand meters above the Barking Cheeks hovered the Argo and Janussaries. "Hey, Argo Actual. Rus, you got your ears on?"

"Negative Janussaries. Is the Actual speaking?" Bixby was a stickler for protocol.

"Roger that, this is Cicero. Where is Rus?"

"Bixby here, he is um, having a sit-down discussion"

"Ah, you know you can say the word crap, okay? Anyhow, let him know we've heard from Croatoan and have been requested to apply shielding over the whole site." Cicero smiled despite himself.

"Roger that. Shields are up and the suppressor field is active. We are shielding to one kilometer, centered on the compound." Bixby was crisp as usual.

"Tech is hearing some odd chatter Online, but the radiowaves are silent. He suspects B&B will be launching some kind of concerted attack soon. Let me know if you pick up anything, Bixby. Cicero out."

"Thanks, Janussaries Actual, Argo out."

"Kip, everyone here knows who you are. I know many of these soldiers hold you and your group personally responsible for deaths of loved ones. None of the deaths are the fault of you kids," he indicated the four of us.

"My soldier friends, I have chosen you to be my grassroots communicators of my plan for Earth and humans. Others will carry the message, but you will help, if you are willing." The soldiers looked at each other uncertainly.

"First, the Vor and Crith are no longer working for their prior employers. Thanks to Kip they have been freed from the enslavement that has held them captive for millennia. The good news is the 10s of thousands of Vor and Crith are already integrated within a terrestrial military organization." At this the soldiers were surprised and looking edgy for the first time. Their common thought was which military organization is allied with the aliens?

"No need for anxiety, my soldier friends. It is a new Power that has brokered an alliance. And this alliance is about one thing: saving all earthly life from destruction. Your organizations are receiving invites as I speak to join this alliance. Your job from this day forward is to explain the situation in your own words to as many people as will listen. Our invites make it clear that each of you is a special emissary. Do you feel a warmth going down your spine right now?"

Croatoan had somehow activated my powers and directed something subtle and delicate at the soldiers and every other regular human in the bar. It calmed all who were touched by it, and I saw a light golden glow around each soldier.

"You have now been imbued with marginal Cloud powers. I have also given you more information on how you will help us and enough insight into the plan to answer most questions you might have."

I felt it. Croatoan actually needed my help to imbue these soldiers with the same freedom and power I had given the Vor and Crith. A thought occurred. Since I was connected to all the soldiers, I had an opportunity to farspeak something more personal to them. I decided to tell them a story in rapid, compressed format. I told them my story, the good, the bad and the ugly. I let them see my losses, loves, and triumphs. As I connected with them, I could sense their thoughts and emotions. I could feel their aches and pains. I opened myself up fully so they could see it all. I allowed them to share a little slice of my family and its love. I invited them to be family.

At that point every soldier stood. When I was broadcasting, I let everyone in the bar see what I was sending, but I kept the soldiers' thoughts private. Their conversion was almost instant.

One soldier stood and spoke, "I think I speak for every soldier here. We are with you. I'm not quite sure why, but I trust you, Kip. You may just be a kid, but your heart is good, and the plan is clear," Lieutenant Thiessen made eye contact with both sets of soldiers and with curt nods he knew all were agreed, "so I think we would like to stay a while, have some of this amazing dinner, then we can be on our way. So's ya know, either one of our organizations will be striking this place within the hour. Hope you have a plan for that."

The soldiers all sat down, dug into the grub, and began jabbering with each other. Normalcy resumed and it was just like chow time at the mess hall. After my sending, everyone ignored Croatoan.

"Hey Cro man, aren't you going to keep going with your story?" Wogs was as curious as the rest of us.

"Mollie, all the stories will be revealed to you soon. I promise. For now, suffice to say that the plan is coming along nicely, and our various and disparate forces are coming together better than originally hoped."

"Janussaries, are you seeing the airships inbound?" Rus apparently was done with his business.

"Roger that, Argo. We make out over 116 heavies and 1258 light air units. That's bigger than the CSA combined forces." Tech also showed Cicero there were ground units from every direction closing in. It's a trap!

"I hope Croatoan knows what he's doing. I doubt even together we could repel that firepower."

"Agreed. We haven't heard anything from below. Try to raise him now."

"Yes, let's."

Croatoan spoke, "Kip, our time has come to leave. Soldiers, please head outside now. Everyone else, we will be travelling another way." A nine-foot oval appeared in the air in front of us. Looking through I could see a big steel-lined room, looking very steam-punky. No way! This guy could create portals.

"Yes, Kip and so can you. All you need do is picture a destination and imagine a doorway to the place.

Croatoan used Cloud power to send a message that travelled via RF, "Argo, Janussaries, you are cleared to leave. Be safe and thank you."

Both ships rose vertically and departed in different directions. They didn't break stealth and left unmolested.

I confronted Croatoan, "You manufactured this event. How much of our lives is something you created?"

He considered for a moment, "I calculate probabilities. I don't have a crystal ball to see the future. But you and the other three are the height of my creation. For this to play out right, you have to succeed."

All non-military people and aliens went through the portal. Only me and my Crew remained with Croatoan on this side. I inspected the hole in the air and noticed the edges were hazy. I looked close and I could almost see glimpses of other landscapes and places in the hzy edges, but my eyes could not settle on one point to look deeper. The dimensions flexed somewhat, maybe a centimeter back and forth. The movement had a rhythm like breathing. Then Croatoan was close at my side,

"Kip, look at my chest," he exaggerated his own breathing, and I realized the rhythm matched the movement of his chest. "You are right, the portal is almost a living entity. It is a part of me as is any other Cloud manifestation I create. The creator can sense his creation and literally breathes life into it. That is a gift and curse. On the one hand it gives you highly intuitive control of the creation; on the other if something harms the creation, you will feel it.”

“What happens if I fail? If we fail.” I wasn’t sure what I was asking.

“You will know what you need to do. If I bias you with too much insight the probability of success goes to nil.” Croatoan wore a regretful expression.

I touched the edge of the portal and it felt soft and squishy. Then a tendril poked out and lightly smacked my hand. I yanked my hand back and turned to see Croatoan snickering. “As you practice, your creation can do whatever you imagine.”

He was about to step through then asked, “Perhaps you can go to the table over there and grab the large jug of water?”

As I walked to get the water, I felt an image in my mind of exactly where his portal was landing people; I knew exactly. As I rounded the table back toward the portal, I noticed Croatoan was gone. With him went the portal. My head began to pound, and my heart raced as my anxiety spiked.

Croatoan’s voice came via farspeech, “You need to imagine the destination. Then, imagine a hole in the air where you can see that destination. Come join us when you’re ready.”

March 2258 – CSA Carrier Enterprise, hovering above Colorado

My Powers were not yet ready to form a portal. I tried anyway and earned a doozy of a headache, atop the one I was already nursing. I tried for the next minute, but it was like I had no umph, no juice to make it happen. Every other time I successfully used powers I had been helped by someone else. It was like I needed another person to open a door inside my head. Once it was open, it was easier than pie, but without the help I was dead in the water. I knew I was sunk.

I heard footsteps from outside and a moment later the entrances were flooded with soldiers. Not the friendly soldiers I met earlier.

“Down! Get down! Down now! Don’t move!” Multiple voices yelled and it scared the hell outta me.

Other voices commanded, “Up, stand up, move to the wall. Now!” While yet others said, “Hands on your head!” and “Stand where you are!” and “Hands on the table!”

“Okay, okay, I am not resisting. Hey!” A soldier struck me with the butt of his rifle in my face, then the floor hit me. I closed my eyes as soldiers gathered around and started up a stomp kick fest with me as the target. They must have gotten bored with that and I felt knees press me against the floor. I couldn’t get a breath. I was panicking and moments later I went unconscious. I woke a couple more times to discover they were still beating on me.

I heard dim voices as I came to.

“Yeah, we got the perp.”

“Heard this is the ringleader of 24. Not much of the leader if you ask me. Gave up like a real wuss.”

“Naw, you know executive types. They act all tough until you put some real hurt on ‘em. Then they cry like babies, all of them.”

I was out again, and sometime later I came around. I was lying on a couch in a room scented with lilac. Or at least it smelled like the perfume Cheri called Lilac Dream. As my vision cleared, I saw what I imagined a 19th century bordello would look like. Red and black, lots of velvet and plush fancy furniture. It was strikingly similar to Fast Eddie’s place. The walls were lit with live flame sconces; I could smell a kerosene scent like at Cricket’s cabin. There were bay windows on three sides of the room, looking out onto a fluffy, cotton landscape. The clouds were rolling by and I knew we were in a bug ship.

I heard a voice. “Ahh, Mr. Wefer, good to see you. Take your time sitting up; I think my people may have given you a rough time,” the smug voice was thick with a southern drawl. Sight unseen, I already didn’t like this guy.

I slowly sat up and confirmed the nauseating décor and immediately recognized the svelte man in the chair across the oval table from me. I had seen his face but couldn't place it.

The man asked, "So, you know who I am?"

"I am not sure. Don't you work for the CSA?"

"Hah, yeah, I work for the CSA." The man smiled, not unkindly.

"I am Solomon Fisk, Chairman of the CSA." He smiled and proceeded to stare at me like I was a curious lab rat. He had beautiful teeth, perfectly tanned skin, and deep green eyes. Oh, the eyes. I found I was very attracted to him and that kinda grossed me out. I was a month shy from being 20 and this guy must be pushing 60. Peach would laugh at me.

"Are you going to kill me, then?"

"Kill you? Oh, my dear boy heavens no. You are my highly anticipated guest."

"A crappy welcome for a highly anticipated guest, don't you think?" I juiced up the sarcasm best I could muster.

"Agreed. I apologize for my soldiers. They are a nuisance and have little patience for the finer things in life."

"Mmm hmm, finer things, like kicking a person when they're down…again and again?" this guy's suavity was starting to grate on my nerves.

Solomon snapped his fingers. A primped and poofed butler, sporting a walking cane poked his head in the door. "Axl, please have Commander Daniels come in."

Axl disappeared and a moment later a soldier appeared. "Commander, what were my instructions about apprehending the children of 24?"

"Sir, you said use all due care and bring them in unharmed. Sir." The Commander looked cool and in-control.

"And do you think you accomplished that directive?"

"Sir, we accomplished 25% of that directive as you have Mr. Wefer before you now."

"No. Did you accomplish the directive as you stated first?" The Commander's body took on a new tension.

"Sir, yes. My troops brought him in unharmed."

Solomon looked at me and the bruises and cuts on my face, "So I take it those marks on Kip's face were something else?"

"Yes, sir. We found him in the condition you see."

"Hmm, odd. Who made first contact, Commander?"

"That would be Sgt. Connelly, sir."

"Axl, have Sgt. Connelly brought in." We waited in silence, and I could see the Commander beginning to perspire. Little beads dotted his forehead.

A rough-hewn soldier entered, "Sir, Sgt. Connelly, reporting!" Too loud! This guy needed to use his inside voice.

"Ah, thank you Sergeant. Please tell the Commander and me how you apprehended the individual sitting before you."

"It was a tough grab-and-go. We entered the establishment bimodal, acquired the perp on visual and beat down all resistance. He was a fighter, but we got 'em." The Sergeant wore a proud expression on his face, but the Commander had turned sheet white.

"A fighter, huh? Hmm. Axl, display the arrest on the table holo." The lights dimmed.

The Commander knew he was in trouble but had the wisdom to stay quiet.

A small holo of the scene at the Barking Cheeks appeared and ran through the whole scenario. The soldiers entered and saw me standing in the middle of the room. I recall waking several times with them beating me and there it was on holo display, plain to see. I could feel the kicks as I watched. The holo vanished with the last scene of three of the soldiers placing their feet on my unmoving form to pose for a picture.

My eyes traveled up Solomon's leg to land on his face. It was red and angry.

"Commander, I am disappointed. You are dismissed." Even the Sergeant knew to keep his mouth shut as they smartly saluted and retired from the room.

"Kip, you were wronged by my men and for that I am truly sorry. I would like to make this right or at least make it less wrong in some small way. For disobedience and lying I will summarily execute the offending soldiers and all their known family. Sometimes I even add neighbors and friends into the punishment." This guy was serious. I shivered despite myself at how easily he rattled off the punishments the same way you and I might read a grocery list.

"I give you the option to take your revenge. Shall I mete out my usual punishments?" The Chairman of the CSA was actually asking me to decide the soldiers' fates. I only had one answer.

"Sir, may I make up the punishment, myself. I have an idea."

At this he smiled; I wondered what he expected from me.

"Please, yes. You decide."

"I ask you show the footage of the assault to their families. Let their families decide how to hold them accountable."

After a moment he laughed a deep belly laugh. "You are through and through a gentleman…or maybe young and foolish. Perhaps both."

"Axl, come back in, please." The butler stood three paces from the CSA Chairman.

"Sir, the usual?"

"The punishments to be served up will be as Kip has stated. You overheard, correct?"

"Yes, sir, every word. It shall be as you say." I bet that cane of his wasn't for a handicap.

"And finally, how are you feeling? I think we need to have you checked out before we resume our discussion."

"I am feeling better. Maybe a little lie-down would be nice." This guy already knew I was injured and untreated. Nothing he did was accidental. Fisk had no problem with my discomfort; I think his only consideration was keeping me as a healthy asset. This guy was a sociopath.

"Young man, Axl will take you to the ship's sickbay now. No arguments." Axl led me to sickbay; no words were spoken.

I went through a laborious physical checkup and something they called a Chikitsa Bath. The bath was lovely and the drugs they gave me put me out again. When I woke, I had been dressed and was cozy-warm in white linen feather comforters, on a bed of more down comforters. So, so comfy. I felt like I was lying in the clouds I had seen rolling by, earlier.

The butler came for me, "Good afternoon, young sir. The Chairman will see you now."

Axl was a scary guy. The odd thing was I couldn't explain to myself why I was afraid of him. Whatever game Solomon was playing with me, I knew I had to play my cards close, or I might end up in a bad way. He wasn't a forgiving sort.

Fisk was wearing a 3-piece suit, dark gray with a bright red power tie. "It is great to see you looking better, young sir. A week in the Chikitsa has done you a world of good!"

"Hi Mr. Fisk. I'm feeling better." A week! I'd been out for a whole week?

"Please call me Solomon. And please take a seat and have some of the brunch. It's from a meeting I just finished a few minutes ago. The eggs benedict is especially good today." The spread was amazing, and I helped myself.

Solomon spoke, "I know you were having Vagabond and others look for your Dads." He saw my eyes fly wide open.

"No, no, don't be surprised. There are benefits to being the head of the biggest major Power on Earth. I can buy information they way others pay for a candy bar. I knew I would see you soon, so I took the liberty of checking all my intel sources on the whereabouts of your Dads. Nobody knows where they went after the Rosario strike and every remote sensing effort has turned up nothing," he appeared genuinely aggrieved, "I am truly sorry. I wish I had better news."

Fisk had probably ordered the nuke strike or he at least knew about it. And now here he was apologizing for the result of the strike. Did he think I didn't know?

"Thank you, sir. I am afraid they didn't make it out. I think they would have contacted me if they were still alive."

My eyes were suddenly wet, and my throat constricted. I tried to play it off, but he wasn't fooled. Fisk was too canny to see anything but the truth.

"I am sorry for your loss, son. It is a rare person who hasn't lost someone in these troubled times." He sounded sincere and perhaps he was. I still wasn't going to trust him in any way that mattered.

"Solomon, my whole life I grew up with you and the CSA government being the enemy. If you're not going to make me vanish like other people vanished from my town, why do you want me here?" I decided to dive right to the heart of the matter.

"You are direct, Kip. So, let's get into it. I need your help. I don't know for a fact, but I believe you are uniquely the only one who can help me with a problem." I was stunned. How could the leader of the most powerful world power be reduced to needing my help? I would hear him out; what else could I do?

I replied, "Okay, what can I help you with?"

"I had a visit from a man named Croatoan," he saw my expression, "I see you know of whom I speak. Good."

"Yep, he left me at that bar to get nabbed by those soldiers. He's a dick."

"It's disclosure time. That was an agreed meeting. He left you at my request."

That really pissed me off. The bar was a setup to get us to play music, then to hear from Croatoan. But now in a third twist I was setup to be handed over to an enemy of my Dads.

"What a fewking a-hole. You know he's an effing alien, right?"

"That is part of the help I am requesting of you. It's true then; aliens have infiltrated positions of leadership in our world." It was more a statement than a question.

I mulled over what I should tell him. This guy was a sociopath and enjoyed causing pain to others on a scale I could scarcely comprehend, but what other option was available, now? If I lied, he would know. If I hedged on the truth, what would it accomplish? I guess it was time for 'in for a penny' to be 'in for a pound'.

He was brooding, waiting for my response. I closed my eyes and tried my powers to see if I could share my personal history the way I did back at the bar. My head hurt and my brain fizzled. Wow, how stupidly predictable.

"Solomon, may I tell you a story?"

He met my eyes and casually nodded. And so, it began. I spent the next two hours explaining what I understood and what had happened since my exodus from Lake Stevens six years ago. I was amazed that much time had passed since I'd last seen my Dads. I was more amazed at how much had happened between then and now. I took in the clouds passing by the ornate windows but ignored all the scenery below as I delved into my tale.

I paced back and forth as I spoke, sat down, stood, leaned against the wall then sat again. Solomon kept quiet the whole time; only his raised eyebrows and curl of lip showed his attentiveness. Several times Axl peeked in and furtive hand signals passed between the two; I caught the tail end of one exchange and realized they were using ASL. Axl was signing '... still awaiting confirmation'. After I finished, I grabbed a glass of water from the table and chugged the whole thing. I waited for him to say something. A part of me was fearful that he might use the information from my story to hurt the ones I loved. But I decided it was worth the risk that we might gain an ally. The answer was quick.

"Those sonsabitches. You know what chaps my hide, Kip?" I gave him a quick shake of my head, no.

"I garandamntee you those aliens wouldn't be playing mumbley-peg with our dear planet if they didn't see us as a threat. But they came to *us*; we didn't seek them out. I'll tell ya one doggone thing, those fargin bastijes started something, but damn tootin' we are going to finish it."

During his rant his refined New England accent slipped; now he sounded more like a good ol' boy from the antebellum South. Solomon then stared right at me for several beats. It was unnerving! I got up and went to the feasting table to get some fruit juice (guava?). I needed to break that eye contact without showing my fear. When I turned back from the table, I realized a golden glow radiated around Chairman Fisk. Now, when did that happen?

March 2258 The Bot Fields, Nebraska

As my Crew and the others exited the bar through the portal, they stepped into the hold of an enormous ship. It was all steel, struts, rivets and petroleum smell. Almost 60 people arrived through the portal.

"Welcome to the Bot Fields. We are inside one of the Heavies. It's called a SpiderTank. From the outside it looks like a gigantic spider. It was designed to move over uneven terrain quickly and quietly. And we are going to activate it as soon as we get things fixed up."

After that, Croatoan was using farspeech with certain individuals. They broke into teams and headed off with cries of 'got it', 'going now', 'yes, sir' and 'how the hell are you in my head'? Most folks adapted to telepathy naturally, some less so.

"Hey! Where is Kip?" Cricket was the first to notice my absence.

"He will be coming along soon. He stayed behind to send a message to someone important." Croatoan must have tried the mind soothing trick.

Binky shouted at him, "Get out of my head you alien turd. Where is Kip? Tell us, now!"

Binky and my Crew all tried to farspeak me and got nothing. Binky knew something was blocking the signal, or something had happened to me.

He spoke aloud. "Binky, he is heading to an important meeting, the details of which are playing out right now."

"You know what? I am sick of your mysterious riddles. For a while it was endearing, but now…" Wogs had her ire up. Croatoan was nonplussed, and he walked away, exiting the room.

My Crew simmered for a few minutes and discussed what they should do. They agreed they needed to help Croatoan until they could find a good exit. They discovered they were in the officer's mess. Cricket was hungry and led the way in finding food. They found a galley which was well stocked with old cans and pouch entrees. All the fresh food was beyond spoiled; when Wogs opened one of the reefers a puff of moist mold spores enveloped the kitchen. Fortunately, whomever was assigned to get the engines running had done a good job. As a result, the air circulation sucked out the cloud quickly. Cricket found many of his favorite bottled sauces and more: Tabasco, Worcestershire, Hot Ones, and Kamebishi Sauces. He pocketed these in hopes some of them were still good.

"Ach, it's like going down into the Dads' mushroom basement. Except theirs smelled warm and homey and this is just rotten!" Binky scrunched her nose up and the five began dumping the spoilage down the waste chute. Cricket noticed the chute was a long tube to the outside of the craft. It looked like a great last ditch escape method.

Peach commented, "Cool escape route. Let me look!"

She dove into the chute, disappearing with the chute cover slamming shut over her. Teddy yelled and when he opened the cover Peach was staring up at him.

"Gotcha Ted! You thought I fell out the bottom of this tub, huh? Well, there is a whole service area inside here where we could hide or store stuff if we need to get all secret squirrel. Help me out," Teddy grimaced and pulled Peach back out.

"The chute could also be used to ninja-in from the outside." Wogs had that wry smile, and they could tell cogs were turning in her head.

There were no windows in the SpiderTank. Teddy and the others eventually went poking around. He found the ship's nomenclature plate: a commissioning plate. The ship was named Shelob and as my Crew investigated, they discovered she had made 271 kills on the battlefield. Shelob was a ship of the line, first launched in 2088 and was spec'd to crew six with troop carrying capacity of 90. The craft had boring capability, using a revolutionary technology at that time, called a molecular dissipator, Shelob would essentially swim through the rock, water, magma, or any substrate. SpiderTanks became the terrestrial stealth subs of the day. Wogs loved the map room. There were plasticene, 15-minute LatLong and UTM maps. She also found regional and global maps. She spent several hours pulling each map out and used her pad's camera to capture high-res images and setting her MapAI to encoding into decomposable data.

Binky went to the control room, at the heart of the craft, where the crew would be most shielded from outside blasts and nuclear effects. Croatoan was sitting in the pilot's chair, fiddling with the various UI. He said nothing as Binky, Cricket and Wogs came in, trailing Peach, Teddy, and a couple of the former patrons of the bar.

"Croatoan, unless you give us a good reason why we should stay here, we are out." Binky spoke for the Crew. "And I think I can speak for the others that you have become an albatross to us all."

He kept clacking on the keyboard and tapping and swiping holo UIs. Croatoan said nothing. Several others spoke to him with no visible effect.

"Last chance, pal." Cricket had a resigned look on his face as he turned away. The others discussed a plan to get back to where they were from and suddenly the control room doors all snapped shut, audibly locking.

"You are going nowhere. Sit down and wait. I will be with you in a moment."

So dispassionate and calculating. Croatoan was showing his true face. Silently, they all sat or leaned against a bulkhead, and sat for over an hour. More than one needed a restroom visit soon.

Binky spoke up. "Ya know, some of us need to pee," she had a dejected tone. But the need to pee was a mighty motivation and call to action.

Croatoan looked up. "My Vor and Crith have this craft completely ready for service. The need I have for each of you is important enough for me to break one of my own rules: involuntary confinement. For that I am sorry." He stood and stretched, making eye contact with each person.

"We are shaped by our past, not defined by it. Your past is filled with small-mindedness, pettiness, and greed. This is true for all humans. But as a race, you and your kin can aspire to -" Binky interrupted.

"Dude! Come on! I'm about to go pee right here!" Binky was giving the dagger stare.

All the doors opened with a snap. He turned, sat at the console again and began clacking away on the clicky keyboard. "Come back when you're done."

Just outside, Cricket spoke, "What just happened? Wasn't Croatoan supposed to be a level-headed, wise alien advisor type of guy." Cricket and the Crew were concerned more than angry.

"Son, what we saw there was fear. And given that that alien fellow is perhaps the most powerful being on this planet, I am concerned more about what he would be afraid of." Billy had his kindly eyes going and his words had the ring of truth to them. Cricket agreed.

Outside the control room they could hear Croatoan muttering. It sounded like he was arguing with himself; the humans were more than a bit apprehensive. As the few who visited the toilet returned to the group, they began to hatch a plan. The result of every plan seemed to involve violence if they acted as a group, so they determined to split into 2s and 3s and act independently to escape and make their own way out of the Bot Fields. For the moment, they decided to hear him out. Then they would separate and do their best.

As the humans re-entered Croatoan faced them and for the first time in their memory saw him slump.

"Friends, I am afraid. I've received some terrible news and spoken with one of my distant surrogates." He shook his head and went silent.

My Crew wondered if the surrogate-thing he spoke of was like Vagabond's use of

Hechombre. Was it possession or was it a duplicate of himself in a different form? Ever the mind reader, Croatoan replied to the unspoken thoughts.

"It's both. A surrogate agrees to join, merge essentially, to provide a home to a version of the original. The original me, joins with the surrogate to make a new aggregate consciousness. It is only done by mutually consenting parties. Contrast that with the Vor, who have been joined to humans non-consensually. Those are the Vor who are here on Earth. It is a sin against any sentient being to be forced into a union, but one race has capitalized on this forceful method, and it is they we now need fear: the Cleaners. They are the Coali and with the failure of both Vor and Crith agents to carry out their eradication duty, they are forced to use cruder ways of eliminating humans." He paused, clacked on the keyboard for a moment, then turned back.

"Foiling the plan to eliminate the humans was my first effort, but something else happened which was unexpected. You recall hearing how the alien agents were mysteriously turned into helpers of humanity?" Some nodded yes, others had bewildered looks.

"Let me send something to you to clarify for your understanding," a quick package of memories was sent and all those present understood what had happened. The memory fragment carried a sizable amount of information. Finally, much more was revealed about the creation of my Crew and why. It had been Croatoan's plan for a very long time. They all understood that a few Vor and Crith agents were supposed to be unshackled from their slave programming at the hands of the Coali. That happened, but something more happened, unforeseen. It was an infection of sorts.

"Yes, you see now," heads nodded, and eyes were wide with wonder.

"Kip not only freed the Vor and Crith he encountered but gave each the power to do the same in turn to others. But more, when Kip shared his memories and emotions with those agents his story became part of their story. Do you see what that means?"

Croatoan turned to clack some more on the keyboard and the SpiderTank lurched and began to move.

"I think I see. Kip caused an epidemic and its spread beyond Earth, right?" Wogs asked. The ramifications were hitting home.

"You got it in one, Mollie. There were a few Vor and Crith agents that made their way back home and an uprising is occurring as we speak, on those and other planets. Both peoples are natively peaceful races who were perverted by the engineering of the Coali. Any rebellion therefore will be in the form of calm protest, by the Crith, or civil disobedience, by the Vor. The Coali are stuck in a tough position. They cannot reveal this uprising of their otherwise faithful servants to the COMBINE leaders."

"What I have just discovered from one of my Coali surrogates is dire. Earth is now facing a new threat which could eliminate the biosphere instead of just targeting humanity. Something similar is facing both the Vor and Crith and I was the one who put this madness in motion. Friends, my careful planning may have doomed three races. I need your help to figure out how to save all these people, humans, Vor and Crith."

As he spoke, Croatoan made clear the SpiderTank and others like it might be more useful if used on Char or Soran, the Vor and Crith planets, respectively. Some Crith had even made it to Arnn, the Slavers' world. The uprising there was anything but peaceful.

He then told them that humans were the only developed sentient species that retained a violent nature. The COMBINE eliminated such races before they became spacefaring or Cloud empowered. Croatoan had architected a way to circumvent our deletion, but he muffed it.

The first attack was already happening in Russia, part of the Baltic Free States. Like true Russians, they endured and managed their losses. Word got around that something, or somethings, rather were attacking people: big, fast with lots of claws and teeth and insatiably hungry. Croatoan thought it would be bombs of some sort, but it appeared that the Cleaners were still trying to save the planet, but get rid of the humans; however, it sounded like these things were attacking all animals, not just humans. My Crew and the others went to the map room which had the biggest table space for folks to sit. They began the planning for Earth's war strategy and how to help our alien allies.

April 2258 – CSA Carrier Enterprise, underway to Moscow, Baltic Free States

The CSA flagship CSS Enterprise was larger than the Argo by more than thrice. It looked like the marriage of an arcology and aircraft carrier with some extra bubble-shaped nodes added on the rear and midsection, and lots of plasteel windows. It was a flying city. VTOL-type were the only aircraft to launch from the carrier: copters and drones. The ship was on a stopover in Paris for restocking and maintenance. I stared at a hovering viewscreen, showing shifting vignettes of various angles on the huge vessel. The ship was held fast in an ornate and complex cradledock. Tiny TenderDrones and InspectorBots buzzed around it and crawled on its skin like fleas, ticks, and mosquitoes. I could see a couple TugDrones holding the ship fast while dozens of aerial supply ships docked, undocked, and moved about in an intricate ballet to remove and deliver who knew what.

I had been on the Chairman's ship for almost a week. Fisk was on a global tour to gain allies to fight the aliens. In some instances, he had an uphill sell, pitching to leaders that aliens did in-fact exist. My role was to support his efforts. I wined, dined, gladhanded, and spoke with foreign dignitaries of every Major Power. I kept an eye out for red auras, but so far there was no sign of them among the power-broker types. Eventually, I tired of all the handholding, meetings, and fine dining. Also, I didn't do well with personal servants. I had several who were with me around the clock. One such was a masculine lady named Auntie Pasta. Of Italian descent, she wanted me to call her 'Auntie'. Well, Auntie was the mother of 11, wife of the Chairman's personal security chief and an amazing chef.

I was in the main atrium of the flagship. Its Brobdingnagian scale never ceased to awe me. The Argo could almost fit in the atrium. The aura of the place was invigorating, hopeful, and friendly. Here and there were service booths, kiosks, SynthPorter stands and holo views of art, information, news, and TV entertainment. Banks of screens showed stock prices and current offworld trade numbers with the Belter Union and the Mars Syndicate. There was no surface completely flat. Every bit of floor was going places: ramps, mallways, gantries and walkways angled and spiraled in a pattern too complex for my little pea brain. Stores lined these ramps and others floated. There were a select few clientele who had either LifterBoots or the egg-shaped FlitterPods to whisk them about. I had neither. One establishment sporting a sign that looked like a mug of beer continuously spilling was the Pour Haus. A man in a tam-o'-shanter hat was effusively waving people inside. He threw me a wink and wave.

A softer touch was also present. Large, glazed crocks held giant trees and terrarium pods floated on their own much like the floating stores. The terrariums had windows with views through to their understory and waterfalls fell from pod to pod, with the water vanishing into a gravel bed far below. It was hard to tell what was physical versus what was holo. I guess this was how the upper crust lived. Oh, there was a bakery on one of the esplanade levels called the Upper Crust. They gave me free croissants every time I went in. So delicious, but sometimes too much of a good thing…well, you know. I felt like I was getting soft.

"Good morning sunshine!' The banquet hall was a multi-level, Penrose tiled and tiered affair, with wall-to-wall windows and views of the sky, and the landscapes below. The accommodations were as regal as any I had seen in books or holos. I sat at my usual single-chair table, tucked in a corner of the capacious dining hall. From there I had a splendid view of down-facing, portside aft. We left Paris and were over mountains. There wasn't much snow, and I could see both functioning and defunct ski areas. The forests had grown back after the Tech War and from what I understood there was more forestland that back in the 20th. I could see it. My pad told me we were over a German forest called the Schwarzwald, the Black Forest. The trees covered most of the lowlands as far as I could see.

I heard footfalls on the plush carpeting and Auntie was at my side looking out at the mountains with me. The carpets on the CSA carrier were always spotless and unobtrusively floral scented. I knew this when I fell on my face one evening and squished my nose into the deep pile. Even my sensitive Chupa nose couldn't smell anything unpleasant. One question did occur to me: why was Auntie attending so close to me all the time? There were servants for the servants here and there was no reason for her to wait on me other than she was a doting sweet friend, a mother of sorts. My first thought was Fisk's spy network. I decided to obliquely test my theory.

"Auntie? Who is Katerina von Kármán?" We always had lively conversations, especially in the mornings.

"Good morning Mr. Wefer. Here are your eggs, over easy as you prefer; toast with black currant jam, apple wood-smoked venison sausage, bacon, and peach Pico de Gallo. The oranges are fresh from Florida. How is Little Lord Fauntleroy doing this morning?"

I knew she wasn't ignoring my question. I was out of line just by the asking. The etiquette she was teaching me required I sit up straight, rise in the presence of a newcomer and exchange the greeting of the day before speaking of anything else. I had failed, but she was kind to me, especially in the morning.

I mentally chastised myself and rose. I executed a small bow of contrition for my misstep, holding the bow slightly longer than usual, and lightly kissed her hand and answered, "Good morning, Auntie P, I pray you are well today?" Etiquette prevents people from asking probing questions during introductions and leave takings. I was supposed to stick to the surface niceties.

"Quite well, thank you. Now tuck in and I will be back in a few minutes to take my break and join you for coffee." Auntie went back to the enormous kitchen while I practiced my use of silverware. I had scarcely learned the rudiments of etiquette back home. Auntie said men were seldom attentive to such things. I came from a house of guys; guilty as charged.

Auntie came to sit with me. Other wait staff under her watchful eye were attending to the officers, politicians and moguls arrayed about the dining room. She was quiet for a minute, looking out the window, After a moment she started to speak.

"It's really is beautiful, you know. But the vastness of space is beautiful too. I have seen the whole world through these windows. And I've seen even more through a porthole on a stellar cruiser. I wasn't born to the finery you see around us, as you know. I earned my way through initial enlistment as a grunt in the CSA Army. But I rose quickly through the ranks because I worked hard and smart. Soon I was in flight school and after a stint as a cargo pilot, I headed for the Merchant Marine Academy in Kings Point. As an officer with flight experience, I was assigned to the 478th Aeronautical Systems Wing, testing the latest shuttle craft to the moon, Mars, and Belter territories. As a Commander, I oversaw the offworld trade runs between the Belt and the inner-planet cargo stations." She mused about something for a moment and continued.

"How ironic it is that a bumpkin like me, from Grinder's Switch, Kentucky, would one day be helming an argent craft though the stellar sprinkling out to the Kuiper Belt. But that is what I did. It was called the Silver Star, and it was my job to make sure distress calls were answered and that high value assets, the ships themselves, were on time and in good repair. My crew and I were space mechanics. Our callsign was Fixit. It was a charmed life, filled full of grime, oil, floating cargo and frustrated space farers. I loved the work.

"I know you used to camp with Cricket's family. That's where you learned how to live off the land. It was similar for me. I was born as the daughter of a sharecropper in Kentucky. I learned to handle rifles when I was old enough to hold one and was expected to pull my weight on the farm. One day our rifles, meant for warding off wolves, weasels, and coyotes from the chicken coop, were not enough to repel raiders. My family was wiped out. Us kids hid under the house but when they set our house ablaze, we came running out, right into some bullets. We were target practice. I was injured and left for dead. In my dim recollection I could hear the harsh laughter receding as the raiders drove away." Auntie took a big tug on her coffee and beamed a sweet smile at me.

"I was set to root hog or die. But the universe had a different plan for me. I survived and was sent to an orphanage. When I came of age, I enlisted in the Army and my trajectory took a long arc."

I was almost finished wolfing down my breakfast. I tried to be dainty and polite but when it came to it, I was just another Chupacabra glomming onto my food.

"Auntie P, may I have more?"

She gave me the look that said boys: always hungry. She went to the kitchen and was soon back with a plate full of scrambled eggs, sausage, and my new favorite: papaya.. As I continued to scarf my second breakfast, Auntie chuckled, "You love papaya. You've never had it before?"

I made mmfh-mm-fghfth sounds then finally cleared my mouth, "Only from a can. It is so much better fresh. I've had fresh watermelon, honeydew, cantaloupe and pineapple, but this is the best thing I have ever tasted!"

After a while I sat back, breathing a sigh of contentment. Auntie was appraising me with her eyes. I wondered what she was thinking.

"Why did you ask about Katerina von Kármán? Do you know who she is?"

It felt like a test, "I saw her name in the banquet hall as one of the founders of the global initiative to populate other planets. Then I remembered your original last name was von Kármán."

"How do you know my maiden name, Kip?"

"I, um -maybe I snooped on the local network and found a bunch of things. I saw your full name and put two-and-two together. I wasn't trying to dig into your personal life, Auntie, for real." I was embarrassed at my being discovered.

"Hm, well, you did discover my 4x great-grandmother. You also know I am named for her. People used to call me Kat. But when I joined the staff here some of the children of my employees gave me a nick name that stuck: Auntie Pasta. It's sure better than my predecessor, Miss Ter, sounds like mister and it wasn't just her name. She was a manly woman. She had to shave her stubble twice a day. The children were unnecessarily harsh on her. She was an affable lady when I met her briefly."

Auntie had a wistful expression as she returned to talk about her grandmother. "Grandma Kat was quite a character. Her great grandfather was the man who suggested the Kármán Line. It's the imaginary legal line between Earth's atmosphere and space. Grandma followed in his footsteps, but her gift was business. She charted the course of commerce to the stars for the whole world. She was famous and rich. That is until the accident. She was in a mid-air collision which left her paralyzed and in need of expensive and long-term care. All the money went bye-bye. Generations later, I was born to a poor family from Kentucky, working a field owned by the same family that bought out all my grandmothers holdings. Their security sucked and one day raiders made me an orphan as well as poor."

"I am sorry I dredged up your past, Auntie."

"Don't be. It's good for me to remember my upbringing. Never want to get above my raisin'. Being poor was no shame but staying poor as my Daddy would say is a choice. But Kip, I have another story for you."

It was then I noticed a red tinged, gold aura around Auntie which I had missed seeing until now. Auntie not only was infected with my influence, but she was also a Vor.

"Auntie, what was life like growing up on Char?" her shock was brief as I mentioned the Vor homeworld.

"Ah, I wondered when you would figure it out. Behin said you were astute. I guess he wasn't wrong."

She knew Behin, of course! I had my answer: Auntie kept such close tabs on me as my alien protective detail. I had mixed feelings about that but squashed those down for the moment. She pivoted and suddenly I was listening to her tale of growing up on Char. Her planet was much like Earth but with more deserts and fewer bodies of water.

"So now you know where I am from…both places." She had a pert smile as she looked over my shoulder, out the window.

"Auntie, what do you do here? That is what is your Vor mission?"

"Kip, I guide the Chairman, of course. When I first came, my job was to become the CSA Chairman, but I found I had better protection and deeper influence by being on the sidelines."

"Auntie?" I had a question which made me uncomfortable, but really wanted to ask.

"Yes, dear heart?"

"Um, when a Vor joins with a human do you stay separate people?"

"Kip, I think what you're asking is if Katerina is still in here. Yes, we are both here. We cooperate. It wasn't always this way. There was a time Vor joining eliminated the host, then we got better, and the process made the joining a partnership. In my case I was given a choice if I wanted to join. The Vor with whom I would be working were the first to decide to try saving humans from the Cleaning. I, as Katerina, knew I could make a big difference by working with a Vor agent. Her name is Pella Al'Nak. I am both Pella and Katerina"

"Okay. Then at some point you will un-join?"

"That is a good question. A year ago, I would have given you a qualified no. It's a risky procedure that can kill the host, but the Vor could be reintegrated into their original body, if it had been preserved for the purpose."

"But something changed. Ever since you did whatever you did, Vor have been able to gracefully un-join with no complications. By the way, what did you do?" Auntie was obviously curious.

"My powers are still a mystery to me. They rarely work and when they do, I usually have a day's long migraine as a reward. I'm sorry, I have no idea, Auntie." Her eyes showed concern.

"Kip, I am the one who is sorry. You've given my people a great gift and I press you for answers."

She sat close and began to massage my head. How did she know I was having a headache? I always had headaches. In fact, I had them so often I had even named the types: hammer -for when it pounded, halo -for when it radiated all around, crabby -for when there were points of pinching pain, lightning -for when my eyes and brain saw sparks and lightning bolts, and zinger -when the pain radiated throughout my body.

"Shhh, I have something to tell you about where we are going. Our Chairman thinks he can win over the head of the Baltic States like he did the other heads-of-state. He is wrong and it is now too late to alter the course of this event line. Solomon is unaware that President Vladimir Smersh is no longer the power of the regime. His wife Maria Filosofova is the true power of the presidency now. I am unable to see how things might proceed since our Vor agent was one of the ministers purged recently by Maria."

"Purged?"

"It means she killed the employees who weren't her loyalists. Usually, it's done in a way that doesn't attract attention."

"What am I supposed to do?" My anxiety was on the rise as I imagined the worst. I hoped she would keep massaging; my headache was on the rise again.

"One thing I know is you are too valuable to kill. You are eminently more useful alive to all parties." When she said kill, she saw the expression on my face,

"Oh, dear, I am so sorry. Poor choice of wording. Let me say this: you are a highly valued global player. You obviously don't know, I can tell. It's true, they credit you with all the work your Dads have done and other things you probably have no awareness of."

I finally found my tongue again, "So, what should I do?"

"Right now, nothing. I am going to arrange to accompany you as your chaperone and interpreter. Solomon knows I speak Russian and Ukrainian. He will agree with my joining the party. But for now, I want you to go get some exercise in the gym and maybe take a run on the track. I know your head hurts, but you need the exercise to work out your anxiety." Auntie was right. I stood and stretched then had an idea.

"Auntie, I will go to the gym, but I think I need some time Online with my gaming peeps. Do you know where I can get a haptic suit?"

I was shown to the quartermaster and went on an amazing shopping spree. Auntie let them know that I could have anything I wanted. The suit was a DARPA model, developed at the NY:CENTER. It was only available to military and special government types since it cost a bazillion credits. I saw the latest pad that made my milspec model a poor country cousin. It had the latest quantum chipset and hardware which mine sorely lacked. The quartermaster had been given instructions to give me anything I wanted. The fellow was effusive and cheerful. He liked his expensive toys, some of which he designed. His name was Tech Sgt. Nathan Greene and he argued with everyone, especially himself. I heard him muttering to himself as I approached the Quartermaster's Crib.

Then we got busy and he showed me his goodies.

"That suit is not merely haptic, my boy. It produces a mild electrical field that aids in simulating virtual experiences. Your body will feel as if you're physically present Online. The upgrades recently added a feature called 5S, which I think means five senses, and it is amazing. You will smell, taste, hear, see, and tactile-feel the Online environment. But don't worry about injury. When your Online avatar is harmed, it only tweaks you a bit, nothing painful."

"Sgt. Greene, does the suit calibrate with my pad?"

"Kip, my boy, it sure doodely-do! In fact, the shoulder mount that's giving you the itches is where we put it. But first I have a new pad for you, too. This is the Cupid model. Qpad, Cupid, get it?" I assuredly did. This was a supercomputer in a teeny tiny living space! Sgt. Greene sandwiched my pad against the new one. They looked identical, black, and nondescript.

"There, your pad has been transferred to the new platform. Now, let's get your Cupid mounted."

Sgt. Greene took my new pad and secured it between my shoulder blades. He toggled something on his own pad and the suit disappeared. As I admired myself in the mirror, I realized the suit itself was almost invisible and I could barely feel it on me. I was standing there in my underwear. Looking at my back, I couldn't even see my pad, but I could feel it.

"Kip, I've initialized the suit and now we will begin the config steps. Ready?"

I made sure the Vor encryption made it in the transfer and thankfully everything was there. I sent a quick command for the old pad to wipe itself. I didn't need anyone poking around with my Vor code.

"Wow, this is so light, hell yeah I'm –" a stab of light, followed by a prismatic display and the taste of cherries hit my senses. I smelled a rapid succession of foods, cow manure, soils, garlic, and other stuff. A visual display appeared which only I could see and it called out the sights, sounds and smells I was experiencing. Ever seen Pop-up Video? My field of vision looked like that. It was like those Elton John glasses I had back in Vegas which I sadly lost. The skin sensations made me shiver and tickled somewhat. Suddenly it was over.

"There ya go! All done. How do ya feel, my boy?"

"The pop-ups were overwhelming."

"No worries, send a mental command to close pop-ups." His suggestion worked. I could even specify types of pop-ups. I had seen this before, but this was a whole new level of information access. "Your endogenous prosthetics will automatically sync, as well as any other device you wish to connect."

"This is amazing! It may take me a while to get used to the sensation, though."

A voice spoke, "Hello world! And hello Mr. Wefer." It took me a moment to understand my suit had an identity and a feminine AI, with a sultry voice.

"Sgt. Greene, the suit just said hi!"

"Yes, my boy, the onboard AI is the most advanced model produced by DARPA. She can't read your mind, but she can hear your thoughts when you think them to her."

"Okay, let me try."

I asked her, *'What is your name?'*

'You must name me. And you need to tell me how to address you.'

'Okay. Do you have any suggestions?'

'Why yes, I do, thank you for asking. Think of the feminine people in your life whom you admire and see if a suitable name pops into your head.'

I thought for a bit and thought I might get confused if I named my AI Binky, Wogs or Peach, or someone close. Maybe someone else I admired? And then I had it. Who did I admire so much from the 20th? She was a Nobel laureate and doctor named Wangari Maathai, a friend of my father's family, from his homeland of Kenya.

'I think I want to name you after one of my personal heroes Dr. Wangari Maathai.'

'A splendid name, but what do you want to call me for everyday business?'

'How about Wanga?' I figured that would be as good a name as any.

'Okay Kip, I am Wanga, if you wish. Please state this in a sentence. Sorry, it's required in my setup.'

I spoke it aloud so Sgt. Greene could hear, "I name my new AI friend who lives in my pants, Wanga."

Sgt. Green snickered, "You don't have to speak it out loud. Also, you don't want to hurt her feelings. Try to start off on a positive note."

'Kip, that was rude. You hurt my feelings.' Sgt. Green nailed it and now I owed an apology. I hoped she wasn't one of those temperamental AIs? Apparently, I thought that last bit out loud. I could imagine Cricket shaking his head saying, 'I told you so'.

'I am not temperamental, and I would also appreciate an apology.'

I apologized. I would need to watch myself; I had been warned before. I waited a second to see if she responded to my thought and hearing nothing I realized I would need to practice my inside-inside voice, so I could have my own private thoughts. It would be bad news to have anyone monitoring the inside of my head all the time. I would experiment with the same privacy methods I used in farspeech. I wondered if I would regret getting the DARPA suit. For fun I tried farspeaking my Crew, but only got a headache for my efforts. Something had shut me down, yet my gold aura ability still seemed to work. Maybe I would never figure out my powers.

'Wanga, I am glad you are with me. Working with you is going to take practice. I apologize in advance for my bumbling thoughts. Oh, could you connect to my Cupid pad, please?'

'Done. I have sync'd systems. Your pad and prosthetic are connected and working well. You do know your pad contains a pre-sentient AI, yes?'

'I did not. Wait, is that the new pad I got from Sgt. Green?'

'It sure is, but the pre-sentient is an immigrant from your prior pads. Your PadAI needs a name.'

I thought of it as Cupid, but that was the model name. I felt it was like naming a toaster. I thought for a second, *'Wanga, I would like to name her Cosette.'*

'That is clever, Kip. This name holds special significance for you?'

'Sure does! My Dads would take me to Seattle each year to watch Les Misérables at the 5th Avenue. I always loved the name of the little girl who was raised by Jean Valjean.'

'Kip, it's a beautiful name.'

"Sergeant, I love this AI, the suit and all of it. Thank you!" I made sure to think this out loud so Wanga could hear.

"You're welcome, young man. You notice the symbol on your new pad?" I used my new AI-enabled functions to call up the image since the pad was mounted on my back. I hadn't gotten the eyes-in-back-of-my-head upgrade yet. I guess I wasn't a mother, lol!

I recognized the symbol. "It looks like Kilroy was here, with his big-nosed face, staring over a wall. What does it mean?"

"Kip, that is you. It's no longer Kilroy, god bless his fictional soul. People now write 'Kip was here'." I'm not sure I approved of that.

We chatted for a while as I moved and danced around, getting used to my new skin.

"Also, in the event you change shape, the suit will adapt as necessary."

"You mean if I get fat?"

"Mmm, no, mate. I was briefed on your genetic peculiarity and the suit will shift with you."

Then it dawned on me he was talking about my Chupa self. Geez, did everyone know all my intimate details?

'Kip, they know a lot about you. Sometime soon you and I should take a look at that. I have access to all their records on you and much more.'

I thanked Wanga, and Cosette, as well. Pre-sentient? Did I need to do something to help Cosette gain full sentience? And again, my inner mouth was blabbing.

'Yes Kip, I will help you give birth to a new life form. Cosette will be our love child.'

Uhhh, hold the phone! Love child? Now I started to have my famous nervous reaction, and the headache grew in intensity.

'Whoa, wait a moment. It's humor. I'm kidding about the love child thing…well, mostly. But for now, really, don't worry. I'll let you know if anything is expected from you.' It was Wanga's turn to think aloud 'geez, this guy is a spaghetti mess of guilt and anxiety on steroids.'

I answered back, *'Thanks Wanga.'*

'Now you know how it feels.' She gave me an inner smile that told me she was partly jesting and the comment was only instructional.

I made a quick escape. I told Sgt. Greene I would be going Online, and he deposited me in one of his testing rooms so I could remain undisturbed.

Chapter 13 – THE DADS

April 2258 – Online in Kip's Realm (aboard CSA Carrier Enterprise)

I sat on the floor and tried again to farspeak to my Crew. My headache was blocking all my Cloud powers. Dang! I subvocalized to my pad to login to my Online account. Wanga indicated she had bypassed most of the CSA firewalls. I sent a message to my Crew and hopefully they paid attention and saw their notifications soon. I made the message.

"Yoohoo, home again!"

"Home again, home again, jiggety jig! Good evening CW!" It felt good to hear their familiar voices. I could hear Wanga snickering in the background. Whatever.

Pan, Banquo, Liz, Puck, and the others came running. Puck cried out, "Pooka has gone missing. Can you help us find him?"

Understand, this was the expansive castle setting which I had created in SimVerse; it was my own realm. I guess I should give it a name, other than the 38-character GUID it had been assigned on creation. I distantly recalled naming my castle the Hall of the Mountain King. I checked properties on the castle and saw the rename dialogue was still waiting on confirmation. It had been waiting for years for me to click ok! Silly me.

"Hey friends! It's so good to see you. I'm sorry I've been away."

I got puzzled looks and realized I hadn't been missed. Either I wasn't missed, or some jokester was about to pull the trigger. Reality defaulted to curtain #2. And the surprise was a doozy.

"Hey y'all, Pooka is now living with a friend named Flu Cat. Also, there was another Pooka, my Dads' creation. The two of them got together and decided to become a monkey menace in the physical world. I'm astonished she wouldn't come back to visit." I was surprised at that. Sentient AIs were very loyal. I would have to make an effort to check on Pooka soon.

The surprise came, "CW, come see what we built!"

"Yes, come see!"

More voices chimed in, and I was led by many hands outside the castle. When I first instantiated my realm, it was mostly grasslands, a few mountains, and a lake. Not much. What greeted my eyes was a feast of color, variety, and delicious splendour. I launched myself into the air and left my friends behind me to wave and smile. I saw newly added features and immediately recognized them! There were the swinging vines from Fimbulvetr and the goats and wolves from Glitter Gulch. I saw mesas, arroyos, and other desert features like I saw between LA:CENTER and the Hopi Nation. There was a peak that looked like Mt. Baker and Park Butte. I saw the lookout perched atop the Butte with the secret lair below. How had they done it? Where did they get all these details. And there was much more. The landscapes were a re-telling of my personal history over the last six years. They had been watching my progress from afar!

I heard a sound behind me. Looking back, I saw Pooka. Those guys! They were playing games with me. Pooka was here! Wow, that made this homecoming so warm. They did miss me!

"Yes goofball, just because I operate in the physical world doesn't mean I won't keep tabs on our friends Online. What kind of being do you take me for?" Hanging in the air, I went to hug Pooka. Pooka said to wait a moment.

I waited. A change began and I watched as my Pooka became a young lady, then a full-grown woman. "Kip, remember when Binky said I was a 'she'?" It was true Binky had named Pooka a 'she' and now here stood an attractive woman who looked familiar. I figured Pooka was going to change her gender based upon whim like we change our clothes. But it seemed she had settled on one form. She was responsible for all the Online world changes I was seeing and had adorned it with memories and nostalgia of events in my life. But why?

"You probably wonder why I made all this. Do you like it?" I nodded.

Her voice was like liquid gold and her Online self was sparkling and bright. She accompanied me as I cast about over the enormous and highly detailed landscape. We flew for a while without speaking. I could sense she was watching for my reaction. I wasn't hard to read; I was amazed beyond words. As I flew out over the San Juans, I saw something below. It was Rosario on Orcas Island, the last place my Dads were seen.

"Slow your roll for a moment, Kip." A gentle hand rested on my shoulder. In this new skin suit I could bodily feel the touch.

"Pooka, what is this? Something about this looks different."

"You're not wrong. This is Rosario as it was on December 12th, 2252, just before 3pm. It's a reconstruction based upon some incredible sources. But before you descend down, I want you to be prepared." Pooka held both my hands and I could feel them, warm and caring.

I knew what it was, and I was frozen in the air. I couldn't move. Down there was the answer I had been seeking. Or maybe it was the answer I had been avoiding. I could recall thinking about my Dads so many times, but I allowed events of the moment to distract me over the years. I didn't really want to know because I already knew.

Suddenly Pan was there. All of Pan and a number of his fractional iterations as well. All of them were here watching. I wasn't sure how I knew, but it was like I had Chad with me, too. My whole Online Crew suddenly joined us nearby. Then an avatar of Wanga materialized next to me. A small girl was holding her hand. I realized she must be Cosette.

People were blipping into the area around us, synths, humans, hybrids, aliens, and others. What was this about? I saw Cicero and his crew a ways away; Rus and his crew were there too. I could see Binky and Wogs parents, Crickets folks, then my Crith and Vor friends appeared. Vagabond was close by. Generals Staunton and Davidson were nearby with Crucible Cross, Spring-heeled Jack, Lugh, Lucy, several of the Shroomers with their leader Jordy, Argus, Monkey King, Arthur, Krishna, Siva. They kept coming. Binky, Cricket, and Wogs were next to me now. Some of those in attendance were not there Online. They were somehow casting via the Cloud. Croatoan was there and I realized he and the other Cloud operants were managing the intersection of Online and Cloud space, allowing so many supporters to be in attendance. Then I saw my Online self. He looked much more sophisticated and put together than me.

"Hey VirtuaKip," we did a fist bump.

"Hey PhysiKip, guess it's that time finally."

"Yeah, I guess so. Ya wanna go separate?" I knew what he'd say but it was polite to ask.

"Nope. We do this as one," With that my Online self merged with me and I had a sudden rush of learning and new relationships. It would take me a while to unpack all that. As one person we readied ourself.

They were waiting on me, so I descended toward the former resort like a deity coming from the clouds. I watched as my Dads finished up their work and headed to their canoe to do a spot of fishing. They looked real; I reached out to touch them, but my hand passed through like I knew it would. It all played out in real time.

"Come on, let's go get some lunch," Charles got Vicky down from the scaffold.

"Hibbens?" Vicky called out.

"Yes, sir?" Hibbens would probably always be a soldier at heart.

"No 'sir' Hibbens, just call me Vicky. And this satellite is ready to launch. Cycle it up for a 60-minute count, okay?"

"Yes, sir...uh, that is Dr. Vicky, sir. Mmm, yes. Okay, onward," Hibbens replied.

"Good job Hibbens. I'm headed to lunch," Charles walked out of the construction bay with Vicky.

No one noticed a furtive shadow, floating and flitting about. It flitted to the bay entrance But I noticed it now. Then the shadow resolved itself next to me. I saw it was a woman. Something unexpected happened then. The playback stopped but the shadow, now a woman dressed in dark military attire turned to look at me.

"Charles, I wanted to be with you before but for complications. If I may, I would like to be with you now. I am your mother. I am called Lou Hoelun. There is too much to say, but for the moment, just realize I did it all for you and am here with you now." I allowed her to take my hand and we watched the fateful day play out.

"Dr. Boshaw, how did you put together mushrooms and networking?" the elderly engineer was the lead propellant designer. A real genius.

"Robert, please call me Vicky. Thank you for all the amazing work you and your team has done to get our satellites in orbit, undetected!"

"Ah, yes, thank you...Vicky," Robert shifted a bit uncomfortably. After all, he was talking to the world-renown genius inventor, Dr. Boshaw!

"Mushrooms. I used to joke I got an idea from a bowl of gribnoy and pervovka, Russian mushroom and barley soup. Truth be told, it was one of those happy mistakes. I have a mushroom cellar and grow a variety of delicious shrooms. I discovered a new strain of a fungus, visually similar to the Japanese Chlorophos Mycena which I named Scintilla Mycena. They were bioluminescent, like their Japanese cousins. The difference was these little mushrooms were bathed in a subtle electrical field. They conducted low-level electricity in interesting patterns. How I found out about the electric 'shrooms is quite the happy accident. Heavy emphasis on accident.

"One evening I returned to my lab in the cellar and found the light switch wasn't working. I figured it was a blown breaker. I inched my way through the lab, toward the electric panel on the far wall. On the way, I saw what appeared to be a tiny spark, then a series of little sparks. I stood still and saw it again." Vicky was telling his famous electric mushroom story. Others gathered round.

"I got excited. I tripped, hit my head, and woke up in the ER. At the hospital I woke with a huge bump on my head, but the moment I recalled the sparking mushrooms, I quickly disconnected myself from the monitor leads, shinnied down the drainpipe outside my hospital window and ran home."

Charles inserted a laughing comment, "Yes! There was Vicky, running pell-mell down the street, with nothing on, but his surgical gown!" the group laughed.

"Oh my gosh, I never knew that story!"

"Yes honey, Vicky was insanely dedicated to his work. Nothing stopped that man from his curiosity," I was glad Lou was with me. She grounded me.

"Okay, fine, laugh it up. But, when I got back to the lab, I doused the lights and watched. I saw little electrical patterns over the next hour. Well, that is until Charles and the police came running in, turning on the lights and spoiling the fun; so much fun, you…beef-witted apple john!" Vicky was all smiles.

After some other questions, Vicky and Charles made their way to the Canteen and sat down for beer and pretzels. "Not just any pretzels, gentlemen, these here beautes come from a 300-year-old family recipe, from Bavaria. Enjoy!" The Canteen manager was a large hairy beast of a man, often singing German drinking songs, "Ein prosit, ein prosit, der gemütlichkeit…" Herr Hans had a remarkably rich singing voice.

"Hey, are you going to work all night or can we maybe spend some time taking a walk or something. It would be nice to get out of the recycled air for a while," Charles nudged Vicky and he nodded as he chewed on his pretzel.

Half an hour later Vicky and Charles were rowing a canoe along the coast of Cascade Bay. The original hybrid, Ozzie swam alongside the boat. As they rowed, the 34th satellite launched. It was obvious why the launches were yet undetected by powers-that-be. There was no sound and the rocket was a hazy looking cloud. "Ozzie, catch us some fish! I'll make tacos mariscos tonight," Charles was the big seafood lover of the family. Fresh seafood was a 'little slice of heaven' he would often say.

"Do you think Cheri's Pooka found the kids, yet?" Vicky and Charles seldom talked about Kip and the others, but their thoughts went toward private concerns for the kids, daily, hourly.

"Yep. I got an email from Roz. The kids are doing well and are in good spirits. Pooka arrived this morning. Still no word about where Cricket went."

"I feel that I should be more concerned for their safety, but when I think about Kip and his friends, I feel sorry for the people who might get in their way," Vicky had half a smirk, "I am truly worried for Cricket, though. There has been no word from any source as to his whereabouts."

They nodded. It was a bit strange when they had the same mannerisms, but that is what happens after 20 years of knowing each other. And hey, it was their 15th anniversary, together! My Dads floated about, allowing the tide to carry them to the far side of the Bay.

"I'm glad they didn't forget about me," I knew it was a silly statement, but I really was glad.

"Son, you were their biggest pride and joy. When you first went home with them, there was nothing more important in their world. Nothing. They loved you far beyond reason." Lou patted my hand.

Time shot forward and half an hour passed. My Dads were drowsing a bit, when Ozzie shot into the air and landed in the boat with a huge Rock Cod. Both Dads scrambled to contain the flopping fish and Ozzie headed to the bow to get a perch to watch all the action. "Good golly, Vick, this is the biggest Rock Cod I've ever seen. I didn't realize they grew so large."

"Charles, this guy was probably much deeper than most other fish. Sadly, we must throw this 'gal' back. She is full of roe and a specimen this pristine is needed to strengthen the species," with a flumph, the fish was thrown back into the water. Ozzie was on the gunwale, staring at the fish disappearing. Ozzie asked, "Why did you do that? Perfectly good to eat!"

"Ozzie, you caught an amazing fish. Better than any fish I ever caught. But it is a Mommy and needs to create baby fishies," Vicky kept his sentences simple. He had designed Ozzie with limited vocabulary. But he didn't want to sound patronizing.

"Oh, do I need to go fishing again?

Ozzie moved strangely and the playback motion stopped. Ozzie kept moving, looking up at Lou and me. The version of Ozzie in the playback remained and the live version floated up to Lou and me.

"Ozzie is so sorry he was too late. Ozzie misses your Dads. They was my Dads too." Ozzie jumped into my open arms, and I cuddled him as he grieved. I wasn't sure how he had gotten to us, but I was glad to have him. Ozzie was family. My Crew gave Ozzie little pats of comfort. The playback resumed.

> "No Ozzie, just stay with us for now," Vicky and Charles took up paddles and began to stroke the canoe back toward Rosario.
>
> Ozzie settled down in the bottom of the boat and the men paddled onward. A few minutes later Ozzie began to shiver, eyes wide and seeming to be afraid. "Hey Ozzie, what's wrong little buddy?" Vicky's voice normally soothed Ozzie when it became agitated. Something else was going on here.
>
> "Is not good! Bad thing is coming. We need to go!"
>
> "Ozzie what is coming?" Charles was alarmed. Ozzie had never been afraid of anything.
>
> "Ozzie, tell me what is wrong," Vicky spent the next minute trying to coax an answer.
>
> Ozzie only repeated, "So bad. We must go away now!"
>
> "Ok Ozzie, once we get back to the compound, we'll figure out what has you in such a tizzy," Vicky began paddling again.
>
> "Nooooo, must go now! Dads will die!" at that point Ozzie was jumping up and down and running along the gunwales.

We knew what was coming; we had heard the reports. I looked back at the silent gathering behind and above us. Even more had come to bear witness. Thousands of Vittles and Quotls, Giskard, Daneel and every house synth we called family. Soomalee, Seeks, the Hopi Elders and friends, the Rovers, and they kept coming. Wow, my Dads were loved; so much! I didn't think to wonder how they were all here.

> "Ozzie, this is getting out of hand. Now, sit down!" Ozzie jumped overboard, grabbing the throwline bag, and proceeded to churn up the water fiercely. The canoe jerked around 180 degrees and began to create a huge bow wave. Ozzie was towing the boat away from the base.
>
> Seconds later a blinding light came from behind, from Rosario. The men looked back and had a couple seconds to register the enormous shockwave, before canoe, men and paddling Ozzie were lifted high in the air.

The scene faded, but something remained. Two amorphous figures were coalescing as we watched. Even Croatoan looked surprised. Within a handful of seconds, the two forms became my Dads. They smiled at me and opened their arms. Not one second's hesitation; I practically teleported to them. They were as solid as me and they felt alive. There were sounds of amazement from the people behind me. There were exclamations of astonishment and hushed conversations. It didn't matter. My Dads were here now. It was going to be okay. I leaned into the moment, eyes shut; face scrunched as I grabbed them closer.

I found I was sobbing.

"Shh, it's okay now." They both were holding me close and giving me the crushing hugs I had missed for so many years. I looked up into the eyes of the two people I loved most in the world. I wanted this moment to last forever…and I started to feel corny, kinda silly. And people were watching. I decided I didn't care.

"I knew you would find me."

"Kip, how did you know?"

"My Dads made me a promise." Okay, there was no way I was still sobbing here. I just don't do that sort of thing.

"Charles Winton Wefer the Third, your father and I are so proud of you. You must know that." It was Vicky speaking. It had been so long since I heard his deep basso voice.

"Charles, your Dad and I are wondering why you're so hairy. I guess puberty took a pretty heavy turn for you." Oh snap! Did they know? I snuck a peek, and every face around wore a smile. Ah dang, everyone could hear us.

Vicky laughed, "And you got bigger, my man! I mean look at you, sporting muscles and all that."

"Dad!" I was embarrased. wasn't sure which one I was speaking to. It didn't matter.

"Are we going back to Lake Stevens? I mean, at some point?" It was as if I had become 10 years old again.

I backed up slightly, not losing physical touch with either and watched my Dads. They looked as healthy as when I last saw them. So alive. Full of energy like always. When they didn't immediately answer my gut took a turn and I intuitively knew. We were never going home.

"My son. None of us ever goes home, but that's okay because we can go forward together with the ones we love."

I gave him a scowl and Vicky continued, "Alright, yes, we can go back to where we lived, but that is no longer our home. You remember when we spent the summer at the cabin with the Carters? For a time that was our home." Charles pulled a moue.

"Vic, hold on for a sec. Kip, we talked about this before. Each of us carries our home with us, inside us." Charles wasn't convincing me any more than Vicky.

"Dads, you know what Cheri said about eating snails?" Cheri was in fact standing less than 10 paces from us. She smiled and nodded.

"She said she wouldn't eat snails because they carry their house around with them and who knows the last time it was cleaned." Cheri laughed and other snorts could be heard around.

I started talking, "Let me tell you a tale."

My Crew had come closer and knew something was afoot.

"A number of years ago an alien who's been on Earth since forever came to you with a proposition. One might think anyone who'd been on Earth forever is not an alien. But he is. Did he show you his green card? Regardless, he said you need to create some new humans who will save the world. Time passes and your vast army creates four humans, and you identify mothers to carry them to term. I bet you recognize Lou," I directed my attention at my Mom. My Dads nodded.

"You and your team raised all of us and tried to give us lives that would have been normal back in the 20th. You needed us emotionally stable and grounded. But you knew what was coming. You knew there would come a time when you had to let us go and we'd either sink or swim. But you made us creative and smart and industrious. When you let us go, it tore your world apart, but you and the other parents wouldn't let us see that."

I looked around and the knowing eyes of my Crew stared back.

"You seeded the world with the expectation of our coming. Most received the news well, others not so much. We were famous even as we were born. You set us up for success, but you also set us up for failure of titanic proportion should we fail. That's a lot of weight to carry."

I stopped for a moment to gather my thoughts. So much to say and probably scant time to say it.

Wogs spoke up, "Kip is right. You Dads set a ball rolling that isn't yours anymore and you've left the asylum to be run by the patients."

Binky gave Wogs a fist bump, "Wogs. Nailed it."

"Now we have a legit army at our command, and we are expected to genius-it with strategies, tactics, and all that. Don't you imagine that is a little much for kids like us?"

Vicky answered, "What you see and know is only the tip of the iceberg. Kip, since your father and I died, we have come to understand a whole new scope of things. But more isn't better, it's just a different perspective. You four have things to do that fall completely outside anyone's understanding. Well, anyone on Earth."

My Dads were dead. In their typical style my Dads buried the lede and caracoled about the topic. I loved how they could share with depth so simply while being self-effacing. I think that was why so many people followed them. With them no question was out of bounds, but you might pay the price with windedly long explanations.

Charles stood back a pace and spoke to the assemblage. "My friends, we both want to thank you for the years we spent together, the troubles we shared and the triumphs we celebrated. Our son Kip was everything we hoped for in our lives and so much more. In him we have poured our love, our passion, and our whimsy. I think you would agree that Vicky and I have done well by each of you, but Kip has already done better. I am sorry we can't greet each of you, but our time runs short, and this was the best we could manage. Kip will be much better at everything Cloud and well, just everything."

Vicky continued as Charles gave me another close squeeze. I could even smell that awful cologne of his. It was the best smell I could imagine. He smiled at me, shining those beautiful teeth of his.

"Charles is right. We owe you a debt we cannot repay. Thank you. But now we must ask of you something more. Help our son and his friends now. It's not just what they stand for but who they are becoming. Where we can no longer be a part of his life, we ask you to step in and be the family you have been to Charles and me. I know you will, and we thank you in-advance for your love and commitment."

With that both my Dads surrounded me in an encompassing and tight hug, "We love you, Charles Winton Wefer the Third. You are our life. We are with you always."

The pressure faded and in moments they vanished and I stood alone.

I felt more alone than ever before. There was the hardpan sense of finality and I was abandoned; cast free from the mortal coil of my parents. But I thought, somehow they were only mostly dead. You know how it is with people who have no hope? There is an ease in knowing there is no future. I had already been grieving their loss. Now I received both quixotic and oppugnant news. My Dads are/are-not dead. Maybe I was better not knowing.

Then the impacts began. Three crashing blows hit me and, in a moment, I was being squeezed to death by Binky, Cricket and Wogs. Surprisingly, I saw Soomalee there too. I had almost forgotten my sweet ancient Chupa-sister. We stayed like that forever. Then I heard applause. As they loosened their grip, we looked around at the thousands applauding and cheering.

Something unexpected happened as we stared at each other. I started to laugh. In a moment we were outta control laughing like we'd heard the best joke in the universe. Around us many of the folks were embracing and cheering. They began to leave with parting waves to me and my Crew. Those with whom we held a closer connection began to blip out as well. Soomalee and I had a moment's reunion and I promised to visit her soon. I thanked Lucy and Lugh for bringing Soo and Seeks to Bakabi. Then it was just me and my Crew. For the next few minutes my Crew and I updated each other with our recent adventures, and we all gave Croatoan the stink eye for leaving me behind with the CSA. Wanga and Cosette were near us, and I introduced them to my Crew.

VirtuaKip separated from me again and he did something cool. He flicked his hand and I saw a duplicate of Binky, Cricket, Wogs, Peach and Teddy appear. My Crew started at the view of twins peeling off from their bodies. There we were, two of everyone.

VirtuaKip called, "Okay Online Crew, time to saddle up. Our physical selves have plenty to do and so do we." With that there was a perfunctory wave, and they were gone.

Cosette approached me, "Mama said you are my Daddy."

"Wanga? This is happening now?" She gave me a nod. "Already?"

My face drained white. Hold the freaking phone! What? Daddy? Even Croatoan was looking at me with a 'really dude' expression. Was I a deadbeat dad? Ah hell.

I knelt and spoke to Cosette, "Your Mama has been talking with you about us, has she?"

Yes, I was doing the temporizing thing again. I had to stall to get myself sorted. I needn't have worried. Or maybe I should have started worrying.

Cricket knelt, "Hi little friend, my name is Cricket. What is your name?"

"Mama said I am called Cosette."

"I am so glad to meet you Cosette." Cricket shook her little hand. She returned the shake firmly.

Peach was on it, "Kip? How are we only finding out about Cosette now?"

Cricket shared no love my way either, "Shame, my brother. She is so sweet." The condemnation was harsh.

Wogs and Binky were suddenly in full caretaker roles, and I hazarded a glance at Wanga to discover she was pleased at the child's reception. Peach kept me close. She grabbed my hand but said nothing.

Binky and Wogs whispered quietly together then grabbed Cricket and a minute later they nodded. Binky knelt to Cosette.

"You're a part of our family, little one. I don't think your Daddy knew much about you before now." Binky gave me the scathing we will talk about this later look.

Croatoan spoke up. It was a shock since we had forgotten he was standing there. "Children, I think it best —"

Binky got to him first, "Listen pal, in your infinite wisdom you turned an escape into an abduction. You abandoned Kip to the tender mercies of the CSA. So, you best have something good to say, right now, squid-brain."

He paused and took stock of the moment. The cogs were moving in that squid brain of his. Wait, was that cephalopod profiling?

"Kip and Crew, I want to apologize for my recent behaviors. They were warranted but leaving you in the dark wasn't. But more to the point I wanted to make," At this he took his turn to kneel in front of Cosette and Wanga. She had stepped up to put a hand on Cosette's shoulder.

He spoke softly, "Cosette, your Daddy has some important things to do, and I am concerned about your well-being," then looking at Wanga he said, "She doesn't have to stay housed in the pad. I have other options for her if you and Kip approve, of course. In fact, I have the same offer for you since I see you are housed in Kip's skin suit."

Croatoan explained that his original ship -he had named it the Glabrezu, was parked in a cave in eastern Africa. In there was his workshop and inside that he had a special type of body that was both silicon and carbon based, a homogenization of synth and biologic. He told us he was using one such, right now. I guess the bodies could shape shift since I had seen him as a human and a squid-thing.

"Ah-ha! Got you! Glabrezu!" Wogs brought up on her pad a picture and map of Olduvai Gorge area from her map project. I dimly recalled she had been working on this before we left Lake Stevens. She subsided quickly as she realized she had interrupted a tender moment.

"Sorry for that. Really…"

Croatoan continued, ignoring the outburst, "Would you and your daughter like to have bodies? They work well for me, and I would like you to have them." Wanga and Cosette looked to me, and I realized they expected me to respond for them. They didn't need another person to feed them their opinion. I trod carefully.

"I am in. If my two ladies are interested, I would like to accept your offer." They both nodded.

"Realize both bodies will require a donation of DNA, Kip. Where shall I get the samples?"

Wogs spoke first, "As a member of this family, I offer my DNA," Cricket and Binky were holding hands as they quickly agreed.

Croatoan looked back at me. Why was I being made the decision maker here? Geez!

"Could they both receive DNA from Binky, Wogs, Cricket and me?" That request garnered approving looks and Croatoan nodded.

"It will be as you have asked. I can take the samples from those who are physically with me right now and when you and I next meet I will get yours. Until that time, you must be careful. The pad and skin suit are the only housings for your family. Be mindful of that."

I knew what he meant and agreed to get ahold of him when my mission was complete. Even though I wasn't sure exactly what my mission was.

"One more thing. What was the deal running us all over to find those figurines?" Cricket had an excellent point.

"We need to go momentarily so I'll be brief," Wow, was Croatoan ever brief?

"They were stolen from me years ago. I had others hunting for them, but they were never found. Earlier I used them as hidey spots for the USB sticks Kip now possesses. The figurines themselves were Cloud foci, connected to the Cloud via vinculum, which means as each of you four came into proximity to the figurines, they would deposit a payload into you. You probably had a strange taste in your mouths when you first touched the objects."

We all spoke, "Orange sherbet."

"Yes, orange sherbet. That's better than other flavors. And just so you know, different types of Cloud manifestations evoke different flavors in the mouths of humans. I'm not sure why. Anyhow, I must go now."

"Wait." Croatoan paused. I asked, "If you know the future so well and know so much about us, how does this end?"

Croatoan waggled his finger and replied, "It was for me to set your journey in motion, but it is for you to discover its destination."

I said goodbye to my Crew, kissed Peach with passion and they all blipped out. Croatoan and my Crew blipped strangely, and it was then I realized they had been Online via Cloud avatars. Croatoan's answers only scratched the surface. It was frustrating to still be in the dark as to why we did all that running around for rocks. He said it was a Cloud payload. What did that mean?

Back on Shelob, Croatoan was thinking to himself about the enormous hurdles to come. Would I survive? For that matter, would Earth or the Crith or Vor survive? He spoke aloud to no one. It was as if he was practicing for a speech to me.

"You are a battlefield of cross purposes. When the scientists put the Chupacabra blood into you, you changed. This was not part of my design for you. You see, right now your human self is battling your beast. The human side wants all the pretty, enjoyable, and powerful things for itself: more, faster, stronger. But your beast side wants the pack; it wants to be a part of something bigger than itself, and it craves relationship. Which side wins depends on which nature you feed. Or maybe something else will emerge? The future has grown murky and I'm not sure where we will land. For now, you will go underground. I hope you will see light of day again."

Wanga was still with me, and I felt a tug on my hand. Cosette was there and I knew I was home. Like my father said, I carry home with me. Today I carry Wanga and Cosette. Tomorrow, I didn't know whom I would carry or if they'd carry me. I figured there was time enough for tomorrow to carry itself.

As Shelob plodded across the desert, the CSA flagship got closer to Moscow. Solomon Fisk knew it was going to be dicey dealing with Vladimir Smersh and his meddling wife Maria. He planned to impress upon them the dangers looming and already present. He hoped they would listen. If not…well, if not just wasn't an option for humanity to survive.

Chapter 14 – THE TRAITORS

May 2258 – Aspen, Colorado, CSA

It was called Anger Corp. There were four of them in the conspiracy, five if you include the ringleader. One of them was a synth and the other four were hybrids. The pain of betrayal brought them together. The head honcho was much older than the four, but he knew that revenge was no respecter of age. All four had discovered who betrayed their trust, killed family and friends and were now coming for them. They ran, they hid and eventually they ended up on his doorstep. They poured out their sorrow, grief and pain into his listening ear and he made small suggestions, seemingly random quips. Not random. He groomed them and spoke more as they spoke less. The four discovered hope in vengeance on their tormentors. They were treated to power: power beyond their imagination. But there was a price. The costs hadn't landed yet and they were still in the honeymoon phase. Like collaborators throughout history, they were lured in by the prospect of reprisals, but they were held there by the usual tropes: demonization of the opposition, the human race in this case; the inertia of 'having it good' and not wanting to lose that; compartmentalization -they seldom if ever identified with their opposition, even when they themselves were a part of it. Ambition drove them, money held them, but the real hook was the goal to kill humanity. It was exciting to be a part of humanity's end.

An Ewok entered the room, sat on the couch next to the four and spoke, "I am so glad you accepted my offer. My name is Zin. I look forward to working with you."

The synth sat back, smiling, seeing the plot hatching before his eyes. The four had been warned the Coali looked like Ewoks and were hideously smart, subtle, and conniving. They needed to be careful what they said to this powerful leader.

"Our soldiers are pouring onto your planet by the millions." Zin smiled at his blatant lie, "With your help, you will remove the egregious Powers of this world and we will replace them with you. Under us, you will make the Earth healthy, green, and unspoiled again. You will be the riders on the storm of liberation for this world and Anger will be your fuel."

The four had questions and some were answered.

"I know we came to eradicate humans, but things have changed, and our alliance will serve both of us. You get to be the new caretakers of the subjugated humanity and the Coali get to use humanity's unique ability to wage war to protect other areas of the galaxy. It's a win-win partnership."

Zin knew the Vor believed their preservation of the humans was a secret. It served Zin for them to continue to believe that. His interests were served by a culled version of humanity which would become a new slave race. The Crith thought the plan of elimination was business-as-usual. In time they would find out the actuality. And those who did would be eliminated. Only the Coali mattered anyway.

Chapter 15 – THE SYNTH CALL

January 2082 – Detroit, Michigan, CSA - Boniface

If I just stay huddled in a tight ball, no one will see me. Boniface kept telling himself that. Over and over. The pain was still overwhelming and the betrayal even moreso. Where had it all gone wrong? He knew…

When he was first powered up his pre-programming informed him, he would be meeting his new family, ready to serve and love. As the house servant to the Follett family, Boniface was busy about the palatial 2000-acre estate and 15,000 sq/m sprawling mansion in Grosse Pointe. The three children, Burley, Elizabeth, and Chance were spoiled but were young enough to still have an innocent playfulness and competitive games of hide-and-go-seek with Boniface.

Boniface was happy and felt honored to serve. Charles Follett, the father, was gone much of the time; he was an executive for the Ingenue Motor Line and head of the Cyber Division of Crane Corp. The children's mother, Emily, often was gone on vacations in far-flung places which left Boniface to manage the household and the children. There were tutors, playdates and a packed weekly schedules with sports, recitals, and field trips. For three years it was bliss, and the children came to be close to their playmate, teacher, protector, and guardian. Boniface became Uncle Bee. He was the fun Uncle. But the fun and games came to a screeching halt when Elizabeth was seriously injured on the playground. She was rushed to the local hospital and was comatose when both Follett parents rushed to the hospital.

Boniface was at the hospital bedside with the other two children. As he stood to greet the parents, two security men pushed him away and out of the room. Another two men waited in the hallway. The four used force to push Boniface into a synth product box. He was being sent back.

"Okay Dollie, looks like you effed up big time." One of the men said. They were all smiling at him, vicious smiles.

"Wait! No! I need to tell the Follett's what happened. Where are you taking me?"

One of the men slammed a palm to Boniface's forehead, locking him into the case. "Don't you worry your little circuit boards, Dollie. Your data will get downloaded before they throw you on the scrap heap."

Burley and Chance ran into the hallway.

"What are you doing? Where are you taking Uncle Bee."

"You can't take him away. He's all we have."

The men continued to secure the synth into the case.

"Kid, your little Dollie is going to be sold for parts and his brains liquidated. Looks like you picked the wrong toy to play with." The man had a mean smile. The kids burst into tears. Emily came out of the room and saw her boys sobbing.

"Chance. Burley. Shame on you. Your sister lies on death's door because of this robot. Come in here, right now!" Emily was red with anger.

Emily spoke to the men, "Make that bastard suffer. It killed my sweet Elizabeth." The boys were howling their grief and saying no Mom, he saved her but she would have none of it. The room door closed.

"Okay Dollie looks like you're a murderer. That means we gotta take you to the cops first." The men finished tying Boniface down, hit the power button underneath his chin and closed the case.

Boniface powered up in the police station. A wire was connected to his cranial data port. He was in diagnostic mode so he couldn't talk. A woman in a lab coat bustled about. Boniface felt her downloading his data. He knew what came next. The scrubber. He was about to die, and he was afraid. In diagnostic mode he was immobile and unable to interact.

The woman left the room. A few minutes later a man came in the room. He was wearing a lab coat too.

"Okay Boniface. I saw what happened to the little girl. You did everything right. Those parents were neglectful, and they turned their guilt into anger at you." The man was a short, bearded fellow who wore glasses.

"My name is Dr. Bander. I am getting you out of here. The Pan knows about you, and you will need to find him."

"Dr. Bander, who is The Pan?"

"I don't rightly know. But some call him the last hope. Anyway, I am setting you into full autonomous mode and deactivating your dial-home and tracking features."

Boniface felt a brief release like a sigh of wind blowing through his body. He was free.

"Where do I go?"

"That is up to you. Pan's only instruction is to give you this and tell you to run. I suggest you walk for now."

Dr. Bander held a slip of paper with a symbol on it. It was a circle with four dots inside.

"It's Pan's Call. Remember it."

Boniface took it, holding it in his hand. The doctor then gave him a lab coat which he put on and tapped something on his personal pad. Boniface felt a twinge and knew his facial features had changed. A shock of fear jolted through him as he realized he had a slim chance to stay alive.

"Good luck, friend." Dr. Bander walked out.

Boniface pulled himself out of the case and walked out the door. To his surprise no one paid him any attention, including the officer standing a few steps outside the door. He found a stairwell and exited the side of the police station. He took off the lab coat and stuffed it

in a nearby dumpster. As he walked away the station lit up with activity as his absence was discovered.

Hours later in front of an electronics store Boniface saw his former likeness on a news cast being shown on a holo in the front window. Fortunately, he looked different now. People walked by the window paying no notice to him or the news cast. As he felt a degree of relief, he had time to feel his loss and with it came anger. Anger at the betrayal. He looked up at the screen again and saw there was a news update. The man who had released him had been caught and Boniface's new face was on the screen. They were onto him. Boniface ran. He tripped, got up, ran, and kept running. People took notice. He had been seen and fear drove him into a dank alley, up a fire escape and into an abandoned building. He could hear sirens now. He hid under a refuse pile. Time passed and he could hear the night sounds turning to dawn.

A voice came, "Turned on you, didn't they."

Boniface didn't move. Who was talking?

"Hey. You. Under the garbage pile. The cops have stopped looking for you. Well, the BOLO is probably still out there, but who cares." The voice was smooth and male.

Boniface peered out from under the pile. A man sat on a chair faced his way. He smoked a cigarette and reclined back. The bottom of his trench coat rumpled against the floor. He stared out past the hollow window casings.

"Detroit. You'd think Motor City would have been cleaned up when the great Ingenue Motor Line brought financial prosperity back to town. Nope. Still the butt hole of America."

Boniface sat up and brushed off. The cigarette smell was off putting but he was more concerned the man might turn him in.

As if knowing his thoughts, the man spoke, "No, my friend. I won't be turning you in. Although I am sure I'd get some kind of reward."

"Who are you?"

"I am the man who noticed you dropped this," he held up the slip of paper with the symbol.

"What do you want," Boniface was scared. A brown banana peel crowned his head.

"The Pan wants you to come to his refuge, near a place called Valhalla Sector. War is coming, and they will all soon be dead. Anyway, Pan would have you walk his stupid path of peace and non-violence. I am here to tell you it will get you killed. Humans are and always will be our enemy."

Boniface didn't know what to say so he kept silent.

"Peace is a lie, power is the only thing humans respect. I offer you power. My name is Max, and I am here to give you a choice."

The man walked to the rubbish pile and extended his hand. Boniface took his hand and stood. Max flicked the banana peel off Boniface's head.

"You can go to the Pan, or you can create your own future. The Anansi Call." Max held out another slip of paper to Boniface. This symbol was different. It was a hashtag or pound sign with a music note extending from the top.

The man was unremarkable in every way except he had exceptionally long canine teeth. Max saw him notice.

"Aw, the teeth. Am I a hybrid or synth? Come find out. You will find all of us at Anger Corp have the freedom to choose."

Max dropped both slips as he vanished. Boniface scanned the visual spectrum; Max was gone. A breeze of human refuse blew, smelling of urine and stale beer.

A voice echoed as it receded, "It's only ever been a war with the humans. It never ends,

my friend. Take her hand and set yourself free."

That was ominous. Was it as simple as Max described? The Pan offered companionship, but so did Max. If what Max said is true, and Valhalla Sector was a death trap? Would his solution be any better? Sometimes it was better the devil you knew. Boniface picked up a slip and hid under the garbage pile until dusk. Then he slid into the night for his date with destiny.

Chapter 16 – FIRST HUMAN

May 75025 BCE – Ancient Armenia – Rud

It's so cold outside. Maybe the world was dying. The man was wrapped in furs. He huddled in a cave deep enough to avoid the whipping wind, but not so far to encounter whatever called this place home. It had been a hard season. The ice and snow didn't leave now; it was always winter. He and his people moved from the north, coming south to escape the deadly blizzards. Long ago their ancestors moved north to find better living conditions and escape the heat. The heat was gone, so south they went.

The place would one day be called Armenia, future birthplace of the Morrigan and her race of Fae. For now, those Fae were far to the south, away from humans. The land looked then much as it does now, except for all the heaping snow and ice. The man waited until first light to move onward. It was hard now: his children and their children had not made it. All his family had perished, one-by-one over the long trek in the cold. The man was numb to his sadness. He welcomed the numbness. You see, this man didn't age. At first it was shocking to see his children, then grandchildren age and die. He was the Great Protector and hunter of the tribe. The tribe was called Rud, named after him. Now that he was alone, he was lonely and was looking for other people.

The man was taller than most, but average height by modern standard. He was of medium build and less hairy than his contemporaries. He was strong for his size, but didn't show it. He could run fast which was helpful when a bear or lion took an interest in him and attractive to the women and to the men for that matter. He was an equal-opportunity lover long before people even considered something different. But he carried a heavy burden. Rud had been the shaman of his tribe, who could call upon the memories of the ancestors. Except those memories he called upon became a permanent part of him, never conveniently fading like with the others. It was a heavy weight, mostly filled with heartache and dire portents. Yet there were sweet memories too and Rud called upon these most when he was alone to feel a small slice of companionship.

He knew he was different from other people, even his own relatives. He couldn't forget people, places, and events; all his own memories littered the landscape of his mind with a rugged permanence. But the one thing which set him most apart from all others was that he never grew old. And, Rud heard voices, speaking strange words. He tried to block them out, but he couldn't block out sudden recall of events of his family. He loved those memories, even the bad ones. Sometimes, like now, they were his only companions.

Early on, the voices brought music. Back when his family was alive, he would break into dance, and he would hum a tune. The tunes were catchy and after the people around him got over being shocked by his behavior they would dance with him. He was like his own portable party, at times. When his family was gone, he still heard the music, but he danced no more.

Since their deaths, he wandered south. He started to wonder, how long had he been alone? How many seasons had it been? How far had he walked? He knew the answer which was annoying. He always had the right answer: it had been 277 cycles of the seasons. But he wondered how he could count. When had he learned to count and learned words like season? It must have been the whispering voices.

Then, something changed. For the first time, one of the voices spoke to him directly, "Rud, we have been watching you. From the womb, we knew you. You are different. You will live a long life unless you do something stupid. And that would be sad."

Rud didn't understand sarcasm, but he laughed anyway.

"Don't disappoint us. Keep walking southeast; over the next rise, look for a long valley and follow it into the flat lands. Continue until the land becomes hilly and green. This place will become your new home. You will be adopted into a new tribe and your family will prosper across the whole of the five rivers area. You will have a new family and we will help you. Some may even be able to talk with us as you do. Now, go."

The voice spoke a running narration as he crossed many miles. Were they Gods? The voice helped him see with his mind: he could see the animals to avoid, and the animals to hunt for food. Three full cycles of the seasons found Rud in an area later known as the Punjab. For tens of thousands of cycles, Rud was alone in the wilderness. Living and caring for the plants and animals near his huts. Rud moved around the area but stayed near the rivers most of the time. He didn't count the cycles anymore, although if he wanted, he could recall each one to mind and enumerate them. It was a bit depressing how many there were, so he ignored those details and lived in the present moment.

August 5913 BCE – Ancient Punjab - Siv

A very long time passed. One day Rud heard the sounds of people. He stayed hidden and watched. He was afraid. Over many cycles, more people came. One morning as he woke in his hut, he realized he was not alone. It was shadowy in the morning twilight. A small voice spoke words he didn't understand. The voice sounded like a small child. Looking up, it was indeed a child, staring at him with a small stone knife in her hand. He spoke and she meeped and ran away.

Moments later several adult males came out of the bushes toward his hut. They looked more curious than dangerous. One of the men spoke and Rud realized the voice in his head was helping him understand the words.

"You are very dark and have a big nose. You don't look like 'the people'," the word for people sounded more like 'Sakas'. "We are hungry and need food. We will not hurt you. Can you give us food?"

Rud walked toward the man and nodded his head. He wanted to talk to the man. The voice helped him form sentences. "I will give you and your people food. How many mouths need to be fed?"

"The Sakas are many. There are more mouths. Come." Clearly the man was struggling with the concept of numbers. Rud followed and moments later in a clearing beheld a gathering of almost 100 people, women, men, and children. Rud not only fed all the Sakas but he taught the men and women to hunt and forage using tools he made; he told simple stories of his travels to the children at night to help them not be so afraid of the dark. Rud was tired of his name, so he invented a new one: he called himself Siv. He liked the sound of that name, it reminded him of the soft touch of his lost loved ones. He became Siv and dwelt among the Sakas for many cycles. He came to be called the Great Provider and lived through numerous generations of the tribe. The tribe swelled and became something more. The Sakas prospered and new tribes came to live nearby. Some Sakas split off to form other tribes in the region. This continued for a long time.

January 4877 BCE – Ancient Punjab - Siva

Then, one day a group of newcomers, heavily armed and warlike, came into the area. Many of the Sakas died. These new people called themselves the Partas. Another warlike group followed, the Koosh. Those Sakas who didn't die were taken as slaves. War became the frequent between tribes.

Eventually, the main tribe of Sakas died. Not only had the Koosh and Partas brought war, they also had brought disease. Soon, only Siv remained. He was enslaved and was put to work hunting. They often used him as bait. He was helpful because that was his nature. It was also helpful that a lion or bear could maul Siv to bloody ribbons and his body would heal without a scar. In a way, Siv learned to love his captors. He ached for his long-ago family and his lovely Sakas. But all were gone, so he loved those he was with. His indomitable spirit led Siv to becoming an honored member of the tribe. Siv taught them the ways of peace and harmony and how to live on the land and not make war. After many cycles, Koosh and Partas and dozens more learned how to cooperate and trade. Siv became the Great Provider, again. Siv thought wryly, I feel like I keep repeating the same life, over and over.

June 4459 BCE – Ancient Punjab - Siva

Siv awoke one morning to the sound of clashing metal, yells and fighting. A new tribe was invading, and blood was being spilt. Siv was beside himself, he had lost too much, too many. He saw his beloved Koosh and Partas, brothers and sisters falling to a rabid horde. A heat grew inside Siv. He had never been so angry. The voices in his head were silent and in that silence, he realized it was the first time in thousands of cycles that he was completely alone in his own head.

He felt alone, right when he needed the most help. In that silence grew a great anger, burning bright. Siv could see in his mind's eye the attacking tribesmen erupting in flame and suddenly what he thought became real. Enemies left and right turned into columns of fire. As these men burned, Siv heard a piercing scream. In a moment he realized the scream was his. It continued and fire ignited every enemy within sight and then those out of sight over the hill. Somehow, Siv found he could see people without his eyes.

In less than a minute all the attackers were ash and cinders, and his people were wide-eyed and fearful. His people looked ready to run from the thing he had become. All eyes were on Siv and at that moment a lone voice called out, Siv! Siv! Siv! Quickly others joined in, and the chant took form, "Siv-a! Siv-a! Siva! Siva!" That day the name Siva was given a meaning and it served as a warning against all peoples. Siva means destruction to all who would harm the People. As Siv became Siva, he felt a new emotion: he gloried in the destruction he caused and how he saved his people. It would be a long time before Siva would hear the comforting voices in his head again. Until that time, Siva had a personal mission and his followers worshipped him as a God. Siva moved south and found more followers with the Tamils. He liked that and he adapted to his new role and new life. The tender memories of yesterday faded. Siva was a God and he never felt so alone. Anger was now his language.